MAID OF HONOUR

MAID OF HONOUR

Melinda Hammond

CHIVERS
THORNDIKE

This Large Print book is published by BBC Audiobooks Ltd, Bath, England and by Thorndike Press®, Waterville, Maine, USA.

Published in 2005 in the U.K. by arrangement with Robert Hale Ltd.

Published in 2005 in the U.S. by arrangement with Robert Hale Ltd.

U.K. Hardcover ISBN 1–4056–3349–2 (Chivers Large Print)
U.K. Softcover ISBN 1–4056–3350–6 (Camden Large Print)
U.S. Softcover ISBN 0–7862–7576–6 (Buckinghams)

The text of this Large Print edition is unabridged.
Other aspects of the book may vary from the original edition.

Set in 16 pt. New Times Roman.

Printed in Great Britain on acid-free paper.

British Library Cataloguing in Publication Data available

Library of Congress Cataloging-in-Publication Data

Hammond, Melinda.
    Maid of honour / by Melinda Hammond.
       p.   cm.
    ISBN 0–7862–7576–6 (lg. print : sc : alk. paper)
    1. Sisters—Fiction. 2. Nobility—Fiction. 3. Large type books.
    I. Title.
PR6108.A525M35 2005
823'.92—dc22   2005002610

ONE

'No, no—this is too bad of you! I will not go without you!' Lucilla's eyes, dark with anger, were fixed intently upon her mother.

'No, Lucy, pray do not be difficult. You must see that I cannot go to the Cornholmes tomorrow.' Mrs Chambers was reclining upon a day bed, her smelling salts clutched in one hand. She glanced down at her heavily bandaged foot. 'I agree it is most inconvenient for me to be laid up at this time, but although there is nothing broken, Dr Ribble tells me it is an exceptionally severe sprain of the ankle and needs complete rest.'

'And you will need me here to look after you!' protested Lucy.

Her mother shook her head. 'No, darling. I shall manage perfectly well here. It was agreed that Charlotte should join the Cornholmes at Stock House for the whole of August and since I cannot take her, you must go in my stead. I understand your reluctance, indeed I know you do not find it easy to make new friends, but I do hope you will overcome your shyness on this one occasion, for 'twould be most unseemly for your sister to be unattended, for all she has been a widow these past two years. Dear Charlotte is much too young and beautiful to go alone.' She shifted her gaze to

1

her elder daughter, who was sitting by the window, idly studying her reflection in the glass doors of a nearby bookcase.

Hearing her name, 'dear Charlotte' turned her head, a petulant frown marring her beautiful features.

'I know what it is,' she remarked, 'Lucy is jealous because I am about to receive another offer of marriage, and she has not yet had even one!'

'That is scarcely any wonder, as I am not yet out!' retorted Lucilla, stung.

'And you never *will* get a husband if you continue to spend all your time in the stables. You will end as an old maid, unless you can prevail upon Tom Bancroft to offer for you. He seems to enjoy a privileged position in your eyes!'

'Pray don't be so childish, Charlotte! Since Tom is our neighbour it is no wonder we are such friends, but it is nothing more than that!'

Charlotte smiled with false sweetness.

'Much joy that will be when you are in your dotage!'

'Girls, please!' murmured Mrs Chambers in failing accents. From under her fluttering lashes she glanced at her daughters, wondering the best way to deal with the situation. There was little to mark the two young ladies as sisters. Charlotte at two-and-twenty was undoubtedly the beauty of the family, with a dainty frame and a melting look in her cornflower-blue eyes that men found irresistible. Lucy's trim figure was the envy of her friends, but her fond mama knew that she compared herself unfavourably to Charlotte's ethereal appearance and felt awkward and ungainly next to her. Lucy had been told she resembled her father, but since that gentleman had died when she was still a baby, she could only verify this by studying the portrait of the late Mr Chambers that hung in the dining-room. True, they had the same light-brown hair, not at all as fashionable as Charlotte's guinea-gold curls. There was also a similarity about the blue-grey eyes with their direct, faintly appraising gaze set under dark, naturally curving brows. Apart from this Lucy could trace no likeness. Had she ever thought to enquire, those who remembered her father could have told her that the resemblance was more marked than any portrait could show. It lay in the tilt of the head and enquiring look that Lucy gave when she was puzzled, in the way her blue-grey eyes would suddenly twinkle with merriment, or in the stubborn set of her chin when she was displeased. It was this obstinate look that now made Mrs Chambers sigh inwardly as she regarded her younger child.

She said patiently, 'My dear, when I brought Charlotte back with me from London, I explained to you that Mr Vanderley's attentions had been most marked. The fact

3

that he is to cut short his stay in Town, where everyone is revelling in the Peace Celebrations now that that monster Bonaparte is safely put away on Elba—well, that *he* should prefer a quiet country party at Stock House is a most encouraging sign. Charlotte has every expectation that when they meet again he will make her an offer. Surely you cannot wish to see your sister's happiness blighted because you will not accompany her on a short visit!'

Lucy shrugged. 'I do not see why Charlotte cannot go alone. She is after all a widow, not a girl in her first season.'

'That is just what I shall do, even though Mama says I must not, if you are so disagreeable as to refuse to come with me. And when I am the rich Mrs Vanderley, little sister, do not look to me to help you catch a husband!'

Mrs Chambers quickly put an end to what promised to be a prolonged argument by despatching Charlotte upon an errand. She then commanded Lucy to draw her chair closer that they might talk confidentially.

'It pains me to admit it, Lucy dear,' she began, choosing her words carefully, 'but despite being three years your senior, I am afraid that Charlotte is a little lacking in sense. I know many young women who manage their lives quite successfully and if Lairne had lived I have no doubt that Charlotte would have made him an excellent wife. However, we both know that she is quite unsuited to living alone.'

'She is a pea-goose,' stated Lucy bluntly.

'Let us just say that if I had not insisted that she return here to Templecombe when Lairne died, she would have been the target of every fortune-hunter in Town and heaven knows what might have become of her! So you must see, Lucilla, how anxious I am that she should contract a good marriage.'

'Is this a good match?' countered Lucilla. 'Tom says he's heard Dominic Vanderley is a notorious rake and never seen without an opera dancer on his arm—'

'Nothing of the kind!' Mrs Chambers interrupted her, flushing slightly. 'There has never been any scandal attached to his name, even though he has been a little wild, perhaps. But last season he did not look at another woman once he had seen Charlotte! Several people said to me it would be a match! And until Charlotte is off my hands once more, I cannot set about finding a suitable match for you!'

'Poor Mama! What a trial your daughters must be to you.'

'No, no, but you must see how much it would relieve my mind to know that you were looking after Charlotte. I know I can rely upon your good sense to prevent her from committing any gross folly.'

Lucilla's eyes widened. 'But Mama, whatever do you expect to happen to her at

Stock House? I thought Lord and Lady Cornholme were most respectable—'

'Of course they are!' Mrs Chambers agreed hastily, looking uncomfortable. 'I would not for the world have accepted an invitation from them if they were not of the highest respectability, but Mr Vanderley is no callow youth: he is very much a man of the world and it would not do for him to think Charlotte is unchaperoned . . .'

'You are afraid he might try to bed her rather than wed her!'

'Lucilla! I vow I blush to hear such words on your lips! I daresay you pick up these things from the stables, but I would thank you to remember that you are a young lady and not some low serving wench! Pray let me have no more of this behaviour, or I shall close down the stables and have all the horses sold!'

Knowing this to be an empty threat, Lucilla was not much troubled by her mother's words, but she immediately begged pardon.

'I will *try* to guard my tongue, Mama, but that was indeed what you meant, was it not? Charlotte herself told me Mr Vanderley is considered by some to be dangerous . . .'

'I am sure his intentions towards Charlotte are strictly honourable,' said her mama uneasily, 'but you must admit that your sister is very beautiful, and when passions are running high . . .' she trailed off, spreading her hands expressively.

6

'You need not fear, Mama. I will go to Stock House with Charlotte and I will make it clear to her beau that he can expect nothing from her until she is his wife!'

Mrs Chambers looked anything but reassured by this, but apart from begging Lucy to be sensible, she said nothing more, merely advising her to go and make her peace with Charlotte.

*   *   *

'So you see Tom, we are to go to the Cornholmes after all, and I am to be Charlotte's chaperon!'

Lucilla had ridden over to Mirlow Hall early the following morning and poured out the whole story to her life-long friend. The squire and his wife had welcomed Lucy in their usual friendly way and directed her to the hay-barn, where she found their only son inspecting a new litter of pups from one of his gun-dogs. Tom Bancroft was a fresh-faced youth, scarcely a year older than Lucilla and he heartily entered into her feelings on the matter, although his first reaction to her announcement was scarcely flattering.

'*You,* a chaperon for Charlotte! Why, that's the oddest notion I've ever heard! You'll be in some devilish scrape before the week's out!'

'I will not!'

'Oh yes you will!' he declared frankly. 'Why

you're too shy to say boo to a goose, so how are you going to protect the ravishing Lady Lairne from all her admirers? I'll tell you what, Lucy, I don't wish to upset you, but that fall your mother had must have unsettled her mind.'

'Nothing of the sort, Tom Bancroft! Mama knows she can rely upon me to look after Charlotte. After all, I have reached my twentieth year; it's not as if I'm a baby, even if I have not yet been presented.'

Tom grinned. 'You've as much notion how to go on in society as that pup you are holding!'

Lucy's eyes flashed for a moment, then she laughed.

'You're right, and I'm not half so beautiful! Oh, I wish I was staying here with you, Tom, instead of having to go, but Mama is so worried that Charlotte will do something foolish if she is allowed to go to Stock House on her own!'

'Well, I don't see that. Charlotte's set on marrying him, and if this fellow is as besotted as you say he'll be planning to make her his wife—'

'Yes, but Mama's afraid marriage may not be uppermost in his mind.' Lucilla gave the little pup she was holding a kiss and placed it gently beside its mother, saying with a sigh, 'Oh, it is going to be the most tiresome visit! Short of hanging on to Charlotte's skirts I do not see that I will be able to watch her every minute of the day!'

* * *

'Come up, you sluggard!' Lucy brought her riding crop down heavily upon the mare's rump and the animal responded by breaking into a reluctant canter. After covering a short distance she allowed the creature to resume its favourite pace. As the horse walked on, Lucy gave a sigh of exasperation: if only she had brought her own mare she could have enjoyed riding here! She toyed with the idea of sending for her hack. After all, it was little more than thirty miles to Templecombe, but she decided against it. Mama would not appreciate the trouble or expense of sending another servant to Stock House with the mare. Also, she did not wish to give any offence to her hostess who had kindly offered her the loan of her own horse. She and Charlotte had been with the Cornholmes for three days: upon their arrival Charlotte had been disappointed to discover that Dominic Vanderley and his sister had not yet arrived, but since she was acquainted with almost everyone present, she was soon very much at home. Lucy however, not yet having experienced a season in London, knew no one, and although Lord and Lady Cornholme were extremely kind, Lucy's natural shyness made her feel awkward and uncomfortable amongst so many strangers. A chance remark led Lady Cornholme to offer Lucy the use of her own hack during her stay, which Lucy eagerly accepted and she was now trying out the mare. The other guests considered the hot weather too oppressive for riding and Charlotte had frowned at her sister's eagerness to go out, but Lucy was adamant: since Miss Vanderley and her brother were due to arrive at any moment she felt that this might be her only chance to enjoy herself before she took on the irksome task of chaperon to her elder sister. Lady Cornholme's suggestion that she should take a groom as her escort was politely but firmly rejected and, promising not to leave the Cornholme estate, Lucy rode out alone, happy to be free of company for a few hours.

It did not take Lucy long to realize that her hostess was no bruising rider. Lady Cornholme's hack was a placid, over-weight grey mare with a fixed idea of the proper pace for a lady. Despite this Lucy enjoyed exploring the park and surrounding countryside. Stock House was pleasantly situated amongst the hills between Bath and Bristol. The house itself nestled into the side of a hill, surrounded on three sides by rolling parkland and to the north by thick woods. The western side of the park was the most open, the smooth grass stretching up to the crest of the hill where a line of trees and bushes marked the boundary and the passage of a leafy road. Lucy had

10

skirted round this open space during her exploration, keeping to the boundary and within the cool shelter of the trees, but she now found herself at the western edge of the estate and, having decided it was time to head back to the stables, she set out across the broad expanse of grass. She pushed the mare on, determined to enjoy at least one gallop before going back. The mare lengthened her stride and Lucy felt the familiar thrill of the wind in her face as they sped over the ground. She was about to congratulate herself on her progress when the horse stumbled, lurched forward and Lucy was thrown to the ground. For a few seconds she lay still, gathering her disordered senses. She felt bruised and shaken, but nothing worse. She got up, furious with herself for her carelessness. The mare was standing a few yards off and, as Lucy approached, she threw up her head, ears pricked. Looking over her shoulder, Lucy saw a horse and rider coming towards her. She felt a flush of embarrassment as she realized that the stranger must have been travelling on the road and seen her fall. She turned her attention to the mare as the approaching hoof-beats slowed behind her.

'I saw what happened—are you hurt?'

Lucy shook her head. 'No, but I think the mare—her foreleg, there's blood—' She realized as she tried to speak how much the fall had shaken her.

'Let me look.'

The man jumped down from his horse and handed the reins to Lucy. She watched with approval as he slowly approached the mare, talking reassuringly to the animal as he bent to examine the leg. Lucilla could not resist an envious glance at the big black hunter standing patiently beside her. She put up a hand to smooth the glossy neck and was obliged to stifle the very uncharitable comparisons that sprang to her mind when she looked again at her borrowed hack. She took the opportunity of studying the stranger. He was very tall, his short black hair just visible beneath the edge of his curly-brimmed beaver. A coat of blue superfine fitted snugly over his broad shoulders and a snowy white cravat enhanced a naturally dark complexion. A more experienced eye would have seen at a glance that the stranger's coat came from Weston in Old Bond Street. Her sister could have told her that his plain dress was influenced by Brummell, one of the undoubted leaders of fashion, but Lucy saw only a country gentleman dressed neatly and without ostentation. She looked away quickly as he turned to her.

'Nothing broken, I think, but that's a nasty gash just above the fetlock. Most likely she kicked herself when she stumbled.'

Lucy pulled off her cravat and held it out. 'We could use this until I can get her back to the stable and treat her properly. Perhaps you would be good enough to do it for me. I hate to admit to such weakness, but my hands are shaking . . .'

'That's nothing to be ashamed of, 'tis merely the shock of taking a tumble. It will pass. You are very lucky, this dry weather has made the ground so hard you could have been badly injured by your fall. There'—he stood back to admire his handiwork—'that should hold until you get home. Do you have far to go?'

'I am staying at Stock House. The fence in the distance has a gate leading directly to the stables.' She handed him the reins of his horse, looking up at him for the first time. His aquiline features gave his face a stern, almost fierce appearance, but even as she thought this, the look softened and she was aware of a smile lurking in his brown eyes. Lucy put her head on one side and regarded him questioningly.

'You have grass in your hair,' he explained, reaching out to pull the offending greenery from her curls.

Lucy laughed. 'And dust on my skirts! I am well served. My hostess loaned me her mare and even if the animal is slow she does not deserve to be hurt! I should never have pushed her.'

'A sluggard is she?'

'A veritable snail!' agreed Lucy cordially. She caught up the mare's reins. 'Thank you for

13

your assistance, sir. I must go now if I am to be at Stock House in time for dinner.'

'Then allow me to accompany you as far as the gate, it is not far out of my way.' He fell into step beside her, leading his own horse. 'You are a guest at Stock House, you said; do you make a long stay?'

'For the month. My sister and I arrived a few days ago.'

'And are you enjoying your visit?'

'Mm, yes.'

He noticed her hesitation.

'But not entirely?'

'You see, I am not yet out,' she confided. 'I have not been into society before, only Mama insisted I accompany Charlotte because—well, never mind that! But while my sister knows everyone and just how to go on, I do not feel comfortable yet amongst so many strangers.'

He laughed. 'I am a stranger and we are getting along famously.'

'Yes, but this situation *is quite* different! You came to my assistance; how could I not talk to you? But to be constantly with people one does not know—I feel I can never relax! That is why I was so pleased to be alone for a few hours, especially today, when even more guests are expected and everyone is in a panic just because the gentleman is as rich as Croesus!'

'You sound very disapproving; do you dislike the fellow so much?'

'I have never met him, so I cannot say,

although if he really is the spoilt darling of society I cannot think that I *shall* like him! No, I disapprove of the way everyone talks of him, merely because of his wealth. If I were to believe all I have heard I should be expecting a veritable Adonis! Instead, he will most likely turn out to be an ageing roué! Oh dear—why do you laugh at me? Have I said something I shouldn't?'

'No, no, you have been most entertaining! But you see we have reached Stock House and the gate to the stables is just ahead of us, so I must take my leave of you.'

'Oh, will you not come in? I am sure if you come to the house with me Lady Cornholme will provide some refreshment for you!'

His eyes were alight with laughter, but he replied seriously, 'No, as tempting as it is I must decline your offer and be on my way. *Au revoir,* little one.' He swung nimbly into the saddle. 'Get the mare to her stable and be sure that leg is properly tended, then change into your prettiest gown before you greet your ageing roué!'

The stranger turned his horse and with a final wave he galloped off towards the road. Lucy watched until horse and rider had disappeared into the trees then she turned away to lead the mare across to the stable.

*   *   *

It was almost the dinner hour when Lucy returned to the bedchamber she shared with her sister. She found Charlotte sitting before her glass while Bracey, their maid, put the final touches to her coiffure. Charlotte's disapproving glance fluttered over Lucy.

'And just where have you been, miss? I expected you here a good hour since and have been imagining all sorts of accidents that might have befallen you!'

'I am sorry, Lady Cornholme's mare went lame and I was obliged to walk back. I had at last managed to get the animal to gallop and was just—'

Charlotte waved her hand impatiently, cutting her short. 'Never mind that now! Hurry up and change, or we shall be late for dinner!'

'Shall I fetch out the lemon sprigged muslin, Miss Lucy?' asked Bracey.

'Please do,' Lucy laughed. 'It is after all my *prettiest* dress!'

A severe look from her sister made Lucy stifle her merriment and she scrambled out of her dusty habit. She shot a mischievous look at Charlotte.

'I presume from the excellent equipage I saw in the stable yard that your beau has arrived?'

'Mr Vanderley is not my beau, I would never acknowledge such a vulgar term!' came the stiff reply. 'As a matter of fact Miss Vanderley arrived in the travelling carriage. Her brother

16

preferred to ride and had not arrived when I came up to change for dinner—as you would know if you had not taken it into your head to go galloping all over the country like a hoyden. As it is you had best hurry, or you will crown your incivility by keeping everyone waiting for their dinner!'

While Charlotte tastefully arranged the folds of a fine silk shawl across her arms, Bracey helped Lucy into a muslin gown of pale cream sprigged with tiny lemon flowers and caught in with a lemon sash at the high waistline. The maid did her best to arrange Lucy's tangled curls into order while that young lady hung a locket around her neck on a length of yellow ribbon. Charlotte cast a critical glance over her sister.

'Very suitable, miss, if I may say so,' remarked Bracey, nodding approvingly. 'Yellow was always your colour. Now Miss Charlotte—Lady Lairne I *should* say!—could never wear it, not with her pink and white complexion, but the new blue silk is most becoming, my lady.'

Bracey's judgement on matters of colour was beyond question, and such praise from the old retainer brought a flush of pleasure to Charlotte's cheeks.

'Thank you, Bracey. I cannot deny it is good to be able to wear colours again. My widow's weeds were so dull! Goodness, look at the time! Come, Lucy, or we shall be late!'

17

She flew out of the room with Lucy hurrying to keep up. As they made their way downstairs, Lucy noticed an unusual amount of activity in the hall below. Footmen dashed across the floor with an assortment of trunks and portmanteaux of various shapes and sizes. She wondered idly about the owner of such a mountain of luggage as she followed her sister to the drawing-room, where the rest of the party was already assembled. Charlotte stopped short just inside the doorway. Lucy glanced an enquiry then followed her sister's eyes towards a tall, willowy young man at the very centre of the room. Her critical gaze swept over the gentleman. He was dressed in the very height of fashion, his golden curls arranged in a careful semblance of disarray, the starched points of his collar reaching almost to his cheekbones and beneath his chin frothed the snowy folds of his intricately tied cravat. A bronze-green waistcoat gleamed from beneath the dark coat whose padding imperfectly concealed a pair of rather narrow shoulders, while his canary-yellow pantaloons and gleaming, tasselled Hessians encased legs that Lucy thought too long and thin to be considered shapely.

'Good gracious!' exclaimed Lucy. 'Surely that cannot be the notorious Mr Vanderley!'

'Of course not!' hissed Charlotte. 'How can you be so absurd? For all his wealth, Dominic Vanderley is certainly no leader of fashion!

Hush now, he has seen us!'

The elegant gentleman was bearing down upon them, holding up an eyeglass to observe the young ladies as he approached, his long face wreathed in smiles. Lucy was amazed to find her sister graciously returning his greeting and holding out her hand to him in the friendliest manner.

'Lady Lairne—your most obedient servant!' The gentleman made an elegant bow before fixing his pale-blue eyes once more upon the countess. 'When I discovered your destination I immediately cancelled my engagements, packed my bags and *voilà*, I am here, you see!'

'Indeed, Mr Collingham, this is a most delightful surprise! But how can this be? You made no mention of your visit here when we last met in Town.'

'Ah, then I did not know it was your intention to be here, ma'am! But Lady Cornholme is my aunt, you see, so I came down today. Got here scarce an hour since, in fact, with only one change of clothes to my name.' He waved his hands, inviting them to observe his dress as he said thoughtfully, 'However, I think it will do . . . I only hope the coach with my luggage has arrived! Of course, our dear hostess was delighted to see me. I knew she would not object to putting me up for a few nights. After all, what is one guest more or less amongst so many?'

Remembering the harassed servants

19

struggling to clear the hall, Lucy felt inclined to challenge this view, but she held her peace. Charlotte drew Lucy forward and performed the introduction, explaining to her sister that Mr Arthur Collingham was an acquaintance she had made in London during her last visit there.

'Oh come, ma'am, more than an acquaintance, surely!' protested the gentleman. 'We are firm friends now, are we not?'

The countess blushed, simpered and acknowledged the friendship, and after a few more minutes Mr Collingham sauntered off to give other guests the benefit of his delightful conversation.

'Goodness, what a strange man!' breathed Lucy, watching his retreating form with wide-eyed wonder.

'Nonsense, Lucy, if you had been to Town you would realize that Mr Collingham is a most accomplished gentleman and considered by many to be the current leader of fashion, let me tell you! He is also a most exquisite dancer. It is considered quite an honour to be chosen as his partner.' The countess lowered her eyes modestly and fluttered her fan. 'We have stood up together for many a dance, and I know our appearance has been most favourably remarked.'

'There is no difficulty about that!' replied Lucy. 'You are both so fair I've no doubt you make a perfect couple,' she broke off to greet

Lady Cornholme.

'So, you have met my nephew,' remarked their hostess, smiling. 'I know Lady Lairne is already acquainted with him, but I wonder, Lucy, if you will give me your opinion of the young man?'

Lucy felt the colour rising in her cheeks.

'I should be afraid to do so, ma'am, upon such short acquaintance. But he does seem very—very elegant!' she stammered.

Lady Cornholme's eyes twinkled merrily. 'Well said, my dear! But I have no doubt he will add a certain lustre to our gathering. Would you not agree, my dear sir?' she addressed her husband, who had come up behind her. The gentleman made a wry face.

'Are you speaking of Arthur? A silly young coxcomb, in my opinion, but he's harmless enough and he has a good heart beneath all that frippery!' He beamed down upon the sisters. 'But you, my dears, are a completely different matter! How lovely you both look! I heard of your tumble this afternoon, Lucilla. I trust you did not hurt yourself?'

'Not a bit, sir, but I am sorry to have lamed the mare.'

Lord Cornholme waved away her apologies.

'Put it out of your mind, child. My head groom was most impressed with the way you strapped up that cut. Most impressed!'

'Oh, but I didn't—'

'Lucy!' cried Charlotte, mortified. 'You did

21

not doctor the horse yourself!'

'She did, and expertly too!' laughed their host, 'But there was no need for you to trouble yourself. My grooms would have attended to the whole.'

'Pray do not think it any trouble for Lucy!' put in Charlotte with an angry titter. 'My sister likes nothing better than to be working in the stables alongside the grooms!'

Noting Lucy's embarrassment, Lady Cornholme quickly tried to heal the breach.

'I think it is admirable, my dear,' she told Lucy. 'Since you are so fond of riding it is very sensible to know how to look after your horses, especially so with your poor mama a widow and no one to keep household. But I am forgetting my duties as a hostess! I must introduce Lucy to our other new guests! Miss Vanderley and her brother arrived while you were out, my love. They were obliged to remain in Town for the jubilee celebrations on the first of the month, I believe it was almost a Royal command! Come along, my dears.' She led Lucy and Charlotte across the room to Miss Vanderley, who was one of a large, chattering group. The crowd parted as Lady Cornholme approached and Lucy saw that Miss Vanderley was a tall, vivacious brunette with a pair of lively dark eyes and a ready smile. She looked vaguely familiar and, as her hostess performed the introductions, Lucy wondered if they had met before. Then Lady

Cornholme's voice interrupted her thoughts.

'Come, child, there is someone else you must meet! Mr Vanderley, may I present to you Lady Lairne's younger sister, Miss Lucilla Chambers.'

Lucy turned to greet the gentleman, but the polite words she had planned died on her lips as she found herself looking up into the wickedly teasing eyes of Mr Dominic Vanderley, for he was none other than the stranger who had come to her aid that afternoon.

TWO

Only for a moment Lucy hesitated, then a gleam just as mischievous as the gentleman's twinkled in her own eyes. Mr Vanderley took her hand between his own lean fingers.

'Miss Chambers and I met earlier today,' he announced, 'although I regret that I was unable to render her more than the most trifling assistance.'

Charlotte looked surprised. 'You said nothing of this to me, Lucy.'

Obedient to the pressure on her fingers, Lucy remained silent. Mr Vanderley smiled at the countess.

'Good evening, Lady Lairne. No need to ask how you go on. You are looking more beautiful than ever.'

He greeted Charlotte with an easy familiarity, but Lucy detected none of the blatant admiration that characterized Arthur Collingham's attentions. Charlotte inclined her head, accepting the compliment as her due, but her tone was disapproving as she spoke again to her sister.

'Really, Lucilla, I do think you could have told me . . .'

'Our meeting was so brief we did not introduce ourselves.' Mr Vanderley bent an apologetic look upon Lucy. 'Miss Chambers had no idea of my identity, although when I learned that she was a guest here I regret to say that I fell prey to the temptation of surprising her—a trick for which I hope she will forgive me?'

Lucy could not suppress a smile. She realized he was still holding her fingers and she blushed, pulling her hand free.

'Willingly, sir, since you proved to be so useful to me!'

Charlotte became impatient for this interchange to end: she found she did not care to have her little sister the centre of attention.

'Well, I for one am quite tired of hearing about Lucy's adventures,' she remarked. 'Since it resulted in injury to Lady Cornholme's hack I feel it does not reflect well upon her.'

'Pshaw, nonsense!' cried Lord Cornholme, overhearing this. 'Such an accident could happen to anyone. My only regret is that I have nothing else in my stable suitable for a lady to ride.'

'If I might be permitted to offer a suggestion.'

All eyes turned to Mr Vanderley.

'I have amongst my horses a suitable mount for a lady. I brought her for my sister's pleasure; however, I am sure that Judith would be only too pleased to share her with Miss Chambers.'

'Oh no!' cried Lucy, 'I couldn't possibly—'

Charlotte, realizing that Mr Vanderley's offer had been made purely for her sake, gave him her warmest smile.

'It is very kind of you, sir, to honour my little sister in this way, but I am sure she could not be happy taking Miss Vanderley's horse.'

'But she would be doing me a service,' put in Judith Vanderley, smiling at Lucy. 'I do not care to ride very often, you see, and you know how restive a spirited horse can be if she is left eating her head off in the stable.'

'If—if you think I can be trusted,' stammered Lucy, looking up at Mr Vanderley and blushing furiously.

'I am sure of it,' he told her gravely. 'I was watching you today, before your horse put her foot in that rabbit hole. But perhaps we should ride out together tomorrow and I will give you my final judgement afterwards!'

* * *

Lucy sat through dinner in a daze of happiness. From what she had seen of Mr Vanderley's own horse she had no doubt that the mare she was to borrow would provide her with an excellent ride. Charlotte too was in good spirits. She felt that Mr Vanderley's generosity was a further example of his affection for herself, and when the ladies retired to the drawing-room, she attached herself to Miss Vanderley and conversed with her until the gentlemen joined them. After that there was little time for conversation. The young ladies were persuaded to show their talents upon the pianoforte. Charlotte was happy to oblige and, as she took her place at the instrument, Miss Vanderley beckoned to Lucilla to sit beside her.

'The countess plays well.'

Lucy nodded. 'She has a lovely singing voice, too. No doubt you heard her sing in London, Mr Vanderley?' She looked around at the gentleman, who had drawn up a chair beside them.

'I might have done, but I hear so many.'

His sister rapped his hand with her fan.

'Dominic! Where are your manners?'

'You know I have none, Ju!' he answered with a grin. When she turned her attention once more to the music, he murmured to Lucilla, 'Is that your *prettiest* dress, Miss

26

Chambers?'

Her eyes danced. 'I believe it is a style that appeals to the more *mature* gentleman, sir.'

'Good God, then I must be older than I thought!'

Lucy laughed and Miss Vanderley looked at them suspiciously.

'What is this?' she demanded. 'What joke are you sharing?'

Lucy shook her head, her eyes brimming with laughter, but she was saved from giving an explanation by being called at that moment to take her turn at the piano. She hesitated, her natural reserve making her nervous of performing in front of so many people, but to refuse would be ill-mannered, and not to be thought of. As if sensing her reluctance, Mr Vanderley gave her a reassuring smile.

'Go along, child. Forget the strangers. Play for your friends here!'

He watched her walk away, a little smile still playing about his mouth.

'Come, Dominic. Nursery charms are not for you!'

'Of course not, Judith,' he agreed. 'I am merely enjoying an amusing interlude.'

'And does it amuse you to lend the child my mare?'

'A chivalrous whim, nothing more. You did not object to it.'

She laughed. 'I deduced from the way you pinched my arm that you did not want me to

27

do so! What is it, Dom, a way to ingratiate yourself with the sister?'

'Lady Lairne is undoubtedly a piece of perfection,' he admitted, 'and we enjoyed a pleasant dalliance in Town, but you can scarcely have spent an evening in her company without learning that she hasn't an ounce of wit.'

'I am well aware of it!' replied Judith feelingly. 'Her Ladyship was at my side as soon as we left the dinner-table! Everyone knows Lairne was bowled over by her beauty. Old men can be such fools!'

'Luckily he had the good sense to die before he could get bored with his pretty little ingénue.'

'Rumour has it that you are thinking of filling his shoes.'

Dominic grimaced. 'God forbid! A little flirtation—mayhap even a brief *affaire de coeur*, but I have no plans to marry anyone, least of all a brainless beauty or even—before your suspicious mind can think it, my dear—even her not-so-brainless sister!'

*   *   *

Much to her surprise, the addition of Mr and Miss Vanderley to the house party greatly increased Lucy's enjoyment. Miss Vanderley's friendly manner helped Lucy to overcome her shyness and she began to feel less overshadowed by her sister's beauty. This new-found confidence and the prospect of an enjoyable ride the following day sent Lucy to bed that night with a glow of happy expectation. Charlotte, too, was delighted by the success of the evening. When Bracey had finished helping them both to undress and had seen them safely into bed, Charlotte lay upon her pillows, recounting to Lucy every instance of Mr Vanderley's affections.

'When I write to Mama in the morning I think I can quite safely assure her that a proposal is imminent,' she concluded. 'There could be no mistaking his attentions.'

'Are you sure?' asked Lucy, a note of doubt in her voice. She was very conscious of her promise to her mama and had studiously observed Mr Vanderley's behaviour towards Charlotte. 'I thought Mr Vanderley divided his time mostly between the gentlemen and his sister this evening.'

'What a little innocent you are!' Charlotte gave an indulgent laugh. 'Of course he could not single me out too blatantly; that would give rise to just the sort of gossip that is abhorrent to a gentleman of such breeding and sensibility.'

'But Mama said he flirted outrageously—'

'That was in London, where manners are very different! Goodness, Lucy, how you do take one up!'

'Well, I thought Arthur Collingham was

your most attentive courtier tonight, Charlotte. Doubtless you find his compliments a little tedious, but it was very amusing, watching him follow you around like a hopeful puppy!'

'It is not very kind of you to make fun of Mr Collingham!'

Lucy blinked. 'I am sorry. I meant no harm.'

'Very well, but you will soon come to grief if you mean to laugh in that childish way at everyone you meet. Please try to remember that you are not in the school-room now, Lucilla, and act with a little more dignity.'

Miss Chambers realized that her sister was more than a little put out by her jesting and immediately begged pardon. Charlotte accepted the apology and for a few moments silence reigned in the bedroom before the countess returned to her favourite theme.

'Of course, I shall have to give up my title if I decide to marry Dominic Vanderley, but I shall not object to it. Lairne's family will be quite pleased to be rid of me, I should think, for they never liked the match.'

'Are you in love with him, Charlotte?'

'With whom? Mr Vanderley? Heavens, Lucy, what has that to say to anything?'

'How can you marry him if you do not love him?'

Charlotte tittered. 'Lord, Lucilla, people do not marry for love! Dominic Vanderley would be an excellent match. Any number of caps have been thrown at him, for he is very rich.'

'But so too are you very rich,' Lucy pointed out. 'Mama told me that Lairne's settlement was very generous, so you do not need to marry a wealthy man.'

Charlotte thought this argument quite unworthy of comment.

'It is as much in your interest as mine to hope that he will make me an offer,' she told Lucy. 'As Mrs Vanderley I shall be one of the foremost hostesses in Town and you, my dear Lucy, will be able to make your debut in society under my aegis.' She yawned. 'Who knows, with a little town bronze we may even be able to achieve a splendid match for you!'

Despite her sister's confidence, Lucy's doubts remained and her observations at the breakfast-table the following morning did nothing to alleviate them. She could see nothing in Mr Vanderley's manner to suggest that he favoured Charlotte above any of the other ladies present. By contrast, Mr Collingham was most attentive to Lady Lairne, hovering while she made her selection from the array of dishes on the side tables, escorting her to her chair and pulling his own closer before pouring coffee for the lady. Charlotte thrived upon his assiduous attentions, turning her huge cornflower eyes towards the gentleman and thanking him prettily for his efforts. Even this blatant show of interest by the elegant Mr Collingham did not have any noticeable effect upon Mr Vanderley. He continued to enjoy his breakfast without any signs of jealousy. Lucy silently concluded that Mama and her sister had made too much of his attentions in Town. However, all such thoughts vanished from her mind when the gentleman reminded her that she had promised to ride out with him.

'It promises to be another fine day, Miss Chambers. It would perhaps be best to set out soon before the heat becomes uncomfortable.'

Lucy laid aside her knife and fork.

'If you will allow me a few minutes to change my dress, sir, I will gladly come with you. That is—Charlotte, you do not mind?'

Lady Lairne waved her away.

'Not at all, Lucilla. Lady Cornholme has promised to show me some fashion plates she has received from Town, so I shall not need you.'

Their hostess looked a little concerned.

'You do not think someone should ride with them . . .'

'I am sure you would not ask Lady Lairne to go out on such a day,' put in Mr Collingham earnestly. 'The sun is at its strongest at this time of the year and would be most injurious to the countess's fair skin.' He added, frowning at Mr Vanderley, 'I wonder that anyone should consider riding out on what promises to be a very hot day.'

Lucilla wanted to cry out against this threat

to her proposed treat, but shyness prevented her. As for Mr Vanderley, apart from a brief, contemptuous glance at the gentleman, he ignored the interjection and addressed himself directly to his hostess.

'If you are concerned for the proprieties, ma'am, my groom will be in attendance.'

Lady Cornholme was not completely reassured, but she said no more and Lucy went off to her room to change into her riding habit. Less than twenty minutes later she was accompanying Mr Vanderley to the stables, her muslin morning gown replaced by a serviceable sage-green velvet skirt and short-waisted jacket. Lady Lairne would not have stepped out in such a plain dress, which showed evident signs of much wear, but Lucy paid little thought to her appearance, her interest fixed upon the forthcoming ride.

'Accept my compliments, Miss Chambers,' said the gentleman, as they walked to the stables, 'there are few women of my acquaintance who could have changed so quickly.'

'I had Bracey put everything out in readiness,' she admitted. 'I would have worn it down to breakfast, but I thought you might have changed your mind and not wish to be reminded of our ride.'

'That would be a very ungentlemanly thing to do.'

'Yes, but I would quite understand if you

were regretting your offer. Tom is forever promising something, then wishing he had not.'

'Tom?'

'Tom Bancroft, our neighbour's son at Templecombe. He is so good-natured that he is always putting himself at other people's service, when very often that is not what he wants to do at all! I think he would do better to have a little resolution. People tend to take advantage of a generous nature, do they not, Mr Vanderley?'

'Not being blessed with a, ah—generous nature, I could not say.'

Miss Chambers accepted this without comment and after a moment her companion asked her if she was missing her friend Mr Bancroft.

'Heavens yes!' she replied wistfully. 'At Templecombe we can be out riding every day, never worrying how muddy it is, or whether we will be late for a meal—' She broke off and glanced up at him guiltily. 'That sounds most ungrateful. You must think me very rag-mannered.'

'Not at all. You are fortunate to have such a companion.'

'I know it. We are very much like brother and sister, for we have known each other forever.' She chuckled and added mischievously, 'Charlotte wanted Mama to stop us seeing each other, for she is afraid we will fall in love and that would spoil Mama's plans to take me to London and achieve a good match! Thankfully, Mama has more sense. She knows Tom and I will only ever be very good friends.'

They walked through the archway leading to the yard where Sultan, Mr Vanderley's big hunter was tethered and the groom was leading out a pretty long-tailed grey mare that side-stepped daintily as they approached.

'Well, do you like her?'

Lucy's shining eyes gave him the answer. Waving aside the mounting block he threw her up into the saddle, watching appreciatively as she handled the mare's playful dancing.

'She's beautiful!' declared Lucy. 'What do you call her?'

'Snowfire. Judith's choice, not mine!'

'It is a lovely name for her. I cannot thank you enough for allowing me to ride her: I will try to make sure you don't regret it.'

'From the little I have seen I am sure I will not. You sit well on the horse and your hands are very light. I would not have let you near her if I had not thought you a good horsewoman.'

Lucy blushed. 'Th-thank you, sir. I shall do my best not to let you down.'

He checked the girths and satisfied himself that she was settled comfortably in the saddle before mounting his own horse. They set off across the park with Mr Vanderley's groom at a discreet distance, keeping to a steady pace until they were clear of the trees. Then, with the lightest touch from his master, the big black lengthened his stride to a gallop and Lucy followed on, marvelling at the way the little mare flew over the ground. When at last they drew rein they had reached the park palings and a small gate that took them through to the open fields beyond. Mr Vanderley looked back, his brows raised questioningly.

'She's wonderful,' enthused Lucy, 'I have a lovely bay hack of my own at home, but nothing to compare to Snowfire. She is so light on her feet, and very fast!'

'She needs to be to keep up with Sultan. Judith and I have enjoyed many a gallop on these two, but with the ground so hard and dry we won't overtax them today.' He pointed down the hill. 'I believe there is a ford across the river a few miles in that direction. If we head that way we can rest the horses there before we turn back to Stock House.'

They set their horses on the downhill track. The sun was almost overhead and there was very little shade until they reached the valley road, where the river flowed gently along between tree-lined banks.

'The air feels cooler here by the river. It's a pity those branches are too low to ride in the shade.

'Well, it is certainly too hot in the sun!'

declared Lucy. Slipping from the saddle she led the grey mare into the shade. With a laugh, Dominic Vanderley followed her example and they strolled along the riverbank to the ford, where the groom took charge of the horses while Lucy and her companion rested under a shady tree.

'Do you know, Miss Chambers, I feel I have been gravely misled. I was informed you were a very quiet, reserved young lady.'

Lucy looked up quickly and was relieved to note a faint but definite gleam in his dark eyes, belying his stern countenance.

'Oh dear, ought I not to have dismounted? I thought there could be no harm in it, to rest in the shade for a while.'

'But are you not alarmed, to be here alone with me?'

'Don't be silly,' she laughed at him. 'What possible harm can there be in it?'

He studied her face, an enigmatic look in his eyes.

'I might make love to you.'

'You might try,' she said cordially, 'but I see no reason at all why you should!'

'Has this young neighbour of yours—Tom, is it?—has he never tried to flirt with you?'

'No, of course not. Why on earth should he?'

'I do not see that any man could be in the company of a pretty young lady and *not* do so.'

She laughed. 'Is that what you are doing

now, sir, flirting with me? It is very kind of you, but I would as lief you did not, for I would much prefer to talk sensibly with you. Tom is scarcely a year older than I am and we have known each other forever, I expect that is why he has never flirted with me. Besides, he wishes to join the army. His papa is very much against it, however, and now that Bonaparte is beaten, I expect Tom will be persuaded to stay at home and look after the farm.'

'I have a younger brother who is also army-mad. He is in the Guards.'

'Do you worry about him?'

'Judith does the worrying for all of us!' he returned lightly. 'But even she can be easy for the moment. He is on furlough in London, enjoying himself with the ladies!'

'A family trait, I suspect!'

'Yes, but much easier for Giles, since he is considered the handsome one of the family.'

'But your wealth, Mr Vanderley, makes you *extremely* attractive!'

He threw back his head, laughing.

'Miss Chambers, you are very different from your sister!'

Lucy sighed. 'I know it. Charlotte was ever the beauty of the family. It was no surprise to Mama when Lairne offered for her.'

'And does Mrs Chambers despair of you?'

'Constantly! She was almost relieved that it was not possible to take me to London last year. Poor Charlotte was still in mourning for

Lairne you see, and Mama thought it would be best to wait, but she says I must make my come-out next year, for I shall be twenty in March.'

'In your dotage, in fact!'

'Exactly!' agreed Lucy, her eyes dancing. 'Mama will take me to Town and if I am not respectably settled by the end of the season she says she will wash her hands of me! She need not worry, though, for Charlotte has promised that she will take me under her wing once she is—settled.' She ended lamely, but if her companion noticed her sudden confusion he did not show it, but merely ordered her to get up. She looked up at him questioningly.

'I pray you, Miss Chambers, stand up,' he repeated, nodding approvingly as she obeyed him. 'That's better. Hmm . . . Walk towards the water, then turn—that's a good girl.'

She did as she was told, turning at the water's edge to look at him, a mixture of laughter and puzzlement in her face. He met her eyes, a decided gleam in his own.

'I think your mama is wrong to despair of you, Miss Chambers. Undoubtedly your sister is an exquisite creation—one of the most beautiful women of my acquaintance, in fact— but you have no need to hide in her shadow. Your figure is good, your carriage excellent and your face, not classically beautiful, perhaps, but pretty enough.'

She laughed and dropped a mock curtsy.

'Why, sir, I am overwhelmed by this! So you think I shall pass muster?'

'More than that,' he replied, smiling at her in a way that gave her a strange, light sensation inside, 'you have something your sister lacks. Spirit. Spirit and charm.'

Lucy laughed again, but this time with less certainty. The warm glow in the gentleman's eyes made her pulses race. However, before she could ponder too deeply upon her companion's enigmatic mood, it had passed, and he was on his feet, suggesting that they should continue their ride.

They took the homeward journey at a steady pace, for the full heat of the day now made hurrying a dusty and uncomfortable process. Despite this, she was surprised how quickly the time passed for they soon reached the park, riding gratefully into the shade offered by the long avenue of trees that bordered the drive. She sighed.

'Tired, Miss Chambers?'

'No. A little sad that so enjoyable an outing has to come to an end.'

'I am flattered, but this need not be our only ride. There will be other times.'

Yes, thought Lucy. When you are married to Charlotte, doubtless I shall be permitted to ride with my brother-in-law.

For some reason this picture failed to please her and she brushed it aside, forcing a brief smile.

'Yes, of course.'

When they reached Stock House, Mr Vanderley accompanied his groom to the stables with the horses, leaving Lucy to enter the house alone. She flew up to her room to change out of her dusty habit, informing Bracey who was waiting to help her that it was the best day she had spent at Stock House.

*   *   *

A hot humid night was followed by a grey day, with heavy clouds hanging low over the house, threatening rain. Fearing a sudden downpour, Lady Cornholme was reluctant for Lucy to go out and all thoughts of riding had to be abandoned. She joined her sister and the other guests in the library, where books and conversation were the main entertainment. Watching Mr Vanderley, Lucy could not detect anything but courtesy in his treatment of her sister, but she was uncomfortably aware of Charlotte's repeated attempts to draw the gentleman into conversation. In this she was not entirely successful, and Lucy noted with some relief that Arthur Collingham's willingness to step into the breach prevented Charlotte from feeling hardly treated and kept the countess in a sunny mood. By dinnertime the rain clouds had cleared, giving way to a rosy sunset that promised well for the following day. Lord Cornholme announced

41

that if the dry weather held, they should take the carriages to Lansdown and dine *al fresco*. The suggestion met with universal agreement and, as the candles were lit and the curtains pulled against the clear night sky, Mr Vanderley came up to Lucilla, saying, 'It would seem, Miss Chambers, that we may be able to ride again tomorrow.'

'It is your sister's mare, sir. I am reluctant to usurp her pleasure—'

'You may take her with my goodwill,' Judith Vanderley came up, smiling. 'Dominic's suggestion that I should use the carriage is much more to my liking.'

'Really, Judith, I think our hostess deserves the credit for that idea, not I.'

'Nonsense, 'twas your golden tongue convinced Lady Cornholme to arrange it so!' retorted Miss Vanderley. She turned back to Lucy. 'Is it not a splendid idea? Those of you who wish to use your energies getting hot and dusty may ride and the rest of us will make a more comfortable journey by chaise.'

The general chorus of approval from the other guests set the seal on the proposed trip and Lucy, unaccountably relieved that she would not be riding out alone with Mr Vanderley, retired to her chamber to look forward to the treat.

The following day dawned clear and sunny. Talk at the breakfast-table centred on the forthcoming outing and Lady Cornholme confirmed that everything was in readiness for their departure. Lord Cornholme and most of the gentlemen decided to ride, but although a number of ladies had brought their own hacks to Stock House, only three elected to use them, the others preferring to take their ease in the open carriages. Charlotte was a nervous rider and knew she did not show to advantage in the saddle. Even if a suitable mount could have been found for her she would have refused it—it was much more satisfying to choose from her numerous gowns one that would become her and be most suitable for dining out of doors. After much deliberation she chose a high-waisted dress of powder-blue cotton and a wide-brimmed straw bonnet secured under the chin with a bow of blue ribbon to match her eyes. Dainty sandals and a lace parasol completed the picture and when Mr Collingham remarked to Lucy that the countess was looking more beautiful than ever, Lucy could only agree with him. Mr Collingham's dress of yellow pantaloons, striped waistcoat and lime-green coat proclaimed the fact that he would be travelling in one of the carriages: Lucy did not doubt which particular carriage he would prefer. The party was gathered in the hall and, glancing at her companions, Lucilla noted the bright summer gowns and dashing riding habits of the other ladies. Compared to these Lucy suddenly felt that her own riding dress was very plain. Bracey had coaxed her hair to fall in glossy ringlets beneath the brim of her hat and helped her to arrange the snowy folds of her cravat beneath her chin, but even so she could not believe the others would think of her as anything more than a poor little dab of a girl. She gave herself a mental shake: she was becoming as vain as Charlotte! When had it ever mattered to her how she appeared? The horses were brought round at that moment and all other thoughts were banished from her mind. She settled herself upon Snowfire and brought the mare alongside the open carriage that Charlotte was sharing with Miss Vanderley and Mr Collingham. The gentleman lifted his hat in a salute as she rode up.

'Ah, Miss Chambers. Your energy puts us all to shame!'

'Lady Lairne was telling me how much you love to ride,' said Judith, leaning forward. 'I must say you look very much at home on Snowfire.'

'I am,' smiled Lucy. 'She is so sweet-natured, how can you bear to let anyone else ride her?'

Charlotte gave her sister a superior smile.

'I am sure, Lucy, that when you are a little older you will realize that it is much more graceful to be at one's ease in a carriage.'

Since less than three years separated the sisters, Lucy found this speech highly amusing, and when she saw the answering twinkle in

44

Judith Vanderley's eyes she was obliged to smother the bubble of laughter welling up within her. With a brief word of farewell she drew the mare away to take her place with the other riders at the rear of the cavalcade.

* * *

The party set off shortly before noon, the carriages leading the way down the twisting road to the foot of Stock Hill. This brought them on to the main Bath road, but it had been decided that they would turn away from Bath to skirt around the hill and approach Lansdown from the west. It was not to be expected that all those on horseback would be satisfied with the sedate pace of the carriages, and while a few of the gentlemen gallantly agreed to act as escort, the other riders set off across country.

'Now, Miss Chambers, we may gallop the fidgets out of these animals!'

Mr Vanderley brought Sultan alongside and Lucy laughed, revelling in the feel of the fresh breeze on her face. The horses settled into a steady gallop across the open fields, the pace slackening only when their route took them on the long climb towards Lansdown. Lucilla was soon aware that she and Dominic Vanderley had outstripped the other riders, but as the black showed no signs of slowing she allowed Snowfire to follow on. They cantered upwards, coming to a walk as they climbed the final stretch that brought them on to the high level plain. Bringing his horse to a halt the gentleman glanced back.

'Tired, Miss Chambers, or will you race me to the trees in the distance? Unless I am mistaken, that is where our picnic is to take place.'

'Tired? Of course not!' declared Lucy, shooting past him. 'Catch us if you can!'

She set the mare galloping headlong across the turf, the wind tugging at her hair. She knew the black must be close behind, but she dare not look round. As she approached the trees, she heard the thunder of hooves above the drumming of the mare's pace and had the impression of a black cloud passing by as horse and rider overtook her. The race over, she slowed, laughing, as Mr Vanderley led the way towards a spreading chestnut where they could tether the horses. He jumped down and came over to help Lucy dismount. She kicked her foot free of the stirrup and slid down into his arms. As her feet touched the ground he did not release her but stood staring down into her face, an arrested look in his eyes. Lucy, exhilarated by the ride smiled up at him, exuding such an air of innocent confidence in his friendship that the intense look faded from his face. He let her go, drew her hand on to his arm and led her across to the picnic site where the servants were busy preparing refreshments. They were well in advance of the main party, but Mr Vanderley entertained his companion with well-practised ease until the rest of the party arrived.

*   *   *

Rugs had been spread out on the ground beneath the trees, which provided welcome shade from the sun. Mr Vanderley excused himself and went off to find his sister while Lucy sank down beside Charlotte.

'I knew how it would be if you rode today!' The countess frowned at her. 'You look a veritable hoyden, with your hair so dishevelled and your cheeks so red. Let me tell you, miss, that it is not at all becoming.'

'It was worth it for such a ride!' declared Lucy, her spirits undimmed. 'And what does it matter if I am a little untidy?'

'It matters to me,' pouted Charlotte. 'You are my sister, and I have no wish to be associated with such outlandish behaviour.'

Lucy begged pardon and sat back quietly to enjoy her own thoughts. Having delivered her homily, Charlotte gave her attention to the picnic. Lucy soon realized that her sister was in sparkling mood. She chattered happily with all those around her, but her brightest smiles were for Dominic Vanderley, whom she invited to sit beside her. Lucy thought she detected a slight reluctance on the part of the gentleman, but to refuse the invitation would be to offer an insult to Lady Lairne, and he dutifully took his place beside her. Watching her sister, Lucy was reminded of a queen holding court. Lucy's glance moved to Mr Collingham, who was sitting at the edge of the group with such a woebegone look upon his countenance that it was difficult not to smile. When they had all finished their meal, the party began to break up. A few moved off to stroll a little way across the down, enjoying the excellent views. Others stretched themselves beneath the trees and relaxed in the shade. Mr Vanderley made one of the latter group, but since Charlotte remained beside him, still chattering, Lucy thought his chances of a peaceful interlude quite small. Mr Collingham rose to his feet.

'Lady Lairne,' he addressed Charlotte hesitantly, 'I wonder—it is such a fine day—perhaps you would care to walk a little?'

Lucy's kind heart went out to the young man as Charlotte gave him a considering look.

'I think not, Mr Collingham. It is far too hot for me to venture out of the shade. You have said yourself that the sun can be so injurious to the complexion.'

'Ah yes, I see. Of course, ma'am. How thoughtless of me.'

He turned away, looking so dejected that Lucy jumped up, saying impulsively, 'I would very much like to walk, sir, if you would give me your arm!'

He bowed slightly and smiled, his good manners obliging him to hide his disappointment.

'Very well, Miss Chambers, but you have no parasol; shall I find one for you?'

'There is no need, sir,' she replied cheerfully. 'My complexion was ruined long ago, from all the riding that I do. A little more sun will not harm me!'

As she prepared to walk off with her escort, Lucy looked back to find Mr Vanderley smiling as he watched her from half-closed eyes. Her own ready smile appeared and when the gentleman winked at her in a most conspiratorial fashion she was obliged to look away to stop herself from laughing. Taking Mr Collingham's arm, she led him away from the trees and out across the short springy turf of the down. The gentleman knew his duty and did his best to entertain her with idle conversation, but when there was no danger of being overheard, she interrupted him.

'You should not allow my sister's behaviour to depress you, Mr Collingham.'

Immediately his face assumed its gloomy look.

'Ah, you noticed, then.'

She bit her lip. 'You looked a trifle . . . disappointed,' she told him gravely.

'I had hoped it was not so obvious,' he said. 'During the journey here Lady Lairne was so—so—'

'Flirtatious?' supplied Lucy, but the young man shook his head emphatically.

'Such an angel could never be that! No, she was charming and obliging—nothing could have exceeded her kindness towards me! Yet as soon as we arrived here . . . !' He paused, struggling against the violence of his emotions. As last he continued, 'I should not complain. It was most kind of your sister to allow me to share her carriage and I must not begrudge others a little of her company, but since we have been here—it is as though, as though I no longer exist for her!' he ended bitterly, the words being wrenched from him.

Lucy squeezed his arm. 'She is a wretch to treat you this way! It pains me to speak so of my own sister, but I fear she is making use of you, Mr Collingham.'

'Oh I know that,' he replied miserably.

'And you do not object?'

'How can one object to being of service to such a divine creature?'

Lucy was sceptical, 'Charlotte is nothing more than a pretty ninny-hammer!' she said bluntly.

'No, no, how can you say so! She is a great beauty, and—and quite adorable!'

'But there is very little behind her beautiful face. Because of her looks people let her behave exactly as she pleases! She has been terribly spoiled.'

'But I love her,' he said simply, 'and when it

comes to brains, well, I'm not one of your clever coves, Miss Chambers. I've acquired a little town polish over the last couple of years and I like to think that I am well-versed on matters of fashion, but I'll never amount to very much in the world, you know. I've a comfortable income, not a fortune you understand, like Vanderley, but enough to give your sister all the little luxuries she enjoys.'

'It seems to me, Mr Collingham,' said Lucy, startled, 'that you should be addressing all this to Charlotte, not to me!'

Her companion seemed to shrink, his shoulders hunched and he shook his head miserably.

'Useless!' he uttered. 'She has set her mind on Vanderley, damn him. If it were anyone else I would not feel so bitter, but Vanderley! Why, he's not a fit husband for any woman of delicacy! His affairs are notorious, always conducted in full view of Society! He is a most unsavoury character, Miss Chambers, with the most appalling manners! Sometimes I think I would like to call him to account. And I would do it too,' he added quickly, 'only I've no great liking for firearms and besides, he is accounted an excellent shot.'

'Then you must on no account call him out,' replied Lucy seriously. 'You must win Charlotte by your superior manners and—and little things, such as always being on hand when she needs you. She likes to be pampered

51

and cosseted, you know, with soft words and constant attentions.'

'Yes,' said her companion, brightening, 'and that's something I *can* do better than Dominic Vanderley! You are quite right, Miss Chambers. Thank you.'

Lucy smiled inwardly and wondered what her friend Tom would say if he could see her offering advice to this fashionable man about town. He would probably laugh, as he had done when she had told him why she had to come to Stock House—Lucy suddenly remembered her role of chaperon.

'Oh, heavens!'

'Is there anything wrong, Miss Chambers?'

'Yes—no, that is, I think perhaps we should be turning back!' She tried to sound calm, and forced herself to stroll back towards the trees where they had been sitting. Sympathy had made her offer to accompany Mr Collingham, but by doing so she had achieved the very thing she was meant to prevent, for Mr Vanderley was alone with her sister!

Lucy was relieved to note as they arrived back at the picnic site that Charlotte had been abandoned by her court. This suited Mr Collingham who, leaving Lucilla in the care of her hostess, immediately put his plans into action by providing the countess with an escort.

THREE

Lucilla saw very little of Dominic Vanderley on the return journey, for he devoted his attention to the other members of the party. However, as she did not expect him to dance attendance upon her, she was in no way disappointed. The sheer pleasure of the ride was enjoyment enough for her. The riders kept a more decorous pace beside the carriages as they rode back to Stock House, where the grooms were waiting on the gravelled drive. The gentlemen rode their horses on to the stables, and Lucy was about to do the same when a groom leapt forward to take the reins. Charlotte, alighting from her carriage, hissed a reminder to her sister to behave herself. Glancing round, Lucy realized that the other ladies had already dismounted. Reluctantly she handed Snowfire over to the groom and followed her sister into the house.

'My dears, I shall be glad to take to my bed for an hour!' declared a buxom young matron with laughing eyes. She turned towards Judith. 'I am exhausted from laughing at your audacious brother, Miss Vanderley. He rode beside our carriage for a good half the journey and kept us well amused with his teasing!'

'I hope you gave him a set-down,' replied Judith. 'I know he can be quite outrageous.'

'I am sure we all enjoy a little flirtation,' returned the matron, chuckling. 'Your brother is considered by some to be quite dangerous, but only by those gentlemen jealous of his success, or mothers of impressionable daughters! When a gentleman is as charming as Mr Vanderley I do not know who could have the heart to turn him away.'

Following them upstairs, Lucy smiled inwardly. This was surely a very different Dominic Vanderley to the easy companion who had entertained her so well that afternoon! She was grateful to him for his friendship which, considering the matter, she assumed was because he already thought of her as a sister.

*　　*　　*

The picnic at Lansdown was generally held to have been a great success and was only eclipsed as a topic of conversation by the forthcoming ball that Lady Cornholme had arranged to take place the following Friday, when those guests invited from the neighbouring houses would have the benefit of a full moon for their homeward journey. In the meantime, the hot, dry weather continued, scorching the fields where the last of the harvest was being gathered in. As the days passed, Lucy lost some of her shyness and happily brought out her drawing pad and pencils when she was invited to join a sketching party. It was soon discovered she had some ability at portraits, catching a likeness with just a few lines. The praise of her companions encouraged her to persevere and she found that sitting with pad and pencil was a pleasant way to pass the time, making lightning sketches of her fellow guests while they relaxed in the shady summer-house at the end of the rose garden.

'You have a real talent,' Lady Cornholme told her one evening, admiring a sketch Lucy had just finished of her sister. 'You have captured Lady Lairne beautifully.'

'We shall all be wanting our likeness drawn before the end of the month,' said Miss Vanderley, who was sitting beside Lucy as she worked. 'May I look through your sketchbook, Miss Chambers?'

Lucy handed it to her, flushing slightly.

'They are not perfect. I wish I had the ability to make a full and accurate likeness.'

Mr Vanderely had come up and was standing behind his sister's chair, looking over her shoulder at the sketches.

'You seem to have captured the spirit of your subjects,' he remarked. 'Your sister's rather fragile beauty, for example, and in this one, the hearty good-nature of our host is quite apparent. These are really very good.'

Lucy's flush deepened at his praise.

'Thank you. That is kinder than my poor

drawings deserve—'

'There's one of you, Dominic!' said Judith, coming to an unfinished sketch. It was merely a rough outline, but there could be no mistaking the lean, firm jaw-line, the hawkish look of the nose and eyes. Lucy put out her hand for the pad, but before Miss Vanderley could give it to her, her brother reached down and took it.

'Hmm, do I really look that severe, Ju?'

'Yes, occasionally, dear brother.' Judith realized that Lucy was looking most uncomfortable and she took the pad away from him.

'I am afraid I did not have time to complete it,' murmured Lucy, retrieving her property from Miss Vanderley with a grateful look.

'Well, I think you should,' replied Dominic, his dark eyes quizzing her. 'I should be quite happy to sit for you.'

Lucy murmured a few disjointed phrases as Charlotte came up and laid a proprietorial hand on Mr Vanderley's sleeve.

'Yes, but not now, my dear sir! You have promised to partner me at whist. Do you not remember?'

The little group moved away and Lucy was glad of a few moments alone to compose herself. The unexpected interest in her sketching was very gratifying, but Mr Vanderley's praise had disconcerted her. Perhaps he had been merely teasing her, but she hoped not, for she was surprised to discover how much she wanted his good opinion.

*   *   *

On the day of the ball, the ladies retired early to their rooms to recruit their energies for the forthcoming entertainment, while the servants bustled about, opening up the great ballroom, polishing the chandeliers and putting everything in readiness for the evening. Lucy felt no desire to sleep during the day, but such was the upheaval in the rest of the house that she spent the afternoon curled up on her bed reading a book while Charlotte slumbered, her face covered with an unappetising mixture of cucumber and crushed strawberries, held to be beneficial to fair skins. However, when Bracey arrived to help the sisters dress, she found Lucy reluctant to move.

'Do come along, Miss Lucy, there's a deal to do to make you both presentable for this evening.'

Lucy sighed. 'Do I have to go? I would as lief stay here.'

Charlotte, her face now cleansed of its beautifying pulp, gave a cry of horror.

'You cannot mean it, Lucy! Why, there are any number of people coming tonight, and Lord Cornholme has even arranged for an orchestra to be brought in from Bath! It will be such fun, and very good for you too, Lucy, to practise your dancing before Mama takes you to London next year.'

Lucy spread out her hands. 'But that is just the point!' she cried, 'I am not prepared for a party! By next year Mama will have arranged for me to have new dresses—'

'Ho, miss, and since when have you become so interested in your appearance?' Bracey interrupted her, smiling. 'You was always one who didn't care if she was dressed in rags!'

Lucy flushed. 'Well, nor do I care what I wear in general, but I did not realize—I am not ready for all this society! I only came because Mama insisted Charlotte should not come alone!' She added peevishly, 'if I had known that I would be expected to make a spectacle of myself in front of a host of strangers I should not have come!'

'Now that's childish nonsense, Miss Lucy, and well you know it!' retorted Bracey, adopting the tone she had used when they were recalcitrant infants. 'You dance very prettily, even if you have only done so in the company of your family and close friends, and your manners are perfectly good, when you choose to remember them! Come along now, let me help you into that pretty sprigged muslin and we will see if we can't do something with your hair.'

'I'll tell you what I shall do!' exclaimed Charlotte, in a mood of rare goodwill. 'I will let you wear my green silk. It has always been a trifle big for me and will fit you perfectly, I am sure.'

'Too big for you indeed!' snorted Bracey. 'Since you eat scarcely enough to keep a sparrow alive I'd not be surprised at it, but in truth the only fault is that the skirts are a little too long.'

'And just the right size for Lucy,' added Charlotte. She saw Bracey's doubtful face and added coaxingly, 'it is a very simple gown, and cannot be thought too old for her. In fact, Mama said only days before we left that I should give it to Lucy when she goes to Town next year. And the colour will suit her admirably.'

'It *would* suit you,' murmured Bracey, thoughtfully regarding her younger mistress.

'And I will lend her my pearls to finish it off,' declared Charlotte handsomely. 'There cannot be the least objection to that!'

Bracey nodded. 'Very well, Miss Lucy,' she stated. 'If you will rid yourself of that sulky look that doesn't become you in the least, I will bring in My Lady's green silk.'

'Don't worry, Lucy, you will do very well,' Charlotte coaxed her. 'I remember how nervous I felt at my first grown-up ball, but I know you will enjoy it. I shall persuade Arthur to lead you out for your first dance. He is an excellent dancer and will soon put you in the way of things.'

'I'd rather not,' cried Lucy, growing pale. 'If Mr Collingham is as good as you say he will be sure to find fault with me!'

'Well, I admit I would as lief not give up my dance with him,' admitted her sister, 'for he is such a joy to have as a partner, and you may be sure that there is nothing shows one to greater advantage than to have a good dance partner!'

'Then it is settled,' declared Lucy, her ready humour surfacing, 'I would on no account take away your chance to shine, Charlotte. You shall have Mr Collingham and I will take my chances with the lesser mortals!'

An hour later, Bracey saw her two charges leave the bed-chamber looking, as she told them, a picture of elegance. Charlotte's evening gown of deep rose-pink enhanced the delicate flush of her cheeks and the maidservant knew that her ethereal beauty would as usual draw all eyes when she entered the ballroom. However, she felt confident that Lucy would also have her admirers that evening. The green silk fitted her perfectly, the low neckline displaying her flawless skin, decorated with a single rope of pearls at her throat. Her gold-brown curls had been brushed until they shone and threaded through with a single green ribbon.

'Now, Miss Lucy,' Bracey had challenged her, as they both stared into the long mirror, 'do you dare to say you will make a spectacle of yourself?'

'Do you think Mama would object?'

'Not at all, my dear. There is nothing improper in your dress—and how does she expect you to look after your sister if you do not go to dances and parties with her?' added the handmaid, revealing her grasp of the true situation.

Lucilla smiled at her reflection and shook her head, making the curls dance about her face.

'I do look quite presentable, do I not?'

'You look very pretty!' declared Charlotte, coming up behind her and shaking out the folds of her own gown. 'Now do hurry, Lucy, or we shall be the last downstairs!'

Lucy's confidence rose when Lord Cornholme, in his fatherly way, complimented her on her appearance and led her off to introduce her to a young gentleman for the first dance. After that Lucy never lacked partners and it was quite unnecessary for Charlotte to give up her dance with the elegant Arthur Collingham. It was some time before she saw Mr Vanderley. They passed as he was leading Charlotte out to join a set that was then forming. He smiled at her.

'Enjoying yourself, Miss Chambers?'

She nodded happily, unable to reply before her young partner led her away. There was no respite until the orchestra stopped playing when supper was announced, and Lucy was gratified to discover that no less than three of her previous partners wished to escort her out of the ballroom. Before she could make a choice, a cool voice at her shoulder decided the matter for her.

'I am sorry to disappoint you, gentlemen, but you have had the pleasure of dancing with Miss Chambers, mine must be the honour of taking her in to supper.' Upon these words Mr Vanderley took her elbow and guided her out of the room. Lucy was impressed.

'That was very gallantly said, sir.'

He inclined his head.

'Thank you, ma'am. May I tell you how well you are looking tonight? But doubtless you have already heard that.'

Lucy's eyes twinkled. 'Yes, from several of my partners!'

'If they were not such callow youths, I would be quite jealous.'

She laughed at him. 'Pray don't tease me.'

'You do not believe me?' He looked down at her, his dark eyes glinting. Deep within her, Lucy heard a tiny voice, urging caution, but she ignored it, enjoying the exchange too much to refrain. She fluttered her fan.

'Of course not. Your reputation precedes you, Mr Vanderley. Besides,' she added with her usual candour, 'there are ladies here ten times more beautiful than I could ever be.'

'If that is the case, why am I escorting you into supper?'

'Doubtless the others had already chosen

62

their partners.'

'Minx!' he grinned. 'Look, there's Judith waving to us. Let me take you over to her, then I will bring you a glass of champagne.'

'Well, my dear, are you enjoying your very first ball?' asked Judith Vanderley while her brother strode off in search of refreshments. 'I would guess that you are, from the way your eyes are sparkling.'

'Yes, I am. Very much. All my partners have been very kind and forgave me my errors on the dance floor. Indeed, some of them even wanted to bring me in to supper, only your brother came along and carried me off! Was that not kind of him?'

Miss Vanderley did not reply immediately. She looked thoughtful and after a pause she said slowly, 'Lucy—may I call you that? I hope you will not attach too much import to the things Dominic may say.'

'Oh no. He is forever teasing.'

'That is not quite what I mean. He can be very charming, my dear, but it would not do to take him seriously.'

Lucy laughed. 'You need not worry, Miss Vanderley. I know his reputation, but I assure you he has never shown me anything but the greatest courtesy.' She wanted to add that while he was paying court to her, she need not worry about chaperoning Charlotte, but thought that Miss Vanderley might not approve of this argument.

'I am glad to hear it. And please, call me Judith. I feel we are going to be good friends.'

When Dominic Vanderley returned to the table Lucilla settled down to enjoy her supper, deciding that nothing else was needed to complete her enjoyment.

*   *   *

If Lucy was disappointed that Mr Vanderley did not secure her hand for a dance when supper was over, she did not allow it to spoil her pleasure. The unaccustomed champagne had made her a little light-headed and even when she saw him leading Charlotte out for a second time she thought little of it until she overheard her hostess talking with one of the guests. Lucy was standing by one of the open windows, half-hidden in the shadows when Lady Cornholme walked by with another matron.

'Lady Lairne has hinted that he will propose soon,' she was saying, nodding in the direction of Charlotte and her partner, who were just then leaving the dance-floor.

'Well, they make a very handsome couple,' replied her companion, 'and there is money on both sides. It would be a splendid match for them both.'

'Yes.' Lady Cornholme sounded doubtful. 'But it is said the gentleman cannot resist a pretty woman. Admittedly Lady Lairne is very beautiful, but will she be able to hold his attention?'

The other lady laughed. 'My dear ma'am, if she has any brains at all, once the knot is tied she will not even try. After all, can a leopard change its spots?'

They moved away and Lucy heard no more, but it was enough to bring her to her senses. She had been feeling reckless, exhilarated by all the attention she was receiving. If she was feeling thus, then so too must Charlotte, whose admirers were legion. Lucy knew she must find her sister. Mama was trusting her to look after Charlotte; she must be vigilant! Lucy threaded her way through the crowds, refusing an offer to dance and making her way across the room to the point she had last seen Charlotte. She caught a glimpse of Mr Vanderley's dark head, and pushed on through the crowd in time to see him leaving the ballroom with her sister on his arm.

'Well, miss, now where are you going in such a hurry?' Lord Cornholme was before her, smiling benevolently.

'I am looking for Charlotte, sir. I think she may have left the ballroom.' She looked up at him. 'Are—are all the other rooms open for use this evening, sir?'

'Well'—he considered the matter—'the morning-room is being used for cards, and I think some of our older guests are relaxing in the pink salon.'

'Goodness, sir. Do you have no room where you can slip away from your guests?'

He chuckled.

'Well, I have given orders that the library is not to be used, much to my wife's dismay. One must have a bolt-hole, eh?'

Lucy smiled and mumbled a reply before moving on: she was sure she knew where to find Charlotte.

*   *   *

Lady Lairne was enjoying herself immensely. Arthur Collingham had led her out for the first dance and even praised her neat footwork. Such a compliment from an acknowledged leader of fashion was not to be taken lightly. She had rewarded him with a second dance and even allowed him to take her into supper. Then Mr Vanderley had led her out for a second time, and she had allowed him to flirt with her during the dance: it was the first time he had shown her so much interest since they had met in London. She turned her eyes upon him in a melting look as he murmured ever more outrageous compliments. At the end of the dance, she fluttered her fan and glanced up at him from beneath her lashes.

'La, but it is grown very warm, Mr Vanderley!'

'Then let us find somewhere a little cooler.'

He led her out of the ballroom, into the hall.

'Shall I fetch you more champagne, My Lady?'

'No, no, I vow I am already light-headed! Thank goodness I have you to support me, sir.' She smiled provocatively, leaning closer so that her perfumed breast brushed his arm.

The gentleman smiled: the lady's eyes held an invitation that was not to be resisted. He led her across the hall and into the library, where only one pair of candles burned in the wall sconce. My lady was immediately coy.

'Oh, perhaps we should not be here.'

'But you were too warm, madam. This is much cooler.'

'It is, sir.' She allowed him to lead her to a sofa. 'Let me tell you, sir, that you have neglected me shamefully since we met in Town last year.'

'I have?' He took the fan from her fingers and began to fan her gently.

'Yes! Never a word, and I thought we were such—good friends.' She pouted prettily. 'Did you not miss me?'

'A little.'

'Oh? What did you miss most?'

She looked up at him, lips slightly parted, inviting his kiss. She saw the desire in his eyes, and was triumphant. The slow movement of the fan ceased as his dark head moved towards her.

'Oh. Excuse me!' Lucilla hovered in the doorway, holding aloft a lighted candle and looking at them with her wide, innocent gaze.

Charlotte swung round.

'Whatever are *you* doing here?' she exclaimed crossly.

'Lord Cornholme said if I was tired of dancing I might find something here to read . . .'

Charlotte bit her lip in frustration. She glanced at her companion, but he was leaning back against the sofa, showing no sign of irritation. Indeed, a slight smile played at the corners of his mouth. Lucy came into the room and started to scan the shelves. Her sister tapped her foot impatiently.

'I cannot think that you can be so impolite as to leave the ball-room, Lucy. There must be plenty of partners for you.'

'Oh yes, but I do not wish to be dancing *all* night; I would much rather remain here for a while, and choose a book.' She continued to study the books, pulling out one, then pushing it back into place and moving on. After a few moments, Mr Vanderley rose to his feet.

'I feel I am *de trop* here. Ladies, if you will excuse me.' Hardly had the door closed behind him than Charlotte jumped to her feet with a little scream.

'How dare you come in here, Lucilla! How *dare* you interfere in my plans!'

'How could *you* be so lost to all sense of propriety as to be here alone with him!' Lucy rounded on her sister. 'Mama said you would do something foolish!'

'What would you know of being foolish, little sister? You have no idea how to make a man fall in love with you.'

'Certainly not by letting him make love to you in this secretive way!'

Charlotte flushed. 'We were merely talking.'

'Fiddle! He was going to kiss you!'

'Well, that is none of your business.'

'It is very much my business! It is the reason Mama wanted me to come with you! Charlotte, can't you see that the man is trifling with you? If he wants you, let him do what is honourable.'

'How dare you talk to me of honour! When you spend every spare moment riding all over the countryside like a hoyden! You are merely jealous, Lucy. Jealous because I am about to be married again and you are not.'

'Oh? Has he asked you?'

'No, not yet'—Charlotte walked stiffly to the door—'but he will, and then I shall make you apologize to me!'

'And I will do so, with pleasure!' came the retort, but it was to the air, for Charlotte had flounced out of the room.

Lucy made her way back to the ballroom, feeling very subdued. She had not wanted to enter the library, but she had to keep her promise to Mama, and she knew she had been right to do so. She had felt more than a little embarrassed, but her timely interruption had indeed had the desired effect. She told herself her depression of spirits was because Charlotte was at odds with her, but there was another, deeper reason. Having spoiled his little flirtation, she thought that Dominic Vanderley was likely to be cross with her. Well, it could not be helped, but she would miss his friendship! There was no sign of him when she returned to the ballroom. Lucy wished she could leave, retire to her room, but as long as Charlotte remained she must also stay. She watched her sister, envying the way she could smile and dance as though nothing had happened. At length she slipped out through the open window on to the wide terrace that separated the house from the rose gardens beyond. After the heat of the ballroom the night air was cool, yet still heavy with the scent of roses and Lucy leaned against the balustrade, looking out over the moonlit gardens and drinking in the velvety night air. Voices grew loud then faded away as the guests passed the open windows, and she could see the dark figures of two or three couples strolling further along the terrace.

'Miss Chambers, is it not?' A young gentleman approached. 'Wilshire's the name—friend of Collingham's, don't you know. We was introduced, but, damme, most likely you disremember it!'

'No, no, Mr Wilshire. Of course I remember you.' The gentleman's back was to the light, but she recalled being presented to a rather foppish young man: he had failed to secure her hand for a dance, but she had been too busy to think any more of him, until now. He was standing between Lucy and the window and although his manner was perfectly correct, Lucy found herself edging along the balustrade in an attempt to move away. When the rail behind her ended she turned to find herself at the top of the shallow steps leading to the garden. 'I—I came out for a little air . . .'

'Then allow me to walk with you,' he said, promptly taking her arm and escorting her down the steps. 'Lovely night, ain't it, what with the moon rising over the trees. Very romantic.'

'Have you come far?' Lucy was anxious to turn the gentleman's thoughts to safer channels.

'What? Oh, from Bath. Don't normally attend this sort of party, you know. They're usually full of country dowds, but when I heard Collingham was staying here, well! If *he's* here you know it must be a devilish fashionable squeeze!'

As they strolled along the path, Lucy tried to disengage her hand from the gentleman's arm, but he tightened his grip.

'I really should be getting back—'

Mr Wilshire patted her hand reassuringly.

'Yes, yes, no hurry yet. I thought we might take a look at that pretty little summer-house I can see ahead. What do you say to that?'

'It would be much better to come and look at it in the daylight.'

'Ah, but that would spoil the mood!'

Lucy guessed that Mr Wilshire had been drinking freely, and she resolved to return to the house at the first opportunity. The flagged path that they were taking led directly to the summer-house, a small, stone structure in the form of a temple. The opening was ornamented with a pediment supported on a series of fluted columns that gleamed palely in the moonlight while the interior of the building was in deep shadow. As they approached, Lucy became aware of a faint, smoky fragrance. Possibly some gentleman had come out to enjoy a cigarillo, but as she looked hopefully about her, the gardens were still, deserted.

She pulled her hand free. 'I must go back now.'

'So soon? I thought you would give me your company a little longer.' He turned to look at her, standing closer than Lucy considered necessary. 'The moonlight is shining on your hair—you look like a goddess and I want to worship you here, in your temple!'

His words amused Lucy, but seconds later she had lost all desire to laugh for he had pinned her against one of the columns and was trying to cover her face with hot, passionate kisses. Unfortunately for Mr Wilshire, the lady's struggles hindered his amorous advances but he persevered, holding Lucy in an unrelenting embrace with one hand while the other roved freely over her breasts, ignoring Lucy's protests until he suddenly felt a strong hand grasping his collar. The young man's intricately tied cravat began to choke him, and he was forced to release his grip on the lady. Lucy stepped aside and watched as Dominic Vanderley released his stranglehold on the young man and neatly floored him with a well-placed blow to the chin.

'Let's hope that you will learn some manners before you attend your next party.'

The young man picked himself up, tenderly nursing his jaw.

'Sir!' exclaimed Mr Wilshire, his voice shaking with indignation, 'You will answer to me for this!'

'Do you think to call me out just because you have made a fool of yourself?' responded Mr Vanderley, amused.

'It's a matter of honour!'

'My fine young buck, you don't know the meaning of the word. Do you think it honourable to force your attentions on a young lady? Take yourself off before I give you the finest trimming of your life.'

Mr Wilshire hesitated: even in his angry state he was well aware of his opponent's superior height and powerful frame. Deciding that to prolong the confrontation would only result in further humiliation, the young man turned on his heel and lounged off, determined to quit with all speed the shabbiest party he had ever attended.

'Arrogant young cub!' remarked Mr Vanderley, watching his departure. He turned back to Lucy. 'You are shaking. Come and sit down for a moment. Did that silly pup hurt you?'

'N-no. He startled me a little, I did not expect . . .' Her voice trailed off as he led her into the summer-house and sat down with her on a wooden bench, taking her trembling hands in a reassuring grasp.

'Pretty young ladies should always be wary of walking in the moonlight with a gentleman.'

'I shall certainly not be taken in again!' she replied, her spirit reasserting itself. 'Why that silly young man thought that I would want to be mauled in such a way I just cannot guess!'

'No, I could see you weren't enjoying it.'

She turned towards him, peering through the gloomy shadows in an attempt to see his face.

'Do you mean to tell me you saw everything?' she demanded indignantly, pulling her hands free.

'I am sorry. I was enjoying a little solitude, you see. When I heard voices I merely stepped back here into the shadows.'

'Then why did you not come forward earlier? Surely you must have realized that I did not wish for his attentions!'

'I did realize that, of course, but it has never been *my* practice to disturb a gentleman when he is about to kiss a lady.'

There was a pause.

'Oh. You are referring to my entrance into the library, I suppose. I am sorry if I offended you, but I was there to—to protect my sister's honour.'

'Very noble of you.'

'Well, at least I acted upon the very best of intentions!' she retorted. 'I have no doubt that you were enjoying my discomfiture when Mr Wilshire tried to maul me!'

'I have to confess I was interested to see what he would do.'

'You were—! Well, I hope you were satisfied with what you observed!' declared Lucy furiously.

'Not at all. I thought he handled the situation very ill indeed.'

'I doubt he has had your experience!'

'I think you are right, Miss Chambers, else he would have known that this is the way to kiss a lady.'

In one smooth movement he pulled her into his arms. Lucy lifted her head to protest, only to have her lips crushed beneath his as he kissed her so fiercely that her senses reeled. In the darkness his hands began to caress her, exploring her body through the thin silk, but arousing none of the revulsion caused by Mr Wilshire's embrace. Summoning all her will-power, Lucy at last broke away, catching at his hands and holding them in front of her.

'Undoubtedly Mr Wilshire has much to learn,' she joked, unwilling to let her companion see how much his embrace had affected her. 'Is—is that why you are considered so dangerous?'

He laughed. 'Perhaps.'

Lucy rose and walked about the small summer-house, touching the pieces of furniture that were barely visible in the shadows. She had been here many times in daylight, taking advantage of its cool shelter from the burning sun, but now in the darkness, her body tingling with new and unrecognized sensations, everything was changed—she felt she was exploring a strange world, dangerous and exciting.

'Is it—is it necessary for you, sir, to flirt with every young female who crosses your path?'

In the dim light he watched her, an amused smile lifting the corners of his mouth.

'Not at all. I only flirt with the pretty ones.'

She bobbed a curtsy.

'Then I thank you, sir, for the compliment!'

As he rose from the bench she moved swiftly out into the moonlight.

'I—I think it is time we returned to the ballroom, Mr Vanderley, before our absence is noticed.'

'As you wish.' He took her arm and guided her back along the flagged path towards the terrace. The warm night air was moved by a gentle breeze and Lucy breathed in the sweet heady fragrance of the roses. She had never known their scent so strong. She glanced up at her companion. The moonlight cast deep shadows over his countenance, making it the face of a stranger, then he turned to look at her and she was reassured by his smile.

'Lady Lairne tells me this is your first such ball, Miss Chambers. What do you think of it?'

'At first I did not wish to attend, but I cannot deny I have enjoyed it—the dancing, that is!'

He stopped and turned to look at her, smiling down at her in a way that set her heart pounding again.

'Was it only the dancing you enjoyed?' he laughed and pinched her chin. 'There, child, don't look so distressed. I won't tease you any more, I promise!' He led her on towards the house, saying when they reached the steps, 'I think it would be best if we parted on the terrace.'

Lucy felt an unaccountable disappointment. The brief interlude was over; he had no further use for her. She told herself firmly she had expected nothing else.

'Of course,' she agreed brightly. 'We would not want to be the subject of gossip!'

Head high, she walked on alone into the ballroom. The music had started and the young man who was to be her partner was standing disconsolately at the edge of the room. As she moved towards him his face lit up.

'Miss Chambers! I thought you had deserted me!'

'Not at all!' She summoned up a smile.

He swept her on to the dance-floor where they were soon caught up with the mass of laughing, swirling dancers. As she moved around the room, Lucy tried to keep watch on the long windows, but it was not until the music had ended and her partner was escorting her off the floor that she saw Dominic Vanderley. She was aware of a faint fluttering within her as she watched him moving towards a small alcove where his sister was sitting alone. Lucy's partner led her past the alcove and she kept her eyes averted from the brother and sister, but she could not help overhearing their first words to each other.

'Dominic, you missed our dance! Have you been courting some young beauty in the moonlight?'

'A little harmless flirtation, Ju, nothing more . . .'

FOUR

It was inevitable that when they retired to their bedchamber, after the last carriage had rolled away, Charlotte would want to discuss the ball. With Mr Collingham's assiduous attentions and a host of admirers ever present, Lady Lairne could not but be pleased with the evening, but she was still angry with Lucy for interrupting her *tête-à-tête* with Mr Vanderley.

'Really, Lucy, I cannot imagine what you thought you were about, to interrupt us so rudely,' she complained, as soon as Bracey had retired.

'I was merely doing as Mama bade me, and keeping you out of mischief.'

'Well, I call it a great piece of meddling! I am perfectly capable of handling Dominic Vanderley. If you had not intruded when you did I have no doubt that we would be betrothed by this time!'

'Oh? When I walked in upon you it appeared to me that he was about to kiss you.'

'Well, of course, but it would have been followed by a proposal.'

Remembering events in the summer-house, Lucy was not so sure.

'Oh? Is that how it happens? A man kisses you and *then* proposes? Mama has always told me it should be the reverse.'

'Pray do not joke, Lucilla. You are such a child; you know nothing about these things. Mr Vanderley and I have a—an understanding.'

'But you are not betrothed.'

'Not yet, but I am confident it will happen very soon.'

*　　*　　*

Lucy lay awake in the darkness long after Charlotte had drifted off to sleep. Her mind kept running over the events of the evening, eventually settling on the incident in the rose garden. Something very like a moan broke from her lips and she turned to bury her face in the pillow.

Why don't you admit it, she scolded herself, you are in love with Dominic Vanderley! What a fool you are, Lucy Chambers: you have lost your heart to the first man to flirt with you! The confession brought with it no relief, but when her tears had subsided she tried to consider her situation calmly. She had tried to respond to his advances in a light vein and could only hope that she had succeeded in hiding her true feelings. This gave her some comfort and she resolved sleepily that if at all possible, she would keep her own secret, and never let him know that he had conquered yet one more heart.

The following morning found Lucy and her

host breakfasting alone.

'No stamina, these young people!' declared Lord Cornholme, his merry eyes twinkling at her across the table. 'When I was a young man in London, we would not think of going to bed before dawn, then up again and off to attend a prize fight at noon. Not, of course, that it would be at all the thing for a young lady to attend! But I am surprised that you are the only one to be at breakfast, Lucilla.'

'I am not in the habit of lying a-bed in the mornings, sir, but I think it is a compliment to the excellence of your entertainment, that your guests are so exhausted!'

My Lord laughed heartily at this, called her a saucy little puss and enquired how she intended to spend the morning.

'I thought I might take my pad into the park and do a little sketching. Later in the day it may be too hot to sit outside in comfort.'

'Very true, my dear. If you would like the use of a carriage . . . ?'

'You are very kind, sir, but I would not dream of taking your horses for such a short distance. No, I have a very good pair of walking boots and I shall enjoy the exercise.'

*   *   *

Lucy strode out across the park with her sketching pad tucked under her arm. She had already decided upon an ideal spot high up on the far side of the park and she made her way directly to it, a soft breeze cooling her face as she began the long steady climb. When she reached her chosen viewpoint, she was not disappointed, for not only could she see Stock House and its gardens, but she had an uninterrupted view southwards over the park and on across the river, until the land disappeared into a misty haze on the horizon.

*   *   *

The sun was already climbing high above her and she chose to sit in the shade of a towering beech tree. Lucy leaned against the tree-trunk with her sketch pad resting on her knees. She had planned to take Stock House as her subject, but now she spotted an ancient oak, standing in magnificent isolation. Its lower branches almost swept the ground and its massive form attracted Lucy. She set to work trying to capture its stolid majesty with delicate strokes of her pencil.

'Tired of drawing people, Miss Chambers?'

Lucy jumped. Dominic Vanderley leaned against the beech, looking over her shoulder.

'Oh! Oh, no, that is, I thought I should take advantage of this fine weather.' She continued to work, thankful that her steady pencil gave no indication of how much his presence disturbed her. 'You are perhaps making a tour of the park?'

'No.' He sat down beside her. 'I came to find you.'

'Oh.'

'You sound disappointed.'

'I am.' She kept her voice light. 'I work much better alone.'

'Do you wish me to leave you?'

Yes, she thought, but when she looked into his face she could not utter the word. Quickly she looked away.

'I—no—that is'—she felt his hand on her neck, playing with one of the curls that peeped out from the edge of her bonnet—'I do not think you should be here.'

'May I ask why?'

'Because—you frighten me.'

The hand fell away from her neck. Lucy kept her eyes fixed upon the work in front of her but she knew he was smiling.

'Ah. I see. And if I give you my word that I will sit here quietly and not interrupt you— then may I stay?'

Lucy could not resist it.

'I doubt 'twould be possible for you, sir!'

He laughed.

'*Touché,* Lucilla! No sooner have I decided that you are nothing but a child than you floor me with your sharp words! You constantly surprise me.'

'That is not my intention, Mr Vanderley.'

'I am well aware of that! But I will prove to you that I am as good as my word! Carry on

83

with your sketching, and I shall sit here mute until you are finished.'

Lucy tried to continue, blocking in the area around the great oak, darkening the shadows beneath its boughs, but the tree itself needed concentration. She stole a glance at her companion and encountered such a bland look of patient resignation that she could not help laughing.

'You are abominable!' she told him, throwing down her pencil. 'I shall never finish my drawing while you are sitting there!'

'You could, of course, complete my portrait instead.'

'No, I think not.' Lucy closed her pad. 'I will do no more today.'

'Poor Lucy—have I spoiled your morning?'

His change of tone disconcerted her.

'Pray you, sir, do not call me that.' She put out one hand, as if to ward off some unwelcome thought and he caught her fingers in his own.

'But are we not friends?'

I thought so, once! was her silent cry. She gently pulled her hand free, saying lightly, 'perhaps we shall be, in time.'

She made a move to rise and he jumped up, putting out his hand to help her.

'Thank you.' She looked up into his face and the light she saw burning in his eyes made her suddenly frightened, not of Dominic Vanderley, but of herself. She felt spellbound, unable to look away as he took her in his arms, his mouth coming down to meet hers in a kiss of such tenderness that it took her by surprise and she found herself responding. At length she broke away, guiltily aware that she should not have allowed him to kiss her. When he tried to pull her back into his arms she held him away.

'Please don't! I am sorry, Mr Vanderley, but I—I am not accustomed to—to Society ways and c-cannot indulge you in the kind of—of *flirtation* that you are used to!'

He looked amused. 'My dear, you were doing excellently, and I had the strangest feeling that you were enjoying it! There is no one near; let us try again to see if that was indeed so—'

'No! I am sorry,' cried Lucy, very red and scarcely daring to look up into his laughing face, 'I cannot, *will* not be disloyal to Charlotte!'

'And what has the countess to do with this?'

'She thinks you are going to marry her!'

His embrace slackened: there was a long silence. Glancing up, Lucy saw the frown deepening on the gentleman's brow. When he spoke again, his voice had lost its bantering tone.

'I see. And has Lady Lairne told you I have made her an offer, or spoken to her of marriage?'

'No—no, that is, she thought . . .'

'I know exactly what she thought!' He spoke harshly. 'She thought that because I obliged her with a little flirtation last season—a flirtation she was very keen to encourage, may I add!—that I was on the point of proposing!'

'And why should she think otherwise?' retorted Lucy, nettled. 'Indeed, you were only too willing to renew your attentions at the ball!'

'That, I admit, was an error, but when a lady is throwing out such lures who am I to gainsay her?'

'If you were merely toying with her affections then you are very much to blame!'

'Toying with—!'

He let her go and stepped back, studying her in silence for several moments, an arrested look in his eyes.

'For one who admits to no knowledge of Society, Miss Chambers, you have very decided views of our behaviour!'

Lucy looked away, her cheeks flushed.

'I am sorry if I have offended you, Mr Vanderley, but where my sister's affections are concerned—'

'Do you mean to tell me that Lady Lairne is in love with me?' he demanded, on a note of incredulity.

Lucy looked even more uncomfortable.

'I cannot tell that,' she replied, incurably honest, 'but I know that she expects you to make her an offer.'

'I see.'

She stole a glance at him, her eyes anxiously scanning his grim profile.

'I have spoken out of turn, sir. I apologize—'

'There is no need to be sorry, Miss Chambers. You have pointed out to me a gross error in my conduct, something that everyone else is either too indifferent or too afraid of me to do—with the exception of my sister, of course. She has been telling me for years to mend my ways.' He glanced up at the sky. 'It is growing cloudy. I would offer to escort you back to the house, but under the circumstances I have no doubt you would find my presence unwelcome. Good-day to you!'

With that he turned on his heel and walked away, leaving Lucy with nothing to do but collect her things and follow on. By the time she arrived back at Stock House, the clouds that had been gathering now blotted out the sun, and a faint rumble of thunder growled ominously in the distance.

*   *   *

The storm broke just before dawn the following morning, and after the first torrential downpour the rain continued steadily for the rest of the day, keeping the guests confined within Stock House. Lucy was at pains to ensure that she was always in company, but she need not have troubled:

87

Dominic Vanderley made no attempt to approach her and she had the doubtful satisfaction of observing that he was paying Charlotte a great deal of attention. Lady Lairne was in excellent spirits. She had conveniently banished the incident in the library from her mind and could look back at the ball with equanimity, remembering the host of admirers paying court to her. The occasion was to be remembered, talked over and examined by the guests as they each recalled how wonderful it had been. Lucy did not join in this conversation, feeling that as far as she was concerned the events of the previous two days were best forgotten and when it was suggested that they should while away the rainy afternoon with charades she excused herself, explaining that she was very weary from her late night and escaped to the seclusion of her bed-chamber.

*　　*　　*

When Charlotte came up to change into her evening gown she found Lucy curled up asleep on her bed, an open book beside her. She stirred as Charlotte came in and opened her eyes.

'I'm sorry, did I wake you? Poor Lucy, you are not accustomed to dancing until the early hours, are you? Wake up now, it is nearly time for dinner. What a pity you missed the charades, it was such fun. I admit I thought at first it would be a little childish, and I have never been very good at such games, so when some of the gentlemen took themselves off to play billiards I thought I might prefer to sit out, but Mr Collingham begged me to join in, and everyone else was so obliging, especially Miss Vanderley. Is she not a delightful creature? I am sure she is in favour of the match.'

'What match?'

'Why, between her brother and myself, of course.'

Lucy felt her heart sinking.

'Oh. Has he proposed to you?'

Charlotte shook her head impatiently.

'No, Lucilla, thanks to your untimely intervention, he has not! But his attentions are so marked I have no doubt that he will do so, and very soon. Of course, poor Arthur is quite overset, for I had to tell him why I could only give him two dances last night, but he knows that once I am safely married we may dance together as often as we like, and I must admit I think him a much better dancer than Dominic Vanderley, don't you agree? But of course, you danced with neither of them! Well, there is no comparison, I can tell you, and although Mr Vanderley is acclaimed a great sportsman, he lacks Arthur's grace.'

'Since Mr Collingham is such a paragon, I don't know why you don't marry him!'

remarked Lucy, somewhat acidly.

Charlotte stared at her.

'Marry Arthur?' My dear girl how can you be so absurd! Why, I shall be the envy of everyone when I am Mrs Vanderley, for he is highly regarded, you know, besides being a great friend of the Prince! And such wealth! I am told he has no less than four notable properties in the country, besides the house in London and his estates in the West Indies, and such a vast income that he may do as he pleases! Will he not make me a perfect husband?'

Lucy sat up and stretched.

'Mr Vanderley seems to possess everything you want, Charlotte, but can you make him happy?'

Her sister looked surprised at the question.

'But of course! What a strange question, Lucilla. I fear you are still half-asleep. Come along, my dear, hurry out of that crumpled dress, Bracey will be here any minute to help you change.'

'I am not hungry.'

'But you must come down for dinner.'

'No, I think not. Pray be good enough to make my apologies. You may say I have the headache.'

Charlotte, her mind already on the evening ahead, did not stop to question her sister, but merely shrugged her bare white shoulders.

'Oh very well. I shall ask Lady Cornholme

to have a tray sent up to you, if I remember. Now, I wonder which gown I should wear this evening? I remember Mr Vanderley saying how much he liked me in pink, so perhaps I should wear the satin. Or mayhap the blue. I know he has seen me wear it before, but it does bring out the blue of my eyes, do you not think so? Lucilla—where are you going?'

Feeling a sudden compulsion to escape from her sister's incessant chatter, Lucy was at the door.

'I really do have the headache,' she said, as she went out. 'I am going to ask Bracey to let me have one of her sleeping powders.'

'But Bracey will be coming here any moment . . .' Charlotte's words fell on empty air, and with a shrug she continued her own preparations for dinner.

*   *   *

'Ah, Lady Lairne. I thought to find you here, but where is Lucy?' Lady Cornholme peeped into the room.

'She has gone to ask our maid for a powder, she has the headache, you see. I hope she will be quick about it, for I need Bracey here to help me change!'

'Poor child, I do trust I did the right thing allowing her to stay up until the end of the ball. She has been looking very pale ever since. However, that is not why I came. When I was

91

going through my jewel-box last night I came across this ring. The stones are merely paste, but the setting is unusual, and a very good match for a necklace of your dear Mama's. When we last met she was so taken by it that I intended to make her a present of it when she came here. Of course, now I do not know when I shall be seeing her again, unless it be in London next season, but I wondered if you would take it to her when you return to Templecombe?'

'But of course.' Charlotte held out her hand for the trinket. 'I shall be delighted to give it to her.'

Lady Cornholme thanked her and went back to finish her own toilet, while Charlotte examined the ring: it was a gold setting with a cluster of paste stones shaped like a tiny knot of ribbon. It was too intricate for Charlotte's taste, but she admired the craftsmanship. If Lady Cornholme had not told her she would not have guessed that the stones were not real diamonds. She slipped the ring into her jewel case then tugged violently at the bell-pull to inform Bracey that her services were required urgently.

＊　　　＊　　　＊

It was very late when Lucy awoke the next morning, feeling little refreshed by her night's rest. Charlotte had already dressed and gone downstairs, and Lucy was spared the necessity of following her by the appearance of a maid carrying a breakfast tray that Lady Cornholme had ordered to be sent up. At mid-day Lucilla ventured out of her room and was immediately aware that the house seemed unnaturally quiet. As she descended the stairs she encountered her hostess.

'Lucilla, my dear, I was on my way to see how you go on!' Lady Cornholme enveloped her guest in her good-natured smile. 'Your headache has gone, I hope? Good. It is most likely this thundery weather; it seems we are in for another stormy day! Most of my guests are gathered in the library—you will certainly find your sister there. I'll leave you to make your own way, my dear, if you don't mind, for I promised to go to the kitchens as soon as I could spare a moment. One of the scullery maids had to be turned off yesterday and now Cook is threatening to leave unless he gets more help! Heavens knows what we should do then, with so many people in the house . . .'

The good lady bustled away and Lucy crossed the hall to the library. As she approached the door she could hear the chatter of the guests, and a sudden burst of laughter. It was a world to which she did not belong. Suddenly she was overwhelmed with a desire to be at home. Until recently she had spent all her time living a somewhat solitary existence, quite happy to divide her day between the old school-room and the stables. Upon an impulse she turned away and slipped out of the house, heading for the stable block. For the moment the rain had stopped, although the heavy stormclouds still crowded the sky and Lucy decided against going back for a cloak. She walked through the archway to find the stable-yard deserted. Having completed their morning's work, the stable-lads had gone off to enjoy their unexpected leisure. The wind swirled about the yard, whipping up the loose strands of hay that had escaped from the buildings. Lucy stepped through the nearest door: the air was cool and still, although she could still hear the wind whistling and moaning outside. The familiar smell of horses and straw was comforting and she walked slowly past the boxes, oblivious to the dust that clung to her skirts. She came to Lady Cornholme's hack and the horse turned to greet her, blowing gently. Lucy talked quietly to the mare as she bent to examine the injured leg. The cut was healing well, but it brought back to Lucy unwelcome memories of that first fateful ride. Stifling a sigh she left the mare and wandered on through the stables to the carriage-house. From her previous visits to the stable-yard she knew that the guests' horses were stabled on the far side of the carriage house and she went on past the chaises and travelling carriages to a narrow doorway leading to a row of loose-boxes. It was easy to find the Vanderley horses. Lucy looked about her with admiration at the highly polished saddles set carefully to one side, bridles hung above in orderly rows. Everything reminded her of Dominic Vanderley, the exquisite quality of the leather, the superb horses, all attended by a groom whose standards were as exacting as his master's. Snowfire put her head over the door to greet her, nuzzling for a titbit. Lucy stroked the soft nose.

'Hello, girl,' she murmured, 'where's Sultan? The master's off riding is he? I hope the rain holds off. How I envy him! I would much rather be outside than indoors, even in this weather. Poor Charlotte cannot bear the rain.'

Suddenly the thought came into Lucy's head that everything around her, the gleaming harness, the beautiful horses—even their master—might soon belong to her sister and a wave of jealousy so strong swept over her that Lucy began to tremble, frightened by the violence of her own feelings. As if sensing her agitation, the mare dropped her head against Lucy and with a stifled cry the girl threw her arms about the curved neck, burying her face in the loose warm mane.

'Oh Snowfire, what am I to do!'

Suddenly the mare lifted her head, ears pricked. The moaning of the wind obscured any other noise, but now Dominic

Vanderley stepped into the stable, leading Sultan to his stall. Lucy looked around wildly for some way to escape without being seen: there was none. At first he did not notice her in the dim light, but as he shook the droplets of rain from his hat he looked up, his brows rising. Lucy gestured towards the mare.

'I'm sorry—I came in to see . . .' she trailed off, painfully aware of the frowning look he had fixed upon her. She looked away, but even so she knew he was watching her. With a muttered apology she moved to step past him but he caught her arm. Lucy stopped, her face averted, resisting the temptation to bury her face in his coat and burst into tears. She heard his voice, low and hoarse, the words almost wrenched from him.

'I have made you unhappy. I cannot bear that!'

'Why, sir, I know not what you mean—'

'Lucy, Lucy—let us end this pretence! This is no mere flirtation, we both know that!'

Unable to trust her voice, Lucy shook her head, but she did not resist when he pulled her into his arms and she lifted her face mutely towards him. He kissed her, gently at first then so fiercely that she thought she would swoon from the violence of it. His body pressed against hers, arousing within her such feelings as she had never known, at once exciting and frightening her. At last he lifted his head, his arms remaining firmly around her, binding her to him. She looked up into his eyes, which seemed to glow with a triumphant satisfaction. A shiver of excitement ran through her.

'*Now* will you dare to deny me?'

She shook her head, unable to speak for the tumult of emotions raging within. No man had ever held her so close before, yet she felt no awkward shyness—instead she realized in a detached way that her own limbs were pressed against him of their own accord, but before her brain could regain control of her wayward body he was kissing her again. His hands caressed her and Lucy moaned faintly, her senses swimming as his kisses covered her neck and shoulders. She threw back her head, breathing in the soft familiar smell of the stables and dimly aware of the horses moving quietly in their boxes. Then, from outside, came the sound of voices. Dominic threw up his head, listening. Leaning quietly against him, Lucy looked up at his face, taking in every detail of the strong, lean features. Abruptly he released her.

'It is my groom,' he muttered, 'you had best leave—go back past the carriages.'

Released from his arms, Lucy stood quite still for a moment, unable to comprehend what she should do. Dominic reached out one hand and, threading his fingers though her disordered curls, he drew her to him for one last savage kiss. As he let her go he gave her a little push.

'Go now, sweetheart, before they see you.' He added, in a softer tone, 'Wait for me in the house—I will come to you later. We have much to discuss.'

*　　　*　　　*

Lucy ran into the carriage-house and paused there. Behind her, she could hear Dominic talking to the stable-hands. His voice sounded cheerful, matter-of-fact, as though the earth-shattering moment she had just lived through had never taken place. She decided she dare not return to the house until she had recovered her composure, but neither could she remain in the stables. A large driving coat had been left hanging over the side of an open chaise and this gave her an idea. She pulled the coat over her loose summer gown. It reached nearly to her ankles, but she pulled it tightly about her then slipped quietly out of the stable-yard and through a small wicket-gate into the shrubbery at the side of the house. A fine rain was falling, blown into her face by the blustery wind, but Lucy paid no heed to it. She felt safe from prying eyes in the seclusion of the shrubbery and the driving coat kept her dry, although her thin slippers could not protect her feet from the wet grass. She made her way between the rows of clipped box and yew to the shady avenues of beech and oak that bordered the formal gardens, wandering aimlessly beneath their sheltering branches, trying to understand what had occurred. Only one reasonable explanation presented itself to her, and that was too wonderful, too fantastic for her to dare to believe it.

FIVE

Lady Lairne smiled to herself as she slipped into the morning-room. When Mr Vanderley had entered the library a short while before and discreetly requested a few moments' private conversation with her, Charlotte had known immediately what was to come. Now, as she waited for the gentleman to appear she practised how she would reply to his offer: in the affirmative, naturally, but should it be with a demure smile or a rush of grateful affection? Really, it was difficult to know what he would expect, he was such an unaccountable person—even in London, when his attentions to her had been most marked, she had often been at a loss to understand him and at times she even suspected him of laughing at her. However, when Dominic Vanderley entered the room there was no mockery in his eyes. He had not changed from his riding clothes and his dark hair was still damp from the rain. Although Charlotte would have preferred more formal dress, she could not but be flattered by his impatience. She chose to sit on a chair by the window, where the light would show her to her best advantage and with a smile begged Mr Vanderley to be seated. He shook his head, a grim set to his mouth. Goodness, thought My Lady, could the gentleman be nervous?

'Thank you, ma'am, but I will not sit down. My business will not detain you long, but I thought it important that we should talk.'

Charlotte smiled at him encouragingly: this was not at all the way she had imagined he would make her an offer.

'Lady Lairne, when we were in London last season we struck up a charming friendship, did we not? I confess that I yielded to the temptation to—ah—pay court to such a beautiful woman as yourself, as I did again at the ball the other night. Alas, it is to my shame that I had not until now any reason to resist such temptations. However, for my conduct then I apologize—'

'My dear Mr Vanderley,' Charlotte stopped him, all graciousness, 'you have nothing in the world to apologize for! I assure you I have never found your behaviour in the least unbecoming.'

'You are being too generous, ma'am,' he replied swiftly, 'for I suspect, nay I am sure that my conduct has given rise to hopes that cannot be fulfilled.'

For the first time since the interview began, Charlotte felt uneasy. She watched as the gentleman took a turn about the room, his face dark and brooding. Suddenly he stopped and faced her.

'Let us be blunt! Lady Lairne, in all my dealings with your sex I have tried to act fairly: never have I knowingly led any woman to believe that my attentions would end in marriage—indeed, I have been very careful to conduct my—let us call them affairs—with women of my own circle, those who could be counted upon to know that it was merely a brief *amourette* to be enjoyed and then forgotten. It seems that with regard to yourself, I have erred, gravely.'

'I—I do not think I understand you,' muttered Charlotte, very white.

He drew a chair towards her and sat down, looking directly into her face. He said gently, 'Our time in London was but a sweet little flirtation, nothing else. If you expected anything more, then I am very sorry for it, but it is better that we are honest with each other—indeed, there are now pressing reasons why there should be no misunderstanding between us!'

'I see.' Charlotte rose from her chair, her beautiful face impassive as she digested his words. 'And at the ball, am I to understand that that too was the impulse of the moment? I see. I am honoured, sir, that you have treated me to this frank explanation of your intentions, but there was no need: I have never for one moment considered you as anything more than an amusing acquaintance.'

'Then your forbearance with me now is even more gratifying. With your permission, Lady Lairne, we will conclude this interview and say nothing more of the matter.'

Charlotte regarded his dark head as he bent over her hand.

'Pray sir, be easy. I shall forget that this conversation ever took place.'

'You are very good, ma'am.'

With a final bow Mr Vanderley went out. As the door closed behind him the calm dignity left Charlotte's face. Her blue eyes snapped angrily. The humiliation of it: how could she stay here now, when she had hinted so strongly to Lady Cornholme that an offer was imminent? She took a hasty turn about the room, her lips compressed into a tight, thin line. She stopped before the fireplace, staring at her reflection in the gold-framed mirror that hung above it. Then, with a little cry of rage, she swept her arm along the mantelshelf, sending the display of delicate ornaments crashing to the floor.

It was almost the dinner hour when Lucy turned back towards the house. The rain had ceased but the sky was heavy with dark clouds and the air was ominously still, as if another storm was waiting to break. She slipped into the house by a side door and laid the wet driving cloak across a nearby chest. She hoped to gain the safety of her bed-chamber without meeting anyone, but she had scarcely crossed the hall when Lady Cornholme came bustling down the stairs. At the sight of Lucy she hurried towards her, clucking like a mother hen.

'Lucilla, my dear child, where have you been! It wants but ten minutes to the hour! Lord, child, your hair is wet through!'

'I—was caught in a shower—'

Fortunately for Lucy, who was anxious to avoid more searching questions, Lady Cornholme's main thought was for the dinner and she waved Lucy on, saying, 'Quickly, child, before you catch your death! Upstairs and change your gown. I will have dinner set back by twenty minutes and do what I can to placate Cook, who is bound to say that the sauce will be ruined. Heavens, my servants try my patience! Even now one of the parlour maids is having hysterics because I asked her if she knew anything about the broken figurines in the morning-room! Heaven knows what is happening in this house . . .'

Her hostess went on her way, still muttering, and Lucy sped up the stairs to her room. She found Charlotte sitting before the mirror while the maid put the finishing touches to her elegant coiffure. The gloom from the grey overcast sky had been dispelled by clusters of lighted candles. Lady Lairne glanced at her sister, her blue eyes darkening with disapproval.

'Goodness Lucy, how late you are! No doubt we shall have to wait dinner again for you.'

'I'm sorry. I shall be ready in a moment!' Lucy apologized, scrambling out of her clothes.

'So I should hope!' snapped Charlotte. 'Have you no more sense than to go out on such a day as this? You will catch your death of cold!'

'No I won't, I never catch cold. Hurry, Bracey, help me into my gown. What have you put out for me today?'

'I have laid out the apricot muslin, miss, since it is so hot. You would think all this rain we are having would cool the air but no, it just seems to make it close and sticky! Now if you will only keep still a moment I will brush out your hair.'

'Though what you expect Bracey to do when your hair is so wet I don't know!' put in Charlotte, but despite these doubts the maid had soon tidied Lucy's damp locks into some sort of order. She paused for a moment to cast a critical eye over her handiwork then began to gather up Lucy's discarded clothes. She shook her head over the ruined slippers.

'If you will go out walking in the wet, miss, I wish you would put on some sensible shoes!'

said the maid, making for the door. 'And what's this on your skirts—straw! Miss Lucy, how many times have you been told not to wear your best gowns to the stables! If your dear mother was here I don't know what she'd say to you!'

As the maid went out Lady Lairne paused in the act of draping a silk shawl over her arms.

'You have been to the stables? Whatever can have taken you there on such a day? There was not the slightest possibility of riding today.'

'I—I wanted to see what progress Lady Cornholme's hack was making.'

Some instinct made Charlotte look closely at her sister. Lucy avoided her eyes, but a faint blush covered her cheeks, arousing a sudden suspicion.

'And pray, Lucilla, was that your only reason for going there, or was there perhaps some secret assignation to be kept?'

'Of course not . . .'

'Then why do you colour up so? Come, little sister. Tell me the truth!'

'Really, Charlotte—'

'Don't think of lying to me, Lucilla, for your face gives you away!' declared Charlotte, her own colour heightened, 'I believe you went out to meet someone and since Mama is not here I demand that you tell me his name.'

'Charlotte, believe me, nothing was

arranged!'

'Then you *did* meet someone?'

'Yes,' admitted Lucy unhappily, 'I know it was wrong of me, but I thought there could be no harm in it if I went to see Snowfire. It was sheer chance that he should come in . . .'

Charlotte was very still, her eyes fixed unblinkingly upon Lucilla.

'You were there with Dominic Vanderley?'

Lucy nodded, unable to prevent the glow of happiness shining from her eyes. Charlotte's next words struck her like an icy blast.

'How—dare—you!' she whispered hoarsely. 'How *dare* you bring our family to such a depth of shame! Any slut from the gutters would have more pride than to throw herself at a man in such a way.'

Lucy's cheeked flamed. 'I did not throw myself at anyone! It was not like that at all! It was the briefest of meetings. I have been walking in the garden for I don't know how long—'

'Did he kiss you?'

'Yes, but—' Lucy's reply was interrupted as Charlotte gave a brittle laugh.

'You little fool! And after you presumed to lecture me on my behaviour! Can't you see that he is just playing with you? Doubtless he thought you were lying in wait for him—and he was right, was he not? Did you repulse his advances? No, I thought not! The man is a notorious flirt, Lucy, and it is well known that he cannot resist a pretty face.'

'This was no flirtation.'

'What would you know of it, you little innocent!' retorted Charlotte scornfully. 'The man has broken a dozen hearts—silly girls like yourself who fall for his charm. Nothing will come of it, you know, except perhaps a bastard—a fine reward for Mama, when she has shown so much trust in you!'

'Don't say such things, Charlotte! You know I would never—! Besides, you are wrong about him. I will not believe you.'

Charlotte shrugged and turned away. She opened her jewel-box and began to make her selection.

'Then you are a fool. You are not the first maid to be taken in by a silver tongue.'

'I love him!' declared Lucy. 'And I believe he loves me!'

Charlotte was in the act of choosing a pair of diamond earrings, but at these words her hand remained poised above the box. She gave a tinkling laugh.

'You innocent babe. What has love to do with anything? That is not the way of our world.'

'No!' cried Lucy, her voice breaking. 'Dominic would never treat me so!'

With slow deliberation the countess picked out the paste ring Lady Cornholme had entrusted to her and she slipped it on to her left hand. Outside a rumble of thunder could be heard in the distance.

'If that is so,' she said slowly, turning to face her sister, 'why did he come to me scarce an hour since, immediately after your sordid little episode in the stable? You see, Lucy, I am not at all upset by his actions. No, little sister, Dominic Vanderley is a man of the world and he wants a wife who understands his need to— ah—amuse himself.' She held out her left hand for Lucy to see the ring upon her finger, an angry little smile of triumph curling her lips as she watched Lucy's eyes widen in dismay.

'Yes,' laughed Charlotte, her blue eyes glittering, 'you may well look downcast. Did you think to catch yourself a husband with your hoydenish tricks?' Lucy made no answer, but sat down upon the edge of the bed, ashen-faced. Charlotte continued in a kinder tone, 'You have had a bitter disappointment, my love, but believe me, it is better to put an end to this nonsense now than to let it go on, for you could find yourself ruined by your thoughtless behaviour. And not only yourself, but Mama—think how ashamed she would be if she knew of it!' She rose, shaking out her skirts. 'Doubtless you will not wish to come downstairs for dinner. I shall ask for a tray to be sent up to you.'

'Thank you, I am not hungry'

'No, I can understand that. ' Charlotte cast a final, critical glance at her reflection in the long glass. 'There, that will do. Well, Lucy, do you mean to sit there like a statue all evening? Go to bed, child, you look worn out. I will make your excuses to Lady Cornholme, never fear.' She swept out, closing the door softly behind her. At the head of the stairs she paused, taking long deep breaths to calm herself. Gradually her anger died down: she drew the paste ring from her finger and dropped it into her reticule. Then, adjusting the shawl about her arms, she made her way at a leisurely pace to the drawing-room.

*   *   *

For a long time Lucy remained sitting on the edge of her bed, staring at the door. She wanted to cry, but the tears would not come. At last she stood up and paced the room, the motion providing some relief to her feelings. Gradually the hurt within her turned to anger, then shame. Charlotte was right: she had acted appallingly, with no thought for anyone but herself. What would Mama say when she heard that the daughter she trusted had allowed herself to be seduced? At the thought of her mother Lucy had a sudden longing to be at home, to throw herself upon her mother's mercy, beg her forgiveness and to bury herself in the household chores, never to have to face the world again. All at once the room seemed too hot. She ran to the window and threw up the sash, breathing in the still, humid air. Her room was on the same side of the house as the dining-room and from the open windows below she could hear the faint sounds of voices and laughter. In her imagination she could see Charlotte and Dominic, their heads close together, blonde curls touching sleek black hair as they laughed together over the discomfiture of little Lucilla! She could not bear to face them or anyone in the house again. If only she could go home now, this minute. Jump on a horse and ride away. After all, if Charlotte and Dominic were engaged there was no need for her to stay. The thought came to her as the faintest whisper: why not? She had money in her purse, if she could get to Bath she could buy herself a seat on the night mail and be in Templecombe by the following evening. Lucy felt sure it would work. She would borrow Snowfire—after all, it was in part Dominic Vanderley's fault that she was in this fix, he could not object, and she would see to it that the mare was returned when she reached Bath—no, not Bath, she decided. Once her departure was noticed they would be certain to make their first enquiries there. No, she would go to Keynsham, for had they not seen the mail-coach when they passed through the town on their way to Stock House? The heavy clouds obliterated the last of the evening sun, but she decided that once she reached Fordham and crossed the river, it would then be an easy matter to ride cross-country to reach Keynsham before dark. Anxious to waste no more time, Lucy hunted through the big cupboards until she found her riding habit. Outside, the thunder grew louder and more frequent but Lucy paid no heed: her whole attention was fixed upon flight.

SIX

'Miss Chambers does not join us this evening, ma'am?' Mr Vanderley approached Lady Cornholme as the guests gathered in the drawing-room.

My Lady shook her head.

'Her sister tells me she has the headache. Poor child, I wish I could do something for her, but Lady Lairne says she merely wishes to rest quietly.'

'It's this dashed weather,' put in Lord Cornholme, 'it has been building up for a storm these past few days and the air has been so close and heavy I wonder we don't all have the headache! There's a deal of rain to fall this night, unless I'm very much mistaken.'

'Well, we should not look so gloomy,' replied his wife, smiling. 'The ground is so parched we should be glad of the rain.'

'A gentle shower, perhaps, ma'am, to soak the ground,' said Mr Vanderley, 'but I think My Lord is concerned that a heavy downpour won't drain away.'

'Aye, that's just it,' replied that gentleman. 'The ground is iron-hard and the rain will most likely run above ground until it reaches the river. It's my opinion there'll be flooding before morning.'

'But not here, surely!' objected his lady, growing alarmed.

A number of guests were listening anxiously and Lord Cornholme did his best to allay their fears.

'No, no danger here, of course. We are well above it, but the cottagers at Fordham will be watching the river levels tonight, I'll be bound. But they are well used to this sort of thing and will doubtless have moved their livestock and valuables to higher ground.' Lord Cornholme was relieved when dinner was announced at that moment, and he could turn his attention to the happier duty of shepherding his guests into the dining-room.

*   *   *

Throughout the meal Dominic watched Countess Lairne. She seemed to be in high spirits as she responded to the gallantries of Arthur Collingham, but he thought he could detect a brittle quality in her laughter, and an angry glitter in her blue eyes. He had no opportunity to speak with the lady until dinner was over, and they were gathered once more in the drawing-room. The rain had started again, accompanied by such thunder and lightning that Lady Cornholme ordered lights to be brought in and the curtains pulled against the storm, yet still a sense of unease hung over the room. Mr Vanderley paused as he passed Charlotte's chair.

'Your sister is unwell, ma'am?'

She shot him a haughty look.

'She has the headache, sir.'

'Strange—I had not thought her the sort to be affected by the weather: she was certainly well enough when I saw her this afternoon.'

Charlotte's blue eyes darkened angrily. She rose.

'Perhaps, Mr Vanderley, it was a surfeit of your attentions that affected her!' she retorted, walking away.

Lady Lairne made sure there was no further chance for the gentleman to approach her and she very soon made her excuses and retired. Mr Vanderley watched her leave and a few moments later he slipped quietly out of the room. He made his way upstairs and paused on the upper landing, gripped by a strong sense of foreboding. He knew Lucy and Charlotte shared one of these rooms, but which one? Knowing the rest of the party to be still in the drawing-room, he began knocking on each door in turn. At the third attempt he was rewarded with a response. Lady Lairne's voice called from inside the room, demanding to know who knocked. The gentleman gave his name and waited.

'Go away!'

'I want to see Miss Chambers.'

'No. She—she will not see you.'

'One word, ma'am. No more.'

'She will not. Please go away.'

He cursed under his breath, certain now that something was amiss.

'Open this door, ma'am, or I shall break it open!'

There was a pause. The door opened a little and the countess looked out. She was very pale and shook her head at him, saying in a loud whisper, 'Pray you sir, go away! You cannot enter a lady's bedroom!'

'I can and will!' he replied grimly, pushing his way past her.

The room was in darkness save for a branched candlestick burning on the dressing-table, but, as he entered, a flash of lightning illuminated the scene, showing with devastating clarty the two empty beds, the disordered room and Lucy's discarded clothes still lying on the floor. He turned to Charlotte.

'Where is she?'

'I don't know.'

'You must ring for your servant, have her check the house—'

'No! I—I think she has run away.' Charlotte gave a tiny shrug and held out a note. He took it and went over to the candles, turning the paper to their feeble glow.

'*Dear Charlotte,*' he read, '*Please don't worry about me. I have gone home and shall not embarrass you further.*' He looked up. 'Is that all, you know nothing else?'

'She was not happy here,' muttered the countess defensively. 'She never wished to come.'

Mr Vanderley was busy lighting more of the candles, his face set in grim lines.

'What does she mean when she says she will not embarrass you?'

'You should know that, sir, as well as I!' she shot back at him. 'I thought seducing virgins was not part of your creed!'

For a moment she thought he would strike her and she stepped back, her eyes wide with fear, but as she watched the savage look died out of his face.

'If she has run away because of me I will bring her back. Can you discover what baggage she has taken?'

Charlotte threw out her hands and gave a cursory glance about the room.

'As far as I can tell she has taken nothing.'

'Come woman, you can do better than that!' he declared angrily. 'Check the cupboards—at least you should be able to tell me what she is wearing!'

Charlotte was feeling tired and anxious. She was not used to harsh words and tears sprang to her eyes, but some instinct told her that this gentleman would not appreciate a display of hysterics. With a small sniff she began to look through the cupboard that held most of Lucy's gowns.

'I cannot tell what is missing!' she complained. 'I am not a lady's maid!'

Dominic was at the window, staring out at the rain.

'She could not have set off on foot,' he murmured, 'it has to be carriage or horseback. I am going to the stables to see what I can discover there. You had best tidy this room a little and tell no one of Lucy's flight. With good fortune we may be able to avert a scandal.' He strode out of the room and was halfway down the stairs when a footman came hurrying across the hall.

'Mr Vanderley, sir, your groom has this minute come in and is very wishful to speak to you—he is in the master's office, sir, if you will see him there.'

He followed the servant down to the lower floor where Lord Cornholme had a room set aside for business affairs. There he found his groom restlessly pacing the floor, twisting his cap together between his fingers. At the sight of his master he stopped pacing and almost ran forward.

'Ah, thank goodness they have found you, sir!'

'I was just coming to find you, John. Tell me what is the matter!'

'It's Snowfire, sir. She's gone. At first I thought she might have slipped out of her stable, for you know what some of the younger lads are, they cannot be trusted to fasten a bolt properly, no matter how many times they're told, but when I came to check I found that her saddle's gone, too.' He paused, waiting for the expected torrent of anger to burst upon him. It did not come.

'Well, that's solved one mystery,' muttered Mr Vanderley, thinking quickly. 'Saddle up Sultan, John, and you had best find me an extra riding coat to take with me. I am going upstairs to change. Be ready in ten minutes!'

The groom sped away and Mr Vanderley made his way back to the drawing-room where he drew his sister to one side and explained the situation.

'Make your excuses and retire soon, Ju. Go up to Lady Lairne and stay with her until I get back. I don't trust her to keep silent.'

'I will look after her, never fear,' Judith replied in a low voice. 'I shall ensure the side door is left unlocked for your return. Pray God you can find her and bring her back in safety. Whatever possessed her to run off in weather like this?'

A grim little smile twisted the gentleman's lips but he was saved from answering by the sudden crack of thunder that broke overhead. He went off again, leaving Judith to make what excuses she could to the company for his strange behaviour.

*   *   *

Dominic arrived at the stables barely ten minutes later to find his groom leading Sultan out of his box.

'Who else knows of Snowfire's disappearance, John?' he asked, buttoning his greatcoat.

'No one that I know of, sir,' replied the groom, scratching his head. 'The weather being what it is we bedded them all down early tonight and the lads cleared off to their supper. I was just making a last check when I spotted she were gone.'

'Then I'd like to keep this quiet if I can.'

A conspiratorial gleam shone in the groom's eyes.

'I understand, sir. Trust me to act dumb if anyone comes looking for you!'

Dominic sprang up on to Sultan's back and with a final nod to his groom he guided the great horse out of the stable and across the yard. It was very dark now, the rain slanting down into the faces of horse and rider as they picked their way down the winding drive. The darkness was frequently broken by flashes of lightning, although the thunder was more distant now. When he reached the end of the drive he stopped: to the left the road climbed upwards through Kelston before descending in a sweeping curve towards Bath. To the right it dropped down to run level with the river as far as Fordham before rising again on is way to Bristol.

'Now which way?' he mused, 'Bath, and the main coaching route?'

While he was debating the problem, a figure approached out of the gloom. Shrouded in a long cloak, the fellow plodded on, his head bent against the driving rain so that he did not see the horse and rider until he was almost upon them. Then he looked up touching his hat.

'Evening, sir,' he called cheerfully, 'fine weather for a man to be walking home, ain't it?'

'Have you come far?'

'I've been to Fordham to see m'daughter. She begged me to stay the night, but I says no, Lord Cornholme will be expecting me back tonight, Sally, so tonight I must go.'

'You're one of Lord Cornholme's men?'

'Aye, Sir. Second gardener I've been to His Lordship now for the past ten years.' The fellow peered up through the rain. 'A terrible bad night to be out, sir. Never seen the like. The road's near flooded in places the rain's so heavy. I tried to warn t'other rider, but he wouldn't heed me ...'

'You've seen someone else out tonight?' Mr Vanderley broke in.

'Aye, sir. On a white 'oss he was, looking as

miserable as sin, too.'

'Are you sure it was a man?'

'Now then, sir, how can you be sure of anything in this light? 'Twas someone wrapped in a big cloak, that's all I can say.'

'Which direction? How long past?' came the urgent demand.

'Why, Fordham way, sir,' replied the fellow, pointing back along the road, 'couldn't have been more than ten minutes since.'

Scarcely waiting for the man to finish, Dominic put his heels to Sultan's flanks and the horse leapt forward, setting off along the wet road at a gallop. The gardener turned to watch him go, shaking his head at the antics of the Quality, then he resumed his steady progress towards the house.

Dominic pressed on. Surely there could not be another rider on a white horse out on such a night. She would be heading for Keynsham, he reasoned, and the quickest route home. Sultan stumbled on the wet, uneven surface and his master slackened the pace, uttering a few words of encouragement to the animal. Damn the girl! he thought savagely. Why should he concern himself with her madcap antics? He knew the answer of course: despite her twenty years she was such a child. She used no arts to attract him, yet when she turned her innocent smile upon him, his jaded spirit soared. Over the years he had become cynical, avoiding the fortune-seeking mamas who sought to throw their marriageable daughters in his path, and knowing that the married women on whom he bestowed his favours looked upon him as some sort of prize, to be flaunted. It was a social achievement to be Vanderley's latest flirt, but none of the beauties he had courted had touched his heart, which he had thought invulnerable, until he had come upon this slip of a girl with her artless chatter, indomitable spirit and a sense of humour to match his own. Now the thought of her flying from him, troubled and possibly in danger, made him push Sultan on at breakneck speed through the driving rain.

*   *   *

Darkness was closing in rapidly. The thick clouds and heavy rain made it impossible to see more than a few yards ahead. He knew he must be approaching Fordham when, above the noise of the storm, he could hear the roar of the swollen river. What was it the fellow had said about the road being flooded? He could well believe it, for even now the surface was awash and, as he turned Sultan off the road towards where he guessed the ford should be, all signs of the crossing had disappeared and the river frothed and bubbled out over the road on each side. Sultan stopped, snorting his disapproval: feeling the pressure of his master's heels, the great horse stepped forward gingerly, disliking the cold water that rose above his fetlocks. They cleared the trees and were standing at the edge of the ford itself when Dominic caught his breath. His keen eyes fell on the shadowy-white shape some twenty feet away. It took him a moment to adjust his gaze, then he realized that Snowfire was standing up to her knees in water just downstream of the ford, but although she stood her ground against the waters raging around her she could not find purchase for her hoofs to clamber up on to the bank. A flash of lightning briefly illuminated the scene. He saw the reins stretching from the mare to Lucilla, who was standing on the far bank, the floodwaters tugging at her sodden skirts. With one hand clinging to the slender trunk of a young tree and the other grasping the mare's bridle, she struggled to keep her stand against the elements. He shouted her name, but in the noise of wind and water it was impossible to know if she had heard him. He jumped down and led Sultan through the ford. The waters, though shallow, raced past his legs, threatening to pull him off balance. Cautiously he advanced, the rain lashing down as they reached the centre of the crossing, away from the shelter of the overhanging trees. When they had gained the higher ground on the far side, Dominic secured Sultan's bridle to a low branch and ran to Lucilla.

'Thank G-God you are come!' Her voice

was faint against the storm. 'Snowfire—I can't pull her out—'

'I know. Leave her to me. Get yourself out of the water. Go!' He took the reins from her fingers and moved along the water's edge, calling to the mare. She pricked up her ears at the familiar voice and at his command she began to back upstream, very slowly, carefully pushing against the torrent until she reached the shallower waters of the crossing place. Then, with Dominic encouraging her she scrambled up on to the bank and he led her towards Sultan. Lucilla was crouching against the tree, wrapped in her sodden cloak with her head on her knees, racked by deep, convulsive sobs that shook her whole body. Dominic knelt beside her, one arm around her wet shoulders.

'It's all over,' he said, his mouth close to her ear. 'You're safe now, but we must find shelter. Can you stand?'

He helped her up and she leaned against him, shivering.

'It was the storm,' she said in a stilted voice, gasping to make herself heard. 'We had almost reached the bank when there was a flash, and thunder so loud that it startled Snowfire. She—she lost her f-footing and we both fell. I managed to keep hold of the reins and make the bank, but I—I couldn't pull her out . . .'

'Hush now, you did well to hold her. You're both safe now. Come, you must keep moving.'

He led Lucy and the horses away from the

river, his eyes searching the darkness for some form of shelter. As they moved away from the river the ground became firmer and walking was easier without the thick mud to tug at their feet. The rain continued to lash them as they made their way across an open field. The lightning was infrequent now and the thunder merely a distant rumble, but the occasional flashes were sufficient to show them a small wooden building standing in the corner of the field. They turned their steps towards it, heads bent against the rain as they covered the last few yards that brought them to the square shape of the barn.

'A cow-byre. Not what you are used to, perhaps, but it will provide us with shelter.'

'Anything to get out of this storm!' declared Lucy through chattering teeth.

Dominic opened the door and led the way inside. An oil lamp hung on the inside of the door post and he muttered his thanks to Providence as he reached into his saddle-bag for his tinder-box. Moments later, a comforting light gleamed palely around the barn and the door was securely fastened against the rain. A quick glance around showed them that the barn was partially filled with hay, piled into a golden mound at one end. A hayrack had been fixed to one wall while in another corner a few sacks of turnips were stored. A thick layer of straw covered the floor and the air still held the thick, pungent smell of cattle.

'It would seem the farmer has taken the precaution of moving his animals out of here for tonight. I don't think the water will come this far, but it's very convenient for us.'

There was no reply. Snowfire was trembling pitifully and Lucy was trying to remove the saddle but her fingers were shaking too much to unfasten the buckles. Instead she grasped a handful of hay and began to rub down the mare.

'Let me do that,' Dominic came up to her, 'you can get out of those wet clothes.'

'We must make the horses comfortable first,' she muttered, setting to work with dogged determination.

He did not waste time arguing, but shrugged off his wet greatcoat and set about removing the saddles. He helped Lucy to rub down the animals with handfuls of sweet-smelling hay. Lucy found the activity warmed her chilled limbs and gradually the warmth from the horses filled the barn, providing them with a cosy haven from the heavy rain that drummed on the roof. When the animals had been tended and were tethered to the hayrack with a good supply of fodder, Dominic turned his attention to his companion. Even in the dim light she looked drawn and tired, and she was shivering uncontrollably.

'We must get you out of these wet clothes or you will never be warm. Come, let me help

125

you.'

Lucy made no protest as he began to undress her and Dominic thought wryly that his years of practice had not been wasted as he deftly dealt with buttons, hooks and drawstrings. When he turned to collect the extra great-coat his groom had strapped to his saddle he noticed that his own hands were shaking: not since his first love-affair had any woman excited him so much as this slip of a girl.

'I'm sorry, I didn't think to bring a spare shirt, but this will keep you warm.' He handed her the coat, scarcely looking at her pale slender body as she wrapped herself in its voluminous folds. The rough wool grazed her bare skin but at least it was dry.

'Thank you. That's much better. I—I am sorry to have put you to this trouble.'

Wrapped in the enormous coat she looked ludicrously fragile, her damp hair curling wildly about her head and her eyes sparkling with unshed tears. He fought down an impulse to take her in his arms and turned away to busy himself fetching hay to pile into a thick layer in one corner of the barn.

'You should try to rest: when the rain stops we must find some way to smuggle you back to Stock House.'

Lucy did not move. He looked around to see her standing just as he had left her.

'And you?' she asked him. 'Are you not wet

126

through, coming to rescue me?' He shook his head at her.

'My coat took the worst of it,' he grimaced, glancing down at his feet. 'I've no doubt my boots are ruined, but they are so wet if I take them off now I shall never get them on again.'

She gave a small chuckle and he stepped forward to take her hands.

'That's better. I thought I should never hear you laugh again.'

Lucy felt a sudden constriction in her throat making speech difficult. She gazed up at him silently, acutely aware of his presence, tingling in every nerve with a longing for him to take her in his arms. Gently he pulled her to him, his cheek resting on the top of her head as she clung to him, but as he held her, he felt his self-control slipping away. He buried his face in her damp curls, breathing in the sweet fragrance of her hair, then with one hand he tilted up her chin, covering her mouth with his own. With a groan he crushed Lucy to him, swept her up and carried her over to the makeshift bed of hay. She lay unprotesting as he unwrapped her from the greatcoat and began to cover her body with kisses. Lucy's senses swam: in the near darkness, the fresh clean smell of the hay created a new world, a safe haven where she could give herself up to the present with no thought for past or future. His hands explored her body and she moved instinctively, sensuously beneath his touch. His

127

mouth sought hers, melting her with a warm, passionate, demanding kiss that she returned fervently, knowing that she would deny him nothing.

A sudden noise outside made them pause. A dog began to bark and someone hammered on the barn door.

'What's goin' on in there? Come on, you open this door, now, this minute, d'you 'ear me?'

Dominic gave a sigh.

'The owner of our humble shelter, I suspect,' he murmured, drawing the greatcoat across Lucy and dropping a light kiss upon her brow before going to door. The hammering continued and Dominic called cheerfully, 'Careful, my man! There's no need to break the door down!' He unlatched the door and held it wide. A short, stocky figure stood in the doorway, his coat and hat glistening with the rain. He held aloft a lantern in order to scrutinize the face of this tall trespasser.

'Now then,' the fellow began sternly, 'what be 'ee doin' 'ere? You ain't got no rights to be in my barn. Jip, come 'ere!' The last command was to his dog, a small, black and white shape that had slipped past Dominic and was sniffing at Lucy, wrapped in the greatcoat in one dark corner of the barn.

'My son and I were caught in the storm. The boy got a soaking in the river and we came here to rest and dry off. I'm sure you would

128

not grudge us shelter?' Dominic's tone was friendly and the lantern's light gleamed upon the coins he held out. The farmer relaxed slightly and reached out to take the money.

'Well, now,' he said, his tone much less belligerent, 'I's a God-fearing man, when all's said an' done, and 'twouldn't be Christian to turn you out on a night like this. I only came down 'ere to see 'ow the flood's doin'. I moved me cattle 'igher up, see, out of 'arm's way, but there's me 'ay to think of, see, so as soon as the rain eased a bit I came down 'ere to take a look at it.'

'Yes, well, you can see for yourself your hay is safe, apart from the few handfuls we used for the horses and I think you will agree that I have paid you handsomely for that! If you will grant us the use of your barn for a while longer, we will soon be on our way, and you can bring your cattle back again at day-break.'

'Aye. S'pose I can,' replied the man, glancing thoughtfully around the barn. 'I'll be back soon after dawn and I shall expect you to be gone, but mind—I don't want to find any damage in 'ere! Come up, Jip!'

Assuring the farmer that they would take great care of his property, Dominic bade him goodnight and watched the man and his dog stride off into the night before closing the door upon them.

The interruption brought Lucy back to reality. With chilling clarity she recalled

Charlotte's look of revulsion when she had accused Lucy of throwing herself at Dominic. Perhaps Charlotte was right: Lucy should never have allowed him to kiss her and if the farmer had not come to the barn at that moment, Lucy knew there could have been only one conclusion to their embraces. Suddenly she felt sick with shame. She sat up, drawing the greatcoat firmly about her as Dominic approached. Sensing something of her mood he knelt beside her, but made no attempt to touch her. He spoke gently.

'I'm sorry, child, I never meant for this to happen. Will you not tell me why you were running away?'

Running away. It seemed a lifetime since Lucy had left Stock House, but now as the shock and fear of the storm receded, the anger and pain of Charlotte's disclosure flooded through her again, choking her with emotion. She said haltingly, 'Because of—you and Charlotte.'

'Lucy, pray do not worry your pretty head on that score. When I saw your sister this afternoon she was very understanding. I did not tell her about you, but in any event she could not object—'

Lucilla's misery intensified. She turned away, shutting her eyes tightly to prevent the hot, scalding tears from falling. Dominic's voice was gentle, but the words burned into her heart.

'I want only the best for you, sweetness. I shall dress you in silks, install you in my London house where I can show you off to the world and at night you shall sleep with me between scented sheets—'

'No! please, no more!' She continued in a carefully controlled voice, 'And—and what of Charlotte?'

She could hear the amusement in his voice as he answered.

'My darling, your sister will go her own sweet way. I thought that was understood?'

Lucy clenched her teeth, trying to whip up her anger. How arrogant that he should think he could have them both, Charlotte as his wife and herself as his mistress! Charlotte's words came back to her: *he wants a wife who understands his need to amuse himself.* Very well, but let him amuse himself elsewhere! Screwing up her courage, she knew what must be done.

'Sir—Dominic—I am sorry. This should never have happened. Yet I own I cannot regret it.' Her voice trembled a little. 'I shall remember this night as long as I live.'

'You talk as if we shall not see each other again.'

'We shall not. At least, not in *this* way. If—*when* we meet again, it can only be as friends. No one must ever know of this.'

There was a silence.

'Lucy—sweet life—I do not understand

131

you.'

She shrugged off his touch and rose, trying to distance herself from him.

'I cannot, will not, allow this to happen again.'

Lucy stood with her back to him and Dominic stared at her dark, unyielding shadow, his numbed brain refusing to take in her words. He too rose, suddenly aware of the chill in the air.

'But—in Heaven's name, Lucilla, why?' He felt rather than saw the shake of her head and he continued roughly, 'Did my embraces then mean nothing to you? My apologies, madam, I am undoubtedly a fool! I have always prided myself on my knowledge of women! I could have sworn, nay'—he reached out, seizing her shoulders and dragging her round to face him, gripping her so fiercely she could feel his fingers digging into her flesh through the thick folds of the greatcoat. He stared down at her, the feeble glow from the lantern casting long shadows across his face. Lucy risked one brief glance up and was shocked at the savagery in his eyes. He shook her roughly, saying in a low voice, 'I know you love me!'

'What has love to do with anything?' she retorted, in a bitter echo of her sister's words. She tore herself away. 'Forgive me, sir, if I have offended you, but believe me it is for the best.'

Dominic shook his head, suddenly feeling

very tired.

'Offended me! No, I cannot believe you mean what you are saying, but this is not the time to discuss it further. The rain has stopped and we must get you back to Stock House.'

Turning away, he began to saddle the horses.

SEVEN

The storm had passed, leaving the air still and calm, while in the night sky the heavy black clouds were breaking up, allowing the moon and stars to brighten the glistening landscape with a silvery touch. Neither of the riders heading away from the old wooden barn was in any mood to appreciate the night's beauty. Dominic led the way, moving steadily through the darkness and curtly ordering Lucy to keep close behind him as they crossed the still-swollen waters at the ford. Lucy, her wet clothes rolled into a tight bundle and strapped onto the saddle behind her, followed on silently. The voluminous greatcoat, her only covering against the night, chafed her continuously, but she scarcely noticed it, so deep was her misery. They pressed on, silent save for the creaking of the leather saddles and the steady beat of hoofs upon the wet track.

Everything was in darkness when they reached the stables, but as Dominic rode the black across the stable-yard the glimmer of an oil-lamp shining from a doorway told him his groom was waiting in Sultan's stall. The servant hurried out to take the reins.

'Is all well, master? Snowfire?'

'Behind me. Put them to bed for me, John, and let no one know they have been out this night!'

'Yes, sir.'

Apart from one swift, curious glance the groom ignored the shadowy figure huddled in the greatcoat that his master lifted from Snowfire's back and without another word he closed the door upon them, leaving Dominic and Lucy alone in the yard. They returned to the house by way of the side door, using the candle thoughtfully provided to light their way upstairs. Encumbered by the heavy folds of the coat, Lucy trudged wearily upwards, wondering how much longer her tired limbs would continue to function. They made directly for Charlotte's room, Dominic scarcely waiting for an answer to his knock before entering.

Judith Vanderley was there with Lady Lairne, and two pairs of eyes were fixed anxiously upon him as he strode in. Miss Vanderley was the first to find her voice.

'Dominic, God be praised! And Lucy!'

Charlotte ran forward to greet her sister.

'My dear, thank God you are safe.'

Dominic held out a wet bundle.

'Lucy's clothes,' he said, not without humour.

'I fell into the river,' Lucy explained, observing their astonished faces.

'Poor child.' Judith put her arms about her and walked with her to the bed. 'You must be chilled to the bone. We must get you into bed. I took the precaution of ordering a hot brick, which is already warming the sheets for you. You look worn out, both of you. Dom, you can do no good here. Go and change out of your wet things and wait for me in my room. Lady Lairne and I will take care of Lucy.'

As soon as the door had closed behind him Judith and Charlotte helped Lucy to put on her night-gown and get into bed.

'Poor darling!' crooned Charlotte, smoothing the damp curls from Lucy's pale brow. 'I had no idea that you would be so foolish as to run away—I pray God it will result in nothing worse than a chill for you! But how—?'

'We should let her sleep,' Judith interrupted her quietly, 'the poor child is quite dazed. There will be time enough to talk in the morning.'

'Yes, of course.' Charlotte looked down at her sister.

'Come,' said Judith, 'let us go and find my brother. He will be able to tell us what happened.'

They found Dominic waiting for them in Judith's apartment. He had changed out of his wet and muddied clothes but the night's adventures had left him very weary. However, as they entered he came forward, saying cheerfully, 'I think we shall come about. No one saw me come in with Lucy, so there is no need for anyone to know I had a hand in this. But I am afraid there is a trail of mud across the hall that will need to be explained.'

Judith nodded.

'Of course. We will concoct some story, a sisters' quarrel and Lucy going off in a temper. Will that do, Lady Lairne?'

'Yes, that might work . . .'

'Then you asked for my help, not wishing to alarm Lady Cornholme when Lucy returned soaked through. I think that will do, will it not, Dom?'

'Yes. Very good.'

Charlotte sank down on to a sofa, clasping her hands together. 'I only pray she will take no lasting ill from this night's work. Poor Mama would be heartbroken if she knew of it.'

Judith scarcely heard her: she was watching her brother. He looked tired and drawn, as well he might after a sleepless night, but there was something else in his face that she had not seen there since the death of their father two years before. It was a bleakness, as if something within Dominic himself had

136

suffered. Wondering how best to help him, she took little heed of the countess's next words.

'I have wished a thousand times that I had not said what I did!'

Dominic's tired eyes moved to rest upon her beautiful face. He said wearily, 'And what did you say to her, My Lady, to make her run away?'

Charlotte bit her lip, her gaze shifting anxiously from brother to sister, but neither face gave her any comfort.

'I—I told her we were—betrothed.'

'*What!*'

Dominic's voice made her wince, but she had said too much to stop now. She said pleadingly, 'I was angry after our—our discussion in the morning-room and when Lucy came in, telling me that you loved her . . . I told her you were not serious, that you would make her your mistress—' She broke off, her eyes widening in horror as he advanced towards her, his face thunderous.

'Dominic!' Judith threw herself in his way, clutching at his arm. He stopped, but did not take his eyes off the countess.

'You said that? You told such lies to your own sister? You may let me go now, Ju. You have my word I will not lay a finger upon her!'

Charlotte shrank back still further at the revulsion in his tone. She said sulkily, 'I merely wanted to put an end to her childish infatuation. Of course I did not know she would run away.'

'You might have considered what effect your words would have upon her! Good God, madam, do you know so little of your sister?'

'Perhaps it is that I know a great deal more about you!' she flashed back at him. 'You are notorious for your intrigues—the great Dominic Vanderley! Not all your wealth could restore Lucilla's honour if she became one of your conquests!' She noted the arrested look in his face and continued scathingly, 'Honour—I doubt that word means much to you now, sir, having spent your adult life enjoying every form of dissipation! But you cannot *in honour* be considered a suitable companion for such a sweet innocent as my sister! Why, it disgusts me even to think of such a union!'

There was silence. The countess leaned back upon the sofa, her face pale and her breast heaving with emotion. Judith stood to one side, an unwilling spectator. Following Charlotte's outburst she would have spoken, defending her brother, but Dominic gestured her to silence.

'Why don't you go?' said Charlotte wearily. 'Leave us in peace and allow Lucilla to find a man worthy of her—one who will make her happy.'

'You may rest easy, ma'am. I am leaving in the morning.'

'Dom, no!'

He gave his sister a brief smile.

'Don't worry about me, Ju. There's work a-plenty to occupy me on the estates—tasks you have been nagging me to undertake since I became the master. I shall leave you the carriage, so you need not cut short your own visit.'

Judith spoke as he opened the door. 'And Lucilla?'

He said, without turning, 'When she is well enough, tell her . . . tell her I want only her happiness, and that I shall always be her obedient servant.'

*   *   *

Lucy knew little of the following days: exhaustion and the soaking she had received had left her with a severe chill and her hostess, hearing that she had run off following a quarrel with Charlotte, could not find it in her kind heart to scold the child for her behaviour. Instead she summoned her own doctor to attend Lucy and after receiving his cheerful assurances that a few days' rest was all that was necessary to repair the damage, Lady Cornholme sat down to write a long explanatory letter to Mrs Chambers.

It was two days later when Lucy opened her eyes to find the sun streaming into the room and Charlotte sitting in a chair beside her bed, idly flicking through the pages of a magazine.

When she saw her sister was awake, Lady Lairne threw aside the periodical.

'Oh Lucy, how do you feel?' she asked softly. 'The doctor said I might sit with you for a while. Are you thirsty? Lady Cornholme sent up some lemonade . . .'

'Thank you. How long have I been here?'

'Two days. Can you not remember? I have been so worried about you!'

Lucy frowned. Was the storm only two days past? She fixed her eyes upon Charlotte.

'I remember you and Miss Vanderley were waiting when we got back—who else knows what happened?'

'No one. And thankfully no one is aware of Mr Vanderley's part in it. Everyone thinks you have been in a silly scrape, but nothing worse than that. And with the gentleman out of the way now we can all be easy again.'

'Mr Vanderley has left?'

Charlotte looked a little uncomfortable.

'Why yes,' she replied with forced lightness, 'he left the morning after the storm. He has pressing business to attend to, I believe.' She hesitated, then, 'I'm sorry, Lucilla, if you have a *tendre* for him . . .'

'No!' Lucy interrupted her, a stubborn set to her chin as she forced herself to look at her sister. 'No, I don't love Dominic Vanderley. I was mistaken.'

'Oh my dear! Truly?'

Lucy looked away.

140

'Yes, truly. But when you are married, Charlotte, I would rather not—'

'Oh but I am not going to marry Dominic Vanderley!' Charlotte saw Lucy's look of surprise and blushed faintly. She had been dreading this moment but now Lucy had made it so much easier for her. If she was no longer infatuated with Mr Vanderley there was no need for a full confession. She continued airily. 'Oh no! I could not marry him after the way he behaved towards you.' Charlotte was unable to meet her sister's gaze, yet still some feeling of guilt made her cry out, 'Oh Lucy, Dominic Vanderley is not the man for you! If you had heard the way he spoke to me the night you ran away—he was a positive monster! If his sister had not been there to restrain him I really think he would have struck me! I was very relieved when he left us, I assure you.'

'So it has all come to naught.'

Hearing the desolate note in Lucy's voice, Charlotte threw herself down beside the bed, burying her face in the covers.

'Oh Lucy, forgive me!'

Lucy stared uncomprehendingly at the mass of fair curls.

'Dry your tears, Charlotte. You are not to blame.' Lucy's fingers plucked idly at the bedcovers. 'Is he—does he intend to return here?' Charlotte shook her head.

'You need not fear, love. He is gone for good. Judith Vanderley has remained, but she has her own carriage to take her home at the end of her visit.'

'Then it is all finished.'

Her sister beamed at her, patting her hand.

'Indeed it is. And there is nothing for you to concern yourself with other than getting better. Everyone sends you their best wishes—Lady Cornholme and I agreed between us that it would be best if you had few visitors until you are feeling stronger. Now, as you are awake you should try to take some nourishment. I shall arrange for a tray to be sent up!'

Charlotte hurried away, happily aware that a cloud had been lifted from her shoulders. Lucy was left to her own more sober reflections.

*   *   *

It was several days before Lucy heard Mr Vanderley's name again. Fearful for her guest's health, Lady Cornholme strictly forbade anyone save Lady Lairne to visit the sickroom until Lucilla showed visible signs of improvement. After a week confined to her room, she judged her to be well enough to have visitors. My Lady thought privately that the child looked listless and unhappy, and she wondered just what had caused the quarrel between Lucy and her sister. Her Ladyship had to admit that Charlotte had been most attentive since Lucy's mishap, but she wondered wryly if she would have been quite so assiduous in her duties had Mr Vanderley still been in residence. It had been obvious to both My Lady and her spouse that Lady Lairne had set her cap at that gentleman, and equally plain that Mr Vanderley was not interested in the beautiful widow. Lord Cornholme had given it as his opinion that it was this determined pursuit that had caused Mr Vanderley to fly from the house without so much as a by-your-leave, but Lady Cornholme's kind heart would not allow it. She was quite happy to accept Miss Vanderley's explanation that her brother feared the recent storms may have badly damaged his own extensive lands in Oxfordshire, and had felt compelled to see for himself.

As Lucy's strength returned, Charlotte gladly relinquished her self-imposed role of sick-nurse. She had found the task extremely irksome, but as she was very fond of Lucilla at the bottom of her somewhat shallow heart, she had resolved to do her duty. She was also relieved to think that her sister's infatuation with Dominic Vanderley was short-lived, for after their initial conversation the gentleman's name had not been mentioned again, and Charlotte was content to believe that Lucy's heart as well as her body was on the way to a full recovery. Judith Vanderley was one of her first visitors, but as Lady Lairne was hovering anxiously about her patient, she kept her visit brief, with a promise to look in again. It was almost a week after the storm that they had the opportunity of a private talk. Lucy had just finished her dinner in her room when Miss Vanderley scratched on the door.

'Am I disturbing you? I wondered if you might like a little company.'

'Yes, indeed. Come in.' Lucy smiled, dismissing the maid who had come to collect her tray. Miss Vanderley noticed that she had barely touched her meal. 'How kind of you,' Lucy continued, 'I do hope you have not curtailed your own meal to come here.'

'Not a bit of it,' replied Miss Vanderley, her dark eyes twinkling. 'I merely excused myself from playing cards.'

Lucy grimaced. 'Silver loo, or whist? If Charlotte has her way it will be whist.'

'It is!' laughed Judith. 'No one disagreed when Lady Lairne put forward the suggestion and she has settled down to the game in high good humour with Arthur Collingham as her partner.'

'Charlotte has always been fond of cards.' Lucy paused. 'From the little my sister has told me, I begin to think that Mr Collingham is a most favoured companion.'

Judith considered the matter.

'She is certainly a great deal in his company. She has only to suggest something and he is her most eager advocate.'

'I'm glad,' remarked Lucy, 'for he is a very pleasant gentleman and I believe—nay I am sure he adores Charlotte.' She gave a little sigh. 'I think he could make her happy, if she had not set her heart on—'

'I know,' Judith put in, when Lucy broke off in confusion. 'Your sister was dazzled by the thought of catching the biggest prize of the season! I am well aware that she had set her cap at my brother and I regret to say that Dominic must take a share of the blame! But that is all in the past. I am certain he has learned his lesson. Which brings me on to something I want to say to you.' She noted the wary look upon Lucy's face and hurried on, 'Pray believe me, I have no wish to distress you, but my visit here comes to an end tomorrow, and my brother charged me with a message for you. I am to tell you that he wishes only your happiness and he will always be your most obedient servant.' Judith waited, but Lucy was silent. 'Am I to give him no reply?'

'There is nothing more to be said.'

Judith studied her for a moment, then leaned forward and laid her hand over Lucy's.

'My dear, I do not know what has passed between you and Dominic, but when he left here there was such pain in his face—can you give me no word of encouragement that I may pass on to him?'

She felt a tremor run through Lucy, and when she spoke she seemed almost to be talking to herself.

'It is best that it ends like this, before it is even begun.' She turned her blue-grey eyes upon Judith, who felt a slight shock at the depth of misery they contained. 'Tell your brother I wish him every happiness. I blame him for nothing and I—I hope he can forgive me. It was a mistake that we should ever have met. I'm sorry.'

When Miss Vanderley had gone, Lucy remained staring at the vacant chair beside the bed, feeling that the last ties had been severed. The knowledge gave her no comfort. August was at an end; she could return home and devote herself once more to her beloved horses, but deep within her a tiny voice mocked, saying that her life could never be the same again.

*   *   *

Mrs Chambers came in person to carry her daughters home from Stock House, reproaching herself that she had ever been foolish enough to allow two such silly children to make the visit without her. Upon her arrival, Lady Cornholme came out to greet her with all the warmth of a long friendship and the two ladies spent a long time closeted together in private conversation after Mrs

146

Chambers had greeted her daughters. They set off for Templecombe the next morning with Arthur Collingham riding alongside as escort. Lucy was a little surprised at her mama's calm acceptance of the young gentleman's attendance. She was even more surprised at her suggestion that he should spend a few days with them before making his way back to Town, but she was glad her mother had observed the pleasant young man beneath Mr Collingham's rather foppish appearance. They had been at Templecombe for less than twenty-four hours when he asked for permission to pay his addresses to Lady Lairne. This was not strictly necessary since Charlotte was already a widow, but the gesture delighted Mrs Chambers, who was overjoyed when Charlotte accepted his proposal. Conscious of her erratic behaviour, Charlotte was very anxious to explain her change of heart to her sister. She followed Lucy into her bed-chamber that evening, remarking that no doubt her sister thought her very fickle.

'Of course I never loved Mr Vanderley,' she said airily, 'although I did think I should like to be his wife. However, I now see that we should not suit at all.'

Lucy murmured some inarticulate reply, thinking that her sister sounded very calm, as though they were discussing the choice of a new gown.

'I have no doubt that Arthur and I will deal

extremely well,' Charlotte continued. 'He is so obliging! Indeed, I cannot recall ever having heard him utter a cross word, unlike . . .' she trailed off uncomfortably, but Lucy seemed not to notice. She merely smiled and gave her sister a hug.

'I am sure you will be very happy, Charlotte. Have you agreed upon a date?'

'It is to be in November and you, dear sister, shall be my maid of honour! Mama has decided to bring you out at the same time, so she will be saved the expense of another visit to London next year. Does that not please you, Lucy?'

'Of course.'

'Mama is quite distracted with all the arrangements. I told her we would help as much as we can, but there is such a lot to do, with all the different gowns I shall need! I wonder that she should wish to prepare for both a wedding and a presentation at the same time. Of course, you could ease the burden for her.' Charlotte paused, glancing speculatively at her sister.

'I could? How?'

'You might like to make it a double wedding! Pray don't look so offended;' added Charlotte, laughing, 'but one cannot help noticing that since your return Tom Bancroft has been most attentive!'

'Tom and I are like brother and sister.'

'I doubt if that is how Tom views the

matter! I believe that while we were staying at Stock House, young Mr Bancroft realized just how much he cares for you!'

Lucy shook her head, refusing to talk further on the subject, but privately she feared there was some truth in her sister's words. Her childhood friend had several times hinted that his feelings for her had undergone a change and she knew it was only a matter of time before he proposed to her.

Arthur Collingham had been a constant visitor to Templecombe since their return from Stock House and it was something of a relief to Mrs Chambers when he bore Charlotte away to make her known to his numerous relations. Left to themselves, she hoped that Lucy might unburden herself and tell her Mama just what it was that was troubling her. It was not that Lucy was miserable, for she settled back into her life at Templecombe with every appearance of enjoyment, spending most of her time in the stables, or with Tom, riding over the countryside, yet there was something missing. The sparkle that had always warned her fond Mama of mischief brewing was gone, replaced by a restlessness that Mrs Chambers found far more disturbing. To all solicitous enquiries Lucy merely said that she was feeling a little low following her illness and quickly changed the subject. Tactful questioning of young Mr Bancroft convinced Mrs Chambers that he had not been admitted into Lucy's confidence and she could only hope that the mood would pass.

*   *   *

A diversion came at the beginning of October in the form of an unexpected caller. When Mrs Chambers informed Lucy that she had a visitor, she was intrigued to observe her daughter's reaction.

'A-a visitor, Mama?' she faltered, deathly pale.

'Yes, my dear. Miss Vanderley has called especially to see you. Do go on in, child. I am sure you have much say to each other, and tell Miss Vanderley if she would care to take luncheon with us we would be delighted to have her stay. I shall go and see Cook now!'

Lucy made her way to the small parlour, where she found Judith Vanderley in travelling dress, standing before the tall windows looking out over the rolling countryside. As Lucy entered she turned and walked forward, holding out her hand.

'Lucilla, my dear! I hope you will forgive my calling upon you unannounced, but I am on my way to Wells to stay with friends there and since you were so close, I could not drive by without stopping to enquire after you! How do you go on?'

Lucy murmured a suitable reply and begged her guest to be seated. They exchanged pleasantries, and Lucy tried to appear composed. She dreaded hearing Judith Vanderley mention her brother, yet when this did not happen she could not resist asking after him. Judith's bright smile faded.

'Dominic is very busy with the estate. There is much to do, for he wants to have everything in order before he leaves for Vienna in two weeks.'

'Vienna?'

'He has been invited to join Lord Castlereagh there for the Peace Congress. Perhaps you did not know but he was greatly involved with the Foreign Secretary some years ago. Then our father's illness made it imperative for him to leave his service and take over the management of the estates.' She paused. 'Will you not see him, Lucilla, before he leaves England?'

'It would serve no purpose.'

'It might make you both a little happier.'

'It might also have the opposite effect,' countered Lucy.

Judith looked at her steadily.

'I thought you cared for him.'

Lucy kept her eyes lowered *I do!* she wanted to cry out, *I love him so much my whole body aches for him!* She said, 'If he—if he wishes to see me he may visit me here.'

Judith gave an exasperated sigh.

'You know he will not come without some sign from you! Dominic does not talk of what

151

happened, but I know that in some way you have rejected him. He is a proud man, Lucy. He will not come here to risk another rebuff. But that is not all: my brother is too much the gentleman to force his attentions upon you.'

He did so once, thought Lucy, remembering the first time he had kissed her, the feel of his mouth crushing down on hers, the way her own body had responded. She closed her eyes tightly to fend off the threatening tears.

'There is no reason to shut him out of your life,' Judith urged her. 'Nothing stands between you!'

'You are wrong.' Lucilla rose from her chair, anxious to conclude this painful interview. 'A great deal stands between us. I'm sorry, I cannot—' she stopped, her voice suspended in tears and Judith Vanderley sprang forward to comfort her.

'There, there, my dear. Dry your tears—I will not press you further. If you will not see him that is an end to it. Mayhap it is for the best, but—I pray you will neither of you regret it!'

*   *   *

Lucy lay awake until the early hours, going over the details of Judith Vanderley's visit. She had convinced her guest that there could be no reconciliation and so it must be, for Dominic was leaving England and the faint, scarcely acknowledged hopes she had had of meeting him in Town were dashed. The future for Lucilla Chambers looked very bleak indeed.

Charlotte's wedding was a magnificent event, occasioning no little interest. The story of the beautiful countess, tragically widowed so young and now becoming plain Mrs Collingham had a romantic quality that caught the imagination of London society. Lucy's introduction to the polite world was by comparison a very quiet affair, being quite overshadowed by both the wedding and the continuing Peace Congress, which drew vast numbers of the *haut monde* to Vienna. Mrs Chambers might bemoan the fact that Town was very thin of company but Lucy could not be sorry for it. Privately she breathed a sigh of relief when they were at last on their way home to Templecombe for Christmas. Her mother however was in a less sanguine mood. The day was cold, the carriage draughty and despite every effort by her determined parent, Lucy was leaving Town without a single conquest to her credit.

'I must say, Lucilla, I cannot believe that you made the most of your opportunity in Town. It is not that you are bad-looking—indeed, with your hair now dressed in ringlets you look very well indeed! But even though our visit was so short, I expected to receive at least one offer for your hand. But I shall say no more on that head!'

Lucy said nothing. She gazed steadily out of the window, thinking back over the past few weeks. Following hard upon Charlotte's wedding she had been presented at court and thrown into a whirl of parties and engagements that she had lived through as though in a dream. Nothing had touched her during those weeks, for her innermost feelings had been locked away and she had played her part as debutante perfectly, yet when any gentleman's interest grew too great, she made it plain—quietly yet decisively—that his suit was hopeless. She had retreated into her own safe world, determined never to be hurt again.

'Well, I do not know what is to become of you!' concluded Mrs Chambers. 'Perhaps after all you should marry young Bancroft!'

Lucy's solemn eyes had something of their old twinkle in them as she replied that Tom had not yet proposed to her.

'He will,' returned her mother confidently. 'He was on the point of doing so after your return from Stock House and it needs only the slightest encouragement from you to bring him to the point.' She sighed, ending in a martyred tone, 'Now that all my hopes for you are dashed, I shall not oppose the match. Indeed, I shall be pleased to see you respectably settled, even to the son of the local squire. Ah, Lucilla, you could have done so much better for yourself!'

Lucy turned away to resume her study of

the passing landscape, bare and brown now with the onset of winter. The constant pressure upon her to marry weighed heavily on her spirits. She wanted to be left alone, to live within the shell she had built around herself, yet she knew her mother would not be satisfied until both her daughters were settled.

*   *   *

The winter months passed uneventfully at Templecombe, where Mrs Chambers was content to live quietly with her daughter. Their only contact with the outside world was the occasional meetings with their nearest neighbours, the Bancrofts, and the infrequent letters from Charlotte, who seemed to be enjoying herself immensely in her new role. The income she retained from the late earl's will and Mr Collingham's comfortable independence allowed the couple to live in the first style of elegance and move in the very highest circles. When these letters arrived, Mrs Chambers noted that Lucy would read them quickly, frowning over her sister's closely written scrawl and at the end toss the letter aside, as though she had been searching for something and not found it. As spring approached, Mrs Chambers suggested that Lucy might like to go to Town in March, to spend her birthday with Charlotte. Lucy's appeals to remain quietly at Templecombe touched her mother's heart and she agreed to it, promising to arrange nothing more than a quiet birthday dinner with the Bancrofts to mark the occasion. Lucy tried to show a proper interest in the preparations that were being made, but she found it increasingly difficult to throw off the leaden depression that had settled over her. The end of winter had always been a hopeful time for her in the past, but now she felt imprisoned by the inclement weather and increasingly irritated by the steady pace of life in her mother's house. Gazing out of her rain-washed bedroom window on the morning of her twentieth birthday, Lucy thought that perhaps the day would have been easier to bear if they had gone to stay with Charlotte. With a faint sigh she turned away and went downstairs to join her mother for breakfast, summoning a cheerful appreciation for her mother's gifts to her—a new riding habit and a pearl bracelet to match the necklace she had been given for her presentation. Breakfast finished, Lucy was about to take the riding habit to her room to try it on when the door of the breakfast-room opened to admit Mr Bancroft, his cheeks flushed and a boyish grin splitting his face.

'Good morning, Tom,' Mrs Chambers greeted the newcomer placidly, well used to the young man's presence in her house. 'Have you breakfasted?'

Mr Tom Bancroft stepped forward to take

the hand she extended to him.

'Good day to you, ma'am, and to you, Lucy! Yes, thank you, Mrs Chambers, I took breakfast at home. Happy birthday, Lucy.' He held out a small parcel. 'I've brought you a present. I hope you like them,' he added as she unwrapped her gift. 'Your Mama told me she had ordered a new habit for you and I thought you might like a pair of gloves to match.'

'They're lovely, Tom. Thank you.'

'I hope you don't mind my bursting in on you so early, but I also wanted to tell you the news!'

'Why, what has happened,' cried Mrs Chambers, 'some accident—?'

'No, no, nothing like that! I thought you would not have heard, for I know you take no London papers.'

'Heard what?' cried Lucy impatiently, frowning at her childhood friend.

He turned towards her, his eyes glowing with excitement.

'Bonaparte has escaped! He is at this very moment in Paris, gathering an army together.'

'Impossible!' cried Mrs Chambers, horrified.

The young man shook his head.

'Father brought the news back with him from London last night. It is all over Town. Bonaparte appeared in Lyons a week or so ago, and since then the French have been flocking to his banner. It's war again!'

'But this is terrible!' cried Mrs Chambers, 'are we to have no peace in this world?'

'You need not worry, ma'am,' Tom assured her, 'this time we shall put the fellow away for good!' He could not conceal his excitement as he added, 'Father has at last agreed to let me join up! He has an old friend in Town who has promised to arrange everything. Light infantry, he explained. 'Of course I would have preferred a cavalry regiment but that would have been too costly. I shall be in Flanders by the end of April!' He turned his shining face towards Lucy, reaching out to take her hands in his own. 'Well, Lucy?' he asked, a trifle shyly, 'will you make my happiness complete and agree to marry me now?'

Mrs Chambers held her breath, watching the couple in a silence that seemed to fill the room.

'Yes,' said Lucy, very pale. 'Yes, Tom. I will marry you.'

EIGHT

Lucy's reply was met with a moment of stunned silence. Tom Bancroft had grown so used to his childhood friend evading his hints concerning matrimony that he had not expected his proposal to receive an answer. Mrs Chambers was so astonished by Lucilla's sudden change of mind that she could only stare open-mouthed at her daughter for a full minute.

Tom was the first to recover his wits. With a shaky laugh he said, 'Well, devil take me, that's marvellous! I cannot wait to tell Mama; she will be delighted—in fact it might help to reconcile her to my going away, for she's not at all happy about that, I can tell you!' A sudden doubt came to him and he looked questioningly at Mrs Chambers. 'I'm sorry, should I have approached you first, ma'am? Only I knew *you* would not oppose my suit, and I was so excited, what with the thought of joining up and everything, the words just slipped out!'

'No, no, it is quite all right,' murmured Mrs Chambers faintly. 'Of course, I shall need to speak to your father, but perhaps he would give me a few moments of his time before dinner tonight . . .'

'I am sure of it!' returned Tom, beaming at her. 'Now if you will excuse me, I must go back and tell my parents. They will not believe my good luck—indeed, I can scarcely believe it myself! Thank you, Lucy dearest!'

With that he was gone, leaving the two ladies to stare in silence at the closed door. Mrs Chambers was still looking stunned, but before she could remark upon the turn of events, Lucy mumbled her excuses and fled to the seclusion of her bedchamber.

Dinner at Mirlow Hall that evening was a lively affair: Squire Bancroft and his lady were in excellent spirits, overjoyed by the news that their son was to marry a girl they had always regarded in the light of a daughter. Mrs Chambers too had reconciled herself to the fact that Lucilla would never make a great match and she was only too relieved to think that her younger child would be comfortably settled. The happy couple themselves seemed unusually subdued, but this was put down to shyness on Lucy's part and Tom spent the evening in a daze of contentment, not knowing which pleased him most, his engagement or his forthcoming army career.

'Of course,' remarked the squire, as they sat at dinner, 'if this dashed fellow Bonaparte were not on the loose again I would have no hesitation in agreeing to an early marriage, but as it is young Tom here will more than likely be fighting in France within the next couple of months and will need to concentrate on his duties, without the worry of a young bride to distract him.'

Tom leaned towards Lucy, covering her hand with his own.

'You do understand, don't you Lucy?' he said, squeezing her fingers. 'It would not be right to drag you into Heaven knows what when I shall be but a raw recruit myself.'

Mrs Chambers smiled at them both.

'I know how hard it is to wait for anything

when you are young, but I think you must reconcile yourself to an autumn wedding, my dears.'

The squire nodded his agreement.

'You need not fear the time will pass slowly, Lucilla, for what with the arrangements for the wedding and all the bride-clothes you ladies like to buy, I don't doubt you will find plenty to do.'

'We would like to arrange a little dinner before Tom goes away,' put in Mrs Bancroft. 'Nothing formal of course, just a few close friends, to celebrate the betrothal.'

'That will be delightful, won't it, Lucy?' smiled her fond mama.

Lucilla murmured her agreement and was rewarded with a beaming smile from Squire Bancroft.

'Then that's settled! And why not write to Charlotte, ma'am, to see if she and that young husband of hers would like to join us!'

A flurry of activity during the next week kept everyone at Templecombe busy and Mrs Chambers had little time to consider whether her daughter was truly happy in her engagement. In fact, Lucy was surprised at how little the betrothal changed her life. She still rode out regularly with Tom, whose mind was so full of the army that he had little time to play the lover and Lucy felt a detached amusement at the conscientious peck on the cheek he would deliver as a greeting before

161

launching into a detailed description of some facet of army life that he had just discovered. Lucilla was content to let him talk, refusing to question why she should be satisfied with his very unlover-like attentions. A hurriedly despatched message to Charlotte received a swift response, and an elegant travelling carriage brought Mr and Mrs Collingham to the house two days before the Bancrofts' dinner. The meeting between Mrs Chambers and her elder daughter was both joyous and tearful and the news that Charlotte was in a very delicate condition made her fond mama's happiness complete. Congratulations were uttered, with Arthur hovering proudly about his adored wife, anxiously watching her for signs of tiredness after the long journey. Charlotte, as the centre of attention, was radiant and Lucy could even forgiven her for the patronizing way she congratulated her on the betrothal.

'I really do hope you will be as happy as Arthur and me: such a pity you cannot be married in Town, but perhaps a quiet wedding here would be best; after all, young Tom is only the squire's son . . .'

Lucy allowed her sister to continue, feeling vaguely detached from the talk of marriage: did it really concern her? When she tried to look into the future it was nothing but a blank.

Squire Bancroft had announced that his dinner would be followed by 'a little dancing—

not a ball, you understand, just an impromptu hop for our young people!'

There would not be above two dozen people present, all of them local families whom Lucy had known all her life, and this party brought with it none of the anxieties that had concerned her during her stay in Town. She dressed with care, having the undivided attention of Bracey to help her, for since her marriage Charlotte had employed the services of a fashionable and very expensive French maid. Lucy's cream silk was not new, being one of the evening dresses she had worn in London, but it fitted perfectly and enhanced the warm tones of her skin and the golden sheen of her hair, dressed in long ringlets about her head. The family met in the drawing-room before setting out and Lucy entered to find the Collinghams already there. She glanced in appreciation at Charlotte, looking like some fairy-tale princess in a cloud of powder-blue gauze. Lucy had long since ceased to compare herself with her sister, and now she could readily admire the picture Charlotte presented, the white column of her throat encircled with sapphires and diamonds, while more gems nestled amongst her fair curls. If Lucy considered her to be rather over-dressed for a small country party she said nothing, merely complimenting Charlotte on her glowing good looks.

Charlotte embraced her sister warmly,

feeling in perfect charity with the world.

'Thank you, dearest. Do you like these?' She fingered the sapphire necklace. 'Dear Arthur gave them to me only last week. Was that not too kind of him? He is so good to me.'

'Wonderful,' murmured Lucy, smiling at her brother-in-law, whose high, starched shirt-points reminded her of the blinkers on their carriage horse. 'Together you will put us all to shame!'

'Nonsense!' cried Mrs Chambers, entering the room at that moment in high good humour. 'We shall make a splendid picture!'

'Undoubtedly,' agreed Mr Collingham, 'and I must tell you, ma'am, that you look magnificent!' He stood back, lifting his eyeglass the better to study the elegant lines of the high-waisted burgundy gown and matching turban that Mrs Chambers had chosen to wear. 'Magnificent,' he repeated, 'as fine as any dowager duchess!'

'Thank you, Arthur.' Mrs Chambers smiled, well pleased with his tribute. 'I admit I do not often dress up in all my finery, but then, it is not every day that one's daughter is betrothed!' She brought one hand up to straighten her diamond necklace and a flash of reflected candlelight caught Lucy's attention.

'Is that a new ring, Mama? I have not seen it before.'

Mrs Chambers moved forward, holding out her hand towards Lucy.

'Why, it was a little gift from Lady Cornholme! It is only paste, but you will see how the ribbon-like setting matches my necklace, and when I mentioned the fact to her, she was kind enough to make me a present of it.'

Lucy was staring at the ring, a slight flush mounting to her cheeks, then ebbing away to leave her face ashen.

'I had thought,' she said slowly, 'I am sure I saw such a ring in Charlotte's possession.'

Her sister flushed. 'No—of course not. You must be mistaken,' she began, but her mother was already speaking.

'Lady Cornholme gave the ring to Charlotte last summer while you were at Stock House, for she did not know *then* that I would be coming to fetch you! Have I not mentioned it, Lucy? I suppose not, for I cannot recall wearing it since Charlotte passed it on to me.'

Lucy fixed her eyes steadily upon her sister.

'Oh yes, I am quite sure I have seen it before.'

Mrs Collingham gave an uncertain little laugh.

'Why, I remember now. I *did* wear it once, but it was a jest, Lucy. A silly, foolish jest.' Observing the brief blaze of anger in her sister's eyes, Charlotte sank down on a sofa, one hand to her head, saying in failing accents, 'Arthur dear, pray fetch me a glass of water. I feel quite faint.'

Mrs Chambers was immediately at her side and Lucy was glad of the diversion. Her legs felt very weak and she stumbled to a nearby chair, fearing she might swoon. There could be no mistake. She would never forget the moment when Charlotte had turned to her, her eyes shining in triumph as she held out her left hand to show Lucy the ring. But now Charlotte said it had all been in jest. Was it possible? Perhaps. Lucy cast her mind back to those last few days at Stock House, forcing herself to remember scenes she had carefully locked away for the past seven months. What proof was there that Dominic had asked Charlotte to marry him? No one had ever mentioned an engagement, except Charlotte herself. If only she had found the courage to ask Dominic outright, or even if she had spoken of it to Judith Vanderley, this misunderstanding could have been put right, but now it was too late, too late . . .

A footman came in to announce that the carriage was at the door. Arthur Collingham hung over his wife as she sipped at the water, wondering aloud if it might not be best for Charlotte to remain quietly at Templecombe. She gave him the glass and a tremulous smile.

'No, no, I am fine now. It was just a passing spasm.' She looked at Lucy, her eyes pleading with her. 'I have to be so careful at the moment, you see. Because of the baby.'

Lucilla understood her sister's silent

message and shrugged inwardly. What good would come of opening old wounds, going over old quarrels? She rose.

'If you are sure you feel well enough, Charlotte, let us be gone. We will ask the coachman to drive steadily, will we not, Mama?'

*   *   *

Lucy had little recollection of the rest of the evening, but she was thankful that no one questioned her lack of spirits. The troubles abroad overshadowed the evening and Mr Collingham found that even his adored wife was more subdued than usual. During dinner everyone tried to be cheerful, toasts were drunk to the betrothed couple and speeches made wishing them happiness. Later, the drawing-room was cleared for dancing and the younger members of the party were free to enjoy themselves while their parents talked in low voices of this latest threat to peace. Tom and Lucy joined in the dancing, but the young man soon realized that his partner was not enjoying herself.

'What is it, Lucy? Would you rather we sat out for a while?'

'Yes, thank you, Tom. I am a little tired this evening.'

'No wonder,' he said, leading her to a quiet corner, 'this engagement's meant more work

167

than I bargained for, what with all our neighbours wanting to come and wish us well, and now you've Charlotte and her husband staying with you—I hope she's not putting you out too much, Lucy. She's always been the spoiled one and now I hear she's breeding.' Despite her preoccupation, Lucy laughed.

'Tom! You make her sound like a horse! Charlotte is . . . Charlotte,' she ended lamely. Tom smiled and put his arm about her, giving her a hug.

'Well, don't let her upset you while I'm away. I'm damned if I'll have her coming the great lady over you when we're married!'

'Thank you. When do you have to go away?'

'The day after tomorrow. I must say I shall be glad to be on my way—although I shall miss you, of course, dearest! But the news from France is not good. The king has been forced to fly the country and it seems Bonaparte is as much in control as ever, all those who could have been expected to resist him have welcomed him with open arms! So it will be up to us and the Prussians to show him the door!'

Lucy shivered. 'Tom?'

'Yes, love?'

'Do you truly want to marry me?'

'But of course!' he replied, laughing. 'Why in heaven should you doubt it?'

'If I were to ask you to give up the army, to stay here and marry me, would you do it?'

Tom shook his head at her.

'You wouldn't ask that of me,' he said comfortably, 'I know you too well, Lucy. That is not your way. Just wait here for me, darling, and when this war's over I shall come back and marry you. Then we can live happily ever after.'

He pulled her to him and kissed her. As he drew away, Lucy turned to watch the dancing so that he should not see the disappointment in her eyes. For her there had been no passion in that kiss, no tingling excitement as his lips met hers. That is all finished, she thought dully, I shall never feel that way again.

Like the evening itself, life seemed to stretch interminably before her.

NINE

The young Belgian maid fastened the final hooks on Lucy's dress and went away, leaving her young mistress to study the result in the long mirror. Lucy was wearing her new ball gown, a shimmering creation of emerald satin, her pale skin enhanced by the lustrous sheen of the pearls at her neck and wrist. Pearl drops hung from her ears, peeping out between the dark gold hair that curled down to her neck. Despite the warmth of the summer evening, she shivered. There was a scratching at the door of her apartment, and Charlotte entered.

She looked beautiful in blond lace; even though the soft folds of her gown could not disguise the swell of her body Charlotte was untroubled. She was looking forward to the birth of her first baby in a few months' time.

'Come along Lucy, or we shall be late!' Charlotte swept across the room, picking up Lucy's shawl and handing it to her. Lucy took it mechanically.

'I really don't think I can go.'

'Nonsense. Why should you not?'

'I would as lief remain here and wait for Tom.'

Charlotte reached out to give her sister a little shake.

'You know very well that Tom has agreed to follow us as soon as he can! What purpose would be served by your waiting here? Indeed, what was the point of coming with us if you will not enjoy yourself?'

They had been in Belgium for two weeks: Charlotte had refused to give up her place in Society and rest quietly at home until her baby was born. Thus, when the *haut monde* followed the army to Brussels, Mr and Mrs Collingham were of their number, persuading Mrs Chambers to allow Lucy to accompany them, since Tom was stationed with his regiment just a few miles outside the town.

*   *   *

Following her engagement, life had carried on so much as before at Templecombe that Lucy had found it hard to believe she was promised to Tom Bancroft. Now she gazed thoughtfully at the simple opal ring on her finger. Tom had given it to her on the day he left for London, laughing off Mrs Chambers's assertion that opals were an unlucky choice for a betrothal. Even here in Brussels she could scarcely believe they were truly engaged, for Tom's time was taken up mainly with army matters and their meetings were always brief and hurried. Lucy pushed such selfish thoughts aside and tried to give her attention to her sister.

'Any ball given by the Duchess of Richmond would be splendid,' Charlotte was saying, 'but this one promises to be a very grand affair! I have heard that Wellington is to attend, and the Prince of Orange! Oh Lucy, everyone will be there—it would be too bad of you to miss it.'

Lucy hesitated. The foreboding she felt was so strong that she could not ignore it, yet she knew that Charlotte would say it was merely imagination.

'And Tom has made such efforts to attend, even if it will not be possible for him to stay. If you try to get a message to him it might go astray, then imagine his dismay, to turn up at the ball and find you are not there!' She saw that Lucy had not considered this, and pressed home her advantage. She took Lucy's shawl and draped it over the girl's shoulders. 'Arthur is waiting for us in the carriage below. You know how he hates to be late for anything, and since I do not dance now, you may partner Arthur until Tom arrives, though I've no doubt that you must be dreadfully out of practice!'

*   *   *

Having allowed herself to be persuaded, Lucy followed her sister meekly to the waiting carriage. They found Mr Collingham was pacing up and down beside the horses, trying to curb his impatience. The ladies were handed in, the steps put up and the equipage set off at a smart pace through the streets, only to be caught up some ten minutes later in the crush of vehicles heading for Her Grace of Richmond's ball. Descending from the coach, Lucy glanced at the crowd gathered in the street. It seemed all Brussels had turned out to see the guests of the rich English milord and his lady. Once inside, she felt her old shyness coming over her. Strangers filled each room and she walked very close to Charlotte, offering only mechanical replies when her sister introduced her to her many acquaintances. The dancing was already under way in the grand ballroom, but Lucy refused her brother-in-law's offer to partner her. She preferred to sit with Charlotte and watch the

172

laughing, twirling couples circling the room. Amongst the gentlemen there was a predominance of brightly coloured uniforms. Charlotte pointed out the most notable figures in the room, but even the Prince of Orange failed to impress Lucy. The only figure to attract her interest was the Duke of Wellington, who appeared to be constantly at the centre of a small group of officers and a much larger circle of fluttering, admiring ladies. Lucy watched, intrigued, as uniformed gentlemen came and went from the duke's side, bringing messages for the great man to read and hurrying away to carry out further orders. It seemed to Lucy that despite the music and the gaiety, the threat of war was closer here in the glittering ballroom than at any time since her arrival in Brussels. She glanced towards the door: how long had she been here—an hour, perhaps more? Tom should be arriving soon. He had promised to join them as soon as his duties would allow. She found herself wishing that Charlotte had not arranged for them to be invited. It was, of course, an honour to attend such a brilliant occasion but with battle so imminent Lucy was sure Tom would have preferred to spend a quiet evening at the apartment than 'doing the fancy' as he would put it, with a crowd of strangers. Lucy smiled suddenly, remembering the first time she had seen him in his regimentals. Dear Tom! He had been so proud of his new uniform, and although there was twelve months' difference in their age, she had been profoundly aware of feeling much older than her fiancé. And now, in a few hours, he would be marching off with thousands of other young men to face the French.

Suddenly, Lucy froze. Amongst the strangers that passed before her idle gaze there was one she knew well and her eyes locked upon the familiar figure of Dominic Vanderley. Unable to look away, she took in the broad shoulders encased in a smooth black evening coat, the snowy whiteness of his cravat that emphasized the raven-black hair and dark, almost swarthy complexion. As though aware of her gaze he swung round, his eyes meeting hers in a long, enigmatic stare. He began to move towards her and her heart, which had seemed to stop at the sight of him, now began to pound so heavily she could scarcely breathe. There was no reading the expression on the gentleman's face, but his eyes never left her as he greeted Charlotte and her husband.

'You remember Lucilla, Mr Vanderley?' said Charlotte. 'You may not have heard she is soon to be married.'

'Yes. My sister informed me of it.' Dominic's eyes remained firmly fixed on Lucy's face. She curtsied, murmuring disjointed words of greeting that the gentleman seemed not to hear, for he soon interrupted her.

'They are striking up for the next dance, Miss Chambers. I would be honoured if you would stand up with me.'

Words of refusal came to mind but would not pass her lips. In a daze, Lucy accompanied him to the centre of the room, where they began to dance in silence. It was one of the new waltzes and Lucy tried to concentrate upon her steps and ignore the possessive clasp in which the gentleman held her. Presently he spoke.

'How do you go on?'

'Very well, sir, I thank you.' She kept her eyes fixed on the top button of his waistcoat. 'I understood you were in Vienna.'

'I was until yesterday. I came here to see my brother.'

'Ah yes. He is in the Guards, is he not?'

'Yes,' he affirmed shortly, then: 'Are you happy, Lucilla?'

Startled, she glanced up, and having met his intense gaze she knew the question could not be turned off lightly.

'Tom is a good man. No one could ask for a better husband.'

'That does not answer me!'

She shook her head at him, saying desperately, 'I cannot answer you—not here . . .'

'Then where?' His fingers tightened insistently upon hers. 'Don't refuse me, Lucy! I need to talk to you—nothing more, you have my word on that.'

In a low tone she gave him her direction. 'There is a small garden close by the apartment, I shall be walking there alone tomorrow. At two o'clock.' She felt his grip on her relax.

'I shall be there.'

They spoke no more, and when the dance ended, he escorted her from the dance-floor. There was an officer standing beside Charlotte's chair and Lucy's step faltered as she recognized Tom. Dominic's hand upon her arm steadied her and when they came up she performed the introduction calmly, surprised at her own control.

'Mr Vanderley was a guest at Stock House last year,' Charlotte put in to explain their acquaintance.

Tom put out his hand, saying in his easy manner, 'Of course. How do you do? Mr Collingham tells me you are one of Castlereagh's men. Are you here on business?'

Dominic shook his head.

'A purely personal visit. My brother is a major in the Guards. I would introduce you, but he was obliged to leave early. I believe most of the military will be away shortly.' He nodded towards Tom's uniform. 'Infantry?'

Tom confirmed it, grinning.

'I haven't been with them long, but they're one of the best regiments,' he said proudly. 'Saw a lot of action in the Peninsula.'

They talked on for a few minutes before Mr Vanderley took his leave and Tom nodded approvingly at Lucy.

'He seems a good sort of fellow. Brother in the Guards, did he say? I'll look out for him when I get the chance. Lucy—are you feeling unwell, my dear? You look very pale.'

'No, no, I'm fine, thank you. Just a little tired.'

He gave her an affectionate hug.

'All this gadding about with Charlotte has knocked you up. I don't know how your sister does it, but she seems to thrive on this life.'

'Perhaps you could take me home, Tom,' suggested Lucy, but he shook his head.

'I'm sorry, love, but I can only stay a moment more. I have to get back to my regiment. Something's afoot and we're moving out at dawn. I only rode over to let you know. Don't look so downcast, darling. We'll get this little skirmish over and you and I will have years together!' He grinned. 'Now, I must go. Let me take my leave of Arthur and your sister and you can step downstairs with me if you wish, to see me off.'

At the door, Lucy hugged him oblivious of the wooden-faced footmen lining the hall.

'Oh Tom, please be careful!' she whispered, squeezing her eyes tight to prevent her tears.

'Of course. Come along, my dear, tears and vapours are more in Charlotte's line than yours. You've no need to worry yourself over me! Goodbye, darling Lucy. Wait for me—I'll be calling for you just as soon as we've seen off these Frenchies!'

She watched him stride away, a jaunty spring in his step showing his zest for life, then she made her way slowly upstairs to the ballroom.

*   *   *

The noise of the troops gathering in the streets roused Lucy at dawn the following morning. Trumpets blared, calling the men to arms while the shouted orders and beating drums had scant regard for the early hour. Lucy scrambled out of bed and ran to her window from where she watched the columns forming in the street below: the breechless Highlanders in their kilts and scarlet jackets, the green uniforms of the riflemen and blue coats of the Belgians. Then, to the steady drumbeat, they marched way, laughing and joking in the early morning light. The soldiers marched past her window with the same jauntiness she had noted in Tom's step when he had left the ball. Was she the only one to be appalled by the horror to come? Tom had departed in high spirits the previous night and the military uniforms that had dominated the scene in the early part of the evening had mostly disappeared well before the end of the dancing. The ladies and their civilian escorts tried to enjoy themselves as best they might, but although the music had continued, Lucy felt that the sparkle had gone out of the proceedings. With a sigh she crept back to her bed but sleep eluded her. In a few hours she would be meeting Dominic Vanderley. She knew it must be for the last time, but she could not prevent the thrill of anticipation that gripped her.

Shortly before two o'clock Lucy stepped out of the house to walk the short distance to the small gardens where she had arranged the meeting. The streets were very quiet, basking in the hot afternoon sun with little sign of the early morning activity. There were very few carriages abroad and Lucy was relieved to think that her few acquaintances would be resting indoors after the exertions of the evening. The gardens had once fronted a grand mansion. It had been demolished long ago, but the grounds had been preserved as a leafy retreat from the dusty streets that surrounded them. Lucy followed the winding path past beds of colourful summer flowers, their bright faces turned upwards to the sun. A soft breeze stirred the roses and their scent brought back bitter-sweet memories of the rose-garden at Stock House. The air seemed heavy, and Lucy thought she heard a faint, distant rumble of thunder. One further bend brought her to the centre of the gardens and she found Dominic waiting there. He was sitting on a bench, but when he saw her he rose and came forward to meet her. Studying his face, she thought the hawkish lines more marked than before. There was a tired, strained look about his eyes, but it vanished as he smiled at her.

'Thank God you are punctual. I feared you might not come!' He put out his hand but Lucy hung back, as if afraid of his touch. Noticing the movement he withdrew his hand. 'Pray, believe me, Lucilla, I mean you no harm. Whatever my reputation, I would not make love to you while your affiancéd husband is at war! Shall we sit down, or would you prefer to walk a little?'

'Walk, I think.' She kept her eyes lowered, trying to order her senses. There was relief that he would not force his attentions upon her, yet at the same time his very forbearance made her love him even more.

He fell into step beside her, and unable to bear the silence, Lucy enquired after Miss Vanderley. She felt a slight shock at her own calm tone, which sounded strange and distant to her ears.

'I received a letter from my sister a week ago. She was quite well then.'

'I'm glad. Pray give her my regards when you next see her.'

'I will do that.' He paused. 'May I tell her that you are happy?'

'I am not . . . unhappy.'

180

They walked on in silence, but Lucy could feel the tension building between them.

'When do you plan to marry Bancroft?' he asked at last.

'In the autumn.'

'But why?' Dominic lowered his voice, but could not conceal the savage anger barely suppressed within him. 'Why could you not marry *me*?'

She wanted to tell him of the misunderstanding, that she had thought he wished only to make her his mistress, but the words would not come: she could not bring herself to confess her lack of trust. If only he had forced her to listen.

She said simply, 'You never came to ask me.'

'Dear God!' His harsh, self-mocking laugh chilled her. 'My noble forbearance comes to naught! I thought it would be wrong to press you; I wanted to give you time to yourself. I let Judith be my messenger because I did not want to force an answer from you and by heaven, I knew that if I saw you in person I would never want to let you go again! All that self-denial and you tell me that if I had come, you would have married me! Damnation, woman, do you know what this has cost us?'

Lucy bit her lip, her silent anguish more than matching his own.

'Nay—sweet life, don't cry,' he murmured, holding out his handkerchief. 'Here, take this and dry your tears. God's blood, Lucy! If only you knew how much I want to hold you—! But I fear that if I touch you now I shall never let you go, and what happiness could either of us find, knowing we had served young Bancroft such a trick? You have truly put yourself beyond my reach, have you not? Even I would not stoop so low!'

Lucy took the proffered handkerchief and wiped her eyes, desperately trying to keep control.

'I'm sorry' she said at last, her voice low and not quite steady, 'I should not have come, but I wanted so to see you, to explain . . .'

He interrupted her with a shake of his head, saying wearily, 'There is no need. I remember you telling me that you and the young man had always been close. I am sure he will make you an admirable husband. There is nothing more to say. Will you forgive me if I do not escort you back? I think it best if we part here.' He stopped, turning to face her as he held out his hand. Lucy put out her own, unable to prevent the tumult he caused within her by the mere touch of his fingers.

'Dominic, I—'

'No.' He stopped her, a rueful smile softening his eyes. 'Say nothing more, child, I understand. We must part now, and it will probably be best if our paths do not cross again. I won't ask you to forget me, I am too selfish for that, but believe me, you are still young and the pain will lessen in time.' He lifted her hand, brushing her fingers with his lips. 'God bless you, Lucilla.'

With that he turned away, striding out of her life as suddenly as he had entered it. Lucy remained on the path and watched him walk away. A blackbird had flown to one of the lower branches of a nearby tree and now began to serenade her, but she heard nothing of its sweet song, her attention fixed upon the dark, retreating figure blurred now by the tears that scalded her eyes and ran unheeded over her pale cheeks.

Only when Dominic was out of sight did she turn to retrace her steps, realizing as she wiped her eyes that she was still clutching his handkerchief, his initials expertly embroidered in one corner. She carefully tucked the precious square of linen into her reticule and began to walk slowly back through the gardens. A numbing tiredness had overtaken her. She moved mechanically, hardly aware of her surroundings until she reached the little gate leading on to the streets, where she noticed a thin, crooked figure leaning against the railings. He was watching her idly and she dragged her wandering thoughts together and returned his stare with a look of cold enquiry. The old man's face crumpled into a smile and he removed an old clay pipe from his lips in a gesture of greeting. He was dressed in a shabby British uniform, faded from years of wear. Lucy suddenly realized that one of the old man's legs had been replaced below the knee with a wooden stump.

'Lovely day, missus,' the fellow hailed her, impervious to her haughty looks. 'Our boys'll be sweatin' terrible out there in this 'eat.'

'Yes, but the thunder will bring a break in the weather,' she replied, moving towards the gate.

'Thunder? Lord love you, missus, that ain't no thunder. 'Tis guns you'm 'earing, and no mistake!'

Lucy stopped, her eyes darkening with fear. 'Guns?'

'Aye—and a rare bombardment they Frenchies is givin' us, by the sound of it! But there's no need for you to look so pasty-faced, lady. The duke'll see 'em off. I served under the old man in the Peninsula and he never once let us down.'

Listening to the ominous rumbling that floated across Brussels on the still, hot air, Lucy shuddered.

'I pray you are not mistaken,' she murmured, passing through the gate.

'You trust in the duke, missus!' the old man called after her. 'There's not a Frenchman born can beat *him!*'

*　　　*　　　*

Lucy walked back to her apartment, her

184

wretchedness increased by the knowledge that for the past few hours she had given no thought at all to Tom's safety. The distant cannonade reinforced her guilt and after a subdued dinner in the company of Charlotte and Arthur she made her excuses and retired to her room, where she spent a restless night and awoke to a morning as dismal as her spirit. She took breakfast in her apartment, paying little heed to the traffic beneath her window until Charlotte burst into the room shortly before noon.

'Good, you are dressed! I feared you might be still a-bed!' Charlotte paused, fixing her large blue eyes upon her sister. 'You must pack your things immediately. We are leaving.'

'We are?'

'Yes. It is no longer safe to remain in Brussels. The French are so close they could be here at any time. Arthur has arranged for a coach to collect us. Even that was no easy matter, I can assure you, with nearly every vehicle in the city already requisitioned by the army! We are going to Antwerp to await the outcome of the battle.'

'But we shall learn it that much sooner if we remain here,' Lucy pointed out.

Charlotte shook her head.

'This is no time for funning, Lucilla! We must fly from here. Let me help you pack: I only wish Bracey did not have such a dread of the sea; if she were here it would be done in a trice . . .'

'No, Charlotte. You and Arthur may leave if you wish. I shall stay here.'

'But you cannot!'

Lucy gave a faint smile. 'Oh, but I can,' she replied softly.

'Lucilla, this is madness! Tom would not expect you to take such a risk!'

'There is no risk.' Remembering the old man in the park, Lucy added, 'The duke will bring us through.'

'How can you be so thoughtless?' cried Charlotte, alarmed at the obstinate look in her sister's face. 'I have to consider my baby and I will not risk its safety by remaining here!'

'I do not ask you to do so.'

'But I cannot leave you here alone! Mama entrusted you to my care!'

'If it makes you easier I will pack my things and seek refuge vith one of the other English families that remain. There will be several, I am sure.'

'But—'

'Come along, ladies!' Arthur Collingham came in upon them, anxious to be away. 'The carriage is below and we must go with all speed, for I am told the road to Antwerp grows more congested by the hour.'

'Arthur, Lucy says she will not come!'

'The devil she does!' exclaimed Mr Collingham, looking at his sister-in-law.

'It is true, Arthur. I wish to remain here. I

have no doubt Wellington will win the day.'

'Then you are in the minority!' retorted the gentleman. 'You must see that we cannot leave you alone here, my dear! It would not be right!'

'As I told Charlotte, we have English friends in town. They cannot all be leaving. The Honeywells, for example.'

'Well, yes, as a matter of fact they *are* remaining here,' Arthur admitted, 'but—'

'I am sure they will allow me to stay with them until the danger is past and you return.'

'No. It cannot be thought of. We must stay together.'

'But Arthur, we cannot remain!' cried Charlotte, her cheeks very pale. 'It is too dangerous! Think of the baby! You must get me away!'

Mr Collingham hesitated, an agony of indecision clearly written on his countenance. Charlotte began to cry and Lucy gave him a little push.

'Yes, Arthur, think of the baby. Take Charlotte to Antwerp if you think she will be safer there and pray do not worry about me. I shall be quite safe.'

'Oh very well, but I do not like to leave you here unattended,' he said, as Charlotte coaxed him towards the door. 'If we had time I would take you myself and find you somewhere to stay, but we must be going. Promise me that you will pack up now and go immediately to

187

your English friends. Promise!'

'Yes, yes, I promise! Now go, please.'

Arthur Collingham could not be happy about the situation, but as he later admitted to his wife, short of picking her up and carrying her to the coach there was nothing he could do.

*   *   *

Lucy watched the carriage draw away, carrying Charlotte and her husband out of the city to the relative safety of Antwerp. Even as they drove off the air was rent with a vivid flash of lightning, followed almost immediately by a crack of thunder and for a few minutes torrential rain turned the streets into rivers of mud. There was no point in hurrying to pack: she would send a note to Mrs Honeywell, requesting her assistance. Lucy sat down at the small writing-desk and drew a sheet of paper towards her, but the ink dried on her pen before she could think of anything to write. At last she scribbled a few lines, read them through, then with a sigh of exasperation she crumpled the paper and threw it away. She would remain in the apartment. After all, Charlotte had not taken the Belgian maid with her, and the proprietress was a most respectable woman. Lucy decided that she would not leave, at least not yet. Alone in her room, she tried to occupy herself with a book, but the beating of the rain upon the window distracted her thoughts and she resigned herself to a restless night. Lucy awoke the next morning with the uneasy feeling that something was not quite right. It was unnaturally quiet. At first she thought this was because the rain had ceased and the flow of traffic past her window had died away, leaving only the church bells calling the townspeople to their Sunday devotions. She realized that the house itself was silent, without the usual sounds of feet on the stairs and banging doors that had heralded every other morning. She tugged at the bell-pull, but when this brought no response she threw on her clothes and went downstairs to seek out the proprietress. In the basement she found the landlady busily packing food into a basket. At the sight of Lucy, the woman stopped, looking up guiltily from her task.

'Ah—mademoiselle. M'excuse—there is no one to answer your bell. The girls left last night to return to their families . . .'

'I understand. Is there any hot water? I should like to wash.'

The landlady threw up her hands.

'Mais non, mademoiselle. There was no one to light the fires.'

'Surely that is not a task beyond your capabilities,' observed Lucy drily. 'Is there anything for breakfast?'

'Why yes!' responded the woman, pleased to

be able to answer positively. 'There is a little ham, and some bread. I would have prepared a tray for you myself later . . .' she trailed off, pulling the covers over the obvious abundance of provisions packed into her basket.

'Thank you. I will help myself.'

Searching through the cupboards she put together a tolerable meal and carried it on a tray up to her room. She had no appetite, but forced herself to take a little sustenance, then she tidied her room and tried to keep her mind from the battle taking place a few miles south of Brussels.

A few minutes before noon there was a scratching at the door and Lucy was surprised to find her landlady waiting to speak to her.

'I thought you had left the house, *madame*.'

'*Mademoiselle*—I was indeed on my way, but what I have heard in the street persuaded me to come back for you. You must leave Brussels.'

'I cannot do that.'

'Please, *ma petite!* I have met soldiers—men coming from the battlefield who say the French will be here before nightfall.'

'I cannot leave,' Lucy repeated calmly. 'I am waiting for my fiancé.'

The proprietress looked piteously at Lucy, tears in her faded eyes.

'Perhaps *mademoiselle* does not understand. It is being said that Bonaparte has promised his men whatever they wish from the city! I am afraid for myself, but I am afraid also for you, so young, so pretty . . . will you not come with me? I am going to my brother's farm in the north and from there we will arrange transport to take you to your friends in Antwerp.'

'That is very kind, madam, but I must stay in Brussels. I will seek refuge with English friends. I should have done so yesterday, but I could not then bring myself to impose upon them.'

The older woman shrugged.

'Then go quickly, *mademoiselle*. And God bless you. I admire such devotion. He is a fortunate young man, your fiancé.'

'A lucky man indeed,' murmured Lucy, as she shut the door on the landlady's retreating figure, 'to love a woman such as I! They think I wait here for news of Tom. In fact, I remain because I no longer care what becomes of me!' This bitter declaration released the pent-up emotions that Lucy had kept under control for so long and with a wail of anguish she threw herself on the bed, sobbing brokenly.

TEN

By Sunday afternoon, Brussels was in turmoil. A steady stream of people—soldiers and civilians, poured into the city from the south, seeking refuge and adding to the panic with tales of a French victory. At one point towards evening a complete regiment of cavalry swept in from the battlefield and galloped through the streets with swords drawn, overturning everything in their frenzy. Lucy's grief had gradually subsided and her practical nature began to reassert itself. The landlady's words rang in her head with awful clarity: Bonaparte's soldiers running unchecked in the city! Lucy was well aware of the fate of any lady in those circumstances. She thought of the old soldier's confidence that the Allies would win: Lucy wondered if he, too, was amongst those filling the roads and waterways between Brussels and Antwerp. She had a sudden burst of confidence that he would not be of their number and was unaccountably cheered. Leaning from the window she called for news to a solitary officer riding past.

'When I came from the field this morning we were holding the French,' he told her. 'We were defending a ridge of high ground just south of a little place called Waterloo. With any luck our boys will still be there by the time I get back to them!' He grinned up at her, waving his hat in a final salute as he trotted away and Lucy closed the window, wishing the unknown soldier all the luck in the world.

*   *   *

Lucy knew she should leave the empty house

and seek out some English acquaintance in the city. Refusing to panic, she calmly sorted her belongings and began to pack a few essentials into a single large portmanteau. The sound of a door banging somewhere below made her pause, her heart pounding furiously as she became dreadfully aware of her isolation. Swiftly she crossed the room and turned the key in the lock, then she ran to the window and peeped out. The confused bustle in the street below had not diminished, but thankfully she saw no sign of French uniforms amongst the throng. However, the closed and shuttered buildings around her brought a new fear. Could it be looters she could hear moving about in the rooms below? Footsteps sounded on the wooden stairs and she looked about her for some sort of weapon. The short, thick poker lying in the hearth was all that was to hand and she picked it up, drawing some comfort from the cold metal. The footsteps stopped outside her room. Lucy backed against the far wall as someone tried the door, then a dear, familiar voice called her name. With something like a sob she ran to unlock the door.

Dominic Vanderley caught her as she almost fell into his arms.

'Thank God!' she cried, her voice muffled against his coat, 'I thought it might be the French, or—or—'

'Hush, sweetheart,' he murmured, gently

prising the poker from her shaking fingers. 'Let me take this, you won't need it, I promise you.'

He guided her back into the room, closing the door behind them and continuing to hold her until the terror had passed. When at last she could think a little more clearly, she gently released herself from his arms.

'How—why did you come here? Do you not wish to leave Brussels?'

'Not now. I did indeed set off for Antwerp yesterday, but meeting your sister on the road I learned that you had remained behind. Why did you not go with them?'

She shrugged. 'For what?' she said flatly. 'Life has little value for me now.'

'Don't talk like a fool!' he retorted angrily. 'That is an insult to all who care for you!'

Lucy hung her head. 'Yes, of course. I beg your pardon.'

'I am going to take you to the Hotel St George; Madam Lebeque has room and to spare with this sudden exodus. You will be safe there. How Collingham came to abandon you in such a fashion I don't know.'

'I refused to go. What *could* he do?'

'Put you over his shoulder and carry you out! You may smile, my girl, but to leave you here alone, to face God knows what dangers—!'

'Is that why you came back,' she asked him, 'to find me?'

Their eyes met in a long look that said much more than any words. Dominic turned away, breaking the spell.

'Is that your bag? Good. It is time to leave. I have stabled my horse and walked here. The roads around Brussels are so choked with traffic it took me all day to get back here and the poor animal is exhausted. It is but a few streets. Can you walk?'

'Of course.'

He picked up the portmanteau and they let themselves out of the building and walked together through the warm evening streets. There was no sound of gunfire, but when Lucy mentioned this fact to her companion he soon put an end to her hopes by pointing out that the wind was blowing from the north and would thus carry any sound from the battlefield away from the city. There was an unreality about the streets, for as they drew closer to the market-place they found groups of townspeople gathered outside the inns, drinking and talking as if it were any ordinary Sunday evening, while the baggage trains and carriages of wounded soldiers trundled through the city. Dominic stepped into the street and hailed an officer riding by. The two men spoke for some minutes while Lucy waited anxiously at the edge of the road.

'Well, is there news?' she asked, when at length the officer rode on.

'No, only confusion. Although he seemed to

195

think we could yet win the day. I am hopeful that we shall soon know the outcome.'

They continued to the Hotel St George where they were met by Madame Lebeque, a large, homely Bruxelloise who did not wait for an introduction but immediately swept Lucy into a crushing embrace, crying out at the sickly pallor of her new guest. *Madame's* shrewd, twinkling eyes travelled from Dominic to Lucy and back again as he introduced her, but she said nothing, merely guiding Lucy into a cheerful sitting-room and calling to her maid to bring hot food for the English milady.

'For I have not a doubt,' she said, gently but firmly pushing Lucy down into a comfortable chair, 'that you have not eaten all day.'

Dominic nodded. 'Thank you, *madame*. I know I leave Miss Chambers in safe hands.'

'You are not staying?' cried Lucy, 'But I thought—'

Madame Lebeque bethought herself of matters requiring her attention elsewhere and tactfully withdrew. Dominic walked to the window.

'I am staying with Colonel Jones, the Military Commander here in Brussels,' he told her, staring out of the window. 'You must not be afraid. The colonel will be one of the first to know if there is a French victory and I will arrange for you to be escorted safely out of the city.'

She rose from the chair and came to stand

beside him.

'And if the French are beaten?'

'Then you will not require my services.' He turned towards her, his face a cold mask. 'I shall remain in Brussels until I have news of my brother, but it is unlikely that you and I will meet again.'

He held out his hand and Lucy, gathering up all her strength, gave him her own. *This cannot happen!* The words ran silently through her. *How many times must we say goodbye? How can we stand here in this way, like distant acquaintances mouthing our civilities?*

Aloud, she said, 'Goodbye Mr Vanderley. I do hope you find your brother safe.'

He pressed her fingers. 'Thank you. Goodbye.'

He was gone and Lucy returned to her chair, her whole body shaking. It was for the best, this parting. She knew that, but the knowledge did not make it any easier to bear. When Madame Lebeque returned with a tray a few minutes later she found her guest sitting motionless and grey-faced in her chair and drew her own conclusions. Tucking a rug around Lucy, she sat down beside her, the tray upon her own lap and began to coax her guest to eat.

*   *   *

'Ah, *mademoiselle,* such news!'

Lucy raised herself on one elbow as Madame Lebeque bustled into the bedroom, her round face creased with smiles.

'It is over!' The good lady helped Lucy to sit up and plumped up her pillows. 'The French are beaten and all of Brussels celebrates!'

'Truly?'

'Mais oui, Mademoiselle! Monsieur Vanderley sent us word more than an hour past, but you were sleeping soundly then and I would not wake you. But is it not good news? The fighting is finished!'

'Yes.' Lucy tried to think what this would mean: there would be hundreds dead— thousands, perhaps, but the survivors would be coming back to their families—the fathers, sons, husbands.

'Tom!' She threw back the bed-covers. 'I must go—he will be trying to find me—'

'Hush child! Where would you go at such an early hour?' cried *madame,* much alarmed.

'To my old apartment! He will be looking for me there!'

'No, no, you must go back to bed,' insisted her hostess, gently pushing her back against the pillows. 'You will do nothing until you have broken your fast. If you wish, I will send a servant to your rooms with a message.'

'But you don't understand, the building will be empty!'

'Then he shall fix a note to the door to tell anyone who calls your new direction,' returned *madame,* unruffled. 'There is no need for you to distress yourself, *mademoiselle.* These matters are easily resolved.'

Lucy sank back, reassured by such a practical approach and consented to remain in bed for the rest of the morning. By the afternoon, however, there was still no word from Tom and Lucy began to grow restless. Refusing Madame Lebeque's offer to send out a servant for news, Lucy took her shawl and ventured forth herself. Her hostess had insisted upon sending a footman with her and Lucy was glad of his escort through streets crowded with troops and carriages. Her first thought was to seek out the Military Commander, but as she approached his quarters she found the street filled with others who had the same idea, with crowds pressing around the door. She abandoned the attempt and went back towards the market-square, enquiring of any officers she met if they had news of Tom's regiment. Each time her question was met with a blank stare and a shake of the head and she had grown quite despondent by the time she came upon a small group sitting outside one of the inns of the market-place. Again the blank stares, but just as Lucy was about to turn away, one man raised his hand.

'Just a minute—were they not deployed near Hougoumont? I remember hearing something of a light infantry brigade being used in the final skirmish with the Imperial Guard. Suffered for it, too, I wouldn't wonder, for that was Boney's best troops.'

'But what would happen to the wounded—would they bring them here, to Brussels?'

'I doubt it, miss,' opined one officer. 'It's more likely they'd take 'em to one of the field hospitals.'

'Where they say you suffer worse than on the battlefield,' muttered another, only to be silenced by a dig in the ribs from his neighbour, who addressed Lucy in a sympathetic tone.

'I know it's hard to bear the waiting, miss, but your best course would be to go home until things are more settled. If your man's alive he'll find you out and if not'—he shrugged—'well, there's little you or anyone can do for him.'

Silently Lucy nodded and turned away to retrace her steps to the *hotel*. A carriage rumbled by, horses and bodywork spattered with mud and came to a halt before an elegant town house, where four liveried footmen were waiting. They lifted down from the coach a soldier wrapped in a blanket and tenderly carried him inside.

'One of the lucky ones,' murmured Lucy, as the little group disappeared into the house. She walked on, her brow wrinkled in thought. By the time she reached the *hotel* she had decided upon a plan of action which she immediately put to her hostess. Madame Lebeque was horrified.

'You wish to search for your fiancé? No, no, *c'est impossible!'* cried the good lady, most distressed. 'It is much better that you wait here for news.'

'No, *madame*, I am decided. I must go now to try if I can hire a carriage to take me out of town, for if Tom is wounded I want to bring him back with me and, with your permission, Madame Lebeque, to nurse him here.'

'Of course, of course—there can be no difficulty about that, but to go now, so late in the day . . .'

'There are a few hours of daylight left, four—perhaps more.' Lucy turned her steady gaze upon the older woman. 'I *will* go, *madame.*'

'Yes, I believe you will. But at least let me give you my own carriage. Your money will be better saved for later. You might need to pay for your information. If I weren't so big and slow I would come with you myself, but my coachman is a good, honest fellow and can be depended upon to do his best for you.'

Lucy clasped the soft plump hands in her own and squeezed them gratefully.

'Thank you, *madame.*' She ran off to collect her warmest cloak and to put what little money she had into her reticule while Madame Lebeque gave orders for her carriage to be brought to the house.

*   *   *

South of Brussels the road was choked with
soldiers, baggage carts and wagons. Several
times Lucy's driver was forced to stop while
broken vehicles were cleared from the path
and the press of traffic made progress
necessarily slow. The road ran through the
Forest of Soignes, where they came to a small
village. Lucy's hopes rose and from her
carriage she hailed a passing officer.

'What place is this?'

The officer stopped, touching his cap to her.

'Waterloo, ma'am. Are you looking for
someone?'

Lucy began eagerly to explain but the man
stopped her.

'The infantry lost a lot of men, miss, and I
doubt if they have yet brought all the living
from the battlefield. It would be a dashed
unpleasant job searching every field hospital
for one soldier.'

'But I must find him!'

The officer regarded her with a kindly eye.

'This is no place for a young lady like
yourself. If the young man you seek is alive he
will get back to you. Turn your carriage
around, miss, and let our lads get on with the
job of sorting out the dead from the living. You
would only be in the way.'

Lucy listened in silence, her eyes downcast

202

and her fingers twisting the opal ring around her finger. When the man had finished she thanked him for his advice, but with an obstinate set to her chin she ordered her coachman to drive on. Further enquiries brought the information that many of the injured had been taken to Mont St Jean, a mile or so further south. When they arrived there, however, the harassed officers had little time for Lucy's persistent questions. Fortunately, one of the less seriously wounded officers overheard her conversation and followed her back to her carriage.

'Bancroft, did you say the name was? There was a Bancroft in Adam's regiment, light infantry,' he added helpfully. Lucy turned to the man eagerly, but he shook his head at her, warning her not to be too hopeful. 'They were in the thick of it yesterday, but I've seen none of them brought in here. It's likely they have a field hospital closer at hand, so to speak.' He pointed in a southerly direction. 'Take the Nivelles road at the next crossroads and about a mile from there you will find a big country house, Hougoumont. At least, it is probably little more than a ruin by this time, for that's where so many of our brave lads fought and died to keep Boney from winning the day! The light infantry engaged the enemy in the hollow to the east of the house, and if there's any of 'em left alive, you may well find 'em there.'

'Thank you, sir, I—'

'I don't know that you have cause to thank me for sending you to such a place,' said the officer, cutting her short. 'It's a strong stomach you'll be needing!'

'I shall manage,' replied Lucy, climbing back into her carriage.

They drove on, past scenes of such destruction that Lucy scarcely dared to look out of the window. On each side lay broken and twisted vehicles, the horses left to die in their traces. Soon they came to the burned-out shell of a large house—Hougoumont. At the edge of the road, horses and men lay where they had fallen together with the wreckage of wagons and gun carriages. As Lucy alighted, the mingled smell of smoke, gunpowder and death threatened to overwhelm her.

'Will *mademoiselle* not go back?' asked her driver, seeing her pale face, but Lucy resolutely shook her head and beckoned to him to accompany her to where weary soldiers were piling up the bodies while a group of peasants dug a large pit. Observing their approach, one of the soldiers paused and came toward them. Lucy fixed her eyes upon him, concentrating on the living that she might not see the horror of the dead lying everywhere about her. In answer to her question, the soldier told her there was a field hospital nearby, but they had passed the turning.

'You must go back and take the little road leading towards La Haye Saint. It is not far.'

Lucy turned to go, then stopped.

'Who was fighting here?'

'British Guards, mum,' returned the soldier, a touch of pride creeping into his voice. His arm swept around to indicate the trees standing before the blackened ruins of the house. 'They say that wood was taken and retaken three times. The Guards suffered terrible losses there, terrible losses, but they didn't yield and we reckoned two thousand bodies in that orchard before we lost count of 'em, men and officers alike.'

'Do—do you know anything of a Major Vanderley?'

The soldier thought for a moment then shook his head.

'I disremember hearing that name, mum, but then, there was so many charred bodies in there, 'twas impossible to tell who they was!'

With a brief word of thanks, Lucy made her way back to the carriage. The coachman, muttering prayers beneath his breath, turned the horses and drove back until they came to a narrow turning leading eastwards. The ruins of Hougoumont were still visible, but as the coach rumbled on a far more terrible sight met Lucy's eyes. She ordered the driver to stop and some inward compulsion made her step down on to the road. To the south, the ground fell away and opened out on to a small plain, where some of the heaviest fighting of the previous day had taken place. It seemed to

Lucy that the full horror of the battle was spread below her. The ground was covered with the dead, men and horses entangled in a nightmare pattern, the garish colours of the uniforms dulled by mud and gun-smoke and dried blood. Scores of French cavalry had died attacking the British squares, yet the men who had shot them down now lay dead in the very formations they had fought so hard to maintain. That anyone could come out of the battle alive seemed to Lucy to be nothing less than a miracle. A movement caught her eye and she saw grey-cloaked women moving amongst the dead, stealing rings and watches, even pulling teeth from the corpses to sell in the markets of Brussels and London. Anger and nausea welled up within her. She wanted to drive off the harridans, but she knew it would be a futile gesture. They would return as soon as she had gone, if her opposition did not result in her own murder. Lucy turned away, clinging desperately to the carriage wheel as sickness overwhelmed her. The driver hovered nearby, muttering prayers and begging her to return to Brussels.

'It will be dark soon, *mademoiselle*,' he whispered imploringly.

Lucy took a few moments to recover herself. She was trembling as she pulled herself wearily back into the coach.

'We go on,' she told him. 'If necessary we shall stay here until morning!'

206

There was less than an hour of daylight left when they arrived at the huddle of tents where tired medical officers moved from one man to another, repairing as best they could the torn and lacerated bodies. The surrounding area was crowded with men awaiting treatment. They watched Lucy's arrival with dull, lifeless eyes. Her glance skimmed over them, searching for a familiar face. Finding none she left the coach and headed for the nearest tent. Inside, a tall man in a bloodied apron was attending to the wounded, but as Lucy entered he came over to her, asking if he could help. She noticed his eyes, red-rimmed with tiredness but with a kindly look that reassured her.

'I am looking for an infantryman—Thomas Bancroft.' She gave him details of Tom's regiment and the surgeon looked blankly at her for a few moments while his tired brain made sense of her words.

'Bancroft? I remember no one of that name, but names mean very little to us here—I have lost track of the men I have treated today. Look about you—if you don't see the face you want here, try another tent. That's the best I can do for you. But prepare yourself, ma'am, this is not a pleasant place! My men are busy enough without you going off into a swoon!' With this warning he went back to his work and Lucy glanced at the long lines of soldiers lying on makeshift beds upon the floor. None looked at all like Tom. Outside again, Lucy was fortunate enough to find an orderly who thought he recognized the name and directed her to the biggest tent, standing a little apart from the others. Lucy hurried forward, not daring to imagine what she might find. She stepped through the opening and paused for her eyes to adjust to the gloom. There was a sickening stench inside, a mixture of canvas, dirt, sweat and blood. The coachman whimpered and Lucy rounded on him savagely, ordering him to wait for her outside. She dragged a handkerchief from her reticule and held it over her mouth, standing aside to allow two men to pass, carrying a bundle between them. As they went by she realized that they were carrying the remains of a man: both legs were missing, blown away in battle or amputated here—not that it mattered now. Gathering all her strength she walked slowly past the wounded, glancing quickly at the gaunt faces, fearing she might recognize one. She felt her flesh begin to crawl.

'Oh God,' she whispered, the handkerchief still pressed to her face. 'Oh God, these men are here to die!'

She found Tom lying at the end of the second row. Someone had inexpertly wiped the grime and powder from his face and he looked little more than a boy lying motionless beneath the grubby blanket. His noisy, shallow breathing was the only sign of life. Lucy fell on her knees beside him and gently smoothed his hair back from his face. The movement roused him and he opened his eyes. He gazed blankly at her for a few minutes, then smiled.

'Lucy. I prayed I would see you again.'

She smiled back at him. 'I'm going to take you back with me.'

'There's not much to take back,' he joked bravely, but Lucy saw the sudden anguish in his eyes. 'I've lost a leg, Lucy. Cannonball. They won't tell me what else, but I think it ripped me open.'

'When we get you to Brussels I will have the best doctors to look after you . . .'

'No, it's too late. I know I shall never leave here. But I don't mind that now I've seen you.' He struggled to free one hand from the blanket and grasped Lucy's fingers. His flesh was very cold. 'Thank you for coming. Tell Father—and Mama—that I love them . . .'

He was staring at the handkerchief still clutched in her right hand and to her horror Lucy realized it was the one Dominic had given her. Even in the dull light the initials stood out boldly on the corner of the linen that had escaped from her fingers. Her eyes flew to Tom's face, but he merely smiled at her.

'I should never have asked you to marry me,' he told her, his voice weakening. 'Should have stayed friends . . .'

'But I do love you, Tom,' she said, her face very close to his, 'perhaps more as a brother

209

than a husband, but I shall always love you!'

He pressed her fingers but even that small effort seemed to tire him and he closed his eyes again.

'Dry your tears,' he said, frowning with the effort it cost him to speak, 'it—doesn't hurt—now. Kiss me, Lucy, then—go—and be happy.'

She brought her face closer, her tears falling on to his cheek as she kissed him. As she drew back he gave a sigh and closed his eyes, a tiny peaceful smile lifting the corners of his mouth. Only when the fingers gripping her hand fell away did she realize he had stopped breathing.

ELEVEN

The coachman cursed as the wheels once more ran off the edge of the road, sending the carriage lurching to one side. He steadied the horses and brought the vehicle back on to the road before calling down to his passenger.

'It is no good, *mademoiselle.* It is getting too dark and the verges are so turned to mud there is no knowing where it is safe to drive.'

'Then we must find somewhere to stay for the night. We cannot be far from Mont St Jean, perhaps there will be an inn that will accommodate us.'

The coachman set off again, shaking his head miserably. The chances of finding any house not full to the attics with military men were very slim, but to drive back to Brussels in the dark was almost an impossibility. The stretches of road that were not filled with slow-moving vehicles were scattered with wreckage and so full of ruts it was dangerous to go above a snail's pace. The lights of Mont St Jean twinkled in the distance, but before they reached the village they found a small wayside inn, torches flaring invitingly on either side of the entrance. The carriage came to a halt and Lucy climbed out, more than a little stiff from the journey. The inn was a long, low building, freshly white-washed and through the open windows she could hear the chink of glasses and much laughter—a sound she had scarcely expected to hear again. The landlord came out to greet her with the offer of refreshment, but when she told him she desired a room for the night, he threw out his hands and began to speak volubly in a mixture of French and Flemish.

'I understand that your house is full of soldiers,' said Lucy, when at length the man paused for breath, 'but is there no other lady staying here who would share a room with me? A bed on the floor would suffice . . .'

'*Mais non, madame,*' began the landlord, but Lucy was already entering the inn.

The door led directly into the tap-room which was crowded with military men—officers, she guessed, although in the hot, low-ceilinged room most had removed their jackets and sat about in shirts and breeches. The landlord followed her inside, still talking, but he was interrupted by a tall, red-faced man who came forward as Lucy entered.

'Quiet, Gaston, your barbaric tongue will frighten off our lovely visitor. What can we do for you, my lady?'

Lucy hesitated. After the cool night air, the brightness and warmth of the inn made it difficult for her to concentrate. 'I am in need of a room . . .'

'Oho!' The red-faced fellow looked around, winking at his companions. 'If it's a room you want, you may share mine, and willingly!' He laughed and looked about him, inviting his companions to share his jest. The landlord muttered that such ribaldry was out of place before a lady, but no one heeded him in the general merriment. Then through the noise came a cheerful, authoritative voice.

'Now then, lads! What's afoot? Am I to be excluded from the joke?'

A tall officer with a mop of unruly black hair and dashing side-whiskers elbowed his way through the crowd to stand before Lucy. She looked up to find herself being studied by a pair of humorous brown eyes. He summed up the situation and immediately took command.

'Gaston! A glass of wine for the lady and jump to it, man! Come, ma'am, let us move apart from these ruffians and you can tell me what it is you require.'

'You may trust Giles to come in as soon as a pretty face appears!' joked one of the crowd, but they parted good-naturedly to allow the officer to escort Lucy to an empty window-seat.

'You must forgive my friends,' he told her, smiling. 'They are in high good humour tonight, and it is no wonder, after the past few days! Now, tell me how I may help you.'

The landlord appeared with the wine and Lucy fortified herself with a sip before speaking. She was amazed at her own temerity, but the scenes she had witnessed during the day had robbed her of her natural shyness and she was only aware of exhaustion and a desperate need to rest.

'The darkness forces me to break my journey to Brussels and I am thus in need of a room for the night.'

The handsome officer laughed.

'Then there is not the least difficulty!' he cried gaily, 'I will gladly give up my room to you!'

Lucy knew that she should protest at this generosity, make some little show of reluctance, which the gentleman would then be at pains to overcome, but she was too tired to dissemble and merely nodded gratefully. The officer beamed back at her, his dark eyes warm with goodwill.

'Then if you will allow me, madam,' he said gallantly, 'my brother and I are about to dine privately above-stairs, and we would be honoured to have you join us. And while we are enjoying our meal,' he added persuasively, 'our rascally landlord can move my things out of the bedroom. I'll have him make up an extra bed there for his daughter—I feel sure you would be more comfortable with another female to keep you company.'

Despite the horrors she had endured, Lucy smiled.

'Indeed, sir, you seem to think of everything.'

'Years of practice, ma'am,' he replied audaciously. 'Now, if you have finished your wine, I will escort you in to dinner . . .'

Lucy allowed herself to be guided across the tap-room, pausing only to consult the landlord about the coachman and carriage, still waiting for her at the roadside.

'Aye, and while you are seeing them safely stowed for the night,' added the officer, 'ask your good wife to set another place at my table for the lady. Our host is a very good sort,' he continued, as they made their way up the narrow stairs, 'and you may rely upon him to make you comfortable here—by Jove, do you know, we have not yet introduced ourselves? I trust you will forgive the irregularity, ma'am, but you will agree that the circumstances are somewhat unusual.' They had reached the top of the stairs and he stepped back a pace in the narrow passage to execute an elegant bow. 'Allow me to introduce myself. Major Giles Vanderley, ma'am, at your service!'

'Oh!'

'What is it ma'am, are you ill?'

'Oh no—I cannot—'

With the gentleman's concerned gaze upon her, Lucilla realized too late how remiss she had been not to discover her companion's identity before agreeing to dine with him. Surely if she had not been so weary she would have seen the likeness, for it seemed obvious now: had not the man's friends called him Giles? And he had told her he was dining with his brother! Taking a long, steadying breath Lucy told him her name. There was no sign of recognition, and she scolded herself inwardly for the disappointment she felt. There was no reason why Dominic should ever have mentioned her.

Major Vanderley held open the door of the private room and, as she entered, her heart lurched to hear a familiar voice.

'Devil take you, Giles! You have been an age fetching that wine!' Dominic Vanderley was sitting at his ease by the hearth, his long legs encased in buckskins and top-boots which rested negligently on the empty fire-dogs, and he had removed his coat to display an elegantly embroidered blue waistcoat. He glanced around as he spoke and his astonishment when he saw Miss Chambers was so apparent that she could not resist a faint smile. He jumped up at once and came towards her, directing a questioning look at his brother.

'How do you do, Mr Vanderley.' Lucy's quiet voice forestalled any explanation. 'I am sorry to interrupt your dinner, but your brother has rescued me from what promised to be an uncomfortable night spent sleeping in my carriage.'

'Delighted to be of service to you, Miss Chambers, as always,' replied Dominic, raising her fingers to his lips.

'By all the—! You are acquainted!' cried Giles, looking from one to the other in astonishment.

'Yes. We have met before,' replied Lucy, flushing slightly. 'I am sorry if you think I misled you, Major, but truly I had no idea who you were when I accepted your invitation.'

'I can well believe that! And I would like to know what the devil brings you here!'

Mr Vanderley's harsh words brought her anxious gaze to his face. He said gently, 'Come and sit down, child. You look worn out.'

His concern almost overset her, but she fought back her tears to explain her presence so far from Brussels.

'I was searching for Tom. My fiancé was an infantryman,' she said, with a fleeting glance at the major. 'I learned that he had been fighting

216

near La Haye Saint. I was—fortunate enough to find him and—and to speak to him before . . . he died this afternoon.'

'Oh my dear, I am so sorry!' Dominic laid one hand upon her shoulder.

'Aye, we have lost a lot of good men,' said Giles, his face suddenly grave. 'Most of my comrades were killed at Hougoumont, yet I came out of it with barely a scratch!' He laughed bitterly. 'It makes one wonder what God's playing at!' He caught Dominic's warning glance and broke off, continuing after a tiny pause in a lighter tone, 'But never mind that! I forgot to bring up another bottle of wine, Dom. I'd better go back and see what I can find in our host's cellar!'

As the major lounged out, Dominic knelt beside Lucy's chair, taking her hands between his own.

'Will you tell me?' he asked quietly.

She shook her head. 'Thank you, but no. Not yet, I cannot.'

He did not move and they remained in silence until the reappearance of Giles with the landlady gave their thoughts another turn. When a place had been set for her, Lucy sat down between the brothers and began to eat, surprised to discover she was very hungry. Dominic and the major kept up a flow of small talk that soothed any uneasiness she might have felt at being alone with two gentlemen. For the most part she dined in silence, scarcely noticing what she was eating and too tired to join in the conversation.

'You will be going back to England now, Giles?' Dominic pushed away his empty plate.

'I doubt it. I have heard a rumour that we shall soon be in Paris. Will you be there, Dom?'

'Perhaps. When I have finished my work in Vienna I shall become a gentleman of leisure once more. I may yet go home. There's much I can do there.' He rose from the table. 'Come, it is nearly midnight and time we allowed our guest to retire. Poor Lucy, you are falling asleep over your coffee.'

She summoned a wan smile.

'I confess I am a little tired!'

'I have given up my room to Miss Chambers,' explained the major, 'so I have had Gaston put another bed in your room, Dominic. I trust you do not snore?'

'Of course not,' replied Mr Vanderley, keeping his eyes on Lucy's face. 'Giles, pray you go and find Gaston and bid him remove these dishes.'

Major Vanderley looked surprised.

'Eh? Oh, yes, of course!' He glanced from Dominic to Lucy. 'I'll see what I can do.'

'You always seem to be coming to my aid,' remarked Lucy, when they were alone.

Dominic led her away from the table and installed her in a comfortable armchair near the window. Outside, the darkness was complete now and the small room glowed in the soft light of the oil lamps.

'I could wish it were in happier circumstances! My dear—'

She lifted her hand. A small gesture, but Dominic saw it and was silent.

'Tom knew,' she said presently. 'He knew we should not marry, that we did not love each other in *that* way. And I don't think he was merely saying it because he was dying and wanted to make things easier for me.' She fixed her eyes anxiously upon Dominic, willing him to understand. She repeated the words the major had used earlier: 'It makes one wonder what God is playing at.'

Silently she began to cry and, dropping to his knees before her, Dominic pulled her into his arms, holding her tightly as grief racked her tired body: tears for the horrors she had seen that day: for Tom, for the survivors, for herself.

At last the tears subsided and when he had dried her eyes, Dominic escorted her across the narrow corridor to a small room set out with a single bed and a small truckle-bed made up in one corner. With a murmured goodnight he left her, only to reappear moments later with a cotton night-shirt which he held out to her.

'You have no night-clothes, so I will leave you this.' He grinned. 'It will be a little large, but very proper, I assure you! Gaston tells me his daughter will be here soon and she will bring you anything else you require.'

'Thank you. You have been most kind.'

He went out, leaving her with the single candle to light her to bed. She undressed and put on the borrowed night-shirt. It was far too big and hung about her slim body in heavy folds, yet she felt a certain comfort from wearing it, knowing it was Dominic's. A young woman entered the room, announcing in halting French that she had come to sleep in milady's room. Lucy showed her the truckle-bed and with the minimum of fuss the servant threw off her dress and lay down upon the bed in her shift. Lucy slipped between the cool cotton sheets and, within minutes of snuffing out the candle, she was asleep.

Lucilla slept late into the morning and awoke to the unfamiliar sound of bird-song outside her window. During her stay in Brussels she had become used to the sounds of the town, the clatter of wagons and cries from the street vendors that heralded each new day. For a few happy moments she thought she was back at Templecombe, until she opened her eyes and reality descended upon her like a heavy cloud. Rising from her bed, she noted that the landlord's daughter had already departed and Lucy made haste to get dressed, tidying her hair as best she could with the aid of the small mirror thoughtfully provided by her host. There was no one in the private parlour when she entered, but three places had been set at the table, two of which bore signs that the gentlemen had already broken their fast. She was just finishing her own slight breakfast when Major Vanderley came in.

'Good morning, Miss Chambers, I trust you had a comfortable night?'

'Yes, thank you.' She glanced at his uniform. 'You are on duty?'

'Soon, but I have time to enjoy a cup of coffee with you first!' He sat down at the table, watching Lucy as she poured the coffee. 'You will be returning to Brussels today?'

'Yes. I have lodgings there. My poor hostess will be wondering what has become of me!'

'What will you do?'

'I'm not sure. I must wait there for my sister and her husband. They went to Antwerp, you see.'

'And then you will return to England?'

Lucy nodded. 'I must. Tom's parents will be anxious. They will want to know of our last meeting.' Tears suspended her voice; the major waited in silence until she had composed herself. 'I'm sorry, I must not burden you with my small sorrow when you have lost so many good friends.'

He reached across the table and took her hand.

'Everyone suffers in war, my dear. Try to comfort yourself with the knowledge that you at least were with your fiancé when he died. Most faced the end alone.'

'Thank you, Major. I'll not forget it.'

Dominic Vanderley came in to see them holding hands across the table. Giles, glancing up at that moment, caught sight of his brother's face and his brows drew together slightly. Giving Lucy's hand a friendly squeeze he sat back in his chair and finished his coffee.

'I must go,' he said, rising. 'I leave our visitor in your hands, Dominic. Take good care of her!' Coming round the table he picked up Lucy's fingers and raised them to his lips, a smile gleaming in his eyes. 'I will say *au revoir*, Miss Chambers, for I feel sure we shall meet again!'

'Goodbye, Major, and thank you.'

'I have given orders for your carriage to be at the door in twenty minutes,' said Dominic, when the major had gone. 'Can you be ready to leave by then?'

Lucy was puzzled at his curt tone, but she answered evenly, 'Yes, sir. I have only to collect my hat and cloak. I will fetch them now—'

'Wait!'

She stopped, looking up at him with some surprise. He frowned at her.

'Why were you holding my brother's hand?' When she did not answer he continued roughly, 'I am led to believe, Miss Chambers, that Giles is very attractive to your sex.'

She stared at him. 'You think your brother was—was flirting with me—that I would allow him to do so when only yesterday—!' She broke off, anger and dismay choking her. Blindly, she made for the door.

'Lucy, wait!' He caught her as she passed him, the anger gone now from his voice. 'Lucy, forgive me! Of course I do not believe that either of you would be so insensitive! It is my cursed temper, my dear! I get so damnably jealous when I think of you with anyone!'

She leaned against him.

'Oh Dominic, you have no need to do so!' Looking up, she saw in his eyes such warmth that her pulses raced and she made no protest as he bent his head towards her, locking his lips upon her own in a long kiss.

'I'm sorry,' he muttered, crushing her to him. 'God forgive me, I don't know how I will live without you! I have to return to Vienna at the end of the week. Come with me!'

She held him away, gazing up, her eyes shining with such tenderness that he felt his passion for her growing dangerously.

'I can't' she said softly, tracing the outline of his jaw with one finger. 'I must go back to England, at least for a while.'

'I won't lose you again!' he muttered; savagely kissing her once more.

'You won't lose me, Dominic,' she assured him when she could speak. 'But I must go back.'

She drew away from him, for his closeness made it difficult for her to explain.

'I do not think I ever really considered the future as Tom's wife. I loved him like a brother, you see. Tom understood that, I *believe* he understood that. But I must go back—not for my sake or his, but for our families. There must be a period of mourning. Please say you understand.'

He took her hands.

'Of course. I cannot bear to leave you, but I understand. Would you like me to come with you to Brussels?'

'Thank you, but no. It is better that I return alone.'

'I will write to you—'

She put a finger to his lips, interrupting him.

'No, no contact until I am completely free. I owe Tom that much, I think. You will finish your work in Vienna, I shall do my duty at home and then . . .'

He pulled her close.

'And then, sweet life, let no man try to keep us apart!'

TWELVE

High above the English countryside the June sun shone down ceaselessly, scorching the plants, drying up the streams and making travelling in a closed carriage very uncomfortable. Inside the carriage, Mrs Chambers fanned herself vigorously as she stared out of the window.

'We should be able to see Stock House any moment now, Lucy—there it is! Thank goodness the journey is almost at an end!'

Lucilla fixed her eyes on the creamy stone building, visible for a brief moment before the carriage entered the shady tree-lined avenue leading to the house.

This is where it all began, she thought. Was it only two summers past? It seemed a lifetime.

It was a full year since she had said goodbye to Dominic at the inn outside Brussels. She had returned to the town to find Charlotte and Arthur anxiousy searching for her and they had made their way to England with all speed, Charlotte having decided that the excitement of life abroad was too much for her delicate condition. Safely back at Templecombe, Lucilla had met with fortitude the harrowing interviews with Squire Bancroft and his lady. In England, the death of her childhood friend was much more real to Lucy. During the day there were constant memories to be faced, and at night she relived the horrors of the battlefield in her dreams. The months had passed without word from Dominic and his image faded until it took on a dream-like quality. Lucy had insisted that they should not write, but there were days when her soul ached to know where he was, and if he was thinking of her. Lady Cornholme's invitation for Mrs Chambers and her daughter to visit Stock House promised a welcome change of scene, yet as the carriage bowled along the drive Lucy found that she was trembling, fearful she would have to encamedure even more painful memories.

Their hosts came out to meet them as the carriage pulled up, greeting them with all the warmth and affection of old friends.

'Well, Lucilla, let me look at you!' cried Lord Cornholme, holding her at arm's length while he studied her face. 'Hmm, you are a little paler than I remember, but even prettier! And I see you have brought your own mare with you this time, as I suggested.' He nodded to Lucy's groom, following behind the carriage with her bay. 'Come along inside, my dears. Lucy, there is someone here who is most anxious to see you!'

He led the way into the inner hall, where Lucy found Judith Vanderley waiting to greet her.

'My dear Miss Chambers!' Miss Vanderley

smiled, coming forward to embrace her warmly. 'How do you go on? It is such a time since we met!' She linked her arm through Lucy's. 'If Lady Cornholme does not object, I will show you to your room. We have so much to talk about.'

Receiving a nod from her hostess, the two young women made their way upstairs.

'We have rooms on the other side of the house this time,' explained Miss Vanderley, as they made their way along a wide corridor, 'with the most wonderful southerly views.' She stopped and threw open one of the doors. 'This is your room; mine is just a few doors along.'

'It is a lovely room! I had no idea you would be here.'

'I did not know myself until a week past!' replied Judith. 'At first I declined Lady Cornholme's invitation, for I am expecting Giles back from the Continent at any time, but in the end I decided to come, and I have left a message for Giles, telling him my direction. Lady Cornholme gave me permission to invite him to join us here. By the by, Giles wrote to tell me he had met you in Brussels. I should like to have been there myself, but Dominic would not permit it. He told me he needed me to run things here in England, but I think he considered the situation too dangerous. He was in Brussels himself for a few days, I believe, before he was obliged to return to

Vienna.' She looked closely at Lucy, 'He did not mention seeing you there.'

'No. I—um—is he still abroad?'

'Yes, he has written to me from most of the capitals of Europe! Goodness only knows when he means to return!' After a pause, she continued, 'Giles told me you were in Brussels throughout the fighting. I understand the French came very close. Were you frightened?'

'Yes, at times.'

'Your fiancé died in the battle did he not?' Judith's tone was compassionate. 'I was most sorry to hear of it.'

'Thank you. It—it was a great sadness to us all.'

Judith looked as if she would say more, but she was interrupted as the servants entered with Lucy's trunk and the moment passed.

At dinner that evening Lucy was relieved to discover that they were the only guests at Stock House. Lady Cornholme was anxious that they should not be disappointed by the small numbers, but Mrs Chambers made haste to reassure her.

'We are very quiet ourselves at Templecombe,' she told her hostess, 'and a small party is just what we like best, is it not, Lucilla?'

'And there is no reason why we should not enjoy ourselves,' added Lord Cornholme. 'I am sure these two accomplished young ladies will find plenty to amuse them. Which reminds me, Lucilla: when you were last here you left behind your sketching pad. Did you not miss it? I am sorry to say that by some oversight it was never sent on to you, but now that I have it in mind, I will have it sent up to your room!'

Later that night, Lucy sat on her bed with the drawing pad upon her knees, slowly turning the pages. She had given away many of her sketches, her subjects anxious to take away the likeness to show their friends, but there were enough to remind her of her last visit to Stock House. The outline sketch of the great oak, for instance, and the elegant little drawing of Charlotte. Spoiled, selfish Charlotte who must have her way at all costs. If only she had not deceived her with that silly ring—how different life might have been! Lucy sighed and turned the page to find herself staring at the incomplete portrait of Dominic Vanderley. She knew now why she had never been able to finish it: the features were too harsh, a good likeness of his countenance in repose, perhaps, but she had wanted to capture another side of him, the kindly gleam in his eyes when he teased her, the smile that hinted at a joke shared. Suddenly the faded image in her mind sharpened to such clarity that for a few seconds she could almost believe he was standing beside her, that if she looked round she would find him smiling down at her. She could not resist looking over her shoulder, then scolded herself for being fanciful, yet the feeling that he was near persisted, nurturing the tiny seeds of hope that had lain dormant within her for so long.

By the end of the first week Lucy and Judith had cemented their friendship. They explored the countryside together on horseback, discovered a great many common interests and filled their evenings with cards, books and music. It was therefore no surprise that Judith should let her be the first to share her good news.

'Lucy, I have this minute received a letter from Giles!' exclaimed Miss Vanderley, coming into Lucy's bedroom before dinner one evening. 'He says he hopes to be with us by tomorrow!'

Judith sat down to dinner that night in a mood of pleasurable anticipation, but Lucy found herself looking forward to the major's arrival with mixed feelings. She had given her family only the barest outline of what had happened in Belgium and had made no mention of Dominic's part in it, wishing to avoid painful explanations and the inevitable speculation. Now, she thought it unlikely that the truth could be avoided.

Major Vanderley duly arrived in time for dinner the following evening. He had left off his uniform, but even in a simply-cut riding coat Lucy thought he looked very much the soldier. He greeted Lucy with all the ease of long friendship, taking her hand and smiling down at her in a way that reminded her very much of Dominic.

'Ah, Miss Chambers. How do you go on? I am glad to have this opportunity to meet you again, but this time in happier circumstances. Belgium seems such a lifetime ago, does it not—but I don't wish to awaken painful memories for you!' He lowered his voice. 'I made but the briefest mention to Judith of our meeting in Brussels, I thought you would prefer that.'

'Yes—thank you, Major.'

'Well then, let us begin our acquaintance from this moment; after all, we have not until now been properly introduced!'

'No indeed,' she replied, smiling. 'But now that that has been rectified I am very happy to see you again!'

'And have you any news of Dominic?' asked Judith, as they went in to dinner.

'Devil a bit!' he exclaimed, laughing. 'The last I heard he was enjoying himself in Rome. Never know where he's going to pop up next!'

Lucy heard the words with a faint chill of disappointment. It had been her suggestion there should be no contact: it was only to be expected that a man like Dominic Vanderley would find solace with other women during their separation and a little voice within her whispered that it was just possible he had forgotten her.

231

*   *   *

'Lucy, my dear! Giles and I are going to drive into Bath today. Do say you will come with us!'

Across the breakfast-table Lucy returned Judith's smile 'Thank you, but no. I have other plans for this morning.'

'But I made sure you would like to come,' Judith coaxed her. 'We are going to visit the Abbey and try the waters in the Pump Room, though Lady Cornholme assured me they are quite horrid!'

Lucy laughed but resolutely shook her head.

'I am sure you and Giles have a great deal to talk about and will not miss me! It is such a fine day I am going to the park, to try if I can to finish a sketch I started years ago!'

*   *   *

Gazing out across the park in the summer sunshine, Lucy felt as if time had stood still in this place: nothing had changed, the trees looked as strong and green as they had done the last time she had rested under this same beech tree, and the great oak spreading out its massive branches in silent majesty had a timeless quality that she now sought to capture with her pencil. She worked on as the sun climbed higher, the welcome shade of the beech tree protecting her from the burning heat. A movement on the far side of the park

232

caught her attention and she stopped, pencil poised, as she watched the dark shape of a horse and rider crossing the open land towards her. She became aware of a dizzy lightness within her: surely she recognized the big black stallion that was approaching her with alarming speed, and the rider, bent low over the black's powerful neck. Pencil and pad slipped unheeded to the ground as she jumped up, running forward a few steps as the stallion covered the last yards between them. Dominic Vanderley reined in his horse and sat looking down at her, frowning slightly as if unsure of his welcome. His dark coat was unbuttoned and his boots were grey with dust from the roads: he looked larger than she remembered, his tall frame blocking out the sun.

'Oh'—her voice caught on a sob—'I knew you would come!'

Dominic slid down from Sultan's back and caught Lucy in his arms. She threw back her head, such a glow of happiness shining from her eyes that he felt momentarily unable to breathe.

'I could stay away no longer!' he told her, his voice not quite steady. 'Thirteen months, and to me it seemed thirteen years!'

'A lifetime!' she murmured, her cheek pressed against his comfortingly firm shoulder.

He kissed her hair, murmuring, 'Oh that I should love a bright, particular star!'

She looked up just as he bent his head

towards her, fastening his mouth on hers in a long, lingering kiss. When he released her she remained within his arms, gazing silently up at the harsh, lean face. The dark eyes seemed to look into her very soul and sent a shiver through her. There was so much to say, so many questions to ask him, yet she was afraid to break the spell. Dominic's arms tightened around her, holding her even closer and they kissed again, Lucy feeling the tug of excitement as she pressed against him. When at last she could speak she leaned against him, feeling the heavy thud of his heartbeat against her cheek.

'I have waited for ever for this moment! How long have you been in England?'

'Three days.' He planted a kiss on the top of her head. 'I have yet to go home. I wanted to see you first and called at Templecombe. Your butler gave me your direction.'

'Judith is here, and your brother.'

'So Lady Cornholme informed me.' He grinned. 'She thought it only natural that I should come in search of them, and without waiting for any explanation she has invited me to stay. Was ever a man so fortunate?'

'How long will you stay?'

'Forever if you'll have me!'

She smiled at him. 'Be serious, Dominic!'

He kissed her.

'How can I be serious when you look up at me so adorably? Very well, I have business in

London that requires my attention, but not quite yet. I have a few days at my disposal.'

She felt a tug of disappointment. Only a few days, and so much time to make up! She put her hand on his chest and looked up at him anxiously.

'Dominic, before we go on, I must tell you—pray, Dominic, do not be angry, but—Charlotte lied to me. When we were here last. She—she told me you were going to marry her!'

He looked grave. 'I know. She told me of it, the night I brought you back from the flood. It was a damned silly lie to tell you.'

Lucy grasped his hands, her eyes fixed anxiously on his face. 'But I did not *know* it was a lie, Dominic, until after I was engaged to Tom! Charlotte said she—she had jilted you. Oh please do not be too angry with her! She thought it no longer mattered . . . But I want you to know why I told Judith there was no hope. Are you very angry with me?'

'No, love. I'm not angry, not now. That is all in the past.' The harsh features relaxed. 'Dearest Lucy, say now that you will marry me!' He fixed his eyes on her face. 'This time I have come to you in person. No letters, no go-betweens—just a weary traveller waiting for you to make him the happiest of men. You do not answer'—he stared at her, saying roughly, 'if you dare to say you are not sure—'

'No, no, of course not!' she laughed a little

235

uncertainly, putting her fingers to his lips to stop his speech. He covered her hand with his own, imprisoning it against his mouth. She watched him tenderly. 'I have imagined this moment for so long, waited for you, prayed for you—it is hard to believe it's at an end . . .'

'This is not the end, sweet life,' he told her, taking her in his arms again, 'this is only the beginning!'

Richard Montanari is the *Sunday Times* top ten bestselling author of *The Devil's Garden, Play Dead, The Rosary Girls, The Skin Gods* and *Broken Angels,* as well as the internationally acclaimed thriller *Kiss of Evil.* He lives in Cleveland, Ohio.

www.richardmontanari.com

THE ECHO MAN

In Philadelphia the mutilated body of a man is found in one of the poorest neighbourhoods of the city. The victim has been viciously tortured to death. It's the work of a sick mind in free fall. Homicide detectives Kevin Byrne and Jessica Balzano investigate and soon realise that their crime scene is linked to the past. Eight years ago, another body was found in the same place, in the same position, killed in the same manner. That case was never closed. Apart from their killer's unusual calling cards, the crime scene photos — past and present — are identical. As another brutalised body appears, then another, it becomes clear that someone is recreating unsolved murders from Philadelphia's past and the killer is closer than they think . . .

RICHARD MONTANARI

THE ECHO MAN

Complete and Unabridged

CHARNWOOD
Leicester

First published in Great Britain in 2011 by
William Heinemann, London

First Charnwood Edition
published 2011
by arrangement with
William Heinemann
The Random House Group Limited, London

British Library CIP Data

Montanari, Richard.
  The echo man.
  1. Byrne, Kevin (Fictitious character)- -Fiction.
  2. Balzano, Jessica (Fictitious character)- -Fiction.
  3. Police- -Pennsylvania- -Philadelphia- -Fiction.
  4. Detective and mystery stories 5. Large type books.
  I. Title
  813.6–dc22

  ISBN 978–1–4448–0908–4

Published by
F. A. Thorpe (Publishing)
Anstey, Leicestershire

Set by Words & Graphics Ltd.
Anstey, Leicestershire
Printed and bound in Great Britain by
T. J. International Ltd., Padstow, Cornwall

This book is printed on acid-free paper

MAN
All seems evil until I
Sleepless would lie down and die.

ECHO
Lie down and die.

— William Butler Yeats
Man and the Echo

PROLOGUE

For every light there is shadow. For every sound, silence.

From the moment he got the call Detective Kevin Francis Byrne had a premonition this night would forever change his life, that he was headed to a place marked by a profound evil, leaving only darkness in its wake.

'You ready?'

Byrne glanced at Jimmy. Detective Jimmy Purify, sitting in the passenger seat of the bashed and battered department-issue Ford, was just a few years older than Byrne, but something in the man's eyes held deep wisdom, a hard-won experience that transcended time spent on the job and spoke instead of time earned. They'd known each other a long time, but this was their first full tour as partners.

'I'm ready,' Byrne said.

He wasn't.

They got out of the car and walked to the front entrance of the sprawling, well-tended Chestnut Hill mansion. Here, in this exclusive section of the northwest part of the city, there was history at every turn, a neighborhood designed at a time when Philadelphia was second only to London as the largest English-speaking city in the world.

The first officer on the scene, a rookie named Timothy Meehan, stood inside the foyer, cloistered by coats and hats and scarves perfumed with age, just beyond the reach of the cold autumn wind cutting across the grounds.

Byrne had been in Officer Meehan's shoes a handful of years earlier and remembered well how he'd felt when detectives arrived, the tangle of envy and relief and admiration. Chances were slight that Meehan would one day do the job Byrne was about to do. It took a certain breed to stay in the trenches, especially in a city like Philly, and most uniformed cops, at least the smart ones, moved on.

Byrne signed the crime-scene log and stepped into the warmth of the atrium, taking in the sights, the sounds, the smells. He would never again enter this scene for the first time, never again breathe an air so red with violence. Looking into the kitchen, he saw a blood-splattered killing room, scarlet murals on pebbled white tile, the torn flesh of the victim jigsawed on the floor.

While Jimmy called for the medical examiner and crime-scene unit, Byrne walked to the end of the entrance hall. The officer standing there was a veteran patrolman, a man of fifty, a man content to live without ambition. At that moment Byrne envied him. The cop nodded toward the room on the other side of the corridor.

And that was when Kevin Byrne heard the music.

★   ★   ★

2

She sat in a chair on the opposite side of the room. The walls were covered with a forest-green silk; the floor with an exquisite burgundy Persian. The furniture was sturdy, in the Queen Anne style. The air smelled of jasmine and leather.

Byrne knew the room had been cleared, but he scanned every inch of it anyway. In one corner stood an antique curio case with beveled glass doors, its shelves arrayed with small porcelain figurines. In another corner leaned a beautiful cello. Candlelight shimmered on its golden surface.

The woman was slender and elegant, in her late twenties. She had burnished russet hair down to her shoulders, eyes the color of soft copper. She wore a long black gown, sling-back heels, pearls. Her makeup was a bit garish — theatrical, some might say — but it flattered her delicate features, her lucent skin.

When Byrne stepped fully into the room the woman looked his way, as if she had been expecting him, as if he might be a guest for Thanksgiving dinner, some discomfited cousin just in from Allentown or Ashtabula. But he was neither. He was there to arrest her.

'Can you hear it?' the woman asked. Her voice was almost adolescent in its pitch and resonance.

Byrne glanced at the crystal CD case resting on a small wooden easel atop the expensive stereo component. *Chopin: Nocturne in G Major.* Then he looked more closely at the cello. There was fresh blood on the strings and fingerboard, as well as on the bow lying on the

3

floor. Afterwards, she had played.

The woman closed her eyes. 'Listen,' she said. 'The blue notes.'

Byrne listened. He has never forgotten the melody, the way it both lifted and shattered his heart.

Moments later the music stopped. Byrne waited for the last note to feather into silence. 'I'm going to need you to stand up now, ma'am,' he said.

When the woman opened her eyes Byrne felt something flicker in his chest. In his time on the streets of Philadelphia he had met all types of people, from soulless drug dealers, to oily con men, to smash-and-grab artists, to hopped-up joyriding kids. But never before had he encountered anyone so detached from the crime they had just committed. In her light brown eyes Byrne saw demons caper from shadow to shadow.

The woman rose, turned to the side, put her hands behind her back. Byrne took out his handcuffs, slipped them over her slender white wrists, and clicked them shut.

She turned to face him. They stood in silence now, just a few inches apart, strangers not only to each other, but to this grim pageant and all that was to come.

'I'm scared,' she said.

Byrne wanted to tell her that he understood. He wanted to say that we all have moments of rage, moments when the walls of sanity tremble and crack. He wanted to tell her that she would pay for her crime, probably for the rest of her life

4

— perhaps even *with* her life — but that while she was in his care she would be treated with dignity and respect.

He did not say these things.

'My name is Detective Kevin Byrne,' he said. 'It's going to be all right.'

It was November 1, 1990.

Nothing has been right since.

ONE

ALLEGRO

1

SUNDAY, OCTOBER 24

Can you hear it?

Listen closely. There, beneath the clatter of the lane, beneath the ceaseless hum of man and machine, you will hear the sound of the slaughter, the screaming of peasants in the moment before death, the plea of an emperor with a sword at his throat.

Can you hear it?

Step onto hallowed ground, where madness has made the soil luxuriant with blood, and you will hear it: Nanjing, Thessaloniki, Warsaw.

If you listen closely you will realize it is always there, never fully silenced, not by prayer, by law, by time. The history of the world, and its annals of crime, is the slow, sepulchral music of the dead.

There.

Can you hear it?

I hear it. I am the one who walks in shadow, ears tuned to the night. I am the one who hides in rooms where murder is done, rooms that will never again be quieted, each corner now and forever sheltering a whispering ghost. I hear fingernails scratching granite walls, the drip of blood onto scarred tile, the hiss of air drawn into a mortal chest wound. Sometimes it all becomes too much, too loud, and I must let it out.

I am the Echo Man.
I hear it all.

★ ★ ★

On Sunday morning I rise early, shower, take my breakfast at home. I step onto the street. It is a glorious fall day. The sky is clear and crystalline blue, the air holds the faint smell of decaying leaves.

As I walk down Pine Street I feel the weight of the three killing instruments at the small of my back. I study the eyes of passersby, or at least those who will meet my gaze. Every so often I pause, eavesdrop, gathering the sounds of the past. In Philadelphia Death has lingered in so many places. I collect its spectral sounds the way some men collect fine art, or war souvenirs, or lovers.

Like many who have toiled in the arts over the centuries my work has gone largely unnoticed. That is about to change. This will be my magnum opus, that by which all such works are judged forever. It has already begun.

I turn up my collar and continue down the lane.

Zig, zig, zig.

I rattle through the crowded streets like a white skeleton.

★ ★ ★

At just after eight a.m. I enter Fitler Square, finding the expected gathering — bikers, joggers, the homeless who have dragged themselves here from a nearby passageway. Some of these homeless creatures will not live through the winter. Soon I will hear their last breaths.

I stand near the ram sculpture at the eastern end of the square, watching, waiting. Within minutes I see them, mother and daughter.

They are just what I need.

★   ★   ★

I walk across the square, sit on a bench, take out my newspaper, halve and quarter it. The killing instruments are uncomfortable at my back. I shift my weight as the sounds amass: the flap and squawk of pigeons congregating around a man eating a bagel, a taxi's rude horn, the hard thump of a bass speaker. Looking at my watch, I see that time is short. Soon my mind will be full of screams and I will be unable to do what is necessary.

I glance at the young mother and her baby, catch the woman's eye, smile.

'Good morning,' I say.

The woman smiles back. 'Hi.'

The baby is in an expensive jogging stroller, the kind with a rainproof hood and mesh shopping basket beneath. I rise, cross the path, glance inside the pram. It's a girl, dressed in a pink flannel one-piece and matching hat, swaddled in a snow-white blanket. Bright plastic stars dangle overhead.

'And who is this little movie star?' I ask.

The woman beams. 'This is Ashley.'

'Ashley. She is beautiful.'

'Thank you.'

I am careful not to get too close. Not yet. 'How old is she?'

'She's four months.'

'Four months is a great age,' I reply with a wink. 'I may have peaked around four months.'

The woman laughs.

I'm in.

I glance at the stroller. The baby smiles at me. In her angelic face I see so much. But sight does not drive me. The world is crammed full of beautiful images, breathtaking vistas, all mostly forgotten by the time the next vista presents itself. I have stood before the Taj Mahal, Westminster Abbey, the Grand Canyon. I once spent an afternoon in front of Picasso's Guernica. All these glorious images faded into the dim corners of memory within a relatively short period of time. Yet I recall with exquisite clarity the first time I heard someone scream in anguish, the yelp of a dog struck by a car, the dying breath of a young police officer bleeding out on a hot sidewalk.

'Is she sleeping through the night yet?'

'Not quite,' the woman says.

'My daughter slept through the night at two months. Never had a problem with her at all.'

'Lucky.'

I reach slowly into my right coat pocket, palm what I need, draw it out. The mother stands just a few feet away, on my left. She does not see what I have in my hand.

The baby kicks her feet, bunching her blanket.

12

I wait. I am nothing if not patient. I need the little one to be tranquil and still. Soon she calms, her bright blue eyes scanning the sky.

With my right hand I reach out, slowly, not wanting to alarm the mother. I place a finger into the center of the baby's left palm. She closes her tiny fist around my finger and gurgles. Then, as I had hoped, she begins to coo.

All other sounds cease. In that moment it is just the baby, and this sacred respite from the dissonance that fills my waking hours.

I touch the Record button, keeping the microphone near the little girl's mouth for a few seconds, gathering the sounds, collecting a moment which would otherwise be gone in an instant.

Time slows, lengthens, like a lingering coda.

I withdraw my hand. I do not want to stay too long, nor alert the mother to any danger. I have a full day ahead of me, and cannot be deterred.

'She has your eyes,' I say.

The little girl does not, and it is obvious. But no mother ever refuses such a compliment.

'Thank you.'

I glance at the sky, at the buildings that surround Fitler Square. It is time. 'Well, it was lovely talking to you.'

'You, too,' replies the woman. 'Enjoy your day.'

'Thank you,' I say. 'I'm sure I will.'

I reach out, take one of the baby's tiny hands in mine, give it a little shake. 'It was nice meeting you, little Ashley.'

Mother and daughter giggle.

13

I am safe.

A few moments later, as I walk up Twenty-third Street, toward Delancey, I pull out the digital recorder, insert the mini-plug for the earbuds, play back the recording. Good quality, a minimum of background noise. The baby's voice is precious and clear.

As I slip into the van and head to South Philadelphia I think about this morning, how everything is falling into place.

Harmony and melody live inside me, side by side, violent storms on a sun-blessed shore.

I have captured the beginning of life.

Now I will record its end.

2

'My name is Paulette, and I'm an Alcoholic.'

'Hi, Paulette.'

She looked out over the group. The meeting was larger than it had been the previous week, nearly doubled in size from the first time she attended the Second Verse group at the Trinity United Methodist Church nearly a month earlier. Before that she had been to three meetings at three different places — North Philly, West Philly, South Philly — but, as she soon learned, most people who attend AA meetings regularly find a group, and a vibe, with which they are comfortable, and stay with it.

There were twenty or so people sitting in a loose circle, equally divided between men and women, young and old, nervous and calm. The youngest person was a woman around twenty; the oldest, a man in his seventies, sitting in a wheelchair. It was also a diverse group — black, white, Hispanic, Asian. Addiction, of course, had no prejudice, no gender or age issues. The size of the group indicated that the holidays were rapidly approaching, and if anything pressed the glowing red buttons of inadequacy, resentment, and rage, it was the holidays.

The coffee, as always, was crap.

'Some of you have probably seen me here before,' she began, trying to affect a tone of lightness and cheer. 'Ah, who the hell am I kidding? Maybe I'm wrong about that. Maybe it's ego, right? Maybe I think I'm the shit, and no one else does. Maybe that's the *problem*. Anyway, today is the first time I've really had the balls to speak. So, here I am, and you have me. At least for a little while. Lucky you.'

As she told her story, she scanned the faces. There was a kid in his mid-twenties on the right — killer blue eyes, ripped jeans, a multicolor Ed Hardy T-shirt, biceps of note. More than once she looked over at him and saw him scanning her body. He may have been an alcoholic but he was still most definitely on the make. Next to him was a woman in her fifties, a few decades of heavy use mapped in the broken veins on her face and neck. She rolled a sweaty cellphone over and over in her hands, tapped one foot to some long-silenced beat. A few chairs down from her was a petite blonde in a green Temple University sweatshirt, athletic and toned, the weight of the world just a snowflake on her shoulder. Next to her sat Nestor, the group leader. Nestor had opened the meeting with his own short and sad tale, then asked if there was anyone else who wanted to talk.

My name is Paulette.

When she finished her story everyone clapped politely. After that other people rose, talked, cried. More applause.

When all their stories were exhausted, every emotion wrung, Nestor reached out his hands to either side. 'Let's give thanks and praise.'

They joined hands, said a short prayer, and the meeting was over.

16

'It's not as easy as it looks, is it?'

She turned around. It was Killer Blue Eyes. At just after noon they stood outside the main church doors, between a pair of emaciated brown evergreens, already struggling through the season.

'I don't know,' she replied. 'It looked pretty hard to begin with.'

Killer Blue Eyes laughed. He had put on a short cognac leather jacket. A pair of amber Serengeti sunglasses were clipped to the neck of his T-shirt. He wore thick-soled black boots.

'Yeah. I guess you're right,' he said. He clasped his hands in front of him, rocked back slightly on his heels. His good-guy, not-to-worry pose. 'It's been a while since I've done it for the first time.' He held out his hand. 'Your name is Paulette, right?'

'And I'm an alcoholic.'

Killer Blue Eyes laughed again. 'I'm Danny. Me too.'

'Nice to meet you, Danny.' They shook hands.

'I *can* tell you this, though,' he continued, unasked. 'It gets easier.'

'The sobriety part?'

'I wish I could say that. What I meant was the *talking* part. Once you get comfortable with the group it gets a little easier to tell your stories.'

'Stories?' she asked. 'Plural? I thought I was done.'

'You're not done,' he said. 'It's a process. It goes on for a long time.'

17

'Okay. Like, how long?'

'Did you see that guy in the red flannel shirt?'

Danny was talking about the older man, the guy in his seventies, the guy in the wheelchair. 'What about him?'

'He's been coming to meetings for thirty-six years.'

'*Jesus*. He hasn't had a drink in thirty-six years?'

'That's what he says.'

'And he still wants one?'

'So he says.'

Danny looked at his watch, an oversized Fossil chronograph. The move looked just slightly less calculated and rehearsed than it probably was. 'You know, I don't have to be at work for a couple of hours. Can I buy you a cup of coffee?'

She looked appropriately suspicious. 'I don't know.'

Danny put up both hands. 'No strings. Just coffee.'

She smiled. 'Irish?'

'Bad Paulette. Bad, *bad* Paulette.'

She laughed. 'Let's go.'

★　★　★

They picked a place on Germantown Avenue, sat at a table near the window, small-talked — movies, fashion, the economy. She had a fruit salad. He had coffee and a cheeseburger. Neither would rate Zagat's.

After fifteen minutes or so she held up her iPhone, tapped the touch screen. She did not dial a number, did not send a text or an email, did not make an entry onto her contact list or schedule something in iCal. Instead, she took a picture of Killer Blue Eyes, having earlier in the day deselected the option that attached the sound of a clicking camera to the operation. When she was done she looked at the cellphone's screen in mock frustration, as if something was wrong. Nothing was wrong. The photograph, which the young man could not see, was perfect.

'Problem?' he asked.

She shook her head. 'No. It's just that I can never get much of a signal around here.'

'Maybe you can get a signal outside,' Danny said. He stood up, slipped on his jacket. 'Want to give it a shot?'

She hit one more button, waited until the progress bar made its way fully to the right, and said: 'Sure.'

'Come on,' Danny said. 'I'll get the check.'

* * *

They walked slowly down the street, wordlessly window browsing.

'Don't you have to make that call?' Danny asked.

She shook her head. 'Not really. It's just my mother. She's just going to give me shit about what a loser I am. I can wait.'

'We might be related,' Danny said. 'Like *closely* related. I think we have the same mother.'

'I thought you looked familiar.'

19

Danny looked around. 'So, where are you parked?'

'Just up this way.'

'Would you like me to walk you to your car?'

She stopped. 'Oh *no*.'

'What?'

'You're not a gentleman, are you?' she accused him flirtatiously.

Danny raised a hand, three fingers up, Boy Scout style. 'I swear to God I'm not.'

She laughed. 'Sure.'

They turned the corner into a dim alleyway, heading toward the parking lot. Before they took three steps she saw the glint of the revolver.

With a strong forearm Danny slammed her against the bricks and brought his face very close to hers.

'You see that red Sebring over there?' he whispered, nodding toward the Chrysler parked near the end of the alley. 'Here's what we're going to do. We're going to walk over there and you're going to get in that car. If you give me any trouble, make a single sound, so help me God I will shoot you in the fucking face. Do you hear me?'

'Yes.'

'Do you doubt what I say?'

She shook her head.

'I want you to say it out loud. I want you to say 'I understand, Danny.''

'I understand, Danny.'

'Good. Good,' he said. '*Paulette*.' He kept a hand on her, leaned away. 'You know, you've got great tits. You wear this loose shit to hide them,

20

but I can tell. *And* you're a goddamn drunk. Do you know what a plus that is?'

She just stared.

'Me? I've never had a drink in my life. I just have this weakness for weak women. Always have.'

He ran his left hand slowly over her right hip, his other hand remaining on the butt of the gun. He smiled.

'I think we're going to do it right here. What do you think of that?'

'You won't hurt me?'

'No,' he said. 'But admit it, *Paulette*. There *is* something exciting about doing it in public. Especially with a total stranger.' He pulled down his zipper. 'But that's why you drink, isn't it? Because you hate yourself? Because you're a whore?'

She didn't know if it was really a question. She remained silent. He continued.

'Of course it is. And you know what? I bet you've gotten plenty loaded over the years, and fucked plenty of guys in alleys. Right?'

This was definitely a question. When she didn't answer he took the revolver from his waistband and stuck it between her legs. Hard.

'Answer . . . the fucking . . . *question*.'

'Yes.'

He ran the barrel of the gun up and down, applying even more pressure. 'Say it.'

'I've fucked a lot of guys in alleys.'

'And you loved it.'

'And I loved it.'

'Because you're a fucking whore.'

21

'Because I'm a fucking whore.'

'I thought so.' He slipped the gun back into his waistband. 'You know that other girl? She gave me a hard time. She didn't have to die.'

'The other girl?'

'The redhead. The fat one. *Marcy* something, the papers said. Smelled like a cheap slut. Which she was, of course.'

He leaned in, sniffed her hair.

'You don't smell cheap,' he said. 'You smell good.'

A shadow crawled slowly across the ground, pooling at their feet. Danny noticed, spun around.

Behind him, a few paces away, stood the petite blonde from the AA meeting, the one wearing the green Temple University hooded sweatshirt. In her hand was a Glock 17, pointed at the center of Danny's chest.

'My name is Nicci,' the blonde said. 'And I'm a police officer.'

'Hi, Nicci!' Detective Jessica Balzano responded.

During the previous three weeks, on her undercover assignment to catch the AA Killer, Jessica had been Paulette. No last name. Just Paulette. She discovered early on in the assignment that no one had a last name at AA.

Behind Detective Nicolette Malone stood two other detectives, as well as a veteran patrolman named Stan Keegan. At either end of the alley were a pair of sector cars.

Danny looked at Jessica, his hands trembling now. 'You're a *cop?*'

Jessica stepped back, drew her own weapon

from a holster at the small of her back, leveled it. 'Put your hands behind your head and interlace your fingers.'

Danny hesitated, his eyes shifting from side to side.

'Do it *now*.'

Danny froze.

'Suit yourself,' Jessica said. 'But if you don't do what I tell you to do, you will die where you stand. In an Ed Hardy T-shirt, no less. *With* your zipper down. Your call.'

The suspect, whose real name was Lucas Anthony Thompson, seemed to realize his two choices. He was leaving this alley either in handcuffs or on a gurney. In an instant his will was broken. His shoulders sagged. He put his hands on top of his head, fingers interlaced.

Jessica had seen it a hundred times. And it never failed to warm her heart.

Gotcha.

Nicci Malone stepped forward, pulled the weapon from the suspect's waistband, handed it to Officer Keegan, who put it in an evidence bag. Nicci then swept the suspect's legs from beneath him. He hit the ground hard, face down. An instant later Nicci dropped a knee into the center of Thompson's back, cuffed him.

'It's almost impossible you're this fucking stupid,' Nicci said.

Jessica holstered her gun, stepped forward. Each grabbing an arm, the two detectives pulled the suspect roughly to his feet.

'You are under arrest for the murder of Marcia Jane Kimmelman,' Jessica said. She read him his

Miranda rights. 'Do you understand these rights?'

Thompson nodded, still dazed.

'You have to answer out loud,' she said. 'You have to say 'yes.''

'Yes.'

'Actually, I want you to say, 'Yes, I understand, Detective Goddess Balzano.''

Thompson didn't say it. He was still a bit stunned.

Ah, well, Jessica thought. *Worth a shot.* She reached into her pocket, pulled out the small digital recorder. She rewound the recording, clicked PLAY.

You know that other girl? She gave me a hard time. She didn't have to die.

Jessica clicked off the recorder. Thompson hung his head.

They had plenty with which to charge him. An eyewitness, a good sampling of DNA, ballistics. The recording was just icing on the cake. The DA's office loved recordings. Sometimes a recording made all the difference in the world.

As uniformed officers led Thompson away, Officer Stan Keegan leaned against the brick wall, crossed his arms over his kettle-drum chest, a Cheshire-cat grin on his face.

'What's so funny?' Jessica asked.

'You two,' he said, nodding at her and Nicci. 'I'm just trying to figure out which one of you is Batman and which one is Robin.'

'Batman? Dream *on*, mortal,' Jessica said. 'I'm Wonder Woman.'

'And I'm She Hulk,' Nicci added.

The two women bumped fists.

★　　★　　★

There was a young man standing next to the sector car, talking to one of the uniformed officers. He was tall, dark-haired, lanky, and had about him a nervous energy. He carried an expensive-looking digital video camera. Jessica soon realized who he was, and what he was doing there.

She had gotten the memo the week before, and had forgotten all about it. Somebody from Penn State was making a documentary about the homicide unit — a day-in-the-life sort of thing — and the directive from high on high was to cooperate. The memo said the filmmaker would be there for a week.

As Jessica approached, the young man noticed her. He smoothed his hair with his free hand, stood a little taller.

'Hi,' he said. 'I'm David Albrecht.'

'Jessica Balzano.'

They shook hands. David Albrecht wore a gold crucifix around his neck, along with a Nittany Lions long-sleeved T-shirt. He was cleanshaven, save for a sparse bleached-white soul patch beneath his lower lip. It was the only thing keeping his face from being feminine.

'I'd know you anywhere,' he said. He pumped her arm with a little too much enthusiasm.

'Really? And why is that?' Jessica asked, retrieving her limb before it was shaken off.

Albrecht smiled. 'I do my research. You were in that *Philadelphia Magazine* feature a few years ago, the one about the 'new breed' of female

25

detective. Remember that?'

Jessica remembered the article well. She had fought against it but had lost the battle. She was not crazy about having details of her personal life made public. Police officers, especially detectives, were big enough targets for crazies as it was.

'I remember,' Jessica said.

'And I followed the Rosary Killer case pretty closely.'

'I see.'

'Of course, I was in high school then,' Albrecht said. 'I went to a Catholic school. We were all pretty mesmerized by the story.'

High school, Jessica thought. *This kid was in* high school *then*. It seemed like yesterday to her.

'By the way, that was a great photo of you on the cover of the mag,' he added. 'Real Lara Croft. You were kind of a pinup for a lot of the guys at my school for a while.'

'So, you're making a movie?' Jessica asked, hoping to get off the subject of the article.

'Gonna try. Making a feature is a lot different from making a short. I've done mainly webisodes so far.'

Jessica wasn't really sure what a webisode was.

'You should stop by my site and check some of them out,' Albrecht said. 'I think you'll like them.'

He handed her a card bearing his name and a website address.

Jessica did the polite thing, scanning the card before putting it into her pocket. 'Well,' she said. 'It was great meeting you, David. Anything you need.' She didn't mean it, of course. She pointed at the just-arrived police transport van. 'I've got to get this started.'

Albrecht held up a hand. 'No sweat. Just wanted to introduce myself.' He smoothed his hair again. 'I'll be around, but you won't even notice me. I promise not to get in your way. I'm a mouse.'

A mouse, Jessica thought. *We'll see about that.*

★ ★ ★

Two hours later, with paperwork completed, reports filed, and suspect delivered to the police administration building at Eighth and Race Streets — commonly known as the Roundhouse — the team met at a restaurant called the Hot Potato Café on Girard Avenue.

In addition to Jessica and Nicci Malone there was veteran detective Nick Palladino, as well as a relatively new detective in the unit, Dennis Stansfield. Stansfield was in his early forties and was God's gift to women, at least in his own mind. His clearance-rack suits never quite fit, he wore too much cologne and, among his many annoying habits, he seemed to be in constant motion, as if he always had somewhere else to be, something else to do that was far more important than talking to you.

He had only been with the unit for a few months and had yet to make a friend. No one wanted to work with him. His abrasive personality was only one of the reasons. His sloppy work habits, and his uncanny ability to get a witness to clam up immediately, were two others.

Jessica and Nicci held down one side of the table, while Stansfield and Nick Palladino sat on the other.

Nick Palladino — whom everyone called Dino — was a lifer, a South Philly boy with a knack for sniffing out con men and thieves, two categories of criminal of which the city of Philadelphia had no shortage.

They were all on duty for a few more hours, so it was coffee and Cokes for now. They lifted a glass to their day.

Lucas Anthony Thompson, 26, late of Port Richmond, currently a guest of Hotel Homicide, stood accused in the aggravated murder and sexual assault of a young woman named Marcia Jane Kimmelman. According to witnesses, the two had met at an AA meeting in West Philly but, because last names were never used, no one knew who Thompson was. They had a general description, but that was about it.

Marcia's body had been found in a vacant lot on Baltimore Avenue near 47th Street. She had been sexually assaulted, shot once in the head with a .38 at close range. Three months later Thompson met and attacked a young woman after a meeting in Kingessing, but the woman, a secretary for Comcast named Bonnie Silvera, survived. DNA found in semen left behind by her attacker matched that of Marcia Kimmelman's killer. Bonnie Silvera gave police a highly detailed description of Thompson, and there began an undercover operation that ultimately involved a dozen detectives and brought them to more than six districts.

'So how'd you ID him?' Dino asked.

Nicci deferred to Jessica. 'Talk to the mastermind.'

'Well, we had a little help from the Audio Visual Unit on this one,' Jessica said. 'But when Thompson and I were sitting in that coffee shop I took his picture with my cellphone. Then I sent the photo via SMS to Nicci's phone. Nicci and two uniforms were out in the van, about half a block away, with Bonnie Silvera. A few seconds later Nicci got the photo, opened it, showed it to Bonnie. The witness made the positive ID, Nicci sent me a text, letting me know we were on, and we knew we had him.'

'That was *your* play?' Dino asked.

Jessica blew on her nails, buffed them dramatically on her blouse.

'My God, you are a dangerous woman,' Dino said.

'Tell the world.'

'I should tell your husband.'

'Like he doesn't know,' Jessica said. 'Right now he's painting the fence behind our house. I'm going to let him draw me a bubble bath later.'

Detective Dennis Stansfield, perhaps feeling left out, piped in. 'You know, I read in a recent survey that, in her lifetime, the average American woman receives 26.5 miles of cock.'

If there was one thing Jessica hated, it was a cop who found a way to make a sex joke after hearing about a rape. Even worse, a rape/murder. Rape had nothing to do with sex. Rape was about violence and power.

Stansfield glanced over at Jessica. It seemed that she had gotten the assignment to be the flustered, blushing female officer in his presence, the one ill at ease in the wake of his shabby jokes. Was he kidding? Jessica had been born and raised in South Philly, and had grown up around cops. She was swearing like a longshoreman by the time she was five. She had even gotten to like the taste of soap.

'Twenty-six miles, huh?' Jessica asked.

'Twenty-six point *five*,' Stansfield replied.

Jessica looked at Nicci, at Dino, back at Stansfield. Dino looked at the table. He didn't know exactly what was coming, but he knew *something*.

'So, let me get this straight,' Jessica said, squaring off.

'Sure.'

'Is that 26.5 miles counting each insertion, or all the cocks added up individually?'

Stansfield, all of a sudden, started to redden a bit himself. 'Well, I'm not sure. I don't think the survey said.'

Nothing killed a dirty joke like discussion and analysis. 'Not very scientific, then, is it?'

'Well, it was — '

'Now, if we're counting per insertion,' Jessica continued, unbowed, 'that might be just one hell of a weekend.' She leaned back in her chair, crossed her arms. 'If we're counting each dick just once . . . let's see.' She looked at Nicci, while gesturing to Stansfield. 'How many times does four inches go into twenty-six miles?'

30

'Twenty-six-five,' Nicci added.

'Right,' Jessica said. 'Twenty-six-five.'

Stansfield was now as red as a Roma tomato. 'Four inches? Uh, I don't think so, darlin'.'

Jessica looked behind her, at the woman setting up the next table. 'Hey, Kathy, is there a ruler in the office?' Kathy was one of the owners of the Hot Potato Café.

'Oh yeah,' Kathy said with a wink. A Philly girl herself, she had heard the whole exchange and was probably dying to leap into the fray.

'All right, all right,' Stansfield said.

'Come on, Dennis,' Jessica said. 'Drop that big hot spud on the table.'

Suddenly Stansfield had somewhere else to be. He glanced at his watch, downed his coffee, mumbled his goodbyes, made his exit.

Jessica could ignore the Cro-Magnons of the world on a day like this. A killer was in custody, they had a pile of evidence against him, no civilian or police officer had been injured in the arrest, and a gun was off the street. It didn't get any better than that.

* * *

Twenty minutes later they split up. Jessica walked to her car alone. She knew that she had to keep up a front with her fellow detectives, a shield of hubris and bravado. But the cold truth was that she'd had a gun pointed at her. She knew that everything could have been taken away in the time it took to pull that trigger.

She stepped into a doorway and, making sure

31

she was not observed, closed her eyes, a tidal wave of fear rushing over her. In her mind she saw her husband Vincent, her daughter Sophie, her father Peter. Both Peter Giovanni and Vincent Balzano were cops — her father long retired — and knew the risks, but Jessica envisioned them both standing over her casket at St. Paul's. In her mind she heard the bagpipes.

Jess, she thought. *Don't go there. If you go there, you might never come back.*

On the other hand, after all was said and done, she was tough, wasn't she? She was PPD. She was her father's daughter.

Fuck it all, she was *dangerous.*

By the time she reached her car her legs were steady. Before she could open the door she noticed someone across the street. It was David Albrecht. He had the camera on his shoulder. He was filming her.

Here we go, Jessica thought. It's going to be a long week.

She got in her car, started it. Her cellphone rang. She answered, and learned something she'd always suspected.

She wasn't the only dangerous female in her family.

3

I hear a truck pull into the driveway. A few
moments later, a knock at the door. I open it. In
front of me stands a man of forty, just beginning
to paunch. He is wearing a red windbreaker,
paint-splattered jeans, a pair of soiled running
shoes with frayed laces. In his hand is a
clipboard.

'Mr. Marcato?' the man asks.

Marcato. The name makes me smile.

'Yes.' I extend my hand. The man's skin is
rough, calloused, stained. He reeks of cigarettes
and turpentine.

'I'm Kenny Beckman,' he says. 'We spoke on
the phone.'

'Of course. Please come in.'

Except for a few plastic trash barrels and dusty
glass display cases, the space is empty.

'Man, what's that smell?' Beckman asks.

'It's coming from next door. There used to be
a sausage shop there and I think they left some
meat to rot. I intend to speak to them about it.'

'You better. You're not gonna do any business
in here if it smells like this.'

'I understand.' I gesture at the room. 'As you
can see, we're going to need quite a bit of work
here.'

'You can say that again.'

Beckman walks around the room, touching
the moldering drywall, fingering the dust-caked

33

sills, shining a flashlight along the baseboards. He produces a measuring tape, takes a few dimensions, jots them on the clipboard. I watch him carefully, calculating his speed and agility.

A minute or so later: 'You've got a pretty good sag in the floor joists.' He bounces a few times, driving home his point. The parched joists creak beneath his weight. 'The first thing we're going to need to do is shore that up. You really can't do too much else with the floor out of level.'

'Whatever is necessary to bring this up to code.'

Beckman looks around the room again, perhaps in preparation for his closing. 'Well, you've got a ways to go, but I think we can handle it.'

'Good. I'd like to get started right away.'

'Sounds like a plan.'

'And by the way, you've come highly recommended.'

'Oh yeah? Who recommended me? If you don't mind me asking.'

'I'm not sure I recall. It was a while ago.'

'How long?'

'March 21, 2002.'

At the mention of the date Kenneth Beckman tenses. He takes a step backward, glances at the door. 'I'm sorry? 2002? Is that what you said?'

'Yes.'

'March of 2002?'

'Yes.'

Another glance at the door. 'That's not possible.'

'And why is that?'

34

'Well, for one thing, I wasn't even in business then.'

'I can explain,' I say. 'Let me show you something.' I gesture to the dark hallway leading to the back room of the first floor. Beckman takes a moment, perhaps sensing that something is slightly off kilter, like a radio that cannot quite find a signal. But he clearly needs the work, even if it is for a weird man who speaks in riddles.

We head down the hallway. When we reach the door I push it open. The smell is a lot stronger here.

'Fuck!' Beckman exclaims, recoiling. He reaches into his back pocket, takes out a soiled handkerchief, brings it to his mouth. 'What the hell is that?'

The small square room is spotless. There are two steel tables at the center, both bolted to the floor. The night-black walls have been expensively soundproofed; the drop ceiling is made of acoustic tile purchased by mail order from a Swiss company specializing in outfitting the finest recording studios in the world. Above the tables is a microphone. The floor is a high-gloss enamel, painted red in the name of practicality. Beneath the tables is a drain hole.

On one of the tables rests a figure, supine beneath a white plastic sheet pulled up to the neck.

When Beckman sees the corpse, and recognizes it for what it is, his knees trick.

I turn to the wall, unpin a photograph, a clipping from a newspaper. It is the only adornment in the room. 'She was pretty,' I say.

'Not beautiful, not in the Grace Kelly sense, but pretty beneath the coarseness of all this paint.' I hold up the picture. 'Don't you think?'

In the pitiless fluorescent light Beckman's face contorts with fear.

'Tell me what happened,' I say. 'Don't you think it's time?'

Beckman retreats, waving a forefinger in the air. 'You're fucking nuts, man. Fucking psycho. I'm outta here.' He turns and tries the knob on the door. Locked. He pulls and pushes, pulls and pushes. It is a mounting frenzy, with no success. 'Open the goddamn door!'

Instead of unlocking the door, I step forward, remove the sheet from the figure on the table. The body underneath has begun to decompose, its eyes now descended into their sockets, its skin fallen sallow, the color of overripe corn. The form is still recognizable as human, albeit emaciated and on the precipice of putrefaction. The hands are gray and shriveled, fingers stiff in supplication. I do not gag at the sick-sweet smell. In fact, I have begun to anticipate it with some measure of desire.

I pry back the index finger on the corpse's left hand. There is a small tattoo of a swan. I look at Kenneth Beckman, and say, in my best broken Italian:

'Benvenuto al carnevale!'

Welcome to the carnival.

Beckman staggers against the wall, horrified by the sight, the fresh surge of decay in the air. He tries to speak, but the words bottleneck in his throat.

I lift the Taser and place it to the side of Beckman's chest. Blue lightning strikes. The man folds to the floor.

For a moment the room is silent.

As silent as a womb.

⋆ ⋆ ⋆

I take the three killing instruments out of their sheaths, lay them on the table, next to the salon-quality hair trimmer. I open the hidden cabinet concealed behind a door that has a touch latch, revealing the recording equipment. The sight of the matte-black finish on the six components, free of dust and static, fills me with an almost sexual sensation. The warmth coming off the components — I always warm everything up at least an hour before a session — coats me in a thin layer of perspiration. Or maybe that is just anticipation.

Beckman is shackled to the table with tape over his mouth. His head is held in place by a neurosurgical clamp, a precision device used to fix a patient's head to a table during stereotactic procedures for the placement of electrodes, an operation requiring rigid immobilization. A year ago I ordered the apparatus from a German firm, paying by international money order, receiving the product through a series of remailers.

I slip on a surgical gown, stand next to the table, open the straight razor. With the index finger of my left hand I probe the soft skin on the man's forehead. Beckman howls into his gag, but the sound is muffled.

That is about to change.

With a steady hand I make the first cut across the forehead, just beneath the hairline, taking my time. I watch the skin bisect slowly, revealing the glossy pink tissue beneath. The surgical clamp does its job well. The man cannot move his head at all. With a foot pedal I press Record, then remove the gag.

The man gulps air, pink foam leaking from the corners of his mouth. He has severed the tip of his tongue.

He begins to scream.

I monitor the sound levels, make a few adjustments. Beckman continues to shriek, blood running down both sides of his face now, onto the polished stainless steel of the table, onto the dry enamel of the floor.

A few minutes later I blot the blood on Beckman's forehead, clean it with an alcohol pad. I go to work on the man's right ear. When I am finished I take out a measuring tape, measure down from the cut on the forehead, mark the spot with a red felt-tip pen, then take the second killing instrument in hand, hold it to the light. The carbon tip is a dark, lustrous blue.

One final check of the sound levels and I set about my penultimate task. Slowly, deliberately — largo, one might say — I proceed, knowing that just a few feet away, on the other side of the outside wall, the city of Philadelphia is passing by, oblivious to the symphony being composed inside this common looking building.

Then again, has not the greatest art in history

come from humble surroundings?

Zig, zig, zag.

I am Death in cadence.

When the power drill reaches its full RPM, and the razor-sharp bit nears the skin covering the frontal bone, in an area just above the right eye, Kenneth Arnold Beckman's screams reach a majestic volume, a second octave. The voice is off key, but that can be fixed later. For now, there is no need to hurry. No need at all.

In fact, we have all day.

4

Sophie Balzano sat at one end of the long couch, looking even smaller than usual.

Jessica stepped into the outer office, talked to the secretary, then entered the main office, where she chatted with one of Sophie's Sunday-school teachers. Jessica soon returned, sat next to her daughter. Sophie did not take her stare off her own shoes.

'Want to tell me what happened?' Jessica asked.

Sophie shrugged, looked out the window. Her hair was long, pulled back into a cat's-eye barrette. At seven, she was a little smaller than her friends, but she was fast and smart. Jessica was five-eight in her stocking feet, and had grown to that height somewhere during the summer between sixth and seventh grade. She wondered if the same would happen for her daughter.

'Honey? You have to tell Mommy what happened. We'll make it better, but I have to know what happened. Your teacher said you were in a fight. Is that true?'

Sophie nodded.

'Are you okay?'

Sophie nodded again, although this time a little more slowly. 'I'm all right.'

'We'll talk in the car?'

'Okay.'

As they walked out of the school, Jessica saw some of the other kids whispering to each other. Even in this day and age, it seemed, a playground fight still generated gossip.

They left the school grounds, headed down Academy Road. When they made the turn onto Grant Avenue and the traffic halted for some construction works, Jessica asked, 'Can you tell me what the fight was about?'

'It was about Brendan.'

'Brendan Hurley?'

'Yes.'

Brendan Hurley was a boy in Sophie's class. Thin and quiet and bespectacled, Brendan was bully-bait if Jessica had ever seen it. Beyond that, Jessica didn't know a lot about him. Except that on the previous Valentine's Day Brendan had given Sophie a card. A big *glittery* card.

'What about Brendan?' Jessica asked.

'I don't know,' she said. 'I think he might be . . . '

Traffic began to move. They pulled off the boulevard, onto Torresdale Avenue.

'What, sweetie? You think Brendan might be what?'

Sophie looked out the window, then at her mother. 'I think he might be G-A-E.'

Oh boy, Jessica thought. She had been prepared for a lot of things. The talk about sharing, the talk about race and class, the talk about money, even the talk about religion. Jessica was woefully unprepared for the talk about gender identity. The fact that Sophie spelled the word out instead of saying it — indicating that, to Sophie, and her classmates, the word belonged in that special classification of profanities not to be uttered — spoke volumes. 'I see,' was all that Jessica could come up with at that moment. She decided not to correct her daughter's spelling at this time. 'What makes you say that?'

Sophie straightened her skirt. This was clearly difficult for her. 'He kind of runs like a girl,' she said. 'And throws like a girl.'

'Okay.'

'But so do I, right?'

'Yes, you do.'

'So it's not a bad thing.'

'No, it's not a bad thing at all.'

They pulled into their driveway, cut the engine. Jessica soon realized that she had no idea how much Sophie knew about sexual orientation. Even thinking about the words 'sexual orientation' in connection with her little girl freaked her completely out.

'So, what happened?' Jessica asked.

'Well, this girl was saying mean things about Brendan.'

'Who is this girl?'

'Monica,' Sophie said. 'Monica Quagliata.'

'Is she in your grade?'

'No,' Sophie said. 'She's in third. She's pretty big.' Consciously or subconsciously, Sophie balled her fists.

'What did you say to her?'

'I told her to stop saying those things. Then she pushed me and called me a skank.'

That *bitch*, Jessica thought. She secretly

hoped that Sophie had cleaned the little shit's clock. 'What did you do then?'

'I pushed her back. She fell down. Everyone laughed.'

'Did Brendan laugh?'

'No,' Sophie said. 'Brendan is afraid of Monica Quagliata. *Everyone*'s afraid of Monica Quagliata.'

'But not you.'

Sophie glanced out the window. It had begun to rain. She traced her finger on the misting glass, then looked back at her mother. 'No,' she said. 'Not me.'

Yes, Jessica thought. *My tough little girl*. 'I want you to listen, okay, honey?'

Sophie sat up straight. 'Is this going to be one of our talks?'

Jessica almost laughed. She checked herself at the last second. 'Yes. I guess it is.'

'Okay.'

'I want you to remember that fighting is always the last resort, okay? If you have to defend yourself, it's all right. Every single time. But sometimes we need to take care of people who can't take care of themselves. Do you understand what I mean?'

Sophie nodded, but looked confused. 'What about you, Mom? You used to fight all the time.'

Ah, crap, Jessica thought. *Logic from a seven-year-old*.

After Sophie was born, Jessica had discovered boxing as an exercise and weight-loss regimen. For some reason she took to it, even going so far as to take a few amateur bouts before letting her great uncle Vittorio talk her into turning pro.

Although those days were probably behind her — unless there was a Senior Tour for female boxers closing in on thirty-five — she had begun to visit Joe Hand's Gym in anticipation of a series of exhibition bouts planned to raise money for the Police Athletic League.

None of that training helped her at this moment, however, a moment when she was faced with explaining the difference between fighting and boxing.

Then Jessica saw a shadow in her side mirror.

Vincent was walking up the drive, carrying a pizza from Santucci's. With his caramel eyes, long lashes and muscular physique, he still made Jessica's heart flutter, at least on those days when she didn't want to kill him. Sometimes he dressed in suits and ties, cleanshaven, his dark hair swept back. Other days he was scruffy. Today was a scruffy day. Jessica was, and always had been, a pushover for scruff. She had to admit it. Detective Vincent Balzano looked pretty damned good for a married man.

'Sweetie?' Jessica asked.

'Yeah, mom?'

'That thing we were talking about? About fighting versus boxing?'

'What about it?'

Jessica reached over, patted her daughter's hand. 'Ask your father.'

* * *

They had lived in the Lexington Park section of Northeast Philadelphia for more than five years,

44

just a few blocks from Roosevelt Boulevard. On a good day it would take Jessica forty-five minutes to get to the Roundhouse. On a bad day — most days — even longer. But all that was about to change.

She and Vincent had just closed on a vacant trinity in South Philly, a three-story row house belonging to old friends, which was how many houses in the neighborhood changed hands. Rare was the property that made it to the classifieds.

They would be living in the shadow of their new church, Sacred Heart of Jesus, where Sophie would be starting school. New friends, new teachers. Jessica wondered what the effect on her little girl was going to be.

Jessica's father, Peter Giovanni, one of the most decorated cops in PPD history, still lived in the South Philadelphia house in which Jessica had grown up — at Sixth and Catharine. He was still vibrant and active, very much involved in the community, but he was getting on in years, and the trip for him to see his only granddaughter would eventually become a burden. For this, and for so many other reasons, they were moving back to South Philly.

With her daughter fast asleep, and her husband ensconced in the basement with his brothers, Jessica stood at the top of the narrow stairs to the attic.

It seemed as if her entire life was in these boxes, these cramped and angled rooms. Photographs, keepsakes, awards, birth and death certificates, diplomas.

She picked up one of the boxes, a white Strawbridge's gift box with a piece of green yarn around it. It was the yarn with which her mother used to tie her hair in autumn, after the summer sun had made her brunette hair turn auburn.

Jessica slid off the yarn, opened the box: a faux-pearl mirror compact, a small leather change purse, a stack of Polaroids. Jessica felt the familiar pangs of pain and grief and loss, even though it had been more than twenty-five years since her mother had died. She slipped the yarn back around the box, put it by the stairs, gave the room one last survey.

She had been a cop for a long time, had seen just about everything. There wasn't too much that unnerved her.

This did.

They were moving back to the city.

5

'Fuckin' city,' the man said. 'First my car gets booted, then they tow it, then I hadda go down to PPA and spend two hours standing around with a bunch of smelly lowlifes. Then I hadda go down to Ninth and Filbert. *Then* they tell me I owe three-hunna-ninety dollars in tickets. Three-hunna-ninety *dollars*.'

The man slammed back his drink, washed it down with a mouthful of beer.

'Fuckin' city. Fuckin' PPA. Buncha Nazis is what they are. Fuckin' racket.'

Detective Kevin Byrne glanced at his watch. It was 11:45 p.m. His city was coming alive. The guy next to him had come alive after his third Jim Beam. The man migrated from tales of woe that began with his wife (fat and loud and lazy) to his two sons (ditto on the lazy, no data on body type) to his car (a Prism not really worth getting out of hock) and his ongoing war with the Philadelphia Parking Authority. The PPA had few fans in the city. Without them, though, the city would be chaos.

They were sitting at the bar in a corner tavern in Kensington, a hole in the wall called The Well. The place was half-full. Kool and the Gang were on the juke; an ESPN wrap-up of the day's sports was on the television over the bar.

Byrne slipped in the earbuds, blotting out the *Parking Wars* victim, looked at the screen on his

47

iPod, dialed down to his classic blues playlist. The jukebox in the bar was now playing something by the Commodores, but here, inside Byrne's head, it was 1957, and Muddy Waters was going down to Louisiana, saying something about a mojo hand.

Byrne nodded to the bartender, the bartender nodded back. Byrne had never been to this tavern before, but the barkeep was a pro at what he did, as was Byrne.

Byrne had grown up in Philadelphia, was a Two-Streeter for life, had seen the city's best days and its worst. Well, maybe not its best. It was, after all, the place where the Declaration of Independence had been signed, the place where the Founding Fathers had gathered and hammered out the rules by which Americans, at least to some small degree, still lived.

On the other hand, the Phillies had won the World Series in 2008, and for a Phillies fan that trumped some faded old document any day.

In his time on the job Byrne had investigated thousands of crimes, worked hundreds of homicides, had spent nearly half his life among the dead, the broken, the forgotten.

What was the Thomas de Quincy quote?

If once a man indulges himself in murder, very soon he comes to think little of robbing; and from robbing he comes next to drinking and Sabbath-breaking, and from that to incivility and procrastination.

Byrne had his own word for it.

Slippage.

To Kevin Byrne, slippage was about accepting

levels of behavior that previous generations would have considered unthinkable, standards that had slowly become the norm, new lows from which the cycle could begin again, inching ever downward.

Lately he found himself thinking obsessively about all the innocent, the unavenged. He thought about the short, inconsequential life of Kitty Jo Morris, aged three, scalded to death by her mother's boyfriend, a man angered over the little girl's habit of taking the remote from the living room; of Bonita Alvarez, not quite eleven, who was pushed from the roof of a three-story building in North Philly for hiding one of her older sister's Rice Krispie treats in the broom closet; of Max Pearlman, aged eighteen months, left in a car overnight in January while his father smoked crack underneath the Platt Bridge.

No headlines here. No NBC White Paper specials on the state of the American family. Just a little less space in the graveyards. Just a little slip.

Now, in Byrne's head, it was 1970, Blues legend Willie Dixon was proclaiming that he ain't superstitious. Neither was Kevin Byrne. He had seen too much to believe in anything but good and evil.

And evil is in the house, Byrne thought as he considered the man sitting across the bar from him at that moment, a man who had the blood of at least two people on his hands, a murderer named Eduardo Robles.

★ ★ ★

On a hot summer afternoon in 2007, Eduardo Robles and his girlfriend were walking down a street in Fishtown. According to Robles, at around 1:30 p.m. a car cruised slowly by, the deep bass of a rap song rattling the windows of nearby buildings. Someone in that car pointed a gun out the window and fired. Robles's girlfriend, a seventeen-year-old named Lina Laskaris, was struck three times.

Robles called 911, and when he arrived at the police station, after having his statement taken by a patrol officer on the street, a divisional detective assumed that the young man was a suspect, not a witness. The detective cuffed Robles and stuck him in a holding cell.

Byrne got the call at eleven p.m. When Robles arrived at the Roundhouse — nearly ten hours after the incident — Byrne removed the cuffs, sat Robles down in one of the interrogation rooms. Robles said he was hungry and thirsty. Byrne sent out for hoagies and Mountain Dew, then began to question Robles.

They danced.

At three o'clock the next morning Robles rolled, and admitted it had been he who'd shot Lina Laskaris. Byrne arrested Robles for murder at 3:06 a.m., read him his Miranda warnings.

The problem with the case was that, according to the law, the police had six hours to determine someone's status as a witness or a suspect.

Three days later the grand jury came back with a no-bill because they believed, rightly so, that the arrest had begun the moment Robles was mistakenly put in cuffs at the station house.

In that moment Robles went from witness to suspect, and the clock began to tick.

Five days after killing his girlfriend in cold blood, Eduardo Robles was a free man, courtesy of the astonishingly incompetent work of a divisional detective who, incredibly, due to some unfathomable political connection, had recently been rewarded for his incompetence with a job in the Homicide Unit, at an increase in pay.

That man's name was Detective Dennis Stansfield.

Robles went back to the life and within months was involved in the murder of a man named Samuel Reese, a night clerk at a bodega in Chinatown. Police believed that Robles shot Reese twice, took the surveillance disk from the recorder in the back room, and walked out with sixty-six dollars and a can of brake fluid.

It was all circumstantial — no ballistics, no physical evidence, shaky witness accounts — nothing that would stand up in court. In terms of the reality of the law, bullshit.

Byrne had spent the past two days building a case against Robles, but it was not going well. Although they had not found the murder weapon, Byrne interviewed four people who could put Robles in that bodega at that time. None of them were willing to talk to police, at least not on the record. Byrne had seen the fear in their eyes. But he also knew that talking to a cop on the street corner, or in your living room, or even at your place of business was one thing. Talking to a district attorney in front of a grand jury, under oath, was something else. Everyone

51

called to testify would understand that committing perjury in front of a grand jury carried a prison term of five months, twenty-nine days. And that was for each lie.

In the morning Byrne would meet with Michael Drummond, the assistant district attorney assigned to the Robles case. If they could get four people to implicate Robles, they might be able to get a search warrant for Robles's car and apartment, perhaps finding something that would create a daisy chain, and the evidence would roll in.

Or maybe it wouldn't get that far. Maybe something would happen to Robles.

You never knew about such things in a city like Philadelphia.

Were the police partially responsible for the death of Samuel Reese? In this case they were. Robles should never have gotten back on the street.

Slippage.

On the day Robles was arrested, Byrne visited Lina Laskaris's grandmother. Anna Laskaris was a Greek immigrant in her early seventies. She had raised Lina alone. Byrne told the woman that the man responsible for Lina's death was being brought to justice. He remembered the woman's tears, how she held him, how her hair smelled of cinnamon. She was making *pantespani*.

What Byrne remembered most was that Anna Laskaris had trusted him, and he had let her down.

Byrne now caught a glimpse of himself in the filmy mirror behind the bar. He wore a ball cap, and the glasses he had been forced to start wearing lately. If Robles had not been drinking he might have recognized Byrne. But Byrne was probably just a blur in the near distance to Robles, as well as to everyone else in the bar. This was no upscale Center City watering hole. This place was for hard drinkers, for hard men.

At 12:30 Robles stumbled out of the bar. He got into his car and drove down Frankford Avenue. When Robles reached York Street he turned east, drove a few blocks, parked.

Byrne sat in his car across the street, and watched. Robles got out of his car, stopped twice to talk to people. He was looking to score. Within minutes a man approached.

Robles and the other man walked, a little unsteadily, down the alley. A moment later Byrne saw light flare against the dirty brick wall of the alley. Robles was hitting the rock.

Byrne got out of his car, looked both ways up the street. Deserted. They were alone. Philadelphia was once again sliding into slumber, except for those who moved silently through the harbor of night.

Byrne stepped into shadow. From somewhere, perhaps deep inside him, a long-forgotten melody began to play.

It sounded like a requiem.

6

The early morning run through Pennypack Park
had become a sacrament, one that Jessica was
not quite ready to relinquish. The people she saw
every morning were not just part of the
landscape but part of her life.

There was the older woman, always meticulously turned out in 1960s pillbox chic, who
walked her four Jack Russell terriers every
morning, the dogs in possession of a wardrobe
more extensive and seasonal than Jessica's. There
was the *tai chi* group who, rain or shine,
performed their morning rituals on the baseball
diamond near Holme Avenue. Then there were
her buddies, the two Russians, half-brothers,
both named Ivan. They were well into their
sixties, but incredibly fit, as well as shockingly
hirsute, given to jogging in their matching
limegreen Speedos in summer. For half-brothers
they looked almost identically alike. At times
Jessica could not tell them apart, but it didn't
really matter. When she saw one of them she
simply said, 'Good morning, Ivan.' She always
got a smile.

When she and Vincent and Sophie moved to
South Philly there would still be a few places for
her to jog, but it would be a long time before
Jessica could run again without caution, like she

54

could here. Here, where her route and path were well worn, she could sort things out. It was this she would miss most of all.

She rounded the bend, ran up the incline, thought about Marcia Kimmelman, and what had been done to her. She thought about Lucas Anthony Thompson, and the startled look in his eyes when he'd realized it was over, the moment the cuffs clicked shut on his wrists and he was yanked to his feet, dirt and gravel on his face, his clothing. Jessica had to admit she liked the dirt-and-gravel part, always had. Mud, weather permitting, was even better.

With this comforting image in mind she turned the corner, onto her street, and saw someone standing at the end of her driveway. A man in a dark suit. It was Dennis Stansfield.

Jessica let her feelings morph from apprehension to annoyance. What the hell was this jackass doing at her house?

She slowed to a walk for the last one hundred feet, catching her breath. She approached the man, who seemed to realize he was out of place.

'Detective,' Jessica said, suddenly conscious of her appearance. She wore loose sweatpants and a tight tank top, a sports bra beneath. She had worked up a sweat and taken off her fleece hoodie, tied it around her waist. She saw Stansfield's stare do a quick inventory of her body, then find her eyes. Jessica took a moment, caught the rest of her breath, drilling the look right back. Stansfield flinched first, looking away.

'Good morning,' he said.

Jessica had the option of putting her hoodie

back on, zipping it up, but that would be telling Stansfield that she had a problem. She had no problems. Not one. She put her hands on her hips. 'What's up?'

Stansfield turned back to her, clearly doing his best to look at her face. 'The boss said Detective Burns might not be back today, and that if it was okay with you — '

'Byrne,' Jessica said. 'His name is Kevin Byrne.' Jessica wondered if Stansfield was intentionally busting her chops or was really that clueless. Right now it was a toss-up. It wasn't that Kevin was Superman, but he did have a reputation within the unit, if not the entire department. Jessica and Byrne had worked some high-profile cases over the past few years, and unless you were a rookie you had to know who he was. Plus, Byrne was off cleaning up Stansfield's mess, and this could not possibly have been lost on the man.

'Byrne,' Stansfield said, correcting himself. 'Sorry. The boss said that he might not be done with the grand jury today, and that we should partner up for the duration. At least until Detective Byrne gets back.' He shuffled his feet. 'If that's all right with you.'

Jessica didn't remember anyone asking what her thoughts were on the subject. 'You have the notification sheet?'

Stansfield reached into his suit-coat pocket, retrieved the form, held it up.

As he did this, Jessica glanced at the house. She saw a shadow near the window in the front bedroom, saw the curtains part a few inches. It was Vincent. Jessica might have been a police officer, and even when she jogged these days she was armed — at that moment she had the sweetest little Browning .25 at the small of her back — but when Vincent saw her talking to someone in front of the house, someone he didn't know, his antennae went up. The number of police officers killed had risen sharply over the past few years, and neither Jessica nor Vincent ever let down their guards.

Jessica nodded, almost imperceptibly, and, a few seconds later, the curtain closed. She turned back to Stansfield.

'All in a day, detective,' Jessica said. 'Let's partner up.'

The twisted, phony smile on Stansfield's face all but shouted his disappointment at her tepid response. 'That's good news,' he said. 'Because we have a job.'

We, Jessica thought. What a true delight this was going to be. She knew she was up on the wheel. The wheel was the roster of detectives on the Line Squad. When you caught a new case you went to the end of the line, worked the case, slowly making your way back to the top. When you reached the number one position, regardless how many cases you had on your plate, you were up again. Rare was the day in the unit where you cleared your cases when a new body fell.

'All right,' she said. 'Let me a grab a shower. I'll be out in ten minutes.'

Two things immediately registered on Stansfield's face. One, the idea of her taking a shower. Two, the fact that he hadn't been invited in.

57

The crime scene was at the northern end of the Pennsport section of South Philadelphia. Pennsport was a working-class neighborhood, bounded by Passyunk Square to the west, the Delaware River to the east, Queen Village to the north, Whitman to the south.

One of the oldest sections of the city, Pennsport had been slow in the development of new projects, with some of the homes dating back to 1815. It was quite possible to have a new block of row houses bookended by structures that had been built when James Madison was president of the United States.

When Jessica and Stansfield pulled up to the crime scene — a boarded-up storefront near the corner of Fifth and Federal Streets — a sector car was parked diagonally across the street. Both Federal and Fifth were one-way streets and at either end of the block stood a pair of uniformed officers, diverting traffic. The Crime Scene Unit had not yet arrived, so there was no tape ringing the perimeter yet. Budget cuts had forced the city to curtail new hires, to postpone updating equipment, and these days there could be a two-hour or longer lag in the arrival of key crime scene personnel.

But while CSU was not yet there, David Albrecht was, camera in hand.

'Morning!' he shouted from across the street.

Great, Jessica thought. *Another morning person.* Her husband and Sophie were morning people. Everyone around her was a morning person.

Except Byrne. It was one of the reasons they worked so well together. On most days they grunted at each other until noon.

Jessica waved at David Albrecht, who promptly put up his camera and filmed the gesture. Then Jessica glanced at Dennis Stansfield. Stansfield, seeing he was on camera, buttoned his coat, sucked in his gut, and tried to look official.

★   ★   ★

They signed onto the log. The uniformed officer pointed down the alley.

'Inside or outside?' Jessica asked.

'Inside,' he said. 'But just.'

The scene was the rear entrance to a closed-up independent shoe store called All Soles. In the back were steps leading down to the basement, a door through which the various retail establishments that had been located there over the years received their shipments. The small area behind the store was littered with fast-food trash, discarded tires, the sort of urban detritus that people found too time-consuming to put in the Dumpster that was located just a few feet away.

Jessica and Stansfield stopped at the top of the steps. There was an iron handrail leading down. Just as Jessica made a mental note to ask CSU to dust the railing, Stansfield put his hand on it, striking a macho pose, lording his gold badge over the gathering personnel.

'Um, detective?' Jessica said.

Stansfield looked over. Jessica pointed at his hand. Stansfield realized that he was possibly contaminating the site, and withdrew his hand as if he were grabbing a red-hot poker.

Jessica turned her attention to the entrance to the crime scene.

There were four steps. She scanned the immediate area, saw no blood trail. The door was open just a few inches. She walked down the stairs, edged open the door, Stansfield a little too close behind her. His cologne was nauseating. It would soon become welcome.

'Holy shit,' said Stansfield.

The victim was a white male of undeterminable age — undeterminable partly because they could not see all of his face. He was lying in the middle of the small dusty storage room, amid cardboard boxes, plastic buckets, wooden forklift pallets. Jessica immediately saw the deep purple bruises on his wrists and ankles. The victim, it appeared, had been shackled. There was no blood, no sign of struggle in this room.

But two things gave her pause. First, the victim's forehead and eyes were wrapped in a band of white paper. The paper was about five inches wide and completely encircled the man's head. Across the top of the band was a streak of brown, a straight line drawn in what could have been dried blood. Beneath it was another spot, this one a nearly perfect oval about an inch wide. The paper overlapped at the left side of the man's head. It appeared to be sealed with red sealing wax. The right side had another smear of blood, which looked to be in the shape of a figure eight.

But that wasn't the worst of it.

The victim's body was completely nude. It appeared to have been shaved clean, head to toe. Pubic hair, chest hair, arm hair, leg hair — gone. The body's scraped and abraded skin indicated that it had been shaved roughly, violently, perhaps in the past day or so. There appeared to be no new growth.

The sight was so grotesque that it took Jessica a moment to take it all in. She had seen quite a bit. Never anything like this. The indignities of homicide were legion, but there was something about the final degradation of being left naked that made it all worse, a communiqué from the killer to the rest of the world that the humiliation of violent death was not the last word. For the most part, you didn't just die in this life. You were *found* dead.

Jessica took the lead, more out of instinct than from any sense of duty. Hers was a boys' world and the sooner you peed in the corners, the better. She had long since turned the word *bitch* from an epithet to a badge, an emblem as golden as her shield.

Stansfield cleared his throat. 'I'll, uh, get started on a canvass,' he said, and quickly took his leave.

There were some homicide detectives who liked the *idea* of being a homicide detective — the prestige, the pay, the cachet of being one of the chosen — but couldn't stand being at a crime scene. Apparently, Stansfield was just such a detective. *Just as well*, Jessica thought.

She crouched next to the victim, placed two fingers on his neck, checking for a pulse. She found none. She examined the front of the body, looking for some sort of entrance or exit wound. No holes, no blood.

She heard voices outside. She looked up to see Tom Weyrich coming down the steps, his gear in his hand, his photographer in tow. Weyrich was an investigator for the medical examiner's office with almost twenty years on the job.

'Top of the morning, Tom.'

Weyrich was in his early fifties, with a dry wit and a reputation as a thorough and exacting investigator. When Jessica had met him five years earlier he had been a meticulous and classically attired man. Now his mustache was irregularly trimmed, his eyes red and tired. Jessica knew that Weyrich's wife had recently died after a long fight with cancer. Tom Weyrich had taken it hard. Today he appeared to be running on fumes. His slacks were pressed, but Jessica noted that his shirt had probably been slept in.

'Had that double up in Torresdale,' Weyrich said, running his hands over his face, trying to wring out the exhaustion. 'Got out of there about two hours ago.'

'No rest for the righteous.'

'I wouldn't know.'

Weyrich stepped fully inside, saw the body. 'Good God.' Somewhere beneath the trash and shredded cardboard an animal scurried. 'Give me a good old execution-style two taps to the back of the head any day,' he added. 'I never thought I'd miss the crack wars.'

'Yeah,' Jessica said. 'Good times.'

Weyrich tucked his tie into his shirt, buttoned

his suit coat, snapped on a pair of gloves. He went about his business. Jessica watched him, wondering how many times he had done this, how many times he had placed his hands on the cold flesh of the dead. She wondered what it was like for him, sleeping alone these days, and how he, more than anyone, needed to sense the warm flesh of the living. When Jessica and Vincent had been temporarily separated a few years earlier, it had been the thing she'd missed the most, the daily intimate contact with the warmth of another human being.

Jessica stepped outside, waited. She saw David Albrecht across the street, getting exterior shots of the building. Behind him, Jessica saw his sparkling new van, which had his website address painted on the side. It also had what Jessica figured was the title of his movie.

Coming soon: AREA 5292

Clever, Jessica thought. It was obviously a play on Area 51, the area in southern Nevada central to UFO conspiracy theories. The number 5292 was PPD parlance for a dead body.

Fifteen minutes later Tom Weyrich emerged.

'Bringing all my training to bear,' he began, 'I would conclude that this is a deceased person.'

'I knew I should have gone to a better school,' Jessica said. 'COD?'

'Can't even give you a presumptive cause of death until we unwrap his head.'

'Ready?' Jessica asked.

'As ever.'

They stepped back inside the storage room. Jessica snapped on latex gloves. Of late they were bright purple. They knelt down on either side of the body.

The band of paper was fastened with a small wad of sealing wax. The wax was a glossy crimson. Jessica knew this would be a delicate operation, if she wanted to preserve the sample.

She took out her knife — a four-inch serrated Gerber that she always carried in a sheath around her ankle, at least when she was wearing jeans — and slipped it under the circle of hard wax. She pried it gently. At first it looked as if it might split in two, but then she got lucky. The specimen fell off in one piece. She placed it into an evidence bag. With Weyrich holding the opposite side of the paper band, they unveiled the victim's face.

It was a horror mask.

Jessica estimated the victim to be about thirty-five to forty, although most of the lividity was gone and the skin had begun to sag.

Across the upper portion of the victim's forehead was a single laceration, running laterally, perhaps four or five inches in length. The cut did not appear to be very deep, splitting just the skin in a deep violet streak, not deep enough to reach bone. It appeared to have been made with either a razor blade or a very sharp knife.

Just above the right eye was a small puncture wound, the diameter of an ice pick or a knitting needle. This too seemed shallow. Neither wound appeared to be fatal. The victim's right ear looked to be mutilated, with cuts along the top and side, all the way down to the lobe, which was missing.

Around the neck was a deep welt. Death appeared to be a result of strangulation.

'You think that's the COD?' Jessica asked, even though she knew that the cause of death could not be conclusively determined until an autopsy had been performed.

'Hard to tell,' Weyrich said. 'But there is petechiae in the sclera of his eyes. It's a pretty good bet.'

'Let's see, he was stabbed, slashed and strangled,' Jessica said. 'Real hat trick.'

'And that's just the stuff we know about. He might have been poisoned.'

Jessica poked around the small room, carefully overturning boxes and shipping pallets. She found no clothing, no ID, nothing to indicate who this victim might be.

When she stepped outside a few minutes later she saw Detective Joshua Bontrager walking across Federal Street, clipping his badge to his jacket pocket.

Josh Bontrager had only been in the unit a few years but he had developed into a good investigator. Josh was unique in a number of ways, not the least of which was the fact that he had grown up Amish in rural Pennsylvania before making his way to Philadelphia and the police force, where he spent a few years in various units before being called into the homicide unit for a special investigation. Josh was in his mid-thirties, country-boy blond, deceptively fit and agile. He did not bring a lot of street smarts to the job — most of the streets on which he'd grown up had been barely paved

— or any sort of scientific logic, but rather an innate kindness, an affability that completely disarmed all but the most hardened criminal.

There were some in the unit who felt that Josh Bontrager was a country bumpkin who had no business in one of the most respected elite urban homicide divisions in the country. But Jessica knew that you underestimated him at your own peril, especially if you had something to hide.

Bontrager crossed the alley to Jessica's side, lowered his voice. 'So, how do you like working with Stansfield?'

'Well, aside from the racism, sexism, homophobia and completely exaggerated sense of self-worth, it's a blast.'

Bontrager laughed. 'That bad?'

'Nah. Those are the highlights.'

'How come no one seems to like him?'

Jessica explained the Eduardo Robles case, including Stansfield's monumental fuck-up — a fuck-up that to all intents and purposes had led to the death of Samuel Reese.

'You'd think he would have known better,' Bontrager said.

'You'd think.'

'And we definitely like this Robles guy for that second body?'

'Yeah,' Jessica said. 'Kevin's at the grand jury today.'

Bontrager nodded. 'So, for messing up royally Stansfield gets a promotion *and* a kick in pay?'

'The brass works in mysterious ways.'

Bontrager put his hands in his pockets, rocked on his heels. 'Well, until Kevin is back, if you want another partner next time you're up on the wheel, let me know.'

'Thanks, Josh. I will.' She held up a folder. 'Write me up?'

'Sure.'

He took the folder from her, extracted a body chart, clipped it to a clipboard. The body chart was a standard police-department form that had four outlines of the human body drawn on it, front and back, left and right side, as well as space for the rudimentary details of the crime scene. It was the first and most referred-to form in the binder that would be dedicated to the case.

The two detectives stepped inside. Jessica spoke while Josh Bontrager wrote.

'We have a Caucasian male, aged thirty to forty-five years. There is a single laceration across the forehead, what appears to be a puncture wound above the right eye. The victim's right ear is mutilated. A portion of the ear lobe is missing. There is a ligature mark across the base of the neck.'

Bontrager went over the form, marking these areas on the figure.

'The victim is nude. The body looks to have been recently shaved from head to toe. He is barefoot. There are bruises on the wrists and ankles, which indicate the victim may have been restrained.'

Jessica continued to describe the scene, her path now forever crossed with that of this dead man, a dead man with no name.

★   ★   ★

Twenty minutes later, with Josh Bontrager back at the Roundhouse, and Dennis Stansfield still on canvass, Jessica paused at the top of the stairs. She turned 360 degrees, scanning the landscape. Directly behind the store was a double vacant lot, a parcel where a pair of buildings had recently been razed. There were still piles of concrete, bricks, lumber. There was no fence. To the right was a block of row houses. To the left was the rear of some sort of commercial building, with no windows overlooking the alley. If someone were to have seen anyone entering the rear of the crime scene, they would have had to have been in a back room of one of the row houses, or in the vacant lot. The view from across the street was partially obscured by the large piles of debris.

Jessica approached the responding officer, who stood at the mouth of the alley with the crime-scene log. One of his duties was to sign everyone in and out.

'Who found the body?' Jessica asked him.

'It was an anonymous tip,' the officer said. 'Came into 911 around six o'clock this morning.'

Anonymous, Jessica thought. A million and a half people in her city, and they were all anonymous. Until it was one of their own.

7

He awoke, dreambound, still in the hypnotic thrall of troubled sleep. This morning, in his final reverie, as the light of day filtered through the blinds, Kevin Byrne stood in the defendant's well of a cavernous courtroom that was lit by a sea of votive candles. He could not see the members of the jury but he knew who they were. They were the silent victims. And there were more than twelve. There were thousands, each holding one light.

Byrne got out of bed, staggered to the kitchen, splashed cold water on his face. He'd gotten four hours of sleep; three the night before. Over the past few months his insomnia had become acute, a routine part of his life so ingrained that he could not imagine living any other way. Nevertheless, he had an appointment — doctor's orders and against his will — with a neurologist at the University of Pennsylvania Sleep Clinic.

He took a long hot shower, rinsing off the previous night. He toweled, dressed, pulling a fresh shirt out of the dry-cleaning bag. He put on a new suit, his favorite tie, then sat at his small dinette table, sipped his coffee. He glanced at the Sleep Clinic questionnaire. All one hundred sixty probing questions.

Question 87: Do you snore?

If I could get someone to sleep with me, I

might be able to answer that, he thought.

Then Byrne remembered his little experiment. The night before, at around two a.m., when he'd found that he couldn't drift off, he'd dug out his small Sony digital recorder.

He got back in bed, took two Ambien, turned on the recorder, flipped off the light, and closed his eyes. Four hours later he awoke.

And now he had the results of his experiment. He poured more coffee, played the recording from the beginning. At first he heard some rustling, the settling of the unit on the night-stand. Then he heard himself turn off the lamp, a little more rustling, then a bump of the table, which was so loud that it made him jump. He turned down the volume. Then, for the next five minutes or so, he heard nothing but white noise, the occasional car passing by his apartment.

Byrne listened to this rhythmic breathing awhile, which seemed to get slower and slower. Then he heard the first snort. It sounded like a backfire. Or maybe a pissed-off Rottweiler.

Great, he thought. So he *did* snore. Not constantly, but about fifteen minutes into the recording he began to snore again, loudly for a few minutes, then not at all, then loudly again. He stared at the recorder, thinking:

What the fuck am I doing?

The answer? Sitting in his small dining room, barely awake, listening to a recording of himself sleeping. Did it get dumber than this?

Man, he had to get a life.

He pressed the fast-forward button, and every time he came across a sound he stopped, rewound for a few seconds, played it back.

Byrne was just about to give up on the experiment when he heard something that sounded different. He hit Stop, then Play.

'You know,' came his voice from the recorder.

What?

Rewind.

'*You know.*'

He let it run. Soon there was another noise, the sound of the lamp clicking on, and his voice saying, clear as a bell:

'*2:52.*'

Then there was the snap of the lamp being turned off, more rustling, then silence for the rest of the recording. Although he had no memory of it, he must have awakened, turned on the light, looked at the clock, spoken the time aloud, and gone back to sleep.

Except there was no clock in his bedroom. And his watch and cellphone were always on the dresser.

So how did he know what time it was?

Byrne played it all back, one last time, just to be certain that he was not imagining all of it. He was not.

2:52.

You know.

★ ★ ★

As Byrne waited in the park, he thought about another moment in this place, a time when his heart had been intact. His daughter Colleen had been four years old, and was trying desperately

71

to get a kite in the air. She ran in circles, back and forth, her blonde hair trailing, arms raised high, repeatedly getting tangled in the string. She stamped her feet, shook a fist at the sky, untangled herself, tried again and again. But she never asked him for help. Not once.

It seemed as if it were just a few weeks ago. But it was not. It was a long time ago. Somehow, Colleen, who had been deaf since birth, the result of a condition called *Mondini Dysplasia*, was going to Gallaudet University, the country's first and most preeminent college for deaf and hard-of-hearing undergraduate students.

Today she was off on an overnighter to the Gallaudet campus in Washington D.C. with her friend Lauren, ostensibly to scope out the campus and the possibilities for living quarters, but quite possibly to scope out the nightlife and the young men. Byrne knew the tuition fees were steep, but he had been saving and investing for a long time, and Colleen had a partial scholarship.

Byrne had wanted Colleen to stay nearer to Philadelphia, but it had been ages since he had been able to talk her out of anything once she set her mind to it.

He had never met Lauren, but Colleen had good taste in friends. He hoped Lauren was sensible too, and that he wouldn't be getting a phone call from the D.C. police telling him that the two of them had been picked up at some out-of-control frat kegger.

Byrne sensed someone approaching on his right. He looked around to see his daughter walking across the square, dressed in a navy blue suit. She didn't look like a college student, she looked like a businesswoman. Had he missed something? Had he been asleep for four years?

She looked heart-stoppingly beautiful, but something was wrong. She was holding hands with a guy who had to be at least thirty. And they weren't just holding hands, they were doing that wrap-around-at-the-wrist thing, and brushing up against each other as they walked.

When they got closer Byrne saw that the kid was younger than he had first thought, perhaps around twenty-two, which was still far too old and worldly for his taste.

Unfortunately, in matters such as these Kevin Byrne's taste didn't matter in the least.

Colleen let go of the guy and kissed Byrne on the cheek. She was wearing perfume. This was getting worse by the second.

'Dad, I'd like you to meet my friend Laurent,' Colleen signed.

Of course, Byrne thought. It wasn't Lauren. It wasn't even a girl. It was *Laurent*. His daughter was going on an overnighter with a *man*.

'How are you?' Byrne asked, not meaning it or caring, extending his hand. The kid shook his hand. Good grip, not too firm. Byrne thought about taking the kid to the ground and cuffing him, arresting him for daring to touch Colleen Byrne right in front of him, for daring to think of his only daughter as a woman. He put the impulse on hold for the moment.

'I'm quite well, sir. It's a pleasure to meet you.' Not only was Laurent a guy, he had an accent.

'You're French?' Byrne asked.

73

'French Canadian,' Laurent said.

Close enough, Byrne thought. His daughter was being romanced by a *foreigner*.

They chatted about nothing at all for a while, the sorts of things young men talk about while on the one hand trying to impress a girl's father and on the other trying not to embarrass the girl. As Byrne recalled, it was always a delicate balancing act. The kid was doing all right, Byrne thought, seeing as the routine was complicated by his having to speak out loud to Byrne, and sign everything to Colleen.

When the small talk was exhausted, Laurent said: 'Well, I know you two have things to talk about. I'll leave you to it.'

Laurent wandered a few feet off. Byrne could see the young man's shoulders relax, heard a loud sigh of relief.

Byrne understood. Maybe the kid was okay.

Colleen looked at her father, both eyebrows raised. *What do you think?*

Byrne butterflied a hand, smiled. *Eh.*

Colleen gave him a pretty good shot on the upper arm.

Byrne reached into his pocket, handed Colleen the check that was discreetly contained in a small envelope. Colleen spirited it away in her purse.

'Thanks, Dad. A couple of weeks, tops.'

Byrne waved another hand. 'How many times have I told you that you don't have to pay me back?'

'And yet I will.'

Byrne glanced at Laurent, then back. 'Can I

ask you something?' he signed. He had learned to sign when Colleen was about seven and had taken to it surprisingly well, considering what a lousy student he had been in school. As Colleen got older and a lot of their communication became nonverbal, relying on body language and expression, he stopped studying. He could hold his own, but found himself completely lost around two or more deaf people blazing away.

'Sure,' Colleen signed. 'What is it?'

'Are you in love with this guy?'

Colleen gave him the look. Her mother's look. The one that said *you just encountered a wall, and if you have any thoughts or dreams or hopes of getting over it you better have a ladder, a rope, and rappeling hooks.*

She touched his cheek, and the battle was over. 'I'm in love with *you*,' she signed.

How did she manage to do this? Her mother had done the same thing to him two decades earlier. In his time on the job he had been shot on two different occasions. The impact of those two incidents was nothing compared to a single look from his ex-wife or daughter.

'Why don't you just ask me the question you're dying to ask?' she signed.

Byrne did his best to look confused. 'I don't know what you're talking about.'

Colleen rolled her eyes. 'I'll just go ahead and answer the question anyway. The one you were not going to ask me.'

Byrne shrugged. *Whatever.*

'No, we're not staying in the same room, Dad. Okay? Laurent's aunt has a big house in Stanton

75

Park, and there are a million extra bedrooms. That's where I'll be sleeping. Locks on the door, guard dogs around the bed, honor and virtue intact.'

Byrne smiled.

Suddenly, the world was once again a wonderful place.

★　★　★

Byrne stopped at the Starbuck's on Walnut Street. As he was paying, his cellphone vibrated in his pocket. He took it out, checked the screen. It was a text message from Michael Drummond, the assistant district attorney handling the Eduardo Robles grand jury investigation.

Where are you?

Byrne texted Drummond his location. A few seconds later he received a reply.

Meet me at Marathon.

★　★　★

Ten minutes later Byrne stood in front of the restaurant at 18th and Walnut. He looked up the street, saw Drummond approaching, talking on his cellphone. Michael Drummond was in his mid-thirties, trim and athletic, well-dressed. He looked like the archetypal Philadelphia defense attorney, yet he had somehow stayed in the prosecutor's office for almost ten years. That was about to change. After being courted for years by every high-powered defense firm in the city, he was finally moving on. There was a going-away party scheduled for him at Finnigan's Wake in a few days, a soirée at which Drummond would announce which white-shoe firm he had chosen.

'Counselor,' Byrne said. They shook hands.

'Good morning, detective.'

'How does it look today?'

Drummond smiled. 'Do you remember the tiger scene in *Gladiator*?'

'Sure.'

'Something along those lines.'

'I'm just a flatfoot,' Byrne said. 'You might have to explain that one to me.'

Drummond looked over Byrne's shoulder, then over his own. He turned back. 'Eddie Robles is missing.'

Byrne just stared at Drummond, trying to keep all expression from his face. 'Is that a fact?'

'Facts are my life,' Drummond said. 'I called over there this morning, and Robles's mother said Robles didn't come home last night. She said his bed is still made.'

'This guy has two bodies on him and he lives with his mother?'

'That does have a little bit of a Norman Bates vibe to it, now that you mention it.'

'We don't really need him to indict him, do we?' The question was rhetorical. The DA, as the saying went, could indict a ham sandwich. The sandwich did not need to be present.

'No,' Drummond said. 'But the jury is hearing another case today. That triple at the Fontana.'

The Fontana was a recently opened luxury condominium in Northern Liberties, a 100-million-dollar renovation project that had taken

77

more than four years to complete. Three people had been shot, gangland style, in one of the units. It turned out that one of the victims was a former debutante who'd had a secret life that involved exotic dancing, drug dealing, and trysts with local sports celebrities. It was about as lurid as it got, which meant the story went viral within hours.

As of that morning, police had seven suspects in custody. The singing at the Roundhouse would commence shortly. Which meant that players for the Sixers, Eagles, Phillies, and Flyers were all sweating big time.

'I've got some serious time on this,' Byrne said. He knew that he had to play the game, and he was as good as anybody at it. Probably better.

'I know, Kevin. And I apologize. The Fontana case is high priority, and you know how things go. People forget, people run, people mysteriously disappear. Especially with a drug-homicide case.'

Byrne understood. The passions on a shocking and bloody case such as the Fontana ran high.

'What are we looking at?' he asked.

Drummond checked his BlackBerry. 'The jury will be back on Robles in three days when they meet again. I promise.'

It might not matter. Byrne knew that Philadelphia had a way of solving its own problems.

'Thanks for meeting with me, Michael.'

'Not a problem. Are you coming to my party?'

'Wouldn't miss it.'

They shook hands again. 'Don't worry about a

thing, Kevin. Not a thing. Eddie Robles is history.'

Byrne just stared, impassive. 'Keep me posted.'

★ ★ ★

Byrne thought about heading to the Round-house, but he wasn't expected for a while. He had to think. He drove to York Street, parked across from the alley down which Eduardo Robles had walked.

Eddie Robles is missing.

Byrne got out of the car, looked up and down the street. A half-block away he found what he was looking for, something that he had not noticed before.

There, high above the sidewalk, glancing indifferently down at the street, was a police camera.

8

The Homicide Unit at the Roundhouse was a study in controlled bedlam. There were ninety detectives in the unit, working three shifts, seven days a week. The first floor was a winding labyrinthine warren of half-round rooms which made it a real challenge to place desks, file cabinets, computer tables — in other words, everything that might be needed in an office. Not that anyone went out of their way to give even a simple nod to the concept of decor in this place.

But there was a system, and that system worked. Philly Homicide had one of the highest solve rates of any homicide division in the country.

At noon, with most of the detectives at lunch or on the street, Jessica looked up to see Dana Westbrook crossing the room.

Sergeant Dana Westbrook was the new day-work supervisor, taking over for the retired Ike Buchanan. In her late forties, Westbrook was the daughter of a retired police inspector, and had been raised in Kensington. She was a Marine veteran of Desert Storm.

At first glance she was not the most intimidating figure. With her bobbed cut, just turning gray, and measuring in at just over five-four, she towered over no one. But she was in great physical shape, still adhered to the

Marine circuit-workout four days a week, and could outrun and outperform women on the force half her age, as well as many of the men.

Being a woman in what was still and would probably always be a boys' club, her military training came in handy.

As in all police departments, indeed any paramilitary organization, there was a chain of command. From the commissioner to deputy commissioner, from chief inspector to staff inspector to captain, all the way to lieutenant and sergeant, then detective, officer, and recruit, it was a highly regimented institution. And shit, as they say in the military, doesn't flow uphill.

From day one, Dana Westbrook took a lot of shit.

When a call came in during day work — the eight a.m. to four p.m. shift — the desk detective took the information and brought it to the supervisor on duty. It was then the supervisor's job to initiate and coordinate the first crucial hours of the investigation. A lot of this involved telling men — some of whom had been in homicide for more than twenty years, all of whom had their own way of doing things, certainly their own pace and rhythms — where to go, who to talk to, when to come back. It involved judging their fieldwork, sometimes calling them on the carpet.

For male homicide detectives, who felt as if they were the Chosen, having someone tell them what to do was not an easy pill to swallow. To be told by a woman? This made the medicine bitter indeed.

Westbrook sat next to Jessica, opened a new file, clicked her pen. Jessica gave her the basic details, starting with the anonymous 911 call. Westbrook made her notes.

'Any sign of forced entry to the building?' Westbrook asked.

'Not sure. The place has probably been broken into many times, but there was no new splintering on the jamb.'

'What about vehicles parked near the scene?'

Jessica noticed for the first time that, besides her modest earrings, Dana Westbrook had four empty piercings in her right ear. 'We're running plates in a two-block radius, along with the vehicles parked in the school parking lot, cross-referencing the owners with wants and warrants. Nothing so far.'

Westbrook nodded, made a note of it.

'And we could also take a look at some of the footage our budding Oscar winner took. I saw Albrecht getting some shots of the crowd across the street.'

'Good idea,' Westbrook said.

Sometimes a criminal, especially one guilty of murder, returned to the scene. Police were always aware that a crowd at a crime scene, or one gathered at a funeral, might contain the person they sought.

'And speaking of Albrecht, how much access does this kid get?' Jessica asked.

'Within reason,' Westbrook replied. 'He doesn't get inside the ME's office, of course. Or a hospital.'

'And why are we doing this, again?'

'He's the deputy commissioner's wife's cousin's son. Or something like that. He's plugged in, let's just put it that way. The deputy commissioner is a Penn State grad, you know.'

'Is Albrecht allowed to film a crime scene?'

'Well, word is, the brass is going to see a rough cut of this film and has final approval over it all. If anything compromises an ongoing investigation or is blatantly disrespectful to a victim or a victim's family it won't see the light of day. You can count on that.'

'So, we have the right to chuck him off a scene?'

'Absolutely,' Westbrook said. 'Just make sure Kevin doesn't do it when you're going seventy on I-95.'

Jessica smiled. It hadn't taken long for Sergeant Dana Westbrook to get up to speed. 'I'll make a note.'

Westbrook stood. 'Keep me in the loop.'

'You got it, boss.'

Until they got an ID on the victim there wasn't too much they could do. The faster you got an ID, the faster you could get information such as where the victim lived, worked, went to school, played, and the faster you could begin to collect witness statements. Once identification was made, a person was also run through the various databases, specifically the National Crime Information Center and its local version, the Philadelphia Crime Information Center.

The victim was fingerprinted as soon as the body got to the morgue, but all you could do before identification was canvass the area around the crime scene, process any forensic material, and hope for the best. If they couldn't ID the victim, the best hope was that by the next day someone would have heard the news about the body and would start making calls about their husband, brother, son.

After finishing her initial report, Jessica would head back to the scene. People working early shifts would be getting home soon and just might have something to tell her.

She made a note to ask Kevin to reach out to a friend of his, a detective who worked out of South Detectives. The more eyes and ears on a homicide, especially at this stage, the better. Divisional detectives knew their turf and their criminals better than anyone.

Before she could do that she sensed someone nearby. She turned. Dennis Stansfield stood behind her. He was like a virus that she couldn't seem to shake.

'Can I help you with something, detective?' Jessica asked.

Stansfield pointed to the notepad on the desk. 'I didn't mean to look over your shoulder.'

'And yet?'

'Well, lately I've heard some things about him.'

'Him?'

'Yeah. Detective Byrne.'

Jessica closed the folder on her desk, closed her notebook. She spun her chair around, stood up. She was not going to talk to this guy while she was sitting down. 'Like what sort of things?'

Stansfield glanced around the duty room, looked back, lowered his voice. 'Well, like maybe his heart's not in it anymore.'

'Really?'

'Yeah, and like maybe he's looking for the door. Like maybe he's not quite the cop he used to be.'

Jessica nodded. 'Interesting.'

'I'm just saying, you know? This is what I've heard. And from more than one person.'

'Well, *Dennis*,' Jessica said. 'Maybe you're right.'

Stansfield looked surprised. 'I am?'

'Yeah. Can I tell him you said this? I'm sure he'd like to hear it, seeing as it's going around.'

'Well, I'd really prefer you didn't,' Stansfield said. 'See, I was just saying that — '

'Then again, why don't you tell him yourself?'

'What do you mean?'

'He's right behind you.'

Stansfield spun around to find Kevin Byrne, who loomed over him by about five inches, standing there. It looked for a moment as though Stansfield was going to extend his hand in greeting. It looked for a moment as though Byrne was going to throw Stansfield out a window. Both men then thought better of it.

'Detective,' was all that Stansfield managed.

Byrne stared at him until Stansfield got really interested in the time of day. He glanced at his watch, then back at Jessica.

'I'm going to follow up on the owner of the building,' Stansfield said. 'I'm mobile if you need me.'

'Yeah,' Jessica said when Stansfield was out of earshot. 'That'll happen.' She turned to Byrne.

85

'Done with the grand jury already?'

Byrne shook his head. 'Postponed. They're hearing the Fontana case today.'

'Did Drummond tell you when you're back on?'

'Maybe next week.'

'Sucks.' The longer it went on, the more likely that people were going to catch amnesia.

Byrne pointed across the room, at the departing Stansfield. 'When did he go on day work?'

'Today,' Jessica said. 'The boss put him with me this morning. I caught a case.'

Jessica filled Byrne in on what they had found. They did not have crime-scene photographs yet, but Jessica had taken a few still pictures on her cellphone. She made it a practice never to print off any crime-scene photographs that she took with her own camera, even though there were no rules against it. It just made it a little too likely that personal photographs would get mixed in with official photographs, and things like that were what defense attorneys lived for. Photo-Shop had changed everything.

Byrne stared at the images for a full minute, scrolling through them one by one.

'No ID yet?' he asked.

'Not yet,' Jessica said. 'Body's still on scene.'

Byrne handed back the phone. 'Any witnesses?'

'Nothing. I'm heading back there in a few minutes.'

Byrne looked across the room. David Albrecht sat at one of the desks, playing back footage on his camera's viewfinder.

'Who's the kid with the camera?'

Jessica explained David Albrecht's presence.

'Great,' Byrne said. 'Just what we need.'

Byrne checked the body chart, taking in the general details of the wounds to the victim, the placement of the body. 'Want some company?'

'I'll drive,' Jessica said.

'Let me get my stuff out of my car.'

In the rear parking lot they stopped at Byrne's car. It was a Kia Sedona minivan. Jessica had never seen it before.

'When did you get this?'

'It's a loaner from my cousin Patrick. Colleen is going to be moving soon and we're trying to keep the costs down. I'm bringing some of her stuff to a storage locker this week.'

'Do you like it?'

'Oh yeah,' Byrne said. 'Kias are true babe magnets. Had a few college cheerleaders flash me the other day.'

Byrne unlocked the passenger door, reached in, grabbed some things from the back seat. When he closed the door and turned around, Jessica did a double take.

Kevin Byrne had a stylish leather messenger bag over his shoulder.

'Oh my God,' Jessica said.

'What?'

'Hang on.' Jessica took out her cellphone, opened it, pantomimed dialing a long phone number. A *really* long phone number. She held up a finger. 'Hi, is this Hell?'

Byrne shook his head.

'Yes,' Jessica continued. 'I was calling to get the current temperature. What's that you say? Five below? Snow squalls expected?'

'Funny stuff,' Byrne said. 'Let me get a table so I can catch the whole act.'

Jessica smiled, closed her phone. She leaned against the car, crossed her arms. 'I can't believe it. Kevin Byrne carrying a purse. I am *so* blogging about this.'

'It's a man bag.'

'Ah.'

'And it's a Tumi. Tumi makes good stuff.'

'There's no question about that,' Jessica said. 'I have a Tumi purse myself.'

'This isn't a purse, okay? It's a — '

'Man bag,' Jessica said.

'And, just for the record, I never want to hear the words *metro* and *sexual* in the same sentence. Okay?'

'Promise,' Jessica said. Her fingers were secretly crossed behind her back. 'So, what made you decide to do this?'

Byrne leaned closer. 'It's just getting harder and harder to leave the house, you know? You have to have your keys, your cellphone, your pager, your sunglasses, your regular glasses, your iPod — '

'Wait. You have an iPod?'

'Yes, I have an iPod. What's so odd about that?'

'Well, for one thing, you still buy vinyl records. I just figured in a few years you'd make the giant leap to audiocassettes. Maybe even CDs one day.'

'I buy vinyl because it's collectible. Especially the old blues.'

'Okay.'

'Remember your uniform days when everything went on your belt? And what didn't go on your belt fitted in your shirt pocket?'

'I remember. But keep in mind there's even less room up there for female cops.'

'I'm a detective,' Byrne said. 'I've noticed that.'

He took a few steps back, gestured to the cut of his new suit, which Jessica had to admit looked pretty good on him. It was a charcoal gray two-button.

'Think about it,' he said. 'If I put all that stuff in my pockets it would ruin the line.'

'The line?' Jessica put her hand on the butt of her weapon. 'Okay, who are you and what have you done with my partner?'

Byrne laughed.

'Well, now that you carry a bag,' Jessica continued, 'you should keep in mind one of the first things they taught us at the academy.'

'I may be older than slate, but I seem to recall going to that academy myself. Over on State Road, right?'

'That's the one,' Jessica said. 'But what I meant by 'us' was, well, *women*.'

Byrne braced himself, said nothing.

'They taught us to never, ever, carry your weapon in a purse.'

There was that word again. Byrne looked at the sky, back at Jessica. 'This is going to go on for a while, isn't it?'

'Oh yeah.'

★ ★ ★

The CSU team was still processing the scene on Federal Street, which now had crime-scene tape crossing both ends of the alley. As always, a crowd had gathered to watch the proceedings. It always amazed Jessica how no one ever saw anything, heard anything, witnessed anything, but as soon as the investigation got underway, as soon as there was some sort of urban circus to attend, everyone was suddenly available to gawk and rubberneck, conveniently off work and out of school.

When Jessica and Byrne came around the corner there was a meeting of supervisors. Among them was ADA Michael Drummond.

'Counselor,' Byrne said.

'Twice in one day,' Drummond replied. 'People will talk.' He turned to Jessica. 'Nice to see you, Jess.'

'Always a pleasure,' Jessica said. 'But what brings you out here?'

'I've got court in about an hour, but these were orders from Valhalla. New DA, new initiatives. Anything that happens this close to a school gets priority. My boss wants to watch this one from the beginning. He barks, I fetch.'

'Gotcha.'

'Copy me in on everything?' Drummond asked.

'Not a problem,' Jessica said.

Jessica and Byrne watched as Drummond crossed the street, positioning himself far from the crime scene. Jessica knew why. If an ADA was close to the action, he might witness something, and therefore be called as a witness on his own case, which was grounds for dismissal. It was a game they all knew how to play.

Jessica watched as Byrne walked up to the mouth of the alley, spoke to the uniformed officer. The uniform pointed to the two buildings behind the crime scene, nodded his head. Byrne took out his notebook, began to jot down details.

Jessica had seen it before.

Murder had been done here, and Kevin Byrne was in his element.

9

Byrne walked down the alley, his senses on high alert, his adrenalin surging. It was odd, to say the least. No matter how fatigued he was — today, on a 1 to 10, he would clock in at a bone-weary 7 — it all seemed to melt away when he got to a crime scene. Crime scenes were crack for investigators. Addictive, euphoric, replenishing, ultimately depleting. There was no other feeling like it. The best meal, the finest wine, even soul-shaking sex did not come close.

Okay, Byrne thought. *Maybe sex.*

He took in the approach to the area where the body had been found. The air was suffused with the stench of rotting fruit coming from the Dumpster a few yards away, and the unmistakable aroma of death coming from the shoe store.

He walked down the stairs, opened the door. Although the smell was almost overpowering in here, it was not the first thing he sensed. Instead, that was a feeling, an impression that he had just stepped across the boundary of a killer's mind, had just become an interloper in a realm of madness.

There is a pairing, a balance, a partnership.

Byrne stopped, waiting for more. Nothing. Not yet.

In addition to his upcoming appointment with the sleep-study clinic, he had his annual MRI screening. He'd had yearly MRIs for the past five years, ever since he had been nearly fatally injured in a shooting. He knew everyone in the hospital radiology department, and the mood was always light-hearted when he went there, but they all knew what it was about. There was, and always would be, a possibility of a brain tumor. He'd read all the books on symptoms and signs — blackouts, voices in your head, sometimes unexplained smells.

In a separate incident, many years earlier, he had confronted a suspect in a bar beneath the Walt Whitman Bridge. During the course of the arrest Byrne had plunged into the frigid Delaware River, locked in combat with the suspect. When he was pulled out of the water Byrne was declared dead. One full minute later he came to.

Not long after that the visions had started. They were never full-blown apparitions. He did not show up at a scene, close his eyes, and see any sort of recreation of the crime in Technicolor and THX audio. Instead, it was more of a feeling. Sometimes it crossed over into the dominion of sense and sensation, but mostly he got a feel for the victim, the perpetrator. A thought, a dream, a desire, a habit.

Byrne had been to group-therapy sessions of every kind, even going to a regression-therapy group that tried to take him back to that moment when he'd plunged into the river, an attempt to bring him back to the person he had been before the incident. Byrne now knew that was impossible.

The visions had diminished over the ensuing

years as had the accompanying migraines. These days they were few and far between.

He had not had anything close to a full-blown migraine lately, but he knew something was happening inside him. More than once, in the last few months, he had experienced something . . . not pain, more of a presence, a thickness in his head, along with a slight blurring of vision. And with these feelings came the clearest inner visions he'd ever had, now accompanied by sounds. Then, sometimes, a blackout.

He was still undecided on whether or not to mention these things to his doctor. Telling a doctor something like this only led to more tests.

★   ★   ★

He stepped into the room where a dead man lay on the floor. Byrne's heart picked up a beat, quickening with the knowledge that a killer had stood in this spot no more than twenty-four hours earlier, breathing the same air.

Just when he was about to begin his routine, a warm sensation filled his head. He held onto the door jamb for a second, attempting to ride it out. With the warmth came the knowledge of . . .

. . . *something that has burned for many years, a feeling of loss and desire, a dark passion that will forever be unfulfilled, a love story unwritten, unwritable, the hunger to create a legacy . . .*

Byrne knelt down, snapped on a latex glove, then instantly thought better of it. He removed the glove. He needed the feel of the flesh. A dialogue happened between the skin of the dead and his senses. A superior officer, or a representative of the medical examiner's office would surely object. That didn't matter at the moment. He was alone with the dead, alone with what had happened in this room, alone with the rage that drove someone to brutally take a life.

Alone with himself.

Kevin Byrne reached out and touched a finger to the dead man's lips. He closed his eyes, listened, and the dead man spoke.

10

Jessica and Byrne spent the next hour separately canvassing the neighborhood for a second time. They learned a great deal about cheating spouses, lazy landlords, illegal parking, possible international drug cartels, alien invasions, more illegal parking, and — a fan favorite — government conspiracies. In other words, nothing.

At three o'clock Jessica met Byrne back at the corner of Fifth and Federal to compare notes.

'Jess,' Byrne said, pointing down the street.

Jessica turned and saw two figures sitting in a vacant lot, sandwiched between a pair of old row houses. The detectives were being observed.

Jessica and Byrne walked a half-block up Federal. David Albrecht, who had just returned from getting some high-angle shots from nearby rooftops, followed, but kept his distance.

Two older men sat on lawn chairs across the street from the ball field. They had racing forms on their laps, along with the sports sections of that morning's *Inquirer*. They were in their late seventies and had their chairs positioned in such a way that each could see what was approaching but still be close enough to converse. Jessica had the distinct feeling they didn't miss much.

One of the guys wore at least three cardigans, each a slightly different shade of maroon. The other wore a fishing hat with a button saying *Kiss Me I'm Italian* on it, a button so old that most of the letters were rubbed off. Now, from a few feet away, it looked like *Kiss It*. Jessica wondered if that wasn't on purpose. She showed her badge, introducing herself and Kevin Byrne.

When the men saw they were police officers they sat a little straighter.

Jessica asked: 'You fellows out here every day?'

'Every morning, every afternoon,' Cardigans said. 'Rain or shine. 'Cept when it rains, then we sit over there.' He pointed to an old storefront with a metal awning.

'In winter we meet at Mulroney's,' added Fishing Hat.

Mulroney's was a tavern on the other side of the playground, a fixture that had been around since sometime during the Truman administration.

Jessica asked the men what, if anything, they had seen the previous day. After a brief rundown of the day's events — a *Philadelphia Inquirer* delivery truck got a flat tire, some idiot on a cellphone was yelling at his wife or girlfriend and almost walked into the traffic on Federal, a dog came up and snatched one of their lunch bags right from under the chair — they got around to what they had seen at or near the crime-scene building.

Nothing.

'You didn't see anybody doing anything suspicious, anybody you haven't seen in the neighborhood before?' Byrne asked.

'Nah,' Cardigans said. 'We're the only suspicious characters around here.'

Jessica jotted down the meager information.

'You guys got here pretty quick earlier this morning,' Cardigans said.

'We were on a donut run around the corner,' Jessica said. 'It was on the way.'

Cardigans smiled. He liked her.

'Not like the last time,' Fishing Hat interjected.

Jessica glanced over at Byrne, back. 'I'm sorry?' she said. 'The last time?'

'Yeah. That other one?'

'The other one.'

'The other *dead* one they found in there.' Fishing Hat pointed to the crime-scene building, saying all this like it was common knowledge, worldwide.

'There was another victim found in that building?' Jessica asked.

'Oh, yeah,' he said. 'Place is a slaughterhouse. A regular abbytwar.'

Jessica figured he meant *abattoir*. She stole another glance at Byrne. This was getting better by the minute. Or worse. 'When was this again?'

'2002,' Fishing Hat said. 'Spring of 2002.'

'Nah,' Cardigans said. 'It was '04.'

Fishing Hat looked over, as if the other man had just told him the pope was a woman. '2004? What are you, drunk? It was 2002. March 21st. Mickey Quindlen's grandson broke his arm on the playground. My wife's brother came in from Cinnaminson, rammed his fucking car into the house.' He looked at Jessica. 'Excuse my German.'

'I speak German,' Jessica said.

'Uniforms came around noon. Suits didn't

show up until midnight. I believe I can say all this without fear of contraception.'

Cardigans nodded, acquiescing.

'Uniforms? Suits?' Jessica asked. 'Did you used to be a cop?'

'Cop? Nah. I worked the docks, forty-one years. I just like that *Law and Order* show. The guy with the big teeth says that kind of stuff all the time.'

'He's dead now,' Cardigans said.

Fishing Hat looked at his friend. 'He is? Since when?'

'Long time now.'

'He ain't dead on the show.'

'No. Not on the show he ain't. Just in real life.'

'Damn.'

'Yeah.'

A respectful silence fell over the group for a moment.

'He was a longshoreman, too,' Fishing Hat said then, crooking a thumb at his buddy. 'Back in the day, we were all over. *All* over. Oregon Avenue, up to South Street, Front Street, Third Street. Not like now. Now I got a lawyer living next door to me. A *lawyer*. There goes the neighborhood.'

Jessica made a few more notes as Cardigans looked closely at Byrne. 'You look familiar,' Cardigans said. 'You ever work the docks?'

'My father did,' Byrne said. 'Thirty-five years.'

Cardigans snapped his fingers. 'Paddy Byrne.'

Byrne nodded.

'You look just like him.' He turned to Fishing Hat. 'Did you know Paddy?'

Fishing Hat shook his head.

'This guy was a legend on Pier 96.' He turned back to Byrne. 'How is he these days?'

'He's good,' Byrne said. 'Thanks for asking.'

'So how come you didn't follow in his footsteps? Get an honest job?'

'The docks are too dangerous for me,' Byrne said. 'And I prefer a higher class of criminal.'

Cardigans laughed. 'Yeah. You're Paddy's boy.'

'So, what else can you tell me about this other victim?' Jessica asked, trying to bring the conversation back around.

Both men shrugged in tandem. 'Not much, 'cept that it was a woman,' Fishing Hat said. 'They locked the place up for years. Guy who owned it couldn't even go back in there. Said he was afraid of ghosts or something. He sold it to some guy from Pittsburgh, who sold it to someone else.'

Jessica looked around. 'What's the neighborhood, guys?'

'Some say Queen Village but they don't know shit.'

'What do *you* say?'

'We say Pennsport. Because it *is* Pennsport. We're south of *Washington*, for Chrissake.'

'Did a detective talk to you guys about that case back in '02?' Jessica asked.

'Just me,' Cardigans said.

'Do you remember their names? The detectives?'

Cardigans shook his head.

'He don't remember his kids' names,' Fishing Hat said. 'And he's only got four of 'em.'

'Did you know the victim?'

'No. I heard she was a real hot number, though. Damn shame.'

The information would be easy enough to find, but probably wasn't relevant. Jessica thanked the two men, got their contact information — names, addresses, phone numbers — and gave them both a business card, along with the standard request for them to call if they thought of anything else.

'You come back anytime,' Fishing Hat said. 'We always have time to talk to pretty young girls.'

Jessica smiled. *Pretty young girls.* She'd come back tomorrow.

* * *

Jessica and Byrne returned to the Roundhouse, collated their witness statements, putting them in the binder. While they waited for the coroner's preliminary reports, as well as any forensic findings, they turned their attention to other matters of importance.

They each had a case on which they were working. Both cases had stalled, and there was no worse feeling for a homicide detective than the sense that an investigation was slipping away from them. While Byrne made calls to the four witnesses he needed for the grand-jury probe of Eduardo Robles, just to keep the pot simmering, Jessica looked up some addresses, trying to align the witnesses in another case.

Two weeks earlier a gun had been left at the

scene of a drug-related homicide. The weapon had been traced back to a woman named Patricia Lentz, a known drug addict and prostitute.

The Lentz apartment was on North 19th Street near Cecil B. Moore. When Jessica and Byrne arrived, they found the door open, TV blasting, something burning on the stove. The first floor was a haze of vile smoke, a landfill of soiled mattresses, broken furniture, spent crack vials and empty liquor bottles.

They found Patricia Lentz passed out beneath a pile of clothing in the basement. At first Jessica did not think she was going to find a pulse. But the woman had just passed out and, once she'd been revived by paramedics, was taken into custody without incident.

Whereas the suspect was in custody, her apartment had not yet been cleared. Jessica was quite familiar with the layout of these row houses and knew there were two more rooms upstairs. While Byrne turned the barely coherent woman over to the uniformed officers for transport to the Roundhouse, Jessica continued upstairs. She cleared the first small bedroom, and the bathroom. When she walked into the second bedroom she found there was a closet. She eased open the door.

Jessica froze. There, on the floor in front of her, partially hidden by a plastic garbage bag bursting at the seams with rotting trash, was a little boy. No more than two years old. A dark-haired little boy dressed in a ragged T-shirt and diaper. It appeared that he had crawled beneath the garbage for warmth.

Reaching down into the closet, she picked up the boy. He was shivering with fear, miserable in his soiled diaper. There were rashes on his arms and legs.

'It's okay, little man,' Jessica said. 'It's okay.'

On the way out of the house, Jessica found a pile of papers on a card table near the front door. They were mostly unpaid bills, flyers for pizza and Chinese takeout, shut-off notices. Also on the table was a photograph of an infant lying on a dirty bed sheet. Jessica could not mistake those eyes. It was the little boy she had in her arms. She flipped the picture over. It read *Carlos age three months*.

His name was Carlos.

Jessica brought the boy back to the Roundhouse to await a representative from the Department of Human Services. She had stopped along the way and bought diapers, wipes, lotion, powder. It had been a long time since she had done these things with Sophie, but it was like riding a bike: she hadn't forgotten.

Cleaned up, shiny and combed, Carlos sat at one of the desks, on top of a pile of phone books, secured to the chair with an empty ammunition belt. Someone found a Philadelphia Eagles child's sweatshirt. It was a little too big, so they rolled up the sleeves and Scotch-taped them gently around the boy's wrists.

The boy's mother, Patricia Lentz, was booked on first-degree murder charges, and the case was a lock. They had the murder weapon, ballistics matched, and Lentz would not be coming back for a long time. Carlos would have children of his own by the time she got out.

'What's going on with Carlos?' Byrne asked, bringing Jessica back to the present and the new case at hand.

Jessica had to take a second. The last thing you wanted to do in this room, even with your partner, who knew you better than anyone in your life, was display any emotion besides anger.

'Nothing,' Jessica said. 'They still haven't been able to find Patricia Lentz's sister. Word is that she's an even bigger crackhead.'

Jessica knew it was no secret, especially to Kevin Byrne, that she and Vincent had been trying for two years to have another child. Sophie was now seven, and the longer they waited, well, all the books said you really didn't want too much of an age gap between siblings. The very notion of undertaking the monumental task of adopting Carlos was, of course, a ridiculous idea. During daylight hours, anyway. But when Jessica lay awake in the middle of the night it all seemed possible. Then the sun would come up again and she realized it would never happen.

'How is he doing?' Byrne asked.

'Good, I guess,' Jessica said. She really didn't know if that was true or not, but it was the only answer she had.

'If you want, we can stop in at the Department of Human Services and check on him.'

The sooner Jessica let go, the better it would be. Still, she knew what she was going to say. 'Sure. That would be good.'

Before they could discuss it further, Nicci Malone poked her head into the duty room. 'Kevin, you have a call.'

Byrne crossed the room, hit a button, answered. A few moments later he pulled out his notebook, wrote something in it, punched a fist through the air. It was clearly good news. Jessica needed some good news.

Byrne hung up, grabbed his coat. 'That was the ID Unit.'

The ID Unit processed latent fingerprints.

'Are we on?' Jessica asked.

'We are,' Byrne said. 'Our cleanshaven dead man has a name. Kenneth Arnold Beckman.'

11

The Beckman house was a gaunt and peeling postwar row house on West Tioga Street, in the Nicetown area of North Philadelphia. Nicetown was a blue-collar section of the city that was slowly recovering after three decades of slow decline, a slide culminating in the Tastykake company moving out of the area in 2007. At one time it was rumored that Trump Entertainment would be building a casino on Hunting Park Avenue. It never happened. The only gambling being done in Nicetown these days was among those residents and store owners debating whether or not to hang onto their property.

Before leaving the Roundhouse, Jessica asked Josh Bontrager to run a check on Kenneth Arnold Beckman. Bontrager would call if there was anything to report.

★   ★   ★

When Jessica and Byrne pulled to a stop in front of the Beckman house, near Schuyler Street, it began to rain. The wind picked up, and when they stepped onto the porch wet leaves gathered at their feet.

Jessica rang the bell three times before noticing that there was a wire hanging out from the bottom of the rusted panel. The bell didn't work. A quick look at the crumbling porch, with

106

its leaning support pillars and brickwork desperately in need of tuck pointing, explained why. She knocked on the door, gently at first. The second time she knocked harder. Eventually they heard the deadbolts begin to turn. There were three of them.

The woman who answered the door was a hard forty. Her platinum hair was perm-fried, her make-up looked like it had been applied with a paper towel. She wore black Capri pants and battered pink running shoes. A lighted cigarette hung from the corner of her mouth.

Looking Byrne up and down, she tossed a sideways glance at Jessica.

'Are you Mrs. Beckman?' Byrne asked.

'Well, now,' she replied. 'That would depend on two things, wouldn't it?'

'And what would those two things be?'

'Who you are and what the fuck you want.'

Oh boy, Jessica thought. *We've got a real charmer here.*

Byrne took out his ID, badged the woman. She stared at it far too long. Jessica figured this was an attempt on the woman's part to establish some sort of power dynamic. What the woman didn't know was that Kevin Byrne could outlast a glacier. She looked at Jessica, raising a painted-on eyebrow. Jessica reached into her pocket, showed the woman *her* ID. The woman sniffed, turned back to Byrne.

'Well, that answers one of my questions,' she said.

'May we come in?' Byrne asked.

The woman blinked a few times, as if Byrne

107

was speaking another language. 'Can you hear me?' she asked.

'Ma'am?'

'Can you hear my voice?'

'Yes,' Byrne said. 'I can hear your voice.'

'Good. I hear you too. We can talk right here.'

Jessica sensed Byrne's gloves coming off. He pulled out his notebook, flipped a few pages. 'What's your first name, ma'am?'

Pause. 'Sharon.'

'Is your husband Kenneth Arnold Beckman?'

The woman snorted. 'Husband? That's one way of putting it.'

'Are you married to him, ma'am?'

The woman took a long drag on her cigarette. Jessica noted that the nicotine stains on her fingers reached down to her knuckles. She blew out the smoke, and with it her answer. 'Barely.'

'When was the last time you saw him?'

'Why?'

'Right now I just need you to answer the question, ma'am. I'll explain why in a moment.'

Another drag. Jessica estimated that, if they were going to get through the basic questions at this pace, Sharon Beckman would go through a pack and a half. 'Yesterday afternoon.'

'About what time?'

Another sigh. 'About three o'clock.'

'And where was this?'

'It was at the MGM Grand in Vegas. I'm a dancer there.'

Byrne stared, the woman stared. She rolled her eyes.

'It was right about where you're standing,' she

said. 'I think he said something like 'Clean the kitchen, you lazy fucking bitch.' Real Hallmark moment.'

The wind picked up again, blowing a thin cold rain across the porch. Byrne moved a few feet to his right, making sure that Sharon Beckman caught the rain directly in her face.

'Was he alone at the time?'

'Yeah,' Sharon Beckman said, stepping back a foot. 'For once.'

'And he did not come home last night?'

The woman snorted. 'Why break with tradition?'

Byrne pressed on. 'Does anyone else live here?'

'Just my son.'

My *son*, Jessica thought. *Not* our *son*.

'How old is he?'

The woman smiled. Her teeth were the same color as her tobacco-stained knuckles. 'Why, officer. That would be giving away my age.' When Byrne didn't respond, didn't budge, didn't seem to be weak-kneed by the woman's coquettish charms, she repositioned her scowl, hit her cigarette again, and said, 'He's nineteen. I had him when I was six.'

Byrne made the note. He then asked her what the kid's name was. She told him. Jason Crandall.

'Where does your husband work?'

'*Hey*. You writing a fucking book here? My autobiography, maybe?'

'Ma'am, we're just trying to — '

'No. What you need to do is tell me what this is about or we're done here. I know my rights.'

Jessica knew the notification was coming, so she watched the woman's face as she took in the

109

news. You could tell a lot from the initial reaction to the news that a loved one has been killed. Or even one not so loved.

'Mrs. Beckman, your husband was murdered yesterday.'

The woman drew a sharp intake of breath, but other than that betrayed nothing. Except, perhaps, for a slight shake in her hands, which deposited a long cigarette ash on the floor. She stared out at the street for a moment, turned back. 'How did he get it?'

Get it, Jessica thought. Most people said 'What?' or 'Oh my God' or 'No!' or something like that. *How did he get it*? No, not too many people ask how the deceased became deceased. That usually came a bit later in the conversation.

'May we come in, ma'am?' Byrne said. 'It's getting a little nasty out here.'

The news had undone the woman's resolve, as well as her animosity. Without saying a word, she opened the door and stepped to the side.

They entered the house, a standard porchfront-style row house, large by Philly standards, probably measuring around 1500 square feet on three floors. It was quickly degenerating, already long past its sell-by date.

The living room was directly to the left, with a hallway leading to a kitchen and a stairway at the back of the house. The walls were painted a cheerless, faded baby blue. The furniture was worn, mismatched, spring-shocked. A half-eaten Weight Watchers dinner sat on a coffee table, next to an overflowing ashtray. Cat hair covered nearly every surface. The place smelled like

110

microwave popcorn.

Sharon Beckman did not offer them a seat. Jessica would have passed on that offer anyway.

'Ma'am,' Byrne said. 'We're here because your husband was a victim of homicide. We're trying to find out who did this, and bring that person to justice.'

'Yeah? Well, look in the fucking mirror,' the woman spat.

'I understand your anger,' Byrne continued. 'But if there's anything you can think of that might help us, we would really appreciate it.'

The woman lit another Salem off the first cigarette, held them both for a few moments, one in each hand.

'Can you think of anyone who might have had a problem with your husband?' Byrne asked. 'Someone he owed money to? Someone with whom he had a business problem?'

The woman took a full five seconds to answer. Maybe she did have something to hide.

'Do I need a lawyer?' Sharon Beckman asked. She butted out the short cigarette.

'Have you done anything wrong, Mrs. Beckman?' Byrne asked. It was Cop Speak 101. Standard across the world when police arrive at the lawyer moment.

'Plenty,' she said.

Wrong answer, Jessica thought. The woman was trying to be cute, but she didn't realize that a picture was being painted, and every stroke mattered.

'Well, then, I can't answer your question,' Byrne said. 'If you feel the need for counsel at

111

this time, by all means call your attorney. I *can* tell you that you are not suspected of anything. You are a witness, and a very important witness. All we need to do is ask you a few questions. The more you tell us, the likelier it will be that we can find the person who did this to your husband.'

Jessica made another quick perusal of the room. There were no photographs of the Beckmans on the mantel over the bricked-in fireplace, no soft-focus wedding day portraits in tacky gold-painted frames.

'If you'll just bear with us a little longer,' Byrne continued, 'we'll get the information we need, and we'll leave you to your thoughts and your arrangements.'

Sharon Beckman just stared. Byrne led her through the rest of the standard questions, giving her the standard assurances. He concluded by asking her if she had a photograph of her husband.

While Sharon Beckman was in the hallway, going through a legal-sized cardboard box, looking for the photograph, the front door opened.

The kid who entered looked younger than nineteen. Stringy blond hair, surfer cool, hooded, stoned eyes. When he saw Byrne he must have figured him for a cop, and he shoved his right hand deep into his baggy shorts. Dope pocket.

'How ya doin?' the kid mumbled.

'Good, thanks,' Byrne said. 'Are you Jason?'

The kid looked up, shocked, like there was no way that Byrne could have possibly gotten this information. 'Yeah.' Barely audible. The kid leaned back on his heels, as if that might increase the distance between them. Jessica could smell

112

the marijuana on his clothes from ten feet away.

'Kenny's dead,' Sharon Beckman said, walking back into the room, a pair of old snapshots in her hand. She handed them to Jessica.

Jason stared at his mother, blinking. It was as if the words hadn't yet reached his brain. 'Dead?'

'Yeah. Like in not alive anymore?'

Jessica looked at the kid. No reaction.

Over the next few minutes Byrne asked Jason the basic questions, got the expected answers. Jason said he had not seen his stepfather in more than three days.

'Once again, we're sorry for your loss,' Byrne said to them both, putting away his notebook. He dropped a pair of business cards on the cluttered coffee table. 'If you think of anything that might help us, please call.'

* * *

They walked the half-block to the car, adrift on their own thoughts, sizing up the subdued reactions of Beckman's widow and stepson. It was not the usual response they got from notification, to say the least.

The temperature had dropped a few degrees since they had entered the Beckman house. The rain continued, getting colder. For the first time that year, it felt as if it might snow.

* * *

In the parking lot at the Roundhouse they saw Josh Bontrager getting into one of the detective

113

cars. Spotting them, Bontrager closed the door and crossed the lot. Dennis Stansfield, already in the car, wisely stayed put.

'What's up, Josh?' Byrne asked.

'Have you made notification yet?'

'Just did. What do you have?'

'I ran Kenneth Beckman,' Bontrager said. 'A couple of things jumped out.'

'Such as?'

'Well, at one time he was a person of interest.'

Bontrager meant that the deceased had been looked at by the police for some sort of crime.

'What was the job?' Jessica asked.

'A homicide.'

Jessica felt her pulse kick up a notch. 'This guy was looked at for a murder? When was this?'

'2002.'

'How far did the investigation go?'

'They had him in, but I guess he didn't roll,' Bontrager said. 'The detective working the case kept an eye on the guy for a few years, made a few more notes, but then it went cold. Nothing in the file since '06.'

'Who was the victim?'

Bontrager pulled out his notebook. 'A nineteen-year-old girl named Antoinette Chan. Cause of death was multiple blunt-force trauma. Weapon was a claw hammer found at the scene. The weapon had been wiped clean of prints.'

'What was the date?' Jessica asked.

Bontrager flipped a few pages. 'March 21, 2002.'

A cold finger traced a path along Jessica's spine. It was the date that the old codgers had

114

mentioned earlier. She shot a look at Byrne, who also seemed transfixed by the information.

'I'm going to take a ride over to Record Storage, get the whole story,' Bontrager said.

'We'll do it,' Byrne said. 'Check out the next of kin in the Chan family, see where they are, who they are. If they held Beckman responsible they may be worth looking at.'

'No problem.'

Josh Bontrager got into the car, drove away, a stone-faced Dennis Stansfield in the passenger seat.

'What do you think?' Jessica asked.

Byrne took a few moments to answer. He absently ran a finger over the small V-shaped scar located above his right eye, a keloid souvenir of the time he had been grazed by a bullet years ago. Jessica knew this meant the wheels were turning.

'I think we need to see that original file.' He looked at his watch. 'But first I want to have another word with the lovely and talented Mrs. Beckman.' He looked back at Jessica. 'Funny she didn't mention any of this.'

'Right. When I asked her if she knew who might have done this and she said 'Look in the fucking mirror' I didn't really get it. Now I do. She blames the police.'

'What a rarity,' Byrne said. 'And she seemed so nice.'

'Real debutante,' Jessica said. 'I'll run checks on her and the stoned kid. See where they were and what they were doing in March '02.'

'I'll meet you at Record Storage,' Byrne said.

'Call me if she has any wants or warrants. I don't care if Sharon Beckman did just lose her husband. I'd love to toss her in a cage for a while.'

'Oh, please,' Jessica said. 'You just like putting women in handcuffs.'

12

In the first ten minutes after the police left her house, Sharon Beckman found she couldn't move. She stood by the front door, paralyzed.

Jason went back out. God only knew what he did these days. What Jason had not told the cops was that the last time he had seen Kenny the two had gotten into a fist fight. The last thing Jason had said to his stepfather was 'If you ever touch me again I'm going to fucking kill you.'

That was not something you told the police. *She* knew Jason would never do anything like that, but *they* didn't.

The house was quiet.

Kenny was dead.

Sharon knew she was supposed to be feeling something, something akin to grief, something like heartache, but she didn't. All she felt was a faint cold fear. And the knowledge that she had to move. Fast.

From right when she'd first met Kenny, Sharon had known it was all going to fall apart one day. It wasn't like she didn't know who he was when they'd met, what kind of life she was getting into. She was no angel herself. But eight years ago, when Kenny had robbed all those houses and put himself on the police radar, she'd known a day like this would come.

When she had set fire to the house on Lenox Avenue, back in 2002, destroying all that evidence, she'd known she'd pay for it some day. Today. She had been a little sorry that the whole block had gone up in flames, but no one had got hurt. She didn't lose much sleep over it. There was no love lost between her and her neighbors on Lenox Avenue anyway. *Fucking lowlife crackheads.*

She turned around three times in the living room, trying to organize her thoughts, trying to think straight.

She should have left a long time ago. When cops followed up on things it was a clear sign that they had you in their sights. Cops always knew a lot more than they let on. It was like those jobs she used to go on with her father when she was small. Her dad would work on somebody's plumbing, and when he was all done he'd turn the water back on and slide a sheet of newspaper under the pipes. If one drop of water fell, blotting out on the paper, the job was shit. Her father would always tear it out and start over. If there was one solitary drop there was certain to be more.

Same thing with cops.

Drip, drip, drip.

Then they had you.

Kenny had put all the new stolen merchandise into a storage locker on Linden Avenue. He'd learned the first time not to keep anything in the house. They both had. She wasn't sure what he had in there these days and that was fine with her. The less she knew, the better.

Sharon also knew what Kenny had done to that girl in 2002, even as she tried hard to block it out of her mind. Of course, there wasn't a jury in the world that would give a shit. They had gotten away with it once, but now that Kenny was dead everything was going to fall on her like a load of bricks. There was no way she could deal with this on her own. She knew at least a dozen people who might have wanted to do Kenny in, a dozen people who'd had a beef with him, and once the police realized this they were going to see her as a link. It was only a matter of time until they revisited the Antoinette Chan case. She knew how hard cops worked on burglaries. They didn't give up until they had you in a jail cell.

Murder?

Forget it.

Sharon ran upstairs. She would load the car with what she could, go find Jason. She would get the keys to the Master lock that was on the door at the storage locker, throw them in the Delaware River, and she and her son would be long gone.

But where would they go? They couldn't go to her sister's in Toledo. That would be the first place they'd look. She had exactly eight hundred twenty-six dollars to her name. Plus whatever was in the coin jar, plus whatever was in the gas tank.

Sharon was only forty-four. Still young. Still had her looks, or whatever looks she'd had to begin with. She'd start a new life. Meet a man with a real job.

Kenny was dead.

Before she could get her things out of the

drawers in the upstairs bedroom she heard a noise.

'Jason?' No answer.

She listened for a few more moments, heard nothing. Must have been the brats next door, she thought. One day they'd thrown a basketball against an adjoining wall for three straight hours. She wouldn't miss them.

She grabbed her two battered suitcases from the top shelf of the bedroom closet, began to stuff them with clothing. She soon realized she would need some big plastic garbage bags to take it all.

Sharon ran down the stairs, her mind racing in a hundred different directions. When she turned the corner toward the kitchen she saw the shadow on the wall. She stopped, spun around, her heart pounding.

'Jason, we — '

It wasn't Jason.

13

The building at 31st and Market streets where old police records were kept had once been the offices and publishing plant of the *Evening Bulletin*. The *Bulletin*, published from 1847 to 1982, was at one time the largest evening newspaper in the United States.

Now the massive and deceptively benign-looking building was fenced and sealed like Fort Knox, with concertina wire ringing the exposed public areas. The enormous brick wall that faced the parking lot rose more than four stories and boasted only five small windows near the roofline. A dozen or so parking-lot lights jutted from the wall like rusted bowsprits.

Jessica signed in at the gate, drove in, parked. She was about twenty minutes late, but had not spotted Byrne's van. She decided to wait in the car.

Before leaving the Roundhouse she had run Sharon Beckman and Jason Crandall through the databases. The kid had a misdemeanor possession charge from last year, a charge that was dropped when Jason did community service.

Sharon Beckman had no record.

Jessica thought about how the case was developing. The bizarre condition of Kenneth Beckman's corpse was still a mystery and indicated something that festered deep in the heart of the killer, something personal and

121

twisted. She thought about the paper band wrapped around the victim's head, the way the cut traversed the forehead, the way the —

There was a loud sound, inches from her left ear, a cracking noise that made her jump. She spun in her seat, her hand automatically unsnapping her holster.

Byrne had tapped her window with his ring. Jessica slowly rolled down the window, making him wait in the drizzling rain.

'This is how people get shot, you know,' Jessica said.

'I could use the rest.'

She took her time getting out of the car, driving home her point. A minute later they entered the building, walked over to the elevators, shaking off the rain.

'Did you talk to Sharon Beckman again?' Jessica asked.

Byrne shook his head. 'She wasn't home,' Byrne said. 'Neither was Spicoli.'

Referencing the Sean Penn role in *Fast Times at Ridgemont High*, Byrne was, of course, referring to Jason Crandall. Jessica had no idea where Kevin Byrne's frame of cultural references began and ended.

★ ★ ★

In the extensive basement were records for thousands of crimes, some going back two hundred years, the residue of a city's shame: names, dates, weapons, wounds, witnesses. What was absent was the evidence of loss. There was

122

no record to be found here of a father's tears, a son's loneliness, or a grandmother's empty Sundays.

Instead, here were block after block of huge steel shelving racks, some reaching twenty feet high, each packed firm with thousands of cardboard boxes, each box tagged with a white label detailing name of the deceased, case number, and year.

They split up the Beckman files. Byrne read the witness statements and forensic reports, while Jessica went through the original police reports and the notes written by the lead detective.

Just inside the binder was a picture of Antoinette Chan. She'd been a pretty girl, with flawless skin and a beguiling smile. Jessica moved on to the police report on Beckman.

Kenneth Arnold Beckman, born in 1970, was originally from the Brewerytown area of Philadelphia. At the time of Antoinette Chan's murder he had worked as a handyman for a pair of apartment complexes in Camden, and had lived in the Nicetown/Tioga area on Lenox Avenue.

By the age of twenty-nine he had been arrested five times for breaking and entering, twice convicted of possession of stolen merchandise.

In 2001 Beckman took his ten-year-old stepson Jason trick-or-treating on North 18th Street between Westmoreland and Venango. They went door to door, with Beckman accompanying the boy to each stoop. Some of the people in the neighborhood later remarked about how Beckman hovered a little too close to the door, how he seemed to be looking into the houses with a little too much interest as the little boy received his candy.

Over the next five months there were six burglaries in the neighborhood, all occurring during daylight hours when the residents were at work. Each time the same sort of items were stolen: cameras, jewelry, cash, MP3 players. Nothing too big to fit in a pillowcase.

A pair of astute divisional detectives noticed the pattern and created a photo lineup of people living in a one-mile radius of the break-ins who had a criminal history of burglaries. One of the people in that lineup was Kenneth Beckman.

After getting positive IDs of Beckman as someone who had come to neighborhood houses on Halloween, the detectives placed him under surveillance. Within a few days they followed him to a pawnshop in Chinatown, a known address for fencing stolen items. In forty-eight hours they set up a sting operation, with a detective posing as an employee of the shop. But Beckman, perhaps sensing a problem, never returned.

In mid-March 2002 they received a call from a young woman they had spoken to earlier, a woman named Antoinette Chan, the daughter of one of the burglary victims. She said she had gone down to her basement for the first time in a few weeks to do laundry and had seen a shoe print in the small lavatory off the furnace room. Whoever had broken into her house had come through the basement window. It appeared that the burglar had made a comfort stop. The original investigators had never looked in the lavatory.

The shoe print matched a size twelve Frye boot. Surveillance photos of Kenneth Beckman revealed him wearing the exact model.

Detectives visited Beckman's place of employment, only to discover that he had left.

When detectives arrived at the Beckman house on Lenox Avenue, search warrant in hand, they found a pair of PFD ladder trucks on the scene, and the block of row houses — four in all — ablaze. The old wooden structures burned to the ground in a matter of hours.

Across the street, sitting on a curb, smoking a cigarette, was Sharon Beckman. There was little doubt in anyone's mind about who had started the blaze, and no doubt at all why. Unfortunately for the investigators, there was no direct evidence. Sharon was not formally questioned or charged.

According to police, later that night Kenneth Beckman kidnapped Antoinette Chan, brought her to a location in South Philly and bludgeoned her to death. When Beckman was found in a motel in Allentown three days later and brought in for questioning, he dummied up and requested a lawyer.

Without any witnesses, and without any opportunity to search his house, all charges against Kenneth Arnold Beckman were dropped.

And now he was dead.

Jessica opened the folder with the crime-scene photos and felt her heart leap. 'Holy *shit*.'

'What?' Byrne asked.

Jessica put two of the Antoinette Chan crime-scene photos on the table, took out her iPhone, opened the photos folder, swiped over to her most recent photographs. She put the phone on the table, next to the printed pictures.

There was no mistake.

The man they had found dead that morning, Kenneth Arnold Beckman, the lead suspect in an eight-year-old murder case — that case being the bludgeoning to death of a young woman named Antoinette Chan — was posed inside a building on Federal, the same place where Antoinette Chan had been found.

Eight years before it became the Beckman crime scene it had been the Chan crime scene.

'The suspect in an unsolved homicide gets murdered himself and placed in the same location as his victim,' Jessica summed up.

'Yep,' Byrne said.

'As in *exactly* the same place. Posed in *exactly* the same position as the original victim.' She held up both the photograph and her cellphone. 'Kevin, these are absolutely identical crime-scene photos, only the second murder, our murder, was eight years later.'

'Eight and change, but yeah,' Byrne said. 'These are the facts as we know them.'

The two detectives looked at each other, knowing that this case had just crossed the line. It was now more than a vendetta murder, more than some act committed in the fiery grip of passion.

Jessica glanced again at the photographs.

126

Some inner bell began to peal. In Philadelphia's history, any large city's history, there were many unsolved murders, victims of insanity and fury who for years went unavenged, evil echoing across time.

There was just such a legacy in the City of Brotherly Love, shame and guilt and madness that ran beneath the cobblestone streets like a blood river. Staring at photographs taken eight years apart, at the ragged flesh of two victims connected in a way neither she nor her partner yet understood, Detective Jessica Balzano wondered how much of this history they were about to see.

14

I float in darkness. I have always been nocturnal, eluding sleep, embraced by waking dreams.

Here the screams are scuttled and still. It is a place of repose and reflection, a place of wintry silence. For many years I have felt at home here.

I place the body on the ground. It is the third note. There are eight in this measure. Harmony and melody. I prop the leg against the low headstone. The music swells as I leap into the air, bringing down my full weight. The bone snaps. The sound echoes across the wet granite, the moonlit grass. I take the recorder in my hand, play back the sound. The cracking of bone is bright percussion.

I move among the dead, listening. The departed speak softly to me, études of grace and humility. Soon my movements become fluid, an exaltation of this moment, a dance of death. Le danse macabre. Around and around I twirl. I am free here.

Death at midnight plays a dance-tune,
Zig, zig, zag, on his violin.

I spin among the deceased, thinking about the next days, days leading up to All Hallow's Eve, when all the world's departed will rejoice.

Soon we will dance, the detective and I. We

will dance, and in our embrace we will find that we are of the same heart, the same mind, two damaged souls sipping from a tarnished cup of blood.

TWO

SCHERZO

15

Lucinda Doucette looked at the bathroom floor, thinking:

I live in a world full of pigs.

Le Jardin, a modern 300-room hotel near Seventeenth and Sansom streets, in the heart of Center City, was a monolithic gray edifice with angular black wrought-iron railings around its seventy balconies, a model of European modernity at the corner of what was now being considered Philadelphia's new French Quarter. Managed by a Belgian multinational firm that also managed properties in Paris, Monaco and London, Le Jardin, which had been completely renovated in 2005, catered to the upscale business and leisure traveler, with its highly polished mahogany trim, its frosted French doors, its expensive French amenities.

In addition to the guest rooms there were six suites on the penultimate floor, all of them with views of the city, along with a presidential suite on the top floor that had breathtaking views of the Delaware River and beyond.

For Lucinda Doucette, along with everyone else who worked in hotel housekeeping, the views were less than scenic, although sometimes just as breathtaking in their own right.

Like all hotels, Le Jardin lived and died by its

'star' ratings — Orbitz, Hotels.com, Expedia, Hotwire, Priceline.

And while the management looked to online sites for input and feedback, there were only two accommodation ratings that really mattered: Mobil and AAA.

Mobil 'shopped' hotels every few years. The American Automobile Association, on the other hand, was far more exacting, some might say stingy, with their Diamond ratings, and thus were the most feared and respected of all the organizations on whose assessment of accommodations, dining, and travel the success of any hotel depended. Disappoint AAA, and the drop in business was palpable within months.

What it all boiled down to was comfort, staff, accommodation, and cleanliness.

Le Jardin was rightfully considered an upscale establishment, consistently rated at four stars, and this was something the management guarded fiercely.

Lucy Doucette had worked in housekeeping at Le Jardin for just over a year, starting a few days after her eighteenth birthday. When she first got on staff she found herself visiting the various travel websites with some regularity, checking the guest reviews, the user opinions, especially in the area of cleanliness. Granted, if she wasn't doing her job, she would certainly have heard about it from the director of housekeeping, a chilly, no-nonsense woman named Audrey Balcombe who, it was rumored, held a Master's Degree in communications from the *Université d'Avignon* and had apprenticed as a hotelier with Kurt

Wachtveitl, the legendary former general manager of the Mandarin Oriental, Bangkok.

Still, Lucy took pride in what she did, and wanted to hear about it, good or bad, from the guests themselves. One review on tripadvisor.com had given Le Jardin a single star (there was no option for zero stars, or this guest reviewer certainly would have used it) in the area of cleanliness, going so far as to compare the hotel to a locker room at an inner-city YMCA. The reviewer complained specifically about entering the bathroom upon checking in, only to find the toilet unflushed. Lucy thought that the guy who'd written and uploaded the review, not the toilet, was the one full of shit — there was virtually no chance of this ever happening — but nonetheless, for the next two weeks, she worked doubly hard on her floor, the twelfth floor, checking and then rechecking the toilets before clearing the rooms for the arriving guests.

Most of the time her work ethic was its own reward — God knew the pay was not — but sometimes, not often, there were unexpected perks.

One guest, about five months earlier — an elderly, refined man — stayed for six days and when he checked out he left Lucy a one-hundred-dollar tip beneath the pillow, along with a note that said *To the girl with the haunted eyes: Good job.*

Haunted eyes, Lucy thought at the time. She wore sunglasses to and from work for weeks afterward.

Right now Lucy wanted to choke the man

staying in 1212. In addition to the spilled coffee on the chair, the stained pillowcases, the broken beer bottles in the tub, the overturned breakfast tray, the hair-clogged sink, and the shampoo and conditioner bottles which had somehow ended up under the bed along with two pairs of stained and streaked underwear, every towel was soaking wet and had been piled on the floor. And although she was used to this, this time it was particularly gross. In one of the towels was a copious amount of what looked like vomit.

Jesus, what a pig.

Time to move. Lucy had four more rooms to clean before her lunch break and less than two hours to do it. Management knew exactly when she clocked into a room. If she took longer than forty minutes, they noticed.

In a given day, each room attendant had fourteen rooms to clean. If you were fast — and Lucy, at nineteen, had energy to burn — you could buy 'credits,' or other rooms to clean. Lucy often did. She was good at her job. She did not engage the guests in a lot of small talk in the hallways, she was always courteous and polite, and with a little make-up she was not that hard to look at. With her cornflower-blue eyes, her butterscotch hair and slender figure, she never had a problem fitting into her uniform and more than once had caught the male guests following her movement down the long hallways at the hotel.

Although the work was not particularly demanding, it was mentally taxing. The difference between a three-and-a-half-star and a

136

four-star hotel was often in the attitude and the details.

Some things were out of the control of the employees — the quality of the linens and towels, for instance, or whether or not to include mouthwash in the bathroom, or services like an evening turn-down — while other things were clearly in the purview of the 'ladies' in housekeeping.

Today there was a convention checking into the hotel, booked for three days. Something called *Société Poursuite*, a group of people, as Lucy understood it, who looked into unsolved murders as some sort of strange hobby. They had purchased a third of all the rooms, including the entire twelfth floor.

Using her finely tuned sense of logic, Lucy deduced that the word *Société* meant Society. She just hoped the other word didn't stand for Pig.

★   ★   ★

As she finished Room 1210, Lucy thought about her lunchtime appointment that day.

She had seen so many so-called professionals in the past nine years, so many people who thought they knew what was wrong with her. She had even taken part in a pilot program on regression therapy at the University of Pennsylvania Hospital. Despite Lucy having no money to pay for the treatment, after three separate interviews they had agreed to take her. It hadn't gone well. For five straight days she'd sat in a

137

group of eight people who'd pretty much talked about how, in previous lives, they were raped by Attila the Hun or played footsie with Marie Antoinette, or swapped spit with John the Baptist's severed head. *Yuck.* They had not really understood her problem. Lucy had yet to meet anyone who did.

She did meet some nice people there. The man who died and was brought back to life. The woman who was hit in the head and wandered around the city for three whole months, not knowing who she was.

Lucy had also been to a behavioral psychologist — exactly ten times. Her medical benefits at the hotel allowed her to see someone in the mental health field ten times in a calendar year, paying only her copay, which was twenty-five dollars. She could barely afford that.

Today, if she was lucky, all that was going to change. Today she was going to see the Dreamweaver.

She had found his card just sitting on her cart one day, probably tossed there by a passing guest. For some reason she had put it in her pocket and kept it. Just a week earlier she'd called the number out of the blue and had a brief conversation with the man, who had told her what he did.

He said he helped people explore their dreams. He claimed he could make her nightmares go away. She had made an appointment with him, an appointment for today at noon.

Lucy smoothed the top of the bedspread,

scanned the room. Perfect. But while the room was finished, she was not.

She walked to the closet, stepped inside, and closed the door. She sat down, took the blindfold out of her pocket, wrapped it around her eyes, and tied it at the back of her head.

The darkness drew silently around her, and she welcomed it.

It had been this way for nine years, ever since the ground trembled beneath her feet, the devil had taken her hand, and three days of her life had been stolen.

⋆ ⋆ ⋆

While Lucy Doucette sat in the closet, the ghosts of her past swirling around her, a man entered the hotel lobby, twelve floors below.

As with many who were on their way to Le Jardin this day, his interests ran to the morbid, the darker sides of human nature, the bleak and terrifying landscapes of the sociopathic mind. His specific interests were the kidnapping and murder of young girls, the mindset of the pedophile.

He would be renting Room 1208. The room had a history, a sinister fable with which the man was intimate.

Room 1208 was, of course, on the twelfth floor.

Lucinda Doucette's floor.

16

At just after ten o'clock Jessica and Byrne got a call from the Medical Examiner's office. The Kenneth Beckman autopsy had been scheduled for nine o'clock that morning, but Tom Weyrich's message said there was something he wanted the detectives to see before the doctor started the cut.

On the way to the ME's office Jessica made a call to the Department of Human Services. She was told that Carlos had slept through the night — for the first time in two weeks — and was up and playing. Jessica hung up, revisited by the feeling of paralysis, the feeling that, if she didn't make a move on this, Carlos would slip into the system. She had wanted to discuss adoption with Vincent but with the upcoming move on top of them and all the stress involved with that, she had not seen an opening.

Maybe she would bring it up tonight, she thought. Maybe she would soften Vincent up with a night of inebriated, lamp-smashing sex.

★ ★ ★

The Philadelphia Medical Examiner's Office was located on University Avenue. The purview of the office, among other things, was to investigate and determine the cause in all sudden, violent deaths in Philadelphia County, including homicides, suicides, accidents, and drug-related deaths.

In recent years, the MEO had investigated an average of six thousand cases of death annually, of which almost fifty percent required a post-mortem examination. Other functions of the MEO included positive identification, preparation of autopsy reports, and expert testimony in court, as well as grief assistance for family members.

While Jessica and Byrne waited in the intake room next to the autopsy theaters, they were ser-enaded by the constant zap of insects, courtesy of the large rectangular blue bug light on the wall. The continuous drone of bugs, mostly blowflies, being flash-fried was maddening.

Jessica checked the schedule on the wall. It included the autopsies performed the previous week. Tom Weyrich approached them.

'I don't get it, Tom,' Jessica said. 'There're twelve autopsies and only eleven names.'

'You don't want to know,' Weyrich said.

'See, now I *have* to know,' Jessica said. 'It's my naturally curious nature.'

Weyrich ran his hand over his chin. Jessica noticed that he had cut himself no fewer than four times while shaving that morning. 'You sure?'

'Dish it.'

'Okay, last week we get a call from Penn. It seems someone threw an internal organ onto the front steps of Tanenbaum Hall.'

The Nicole E. Tanenbaum Hall was on the campus of the University of Pennsylvania and contained, among other things, the Biddle Law Library.

'Somebody threw body parts?'

Weyrich nodded. 'What a world, huh?'

141

'What a *city*.'

'We still had to treat it like normal John Doe remains. We ran all our standard pathology tests, did a standard cut.'

'I still don't understand why there's no name on the sheet. Is it because you haven't been able to make an ID on the remains?' Jessica asked.

'Yes and no.'

'Tom.'

'It was a cow stomach.'

Jessica looked at Byrne. Byrne smiled, shook his head.

'One question,' Jessica said.

'Sure.'

'Is it still a John Doe, or is it now an Elsie Doe?'

'Laugh it up,' Weyrich said. 'This job put both my kids through Villanova.'

Jessica lifted both hands in surrender.

'I have something to show you,' Weyrich said.

He wheeled a body into the center of the intake room.

★   ★   ★

The body of Kenneth Arnold Beckman rested on the gleaming stainless steel table, face up, covered to just below the chest with a sheet.

Weyrich directed the overhead light to the victim's right hand. He slipped on a glove, gently pried back the fingers.

'I wanted you to see this,' he said.

There, on the pad of the right index finger, was a small drawing, measuring approximately

142

half an inch by one inch.

'What is that?' Jessica asked.

'It's a tattoo, believe it or not.'

'On his finger?'

'On his finger,' Weyrich said. 'When they cleaned him up to print him they found it.'

Jessica berated herself for not seeing it at the scene. She put on her glasses, looked closely. It looked like a highly stylized drawing of a lion. The colors were bright and primary, the outlines thick, the overall effect not unlike that of an illustration in a child's coloring book.

'I've read this guy's sheet,' Jessica said. 'He didn't strike me as the cartoon type.'

'It takes *all* types,' Weyrich said. 'I've taken a sample and sent it to the lab. They should be able to tell us the type of ink fairly soon.'

'You took a sample?' Jessica asked. 'A skin sample?'

'This is not a regular tattoo. It's a temporary tattoo.'

Jessica looked again. At this distance, and with skin art this size, she really couldn't tell the difference.

Weyrich handed her a large magnifying glass. Jessica looked again at the image of the lion. The ink, and its rich color, stood in bright contrast to the blood-leached pallor of the dead man's skin.

'It's not still wet, is it?'

'No,' Weyrich said. 'But it is new. I'd say it's been there less than seventy-two hours.'

When Jessica had been small, she used to go to a variety store in South Philly and buy little tattoos that she could apply simply by getting wet and pressing them on her skin. They usually washed off with one or two runs through the sprinkler, or a single dip in a pool.

'Does he have any other tattoos?'

'Surprisingly, no,' Weyrich said.

'Why do you think this is relevant?'

Weyrich directed Jessica to look with the magnifying glass at an area on the victim's left shoulder. Jessica repositioned the glass and saw a slight smudge there, a smear no more than a quarter-inch square or so in size. It was the same color as the yellow in the lion tattoo.

'I think this was done at the same time,' Weyrich said. 'I think the doer may have applied the tattoo, then made this smudge when he turned the body over.'

Jessica looked closely. There were no ridge marks. It was not a fingerprint, indicating that the killer might have worn gloves.

'Which brings us to the two other pieces of artwork on the body,' Weyrich said. He pulled down the sheet to reveal a section just above the rib cage on the right side. There were the two unmistakable marks left by a Taser, deep purple bruises looking like a vampire's bite.

'He was Tasered,' Jessica said.

Weyrich nodded. Jessica calculated the planning involved in this homicide. The cutting of the man's forehead, the measured puncture wound, the shaving of the entire body. It removed the crime from any heat of passion, certainly. This was cold, deliberate, calculated.

'What about the shaving?' Jessica asked.

'I think it was done pre-mortem, without

144

benefit of any emollient or shaving cream.' Weyrich pointed to a few areas where the skin was deeply abraded. 'I believe it was done quickly with a hair trimmer, as opposed to a rotary-style shaver, which means he had to press a little harder. Still, he didn't get it all.'

Jessica made notes. Byrne just listened. This was their usual routine at the ME's office.

Weyrich then moved the glass to the victim's forehead. He pointed to the lateral laceration at the top. In the brutal light it looked like a mortal wound, as though the killer had been attempting to take off the top of Kenneth Beckman's head.

'This was done with a straight razor or a scalpel,' he said. 'Our guy took care not to cut too deeply. There is some level of skill here. The cut on the right ear was not nearly so clean.'

Jessica looked at the victim's ear. It had congealed into a scabrous brown mass. 'Can we tell if the cutter is right-handed or left-handed?' she asked.

'Not from this wound, I'm afraid. If he is right-handed, he would most likely start at the left side and draw right. That would be the most natural movement. But only if he was straddling the body.' Weyrich leaned over the cadaver and mimicked the motion of drawing a blade over the victim's forehead from left to right. 'Now, if he was up here . . . ' Weyrich moved to the head of the table, putting the top of the victim's head near his waist. 'He could achieve the same result as a left-hander, drawing the blade right to left.'

'And this was done while the victim was still alive?' Byrne said.

'Yes.'

'How did he keep him still?'

'As well you might ask.' Weyrich pointed out four areas where there were small plum-colored bruises. On either side of the forehead, just above the temple, were contact marks in a circular shape, about a half-inch in diameter. There were also marks on either side of the lower jaw. 'His head was held in place at these four points.'

'With some kind of vice grip?' Byrne asked.

'A little more finesse than that, I believe. And a lot more expensive. I think it may have been a device similar to a surgical clamp. Whenever there is any cranial surgery performed, it is imperative, of course, that the patient be immobilized. Fortunately, we do not have that problem in *this* office. Our patients tend not to fidget much.'

'Do you think our boy has some medical training?'

'Could be.'

Jessica studied the bruises, thought about the horror of having one's head locked into a device. 'Where do you get an item like that?'

'It's pretty specialized. And expensive. I'll get you a list of medical suppliers.'

Jessica made a note to follow up.

'One other thing,' Weyrich said. He pointed at the puncture wound in the forehead. He handed back the magnifying glass to Jessica. She looked at the wound. 'What am I looking for?'

'See the area right around the puncture? The coloration?'

Under magnification the puncture did not look like such a clean wound, but rather twisted, shredded tissue, exploding outward like a tiny lava eruption. Jessica saw a small ring around the puncture that appeared to be red. An unnaturally *bright* shade of red. 'This is not dried blood, I take it.'

'No,' Weyrich said. 'That would be much darker. This was made with a Magic Marker of some sort. Maybe a felt-tip marker.'

Jessica looked up at Byrne, then back. 'A Magic Marker?'

Weyrich nodded.

'You're saying the killer marked the spot first?'

Weyrich nodded, politely smug in his findings. 'I've seen stranger things.'

'Why would he do something like that?'

Weyrich took the magnifying glass back, pulled the sheet over the body. 'That's above my pay grade, detective,' he said. 'You are the *chef de partie* here. I'm only the *commis*.'

* * *

When they stepped out of the MEO, David Albrecht was waiting for them. For any number of reasons he had not been allowed inside the morgue.

'What did I miss?' Albrecht asked.

'Bunch of dead people,' Byrne said. 'I yelled 'action,' but nobody moved.'

David Albrecht soon dialed into the fact that he wasn't going to get anything out of Kevin Byrne on this matter. He turned to Jessica.

147

'Where to?' he asked.

'We're going to grab some coffee,' Jessica said. 'You're welcome to join us.'

'Thanks.'

'You can get some shots of us looking at a menu, putting cream in coffee, fighting over the check,' Byrne said.

Albrecht laughed. 'Okay, okay. I'll just ramp up the suspense in post.'

Byrne smiled, winked at Jessica. It wasn't a thaw, but it was a start. Jessica knew that Byrne was not particularly keen on being followed around with a camera. Neither was she.

Albrecht left his van at the ME's office and traveled with the detectives. They drove down University Avenue.

'So, are you getting what you want?' Jessica asked.

'Pretty much,' Albrecht said. 'I was at the district attorney's office earlier this morning. I'm running two story lines at the same time. I'm shooting two of the DAs at work as well. I don't think it's ever been done before.'

'You mean following both police detectives and district attorneys?' Byrne asked.

'Exactly.'

'You mean like every episode of *Law and Order*?'

Albrecht went quiet.

'I'm sure you'll put your own stamp on it,' Jessica said, shooting Byrne a look.

★ ★ ★

148

They stopped at a coffee shop on Spruce Street. Albrecht, sitting two booths away, really did get footage of them looking at menus. On the second cup, he put down the camera and pulled up a chair to the booth.

'So we're not your only stars?' Byrne asked.

'No,' Albrecht said, smiling. 'I am painting a vast and varied canvas.'

'I've been meaning to ask you,' Byrne said. 'Did you shoot any footage of the crowd at the Federal Street scene?'

'Yeah,' Albrecht said. 'It came out good.'

'We'd like to take a look at it, if you don't mind. Maybe our bad guy showed up to gloat.'

'Right, right,' Albrecht said, nodding. 'I'll get that on a disk right away.'

'We'd appreciate it.'

The waitress came over with three cups of espresso. They weren't for the table. They were all for Albrecht. Jessica and Byrne exchanged a glance.

Albrecht saw the look, shrugged. 'Well, you know the old saying. *Sleep is a symptom of caffeine deprivation.*' He knocked back one of the small cups in a single gulp.

Byrne tapped the DV camera on the seat next to him. 'So tell me, how did you get into this?'

Albrecht stirred sugar into his second cup of espresso. 'Well, it was probably my dad. He used to take me to the movies a lot when I was a kid. He was big in the arts, you know. For some reason I gravitated to documentaries at a young age.'

'Do you remember the film you liked the most?'

'I think the movie that did it for me was called *In the Shadow of the Stars*.' He looked between Jessica and Byrne. 'Did either of you ever see it?'

Jessica had not. She told him so.

'That was the documentary on the choristers in the opera?' Byrne asked.

'Yes!' Albrecht said. He looked around. 'Sorry. That was loud, wasn't it?'

Byrne smiled. 'Not in this place.'

'Well, when I saw that — at the ripe old age of seven — I saw the possibilities of making movies about regular people. Nothing bores me more than celebrity. I never watch television.'

'That movie seems a little highbrow for a kid,' Byrne said.

Albrecht downed a second espresso, nodded. 'Like I said, my dad was big into the arts. I think we saw that film at a fundraiser. I was never the same afterwards. I was especially impressed with the music. The possibilities of sound editing in particular.'

Jessica suddenly made the connection. 'Wait a minute. Your father was Jonas Albrecht?'

'Yes.'

For more than twenty-five years Jonas Albrecht had been a force of nature in Philadelphia arts, business, and politics — one of the directors of the prestigious Pennsylvania Society. He was a wealthy man, having made his fortune in real estate. He founded a number of organizations, and was deeply involved with the Philadelphia Orchestra until he was tragically killed in a violent carjacking in 2003. Jessica had been on the force at the time, but it was before she had joined the homicide unit. She wasn't sure if the case had ever been closed.

'It was a terrible tragedy,' Byrne said. 'We're sorry for your loss.'

Albrecht nodded. 'Thank you.'

We are the sum of our experiences, Jessica thought. David Albrecht might not be doing what he was doing now if it had not been for the terrible tragedy that had befallen his father. It had taken Jessica a long time to realize that, if it were not for her own life's tragedies, among which was her brother Michael's death in Kuwait in 1991, her life might have taken another path. She had been headed to law school until that fateful day. It was Michael who had been going to follow in their father's footsteps and join the force. Life takes its turns.

While Byrne and David Albrecht talked documentary film — not one of Jessica's strong suits, she'd been halfway through *This is Spinal Tap* before she'd realized it was a spoof — she got on her iPhone, did a search for tattoo parlors in Philadelphia. She called a few of them and was told that they did not handle things like temporary tattoos. The last place she called, an emporium on South Street, mentioned a parlor that had recently opened on Chestnut, a place called Ephemera. The girl said they did temporary tattooing and had a good reputation.

★   ★   ★

Ephemera was on the second floor of a row house converted into retail space. The first floor was a retail shop selling Asian specialty foods.

While David Albrecht shot some exteriors of the building, Jessica and Byrne climbed the narrow stairwell, opened the frosted-glass door.

The front parlor was lit with dozens of candles. The walls were covered in tapestries of magenta and gold. There was no furniture, no stools, just pillows. It smelled of rich incense. There were no customers in the waiting area.

A few moments later a woman walked through the curtains and greeted them. She was Indian, elfin and delicate, about forty. She wore a turquoise silk *kurti* and black slacks. 'My name is Dalaja,' she said. 'How may I help you?'

Jessica took out her ID, showed it to the woman. She then introduced herself and Byrne.

'Is there something wrong?' Dalaja asked.

'No,' Jessica said. 'We just have a couple of questions, if you have a few moments.'

'Yes, of course.'

Dalaja gestured to the large pillows in front of the window overlooking Chestnut Street. Jessica and Byrne sat down. Well, *sat* was a loose term for Byrne's action. For a man his size, the best Byrne could do was aim himself at the pillow, then fall onto it.

'Would you like some tea?' the woman asked when they were settled.

'I'm fine, thanks,' Jessica said.

'Would a cup of Masala chai be too much trouble?' Byrne asked.

The woman smiled. 'Not at all. But it will take a few minutes.'

'No problem.'

Dalaja disappeared into the back room.

'Masala chai?' Jessica asked softly.

'What about it?'

'Do you have some sort of secret life I don't know about?'

'Well, if I told you it wouldn't be secret, would it?'

Jessica looked around the room. There were glass shelves on the far wall, each featuring a stack of brightly hued clothing. Another glass rack held carved artifacts and jewelry. The sound of modern Indian music floated softly from behind the curtain.

The woman soon emerged from the back room, sat on a large pillow opposite them. She was so light that she barely made an impression on the pillow. It was as if she floated above it. 'The tea will be ready shortly.'

'Thanks,' Byrne said.

'First, if you don't mind, can you tell me what you do here?' Jessica asked.

'This is a Mehndi parlor.'

'Could you spell that for me?' Jessica asked.

Dalaja did, giving her a few alternate spellings. Jessica wrote it all down. 'I'm not sure I know what that means.'

'Mehndi is a type of skin decoration practiced throughout South Asia, Southeast Asia, North Africa, the Horn of Africa.'

'These are temporary tattoos?'

'Technically no. Tattoos, by definition, are permanent, applied under the skin. Mehndi is temporary, and rests atop the skin.'

'What is it made out of?'

'Mehndi is applied with henna. It is mostly drawn on the palms of the hands and the feet, where the levels of keratin in the skin are highest.'

'And how long does it last?'

'Anywhere from a few days to a few months, depending on the henna paste and where the decoration is placed on the body.'

A young Indian woman came out of the back with a cup of tea on an ornate black lacquered tray. She was about nineteen, and wore traditional South Asian clothing. She was stunningly beautiful. Jessica went back to her notes, but, after a few seconds, noticed that the girl was still standing in front of them. Jesssica glanced at Byrne. He was looking at the girl with his mouth open, not moving, not speaking. She was that beautiful.

'Kevin.'

'Right,' he said finally, closing his mouth and taking the cup and saucer. 'Thank you.'

The girl smiled and, without a word, withdrew to the back room.

When she was gone, their hostess reached onto a nearby table and picked up a beautifully bound leather notebook. She handed the book to Jessica, who riffled the pages. The designs were intricate and skillfully drawn. Page after page of complex artwork in a rainbow of colors, drawn mostly on hands and feet.

'I'm afraid what we're inquiring about is a little different,' Jessica said. 'A little less . . . ornate.'

'I see.'

Jessica then caught the aroma of the tea — ginger and honey — and wished she had taken the woman up on her offer.

'May I show you a photograph?' Jessica asked.

'By all means.'

Jessica pulled out her iPhone, enlarged the photograph of the lion tattoo on Kenneth Beckman's finger.

'Oh, I see,' the woman said. 'This *is* different.'

'Do you know what it is?'

Dalaja nodded. 'This is very small, is it not?'

'Yes,' Jessica said. 'Maybe one inch long.'

'It appears to be a style of temporary body art called a transfer. Relatively inexpensive. And the quality, well . . . '

It was true. By comparison with the photographs in the leather-bound notebook the lion tattoo looked like it had been drawn with a crayon.

'I take it you do not offer this service or sell items like this,' Jessica said.

'We do not. But I believe I can point you in the right direction.'

'That would be great.'

'If you will excuse me for a moment.'

The woman rose, seemingly without effort. She stepped into the back room. She returned a few minutes later with pages from a color printer.

'I believe this is what you are looking for.'

She handed a page to Jessica. On it was an exact replica of the lion transfer tattoo.

'Wow,' Jessica said. 'That's it.'

Dalaja handed her a second sheet. 'At the top

is the website from which I downloaded the image. There are ten others here on the page, but the first company, called World Ink, is the largest. I did not find that exact image on any of the others, but that is not to say it is not sold elsewhere.'

Jessica and Byrne got to their feet.

'The chai was delicious,' Byrne said. 'Thanks very much.'

'You are most welcome,' the woman replied. 'Is there anything else I can do for you?'

'I believe that is it for now,' Jessica said.

'Then, for now, *alvida*.' She spun on her heels and walked toward the back room without making a sound.

*   *   *

Back at the Roundhouse, Jessica got on the Internet and visited World Ink. In addition to transfer tattoos, the company sold a lot of specialty items, such as pocket calendars, paint sheets, and customized scratch-and-win cards.

But it was the stock tattoos in which Jessica was interested. And they had hundreds, maybe thousands of designs. Angels, cars, flags, flowers, sports, holiday-themed, myth and fairy-tale, as well as religious and tribal symbols.

Six pages deep into the online catalog she found the lion design. It was in a collection called TinyToos, and was a perfect match. She took out her cellphone, clicked over to the photograph of Kenneth Beckman's body. There could be no doubt. Unless the victim had put

156

this tattoo on himself — and Jessica had a problem seeing Beckman doing this, it seemed inconsistent with his personality — someone had done it for him. Quite possibly the person who'd strangled and mutilated him.

Byrne already had three calls in to Sharon Beckman to ask if her husband had a tattoo on his finger.

Jessica got on the phone to World Ink, and after a few minutes of *press one, press five, press two*, she pressed *0* until a human being picked up the phone. She identified herself and in short order was passed over to the website-catalog sales manager.

Jessica explained the bare minimum. After a little hemming and hawing, the man told her that they would be happy to help, but he was going to have to get clearance and they would need some kind of request on paper. Jessica asked the man if a fax on a PPD letterhead would suffice, and he said it would. Jessica scratched a few more notes, hung up the phone. She caught Byrne's attention, gave him the highlights. She held up the photo of the lion tattoo.

'This design is exclusive to this company,' she said. 'It's an original design. That's not to say that our guy bought it from them, or didn't duplicate it himself — the guy at World Ink said it was fairly easy to do with a scanner, PhotoShop, and the right supplies — but considering the way these tattoos are applied, I think it's a safe bet that Kenneth Beckman did not apply the tattoo himself. Even if it has nothing to do with the case, we can be pretty sure someone did it for him.'

'Like, for instance, our bad boy.'

'Could be. Now, if it *was* him, he might have placed an order online with this company. I'm going to fax them a request for a customer list, people who purchased this tattoo.'

'Do you think we'll need the DA's office on this?' Byrne asked.

'Maybe.'

'Let me call Mike Drummond and give him a heads-up.'

While Byrne made the call, Jessica printed off the tattoo of the lion. She heard laughter coming down the hall. She looked up to see Nicci Malone — a love-struck, schoolgirl-in-distress Nicci Malone — enter the duty room with Detective Russell Diaz.

Russell Diaz was the head of a newly formed tactical squad, part of the PPD's Special Investigations Unit, a job originally offered to Kevin Byrne, who had turned it down. The tactical unit was a sort of rapid-response team for high-profile cases involving special circumstances. Diaz had spent ten years with the FBI's Philadelphia field office, but had been traveling too much, he said, and joined the PPD to stay closer to his family. While in the FBI he had worked with Behavioral Science and had consulted with the homicide unit a number of times in the past few years.

Beyond that, Russell Diaz was a specimen. About six feet tall, cut from stone, close-cropped brunette hair, dreamy eyes. He was given to wearing those tight navy blue PPD T-shirts that showed off his biceps. Oddly enough, he seemed not to notice his impact on members of both the same and opposite sexes, along with everything in between. This made him even more appealing.

Tomorrow was his first tour in the new unit.

Diaz noticed Jessica, crossed the room, smiled. 'Hello, detective. Been a while.'

'Too long,' Jessica said. They shook hands. Jessica had worked with Diaz on a joint task force when she'd been in the auto-theft unit. They had taken down an international ring, a gang shipping high-end cars to South America. 'Glad to have you on the team. How is Marta?'

Marta was Diaz's daughter. To Jessica's understanding she was some sort of musical prodigy. The fact that Diaz, long divorced, was raising her alone vaulted him from appealing to unbelievably adorable.

'She's great, thanks. Fourteen going on thirty.'

Jessica glanced down at the stack of papers and books in Diaz's grasp.

'What is this?' Jessica pointed at the book. Diaz handed it to her. It was a copy of *Dante's Inferno*.

'Just a little light reading,' Diaz said, with a smile.

Jessica thumbed through the book. It was anything but light reading. 'You read Italian?'

'Working on it. Marta is going to do her sophomore year in Italy, and I want to be able to sound hip to her friends.'

'Impressive.'

'*Che c'è di nuovo?*' Diaz asked.

159

Jessica smiled. '*Non molto.*'

As far as she could tell, Diaz had asked her what was new and she'd told him 'not much.' Outside of swear words, that was about the extent of Jessica's Italian.

Byrne walked into the duty room. Jessica gestured him over. She introduced the two men.

'Kevin Byrne, Russell Diaz,' she said.

'Good to meet you,' Diaz said. 'I've heard a lot about you.'

'Likewise.'

They batted shoptalk around for a while until Diaz glanced at his watch. 'I'm due back at Arch Street to wrap a few things.' The Philadelphia FBI field office was at 6000 Arch. Diaz gathered his things, including the copy of *Dante's Inferno*. He put it all in his duffel, slung it over his broad shoulder. 'Drinks later?'

Standing behind Diaz, Nicci Malone nodded like a bobble-head doll.

★ ★ ★

Jessica and Byrne spent the next hour typing up the witness statements collected from the Federal Street scene, which amounted to little more than *I don't know anything, I didn't hear anything, I didn't see anything.*

'I think you should stay on that tattoo company,' Byrne said. 'I'll see if I can red-light the lab on the brand of paper used to gift-wrap Beckman's head.'

'Sounds like a plan,' Jessica said.

In the background the duty-room phone rang.

160

Out of habit, Jessica and Byrne both looked at the assignment desk, which was positioned more or less in the middle of the cluttered room. Nick Palladino was up on the wheel. They saw him reach into the desk for a notification form, which could only mean one thing.

The homicide unit was contacted every time there was a suspicious death. Some turned out to be accidents, some turned out to be suicides. But every time a non-hospital, non-hospice death occurred, anywhere in the county of Philadelphia, only one phone rang.

Jessica and Byrne turned their attention back to the case, to each other. Or tried to.

A few minutes later, out of the corner of her eye, Jessica noticed someone crossing the duty room. It was Nick Palladino. He was heading straight for Jessica and Byrne, a dour look on his face. For the most part, Dino was a pretty affable guy, even-tempered, at least for a South Philly Italian. Except when he was on a job. Then he was all business.

This was one of those times.

'Please don't tell me we have another body on this case,' Jessica said. 'We don't have another body on this case, do we, Dino?'

'No,' Nick Palladino said, slipping on his coat. 'We don't.' He grabbed a set of keys off the rack, along with a two-way handset. 'We have two.'

17

Lucy Doucette made the six blocks in just under four minutes. It might have been a record. On the way she outpaced two SEPTA buses and just barely dodged an SUV that ran the light on Eighteenth Street. She'd been dodging traffic since she was three. It didn't slow her down a bit.

★ ★ ★

The address was a three-story brick building off Cherry Street. A small plaque next to the door identified it as Tillman Towers. It was hardly a tower. A rusted air conditioner hung precariously overhead; the steps leading up to the door looked to be leaning at a ten-degree angle to the right. She looked at the bottom of the plaque. It said *ENTRANCE TO 106 AROUND BACK*. She walked down an alley, turned the corner and saw a small door, painted red. On it was a symbol that matched the symbol on the card, a highly stylized golden key.

She looked for a buzzer or doorbell and, seeing none, pushed on the door. It opened. Ahead was a long dimly lit hallway.

Lucy started down the corridor, surrounded by the smells of old buildings — bacon fat, wet dog, fruity room deodorizers, with top notes of soiled diaper. She had long ago developed a keen sense of smell — it was something that really helped in her business: sometimes some really funky things lurked in the craziest places in hotel rooms, and being able to root them out and dispose of them, by any means necessary, was a real plus.

When she got to number 106 at the end of the hallway the door was slightly ajar. She knocked on the door jamb and, out of long-ingrained habit, almost called out 'Housekeeping.' She stopped herself at the last second.

She knocked again. 'Hello?'

No response.

She took a deep breath and stepped into the room.

The space was small and cramped, with stacks of old leather-bound books in the corners reaching nearly to the ceiling. In the center were two upholstered chairs of differing style and vintage. In here she tasted long-boiled coffee on the back of her tongue.

'Hello.' The voice came from behind her.

Lucy spun around, her heart leaping. Behind her stood a compact man somewhere in his forties or fifties. He was of average height, but lean and wiry. His white shirt, which had yellowed around the collar and cuffs, appeared to be a few sizes too large. His navy blue suit coat was shiny and worn, his shoes dusty. But what struck Lucy most were his eyes. He had the dark, shiny eyes of a fierce terrier.

'Hello,' she replied, the word coming out squeaky. She hated it when her voice did this. 'I'm Lucy Doucette.'

'I know.'

In contrast to her own, his voice was soft and assured. Lucy had the feeling that he had never shouted in his life.

He took her hand in his but didn't shake it, not like an ordinary handshake. Instead, he just held it for a moment, not taking his eyes from hers. For a moment the rest of the room dissolved away, like something glimpsed through a shower curtain. His lack of physical size belied this powerful touch.

He let go of her hand, eased his own hands back down to his sides.

'What should I call you?' Lucy asked as everything now shimmered back into focus.

The man smiled a thin smile, a light that didn't fully reach his eyes. 'My name is Adrian Costa,' he said. 'You may call me Adrian or Mr. Costa, whichever makes you more comfortable.'

He gestured to the large upholstered avocado chair. Lucy saw the dust on the arms. She wanted to vacuum it.

'I'm of a mind to call you *Mr. Costa* for now,' she said. 'If that's okay.'

'As you wish.'

Lucy sat down. The chair was a lot more comfortable than it looked. It looked a little spring-busted, if the truth were to be told. Lucy had grown up with third-hand furniture, living in drafty rental houses and second-floor apartments situated above everything from bowling alleys to taverns to Chinese restaurants, places where none of the furniture matched, where nothing ever sat level on the floor. Lucy never knew whether it was the floors that were out of whack or that the tables and chairs were short-legged, but she recalled always having to put a matchbook or two under the table legs so her pencils didn't roll off when she was doing her homework. She also remembered many nights when she and her mother would walk the streets of her hometown on the night before trash day, looking for usable items with which her mother could furnish their house, or try to turn around and sell or trade for drugs. They used to call it shopping at Lawn Mart.

'What do you know about hypnotism?' Mr. Costa asked.

Lucy didn't have to think too long about this one. She didn't know much, just the things she'd seen in spooky movies, or the comedies where people got hypnotized and walked around like chickens. Lucy truly hoped she wasn't going to walk around like a chicken. She told Mr. Costa just that.

'Don't worry,' Mr. Costa said. He steepled his fingers. Lucy noticed that there were indentations on six of his fingers, as though he had recently taken off six rings. 'What I do is give you the skills you need to achieve your goal,' he added. 'Do you have a goal, Lucy Doucette? A purpose in coming to see me?'

If you only knew, mister. She tried to answer with a calm, measured response. 'Oh yes.'

'Good. Here we focus on subconscious behaviors and see how they influence your conscious life. The methods I use are tried and true. They go back to Victorian times.'

165

'So, the acting-like-a-chicken business is definitely out?'

Mr. Costa nodded. 'The stage hypnotist wants to give the impression that the subject is out of control,' he said. 'What I do is just the opposite. I want to give you *back* control. Control of your life. The way I do that is to help you to relax as deeply as possible so you can enter a suggestible state, a state where your memories — things you may have forgotten — can be recalled with ease, and therefore be understood and dealt with.'

'Okay,' Lucy said. She hoped she sounded more confident than she felt. 'But there is something I need to know before we go any further. If that's okay.'

'Of course.'

'How much is all this going to cost?'

There. She'd just blurted it out. By the time she was five or six years old she had already learned to shop at the grocery store and drug store, to talk to the people from the phone and electric companies, usually wielding her little-girl charms to forestall a shut-off of services.

Mr. Costa smiled his nick of a smile again. 'You won't owe me anything for now. Let's see where the road takes us. Then we'll talk about the toll.'

Lucy was more than a little surprised. 'Well, Mr. Costa, I appreciate this, I truly do. But I'm a girl who doesn't like surprises. Never have. I'd hate to get to the end of all this and find that I owe you thousands and thousands of dollars or something. It wouldn't be fair to either of us. I couldn't pay you and you'd be really mad.'

Another pause. 'Firstly, I never get angry. I've never found it to be productive. Have you?'

The truth was, she never *had* found it to be productive. Of course, that had never stopped her. 'No. I suppose not.'

'Secondly, when we have completed our third and last session, if you find then that you are satisfied with my services, that you have received true value, I want you to pay me whatever you feel is right.' He gestured to the room around them. 'As you can see, I live a modest existence.'

Lucy looked closely at the walls for the first time, at the cobwebs near the ceiling, at the thin layer of dust everywhere, at the crosshatched lines in the plaster. Once again, her desire to start cleaning was nearly physical. Then she looked closely at the photographs mounted haphazardly on the walls, dozens and dozens of them, many in chipped enamel frames, some staggered behind cracked and spider-webbed glass. They all seemed to be snapshots of similar subjects — travel-type pictures of pavilions and gazebos and gingerbread exhibition halls, places that appeared to be small-town centers, ringed by vendors with brightly colored carts, public benches sporting ads for local concerns. One frame featured a band shell in the shape of a large pumpkin. Another showed what might have been a Civil War re-enactment in progress. A number of the photographs were pictures of a younger Mr. Costa, holding a violin.

'Have you been to all these places?' Lucy asked.

'I have indeed.'

167

Mr. Costa crossed the room to the far wall, the wall opposite the window. There was a velvet curtain there that took up most of the width of the room. He reached behind the right side of the curtain, took hold of a frayed golden rope and pulled it gently.

Behind the curtain was a large booth, perhaps six feet wide and just as tall. It had no window, like a typical booth you might see at a carnival or in front of a theater, but rather a single door crudely cut into the front, a door with a red crystal doorknob. Above the door was a carved scroll, painted to resemble a dark purple sky with billowy clouds. Peering out from behind one of the clouds was a silvery autumn moon, with just the hint of glitter. Down each side of the booth, next to the doorway, were the words *The Dreamweaver*. Across the door, over what looked to be a round portal which showed only darkness, was another legend, this one in a gilded script:

What do you dream?

'That's pretty cool,' Lucy said. And it was true. Lucy Doucette was a small-town girl, one who'd grown up terribly poor. Her entertainment, when her mother was sober enough to take her places, and many times when she was not, had been small-town entertainment — county fairs, local home days, carnivals, parades, festivals, sometimes even wakes if they were held in the park. If there was no cover charge, and it was bright, loud, and festive, Lucy's mother would park her daughter on a bench, returning every so often a little drunker, or a little more stoned, with a corn dog, elephant ear, or funnel cake in

168

her hand. Many times these treats were cold, half-eaten, and it wasn't until years later that Lucy figured out that these were probably items of discarded food. Somehow that knowledge did not make them taste bad, even in retrospect. When you're four years old, cotton candy, even someone else's cotton candy, was the best thing in the world.

Mr. Costa closed the curtain, crossed the room, sat down across from Lucy. 'Shall we begin?'

'Sure,' Lucy said. She took a deep breath, tried to relax her shoulders. It wasn't easy. There was a tension that had settled upon her when she was small and, although there were days when she felt it was easing, it had never gone away completely. She looked up at the Dreamweaver, at his bright little-dog eyes. 'Let's begin.'

'Today, in our first session, we are going to go back to a specific time in your life. The time you can't seem to remember. Okay?'

Lucy felt her hands begin to shake. She knit them together in her lap. 'Okay.'

'But you are not going to re-experience this event. There is no need to be concerned with that. Instead, it will be more like you are observing it.'

'Observing? Like, watching it?'

'Yes,' Mr. Costa said. 'Exactly. Like watching it from above.'

'Like I'm flying?'

'Like you're flying.'

'Very cool,' she said. 'What do I do?'

'You needn't do anything except close your eyes and listen to the sound of my voice.'

* ★ *

'You know, I have to tell you something,' Lucy began. 'In fact, I was going to tell you this when I first walked in.'

'What is that?'

'I don't really think I'm the kind of person who can be hypnotized.'

'Why do you say that?'

Lucy shrugged. 'I don't know. I think I'm too intense, you know? I hardly ever sleep, I'm always nervous. Do other people ever say that?'

'Of course.'

'I'm sure that there are some people who just can't seem to — '

Mr. Costa held up a finger, stopping her. The finger had a ring on it. In fact, all of his rings seemed to be back. All six of them.

When had he done that?

'I hate to interrupt you, but I'm afraid our session is complete for today.'

Lucy wasn't sure she understood. 'What are you saying? Are you saying — '

'Yes.'

Lucy took a few moments, letting the news sink in. She had actually been hypnotized for a while.

She stood up, grabbed her purse, walked toward the door, feeling a little dizzy. She held onto the doorjamb to steady herself. Suddenly Mr. Costa was next to her again. He was light on his feet.

'Are you all right?' he asked.

'Yes,' Lucy said. 'Kinda.'

Mr. Costa nodded. 'Shall we say tomorrow,

170

then? Just at midday?'

'Sure,' Lucy said, suddenly realizing she felt pretty good after all. As in *really* good. Like she'd taken a brief nap.

'I believe you made some progress today,' Mr. Costa said.

Pipe smoke.

'I did?'

'Yes,' he replied. He took off his bifocals, slipped them into an inside pocket of his suit coat. 'I don't believe it was anything like a breakthrough — that may never happen, I'm afraid — but you may have opened a door. Just the slightest bit.'

Pipe smoke and apples.

'A door?' Lucy asked.

'A door to your subconscious. A portal to what happened to you nine years ago.'

Had she told him it was nine years? She didn't remember doing that.

Mr. Costa put his hand on the doorknob. 'One last thing for today,' he said. 'Does the hotel in which you work have notepads in the rooms?'

'Notepads?'

'Notepads with the hotel logo. For the guests.'

'Yes,' Lucy said. She'd only placed a million of these pads — two inches from the left edge of the desk, pen at a forty-five-degree angle across the center.

'Excellent. Please bring one of these pads with you next time,' Mr. Costa said. 'Can you do that?'

'Sure,' Lucy said. 'I'll bring one.'

Mr. Costa opened the door. 'Until tomorrow, my dear Lucinda.'

On the way through the door Lucy glanced at the small picture on the wall next to the casing, just above the grimy light switch. She only saw it for a fleeting moment but that was long enough to see that it was a photograph of another gazebo, this one a rather dilapidated pergola overgrown with ivy. It was only after she'd stepped through the doorway and the door had closed behind her that she realized she knew the house in the background of that photograph, the wreck of a bungalow with its slanted porch and rusted gutters and broken brick walk.

It was the house she had grown up in.

18

It is said of Mozart that he could never sit still for his barber running instead to his clavier every time he had an idea, forcing the man tasked with tonsorial duties to chase after him, ribbons in hand.

I understand. Sometimes, when the music of the dead is loud, I cannot sit still, I must go out and begin the hunt anew.

For now I watch and wait, idling, my killing instruments at the ready.

I survey the ground before me. The cemetery looks so different in the daytime. No glowering ghouls, no hovering apparitions. Just the dead. Just a chorus of plaintive voices asking for justice, for answers, for truth.

I watch the people scramble callously about, the decaying dead underfoot, souls trampled beneath the weight of duty. We all know why we are here.

There. From the other side.

Can you hear it?

It is the rooster, a fresh voice in the choir.

The carnivale has come to town.

19

Mount Olive was an old cemetery in West Philadelphia, the final resting place of hundreds of Civil War dead as well as of some of Philadelphia's most famous and infamous citizens.

As with other areas of the City of Brotherly Love, including the design and layout of Benjamin Franklin Parkway with its similarity to the Champs Elysées, the concept of the pastoral graveyard was based on a Parisian model.

Framed on three sides by residential neighborhoods, Mount Olive was bordered to the northwest by Fairmount Park. Incorporated in the mid-1800s, it was a non-sectarian graveyard that at one time had been nearly four hundred acres in area. It was established at a time when older, smaller urban graveyards, located in city blocks and alongside churches, had stood in the way of Philadelphia's booming development, and over the course of many years a number of the interred had been moved to Mount Olive. But even though the cemetery was a National Historic Landmark and on the Philadelphia Register of Historic Places, over the years it had become the victim of vandalism, dumping, and theft. And now, with many of the families of the dead having moved away, some areas of the graveyard had fallen into a state of disrepair.

Jessica and Byrne stood on Kingsessing Avenue. Two sector cars were already on the

174

scene, as well as a departmental sedan and a van from the Crime Scene Unit.

A second team had already been dispatched to the other crime scene. The location of the second body was a parking lot in Northern Liberties. Nicci Malone would be the lead investigator on that case. Jessica and Byrne would be briefed by phone by Dana Westbrook.

David Albrecht appeared from behind a grove of trees at the northern end of the graveyard. He shouldered his camera, took shots of the mausoleum, the grounds, the arriving personnel. After a few minutes he approached Jessica and Byrne.

'I should have asked about this before,' he said. 'Is it okay to shoot here?'

'I don't see why not,' Jessica said. 'As long as you hang back until CSU has done its job.'

'I don't want to disrespect the dead.'

'I think it's okay.'

Albrecht looked out over the grounds. He pointed to a small monument. It was a single headstone, carved in Georgia gray granite. 'That's my father's grave,' he said. He shrugged, perhaps a bit apologetically. 'I haven't been here in a while. I guess I should probably pay a visit.'

The three of them fell silent for a moment. Finally Byrne broke the calm. 'We're going to be here for a while, David. Take your time.'

'Okay,' Albrecht said. 'Thanks.'

He put the camera at his side, traversed the grounds, stopped at the monument. He crossed himself, bowed his head.

Jessica scanned the area. On the corner,

175

talking to a man Jessica assumed worked for the cemetery, was Josh Bontrager. When the other man left, Bontrager noticed Jessica and Byrne, waved them over.

'What do you have?' Byrne asked.

'Female DOA,' Bontrager said, pointing over his shoulder. Jessica could see a sheet-covered form about twenty yards away. Next to the body stood a CSU officer. Because the potential crime scene was so large, a wide area had been taped off around the body, the sheet that covered it secured with stakes driven into the ground.

'Do we know how long the body has been here?' Byrne asked.

'Not too long.' Bontrager took out his notepad. 'There's a service here later today, and the guy who does the digging found the body about six this morning. He said he was here late yesterday afternoon and he went by the plot, didn't see anything. So the dump occurred sometime between four yesterday afternoon and six this morning.'

Byrne looked at the fences. 'How secure is this place?'

'Not very secure at all,' Bontrager said. He gestured toward the area bordering the two main streets. 'I walked two sides of it when I got here. Lots of places where you can get in and not be seen. Lots of tree cover.'

'Did the man who works here move or touch anything?'

'He says no. As you might imagine, he's not particularly disturbed by the sight of dead bodies. But a homicide victim is another story.

176

He said he saw the body, lit a cigarette, hit the flask of tequila he's not supposed to have, and called his boss.'

'Did he leave the area after the call?'

'Again, he says no. I'm inclined to believe him.'

'Is the body near a plot?' Jessica asked.

'Right on top of one,' Bontrager said.

'Any ID on the victim?'

'No,' Bontrager said. 'Not yet, anyway. I haven't done a full search of the area.'

Byrne took another look around. 'Is this our bad guy, Josh?'

'Oh yeah. This is our bad guy,' Bontrager replied. 'No doubt about it.'

'All right,' Byrne said. 'Let's go look at a dead body in a cemetery.'

The three of them walked onto the grounds, down a narrow weed-grown path between headstones that dated from the mid-1800s. Every tenth site or so had been tended to some degree, with the grass trimmed around the stone, plastic flowers placed. Most of the grave sites were criminally unkempt.

When they reached the top of the rise Jessica glanced over her shoulder. The place was beginning to teem. She noticed that there were now a half-dozen more people, including representatives from the DA's office. The fact that the DA had a presence let the detectives know what priority these killings were being given.

* * *

The three detectives gathered around the site. Josh Bontrager looked at Jessica, then at Byrne. He crouched down next to the body. Jessica nodded. Bontrager drew back the sheet.

'Ah, Christ,' Byrne said. He spoke for everyone.

As with the previous victim, the middle-aged female's body was nude, shaved clean of all hair, as was her head. Jessica immediately noticed the bruises around her ankles. She had been shackled.

Wrapped around the victim's head was a white paper band, identical to the one that they had found wrapped around Kenneth Beckman's head. There was a red wax seal. Also identical were the blood patterns. One lateral slash to the forehead. Beneath it and to the left was another splotch, in a circular pattern. The area near the right ear was marked with blood in a figure eight.

If these were the similarities to the condition in which Kenneth Beckman had been found, there was a difference. This victim was lying on her side, behind the grave marker. One foot was resting on top of the marker. The other leg, the left leg, was bent completely back at an impossible angle. Jessica saw the bone protruding from the victim's thigh.

'ME's been here?' Byrne asked.

'Not yet.'

'Pictures taken?'

Bontrager nodded, pointed to the CSU officer who was leaning against a nearby tree and smoking a cigarette. 'Video, too.'

Jessica looked at the headstone. The victim's right leg extended toward the grave marker, which was half covered in debris and dead grass. The foot rested directly over the center.

'Kevin. Give me a hand here.'

Both detectives snapped on latex gloves. They knelt on either side of the body and gently lifted the victim's right leg, moving it just a few inches, being careful not to disturb any of the area next to the grave. They lowered the victim's leg gently. Jessica looked at the grave marker. It was not nearly as old as the ones that surrounded it, looking as though it had been positioned no more than a few years earlier. A shift in the ground had lowered it a few inches so that the marker's engraving was now covered in dirt.

Byrne motioned to the CSU officer standing nearby, who tossed away his cigarette, walked over and took a number of additional pictures. When he was finished, Byrne took out a pocket knife and began to scrape away the mud. The first thing to be revealed was a carving, one with which Jessica was not familiar. It did not appear to be a Catholic or Christian symbol — praying hands, an angel, a crucifix. As they cleared away more dirt, Jessica thought the symbol was beginning to look like a flower, a red flower with narrow petals.

Byrne brushed away the last of the mud and revealed that it wasn't a flower at all but rather a Chinese character. Beneath it, running vertically, were three other characters, all red.

A few minutes later they had the bottom of the headstone cleared of dirt, and saw what they were looking for. The person interred in this space had died on March 21, 2002.

Her name was Antoinette Chan.

Jessica looked at Byrne, a bolt of electricity passing between them.

Across town, a man had been found murdered, his head wrapped in a band of white paper. A man named Kenneth Beckman. Here in West Philadelphia, a second body is found, its head too wrapped in white paper. This victim, still unidentified, is found on the grave of a young woman who was also murdered.

Murdered, it is believed, by Kenneth Beckman.

'Let's check her hands,' Byrne said.

Byrne lifted the victim's right hand, checked it. Nothing. He circled the body, gently lifted her left hand. There, on the index finger, was a small tattoo. Instead of a lion, this time it was a rooster.

Jessica took a few photographs, her heart starting to race. She glanced over at Byrne. He wore an expression she had come to know well over the years, one that barely contained a cold rage.

Byrne squatted next to the body and began to undo the paper that wrapped the victim's head.

'Kevin, the ME's office is on the way,' Jessica said. 'You should wait.'

'Yeah, well, I should be living in Cazumel with the Corr sisters, too,' Byrne said. 'I don't see either of these things happening.'

Byrne gently unwrapped the victim's head, carefully removing the wax seal first and dropping it into a small evidence bag. The first thing that Jessica noticed when the paper was removed was that the laceration across the forehead, and the puncture wound, were in almost the same places as they'd been with the first victim.

The second thing Jessica noticed was that the dead woman was Sharon Beckman.

20

The feelings coursed through Byrne, sensations that grew exponentially. He paced like an animal.

He stepped behind a tree as the feeling surged, filling his head like an onrush of water from a broken dam. It was followed by a moment of vertigo. He steadied himself, tried to wait it out, trying not to notice as . . .

. . . *the man walks across the cemetery in darkness . . . he is strong . . . the dead weight of Sharon Beckman's body is nothing to him . . . he does not search for the grave site, he knows where it is. He is familiar with this cemetery, all cemeteries. He places her on the ground, steels himself. He is not quite finished. He leaps into the air, and bears down with great force, breaking the dead woman's leg, positioning it back because it means something to him and . . .*

Byrne opened his eyes, got his bearings. He had forgotten where he was, what he was doing.

This was getting bad.

★ ★ ★

The crime scene swarmed with people. Byrne glanced at his watch. It had only been ten seconds. It felt like an hour.

He walked back to the grave site. Information had trickled in about the second body. This had been found in a Dumpster behind a building at Second and Poplar. According to the initial report the victim, a middle-aged male, had been found nude, his forehead wrapped in white paper, his body clean of all hair.

Three bodies in two days. This case was about to break wide open. Wall-to-wall TV and print news, perhaps even national attention. There was a ghoul on the streets of Philadelphia, a monster who was strangling people, shaving their bodies and marking their flesh. When they had found Kenneth Beckman's body they had all hoped that it was an isolated incident, that it was some sort of personal vendetta. It was not. It was bigger than that. There were now three corpses, and everyone had the nasty feeling that there would be more.

Byrne approached Jessica. 'I have that MRI. I have to go.'

'We've got this covered,' Jessica said. 'Don't worry.'

Byrne did not want to leave. The first two hours were the most critical time of a homicide investigation. After that, memories faded, people thought better of getting involved, forensic evidence had a way of giving itself back to nature. Although neither he nor Jessica were the lead investigator on this case, every warm body was critical.

'Kevin,' Jessica said. 'Go to your appointment.'

'I want to stop by the other scene first. This is out of control.'

'I'll go,' Jessica said. 'You don't have to — '

But Byrne was already on his way. He held his

cellphone up as he walked back to the car. 'Call me,' he said.

Leaving the cemetery, Byrne saw the names of the dead carved in time-weathered stone, dates marking fleeting lives, parentheses of birth and death. Out of respect, out of the disquieting knowledge that one day someone would be walking on his final resting place, he did his best to avoid stepping on the graves.

21

At first it is a muffled sound, like that of a wounded animal. I hear it the moment I step inside the room. It soon becomes crystal clear.

I will not be here long. I have much to do. I may be a poor cartwright, but my marchioness awaits.

⋆ ⋆ ⋆

I am not alone in this room. There are others here. We are all part of something, fractions of a whole. They talk to me, to each other, but I don't hear them. I hear what happened here years ago.

I stand in the corner, close my eyes. The scene unfolds, like a stage play viewed through frosted glass, two figures forever mired in a dark and terrible vignette.

⋆ ⋆ ⋆

She is a shy girl, no more than eleven. She has long blonde hair, woven into a braid.

'Who are you? Are you a friend of my mom's?'

'Yes. We are old friends.'

'You shouldn't be here.'

'It's okay. I like your dress. It is very pretty.'

'Thank you.'

'I have a prettier dress. One made especially for you.'

'For me?'

'Oh yes. It is your favorite color.'

'Blue?'

'A very pretty blue.'

'Can I see it?'

'In time.'

'Where do you know my mom from?'

'We work together.'

'My mom doesn't work anymore.'

'This was from before. From a long time ago.'

'Okay.'

'Do you know the story of Eve?'

'Eve?'

'Yes. Eve in the Garden of Eden. Eve who was tempted by an apple.'

The blade removed from its sheath the creak of worn leather the sound of a little heart beating in fear —

'I don't want you here anymore.'

'I won't hurt you.'

'I want you to leave, mister.'

'Don't you want your pretty new dress?'

'No.'

The blade shimmers in the bright afternoon sunlight —

'I'm going to get my sister. I want you to leave now.'

The blade flutters and darts soaring high into the air —

'Eve.'

★   ★   ★

The neighbors say they heard one scream that day, an unearthly wail that cooled the blood in their veins.

I hear it, too.

It is a sound that began a thousand millennia ago, a red wind that has blown through the ages, finding cracks in the world, a breeze that became a howling sirocco here, in the soul of a killer, in the festering heart of Room 1208.

22

Lucy walked down Eighteenth Street in what she had once heard, from one therapist or another, was a fugue state.

She couldn't get that photograph out of her mind.

That *couldn't* have been her house on Melbourne Road. It wasn't possible. It was just a picture of one of a million bungalows. They all looked alike, didn't they? Especially the crappy ones.

But what about that flag, Luce? Did they all have that raggedy flag hanging off the porch by a rusted nail, that stupid pennant that was supposed to mean Spring? The one you were supposed to change every three months but no one ever did, not once in all the time they lived there? They had all of them — Spring, Summer, Fall, Winter, all four seasons, each looking more tattered than the other — but they never changed Spring.

What about *that*, Luce?

What about the Spring flag?

She didn't have an answer, just as she had no idea what had happened during those twenty minutes she couldn't recall. Somehow she must have talked about the day she disappeared. What did she say? And why didn't Mr. Costa *tell* her what she'd said? Wasn't that why she went to see him?

It was all part of the process, she guessed. And she had two more visits to go.

⋆　⋆　⋆

From the time she was six or seven years old, Lucy had been an ace mechanic. Not with cars, necessarily, although she could now do basic maintenance on most cars — changing oil, replacing plugs and belts, the occasional brake job if it didn't involve turning the drums or rotors. No, her forte was small appliances. Bring her a stopped tape player, a cold toaster oven, a dimmed lamp — and a lot of the staff of Le Jardin often did — and she would have it up and running by the end of lunchtime.

She had not gone to a vocational training school, or taken any classes, correspondence or otherwise. It was a natural ability, combined with a necessity of life.

When she was small, on the night forays during which she and her mother picked through trash they would often find all kinds of discarded items — toaster ovens, blenders, tape players. Lucy's mother would haul them back to their apartment, giddy with swag, then pretty much forget about them. Weeks later she would throw them out, and Lucy would rescue them a second time. She started with the easy ones, but eventually got better at repair.

Although she didn't know it, she was practicing reverse engineering.

By the time she was ten, Lucy would go out to dumps, finding her own things to repair. She knew every second-hand dealer in their small towns. Where most kids were reading *Dick and Jane*, Lucy pored over *Sam's Photofact*.

In addition, on her jaunts into the stores Lucy always stole the same color clothes — sweaters, sweatshirts, skirts. She even replaced some of her mother's clothes. Her mother was always falling down, ripping her clothes. Lucy got it down to a science. She could steal a brand new dress and worry the material just enough so that her mother never knew she was wearing a different garment. Her mother was a proud woman in many ways, and it broke Lucy's heart to see her going around in ratty clothes.

On this day, Lucy found herself in the Macy's near City Hall. She made her way over to the children's section, found a sweater that looked to be the right size. She picked up two of them, carried them around for a while. When she got to the women's section she selected a dress, brought it into the dressing room.

Inside she got out her small toolkit and, with her back to the mirrors — she knew all the tricks — removed the electronic tags from one sweater and the dress, affixing them to the second sweater. She slipped the first sweater and the dress into her bag, left the dressing room, replaced the other sweater on the display rack, tarried a bit to make sure that she wasn't being watched, then walked out of the store.

★　★　★

When she arrived back at Le Jardin, with just a few minutes to spare, Lucy could see that the convention guests — the members of *Société Poursuite* — were milling about the lobby. They

190

weren't all guests, of course. It was a convention that attracted a lot of locals, as well as people from all over the tri-state area who drove in for the three days of seminars, lectures and dinners.

In all, over the next few hours there would be ninety-two new guests, and all of them had to be quickly and efficiently processed, greeted with smiles and pleasant repartee, their concerns listened to with rapt attention, their every need anticipated and met, their next three days in the city of Philadelphia — and specifically in Le Jardin — a promised and delivered haven.

Lucy stopped by the Loss Prevention office, picked up her room key.

A door to your subconscious, Mr. Costa had called it. *A portal to what happened to you nine years ago.*

★   ★   ★

Lucy finished her last room, room 1214, at 3:45.

She stepped into the closet, closed the door, sat down. In moments, the darkness embraced her. When she closed her eyes she saw the town of Shanksville, Pennsylvania from above, saw the school on Cornerstone Road, Lake Stonycreek, and the church on Main Street.

★   ★   ★

The Dreamweaver had asked her questions, his silken voice floating above her, behind her, around her, like a warm breeze. Her own voice belonged to a little girl.

191

What day is it, Lucy?
Tuesday.
Is it morning, afternoon, evening?
It's morning. Tuesday morning.
What time?
Around ten. I didn't go to school.
Why not?
Mama was out the night before, and she didn't get up in time.
Where are you?
I am across the street from the church.
Are you alone?
No. Mama's with me. She is wearing her long leather coat. The one with the rip in the right pocket. She is wearing sunglasses. She asked a lady for a cigarette and the lady gave her one.
What happened then?
There was a big bang. It was loud. Even the ground shook.
What did you do?
I don't remember exactly.
Try to remember. Do you smell anything? Taste anything?
I taste milkshake.
What flavor is it?
Chocolate. But it's warm milkshake. I don't like warm milkshake.
What about smell?
I smell smoke, but not like regular smoke. Not like burning leaves, or logs in a fireplace. More like when people burn their plastic garbage bags.
What happens next?
I stand here for a long time, watching the fire and smoke rise up into the sky.

Where is your mother?

Right beside me. Or maybe not.

What do you mean?

Someone is beside me, but I'm not looking at that person. I can't take my eyes off the smoke over the trees. It is making pretty patterns in the sky.

What kind of patterns?

At first it looks like the face of Jesus. Then it looks likes birds.

What happens next?

I reach up my hand for my mother to take me somewhere. Anywhere but here. I'm scared.

Does she take your hand?

I take the person's hand, but as we walk away I realize it can't be my mom.

Why not?

The hand is too big. And rough. It is a man's hand.

Is there anything else you remember?

Yes. We get into a car. And there is a new smell. *Two* new smells.

What are the new smells?

A different kind of smoke. Different from the burning plastic smell. Like from a pipe, I think. A pipe that people smoke. Like *men* smoke.

And what else?

Apples. Empire apples. We have lots of apples in Western Pennsylvania. Especially near the fall.

Do you remember what else happened that day?

The fire. The ground shaking. Being scared.

What about the man? What happened with him?

I don't know.

What about his face? Do you see his face?

When I look at his face it isn't there.

What about the fire? Do you remember what that was? Do you remember what caused the fire?

Yes. I remember, but only because I found out later.

What was it?

It was Flight 93. It was September 11, 2001, and Flight 93 crashed right near Shanksville, Pennsylvania.

★   ★   ★

Lucy looked down at her hands. She had been clenching her fists so tightly that she had eight little red crescents on the palms of her hands. She eased her fists open, stepped out of the closet, looked around. For a few crazy moments she did not know what room she was in. Most people, even people who worked at Le Jardin, would be hard pressed to tell the standard guest rooms apart, their only clues being, perhaps, the view from any given window. But Lucy knew every room on the twelfth floor. It was her floor.

She smoothed out her uniform, stepped into the bathroom, went through the mental checklist in her mind, then checked the entire room.

Done.

She opened the door, stepped into the hall. Two older men were approaching from the elevator. They were probably with the convention. Everyone on the floor this week was with

194

the convention. They nodded to her, smiled. She smiled back, although she didn't feel it inside.

When she reached the business center on the twelfth floor — really just a small niche with computer, fax machine and printer — she sensed another guest coming down the hall. The unwritten rule was that in the hallways, elevators and most public spaces, guests, along with all front-of-the-house personnel, had the right of way. You didn't hide or sidestep from anyone, but if you were any good at your job you knew how to defer with style.

Lucy stepped into the alcove just as the man passed the door of the business center. She did not get a good look at him, just a glimpse of his dark coat.

But she didn't have to see him. It was not her sense of sight that took the floor from beneath her. It was her sense of smell.

There, beneath the hotel smells of cleaning products and filtered, heated air, was another smell, a scent that closed a cold hand over her heart, a smell that unquestionably trailed behind the man who had just passed her in the hallway.

The smell of apples.

She looked down the hall, and knew that he had come out of one of the rooms. Was it 1208? It had to be. She had just cleaned the other two rooms at that end, and they were empty.

Lucy pushed her cart madly down the hall, caught the service elevator to the basement. She left her cart in the basement, ran up the steps toward the service entrance to the first floor. She tried to calm herself as she walked toward the lobby. She didn't know what she would do if she confronted the man, or even who she was looking for.

She stepped into the northern end of the lobby. There were three men in the lobby, none of them wearing or carrying a dark overcoat. Everyone else was staff.

She went out the side door, onto Sansom Street. The sidewalk was crowded. Men, women, children, people making deliveries, cab drivers. She rounded the corner, looked in front of the hotel. Two bellmen were taking bags out of a limo for an elderly couple.

Lucy's heartbeat began to slow. She took a moment, then walked up the drive on the east side of the hotel.

The smell of apples.

It had to be her imagination. Brought on by going to see that crazy old man. She was never going to find out what had happened on those three days. Not really.

She rounded the wall at the back of the hotel, turned the corner.

'Hello, Lucy.'

She stopped, her heart in her throat, her legs all but giving out. She knew the man standing before her. She knew his *face*.

'It's you,' she said.

'Yes, Lucy,' he replied. 'It's Detective Byrne.'

196

23

Jessica spent the early afternoon running data through ViCAP, the Violent Criminal Apprehension Program. Started by the FBI in 1985, ViCAP was a national registry of violent crimes — homicides, sexual assaults, missing persons, and unidentified remains. Case information submitted to ViCAP was available to authorized law-enforcement agencies around the world, and the system allowed investigators to compare their evidence with all other cases in the database and to identify similarities.

Jessica searched the database with the most salient points of the case, those being the signature marks of the shaving of the victims, as well as the use of paper to blindfold them.

She found a similar case from 2006 in Kentucky, where a man had shaved off the hair of three prostitutes before stabbing them to death and dumping their bodies along the banks of the Cumberland River. In this case the man had shaved only the hair on the victims' heads, including their eyebrows — not their entire bodies. There was another 1988 case in Eureka, California of a man who had shaved a strange pattern into the scalps of four victims. The pattern was later identified, through the man's confession, as what he thought were the first four letters of an alien alphabet.

There were many cases of blindfolded victims,

most being execution-style homicides. There were also numerous examples of pre- and post-mortem mutilations. None matched Jessica and Byrne's case.

There were no incidents where all three signatures were present.

Jessica was just about to print off what she needed when all hell broke loose in the duty room. She stood aside as a half-dozen members of the Fugitive Squad ran down the hallway, then through the door to the stairs. They were soon followed by three men wearing US Marshals windbreakers.

Why were the US Marshals there? The purview of the marshal's office, among other things, was the apprehending of fugitives, the transport and managing of prisoners, as well as the protection of witnesses.

Jessica looked across the room to see Dana Westbrook walking toward her. 'What happened?' she asked.

'We had a break.'

Unfortunately, what Westbrook clearly meant was there had been a *prison* break, not a break in Jessica's case.

'From downstairs?' The sub-basement of the Roundhouse was where the PPD holding cells were located. The holding cells were staffed by the county sheriff's office, not the police.

Westbrook shook her head. 'From CF.'

Curran-Fromhold Correctional Facility, on State Road, was a prison in Northeast Philly. In Jessica's entire time on the job she had never heard of a break from CF. 'What happened?'

'It's sketchy right now, but it looks like the prisoner got his hands on a visitor's pass and some street clothes. They've got video of him just waltzing out of the visitor's area.'

The security at CF was tight, which probably meant that the escapee had an accomplice of some sort. Jessica knew the drill. Members of the PPD Fugitive Squad would team up both with US Marshals and with officers from the Pennsylvania State Police. They would scour motels, bus stations, train stations, and of course establish surveillance of the prisoner's residence and those of his known associates. She also knew there was a pretty good chance that a head or two would roll at Curran-Fromhold.

'Fugitive Squad is all over it, and as you can see the marshals are in,' Westbrook said. 'Only a matter of time. Captain wanted me to give you a heads-up, anyway.'

This got Jessica's attention. 'Me? Why?'

'The prisoner? The guy who escaped?'

'What about him?'

'He's your AA Killer suspect. Lucas Anthony Thompson.'

★　★　★

Byrne returned to the Roundhouse at just after three p.m. Jessica had tried to call him twice, got his voicemail both times.

'How did the doctor's appointment go?' she asked.

'Good.'

Jessica just stared. Byrne knew better than to give her the bum's rush on something like this,

199

yet still he tried. Her icy look firmly in place, the moment drew out. Byrne caved in.

'They took the MRI, now they have to read the results. They said they'd call me.'

'When?'

Byrne took a deep breath, realizing he had to play this game or he'd never hear the end of it. 'Maybe tomorrow.'

'You'll let me know the second you hear from them, right?'

'Yes, Mom.'

'Don't make me ground you.'

Jessica told Byrne about Thompson, as well as the scant information she had harvested on ViCAP. Then she gathered her notes, filled him in on the rest of the details regarding the second victim found that day. Black male, mid-fifties, no ID. Initial canvass turned up nothing.

'Has he been printed?' Byrne asked.

'The body's on the way to the morgue now. Boss is going to put Russ Diaz and his team on this. Russ did four years in Behavioral Science, you know. I have a sneaking suspicion we're going to need him.'

'What about the signature?'

'Identical,' Jessica said.

They turned back to the case files on the desk. Three bodies. Three identical MOs. Kenneth and Sharon Beckman were tied to the murder of Antoinette Chan. In the case of serial murder, the first order of business was to try and establish a link between the victims, a commonality that might lead to a denominator they all shared — job, family, circle of friends — and ultimately to the killer. Connecting Kenneth and Sharon Beckman was, of course, easy. They'd see about this new victim.

'I ordered you some garlic prawns, by the way,' Jessica said. 'But it got eaten. You know how Chinese food goes in this place. Like pork in a kennel.'

'I ate at the hospital,' Byrne said. 'But I did bring dessert.' He held up a white bag.

Jessica sat up straight in her chair. *Dessert at lunch!* She beckoned forth the bag. Byrne handed it to her.

Jessica opened the bag and saw that it was an apple fritter from that bakery on Seventeenth she liked.

'What took you to Seventeenth?' she asked.

'I had to pick up a pre-amp from a guy.'

'And a pre-amp would be . . . '

'I'm converting all my old vinyl records to digital. Some of them are old 78s, and I'm trying to clean up the sound.'

Jessica took out the apple fritter, thinking that she couldn't wait for that moment in her life — a moment she fully expected, a moment she fully intended to savor — when she just didn't care about her weight anymore, a moment when she could fully embrace the slide into middle age and obesity.

Or when she got pregnant again. Pregnant would be better.

She bit into the apple fritter. Heaven. 'You can get MRIs as often as you want.'

'We're going to have to give statements, you know.'

Jessica nodded, wiped her lips. She and Byrne had met with Sharon Beckman the day before, and now the woman was the victim of a homicide. Jessica and Byrne had become part of the timeline.

★   ★   ★

The call came at just after four. Nicci Malone and Nick Palladino were at the morgue with the third victim. Jessica put them on speaker.

'We're at the ME's,' Nicci said. 'You wanted me to call?'

'Yeah,' Jessica said. 'Have you checked the victim's hands for tattoos?'

'No. We bagged them at the scene. You want us to check here?'

'Yeah,' Jessica said.

The next minute took somewhere around an hour for Jessica and Byrne. They both paced, neither of them having anything to say. They heard more rustling, then Nicci put the phone back up to her ear.

'Jess?'

'Yeah, Nicci,' Jessica said. 'Is there a tattoo?'

'There is,' Nicci said. 'It's a tattoo of a swan. A tiny blue swan. It's on the index finger of his left hand.'

Someone was on a rampage in the city of Philadelphia and every resource had to be summoned to stop him. The fact that the body of Kenneth Beckman had been found a half-block from an elementary school put two other agencies on alert. Personnel had already

202

been dispatched to Washington Elementary.

Over the next few hours the apparatus of an investigation handling multiple murders would gear up around them. Off-duty detectives would be called in, various sections of the forensic lab would be put on alert.

'Can you take a picture of the tattoo and send it to me?' Jessica asked.

'Sure,' Nicci said.

A few minutes later, Jessica received the image on her cellphone. She put it next to photos of Kenneth and Sharon Beckman that had been taken. The tattoo was in the same style. She got online to the World Ink site, put the word 'swan' in the search box, hit *Enter*. Soon a page came up with six different images of stylized swan tattoos. The third tattoo was a perfect match.

★   ★   ★

Michael Drummond arrived at five-thirty. The ADA had news for them.

'Before I left the office I heard from World Ink's legal department, which, for all I know, might have been a lawyer working out of his car,' Drummond said. He pulled out a fax, handed a copy to Jessica. 'It turns out that you can buy these tattoos à la carte, with a minimum of six tattoos in the order. They searched their database and discovered that, in the past year, they had sold only one package that contained the first two tattoos we found on the victims — the lion and the rooster.'

Drummond pulled out another fax.

203

'They mailed the package to a post-office box in Jersey City, New Jersey, which turned out to be a remailer. From there it went to a USPS box in Allentown.'

This meant that, for the moment, their most promising avenue of the investigation was blocked. Getting information on who rented a PO Box presented a whole new set of challenges. Anytime you dealt with a federal agency the red tape was massive. On this they would have to bring in the postal inspectors.

Drummond glanced at the notes in Jessica's notebook.

'So there's been a third murder,' he said. It was a statement, not a question.

Jessica picked up her iPhone, showed Drummond the photo of the victim, as well as the close-up of the tattoo. Drummond scanned the pictures, then looked at his watch. 'All right. I know where the judges will be drinking in about an hour. I'll catch them between their second and third martinis.' He gathered his papers. 'Speaking of martinis, are you coming to my party, Jess?'

Jessica had forgotten all about it. She hoped it didn't show on her face. 'Of course. Looking forward to it.'

'I'll get on the feds.' Drummond smiled, held up his phone. 'I'll call you later.'

Ten minutes later, with everything printed off, Jessica and Byrne stood in front of the material. There was no question that the tattoos purchased from World Ink were the same tattoos found on the victims.

The bad news was that, according to the material they had just received from Drummond, in the packet of tattoos mailed to their killer there were five other tattoos. Turtle, donkey, elephant, kangaroo, and fish.

Eight tattoos in all. The thought was chilling.

Would there be eight murders?

24

The house in Lexington Park was nearly empty, save for the hundred or so boxes stacked in the attic, upper hallway, living room and kitchen. The furniture was gone. The dining-room chandelier, an heirloom passed down from Jessica's grandmother, had been carefully packed and spirited away, as had all her mother's cut-crystal goblets.

Three dozen people crowded the first floor, eating wings and crab fries from Chickie's and Pete's. Among them were a who's who from the police department, crime lab and district attorney's office. Chits cashed, favors recalled, Jessica had been batting her eyelashes for weeks; Vincent had been twisting arms, sometimes literally, for months.

Also downstairs were Jessica's father Peter Giovanni, most of her cousins, Colleen Byrne and her friend Laurent, Byrne's father Paddy. Just about everyone who could be roped in was in attendance.

Byrne arrived a little late.

★ ★ ★

Jessica and Byrne stood at the top of the stairs, at the entrance to the attic. Before them was arrayed a roomful of boxes.

'Wow,' Byrne said.

'I'm a total pack rat, aren't I?'

Byrne looked around, shrugged. 'It's not that bad. I've seen worse. Remember the old lady on Osage, the one with two hundred cats?'

'Thanks.'

Jessica noticed some hair on Byrne's shoulder. She reached over, brushed it off.

'Did you get a haircut?'

'Yeah,' he said. 'I popped in and got a trim.'

'You *popped in?*'

'Yeah. No good?'

'No, it looks fine. It's just that I've never 'popped in' for a haircut. It takes me four to six weeks to make the decision, then it's another month of doubt, steering committees, estimates, near misses, appointments cancelled at the last second. It's a life-changing event for me.'

'Well, it's pretty much a haircut for me.'

'You have it *so* easy.'

'Oh yeah,' Byrne said. 'My life's a Happy Meal.'

Jessica lifted a few boxes that were, mercifully, light. At least she had taken to labeling things in the past few years. This one read ST. PATRICK'S DAY ORNAMENTS. She did not remember ever buying or displaying St. Patrick's Day ornaments. It looked like she was going to keep them nonetheless, so she could not use them in the future. She put the box by the top of the stairs, turned back.

'Let me ask you something,' she said.

'Shoot.'

'How many times have you moved in the last ten years?'

Byrne thought for a few moments. 'Four times,' he said. 'Why?'

'I don't know. I guess I was just wondering if you're still hanging onto a bunch of completely pointless, useless crap.'

'No,' Byrne said. 'Everything I have is absolutely necessary. I'm a Spartan.'

'Right. You should know that I once talked to Donna about this very thing.'

'Uh-oh.'

In the past few years Jessica and Byrne's ex-wife Donna had become good friends.

'Oh yeah. And she said that when you guys were married, and you moved from the apartment into your house, the first thing you packed was your Roger Ramjet nightlight.'

'Hey! That was a safety issue, okay?'

'Uh-huh. Still have it?'

'I do not,' Byrne said. 'I have a Steve Canyon nightlight now. Roger Ramjet is for kids.'

'Tell you what,' Jessica said. 'I will if you will.'

It was a game they sometimes played — like Truth or Dare, but without the dare. Ninety-nine percent of the time it was light-hearted. Once in a while it was serious. This was not one of those times. Still, there were rules.

'Sure,' Byrne said. 'You're on.'

'Okay. What is the most ludicrous piece of clothing you still own? I mean, something you know you will never wear again, not in a million years, but you just can't bring yourself to part with it?'

'That's an easy one.'

'Really?'

'Oh yeah,' Byrne said. 'A pair of 33-inch waist green velvet pants. Real plum-smugglers.'

Jessica almost laughed. She cleared her throat instead. No laughing was one of the big rules of the game. 'Wow.' It was all she could muster.

'Is that *wow* I once had a 33-inch waist, or *wow* green velvet?'

This was a no-win question. She opted for the velvet.

'Well,' Byrne said. 'I bought them in New York in my Thin Lizzy days. I really wanted to be Phil Lynott. You should have seen me.'

'I would pay good money for that,' Jessica said. 'A lot of women in the department would chip in, too.'

'What about you?'

Jessica glanced at her watch. 'My God. Look at the time.'

'Jess.'

'Okay. When I was nineteen, going to Temple, I had a date with this guy — Richie Randazzo. He invited me to his cousin's wedding in Cheltenham and I saved for three months for the cutest little red dress from Strawbridge's. It's a size four. I still have it.'

'What, you're not a size four?'

'You are the greatest man who has ever lived.'

'As if this were in doubt,' Byrne said. 'One question, though.'

'What?'

'You went out with a guy named Richie Randazzo?'

'If you didn't factor in the mullet, the rusted-out Toronado with the fur-trimmed rearview mirror, and the fact that he drank Southern Comfort and Vernor's, he was kind of cute.'

'At least *I* never had a mullet,' Byrne said. 'Ever.'

'I could always check with Donna, you know.'

Byrne looked at his watch. 'Look at the time.'

Jessica laughed, letting him off the hook. She fell silent for a few moments, looking around the attic. It occurred to her that she would never be back in this room. 'Man.'

'What?'

'My whole life is in these boxes.' She opened a box, took out some photos. On top were pictures of her parents' wedding.

Out of the corner of her eye Jessica saw Byrne turn away for a second, giving her the moment with her memories. Jessica put the photos back.

'So, let me ask you one more thing,' she said.

'Sure.'

Jessica took a few seconds. She hoped that her voice was going to be steady. She put her hand on one of the boxes, the one with the piece of green yarn around it. 'If you have something, some memento that is a part of your life, and you know that the next time you see it, it's going to break your heart, do you keep it? Do you hold onto it anyway? Even though you know it is going to cause you pain the next time you look at it?'

Byrne knew that she was talking about her mother.

'Do you remember her well?' he asked.

Jessica had been five years old when her

210

mother died. Her father had never remarried, had never loved another woman. 'Yeah. Sometimes. Not her face, though. I remember how she smelled. Her shampoo, her perfume. I remember how in summer, when we went to Wildwood, she smelled like Coppertone and cherry Life Savers. And I remember her voice. She always sang with the radio.'

Heaven Must Have Sent You. It was one of her mother's favorites. Jessica hadn't thought of that song in years.

'How about you?' she asked. 'Do you think about your mom a lot?'

'Enough to keep her alive,' Byrne said and leaned against the wall. It was his storytelling pose.

'When I was a kid, and my father used to chew me out, my mother would always run interference, you know? I mean *physically*. She would physically get in between us. She wouldn't make excuses for me, and I always ended up getting punished, but while my father was upbraiding me she would stand with her hands clasped behind her back. I'd look at her hands, and she always had a fifty cent piece for me. My father never knew. I'd have to do my time, but afterwards I always had fifty-cents to blow on a water ice or a comic book when I got paroled.'

Jessica smiled, thinking about anyone — especially Paddy Byrne — intimidating her partner.

'She died on my birthday, you know,' Byrne said.

Jessica *didn't* know. Byrne had never told her this. At that moment she tried to think of

211

something sadder than this, and found herself at a loss. 'I didn't know.'

Byrne nodded. 'You know how you always notice your birthday when you see it printed somewhere, or hear it mentioned in a movie or on television?'

'Yeah,' Jessica said. 'You always turn to the people around you and say *hey . . . that's my birthday.*'

Byrne smiled. 'It's like that for me when I go to the cemetery. I always do a double take when I see the headstone, even though I *know*.' He put his hands in his pockets. 'It will never be my birthday again. It will always be the day she died, no matter how long I live.'

Jessica couldn't think of anything to say. It mattered little, because she had never met a more perceptive person than Kevin Byrne. He always knew when to move things along.

'So, your question?' he asked. 'The one about whether or not to save something, even though you know it will break your heart?'

'What about it?'

Byrne reached into his pocket, pulled something out. It was a fifty-cent piece. Jessica looked at the coin, at her partner. At this moment, his eyes were the deepest emerald she had ever seen.

'It's a strange thing about heartbreak,' Byrne said. 'Sometimes it's the best thing for you. Sometimes it reminds you that your heart is still beating.'

They stood, saying nothing, cosseted in this drafty room full of memory and loss. The silence

212

was shattered by the sound of a breaking dish downstairs. Irish and Italians and booze always led to broken ceramics. Jessica and Byrne smiled at each other, and the moment dissolved.

'Ready for the big bad city?' he asked.

'No.'

Byrne picked up a box, headed for the stairs. He stopped, turned. 'You know, for a South Philly chick, you turned into kind of a wimp.'

'I have a gun in one of these boxes,' Jessica said.

Byrne ran down the steps.

25

By ten o'clock they had everything in the new house. What had seemed like a reasonable amount of goods in the Lexington Park house now filled up every room, every corner, every cabinet. If they put the sofa and two of the dining-room chairs on the roof, they could just about make everything fit.

Byrne stood across the street from the row house. A pair of older teenage girls walked by, reminding him of Lucy Doucette.

When he had first met Lucy at the group regression-therapy sessions she had seemed so lost. He did not know much about her life, but she had told him enough for him to know that she was troubled by a traumatic event in her childhood. He recalled her efforts at the regression-therapy group, her inability to recall anything about the incident. He didn't know if she had been molested or not. Running into her accidentally in the city reminded him how he had promised to look in on her from time to time. He had not.

'Kevin?'

It was a tiny voice. Byrne turned around and saw that it was Jessica's daughter Sophie, bundled up, standing on the sidewalk in front of the porch. The front door was open, and through it Byrne could see Peter Giovanni inside, leaning against the handrail, keeping one eye on his granddaughter. Once a father, always a cop.

Byrne crossed the street. For a long time Jessica had insisted that Sophie should call him Mr. Byrne. It had taken a while for Byrne to change that, and it looked like it had finally taken hold. Byrne got down to Sophie's level, noticing that she wasn't as small as she had been even last year at this time. 'Hey, sweetie.'

'Thanks for helping out.'

'Oh, you're welcome,' Byrne said. 'Do you like your new house?'

'It's small.'

Byrne looked over her shoulder. 'It's not that small. I think it's pretty cool.'

Sophie shrugged. 'It's all right, I guess.'

'Plus your school is only a block away. You can sleep late.'

Sophie giggled. 'You don't know my mom.'

The truth was, he did. He soon realized the folly of his statement.

Sophie glanced up the street. The looming structure of Sacred Heart Parochial School was silhouetted against the carbon-blue night sky. She looked back at Byrne. 'Did you go to Catholic school?'

'Oh yeah,' Byrne said. He wanted to tell her that he still had ruler marks on his knuckles to prove it, but decided against it.

'Did you like it?'

How to answer *this*? 'Well, do you have a kid in your school who is always goofing off, always getting into trouble?'

'Yeah,' Sophie said. 'In my school it's Bobby Tomasello.'

'Well, in *my* school that kid was me.'

'You got into trouble?'

'All the time,' Byrne said.

'Did they make you sit in the corner?'

Byrne smiled at the memory. 'Let me put it this way. Sister Mary Alice ended up putting my desk in the corner. It saved everyone a trip. In fact, I had a corner office in every one of my classrooms.'

Sophie's face softened into an expression that Byrne had seen a thousand times on Jessica's face, a look of compassion and understanding. 'It's all right, Kevin,' she said. 'You turned out okay.'

The jury was still out on that one, Byrne thought. Still, it was nice to hear, even if it was coming from a seven-year-old. Maybe *especially* from a seven-year-old. 'Thanks.'

They fell silent for a moment, listening to the sounds of the party coming from inside the house.

'I like Colleen,' Sophie said.

'Yeah,' Byrne said. 'She's pretty special.'

'She taught me something.'

'Oh yeah?'

Sophie nodded. She thought for a moment, wrinkling her brow, then balled her fists, extended a finger, stopped, thought a bit more, started over. This time she extended her hands, rubbed one palm across the other, lifted the index finger on each hand, bumped fists, and pointed at Byrne.

It was American Sign Language for 'Nice to meet you.'

'*Very* good,' Byrne said. 'Did you just learn that?'

Sophie nodded. 'It took me a few times.'

Byrne smiled. 'It took me *way* more than a few times.'

A few minutes later he kissed Sophie on top of her head, watched her walk back inside. After she was inside, Byrne stood and observed Jessica's family through the window for a while. It had been a long time since he'd been part of something like this.

He thought about Sophie's sign language, how determined she was, how she stayed with it until she got it right. He considered how the oldest sayings were the truest, like that one about the apple not falling far from the tree.

★   ★   ★

Byrne walked down Third Street, got into the van. He had grown up not far from here. He remembered a variety store on the corner. He used to get his water pistols and comic books there, cadging the occasional Baby Ruth and Butterfinger. He remembered a kid who got beat up once in the alley behind the store, a kid who was thought to have molested a little girl from the neighborhood. Byrne had been sitting on the corner with his cousin Patrick when it happened. He remembered the kid screaming. It was the first time he had ever encountered violence like that, the first time he had ever heard someone in so much pain. He believed that all those sounds, all the dark echoes of violence, in many ways remained.

Byrne sat there for a long time, not moving,

217

just rolling the fifty-cent piece over his fingers, the memories of his old neighborhood misting across his mind.

Someone emerged from the shadows just outside the driver's side window of the van. Byrne sat upright. It was Jessica. He rolled down the window.

'What's up?' he asked. 'Ready to move back already?'

'You know the paper that was wrapped around the victims' heads?'

'What about it?'

'We have a make.'

26

The crime lab — officially known as the Forensic Science Center, but never called that — was a massive building that had once been a schoolhouse, located just a few blocks from the Roundhouse at Eighth and Poplar Streets.

The reigning sovereign of the documents section was Sergeant Helmut Rohmer. Hell Rohmer was thirty-five, and a giant, measuring six-four, weighing two-fifty. Besides his strange and eclectic taste in music, which ran from Iron Maiden to Kitty Wells, he was known for his T-shirts — always black, never bearing the same saying twice. He must have had hundreds. He was starting to receive them in the mail, even from people he had helped put away in prison. Today his shirt read:

PADDLE FASTER.
I HEAR BANJOS.

His considerable arms were ringed with rose tattoos, or some variation, which now finished with ivy circling his wrists and ending on the backs of his hands. He was always well-groomed — right down to his oddly manicured fingers. Jessica figured that his manicures had something to do with his sense of the tactile. Hell Rohmer didn't want anything interfering with his sense of touch. He was almost metaphysical in his

219

approach to document forensics. It was one of the reasons why he and Byrne spoke the same language.

'Good evening, sleuths,' Hell said.

'Good evening, alchemist,' Byrne replied.

Hell smiled. 'I have your paper,' he said. 'You can only hide from the Weavemeister for so long.'

On the wall were six enlarged photographs of the paper found on the victims, front and back. The photographs showed the blood that had leached from the lacerations on each of the victim's foreheads, as well as the small dot of blood from the shallow puncture wound. A line, a dot, and the rough figure eight where the ears were mutilated.

'What do we have?' Jessica asked.

Hell picked up a small square of the paper sample, cut from the end of one of the bands. 'This is pricey stuff,' he said, running a finger across the slightly pebbled surface. 'It's beautiful, really. Our boy has exquisite taste.' Hell zoned for a moment, his eyes going a bit unfocused. Hell Rohmer was definitely a touchy-feely sort of guy.

'Hell?'

'Okay. Sorry. The paper is handmade, a hundred percent cotton, acid-free. Which puts it into the same category as about ten thousand brands. I'm not equipped to do a comparison test to determine the make, and I was just about to send it off to the FBI — which, as you know, can take a month or two to get back — when I saw something.' Helmut held up a sample. 'This was cut from the paper we took from the female victim. If you look here, you can see a small segment of a watermark.' Hell held the paper up to a strong light, but not too close. Jessica saw what looked like the portion of a shoulder.

'Is that a cherub of some sort?' Jessica asked.

Hell shook his head. 'The watermark is Venus de Milo. It's not on the other sample, so I'm thinking these were cut from a larger sheet.'

Hell displayed another printout. It was an extreme close-up of the edge of the paper, photographed through a microscope. 'This was cut with a large blade, which is indicated by the slight tearing of the fiber. I think he used a paper cutter, instead of an X-acto blade, scissors, or razor blade. The shearing is consistent front to back, with the fibers pushed downward. Too uniform to have been done by hand.'

Hell pointed to the sample.

'And while this might look white, it is really Felt Light Grey. Deckled on two sides, which leads me to believe it's deckled on four. The band is twenty-four inches long, which leads me to believe it was cut from a sheet that was twenty-four by twenty-six, which is fairly standard in printmaking.'

'This is printmaking paper?'

'Among other things.'

Hell put the sample down, picked up a few pages of computer printouts.

'It's the watermark that jumped out. Without it, we would have had to wait for Washington on this.' He pointed to one of the lines on the printout, highlighted in lime green. 'The manufacturer of this paper is headquartered in

Milan, Italy, and the line is called *Atriana*. Really high-end stuff. Printmaking, mostly, but they make all kinds of multi-use paper — stationery, canvas, vellum, linen. But this stuff is top of the line. One sheet of this paper retails for about seventy dollars.'

'Wow.'

'Yeah,' Hell said. 'And dig this. This company also supplies the paper for the Euro.'

'The currency?'

'The one.'

'They have two distributors in the US,' Hell said. 'As far as I can tell this paper is available at only twenty retail stores across the country. Mostly art supplies and specialty paper shops. Unfortunately — for us, not our bad boy — the paper can be ordered from a dozen online retailers.'

'Are there any stores in Philly that carry it?' Jessica asked.

'No,' Hell said. He smiled, held up a 3 × 5 card with an address on it. 'But there is a store in Doylestown.'

Jessica took the address.

'No applause?'

Jessica clapped.

'Thank you. And now to the wax.' On the table sat a small covered glass dish. The wax seal was inside. 'This is standard candle wax, not sealing wax, which is why it has begun to disintegrate.'

'What's the difference?'

'Well, about five hundred years ago, sealing wax was made primarily of beeswax and something called Venice turpentine, which is an extract of the larch tree. The wax was uncolored in those days, but when the Renaissance hit, folks started to color it with vermilion, and do you really want to know any of this?'

'Maybe one of these days,' Jessica said. 'Right now I'd love to know where our boy bought this. I would like a clear video of him leaving the store, and a copy of his driver's license. Do you have that?'

'No. And what's worse, this candle wax is available at every Rite-Aid, Wal-Mart and Target in the country. But not in this color.'

'What do you mean?'

'Well, what I was getting to, before I was so brusquely interrupted, was that this particular sample was not colored with any old vermilion.'

It took Jessica a second to realize what Hell Rohmer was saying. One look at Byrne told her he'd gotten it as well. She turned back to Hell.

'No.'

'I'm afraid so. The coloring is blood. This is a bad, bad pony, this guy.'

Jessica looked at Byrne just as someone entered the lab and stopped by the door. Hell crossed the room, disappeared from Jessica's line of sight. In the reflection from one of the glass cabinets she saw that the new arrival was Irina Kohl. Irina had with her a few folders, one of which she placed in Hell's hands. Then Jessica saw the diminutive Irina get on her tiptoes and kiss Hell Rohmer flush on the mouth. Hell turned and saw that Jessica could see them in the cabinet's reflection.

The two of them, now red as raspberries, walked back to join Jessica and Byrne.

'Um, you didn't see that,' Hell whispered to Jessica.

'See what?'

Hell winked.

'I'm glad you're here,' Irina said, plowing forward. 'I think we may have something on the murder weapon.'

Irina Kohl worked in the lab's firearms ID unit, which also handled tool marks, and was in her late twenties, a prototypical lab dweller — neat in appearance, precise in manner and speech, probably a little too smart for Mensa. Beneath her lab coat she wore a suit coat, white button-down shirt, and lavender knit tie.

Irina opened a folder, removed some enlargements.

'The wire used as the ligature was made of woven multi-strand titanium.' She pointed to an extreme close-up of the ligature marks on the first two victims. Even to the naked eye the woven characteristics were visible. The flesh bore an imprint of the three-strand weave. 'We found traces of the metal in the wound.'

'What is something like this used for?' Jessica asked.

'There are a lot of uses for it. In general, titanium wire is specified for medical devices, bone screws, orthodontic appliances. In different gauges it is all over the aerospace, medical and marine manufacturing map. It is low-density and has a high resistance to corrosion.'

Irina then picked up a blown-up photograph,

as well as a pair of slides.

'I also found hair samples in the ligature wound on the first two victims. We haven't gotten a crack at the third victim yet.' She pointed to the two slides. 'These are from Sharon Beckman and Kenneth Beckman.'

'Do you think this is our killer's hair?' Jessica asked.

'No,' Irina said. 'I'm afraid not. These samples are definitely not human.'

Jessica looked at Byrne, back. 'Not human as in . . . '

'Well, animal.' Irina pushed up her thick glasses. She scrunched her face, as if smelling something unpleasant. Jessica supposed this was her way of waiting for the conversation to regenerate. She also noted that the woman was wearing two different lipsticks. One shade on her upper lip, one on the lower.

'Well, *duh*, Jess,' Jessica said, berating herself. 'I mean, what else, alien?'

Irina continued, undaunted. 'Domestic animal specifically.'

'We're talking dog or cat?' Jessica asked.

'Not domesti*cated*, necessarily. What I mean is domestic as in cow, sheep, horse.' Irina got a little more animated. 'See, if we're talking the hair of domestic animals there are a number of variations in color and length. However, a lot of these identifiers are pretty general. In order to tell the difference between, say, a dog and a cat, or between a cow and a moose, you really need the root to be present. Which, unfortunately, in this case, we do not have.'

225

She slipped a slide onto the stage of a microscope, clipped it in.

'But we're just getting started.' Irina smiled at Hell. Hell beamed.

Irina then peered into the microscope eyepiece, did a little fine focusing. 'If you take a look here, you can see it.' She stepped back.

Jessica stepped forward, looked through the microscope.

'You see it is quite coarse. The medulla is unbroken,' Irina said. 'The pigment is fine and evenly distributed.'

'Yeah,' Jessica said. 'I was just going to say that about the medulla.' The image she saw looked like a long dark brown tube. She might just as well have been looking at a Tootsie Roll. Hell Rohmer watched Irina, sunny with admiration, seething with forensic lust. Jessica and Byrne had worked with the two of them many times. Hell and Irina liked to have scientifically clueless detectives and other investigators look through microscopes. It validated them as criminalists.

'What tipped me was the ovoid structures,' Irina added.

'Every time,' Jessica said, stepping away from the microscope. 'So what are you saying? I mean, *I* understand it. Tell us for Kevin's benefit.'

Byrne smiled.

'Well, this is not exactly my field,' Irina said. 'So I'm going to send this out. We should know something by tomorrow at the latest.'

Jessica handed Irina a card with her cellphone number on it. 'Call me the second you have it.'

'Will do,' Irina said. 'And our freaky killer

226

better get some game.'

'Why's that?'

Irina smiled. Jessica saw her hand covertly brush up against Hell Rohmer's hand. 'We're about to make his life awfully uncomfortable.'

★   ★   ★

On the way out to the car Jessica thought about the lab and the curious creatures who toiled within. Physical evidence was, as they say, a silent witness to every misdeed, always present at crime scenes due to the simple phenomenon of transference. No individual can enter or leave any enclosed area without picking up or leaving behind innumerable items of physical evidence. But the evidence alone has little value. Only after it has been detected, collected, analyzed, interpreted and presented will it yield meaning and context.

As a rule, criminals have no idea who the people are who plug away in forensic labs all over the world and how dedicated they are to rooting out the truth. If they did know, they wouldn't be so cavalier about leaving at their crime scenes any one of the million skin cells or hundreds of hairs we shed every day, not to mention saliva, footprints, blood, or fibers from clothing.

As Jessica got into the car she also thought about how her job sometimes resembled an episode of *The X-Files*.

These samples are definitely not human.

227

27

Byrne parked across the street from the Mount Olive Cemetery. He had stopped by the main office, spoken to the night security officer. Considering what had happened there that day, he didn't need a trigger happy ex-PPD freaking out about the man standing in the middle of the graveyard.

He thought about the vision he had gotten when he had been here before. What did it all mean?

He tried to add up the hours of sleep he had missed in the past week, but couldn't. The weight of his exhaustion prevented him from making an accurate accounting.

Byrne laid his head back on the seat. Just for a moment. Just a moment of peace.

Sleep came quickly. In the dream he was in a vast concert hall, the only person sitting in the audience. Onstage was a full philharmonic orchestra. He looked around the elegant surroundings. The floor was slicked with blood. On each seat was a severed finger.

He jumped to his feet as the music swelled, ran up the aisle to the lobby. On one wall of the lobby were two words written in bright red blood:

you know

Byrne ran from the hall, down the sidewalks, where everyone had the face of a victim he knew, a case he had investigated. He found his van in an otherwise empty parking lot. He jumped in, his heart racing fit to burst. He noticed the smell immediately. He turned around to find a decomposing body posed in the back, shaved and hairless, its eyes open, familiar eyes —

Byrne sat upright in the driver's seat, the perspiration slicking his body despite the chill in the air. Outside, the city of Philadelphia was pitch black and silent, the only sounds the occasional car trolling by. Around him the dead were still dead.

He got out of the van, breathing in deeply the cold night air.

You know.

He looked at his watch.

It was 2:52.

28

Lucy spent the morning on autopilot, her emotions racing between approach and avoidance. Neither of these were terms that she had ever used in relationship to her state of mind until she had started seeing psychologists. They had a different way of speaking, those people, a wholly separate dictionary. For instance, you didn't just recall something, you had *declarative memory*. Or when you applied simple logic to problems, and solved them, it was called *fluid intelligence*. And then there was her favorite. If you were the kind of person who defined yourself by your own thoughts or actions, you weren't just confident, or happy in your own skin. No, no, no. You had *independent construals of self*.

Lucy almost laughed. Her inside joke — on those rare occasions when she felt good enough to appreciate a joke, inside or out — was that she was just going through her construal cycle.

Regardless, on this day, in this place, Lucy was all but overcome by her new feelings. The craziest thing had been running into Detective Byrne the day before. She had been so hyper when she saw him that, even though she knew that she knew him, she didn't realize who he was. Until he smiled.

They had met at her regression-therapy

230

sessions. He was the man in the group who had been dead for a whole minute. They'd gone for coffee once, shared their experiences. Well, Lucy had listened mostly, because she didn't really know what had happened to her. Yesterday he had given her his card and told her to call if she ever wanted to talk. She wondered if he could help her. She wondered if he would laugh at her suspicions of the man she thought she'd seen come out of Room 1208. No, he wouldn't laugh, but he *would* probably tell her she was imagining things.

As she worked she looked at her watch every five minutes, for the first time in a long while not really gauging her day by how many rooms she had completed, mentally recording the time she entered and left.

Each room attendant had their own section key, an electronic card similar to a guest key, that allowed them access to their rooms but not to other parts of the hotel. If an attendant said they entered a room at 9:08 and it was really 9:21, management could find it out in a second. A lot of dismissed attendants found out the hard way that computers never lie. The lock didn't say when you left, only when you entered.

Today all the rooms blended together, and Lucy had no idea how long it was taking her to finish each one.

He smelled like apples.

That could have been anything, though. There were a million plausible explanations for this. Lots of people wear dark overcoats. For gosh sake, even Detective Byrne wore a dark overcoat.

Lucy stood at the end of the hallway, near the elevators. She looked down the corridor, at the east wing. In this direction there were eight rooms. Rooms 1201 through 1208. Today she was able to swap this wing with a girl who worked on the seventh floor, promising to fix the girl's portable CD player in exchange for the favor. But it would only be for today. Lucy would have to enter Room 1208 tomorrow. She wasn't looking forward to it.

★   ★   ★

All room attendants got a fifteen-minute break in the morning. Lucy usually spent her time reading in the cafeteria or, if it was a nice day, she would run over to Rittenhouse Square for a full five minutes in the sun. It was amazing what even five minutes in sunlight could do for her mood. Today, she stepped into the small courtyard behind the hotel. She almost got lost in the cloud of cigarette smoke. You weren't supposed to smoke within fifty yards of the building, but no one ever listened and the rule had never been enforced.

When she rounded the corner at the back to the hotel she saw her friend Amanda sitting on a delivery pallet, eating a tangerine.

'Hey, girl,' Amanda said.

'Hi.' Lucy sat down next to Amanda. Amanda Cuaron was everything Lucy was not. Exotic, dark-eyed, a true Latin beauty, always flirting. Whenever Amanda was around Lucy felt like a rubber tulip.

'Hey, I forgot to ask, did you see that guy yesterday?' Amanda asked.

That guy was the Dreamweaver. Mr. Costa. Lucy wasn't sure how much she wanted to tell Amanda. Amanda was her friend and all, but Lucy had never shared secrets with her. She'd never shared her secrets with anyone. 'Yeah,' she said. 'I saw him.'

'How did it go?'

'It went okay.'

Amanda just stared at her — she was not going to get off the hook with such a brief explanation. 'Well? Was he weird? Did he wear a pointy hat and carry a wand?'

'Oh yeah,' Lucy said. 'And he had a long white beard. Didn't I mention the beard?'

Amanda smiled. 'Is he cute?'

Lucy snorted. 'Shut *up*. He's like a hundred years old.'

'Is he cute?'

Lucy just rolled her eyes. 'I'm going to see him again today.' Lucy hadn't realized that she'd made the decision to do this until this second.

Amanda smiled her lascivious smile. 'Mala *chica*.'

They both checked their watches at the same moment. They had another six minutes.

Amanda pointed to the wall next to the delivery bay. There was something carved into the stone. *RL loves TF*.

'I wonder if they're still in love,' Amanda said.

Lucy doubted it. She didn't believe in true love. 'Well, it *is* written in stone.'

Amanda laughed. 'I think that was probably

done back when this place was apartments.'

'When was this an apartment building?'

'I think up until maybe 1999. Something like that,' she said. 'I think it was kind of a famous place, too.'

'How so?'

'Well, mostly because of that little girl. You know about that, don't you?'

'What are you talking about?'

'I'm not a hundred percent sure what happened — you could ask Sergio. He'd definitely know.'

Sergio was an older guy who worked in maintenance. He had been with the building for a long time.

'But, from what I understand, a little girl got killed here,' Amanda added.

Lucy shuddered. 'What do you mean, killed? Like an accident or something?'

'No. Like *killed* killed.'

'What are you saying? She was *murdered*?'

'Yeah.' Amanda wiggled her fingers at Lucy, made spooky Halloween noises. 'They say her ghost walks these very halls.'

'Stop it.'

Amanda giggled. 'You're so easy.'

'How old was the girl?'

Amanda shrugged, peeled off another section of tangerine, offered it to Lucy. Lucy declined. 'Not sure. But not too old, though. Ten or eleven, maybe.'

'How did she . . . you know.'

'How did she die?' Amanda shrugged. 'No idea. But I don't think they ever caught the guy that did it.'

234

As creepy as Lucy already felt today, the feeling had just doubled.

'I think it's one of the cases this bunch of nut jobs who are staying here this week are investigating,' Amanda said. 'Or talking about investigating. God only knows what they do.'

Lucy was speechless for the moment. Amanda stood up, threw her tangerine peels in the nearby Dumpster.

'So, are we on?' Amanda asked.

At first Lucy didn't know what Amanda was talking about. Then she remembered. She had told Amanda that she would go out with her for a drink at Fluid, a dance club on Fourth Street, on Halloween Eve Night — always a crazy time in Philly, to say the least — and, according to Amanda, a ton of cute college guys always showed up. This year they were probably all going to be dressed up like Robert Pattinson.

'Yeah,' Lucy said. 'Why not?'

'Awesome. And you are definitely going to let me do something with your hair. We've got to babe you up, *chica*. Maybe get you laid.'

'*Amanda.*'

Amanda giggled. 'I'll be by your mansion around eight.'

'Cool beans.'

Amanda walked back into the hotel but Lucy stayed put. She couldn't stop thinking about the little girl Amanda had mentioned. *Murdered.* At the place Lucy *worked.* She had to find out more about it, although she wasn't sure why. Maybe because there was a dead zone in her own life. Maybe it was because for the past nine

235

years she had felt a dark kinship with all young girls who had been touched by evil. They were her sisters.

They say her ghost walks these very halls.

Thanks, Amanda, Lucy thought. *Thanks a lot.*

29

Doylestown was a quaint township of about eight thousand in Bucks County. The Ulrich Art Supply store was a standalone building, a converted ivy-veined coach house on North Main Street, across the road from the Mercer Square Shopping Center. The front windows held a display of paints, canvases, brushes, easels. Halloween decorations ringed the window and door.

On the way to Doylestown Jessica and Byrne decided not to approach the store in any official capacity. Because this was the only store within reach of the city that carried the paper used in these homicides, there was a chance that they might tip their hand by approaching the store as law-enforcement officers looking for information. If someone in the store was acquainted with the killer they might get on the phone the minute they left. If Plan A failed, they could always come in with guns and badges blazing.

They watched the store for a few minutes. There was a woman behind the counter, working on a small display rack. No one entered the store and they did not see anyone else working.

'Looks like you're up,' Jessica said.

'I thought *you* were the undercover queen.'

'I am,' Jessica said. 'But I think metrosexual is out of my range.'

'What did we say about that word?'

'Sorry.'

Byrne took a moment, scoping the terrain. 'Who am I again?'

Jessica gave it some thought. 'I'm thinking Bennett Strong.'

Byrne nodded. It was a good choice. Tough but suitably fey, given the venue. 'Where was the show?'

Jessica turned her iPhone so that Byrne could see it. She had searched the web on the way into Doylestown and found a recent print show in Philadelphia. She had also looked up the art supply store's website. There she found the owner's name. Alicia Webster.

Byrne pulled his badge from his belt, along with his weapon and his holster, put it all in the back seat. He took off his jacket.

'Want some hair gel?' Jessica asked.

Byrne just gave her a look.

*   *   *

Alicia Webster was in her mid to late thirties. She wore a beige knit cardigan and black corduroy slacks. Her eyeglasses hung around her neck on a rawhide lace.

She glanced up as Byrne entered the store accompanied by a ring of a bell. 'May I help you?' she asked. Pleasant smile, bright eyes.

Byrne proffered a business card. On it was simply a name — no phone number, no address, no email, no website. He had a stack of them in his briefcase. Ten different names. You never knew.

238

'My name is Bennett Strong,' he said. 'I am the owner of Strong Galleries, New York City.'

The woman's face lit up.

'You are Miss Webster?'

The woman looked surprised that he knew her name.

'I am.' She held up her left hand, wiggled her ring finger. 'But it's Mrs.'

Byrne put a hand to his heart. 'Mea culpa.' He smiled at her. 'Mrs. Of course.'

A blush. 'How can I help you, Mr. Strong?'

'I love your store, by the way. Did I see Kolinsky sables on the way in?' It was something Byrne had seen on the store's website. He knew that the woman carried the brushes.

'Yes,' she said. 'You know your brushes.'

'And now to the point. I recently attended the PortPhilio show in Philadelphia. Did you manage to make it to the affair?'

Say no, Byrne thought. *Please say no.*

'No. I wanted to, but I'm all alone here since my son went back to school. I couldn't get away.'

'It was fabulous.'

The door opened behind them, ringing the bell again. A woman entered the store. Alicia's eyes flicked over to the new customer, then back.

'Anyway, I met a man there, a printmaker, who recommended your shop. He showed me some of his work and it was fantastic.'

'How nice.'

'I would really like to contact him, but I'm afraid I lost his card and I don't remember his name.'

'And he said he purchased supplies here?'

'Yes.'

'He was from Doylestown?'

'I don't know.'

'What did the man look like?'

Shit, Byrne thought. He had no idea what to say. He didn't even know if it *was* a man. He aimed for the middle, culling from a standard profile. 'I'm terrible at these things. But I'd say he was thirty to forty. Medium height and weight. I'm not sure of his hair because he was wearing a ball cap.' This was as vague as Byrne could get. He smiled at Alicia. 'I'm a lot better with remembering women.'

Another blush. 'Well, that's not too much for me to go on.'

'Maybe this will help. During the course of our conversation he mentioned his printmaking technique, and said he was enamored of a certain brand of paper. An Italian paper. Quite expensive.'

'Do you remember the line?'

'I do not. But he showed me a sample and the watermark was Venus de Milo.'

'Atriana.'

Byrne snapped his fingers. 'That's it.'

The woman frowned. 'That's not an item we generally keep in stock. I've only sold a few dozen sheets in the past year or so.'

Alicia turned to her computer, tapped a few keys. In a moment a screen came up. Byrne could see the reflection in her glasses. It was a database program and she had found an entry. She nodded, perhaps remembering the man.

'I'm afraid I can't give you anyone's name.

240

Our mailing list is confidential, of course.'

'Of course.'

'If you'd like, I could take your information and have them get in touch with you.'

'That would be great.'

Just then there was a loud crash at the back of the store. Alicia spun around to see a woman at the rear, next to a toppled display rack of oil paints.

'Shoot!' the woman at the back exclaimed.

'Oh my,' Byrne said. 'Look, why don't you tend to this terribly clumsy woman and I'll stop back in a few minutes. I have to hit the ATM, anyway.'

'That would be fine.'

As Alicia walked to the rear of the store to help Jessica pick up the spilled merchandise, Byrne spun the LCD monitor to face him. His eyes scanned the screen. The problem was that he was not wearing his glasses. The customer's name was a little larger than the rest of the entry. He got that with no problem. It was a company called Marcato LLC.

Beneath that: *Attention JP Novak.* Byrne looked at the bottom. Philadelphia. In between, it was mostly a blur.

He spun the monitor back, turned on his heels, and left the store.

★　★　★

They pulled out of the parking lot and headed back to route 611.

'Did we get it?'

'I got the name,' Byrne said. 'And a partial address.'

'A *partial* address?'

Byrne fell silent.

'You weren't wearing your glasses.'

Byrne plowed forward. He checked the notes that he'd scribbled after leaving the store. 'The paper was purchased by a company called Marcato LLC. Contact name is JP Novak. The address is in Philly. Something something something something Ashingdale Road. Or Arlington. I think the number was 8180 or 5150. Maybe 6160.'

Jessica shook her head. 'You know, those glasses do serve a purpose.'

'I don't see you wearing yours all the time.'

'Mind your own business, Mr. Strong. Now, drive the car and let me start sleuthing.'

★ ★ ★

On the way back to Philadelphia Jessica called in the name. There was no phone listing for a JP Novak, nor anyone with that name in PCIC with a criminal record. They found more than three dozen listings for Novaks with J as an initial: John, Joseph, Jerry, Jerszy, Jacob, Joshua.

She also looked up Marcato and did not find any company with that name, LLC or otherwise. She did find a definition of the word and found that it was Italian for *marked*, and when it was applied to music it meant performing the note with an 'attack' and a sustain of two-thirds of the original written length, followed by an audible counted rest.

242

According to one source the *marcato* sound was 'a rhythmic thrust followed by a decay of the sound.'

Who would name their company this? Jessica wondered.

★ ★ ★

When they returned to the Roundhouse they searched every database for a JP Novak, as well as for Philadelphia streets named Ashingdon or dozens of possible permutations. They asked everyone on the floor if they knew of any Philly streets or courts or lanes by that name or similar names. There were a few close matches but nothing exact.

After twenty minutes of strikeouts Jessica stood, began to peruse the large paper map on the wall. You could only look at a computer screen for so long before going six-eyed with fatigue. Somehow she put her finger on two possibilities.

'Look at this,' she said. 'There's a street in West Philly called Abingdon.'

Byrne shot to his feet. 'That's it.'

'There's also one called Ashingdale.'

'Shit.'

Josh Bontrager grabbed his coat. 'I'll take Ashingdale.'

Jessica and Byrne headed to the door. 'Kevin?'

'What?'

'Bring your glasses.'

30

The addresses on Abingdon Road stopped at 7000, so this eliminated the chance of the address being 8180. Jessica and Byrne drove to the far end of the street, worked back from 5150. This was a body shop called D & K Motor Cars. No one inside knew anyone named Novak, nor a company called Marcato LLC.

The address at 6160 was a gentrified apartment building called the Beau Rive, perhaps at one time a warehouse. The front had recently been stuccoed, and all four apartments in the front had leaded-glass bay windows.

Byrne pulled over, cut the engine.

'Hang on,' Jessica said.

She got out of the car, walked up the steps to the apartment building. She walked into the small lobby and looked at the mailboxes. There were six suites. She scanned the names. The second to last name, in apartment 204, was Joseph Paul Novak.

Bingo.

She tried the buzzer twice. No response.

Jessica walked out of the building, across the street. She got back in the car. 'There's a Joseph Novak in apartment 204. I buzzed. Nothing.'

Byrne checked his side mirror, then did a U-turn, pulling up on the opposite side of the street in front of a Thai takeout. They had not stopped for lunch and the aromas were enticing.

He put the Taurus in park, cut the engine. 'Want to stake it out for a little while?'

'Sure,' Jessica said.

They watched the pedestrian traffic up and down Abingdon Road. After ten minutes or so Jessica got restless. She got out of the car, crossed the street, leaned against a light pole, took out her cell. She pretended to have a conversation. Cellphones were, hands down, the best surveillance prop ever invented.

Finally the door to the Beau Rive opened. The first person to walk out the building was a woman in her sixties, well-dressed and accessorized. When she reached the sidewalk she stopped, rummaged through her purse, then turned around in disgust, stormed back inside. She'd obviously forgotten something.

The second person to emerge was a man. He was black, in his late twenties, in a real hurry. He came out of the door buttoning a white chef's jacket. Jessica leaned back against the lamppost, called out:

'Joseph?'

No reaction. He didn't even acknowledge her. A few minutes later the woman reemerged and walked the other way down the street, a little more urgency to her stride. As a woman who forgot something at home every day, Jessica sympathized.

Jessica then crossed the street, leaned against the car next to Byrne's open window, went back to pretending to be on the phone. Ten long minutes later another man came out of the building.

'This is him,' Jessica said.

'How do you know?'

'I know.'

Jessica walked across the sidewalk, gave her hair a quick fluff. 'Is that *Joseph?*' The man turned around. He was tall, broad-shouldered, in his mid-thirties. He had brown hair nearly to his shoulders, a fashionable one-day growth of beard. He wore a dark overcoat. His skin was alabaster pale.

'Do I know you?' he asked. His posture betrayed neither aggression nor retreat. Instead, he looked pleasantly curious.

Jessica continued toward him. 'We met last year. You're Joseph Novak, right?'

The man offered a half-smile but not one that fully committed himself to this conversation. 'I am. But I must confess I don't remember your name.'

'My name is Jessica Balzano.' She produced her ID, held it up. 'I just need to talk to you for a few moments.'

Joseph Novak looked at her badge, then back into her eyes. In this light his eyes were a pale blue, almost colorless. 'We've never met, have we?'

'No,' Jessica said. 'That was just a bold subterfuge on my part.'

The man smiled. 'Well played. But I can't imagine what it is I could tell you.' He looked over her shoulder. 'Or your partner.'

It was Jessica's turn to smile. She always had to remind herself that she and Byrne were not that hard to make as cops. 'It won't take a minute.'

Novak held up a #10 envelope. 'I just need to

246

post this.' He pointed a half-block away, at a mailbox on the corner. He turned back to Jessica. 'I promise not to run.'

Jessica glanced at the envelope. It did not look like the paper found at the crime scenes. 'In that case, I promise not to chase you.'

Another smile. 'If you'll excuse me.'

'Of course.'

Novak threw one more glance at Byrne, then turned on his heels and walked toward the mailbox. Byrne got out of the car, crossed the street.

'That was good,' he said.

'I know.'

Novak mailed the letter and, as promised, began to walk back up the block. His size and bearing made for a striking silhouette in the afternoon light.

'Why don't you call Josh, tell him where we are?' Byrne said.

Jessica got on her cell, filled Bontrager in. She closed her phone just as Novak returned to the steps in front of his apartment building. Novak turned his attention to Byrne.

'I am Joseph Novak.'

'Kevin Byrne,' Byrne said.

'How can I help?' Novak asked.

Jessica pointed at the door to Beau Rive. 'Do you think we could chat inside? As I said, we won't take up too much of your time.'

Novak did not answer right away. When he saw that these two police officers were not about to leave, he relented. He gestured to the door. 'Please.'

31

At the rear of the building, Joseph Novak's apartment was a large two-bedroom flat with ten-foot ceilings and an open floor plan. The furniture was modern, mostly brushed aluminum and leather. Against one wall, nearly floor-to-ceiling, were CDs in custom-made birch shelves. There had to be a thousand of them. Jessica noticed that they were sectioned off by category: Classical, Electronica, New Age, Jazz. There were also subcategories by composer, artist, era. Brahms, Beethoven, Bach, Enya, Parker, Mingus, Tyner, Mulligan, Chemical Brothers. The effect of sunlight streaming through the windows, playing off the crystal cases in rainbow hues, was dizzying.

Upon entering the apartment Novak immediately crossed the room to the large desk at the other side and lowered the screen on his laptop, clicked it shut.

'We won't take up too much of your time,' Byrne said.

'Not at all,' Novak replied. 'Whatever I can do to help.'

'Do you know why we're here, Mr. Novak?' Byrne asked.

Novak sat at the desk, crossed his long legs. 'I'm afraid I do not.'

Byrne placed a sheet with six photographs on the desk in front of Novak. Kenneth Beckman's picture was in the upper right-hand corner. They decided to start this way, inquiring about Beckman as if they were looking for a witness.

Jessica watched Novak closely as his gaze fell on the photo lineup. If the man instantly recognized Beckman there was no indication.

'Do you recognize any of these people?' Byrne asked.

Novak gave the process a few seconds. 'No,' he said. 'Sorry.'

'No problem.' Byrne left the photo array on the desk. He leaned against the wall near the large window, looking around the room, especially at the rack of complicated-looking electronic equipment and what might have been a sound mixing board.

'May I ask what it is that you do for a living?' Byrne asked.

'I am a recording engineer by trade,' Novak said. 'But I keep my hand in with all aspects of the music world. I review for jazz and classical publications.'

'Interesting,' Byrne said. 'I'm a fan of classic blues, myself.'

Novak smiled. 'I have a small but rather interesting collection of old blues. My treasure is the box set of 78s with early recordings of Mary Johnson, Scrapper Blackwell and Kokomo Arnold.'

'Sweet. Any Roosevelt Sykes?'

'Not yet.'

Jessica stepped forward. In a situation like this, she and her partner liked to tag-team the person they were interviewing. If you split the person's attention it gave your partner the opportunity to look around, checking the small details of the room. One wall had a series of shelves with *objets d'art* on it. Small sculptures, Maori carvings, as well as a unique stainless steel bracelet with a single garnet stone inlaid.

Jessica turned her attention back to the CDs. 'This *is* quite an impressive collection of music you have here,' Jessica said.

'Thank you,' Novak said. 'I've been at it for quite a while. But I did not purchase most of them. Receiving free and promotional CDs for review is one of the perks of being a music critic.'

'What's the downside?'

'Listening to terrible music.'

Jessica scanned the wall. 'So, from all of this music, do you have a favorite composer?'

Novak smiled again. 'I imagine that is like asking an Eskimo if he has a favorite snowflake. If pressed, for me there is Johann Sebastian Bach, and then there is everyone else.'

'I'm sorry to impose, but do you think I might use your restroom?' Jessica asked.

This was another old ploy for investigators. It gave you the opportunity to see a little more of a person's dwelling while they were talking with your partner. Not to mention the opportunity to check out their medicine cabinet and perhaps discover what meds they were taking. Someone's medications could tell you a lot about them. Plus, it was a hard thing for people to say no to.

Novak hesitated. His stare shifted to the hallway, then back. The question hung in the air.

'Yes, of course,' he said finally. 'The second

door on your right.'

'Thanks.'

Jessica walked down the hallway. The kitchen was on the left, the bathroom on the right. At the end of the hall was the bedroom, its door slightly ajar.

Jessica stepped into the bathroom. It was spotless. On one wall was a large print, a black and white photograph of a man conducting an orchestra. The man was dark-haired, darkly handsome. He wore white tie and tails. Jessica looked at the caption: RICCARDO MUTI, 1986. Muti was the Italian conductor who had replaced Eugene Ormandy as the musical director of the Philadelphia Orchestra in 1980.

Jessica peeked into the bamboo wastebasket to the right of the toilet. Empty. She opened the medicine cabinet gently. Gently, because she had once opened a medicine cabinet in a similar situation, without thinking, only to have a few bottles crash loudly into the sink.

In the cabinet were an array of skincare products. No meds. If Joseph Novak took any medications, he did not keep them in his bathroom.

When she had exhausted her search, Jessica flushed the toilet. She washed her hands anyway, to keep up the illusion, and because it was a deeply ingrained habit.

She stepped out of the bathroom, listened. Byrne and Novak were still talking. She stepped to her right, inched open the bedroom door. The bedroom continued the rather industrial look of the apartment. There was a king-size platform

251

bed, a pair of night stands bearing stainless steel lamps with rectangular linen shades.

But it wasn't the furnishings that nearly took Jessica's breath away. The entire room was covered in paper. She had to look closely to believe what she was seeing. At first she thought it might have been some kind of creative wallpaper. It was not. What she'd at first thought was wall-covering was really hundreds and hundreds of photographs, articles, magazine covers, newspaper clippings, drawings. All of them seemed to be about one subject. Murder.

Her eyes were drawn to a large corkboard. To it were pinned a number of tabloid pages. The page on top stopped her cold. It was a tear sheet from the sleazy local newspaper *The Report*. The headline read:

Pummeled in Pennsport!

The article was about a brutal murder in 2002. March 21, 2002 to be exact.

The photograph was of a smiling Antoinette Chan.

Jessica looked back down the hall, saw no one coming. She took her iPhone out of her pocket, stepped fully into the bedroom, and began to photograph the walls, hoping there was enough light. Then she walked back down the hall. She stepped into the living room, held up her phone.

'Detective?'

Both Byrne and Novak turned to look at her.

'I'm sorry to interrupt, but there's a call for you.'

Byrne got up, walked across the living room, took a few steps down the hall. Jessica gestured to the opened bedroom door. Byrne stepped to the opening, took in the room. He stepped back.

Their gazes met in silent understanding. Byrne flicked a glance toward the front door. She would take the door. He would take Novak.

They were out of the living room for just a few seconds, but it was long enough. They heard a loud noise. When they returned, the chair in front of the desk was on its back. Novak was gone.

'*Fuck*,' Byrne yelled.

He went for the window and the fire escape beyond. Jessica ran to the door.

She peeked out into the hallway. It was not that long — there were only four apartments on this floor — and there were stairs at only one end. She hurried over to the elevator. Silence. Novak would not have had time to call the elevator, and make it even one floor. She ran down to the stairs, eased open the door, her hand on the butt of her weapon.

The stairwell was empty.

Jessica moved silently down the stairs, her weapon held out front, low. She turned a corner, carried on circling downward, her ears tuned to the sounds around her. Traffic outside, television noise coming from an apartment on the first floor. No footsteps.

She had to make a decision when she came to the first-floor landing. Continue on to the basement or check the first floor? She opted for the first floor. She eased open the door. It led to a short hallway. The lobby was straight ahead. She still hunted down the hall. When she came to the lobby she saw Joseph Novak sitting uneasily on one of the chairs. His right foot was tapping nervously.

Jessica stepped fully into the lobby and was just about to raise her weapon when she sensed another presence. She looked over. It was Josh Bontrager. He was leaning against the front door, a hoagie in one hand, his weapon in the other. He smiled, winked at Jessica just as Byrne came barreling into view in front of the building.

Byrne entered the lobby, caught his breath. Josh Bontrager ate his sandwich. Jessica stepped forward, holstered her weapon, and took Joseph Novak into custody.

32

Lucy found herself standing in front of the door, the small red door with the tarnished golden key on it. She didn't even remember walking to Cherry Street. All she remembered was clocking out for lunch and then, magically, there she was.

★ ★ ★

Lucy walked down the hallway. It was a lot quieter than it had been the day before, or maybe that was because it was so noisy inside her head.

In a few moments she was in front of the Dreamweaver's door. This time it was closed. She knocked, waited. She heard music coming from inside, some kind of classical music. She didn't know anything about classical music. She knocked again. The music stopped. Then she heard some light footsteps. The door opened.

'Lucinda.'

She was instantly taken aback by his appearance. She might have even made some kind of involuntary noise. Mr. Costa seemed younger. Not younger as in he looked like a younger man, but more animated, quicker in his movements. His hair was combed, parted in a perfectly straight line on the right side. He wore what looked like a fresh white shirt. His shoes were newly polished. He smelled of good soap.

Lucy found herself trembling as she walked into his room. She turned slightly as she passed through the doorway, but found that the photograph — the one she was certain was the one of her house when she'd been growing up, the picture that was hanging just above the light switch — had been replaced with a different photograph, this one of a valley full of flowers and a small cabin with smoke curling out of the chimney.

Had she imagined it?

Mr. Costa closed the door behind her. They walked together into the front room.

If the man looked more youthful, his place also looked improved. He had straightened it up a little. He had even *dusted*.

Mr. Costa gestured to the green chair. Lucy took off her coat, sat down.

'I trust you slept well?' he asked.

'Not really,' Lucy said. 'I'm not sure I slept at all.'

'Understandable.'

'I think maybe you were right.'

'In what way?'

Lucy put down her purse, arranged herself in the chair. It too seemed different. Larger, somehow. She felt like a little kid sitting in it, or maybe Alice through the looking glass. 'When you said I may have opened a door yesterday. I think maybe I did.'

Mr. Costa smiled. 'This is wonderful news. What leads you to think this?'

On the way over, Lucy had debated whether or not to tell Mr. Costa about the man in the hotel. She decided to wait until after this session, to wait and see what, if anything, she got out of it. 'I'm not sure,' she said. 'It's just a feeling.'

The look on Mr. Costa's face indicated that he might not have believed her completely, but that it was okay. Lucy had the feeling that a lot of people said things like this to him — half-truths about their lives, their feelings.

'Are you comfortable?' he asked.

As comfortable as I have ever been, Lucy thought. *For some reason.*

'Yes,' she said. 'I'm fine.'

'Did you bring the notepad with you? The hotel notepad?'

Lucy reached into her bag, took out the notepad. She handed it to Mr. Costa but he put out his hands, palms toward her. 'No, this is for you to write on. Do you have a pen?'

'No,' Lucy said. 'Sorry.'

Mr. Costa reached into his coat pocket, took out a beautiful old fountain pen, uncapped it, handed it to Lucy. 'You will write something on the pad a little later.'

'Okay.'

'Are you ready to begin our session?'

'I am.'

'Now, I want you to close your eyes, and listen to the sound of my voice.'

⋆ ⋆ ⋆

Lucy was not floating above the town this time. This time she was sitting. No, she was kneeling, sort of. She was on her knees but leaning back

257

on her heels. And she was afraid.

Where are you?

I'm in the dark. I have a blindfold on.

Do you know where you are?

No.

Are you inside or outside?

I'm inside. Inside a building.

Is the room large or small?

Small. It feels like a closet or something.

Where is the man?

I don't know.

Has he hurt you in any way?

I don't think so.

Are you alone?

Yes. But I met someone else. A girl.

How old is she?

She's my age.

What can you see?

When I take off the blindfold I see a keyhole in the door. I can see out of the keyhole. There's a table next to the sofa. There's something on it.

What is on the table?

It's shiny. It's kind of oval-shaped.

What is it? What is the shiny object?

It's a badge. A policeman's badge.

What are you wearing?

A dress. He put a dress on me.

What kind of dress?

A spangly dress. A grown-up dress. And he calls me Eve.

Eve? Who is Eve? Someone you know?

No. He means Eve in the Garden of Eden. Eve who was tempted by the apple.

Can you see his face?

No. Not yet. But I can see his hand. He wears a big ring.

What kind of ring?

It looks like a snake. It looks like a ring in the shape of a snake.

Suddenly, in her dream world, Lucy Doucette felt herself falling. She sensed that someone was trying to save her. Someone or something.

No. It was the darkness itself. She reached out —

— a ring in the shape of a snake . . . the snake in the Garden of Eden —

— and let the darkness take her.

33

Joseph Novak sat in Interview A, one of the two cramped and oppressive interrogation rooms at the homicide unit.

They did not have much, and they probably wouldn't have been able to bring him in without his consent, but he'd run. People don't realize that once you run from the police it opens a big can of possibilities. It immediately establishes a hostile relationship. What might once have been a conversation that moved gently from casual to mild inquisitiveness now began with doubt and suspicion.

Even if you had to cut people loose, sometimes you got lucky. A lot of it had to do with the nature of the case itself, the heat generated not only within the department and the district attorney's office but also with the public. If a case broke open in the public consciousness, pressure was brought to bear on law enforcement to produce results, therefore detectives put the pressure on DAs, who worked a little harder on judges, and as a result search warrants and body warrants were granted with a little more leeway. When you searched a house or car you never knew what the search would produce. Warrants were the handmaidens of criminal charges, even when you had no idea what you were looking for.

★ ★ ★

They let Novak simmer in Interview A for a few minutes. Interview A at the unit didn't look anything like the interrogation rooms on TV. On TV the rooms had soft gray walls, dramatic lighting, clean carpeting, expensive furnishings, and were usually the size of an average living room. In reality, at least in Philly homicide, the real room was about six by eight, not much bigger than your average jail cell — which was not an accident of design.

There were no windows, just the two-way mirror, which was not much bigger than a magazine. Then there were the bright fluorescent lights overhead, the bolted-down chairs, and the short-legged table. No matter how often the room was cleaned, or even painted, it held onto the faint odors of urine and bleach. All in all, it was the Philadelphia equivalent of a visit to George Orwell's Room 101. Or so the Homicide Unit hoped.

If you had claustrophobia issues and you heard that door close, the bolt slide on the other side, you started to come apart. More than one tough guy had blurted a confession after an hour or two inside Hotel Homicide.

★ ★ ★

Jessica sat across from Novak. Byrne stood, leaning against the wall next to the observation window. Novak sat dispassionately in the bolted-down chair, his face void of all expression.

261

Byrne put the large file box on the table. It was almost empty but Novak didn't need to know that. Novak glanced at the box, then turned his attention back to Byrne.

'Now, where were we?' Byrne said.

Novak said nothing.

'We were having such a nice conversation. Why did you run?'

Novak still said nothing.

'Where were you heading?'

Silence.

Byrne let the questions float for a few moments, then reached out his hand. Jessica handed him her iPhone. Byrne turned the screen toward Novak and began to scroll through the series of pictures Jessica had taken of Novak's bedroom.

Novak scanned the photos, remained impassive.

'This is quite an interesting collage,' Byrne said.

Novak took a moment. 'Is it common practice for the police to be invited into someone's home, then to take covert photographs?'

'Common?' Byrne asked. 'No, I don't suppose it is.'

'I'm sure there are a number of privacy laws that have been violated here. My attorneys will have a lot of fun with this. Search and seizure, for one.'

'It's my recollection that you invited us into your home, Mr. Novak.' Byrne turned to Jessica. 'Is that how you remember it, detective?'

'It is.'

'There were no jackbooted thugs kicking in your door, no one rappelling down the side of your building and smashing in your windows. Just three people talking, two of whom were invited in.' Byrne tapped the photos on the cellphone screen. 'All of this was in plain view.'

Novak didn't react.

'Anything you'd like to share with us?' Byrne asked.

'Such as?'

'Such as why you have a room dedicated to the history of homicide in the City of Brotherly Love?'

Novak hesitated. 'It's research. I am a fan of true crime stories.'

'As you might imagine, so am I,' Byrne said. He indicated one of the photos. 'I remember many of these. In fact, I worked some of the cases.'

Novak said nothing.

Byrne tapped the iPhone screen, selecting another photograph. This one displayed a section of the room devoted to the Antoinette Chan case. It was a collage of clippings from the original stories in the *Inquirer, Daily News* and the tabloid *Report*, as well as from follow-up stories when Kenneth Beckman had been brought in for questioning.

'I see you are following the Antoinette Chan case,' Byrne said.

Novak crossed his hands in his lap, began to rub a finger over his left fist. A classic self-touch gesture. They were getting into a discomfort zone. 'It is an interesting case. One of many. I have research going back one hundred years. I'm sure you'll agree, this city has no shortage of crimes against persons.'

Byrne held up his hands, surrendering the point. 'You'll get no argument here,' he said. 'But let's talk about current cases first, okay?'

Nothing.

'What did you find interesting about the Chan case?' Byrne asked.

Novak leaned back in his chair, looked down, breaking eye contact with Byrne. A disconnect. 'It was particularly brutal, I thought. The weapon used was a claw hammer, if I remember correctly.'

'That's correct.'

'It seems an intimate act, using such a weapon,' Novak said, looking up briefly, then quickly away. 'A lot of passion.'

'Do you know a man named Kenneth Beckman?' Byrne asked.

'No.'

The answer came way too fast. As soon as it left his lips, Jessica saw that Novak knew it was the wrong move.

'But you went to grade school with him,' Byrne said. 'Little Kenny was in your class from second through sixth grades.'

'He was?'

'No,' Byrne said. 'At least, I don't think he was. The point is, based on your quick answer he *might* have been someone you knew, yet you said no without even giving it a moment's thought. Why was that?'

Novak shifted in his seat. 'This man you're

asking me about — I take it he was in the photo lineup you showed me at my apartment?'

'Yes.'

'I don't know anyone by that name.'

Byrne reached into the box, slid the photo lineup across the table. Novak looked at it, his eyes carefully roaming across the six faces. This was clearly for show. He shook his head.

Byrne jabbed the photo on the iPhone screen, enlarging it. It was a news clipping of the Antoinette Chan case. 'You said you were doing research. What kind of research?'

'I'm writing an opera.'

'An opera?'

'Yes,' Novak said. He shifted his weight again in what Jessica knew to be an uncomfortable steel chair. 'It is an epic story of crime and punishment in this city. It covers more than a hundred years. What you are looking at here is my research.'

'Some of your research into the Antoinette Chan case named Kenneth Beckman as a suspect.'

Novak hesitated. 'I can't remember every person's name. Real names are not important to the theme of my work.'

'What is the theme of your work?'

'Crime, punishment, guilt, redemption.'

'Kenneth Beckman is dead.'

Nothing. No reaction.

'He was murdered,' Byrne continued. 'His body was found at the same crime scene where Antoinette Chan was found.'

Novak remained silent.

265

'Hell of a twist, no?' Byrne said. 'I'm seeing that as the end of the first act.'

Novak looked up, a smug look on his face. It was not the look of someone with nothing to hide but rather of one who has very carefully hidden everything.

'If he was involved in the murder of Antoinette Chan, I might make reference to karma, fate, all that. None of it has anything to do with me.'

'So the name Kenneth Beckman means nothing to you?'

'Nothing.'

'What about the name Sharon Beckman?'

'Is that his wife?'

Byrne just stared.

Novak fashioned a thin smile, shook his head. 'Is this the part where you say 'Did I say *wife*? I didn't say *wife*. How did you know it wasn't his daughter or sister?' Is this where you say these things, detective?' Novak clasped his hands in his lap. 'I saw *Sleuth*. The original film, that is. The one with — '

'Laurence Olivier and Michael Caine.'

This time Novak's look said touché.

'You still haven't answered my question,' Byrne said.

Novak stared at the floor.

'Mr. Novak? Does the name Sharon Beckman mean anything to you?'

Novak looked up. 'No.'

Byrne let the exchange settle for a few moments. Then he removed the clear plastic evidence bag containing the sample of Atriana paper.

'Do you recognize this?' Byrne asked.

Novak took the evidence bag from Byrne, held it up to the fluorescent light. The edge of the distinctive watermark was clear.

'I do.'

'Where do you recognize it from?'

'I'm familiar with the line. It's called Atriana.'

'What is Marcato LLC?'

Pause. 'It's a publishing company.'

'Books? Magazines?'

'Music.'

Byrne nodded. 'And you use this paper?'

'Yes,' Novak said. 'I use the paper to bind special editions.'

'Where would I find a copy of one of these editions?'

'They are all over the world.'

'When was the last time you purchased this paper?' Byrne asked.

'I don't recall.'

'If we search your apartment will we find this paper? Maybe cut into five-inch-wide strips?'

'No,' Novak said. 'All the paper I had was stolen. Someone broke into my house.'

'Oh yeah? When was this?'

'Six months ago.'

'Did you report it to the police?'

'Yes.'

Novak was certainly smart enough to know that they would look this up. He probably would not have said this if it weren't true. 'What else was taken?'

'A watch, an MP3 player.'

'And paper,' Byrne added.

No reply.

Byrne stared at the man for a few moments, as if commiserating with him over the strange state of the world. 'Well, I was at your place this morning, and I have to say that if I had broken in I would've found a few more items of value than just a wristwatch, a Nano, and some paper. Some of your audio equipment would go for more than a few bucks on the corner, don't you think? Pioneer Elite, McIntosh. This is serious jelly.'

'I didn't have all that equipment then.'

'Ah, okay,' Byrne said. 'I'm sure you still have the receipts from when you purchased the equipment, yes? We may want to look at them.'

Novak remained stone-faced. 'I could probably find them.'

'Great,' Byrne said. 'That would help a lot.'

Jessica excused herself, stepped out of the interview room. She got on the phone to West Division detectives, made her request. A few minutes later she got a fax of the incident report. Novak was telling the truth. At least about the break-in. She stepped back into the interview room, handed the fax to Byrne. He read it, looked at Novak.

'It appears you were telling the truth,' Byrne said.

'Imagine that.'

Byrne put the fax into the binder, closed it. 'Yet you know what I find odd?'

'What is that?'

'With all your meticulous research into the Antoinette Chan case, you do not remember

268

the name Kenneth Beckman. His name was in the papers — on television, too.'

Novak shrugged. 'I must have missed it.'

'Imagine that.'

'You can see why we might be interested here, Mr. Novak.' Byrne held up the bag with the paper sample. 'Here is an item belonging to you, and it was found at the scene of a homicide.'

'It was an item *stolen* from me,' Novak said. 'And while the injustice that was done to me pales in comparison to what was done to Mr. Beckman I am just as much a victim in this as he.'

Byrne took it all in, waited a few moments. 'Sounds positively operatic.'

For a few moments Novak said nothing. Then, almost on cue: 'I believe we have reached the point where I should contact my attorney. Among other things, I'm sure he will be interested in the photographs you have of my personal and private property, and how they were obtained.'

Byrne looked at Jessica. She held up her iPhone so that Novak could see the screen. She tapped a few icons and a moment later they all watched the progress bar move left to right. The images had been deleted. Byrne looked back at Novak.

'What photographs?' Byrne asked.

The two men stared at each other for a few seconds.

'We're almost done here,' Byrne finally said. 'If you'll excuse us for a moment.'

Byrne stepped out of the room, closed the

door, slid home the bolt. He bumped a fist with Jessica. They had, of course, printed the images from her iPhone before starting the interview. In addition, while holding up her iPhone in the interview room, she had also taken Joseph Novak's picture.

They met with Dana Westbrook in the coffee room. They watched Novak on the monitor.

'Unfortunately, this is not enough to hold him or get a search warrant,' Westbrook said.

'We have to consider his collage of murder stories, boss.'

'Not against the law last time I checked. If it was, I might be in jail myself. Last night I watched a double feature of *Manhunter* and *The Silence of the Lambs*.' Westbrook checked her watch. They had to be careful about how long they kept Novak. They would soon have to charge him or let him go. They'd all had a refresher course in this recently with the Eduardo Robles fiasco. 'Plus, none of the snapshots would be admissible. No probable cause, and how they were obtained would certainly be explored by any defense attorney.'

Jessica looked back into the room. Novak had not moved a muscle. He sat with his eyes closed, his long legs crossed in front of him.

'Can we put him under surveillance?' Jessica asked.

Westbrook walked back to her office, returned. She had looked at the duty roster. 'I don't have a single warm body available. There may be someone on last-out tonight. I'll talk to the watch commander and see what I can do.'

Anything could happen between now and then, Jessica thought. Still, it was what it was.

'Cut him loose,' Westbrook said.

★ ★ ★

A few minutes later Jessica and Byrne stood in the duty room, watching Novak saunter toward the hallway that led to the elevators.

Before Novak rounded the corner he stopped, as if he'd forgotten something. A few seconds later he spun on his heels, walked briskly back, heading directly for Jessica and Byrne.

What the hell is this? Jessica wondered.

34

As Novak approached, Byrne watched the man's hands. It was a habit he'd acquired as a rookie and he'd never forgotten it. Watch the hands, watch the man.

Novak stopped in front of them. He did not look at Jessica, just at Byrne.

'I just wanted to say I harbor no hard feelings,' Novak said.

This isn't over; Byrne thought. *You might change your mind about that.*

Novak extended his hand.

Byrne had learned a lesson from his father many years earlier, and that was never to refuse to shake a man's hand, even if you think he is the most despicable person on earth. The reason, Paddy Byrne explained to his young son, was that if at some point in the future you needed to take that man down, he would never see you coming.

Byrne reached out.

The two men touched, and Byrne saw . . .

. . . the house bathed in darkness, light coming in the high windows, milk of an autumn moon painting everything in a sulfurous blue.

Four people here. Music plays in the background. Lilting, familiar music, soon buoyed by screams of terror and agony. Now the smell of blood in the air. Blood and jasmine.

At midnight three people stand over a dead

body, blood spreading on the white tile, glossy crimson clouds reflecting faces that . . .

. . . Byrne could not see. Not yet. He held Joseph Novak's hand for an uncomfortable second too long. The gesture was not lost on Novak, who turned quickly and walked out of the duty room.

Byrne had one question circling the disturbing vision in his mind, one question to which he did not really want the answer.

Was this Joseph Novak's memory, or my own?

35

They met in the Boss's office. In the room, besides Dana Westbrook, were Russell Diaz, Nicci Malone, Nick Palladino, Josh Bontrager and Dennis Stansfield.

Byrne drew two triangles on the white board. On the first triangle he wrote a name at the top. Antoinette Chan. At the bottom left he wrote Kenneth Beckman. Bottom right, Sharon Beckman.

'Let's start with Antoinette Chan,' Byrne said. 'Let's say for the sake of argument that Beckman killed her. And let's say that Sharon Beckman was his accomplice, in that she set fire to their house to destroy any evidence. Kenneth Beckman's body was found at the original Chan crime scene. Sharon Beckman's was found on Antoinette Chan's grave. Killer, accomplice and victim, all joined in this triangle, each point completed.'

Byrne moved over to the second triangle. At the top he put a question mark. At the lower left he wrote John Doe. At the lower right, another question mark.

'Now, if our bad boy is some kind of vigilante, righting old wrongs, and his MO is to take out the lead suspect in an unsolved homicide and leave the body at the original crime scene, then move on to an accomplice and dump *that* body on the grave of the original victim, I think we can extrapolate a bit here.'

Byrne pointed at the bottom left of the second triangle.

'Because our John Doe was found on the street, we can assume that he was someone who our guy believes was responsible for a homicide that took place at that location. Who the victim was, and who the accomplice was, we won't know until we track down the original crime. We have to start here. Unless we can turn up a witness, it's the only move.'

Byrne turned to Nicci. 'Nothing on the John Doe's prints yet?'

Nicci shook her head. 'The guy was a crackhead. His fingers are so burned we couldn't get a good print. Still working on it, though.'

Byrne nodded. 'Okay, then we'll have to find a homicide committed at the corner of Second and Poplar.'

There were audible moans around the room. This was going to be a paper chase.

★   ★   ★

Six detectives pored over homicide binders for cases from the past thirty years. Unfortunately, there was no way to search the electronic databases based on where a homicide had been committed, or by status. It all had to be done by hand. It was tedious work, having to read each file. Not all of them had been filled out properly or even legibly. It was almost a peer review of the detectives who had worked in the unit over the past three decades.

Jessica flipped through the books covering 2003 to 2007. Case after case her eyes jumped from the name of the victim to the date, to the crime-scene location. Case after case took her on a grotesque tour of her city, its crimes of violence, its victims and perpetrators. It occurred to her more than once that she had been to virtually all these places, many times, often with her family as a child, or with Sophie and Vincent, blissfully unaware that someone in her city's past had been murdered there.

Every so often Jessica got up and fetched herself a fresh cup of coffee, hoping to keep on mission. The names and addresses all started to blend together, and the danger of finding herself daydreaming carried with it the hazard that she would have no idea how long she had been drifting and therefore no idea how far she needed to go back.

Fresh cup, a quick stretch, and back at it. Mid-2004. The page on which she had stopped told a charming little tale of a man who had shot his wife eleven times for having an affair with the UPS man. Jessica wondered if the guy delivered.

You're getting loopy, Jess.

She flipped a page.

'Here it is!' she shouted, almost before she knew it.

The other five detectives got up, all but ran over to her.

'June 21, 2004. DOA found in a Dumpster near Second and Poplar. Victim's name was Marcellus Palmer.'

A quick scan of the page told them the basics.

Marcellus Palmer had been indigent, forty-one years old. He was found bludgeoned to death, his pockets turned inside out, his shoes missing. Jessica made a mental note, as she assumed Byrne did as well, that the COD was the same as for Antoinette Chan. Bludgeoned. Perhaps the connection was there.

They would have to go to Record Storage to get the full file, but they had made a start.

Jessica looked at the photo clipped to the summary. The new crime scene was literally a few feet from where Palmer's body had been found. It was one of Kevin Byrne's old stomping grounds as a patrolman.

'What's the status?' Bontrager asked.

'Open case,' Jessica said.

'Suspects?'

'The main suspect, also homeless, was a man named Preston Braswell, thirty-one at the time. Never charged.'

Nicci Malone sat down at a computer terminal, typed in the name. A few seconds later she had a hit. And a picture. 'That's him. Preston Braswell is our John Doe.'

The other detectives crowded around the terminal. The photograph on the screen was that of a younger, cleaner version of the John Doe. A positive match.

They now had two separate cases where the original suspect in a homicide case was found murdered and had been dumped in the precise same spot as the original homicide. One of the cases had the accomplice dumped on the grave site of the original victim. They had every reason

277

to believe it was about to happen again. If it hadn't happened already.

Nicci sprang to her feet. Dino helped her with her coat, put on his own. 'We're off to Record Storage,' Dino said. 'Stand by.'

As Nicci and Dino left, Jessica and Byrne returned to the white board. Byrne erased the question mark at the top of the triangle on the right, then replaced it with the name Marcellus Palmer. He then erased the question mark at the lower left, replaced it with the name Preston Braswell.

Jessica took a step back, looked at the growing mountain of evidence connected with these three cases. There were three binders on the desk, each with a thickening group of folders within. She glanced at Byrne.

He was staring at something else.

He was staring at the final question mark on the board.

*   ★   ★

Twenty minutes later they got a call from Nicci Malone. She had the box of files on the 2004 murder of Marcellus Palmer. She was just about to fax over the suspect and witness list. Jessica put the phone on speaker.

'How bad is it?' Jessica asked.

'Put on your Nikes. The initial list has seventy-one names.'

'*Seventy-one?*'

'Yeah. The homeless are a social group,' Nicci said. 'But it looks like there were four men

278

besides Preston Braswell who we liked more than the others. They were all questioned and released. I think we should try to track them down first.'

Before our killer does, Jessica thought.

A few minutes later they received the fax with the four names. Jessica found them all in the system and printed off what information they had on the men, including the most recent photographs.

Because there was no information on where Marcellus Palmer was buried they would have to start on the street.

For years, and with no small sense of irony, many homeless had huddled in the park directly across from the police administration building, in what is known as Franklin Square. In general, the homeless congregate where they are fed. Not much had changed in the past twenty-five years.

The detectives divvied up the names and photographs of the four men, as well as the locations of the shelters. They would work these interviews solo, as there were too many places to visit in teams, and time was short.

Jessica would take Old City.

36

The area beneath the Ben Franklin Bridge, at the interchange with I–95, had long been a refuge for Philadelphia's homeless. For years the police referred to it as The Condos. Jessica parked, found a break in the chain-link fence, made her way beneath the overpass. There were a few dozen people congregated there. Stacked against the fence were stuffed cardboard boxes, bursting plastic bags. Nearby was a stroller with only three wheels. Cups, bottles, milk cartons, fast-food trash. No aluminum cans, of course. Cans were currency.

There were ten or twelve people on the north side of the encampment, mostly men. They glanced up at Jessica, not reacting in any way. Two reasons. One, she was a woman. Two, even though she was clearly a police officer, or at least a representative of the system, she was not coming in all guns blazing, with the obvious intention of uprooting them.

There were three distinct camps, with a few men off on their own. Jessica approached the first group, showed them the photographs. No one admitted recognizing anyone. The same with the second and third groups of men.

As Jessica walked away from the third group, one of the men called out to her. Jessica turned around. It was one of the older guys. He was lying on a thick bed of cardboard.

'Say, darling, you ever been with a homeless man?' He smiled his keyboard grin, broke into a phlegmy cough. The other two men in his posse chuckled. 'Guaranteed to change your *life*. You interested?'

'Sure,' Jessica said. 'All you have to do is take a shower and get a job.'

The man looked shocked. He got back under his blanket, turned on his side. 'You ain't all *that*.'

Jessica smiled, made her way back around the camp, asking the same questions, receiving nothing. The last man pointed to a man on the other side of the embankment, someone Jessica hadn't noticed before. As she approached she saw that the man — who was surrounded by carefully placed trash bags — had his legs covered with what appeared to be a new blanket. As Jessica got closer she saw that it still had its price tag.

★   ★   ★

The man was propped against the fence, reading a paperback. Its cover was missing but Jessica could read the spine. *Great Expectations*.

'Excuse me. Sir?'

He looked up. He was black, somewhere between fifty and seventy. He wore a tattered brown corduroy blazer and a yellowed shirt. His tie, like the blanket, looked new. Jessica wondered if there was a price tag on that, too. His eyes were bright and intelligent.

'Madam.'

281

'May I ask your name?'

'Abraham Coltrane.'

Jessica believed the Abraham part. 'Do you mind if I ask you a few questions?' Jessica held up her badge. The man scanned it.

'Not at all.'

Jessica held up three of the photographs. 'Do you know any of these men?'

Coltrane scanned the pictures. 'I do not. Are they men of leisure, such as myself?'

'They are.'

Abraham Coltrane nodded. Jessica held up the final picture, a photograph of the fourth man believed to have been involved with the 2004 murder of Marcellus Palmer. The man's name was Tyvander Alice. 'What about this man?'

Coltrane looked again. This time Jessica saw the slightest flicker of recognition. 'Again,' he said. 'My regrets.'

'This picture was taken a few years ago.'

'I remember everyone I have ever met, madam.'

She believed he did, which was why she didn't believe the part about him not knowing Tyvander Alice. She took out a five-dollar bill, making sure that the man saw it.

'Nice blanket,' she said.

'It provides.'

Jessica lifted the price tag. 'You have a receipt for this, Mr. Coltrane?'

'It was a gift from one of my many admirers.'

'They gave you a gift with the price tag still on it?'

Coltrane shrugged. 'The young have but a

282

nodding acquaintance with custom, I fear.'

'Thank God the court system still does,' Jessica said. 'They're really big on it. Indictment, prosecution, conviction, incarceration. You might say they are sticklers for tradition.'

Coltrane stared at her for a moment. Jessica saw the man's will begin to fade. 'May I see that photograph again?'

'Of course.' Jessica showed him. He studied it for a moment, rubbing his stubbled chin.

'Now that I've had a moment to reflect, I believe I have made the acquaintance of this gentleman.'

'Is this Tyvander Alice?'

'Tyvander?' he asked. 'No. I knew him by another name. I know him as Hoochie.'

'Hoochie?'

'Yes. An unfortunate and undignified sobriquet based on his love of the lesser vintages, I believe.'

Jessica handed Coltrane the five. The man touched it to his forehead, sniffed it, then spirited it away under his blanket.

Before Jessica could ask another question she saw the blanket move. A few seconds later a Jack Russell terrier poked his snout out. His *gray* snout. The dog blinked a few times, adjusting its eyes to the light.

'And who is this?' Jessica asked.

'This is the irascible Biscuit. He is my oldest friend.' Coltrane patted the dog's head. Jessica saw the blanket bounce up and down with the movement of the pooch's tail. 'Is there anything in the world better than a warm biscuit?'

283

Jessica tried to think of something. She could not. There was as good, but not better. She returned to the business at hand. 'Do you know where I might find Hoochie?'

Coltrane shrugged. ''I wander'd lonely as a cloud that floats on high o'er vales and hills.''

Jessica raised an eyebrow, expecting more. There was no more. 'Bon Jovi?'

Coltrane smiled. 'Wordsworth.'

In other words, the answer was no. Homeless were just that. Jessica took out the photograph of Marcellus Palmer, the original victim found at Second and Poplar in 2004. 'Did you know this gentleman?'

'Oh yes.' Coltrane said. 'Marcellus. We shared many a tankard of kill-devil. But that was a long time ago.'

'Do you know what happened to him?'

Coltrane nodded sadly. 'I heard he came to an unfortunate end. City buried him.'

'Do you know where?'

Coltrane looked up at the concrete embankment. For a moment there was only the sound of the cars passing overhead. 'Now, I *did* know at one time. The recollection seems to be pirouetting just at the edge of my memory.'

Jessica produced another five, held it back. 'Think we could coax it back onto the dance floor?'

'I believe we can.'

The money was gone in an instant.

'Up around Parkwood, I believe.'

Jessica's phone rang. She looked at the screen. It was Byrne.

'Thank you for your time, Mr. Coltrane.'

'Always willing to do my part,' he said.

Jessica took a few steps away, answered her phone.

'Where are you?' she asked.

'Still in West Philly.'

Jessica told him what she had learned from Abraham Coltrane. Byrne filled her in on what she had missed. Two of the other homeless men who had been questioned in the murder of Marcellus Palmer were dead. The third man was long gone. Someone told someone that someone's friend had told someone that he was in Florida. Two *someones* was about the extent of any network worth exploring.

When they met back at the Roundhouse, Jessica checked a roster of the city's graveyards.

There was no cemetery in Parkwood.

37

Finnigan's Wake, the popular Irish pub at Third and Spring Garden Streets, in the Northern Liberties section of the city, was packed with a who's who from the department and the DA's office, as well as defense attorneys, paralegals, FBI agents, commissioners, medical examiner's investigators. As always, everyone clustered with their tribe. David Albrecht was there, shooting from the sidelines. Russ Diaz was with his new team. Tom Weyrich was there, looking a little better than Jessica had seen him look in a long time. Maybe it was the Guinness. Dennis Stansfield stood in the corner with two of his old squad mates.

The jampacked party was held on the second floor, also known as the Lincoln Level. After Abraham Lincoln was assassinated, his body was transported to Philadelphia to lie in state at Independence Hall. That night his body had been kept in a Northern Liberties funeral parlor, and the doors from that establishment became part of the second floor at Finnigan's Wake. More than one pint had been lifted to Honest Abe in this room.

★ ★ ★

As the evening wore on a number of people got up and told their Michael Drummond stories.

286

Like all leaving parties, the first hour's worth of stories were mild, only somewhat ribald recounts of incidents that happened around the office. The second hour, seeing as Michael Drummond was about to become part of the opposition to most of the people in the room, became a little more adventurous, if not down-right drunkenly libelous.

At eleven p.m. Michael Drummond himself took the microphone. Although Drummond was not yet forty, there was a lot of fresh blood in the DA's office and he was referred to as the old man.

'Yes, it's true that I joined the office after an unfortunate incident with a Model A Ford,' he said, drawing polite laughter.

He went on to thank just about everyone he'd ever worked with, on both sides of the aisle, taking particular care to heap praise upon all the judges — men and women in front of whom he would shortly be arguing for the defense — regardless of whether they were at the party or not.

Soon it became time for him to spill the beans. With a clank of a spoon on a crystal glass, he got everyone's undivided attention.

'Folks, I have an announcement to make,' Drummond said.

Everyone quieted down. This was, more or less, the reason they had gathered.

'In two weeks I will start work as a junior partner at Paulson Derry Chambers. Until then, I'm on the job. So watch yourselves.'

A rumble went through the room. Paulson

Derry Chambers was one of the most prominent firms in the city. Everyone expected Mike Drummond to go for the dollar, but a junior partnership at Paulson Derry was like stepping into Valhalla. Applause followed.

'Although I didn't know him personally, I'd like to leave you with the wise words of Pericles,' Drummond added. 'He said: *'What you leave behind is not what is engraved in stone monuments, but what is woven into the lives of others.'*'

'Hear, hear,' someone said.

Everyone raised a glass.

'Here's to old dogs,' a slightly inebriated Nick Palladino added.

Drummond laughed. 'And soft bones.'

Everyone returned to their small groups. The detectives gathered near the tall windows overlooking Spring Garden Street and the view of the Ben Franklin Bridge.

'Ah, *shit*,' Dino said after everyone sat down.

'What?' Jessica asked.

Dino stood up, looked in his pockets, patted himself down like a suspect. 'I can't believe this.'

'What's wrong?'

Deadpan: 'I think I left my lip gloss at home.'

Someone snorted.

Dino pointed at Byrne's man bag, hanging off the back of his chair. 'Hey, Kev. You wouldn't happen to have any in there, would you?'

Muffled laughs around the table. Byrne shook his head. 'I'm a lot bigger than you are, you know that, right?'

'I know,' Dino said. 'But you're also older.'

'By what, five or six months?'

'Still.'

'That just means it will take me a few seconds longer to get across the room.'

Dino held up both hands. 'Just don't hit me with your man bag.'

Byrne shot to his feet.

Nick Palladino ran to the bar.

★   ★   ★

By midnight most of the younger players had moved on or gone home. It was a work night. There were young families waiting. After the midnight hour the floor was left to the serious drinkers.

Jessica, who was just about out the door, stood with Byrne near the elevator. Michael Drummond found them, crossed the room. He'd had his share of cheer, and more.

'Thanks for coming, guys.'

Drummond gave Jessica a brotherly hug, shook Byrne's hand, clapped him on the shoulder.

'You do realize we'll probably go up against each other one of these days,' Byrne said.

Drummond nodded. 'Yeah. I feel like I've gone over to the dark side.'

'The money should help ease your pain.'

Drummond smiled. He glanced at his watch. 'I've got to be up in about three hours,' he said. 'We're moving my mother into an assisted living facility.'

'Do you need another pair of hands?' Byrne asked.

'No, we're good. Thanks.' Drummond slipped on his overcoat. 'I just have to be in Parkwood around six-thirty.'

Jessica looked at Byrne, then back. 'Parkwood?'

'What about it?'

'Well, it's just come up twice in one day.'

'What do you mean?' Drummond asked.

Jessica explained what they had done that afternoon, about Abraham Coltrane's claim that Marcellus Palmer, the 2004 victim found in the Dumpster just a few blocks from where they now stood, was buried in or around Parkwood. Drummond thought for a few moments.

'Well, I'm pretty sure there *used* to be a potter's field in Parkwood,' he said. 'It closed a while back.'

'Closed?'

'Yeah. I think the bodies were disinterred and either moved to other cemeteries or cremated. I think there was supposed to be some kind of development that went in that spot, but nothing ever happened.' Drummond drained his glass, put it on the bar. 'Can you imagine living on top of a former cemetery?'

Jessica felt a chill at the idea. 'Do you know where the cemetery was located?'

Drummond shrugged. 'No idea. Sorry. I might even be wrong about this.'

'Counselor!' someone shouted drunkenly from across the room. 'You're needed for a *voir dire*.'

It was two old-timers from the DA's office. The *voir dire* was a process of jury selection, generally involving the judge and attorneys asking potential jurors about their experiences and beliefs. On the table in front of the two ADAs was one of every different kind of drink in the bar. There had to be fifty full glasses. Drummond looked back at Jessica and Byrne. 'Looks like the night isn't over for me yet. Thanks again for coming.'

Drummond slipped off his coat and staggered across the room.

* * *

Downstairs, a few minutes later, Byrne held the door for Jessica. They stepped out onto Spring Garden Street.

'So, what time do you want to meet me at L & I?' Byrne asked. The License & Inspections division had city-zoning archives going back more than two hundred years. If there had once been a cemetery in or around Parkwood it would be recorded there.

'As soon as they open, detective,' Jessica said.

291

38

THURSDAY, OCTOBER 28

The city's last official potter's field had opened in 1956 in Philadelphia's Northeast. Prior to its opening, the most active potter's field had been in a section now used as a police parking lot at Luzerne Street and Whitaker Avenue, adjoining Philadelphia Municipal Hospital, where it became the final resting place for thousands who died in the 1918 flu epidemic. At various times in the city's history, indigent or unclaimed deceased were buried in a number of places, including Logan Square, Franklin Field, Reyburn Park, even at the corner of 15th and Catharine, just a few blocks from where Jessica had grown up.

These days, in the interest of logistics and expense, many of the unidentified and indigent were being cremated, with remains stored in a room off the morgue at the medical examiner's office.

Jessica and Byrne visited the zoning-archives department of Licenses and Inspections at just after eight a.m. The L & I office was located in the Municipal Services Building at 15th and JFK. What they learned was that there had once been a potter's field located in the Parkwood section of Northeast Philadelphia, a field that had since closed.

They stopped for coffee and got onto I–95 at just after nine a.m.

* ★ ★

The field was located near the intersection of Mechanicsville Road and Dunks Ferry Road at the southern end of Poquessing Valley Park.

On the south side of Dunks Ferry Road were blocks of two-story twin row homes, their fasciae festooned with Halloween decorations ranging from the elaborate (one had a skeleton about to climb down the chimney) to the ordinary (an already dented plastic pumpkin stuck on a gas light).

Jessica and Byrne got out of the car, crossed the road. They walked through the trees into a large open field. Here the ground was rippled — the uneven remnants of graves that had been there a long time.

There were no headstones, no crypts, no vaults, no mausoleum. The field had indeed been closed, the bodies moved or cremated, the area planted over.

Jessica looked at the rutted sod. She considered the generations of kids to come, flying kites, playing kickball, unaware that at one time the ground beneath their feet had held the remnants of the city's homeless, its indigent, its lost.

They walked slowly across the undulating earth, looking for any sign of what had once been there — a buried headstone, a grave marker of any kind, a stake in the ground indicating the

293

boundaries of the cemetery. There was nothing. The earth had long ago begun to reclaim the area with life.

'Was this the only city field in this area?' Jessica asked.

'Yeah,' Byrne said. 'This was it.'

Jessica looked around. Nothing looked promising, at least as it might concern the cases. 'We're wasting our time up here, aren't we?'

Byrne didn't reply. Instead he crouched down, ran his hand over a bare patch of ground. A few moments later he stood, dusted off his hands.

Jessica heard a rustling in the nearby trees. She looked up to see a half-dozen crows perched tenuously on a low branch of a nearby maple. A *murder* of crows, she had once learned, and had ever since thought how odd a term that was. A flock of geese, a herd of cattle, a murder of crows. Soon another black bird landed, rustling the others, who responded with a series of loud caws and flapping wings. One of them took off and swooped toward the low shrubs at the other side of the field. Jessica followed the pattern of flight.

'Kevin,' she said, pointing to the bird before it landed out of sight. They looked at each other, started across the open field.

Before they got halfway they saw it — the unnatural gleam through the greenery, the bright white surface glinting in the sunlight.

They sprinted the last hundred feet or so and found the body lying in a shallow depression.

The victim was black, male, in his forties or fifties. He was nude, his body shaven head to toe. The ground beneath the corpse was not yet overgrown with grass. It was a former grave.

'Mother*fucker*,' Byrne yelled.

He stepped through the scene, taking care not to disturb the surrounding area. He put two fingers to the man's neck. 'Jesus Christ,' he said. 'His body's still *warm*. Let's get everyone and his mother down here. Let's get a K-9 unit.'

Then Byrne gently opened the dead man's hand. There, on the ring finger of his left hand, was the tattoo of a fish.

They both called it in — Byrne contacted the crime-scene unit, Jessica contacted the homicide unit who would then alert the MEO. They spread out to either side of the open field, weapons out. They checked the immediate area, combing the bushes, the scrub, the culverts and ditches, finding nothing.

Later they regrouped at the corner, each lost in their own thoughts. Although they had not immediately located any ID, there was no doubt in either Jessica's or Byrne's mind that the body they'd found — the dead man lying atop a former grave — was that of Tyvander 'Hoochie' Alice.

★   ★   ★

The tactical team hit the block in six cars, a combination of special-investigation detectives and members of the fugitive squad.

Russ Diaz and his squad fanned out north and east, toward the woods. A K-9 unit showed up a few minutes later. The next car brought Dana Westbrook. For the moment, this relatively quiet corner of Northeast Philadelphia — a place that had one time been a place of repose and solitude — was crawling with law-enforcement personnel.

Ten minutes later the dog and his officer came full circle, back to the parking area near the ball diamonds. It probably meant that the killer had parked there, returned after dumping the body, and then left. If that was so, the trail was cold.

★   ★   ★

While CSU processed the crime scene, Jessica and Byrne stood at the top of the hill, watching the choreography unfold below.

Detectives would soon canvass the immediate area. There was a condo development at Mechanicsville and Eddington Roads, a pair of apartments next to it. Maybe someone had seen something. But Jessica doubted it. Their killer was a ghost.

Kenneth Beckman, Sharon Beckman, Preston Braswell, Tyvander Alice.

Four bodies, eight tattoos.

Four to go.

And they didn't have a single solid lead.

★   ★   ★

The team spent the entire afternoon canvassing. The residences in this part of the city were not as tightly packed as they were in the inner city, so the act of interviewing and asking the same questions over and over was a much slower, even more enervating process.

★ ★ ★

They returned to the Roundhouse, followed up on a few weak leads. Nothing. By the end of the tour, the entire unit was exhausted and frustrated. Someone was solving the unsolved crimes in Philadelphia, but they were killing the killers and their accomplices. Someone was shaving these bodies clean, mutilating their faces, and wrapping them in paper. Someone who floated through the city like a phantom.

Jessica sat on the edge of a desk, a cup of cold coffee in her hand. She glanced over at the walk-in closet. Inside were the books of homicide cases dating back more than a hundred years. Inside the books were summaries of hundreds of unsolved cases, cases wherein there were suspects who were never charged with the crime, suspects who never became defendants, defendants who were acquitted for any number of reasons. The books were essentially a list of potential victims for their ghoul.

★ ★ ★

The duty room was mostly empty. The second tour had already begun, and those detectives were on the street, pursuing leads, tracking down witnesses. Jessica was envious.

'Don't you have a family to go home to?' Byrne asked.

'Nah,' Jessica said. 'Although, funny you should mention it, I *have* seen a man and a little girl hanging around my house. I should call the police.'

297

Byrne laughed. 'Speaking of which, how are you adjusting to the new house?'

'Well, besides tripping over the furniture and spinning in place for five minutes because there's nowhere to put a cup of coffee down, it's great.'

'Is it that much smaller?'

Jessica nodded. 'It's a lot like the house I grew up in. Same layout. The only problem is, *I* was a lot smaller then.'

'What, like a size four?'

'Smartass.'

Byrne's phone beeped in his hand. He looked at the screen, read for a moment, smiled.

'It's a text from Colleen,' he said. 'She wanted me to know she got back from D.C. okay.'

Jessica nodded. 'Wow,' she said. 'Colleen in college.'

'Don't remind me.'

Byrne picked up a tall stack of mail that was rubber-banded together on the desk. It looked like two weeks' worth of correspondence, mostly junk. Jessica wanted to mention to her partner that it was probably a good idea to check the inbox once in a while, but she figured he knew this.

As Byrne went through the pile, throwing most of the mail in the trash can, Jessica smelled the perfumed letter before she saw it. The scent was jasmine. Byrne held up the envelope, eyed it, sniffed it. It was the size of a personal note card, maybe four by six inches. Expensive-looking paper.

'A note from an admirer?' Jessica asked.

'As if,' Byrne replied.

'It's the charcoal gray suit, Kevin. I'm telling you.'

Byrne pulled a letter opener off the desk, slit the envelope, extracted the card.

As much as Jessica wanted to pry, she stepped a few feet away, giving her partner a little privacy, shoving everything she needed to take with her into her tote bag. When she looked again at Byrne, he was bone pale. Something was wrong.

'What is it?' Jessica asked.

Byrne remained silent.

'Kevin.'

Byrne waited a few moments, then took Jessica by the arm, led her to the small coffee room, closed the door. He handed her the card. It was printed on a luxurious paper, ivory in color. The scent of jasmine was now much stronger. Jessica put on her glasses, read the note, a brief message written in an elegant hand. The ink was lavender.

My dearest Detective Byrne,
It has been a long time, n'est-ce pas? I wonder how you have fared. Do you think of me? I think of you often. In fact I dreamed of you the other night. It was the first time in years. You looked quite dashing in your dark overcoat and black fedora. You carried an umbrella with a carved ivory handle. Do you carry an umbrella as a rule? No, I would think not.

So tell me. Have you found them yet? The lion and the rooster and the swan? Are there others? You might think they do not play together, but they do. I hope you are well, and that the future brings you every happiness. I am no longer scared.

— C

Jessica was stunned. She read the note a second time, the rich scent filling her head.

'Are you fucking *kidding* me?' she finally said in a loud whisper. 'The lion and the rooster and the swan?'

Byrne remained silent.

'Who the hell sent this, Kevin? Who is *C*?'

Byrne turned the envelope over and over in his hands, searching for words. Words were usually his strong suit. He always chose them carefully. He was good at it.

He told her the story.

39

Jessica looked at her partner. She wasn't sure how long she had been staring at him without saying anything, her mouth open, eyebrows raised. Then all she could muster was one word. 'Wow.'

Byrne said nothing.

'I remember her,' Jessica said. 'I mean, I remember the story. I think my father talked about it. Plus, it was all over the news for a while.' Although she'd been in high school at the time she and her friends had discussed the case, mainly because it involved sex, violence and celebrity.

In November 1990 a woman named Christa-Marie Schönburg, a cellist with the Philadelphia Orchestra, was arrested and charged in the murder of a man named Gabriel Thorne. According to the news reports, Thorne was Christa-Marie's psychiatrist, but there was a great deal of speculation at the time as to whether or not they were romantically involved, even though Thorne had been Christa-Marie's caregiver since she was a child and was three decades her senior. If Jessica remembered correctly, Christa-Marie confessed to second-degree murder, diminished capacity, and was sentenced to twenty-to-life in the women's facility at the State Correctional Institution at Muncy.

'That was your first case?' Jessica asked.

Byrne nodded. 'My first as a lead detective,

yeah. I was partnered with Jimmy.'

Jimmy Purify, his rabbi in the homicide unit, had been Byrne's partner before Jessica.

'I don't understand,' Jessica said. 'Is Christa-Marie still in Muncy?'

'No,' Byrne said. 'She was released a few years ago. The last I heard she's still living in the Chestnut Hill house.'

Jessica decided not to ask her partner why he knew all this. It was not all that uncommon for detectives to keep track of people they had arrested and convicted of crimes. What surprised Jessica was that she had known none of this.

'Have you spoken to her since her release?'

'No.'

'Has she tried to contact you before this?'

'Not that I know of.'

Jessica took a few beats. She looked again at the handwriting on the note. It did not look like the penmanship of someone deranged. 'Is she, how do I put this . . . *better* now?'

Byrne shrugged. 'I don't know. The murder was pretty brutal, and she went through a battery of psychological tests at the time of the hearings. I saw some of the reports. Chronic depression. Borderline bipolar. It never came to anything because she pled out. There never was a trial.'

'Were you called at the hearing?'

'I was.'

'Did you testify?'

Byrne hesitated before answering. Jessica sensed a feeling of regret. 'Yes.'

Jessica tried to arrange the timeline in her mind. 'When was that card postmarked?'

Byrne looked at the envelope. 'Last Thursday.'

Jessica did the math. 'So she sent it — '

'Before the murders.'

Jessica felt her breath catch. She tried to process all this. It wasn't often that she was thrown such a curve. 'Is she capable of something like this? I mean, physically capable?'

Jessica knew that at least part of her question was rhetorical. The woman was a convicted murderer, after all. Obviously she was capable of violence. But violence committed in the throes of rage or passion didn't necessarily lead to cold blooded, well-calculated murder. And then there were the physical elements.

'She's capable,' Byrne said. 'The logistics? She's not a big woman, Jess, and she's obviously a lot older now. I don't think she could have done all this without some help.'

Jessica was silent for a moment. 'Okay. Maybe it's just a coincidence. The lion and the rooster and the swan.'

Byrne just glared.

'Okay, it was worth a shot.' Jessica glanced at her watch. 'Do you want to go now or in the morning?'

'Go where?'

'Kevin. We need to talk to her.'

Byrne took the note card from her, slipped it back into the envelope. 'I should probably talk to her alone.'

Byrne was probably right, but that didn't make Jessica want to go along any less. 'You have to tell the boss, Kevin. You have to share it with the team.'

Byrne glanced around the small, cramped room. There wasn't really anything to look at besides a beaten-up coffee maker and the two-way mirror looking into one of the interview rooms. He looked back at his partner.

'Tomorrow,' he said.

Jessica started to object, but Byrne continued. 'Look, this is connected with the Kenneth Beckman case, and I'm working that case. How it's connected, I have no idea. But if it turns out to be something, I'll post it. If it doesn't, then there's no need to drag all this into the mix.'

'How could it *not* be connected, Kevin? It's not as if Christa-Marie could have just now learned any of this from anyone here. She wrote the note *before* the murders happened.'

'If I tell Dana right now, what is she going to do? Send a couple of detectives to interrogate Christa-Marie? I *know* Christa-Marie. I'm the one Dana would send, anyway. There's no reason to turn this woman's life upside down until we know what this is all about.'

'So you're going to talk to her off the record?'

Byrne said nothing.

Jessica wanted to remind her partner that Christa-Marie Schönburg was a confessed murderer, a woman who had spent more than fifteen years in prison. If he didn't have some sort of as-yet-unidentified emotional attachment to the woman and her case, and he'd heard that a confessed murderer had information on fresh homicides, he'd be charging that way with the cavalry and more.

'Besides,' Byrne began, moving on to his

304

closing argument, 'who's to say I didn't read this note tomorrow? Everyone knows I never open my mail.'

Kevin Byrne's secrets were safe with Jessica, as were hers with him. She trusted his judgment more than anyone else she knew.

'Okay,' Jessica said. 'Where do you want me on this?'

'I'll drive up to Chestnut Hill first thing in the morning. I'll call you after.'

Jessica nodded. They both went silent for a long time.

Finally Jessica asked, 'Are you okay, Kevin?'

Byrne opened the door of the coffee room, glanced out. The duty room was a ghost town. He turned back to his partner and said softly: 'I really don't know.'

★ ★ ★

Twenty minutes later Jessica watched Byrne gather his things, close his briefcase, retrieve his weapon from the file cabinet, grab his coat and keys. He stopped at the door, turned, gave her a sad smile and a wave. As he disappeared around the corner Jessica knew there was something else going on with him, something other than the job, something other than the horror of the four bodies dumped ceremoniously around their city.

Something he wasn't telling her.

40

He sits across the table from me, a trembling wreck of a man. In his hands is an old photograph, its colors long faded, its edges folded and creased.

We have had our coffee, shared our pleasantries. I am not one seduced by nostalgia. It means nothing to me.

'I didn't think you were coming back,' he says.

'But you know why I am here,' I say. 'Don't you?'

He nods.

'Everything has changed now,' I say. 'We can never go back.'

He nods again, this time with a tear in his eye.

I glance at my watch. It is time, and time is short. I stand, bring my coffee cup to the sink, rinse it in scalding water. I dry the cup, return it to the cupboard. I am wearing gloves, but one can never be too careful. I return to the table. We fall silent. There is always a calm before the truth.

'Will it hurt?' he asks.

I listen to the voices of the dead swirling around me. I would love to ask them this question. Alas, I cannot. 'I don't know.'

'It's all so Cho Cho San, is it not?'

'Without the baby,' I say.

'Without the baby.'

A few moments pass. Clouds shade his eyes.

'Remember how it was?' he asks.

'I do. All things were possible then, n'est-ce pas? All futures.'

When I think of those times, I am saddened. I realize how much of it is gone forever, lost in the ductwork of memory. I stand. 'Do you want me to wait?'

He looks at the table for a moment, then at his hands. 'No,' he says softly.

I take the photograph from him, put it into my pocket. At the door I stop, turn. I see myself in the mirror at the end of the hall. It reminds me of the shiny crimson mirror of blood on the floor.

Before leaving I turn up the music. It is not Chopin this time, but rather Holst's Planets Suite, a movement called 'Venus, The Bringer of Peace'.

Peace.

Sometimes, I think, as I step through the door for the last time, the music exalts the moment.

Sometimes it is the other way around.

41

The Penn Sleep Center, part of the University of Pennsylvania Hospital system, was located in a modern steel and glass building on Market Street near 36th.

Byrne crossed the river about six, found a parking space, checked in at the desk, presented his insurance card, sat down, speed-skimmed a copy of *Neurology Today*, one of his all-time favorite magazines. He covertly checked the handful of people scattered around the waiting room. Not surprisingly, everyone looked exhausted, beat-up, dragged-out. He hoped everyone there was a new patient. He didn't want to think they were on their twentieth appointment and still looked this bad.

'Mr. Byrne?'

Byrne looked up. Standing at the end of the long desk was a blonde woman, no more than five feet tall. She was in her early forties and wore pink-rimmed glasses. She was perky and full of energy. Insomniacs hate perky.

Byrne got up, walked over to the bubbly gal in white rayon.

'Hi!' she chirruped. 'How are *you* today?'

'Never better, thanks,' Byrne said. Of course, if that was the case, what the hell was he doing at the hospital? 'How about yourself?'

'Super!' she replied.

Her name tag read Viv. Probably short for Vivacious.

'We're just going to check your height and weight.' She led him over to the digital scale, instructed him to take off his shoes. He stepped on the scale.

'I don't want to know how much I weigh, okay?' Byrne said. 'Lately I've just been . . . I don't know. It's hormonal, I think.'

Viv smiled, zipped her lips in a dramatic gesture, recorded Byrne's weight without a word. 'Now, if you could turn around, we'll check your height.'

Byrne spun around. Viv stepped on a footstool, raised the bar of the stadiometer, then lowered it gently, touching the top of Byrne's head. 'What about height?' she asked. 'Would you like to know how tall you are?'

'I think I can handle my height. Emotionally speaking.'

'You're still six foot, three inches.'

'Good,' Byrne said. 'So I haven't shrunk.'

'Nope. You must be washing in cold water.'

Byrne smiled. He liked Viv, despite her vim.

'Come this way,' she said.

★   ★   ★

In the small, windowless examining room Byrne cruised the two battered magazines, picking up a dozen new 30-minute chicken recipes, along with some tips on how to get puppy stains out of the upholstery.

A few minutes later the doctor came in. She was Asian, about thirty, quite attractive. Pinned to her lab coat was a photo ID. Her name was Michelle Chu.

They got the pleasantries about the weather and the insanity of the people in the indoor parking garage out of the way. Dr. Chu ran through Byrne's history on the computer's LCD monitor. When she had him sufficiently pegged, she turned in her chair, crossed her legs.

'So, how long have you had insomnia?'

'Let me put it this way,' Byrne said. 'It's been so long that I can't remember.'

'Do you have trouble falling asleep or staying asleep?'

'Both.'

'How long, on average, does it take you to fall asleep?'

All night, Byrne thought. But he knew what she meant. 'Maybe an hour.'

'Do you wake up during the night?'

'Yeah. At least a couple of times.'

The doctor made a few more notes, her fingers racing across the keyboard. 'Do you snore?'

Byrne knew the answer to this. He just didn't want to tell her *how* he knew. 'Well, these days I don't really have a steady . . . '

'Bed partner?'

'Yeah,' Byrne said. 'That. Do you think you could write me a prescription for one of those?'

She laughed. 'I could, but I don't think your insurance provider would cover it.'

'You're probably right,' Byrne said. 'I can barely get them to pay for the Ambien.'

Ambien. The magic drug, the magic word. At least around neurologists. He had her attention now.

'How long have you been taking Ambien?'

310

'On and off for as long as I can remember.'

'Do you think you've developed a dependence?'

'Without question.'

Dr. Chu handed him a pre-printed sheet. 'These are some of the sleep-hygiene suggestions we have — '

Byrne held up a hand. 'May I?'

'Absolutely.'

'No alcohol, caffeine, or high-fat foods late at night. No nicotine. Exercise regularly, but not within four hours of bedtime. Go to bed and get out of bed at the same times every day. Turn your alarm clock around so you can't see the time. Keep your bedroom cool, not cold. If you can't fall asleep in ten minutes or so, get out of bed until you feel tired again. Although, if you can't see your clock, I don't know how you're supposed to know it's been ten minutes.'

Dr. Chu stared at him for a few moments. She had stopped typing altogether. 'You seem to know quite a bit about this.'

Byrne shrugged. 'You do something long enough.'

She then typed for a full minute. Byrne just watched. When she was done she said, 'Okay. Hop up on the table, please.'

Byrne stood up, walked over to the paper-lined examining table, slid onto it. He hadn't hopped anywhere in years, if ever. Dr. Chu looked into his eyes, ears, nose, throat. She listened to his heart, lungs. Then she took out a tape measure, measured his neck.

'Hmm,' she said.

Never a good sign. 'I prefer a spread collar,' Byrne said. 'French cuffs.'

'Your neck's circumference is greater than seventeen inches.'

'I work out.'

She sat down, put her stethoscope around her neck. Her face took on a concerned look. Not the *you are in deep shit* look, but concerned. 'You have a few markers for sleep apnea.'

Byrne had heard of it, but he really didn't know anything about it. The doctor explained that apnea was a condition wherein a person stops breathing during the night.

'I stop breathing?'

'Well, we don't know that for sure yet.'

'I'm kind of in the stop-breathing business, you know.'

The doctor smiled. 'This is a little different. I think I should schedule you for a sleep study.' She handed him a brochure. Color pics of smiling, healthy people who looked like they got a lot of sleep.

'Okay.'

'You're willing to give it a shot?'

Anything was better than what he was going through. Except maybe the business about not breathing. 'Sure. I'm in.'

In the waiting room, three of the five people were asleep.

★ ★ ★

Byrne stopped at the American Pub in the Center Square Building on Market Street. The

312

place was lively, and lively was just what was needed. He staked a place at the end of the bar, nursed a Bushmills. At just after ten o'clock his phone rang. He checked the ID, fully prepared to blow it off. It was a 215 exchange, with a familiar prefix. A PPD number. He had to answer.

'This is Kevin.'

'Detective Byrne?'

It was a woman's voice. A young woman's voice. He did not recognize it. 'Yes?'

'It's Lucy.'

It took Byrne a little while to realize who it was. Then he remembered. 'Hi, Lucy. Is something wrong?'

'I need to talk to you.'

'Where are you? I'll come get you.'

A long pause.

'Lucy?'

'I'm in jail.'

★   ★   ★

The Mini-Station was located on South Street between Ninth and Tenth. Originally activated in 1985 to provide weekend coverage from spring to autumn, addressing the issues generated by crowds gravitating to South Street for its clubs, shopping and restaurants, it had since become a seven days a week, twenty-four hours a day, year-round commitment, expanded to cover the entire corridor, which included more than 400 retail premises and nearly eighty establishments with liquor licenses.

313

When Byrne walked in, he immediately spotted an old comrade, P/O Denny Dorgan. Short and brick-solid, Dorgan, who was now in his early forties, still worked the bike patrol.

'Alert the hounds,' Dorgan said. 'We got royalty in the building.'

They shook hands. 'You getting shorter and uglier?' Byrne asked.

'Yeah. It's the supplements my wife is making me take. She thinks it will keep me from straying. Shows you what *she* knows.'

Byrne glanced over at Dorgan's bike, leaning near the front door. 'Good thing you can get heavy-duty shocks on the thing.'

Dorgan laughed, turned and looked at the waif-like girl sitting on the bench behind him. He turned back. 'Friend of yours?'

Byrne looked over at Lucy Doucette. She looked like a lost little kid.

'Yeah,' Byrne said. 'Thanks.'

Byrne wondered what *Dorgan* wondered, whether he thought that Byrne was dallying with a nineteen-year-old. Byrne had long ago stopped being concerned with what people thought. What had happened here was clear. Dorgan had stepped in between a misdemeanor and the law, on Byrne's behalf, and had done it as a favor to a fellow cop. The gesture would go into the books as a small act of kindness, and would one day be repaid. No more, no less. Everything else was squad-car scandal.

★   ★   ★

314

Byrne and Lucy had coffee at a small restaurant on South Street. Lucy told him the story. Or, it seemed to Byrne, the part she could bring herself to tell. She had been detained by security personnel at a kids'-clothing boutique on South. They said she'd attempted to walk out of the store with a pair of children's sweaters. The electronic security tags had been removed and were found underneath one of the sale racks, but Lucy had been observed walking around with the items, items which had not been returned to the racks. She had no sales receipts on her. Lucy had not resisted in the least.

'Did you mean to walk out with these items?'

Lucy buried her face in her hands for a moment. 'Yes. I was stealing them.'

From most people Byrne would have expected vehement denials, tales of mistaken identity and dastardly set-ups. Not Lucy Doucette. He remembered her as a blunt and honest person. Well, she was not *that* honest, apparently.

'I don't understand,' Byrne said. 'Do you have a child? A niece or a nephew that these sweaters were for?'

'No.'

'A friend's child?'

Lucy shrugged. 'Not exactly.'

Byrne watched her, waiting for more.

'It's complicated,' she finally said.

'Do you want to tell me about it?'

Lucy took another second. 'Do I have to tell you now?'

Byrne smiled. 'No.'

The waitress refilled their cups. Byrne

315

considered the young woman in front of him. He remembered how she had appeared in their therapy group. Shy, reluctant, scared. Not much had changed.

'Have you been back to any kind of treatment?' Byrne asked.

'Sort of.'

'What do you mean?'

Lucy told him a story, a story about a man called the Dreamweaver.

'How did you find this . . . Dreamweaver guy?'

Lucy rolled her eyes, tapped her fingers on her coffee cup for a few seconds, embarrassed. 'I found his card in the trash bin on my cart. It was right there, staring at me. It was like the card *wanted* me to find it. Like I was *supposed* to find it.'

Byrne gave Lucy a look, a look he hoped wasn't too scolding or paternal.

'I know, I know,' Lucy said. 'But I've tried everything else. I mean *everything*. And I think it might actually be doing me some good. I think it might be helping.'

'Well, that's what counts,' Byrne said. 'Are you going to see this guy again?'

Lucy nodded. 'One last time. Tomorrow.'

'You'll let me know what happens?'

'Okay.'

★   ★   ★

They stood on the corner of South and Third. The evening had grown cold.

'Do you have a car?' Byrne asked.

316

Lucy shook her head. 'I don't drive.'

Byrne glanced at his van, then back. 'I'm afraid I'm going the other way.' He took out his cellphone, called for a cab. Then he reached into his pocket pulled out a pair of twenties.

'I can't take that,' Lucy said.

'Pay me back someday, then.'

Lucy hesitated, then took the money.

Byrne put a hand on each of her slight shoulders. 'Look. You made a mistake today. That's all. You did the right thing calling me. We'll work it out. I want you to call me tomorrow. Will you promise to do that?'

Lucy nodded. Byrne saw her eyes glisten, but no tears followed. Tough kid. He knew that she had been on her own for a while, although she hadn't brought up her mother this time. Byrne didn't ask. She would tell him what she wanted to tell him. He was the same way.

'Am I going to prison?' she asked.

Byrne smiled. 'No, Lucy. You're not going to prison.' The cab arrived, idled. 'As long as you don't carjack this guy on the way home you should be fine.'

Lucy hugged him, got into the cab.

Byrne watched the cab drive away. Lucy's face was small and pale and frightened in the back window. He couldn't imagine the burden she carried. He'd had the same experience of not knowing what had happened to him or where he had gone for that short period of time when they had declared him dead. But he had been an adult, not a child.

The truth was, Lucy Doucette had a

bogeyman. A bogeyman who had kidnapped her and held her for three long days. Three days of dead zone in her life. A bogeyman who lived in every shadow, stood waiting around every corner.

Byrne had gotten a vision when he hugged her, a sparkling clear image that told him about a man who —

— *dates women with young daughters and comes back years later for the girls . . . something about red magnetic numbers on a refrigerator door . . . four numbers . . .*

1 . . . 2 . . . 0 . . . 8.

Byrne made a mental note to call Lucy the next day.

42

Jessica looked around the bedroom. At least they hadn't broken any lamps. They had, however, knocked everything off one of the night stands. She hoped her mother's Hummels were okay.

Jessica rolled over, gathered the sheets around her. Vincent looked as if he had been hit by a car.

'Hey, sailor.'

'No,' Vincent said. 'No, no, no.'

Jessica ran a finger over his lips. 'What?'

'You are a devil temptress.'

'I told you not to marry me.' She snuggled closer. 'What, are you worn out?'

Vincent caught his breath. Or tried to. He was coated with sweat. He pushed the covers off, remained silent.

'Boy, you macho Italian cops sure talk a good game,' Jessica said. 'Try to get you into round two? *Fuggetaboutit.*'

'Do we have any cigarettes?'

'You don't smoke.'

'I want to start.'

Jessica laughed, got out of bed, went down to the kitchen. She returned with two glasses of wine. If her calculations were correct — and they usually were at times like these, she had managed to get new appliances over the past two years by playing these moments just right — she would start her maneuvers in ten minutes.

On the other hand, this was not about a new

319

washer or dryer. This was about a life. Their life. Sophie's life. And the life of a little boy.

When she slipped back into bed, Vincent was checking his messages on his cellphone. He put the phone down, grabbed his glass of wine. They clinked, sipped, kissed. The moment was right. Jessica said:

'I want to talk to you about something.'

43

The man was stabbed twenty times by his lover. The killer, whose name was Antony — a bit of Shakespearean irony — then proceeded to cut open his own stomach, finally bleeding out on the parkway, not two hundred feet from the steps leading to the art museum. The papers ran stories for nearly a week, the high drama too much for them to resist.

I know what really happened.

The murder victim had simply made a meat dish on Good Friday and Antony, being the devout Vatican I Catholic he was, and this being 1939, could not take the shame and guilt. I know this because I can hear their final argument. It is still in the air.

The voices of the dead are a shrill chorus indeed.

Consider the man stabbed over his Social Security check, his final pleas lingering at Fifth and Jefferson Streets.

Or the teenager shot for his bicycle, forever crying at Kensington and Allegheny, right in front of the check-cashing emporium where the regular customers pass by with smug indifference.

Or the grandmother bludgeoned for her purse at Reese and West Dauphin, her voice to this day howling her husband's name, a man dead for more than thirty-five years.

It is becoming harder to keep them out. When I bring one to the other side, it quiets for a while. But not for long.

★　★　★

I push through the huge rusted gate, drive along the overgrown lane. I park in the pooled darkness, remove my shovels. The voices calm for a moment. All I can hear, as I begin to dig, is the slow, inexorable descent of leaves falling from the trees.

44

Byrne couldn't sleep. The images of the four corpses rode a slow carousel in his mind. He got up, poured himself an inch of bourbon, flipped on the computer, logged onto the Net, launched a web browser. He cruised the headlines on philly.com, visited a few other sites, not really reading or comprehending.

Have you found them yet? The lion and the rooster and the swan? Are there others? You might think they do not play together; but they do.

He got onto YouTube. Once there, he typed in Christa-Marie Schönburg's name. Even before he was done typing, a drop-down window opened, listing a number of possibilities.

CHRISTA-MARIE SCHÖNBURG BACH
CHRISTA-MARIE SCHÖNBURG HAYDN
CHRISTA-MARIE SCHÖNBURG ELGAR
CHRISTA-MARIE SCHÖNBURG BRAHMS

Byrne had no idea where to begin. In fact, he really had no idea what he was doing, or exactly what he was looking for. On the surface he imagined he was looking for a portal, admittedly obscure, to the case. Something that might trigger something else. Something that might begin to explain Christa-Marie's impenetrable note to him.

Or maybe he was looking for a young detective who had walked into a house in Chestnut Hill in 1990 and there began a long, dark odyssey of bloodshed and tears and misery. Maybe he was really looking for the man he used to be.

The final entry on the list was:

CHRISTA-MARIE SCHÖNBURG INTERVIEW

Byrne selected it. It was three minutes long, recorded on a PBS show in 1988. Christa-Marie was at the height of her fame and talent. She looked beautiful in a simple white dress, drop earrings. As she answered questions about her playing, her celebrity at such a young age, and what it was like to play for Riccardo Muti, she vacillated between confident career woman, shy schoolgirl, enigmatic artiste. More than once she blushed, and put her hair behind one ear. Byrne had always thought her an attractive woman, but here she was stunning.

When the interview was complete Byrne clicked on the Bach entry. The browser took him to a page that linked to a number of other Christa-Marie Schönburg videos. Her entire public life was shown in freeze-frames down the right-hand side of the page — bright gowns and brighter lights.

He clicked on *Bach Cello Suite No. 1*. It was a montage video, all still photographs. The photographs in the montage, one slowly dissolving into the next, showed Christa-Marie at a number of ages, a variety of poses and settings: in a studio, smiling at the camera, a side view on stage, a low-angle photograph of her at nineteen, a look of intense concentration on her

324

face. The last photograph was Christa-Marie at nine years old, a cello leaning against the wall next to her, almost twice her size.

Byrne spent most of the next hour watching the YouTube offerings. Many were collage-type videos, assembled by fans, but there were also live performances. The last video was Christa-Marie and a pianist in a studio, playing Beethoven's *Sonata No. 3 in A*. At the halfway point, in close-up, Christa-Marie looked up, straight at the lens, straight at Byrne.

When the piece finished, Byrne went to the kitchen, took two Vicodin, chased it with a swig of Wild Turkey. Probably not the prescribed way, but you had to go with what worked, right?

He looked out the window at the empty street below. In the distance was the glow of Center City. There was another body out there, another body waiting to be discovered, a raw, abraded corpse with a strip of blood-streaked paper around its head.

He glanced at the kitchen clock, although he didn't need to.

It was 2:52.

Byrne grabbed his coat, his keys, and went back out into the night.

45

Lucy sat on the fire escape, wrapped in her dark blue afghan, one of the few things that had survived her childhood, one of the few things that she could stuff into a nylon duffel bag and take with her when she moved on, which she had done so many times in the past two years that she had nearly lost count.

She looked in the window. She had rented this room, a third-floor room in a trinity on Fourth Street, about two months earlier. The family was very nice. An elderly couple with no children, they had welcomed her like a granddaughter, and for the first two weeks had invited her to dinner every night.

Lucy, having had no experience with real family life, had begged off with a variety of excuses until the couple — Tilly and Oscar Walters — had gotten the hint.

The night was calm, the sky was clear, and for the first time in a long while she could see a few stars. Maybe they had been there all the time and she had forgotten to look. Perhaps the darkness was inside her, had made its nest in her soul, and refused to leave, refused to let up.

She wrapped the afghan more tightly around her, but she wasn't really all that cold. Maybe it was all those years in drafty apartments, all those years when the heat was turned off, all those years huddling around an electric stove in winter until the electricity too was turned off.

Since the day the plane came out of the sky, she had tried everything to make the feeling go away. Drugs, alcohol, men, religion, yoga, all manner of self-destruction and abuse. Men. Quite often the men she chose — boys, really — filled in any small gaps in the abuse, making her hell complete.

And now she was in trouble. She always knew she would eventually get caught shoplifting, even though she was good at it. Her mother had sent her into stores from the time she was only three years old. In the first few years she was only the diversion, doing the little-cutie bit to distract store owners while her mother boosted cigarettes or alcohol or, once in a great while, a treat for Lucy.

But today she had gotten caught, and she was going to go to jail. Even though Detective Byrne said that wasn't going to happen, she wasn't so sure. She had wanted to tell him about the man in 1208, but for some reason she couldn't bring herself to do it.

And now, sitting on this rusting fire escape, she began to cry. It was the first time for years. She tasted the salt on her lips. She felt pathetic.

It was worse for the little girl who'd been killed. Little Stacy Pennell. Sergio had told her the story.

In 1999 a ten-year-old girl, whose family had lived in Le Jardin when it had been an apartment building, had been down in the laundry room with her older sister Cyndy. Cyndy, whose job it was to watch her runt of a sister, couldn't be

327

bothered, it seemed. When Cyndy wasn't looking, Stacy had grabbed the keys from on top of the dryer and snuck out of the laundry room.

Sergio said that when Stacy got off the elevator she probably did not notice the man standing in the stairwell at the end of the hall, just a few feet from the entrance to the Pennell apartment.

When they found Stacy later she had been brutally murdered, her throat cut from ear to ear. Sergio said her body had bite marks on it.

It had happened in Room 1208.

It couldn't have been coincidence, Lucy thought. It just couldn't. The man in 1208 had been there for a reason. Some other little girl was going to be hurt.

Was the man who killed Stacy Pennell the same man who had kidnapped *her*?

Lucy was suddenly cold. She slipped back inside, shut the window. She walked over to the closet, opened the door, sat down, and waited for the night to embrace her.

Fifteen feet below, in the gloom of the stairwell beneath the fire escape, a man stepped into the shadows and joined Lucinda Doucette in darkness.

46

In the shower Jessica thought about the previous night. Vincent had listened to her entire well-planned speech. He had been surprisingly receptive to the idea of adopting Carlos, considering that he was not the most open-minded person she had ever met.

They made love a second time, this time sweet, married love, and halfway through she saw something in Vincent's dark eyes that told her they might actually do this. Later Vincent told her, in the twilight before sleep, that he wanted to meet Carlos first before even thinking about making any decision, of course. Maybe he wanted to do a little male bonding, Jessica thought. Take the kid to a Flyers game, do a few Jager Bombs, leaf through a copy of the new *Maxim*.

As she was getting dressed, she realized that Vincent had made the bed — a first. She also noticed a flower on her pillow. Granted, it was a silk flower, and Vincent had taken it from the arrangement on the dining-room table. But it was the thought that counted.

★   ★   ★

Marcel's Costume Company was a storefront on Market Street near Third. Established in 1940,

329

Marcel's carried a full line of Halloween outfits, professional make-up, wigs, and accessories. Marcel's also created costumes for local television shows and was quite often hired for supplemental wardrobe for Philadelphia's booming film-production industry.

But today it was all about Halloween. Marcel's was open twenty-four hours a day this week, and even at 7:30 a.m. the store was half full.

When Jessica and Sophie walked in, Jessica saw Rory behind the counter. Rory Bianchi was a kid from the old neighborhood who had always had a crush on Jessica, and ever since ninth grade they'd had the sort of relationship where the flirting went on but never went anywhere.

'The two prettiest girls in Philly,' Rory said. 'In my shop!'

'Hi, Rory!' Sophie said.

'Hey little darlin',' he said. 'Ready for the big night?'

Sophie nodded. A kid in a costume shop. Outside of a candy story, there was nothing cooler. Jessica remembered coming into Marcel's when she was a girl and Wonder Woman had been the rage.

'I have it for you right here,' Rory said.

Of all the costumes available — including Disney characters like Ariel from *The Little Mermaid*, which was Sophie's favorite movie — Sophie had picked something called the Snowflake Fairy. Jessica had tried to explain that Halloween was a fall holiday, but her words had fallen on deaf ears. Unlike her mother, Sophie loved the winter, especially snowflakes. Come

330

December Sophie was endlessly cutting them out of construction paper and dotting the house with them.

'Do you want the wings and the wand, too?' Rory asked.

It was a dumb question, but Jessica looked at Sophie anyway. Sophie seemed to be in a fairy trance, the reflection of white satin in her big brown eyes.

'Sure,' Jessica said.

'I take it you'll want the tiara as well.'

Jessica took out her credit card as fast as she could, in case there was anything else.

★   ★   ★

Sophie floated out to the parking lot, still in a daze, the dress clutched tightly in her hands, as if Monica Quagliata might be lurking behind the next SUV — Monica with designs on the Snowflake Fairy costume.

When they got to the car, Sophie supervised the hanging of the costume on the hook in the back, pronounced it safely stowed for the few-mile journey. She slipped into the seat next to it, buckled in.

Before Jessica could start the car, a family crossed the street in front of them — mom, dad, two boys, two girls. Jessica looked over at Sophie.

'Do most of your friends have brothers and sisters?' Jessica asked. It was a rhetorical question, but one that Jessica needed to ask to get the conversation started.

Sophie didn't give this too much thought. She just nodded.

'Do you ever wish *you* had brothers and sisters?'

A shrug. 'Sometimes.'

'What would you think about having a brother?'

'A brother?'

'Yeah.'

'A *boy*?'

Jessica laughed. 'Yeah. A boy, sweetie.'

Sophie thought for a moment. 'Boys are okay. A little bossy, but okay, I guess.'

★   ★   ★

Jessica dropped Sophie off at school, stopped at Old City Coffee on Church Street. Outside, she picked up an *Inquirer* and a free copy of *The Report*, Philly's sleaziest tabloid — and that was saying something. As expected, the current spate of murders was splashed across the cover.

Philly Noir; the Geometry of Vengeance, screamed the headline.

Jessica tossed the *Report* in the trash, tucked the *Inquirer* under her arm. She got into her car, wondering how Byrne was faring.

Have you found them yet? The lion and the rooster and the swan? Are there others?

What did Christa-Marie Schönburg have to do with all this?

She checked her cellphone. No calls from Byrne.

* ★ ★

The primary role of the Department of Human Services was to intervene and protect neglected, abused or abandoned children, as well as to guarantee their well-being when there were immediate threats or impending dangers in their lives.

The Children and Youth Division provided youth and family-centered services to more than 20,000 children and their families each year.

Although the main offices were located at 1515 Arch Street there were various facilities throughout the city — temporary shelters and foster-care centers.

Jessica arrived at Hosanna House, a standalone brick building on Second Street. She signed in and walked to the day room at the back. She was immediately assaulted by the sound of a dozen toddlers in full morning mania. The place smelled like orange juice and crayons.

Carlos sat at a table with two little girls and a young woman of about twenty. He wore a red cardigan. He looked adorable.

Jessica watched him for a few minutes. Kids were unbelievably resilient, she thought. Just two weeks earlier this little boy's life had been hell on Earth.

But Jessica knew enough, had seen enough cases of abused and neglected children to know that many times there was residual grief and anger and fear. Most of the people she had arrested in the past five years were, almost to a man or woman, products of broken homes.

333

Carlos looked up and saw her. He got out of his chair, rocketed across the room, and threw his arms around her. He ran back, got a piece of paper from the table, ran back to Jessica, handed it to her.

It was a crayon drawing of a room, possibly the living room where Carlos had lived with his mother. There was something that looked like a chair and a table, and a woman in the corner with wild dark hair, eyes the size of her whole head. Patricia Lentz, Carlos's biological mother, had blonde hair, almost white.

It didn't take Jessica long to realize the figure in the drawing just might be her. Right behind her was a bright sun. Jessica's heart felt ready to beat its way out of her chest.

She looked at the table in Carlos's drawing. On the table was something that Jessica had no trouble recognizing. It was a two-year-old boy's rendition of a gun.

Jessica suddenly felt a paralyzing wave of sadness. She fought it.

'Can I have this?' she asked Carlos.

Carlos nodded.

'Stand up tall — let me look at you.'

Carlos stood at attention. His hair was combed, his face scrubbed. His sweater and pants looked new.

'This is a beautiful sweater,' Jessica said.

Carlos giggled, looked down, toyed with a button, perhaps thought better of messing with it. He was two. He knew his limitations.

'Where did you get your new clothes?'

Carlos turned toward the table, held out his

334

tiny hand. Jessica walked over, hand in hand with Carlos. He sat down and tucked into a new drawing.

'Hi,' Jessica said.

The young woman at the plastic picnic table looked up. 'Hi.'

Jessica pointed to the drawing in her hand. 'This is pretty good for a two-year-old. I couldn't draw a straight line then. Still can't.'

The young woman laughed. 'Join the club.' She looked over at Carlos, smoothed his hair. 'He's *such* a beautiful boy.'

'Yes, he is,' Jessica said.

'I'd kill for those eyelashes.'

'Are you a counselor here?'

'No, no,' the young woman said. 'I just help out. I volunteer one day a week.'

Jessica nodded. The young woman had about her an air of competence, but also an air of sadness. Jessica felt the same way about herself sometimes. It was hard to see the things she saw every day and not be affected. Especially the kids. Jessica glanced at her watch. Her tour was starting.

'It was nice talking to you,' Jessica said.

'Same here.'

Jessica extended her hand. 'My name is Jessica, by the way.'

The young woman stood, shook her hand. 'Lucy,' she replied. 'Lucy Doucette.'

47

When Jessica got to her car she felt another wave of melancholy. The drawing that Carlos had given her hit home. It would probably be a long time until those memories passed from his life. Was it too much for her and Vincent to be taking on?

As she unlocked the car door she turned to see someone approaching. It was Martha Reed, the director of Hosanna House. Martha was in her early fifties, plump but energetic, with clever blue eyes that missed nothing.

'Carlos looks well,' Jessica said. 'He looks . . . happy.' It was a stretch, but Jessica couldn't think of anything else to say.

'He's adjusting,' Martha replied. Martha Reed had seen a lot of children in her time.

The woman then rummaged in her bag, took out her BlackBerry. She tapped around, got to her calendar. 'Can you and your husband be here today at around eleven?'

Jessica's heart thundered. They were getting their adoption interview. She'd known this moment was coming, but now that it was here she wondered how she was going to handle it. 'Oh yeah. We'll be here.'

Martha looked around conspiratorially. She lowered her voice. 'Between you and me, it looks really good. I'm not supposed to say that, but it looks good.'

Jessica drove out of the Hosanna House parking lot on a cloud. Before she could turn onto Second Street her cellphone rang in her hand. It was Dana Westbrook.

'Morning, boss. What's going on?'

'I just got the report on the Joseph Novak surveillance.'

'Okay.'

'We had a detective from West on him all night. Experienced guy, used to be in anti-gang, and did some task-force work with DEA. He sat on the apartment his whole tour. He said that from the time he came on until six this morning, there were no lights on in the place, no activity. About eight o'clock this morning he put on a Philadelphia Water Department jacket, grabbed a clipboard, got the super to let him in, and knocked on Novak's door. He got no answer, so he went around back, climbed the fire escape, looked in the window.'

'Was Novak home?'

'He was,' Westbrook said. 'He was sitting at his desk. It looks like, after he left the Roundhouse yesterday, he went home, shredded all of his sheet music and news clippings, and somewhere between six o'clock last night and eight o'clock this morning put a gun in his mouth and pulled the trigger.'

48

The amount of blood was staggering.

Jessica stood next to the stacks of crystal CD cases. The clear boxes were sprayed with blood and brain matter. Bits of shattered skull stuck to the valance over the curtains.

Joseph Novak's body was in the desk chair at an unnatural angle — the force of the blast had twisted his body in two directions. The upper third of his head was missing. *Not missing, exactly*, Jessica thought. It was dispersed around the wall and drapes behind him. The bullet had blasted out the window. There were two CSU officers across the street at that moment searching for the slug.

Was Joseph Novak their killer? He'd seemed unshakeable when he had been in for questioning, but why had he run the previous day? What did he have to hide?

The body was removed at ten a.m.

★　★　★

Jessica watched the CSU officers go through the motions. Now that the body was gone, the apartment-management company would soon contact one of the cleaning crews that specialized in crime-scene cleanup, a mini-growth industry during the past ten years. The world would move on.

The death had all the earmarks of a suicide, so there was probably not going to be a full-blown investigation. The weapon, a Colt Commander, had still been in Joseph Novak's hand when he was found, his finger curled inside the trigger guard.

Jessica would present her report to her boss, who would pass it along to the DA's office, who would then make a ruling. Unless there was any compelling evidence of foul play, this would be ruled a suicide and the homicide division of the PPD would not be involved any further.

But that didn't mean there was not a connection to the serial murders going on in the city.

Jessica got the attention of the two CSU officers who were dusting the doors and table for fingerprints.

'Can you guys give me a few minutes?'

The officers, always ready for a break, set aside what they were doing, walked through the door into the hallway, closed it.

Jessica slipped on gloves, turned the laptop to face the other side of the desk. The screen displayed a default screen saver. She touched the space bar, and in a second the screen came back to life. It was a Word document, with three short sentences.

Zig, zig, zig.
What a saraband!
They all hold hands and dance in circles . . .

Jessica was not familiar with the passage. Was this a suicide note? she wondered. She scrolled down on the trackpad but there was nothing else. The document was just the three lines. She glanced at the corner of the window. It had not been saved.

Was this a work in progress? Was this some sort of message from Joseph Novak, some riddle left behind for friends and family by which they might make some sense of his final, violent act?

Jessica had no idea. As much as she would have liked to take the laptop with her, she had no jurisdiction over it. Not yet, anyway. She would lobby the DA's office to establish a material-witness status for the late Joseph Novak, and perhaps she would get a chance to go through it.

She looked around the place. The silence was thick and oppressive.

Jessica had to be careful about looking through the contents of the computer. The homicide unit had recently received directives from the DA's office about needing court approval for doing anything with a computer that involved clicking a mouse or touching a keyboard. If there was something on the screen to be seen, in plain view, that was one thing. If it involved maximizing a minimized window, launching a program, or visiting a web page located in a history on a browser, that was something else.

A case against a man trafficking in child pornography had recently been tossed because the detective, knowing there were thousands of images on the man's hard drive, had opened a graphics program. It turned out that every time a program was launched, there was a log of the event and a record of the precise time it happened. If the suspect was in custody at that moment, the detective could not claim that the program was already open.

Jessica clicked over to the side bar. There was no harm in looking, as long as she didn't open any files or programs. She glanced at the contents of the drive. There was one file. SARABAND.DOC. That was it. Other than that, there was nothing on the drive. No documents, no spreadsheets, no databases, no photos, music or audio files. It had all the earmarks of a drive that had been recently erased.

Any good computer-forensic lab would be able to tell when a drive had been formatted, and could usually find evidence of the files that were originally on the drive. Jessica was already formulating the case she would make to the DA's office to allow them to do just that.

In the meantime she would get a couple of warm bodies down here to canvass the building, just to see if Joseph Novak had had any visitors earlier in the day. If he had, maybe it could lead to a full-scale investigation of his death as something other than a suicide.

She took out her phone, checked her voicemail. Two messages.

When did she get two messages? Why hadn't it rung? She checked the side of the phone. With an iPhone, the switch to toggle from *silent* to *ring tone* was on the upper left, and was easily activated when you put the phone in your pocket. Too easily. The ringer had been off.

Jessica switched it back on, tapped the first

voicemail message. It was from the man who was hoping to install the awnings on the new house. He wanted two grand. *Dream on.*

The second call was from an unknown caller. She played it.

'*Detective Balzano, this is Joseph Novak.*'

Jessica jumped to her feet. Her skin broke out in gooseflesh. She glanced behind her, at the dark sienna stains on the carpet and walls. She could still smell the cordite in the air, could taste the coppery airborne blood at the back of her throat. Joseph Novak's blood. She was listening to a message from the grave.

'*I want to apologize for my behavior. I can't go on like this. There is more to this than you know. Much more. You don't know him. I cannot live with myself anymore.*'

Jessica paused the message for a moment, paced the living room. Everything she looked at — the books, the CDs, the furniture itself — took on a new meaning.

She stopped pacing, tapped the button, continued the message.

'*I hear him coming down the hall. Look in the cabinet above the range in the kitchen.*'

The message ended.

Jessica put her phone in her pocket, crossed the living room into the compact Pullman kitchen. She opened the cabinets above the range hood. There she found a dozen or so cookbooks — Mexican, Italian, Cajun. She pulled a few of them out, riffled the pages. Nothing. The second-to-last cookbook was labeled *Home Recipes*. She pulled it out. When

342

she did, something fell on the floor. It was a slim leather-bound journal. The cover was worn and creased. She picked it up. Stuck in the front was an old photograph. It was Joseph Novak at fifteen or so, standing next to a beautiful cello. Jessica slipped the picture back in the book, opened it.

It was a diary.

JUNE 22. The competition is this Saturday. But it is more than just a competition for first chair. We both know that. It is a competition for her. It will always be thus.

Jessica flipped ahead to the back of the journal. She read the final entry.

NOVEMBER 1. All Saints Day. It is done. I know now that I will be forever beholden to him. I will never be out of his shadow. For the rest of my life I will do his bidding. My heart is forever broken, forever in his hands.
Zig, zig, zig.
He is death in cadence.

Jessica closed the journal. She needed a warrant to search every square inch of this apartment, and she needed one fast. She put in a call to the DA's office, told them what she had, what she needed. She took the journal, intending to say it had been in plain sight, therefore not covered by the warrant. She stepped outside, locked the door. She told the two CSU officers they could return to the lab. She would call them

343

when and if she needed them.

She walked across the street, grabbed a coffee-to-go at the diner, stepped into the parking lot behind. She called Byrne, got his voicemail. She called Dana Westbrook, gave her a status report. Westbrook said she would send two other detectives from the Special Investigations Unit to aid in the search.

Jessica opened the journal. There was something under the back cover. She peeled it back gently. There was a second photograph there, an old Polaroid, a long shot of a window in a huge stone building. In the window was a figure. It was impossible to see who it was, but it looked like a slender woman. On the back of the photograph was one word scrawled in red pencil.

Hell.

Before Jessica could get the photograph back into the journal she heard someone approaching, footfalls on hard gravel. She turned.

The fist came from nowhere, connecting with the right side of her face in a dull thud. She staggered back, saw stars. The journal flew out of her hands. The second blow was more glancing, but it carried enough force to knock her to the ground. She had enough presence to roll onto the side where she had her weapon holstered.

Through the haze she saw her assailant. White-blond hair, filthy jeans, laceless sneakers. She didn't recognize him. Not by sight, not at first. When he spoke again, she knew. And there was no mistaking those eyes.

'I think we have some unfinished business, Detective Balzano,' Lucas Anthony Thompson

344

said. 'Or should I say Detective *Cunt* Balzano.'

Jessica rolled to her right, worked the Glock from her holster, but she was too slow. Thompson stepped forward, kicked the weapon from her hand.

'You shoulda shot me when you had the fucking chance, bitch. Ain't gonna happen today.'

When Thompson took another step toward her, Jessica saw movement at the back of the parking lot. A shadow slithered along the pavement.

Someone was standing behind Thompson.

And then everything went gray.

49

The Philadelphia Orchestra began life in 1900. Over the next century it held many distinctions, not the least of which was the 'Philadelphia Sound', a legacy that, under conductor Eugene Ormandy, became known for its clarity and skilled execution, its warm tonality and precise timing.

The orchestra also had a unity of artistic leadership virtually unknown in the world of great orchestras, with only seven musical directors in its entire history. Two men, Leopold Stokowski and Eugene Ormandy, held the reins from 1912 to 1980.

It was on the occasion of Ormandy's leaving that the Philadelphia Orchestra found itself at a crossroads and, perhaps in an attempt to modernize its somewhat staid image, turned to a young firebrand, Neapolitan Riccardo Muti, as its new musical director. Darkly handsome, intensely serious to the point of almost never smiling on stage, Muti ushered in a new era, an era dominated by a man whose insistence on the letter of the musical law earned him the nickname — at least around the opera houses of Italy — of *lo scerif*, the sheriff.

In 1981, in a move still discussed in some circles, the orchestra rattled the classical musical world by hiring as its principal cellist a nineteen-year-old named Christa-Marie Schönburg — a tempestuous wunderkind who was taking the world of strings by storm. Within a year her name became as synonymous with the Philadelphia Orchestra's as Muti's, and when the chamber orchestra toured Eastern Europe that summer Christa-Marie Schönburg was the talk of the classical-music universe.

By the time she was twenty-two there was no doubt in the minds of the *cognoscenti* that she would surpass, in technical skill, pure artistry and, indeed, world-wide recognition, the only other woman to capture international fame on the cello, the tragic Jacqueline du Pré, the brilliant cellist whose career was cut short at the age of twenty-eight by multiple sclerosis.

And while Jacqueline du Pré made her most memorable recording with Elgar's *Cello Concerto in E Minor*, Christa-Marie put her imprimatur on the Bach suites.

For nearly a decade, from Vienna's Konzerthaus to Rotterdam's Grote Zaal, from the Royal Festival Hall in London to Avery Fisher Hall in New York City, Christa-Marie Schönburg, with her tensile, passionate music, brought audiences to their feet.

On a cold autumn night in 1990 all of that changed.

Something tragic happened on that night when Christa-Marie returned home after a triumphant performance at the Academy of Music — a benefit attended by many of Philadelphia's elite society, a fund-raiser for Philadelphia's homeless children.

Although details of the last two hours remain unknown, it was believed that Christa-Marie

347

returned to her Chestnut Hill house at approximately 11:45 p.m., delivered there by a car service. A few hours later, according to her housekeeper, there were sounds of an argument in the kitchen, a struggle, then a scream. The housekeeper called the police.

Police arrived at around two-thirty. They found a man named Gabriel Thorne — a psychiatrist who had treated Christa-Marie for many years — sprawled on the kitchen floor, bleeding heavily from wounds to his abdomen and chest, the bloodied knife at his side. He was still alive. They called EMS, who tried to save him at the scene but failed. He was pronounced dead minutes after their arrival. The ME's office would eventually rule that Thorne bled out as a result of multiple stab wounds.

Christa-Marie Schönburg never played another public concert. Because she confessed to the crime there was no show trial, much to the disappointment of the burgeoning cable-TV court shows. Christa-Marie Schönburg was as enigmatic as she was strikingly beautiful, and her relationship with Thorne was, for many years, cause for gossip and speculation.

The last time Byrne saw Christa-Marie Schönburg was at her allocution, when she stood before a judge and admitted her guilt regarding the murder of Dr. Gabriel Thorne.

★   ★   ★

As Byrne drove north he thought of the Chestnut Hill house, how when people heard what had happened they began to gather across the street early the next morning, bringing with them flowers and stuffed animals, even sheet music. It was as if Christa-Marie had been the victim, not the perpetrator.

Byrne had thought of Christa-Marie often. It wasn't just that Christa-Marie Schönburg had been his first case as the lead detective in a homicide. Something else about the woman haunted him. What drew him to her had never been entirely clear to him.

Maybe he would discover what that was today.

50

'I'm fine,' Jessica said.

It was a lie, but she was sticking to it.

The paramedic shone his light into her eyes for the third time, took her blood pressure for the third time, took her pulse for the fifth time.

She had been punched on many occasions in the past — when you box in the ring, it kind of goes with the territory — and this had been a glancing blow, not really that hard. But it had caught her off guard. In the ring, you brace yourself for incoming blows, and the adrenalin that flows naturally at a moment like that works as a sort of neural shock absorber. No one on Earth can be prepared for a sucker punch, which, by definition, comes out of the blue. Her head throbbed a little but her vision was clear, and her energy level was high. She wanted back in the game but they were going to make her sit there like an invalid. She had seen it many times in her years on the job, had even been the purveyor of the unwelcome news to victims of assault.

Just sit there for a moment.

Not so for Vincent Balzano. When the sector cars showed up, she made the call, found Vincent only a dozen blocks away, working an investigation of his own. He broke every speed record getting to the scene. That was the easy part. Calming him down was another matter. At the moment he was pacing like a caged animal. Unfortunately for Vincent Balzano and his Italian temper, he was lacking a convenient punching bag. For now, at least.

Jessica's weapon had been recovered. It had not been fired.

★ ★ ★

All Jessica remembered was hearing other footsteps but she did not know whose they were. She did not mention the journal, which had not been recovered from the scene

'No one said anything?' Westbrook asked.

Jessica shook her head. It hurt. She stopped doing it. 'No. I heard footsteps approaching. I got clocked twice. There was a scuffle. Then I faded out.'

'What kind of scuffle?'

'Not sure. I heard at least two people grunting. Then the ringing in my ears took over.'

'And you did not see the other person?'

'No, but I — '

Jessica suddenly looked at her watch, sprang to her feet. She felt dizzy for a moment, then it passed. Her anger did not.

'What is it?' Vincent asked.

'We missed it. We fucking *missed* it.'

'What?'

'The appointment at the Department of Human Services.'

'Jess.'

'Don't *Jess* me.'

'We'll work it out,' Vincent said. 'Don't worry.'

'Don't *worry*? This is why they turn you down, Vincent. This is the first big test. You don't show, you don't call, it's over.'

Vincent held her close. 'I think you have a pretty good excuse, babe. I think they'll understand.'

'They won't,' Jessica said, wiggling loose. 'Plus, they're not going to place Carlos in a home where his mother is in danger every day.'

'They know we're both cops. They know what we do.'

It all came out. The anger of this brutal case. The inability to conceive for two years. The indignity of being assaulted. All of it.

'You weren't *there*, Vincent. I was there. I saw how Carlos was living. I saw the dog shit and the fucking hypodermic needles all over the place. I saw the cockroaches and rats in the sink, the rotting food. I saw him hiding under a fucking *garbage bag*. You don't know what a hell hole it was, how bad his life was. They are *not* going to hand him over to us so we can make it worse.'

She tried to walk it off. The rage was a breathing thing within her.

Soon Jessica calmed down and let the investigation begin. It was going to be a long day — and it was just getting started.

51

Chestnut Hill was an affluent neighborhood in the Northwest section of Philadelphia, originally part of the German Township laid out by Francis Daniel Pastorius. One of the original 'railroad suburbs,' the area contained a wide variety of nineteenth — and early-twentieth-century residences designed by many of the most prominent Philadelphia architects.

Before leaving Center City, Byrne had called ahead to schedule a time to meet with Christa-Marie. He was directed to Christa-Marie's attorney, a man named Benjamin Curtin. Reluctant at first, Curtin arranged to meet Byrne at the estate at one p.m.

As Byrne turned down St. Andrews Road he saw the house for the second time in his life. He had not been back since the night of the murder.

It was a massive, sprawling Tudor building with a circular driveway accented with cobblestones, a large gabled entrance. To the right, partially hidden by trees, was a stable, next to a pair of tennis courts. A high wrought-iron fence encircled the property.

Byrne parked his van and, even though he was wearing his best suit, suddenly felt underdressed. He also realized that he had been holding his breath. He got out of the vehicle, straightened his tie, smoothed the front of his overcoat, and rang the bell. A few moments later the door was opened by a woman in her sixties. Byrne announced himself, and the woman led him through the high, arched doorway. Ahead was a carved mahogany winding staircase; to the right were thick fluted pillars leading to a formal dining room. To the left was the great room, with a view of the pool and the manicured grounds beyond. Byrne's heels echoed in the massive space. The woman took his coat and led him into a study off the enormous foyer.

The room was darkly paneled, clubby, with a pair of large bookcases built in and a vaulted open-trussed ceiling. A fire burned in the fireplace. The mantel was arrayed with pine cones and other autumn decorations. Above the mantel was a large portrait of Christa-Marie. In the painting she sat in a velvet chair. It had to have been painted right around the time Byrne met her, that dark night in 1990.

A few moments later the door opened and a man entered.

Benjamin Curtin was in his early fifties. He had thick gray hair, swept straight back, a strong jaw. His suit was tailored to perfection and might well have cost what Byrne made in a month. Curtin was probably twenty pounds heavier than he looked.

Byrne introduced himself. He did not produce his identification. He was not there in any official capacity. Not yet.

'It's a pleasure to meet you, detective,' Curtin said, perhaps to remind Byrne what he did for a living. Curtin had a Southern accent. Byrne pegged him as Mississippi money.

'And you, counselor.'

There, Byrne thought. *Everyone knows their jobs.*

'Is Liam still keeping the peace down there?'

Down there, Byrne thought. Curtin made it sound like the boondocks. He was referring to Judge Liam McManus, who everyone knew was going to run for the Philadelphia Supreme Court in a year.

'We're lucky to have him,' Byrne said. 'Rumor is he won't be there for much longer. Next thing you know he'll be living in Chestnut Hill.'

Curtin smiled. But Byrne knew it was his professional smile, not one that held any warmth. The attorney gestured to a chair on the other side of the desk. Both men sat down.

'Can Charlotta get you anything? Coffee? Tea?'

'I'm fine, thanks.'

Curtin nodded. The door behind Byrne was closed.

'So, what brings you here to visit Ms. Schönburg, detective?'

'I'm afraid I can't really get into anything too specific, but I will say that she may have information about an open investigation being conducted by the Philadelphia Police Department.'

Curtin looked slightly amused. 'I'm intrigued.'

'How so?'

'Well, as I'm sure you're aware, Ms. Schönburg no longer lives a public life. She is by no means a recluse, but, as I'm sure you can appreciate, she does not circulate in any of the

355

social circles to which she once belonged.'

'I understand.'

'She has almost constant companionship here, so I'm afraid I don't see how she could possibly be involved in anything that has taken place recently in Philadelphia.'

'That's what I'm here to determine, Mr. Curtin. But I have a few questions before I meet with her.'

'Is she suspected of a crime?'

'No,' Byrne said. 'Absolutely not.'

Curtin stood, walked to the window, looked out. He continued to speak without turning around. 'I must tell you that in the few years she has been out of prison there have been no fewer than a hundred requests for interviews with her. She is still very much the object of fascination not only with people in the world of classical music but also with the basest denizens of the tabloid world.'

'I'm not here to write something for the *Enquirer*,' Byrne said.

Curtin smiled again. Practiced, mirthless, mechanical. 'I understand. What I'm saying is, all these requests have been presented to Christa-Marie and she has categorically turned them all down.'

'She contacted *me*, Mr. Curtin.'

Byrne saw Curtin's shoulders tense. It appeared that he had not known this. 'Of course.'

'I need to ask her a few questions, and I want to know what her general mental state is. Is she lucid?'

356

'Most of the time, yes.'

'I'm not sure what that means.'

'It means that much of the time she is rational and fully functional. She really would not have any problem living on her own, but she chooses to have a full-time psychiatric nurse on the premises.'

Byrne nodded, remained silent.

Curtin walked slowly back to the desk, eased himself into the sumptuous leather chair. He placed his forearms on the desk, leaned forward.

'Christa-Marie has had a hard life, detective. From the outside, one might think she led a life of glamour and privilege and, up until the incident, she *did* enjoy the many rewards of her talent and success. But after that night, from the interrogations and subsequent allocution, to her eighteen months at Convent Hill, to her incarceration at Muncy, she — '

The words dropped like a Scud missile. 'Excuse me?'

Curtin stopped, looked at Byrne.

'You said Convent Hill?' Byrne asked.

'Yes.'

Convent Hill Mental Health Facility was a massive state-run mental hospital in central Pennsylvania. It had been closed under a cloud of suspicion in the early 1990s after nearly one hundred years of operation.

'When was Christa-Marie at Convent Hill?'

'She was there from the time she was sentenced until it closed in 1992.'

'Why was she sent there?'

'She insisted on it.'

357

Byrne's mind reeled. 'You're telling me that Christa-Marie insisted on being sent to Convent Hill? It was her *choice*?'

'Yes. As her attorney I fought against it, of course. But she hired another firm and made it happen.'

'And you say she was there for eighteen months?'

'Yes. From there she went to Muncy.'

Byrne had had no idea that Christa-Marie had spent time at the most notoriously brutal mental-health facility east of Chicago.

While Byrne was absorbing this news a woman walked into the room. She was about forty and wore a smart navy blue suit, white blouse.

'Detective, this is Adele Hancock,' Curtin said. 'She is Christa-Marie's nurse.'

Byrne rose. They shook hands.

Adele Hancock was trim and athletic, had a runner's body, close-cropped gray hair.

'Miss Schönburg will see you now,' the woman said.

Curtin stood, grabbed his coat, his briefcase. He rounded the desk, handed Byrne a linen business card. 'If there is anything else I can do for you, please do not hesitate to call me.'

'I appreciate your time, sir.'

'And give Liam my best.'

Sure, Byrne thought. *At the next curling match.*

Benjamin Curtin nodded to Adele Hancock and took his leave.

★   ★   ★

358

Byrne was led down a long dark-paneled hallway past a room that held a grand piano. On that night twenty years ago he had not visited this wing of the house.

'Is there anything I should know before I meet with her?' Byrne asked.

'No,' Hancock said. 'But I can tell you that she has not spoken of anything else since your call.'

When they reached the end of the hallway, the woman stopped, gestured to the room at the end. Byrne stepped inside. It was a solarium of sorts, an octagonal room walled by misted glass. There were scores of huge tropical plants. Music lilted from unseen speakers.

Have you found them? The lion and the rooster and the swan?

'Hello, detective.'

Byrne turned to the sound of the voice. And saw Christa-Marie Schönburg for the first time in twenty years.

52

Jessica looked out at the throng of police gathered in the parking lot across from Joseph Novak's apartment. There were now two scenes to process — the murder scene, and the scene where a police detective had been assaulted. Out of the crowd walked Nick Palladino, notebook in hand. He spoke to Dana Westbrook for a few moments. Every so often they glanced over at Jessica. Dino did most of the talking. Westbrook did most of the nodding.

Dino came over when they were done, asked after Jessica's well-being. Jessica told him that she was all right. But she could see by the look on his face that things had just gotten worse.

'What's up?' Jessica asked.

Dino told her.

Jessica discovered that she was mistaken about there being two scenes to process. There were three.

★   ★   ★

Lucas Anthony Thompson's body had been found dumped in another parking lot, three blocks away. His body was nude, roughly shaved clean, and there was a band of paper around his head. It appeared that he had been strangled. On one of the fingers of his right hand was a small tattoo of an elephant.

It didn't take long to determine the significance of the crime scene.

Lucas Anthony Thompson's body was found in the parking lot where Marcia Kimmelman's body had been found. It fitted the killer's pattern. Another murderer dumped at the scene of his crime.

There were already two teams watching Thompson's family members. If one of them was an accomplice they would be targeted.

Jessica looked across the lot to see someone trying to get through the police cordon. It was David Albrecht. He wanted to talk to Jessica. The uniformed officer held him back, glanced over.

'Let him through,' Westbrook said.

Albrecht came running up, out of breath.

'What did you want to say?' Westbrook asked.

'I was across the street, getting exterior shots of the building when I saw Detective Balzano come out of the front door.'

Albrecht gasped for breath. He held up a finger.

'Take your time,' Westbrook said. 'Would you like some water?'

Albrecht shook his head, gathered his wind, continued. 'Okay, okay. So I saw Detective Balzano go into the diner, and a few minutes later she came out with a coffee, and walked over here.' He indicated the parking lot, which was now teeming with crime-scene personnel. 'At first, I didn't think there was a shot, you know? I mean, a parking lot is a parking lot, right? Not the most exciting backdrop. We're not talking Robert Flaherty here.'

361

Albrecht looked at Jessica and Dana Westbrook, perhaps expecting a reply or a reaction. None was forthcoming. He continued.

'So anyway, I'm looking at the way the trees back here sort of frame the lot, the way that half-wall sort of provides a horizon, and I saw Detective Balzano pacing back and forth, and I thought it looked pretty good.'

He turned, pointed to his van across the street. 'I set the camera on my tripod, framed the shot, locked it down, then went into the back of the van for a filter. I wanted to use a Circular Polarizer because I wasn't getting much contrast. It took me a few minutes to find it, and when I came back around she was gone. Just papers blowing around in the wind. I looked and saw that her car was still down the block, so I knew she didn't leave. I figured she either went back into the diner or back into the apartment building. I figured I just missed her. Then I looked next to the building and . . . and I saw her lying there.' There was a slight hitch in Albrecht's voice.

'And you didn't see the assailant?' Westbrook asked.

'No, ma'am,' Albrecht said. 'I didn't. Not at first.'

'What do you mean, not at first?'

'I mean I didn't see him *live*.'

Westbrook looked at Jessica, then back at Albrecht. 'I don't know what you mean.'

'I didn't realize I was rolling.'

'Rolling?' Westbrook asked, clearly getting a little agitated.

'Yeah. When I put the camera on the tripod I started shooting. I have to admit, I'm just getting used to this camera. It's brand new. I hit the button by accident. It's a little embarrassing, but that's what happened.'

'What are you saying?' Jessica asked.

'What I'm saying is, I just watched the replay, and I think we have it.'

'Have what?'

David Albrecht held up the camera. 'I think we have footage of the killer.'

53

Christa-Marie Schönburg sat in a large burgundy leather chair, her pale white hands folded in her lap. Even from across the room, the first thing Byrne noticed were her eyes. Not only were they a strikingly deep amber — he had noticed the same thing twenty years earlier — but they had not changed. Two decades, two *difficult* decades of incarceration, psychiatric treatment and dealing with whatever demons had possessed her to begin with had not hardened her eyes in the least. They were a young woman's eyes, still as arresting as they'd been when she was the brightest star in the classical-music firmament.

Her hair had turned a soft, shimmering silver.

She was wearing a black silk pantsuit.

On the table next to her was a pair of reading glasses and an open book.

Byrne crossed the room and found that he was at a loss for words. What power did she have over him?

Christa-Marie stood, still as slender as ever, but standing this close Byrne saw the faint lines that etched her face, her forehead, the papery skin on her hands. Still, with her cascade of silken hair, she was a beautiful woman. Perhaps even more elegant than before.

He had not stood this close to her since the night he had put her in handcuffs.

He took her hand. His first instinct was to lean forward and kiss her on the cheek. He realized at the last instant that this would have been inappropriate, to say the least. Still, the urge was present. She made the decision for him. On tiptoes, she leaned in and grazed his cheek with her lips.

She had been twenty-eight the last time he had seen her. She was now almost fifty. She had escaped, or postponed, so many of the things that can happen to a man or woman in those years. Byrne found himself wondering what he looked like to her, what the landscaping of his face and body by his job and habits and life had done to the image she might have retained from that day in 1990.

Without a word she gestured to the other chair by the windows, perhaps five feet away. Byrne sat down, but for some reason did not sit back. He leaned forward, the way one might do at a job interview. Music played softly in the background. It was a cello piece, with piano.

After a few long minutes Christa-Marie spoke. 'It was her last studio recording, you know.'

'Who?'

'Jackie du Pré,' she said. 'She toured in 1973, and they savaged her. I wonder what they would have said of me.'

After she was sentenced in 1990, Byrne read a few books that had been written about Christa-Marie. The comparisons to Jacqueline du Pré were as specious as they were expected. It was said of Jacqueline du Pré that on her final concert tour, due to her illness, she could no longer feel the strings and had to play by sight. Byrne, having never played an instrument, having never been considered great at anything — he was only world-class at screwing up romantic relationships — could only imagine the horror and heartbreak of something like this happening to someone so gifted.

In Christa-Marie Schönburg's case, her skills had not eroded in the least when she was sent to prison. She was still, at the moment of her incarceration, one of the most celebrated and revered cellists in the world. Here, looking at the woman so many years later, he wondered which fate was worse.

'We came from the conservatories in those days,' she said. 'I went to Prentiss. My teacher was a childhood friend of Ormandy. They might never have found me if not for him.'

Christa-Marie arranged herself on the chair, continued.

'You know, there really weren't all that many women back then. It wasn't until much later that playing in a major orchestra, at least one of the Big Five — Boston, New York, Cleveland, Chicago, Philadelphia — was seen as a job, a full-time job that a woman could do. Gainful employment, as they used to say.'

Byrne remained silent. While he was sitting there he felt his cellphone vibrate three separate times. He couldn't answer. Finally he just said it:

'Christa-Marie, I need to ask you something.'

She sat forward in her chair, expectant. In that instant she looked like a schoolgirl. Byrne held up the note card.

'Why did you write me?'

Instead of answering she looked out the window for a few moments. She looked back. 'Do you know those scrolls on the bottom front of the cello? The holes cut there?'

Byrne glanced at the cello in the corner. He saw what she was talking about. He nodded.

'Do you know what they call those?' she asked.

'No.'

'They're called the F-holes. Can you imagine a group of young students hearing this for the first time?'

Christa-Marie's expression soon changed from one of joyful remembrance to one of longing.

'My happiest years were at Prentiss, you know. There was no pressure. There was just the music. Bernstein once told me that the only thing that mattered was to love the music. It's true.'

She smoothed her hair, ran a hand across her cheek. 'I was just nineteen that first night at the Academy. *Nineteen*. Can you imagine?'

Byrne could not. He told her so.

'It has been so many years since then,' she said.

She fell silent again. Byrne had the feeling that if he did not move forward with his questions he would never again have the opportunity.

'Christa-Marie, I need to talk to you about your letter.'

She glanced at him. 'After all this time, you want to get to business.' She sighed dramatically. 'If we must.'

Byrne held up the note card again. 'I need to know what you were talking about when you

367

wrote me, and asked if I'd 'found them.' If I'd found the lion and the rooster and the swan.'

She stared at him for a long second, then rose from her chair. She walked the short distance between them, knelt before him.

'I can help you,' she said.

Byrne did not answer immediately, hoping she would continue. She did not. 'Help me do what?'

Christa-Marie looked out the window again. In this light, at this short distance, her skin was translucent, the result of a lifetime spent hiding from the sun.

'Do you know the Suzuki method?' she asked.

Byrne had heard of it, but he knew nothing about it. He told her so.

'He focused on song-playing over technique. He allowed students to make music on the first day. It's no different from learning a language.' She leaned in. 'We two speak the language of death, do we not?'

Christa-Marie leaned even closer, as if to share a secret.

'I can help you stop the killings,' she said softly.

The words echoed off the misted glass walls of the solarium.

'The killings?'

'Yes. There will be more, you know. Many more. Before Halloween night at midnight.'

Her tone was flat, emotionless. She talked about murder in the same manner in which she had talked about music earlier.

'Why Halloween midnight?'

Before she answered, Byrne saw the fingers on

368

her left hand move. At first he thought it might have just been some sort of twitch, an involuntary movement brought about by being in one position for an extended period of time. But out of the corner of his eye he saw her fingers curl around an imaginary thing and he realized she was recreating some passage she had once played on the cello. Then, just as suddenly as the movement began, it stopped. She dropped her hands to her lap.

'It is not over until the coda, detective.'

Byrne knew the word. A coda was a final section to a piece of music, generally played with some dramatic urgency — a flourish at the end of a symphony, perhaps. 'I'm not sure what you mean.'

'George Szell would often stand in his office window and see which of his players took their instruments home with them.'

Byrne said nothing, hoping she would return to the moment on her own.

'Easy for the oboist, *n'est-ce pas?*' she added. 'Not so for the bassist.' She sat up on her heels. 'Did you know that the cellist and bassist must each purchase an extra airline ticket for their instruments?'

Byrne hadn't known that.

'The Cavani String Quartet always books for five.'

'Christa-Marie,' Byrne said, hoping that his voice did not sound as if he were pleading. 'I need — '

'Will you come back on Halloween?' she asked, interrupting him. 'I want to show you a special place in the country. We'll make a day of it. We'll have such fun.'

Byrne had to find out what she meant in her note, the references to the animals. But he now knew that getting the information was not going to be easy. Before he could stop himself he said: 'Yes. I'll come back.'

She looked at him as if seeing him for the first time, her expression darkening. 'I can help you stop the killings, Kevin. But first you must do something for me.'

'What is it, Christa-Marie?' he asked. 'What can I do for you?'

Of all the things he expected her to say, what she did say nearly took his breath away. They were probably the last two words he would have expected to hear, two words that would carry his thoughts well into the dark hours of the night.

Christa-Marie Schönburg took his hand in hers, looked deep into his eyes, and said: 'Love me.'

54

Lucy stood in front of the door to Room 1208, her heart pounding. She wanted to go in, but she was afraid, as frightened as she had ever been in her life. She had done a little sleuthing on her own. She knew that everyone on this floor was a member of *Société Poursuite*. The group had a seminar in the Crystal Room that day, a seminar that was scheduled to run from 10:00 a.m. to 3:00 p.m., when they would break for lunch. Lucy figured that the floor would be empty from about 9:30 a.m. until perhaps 2:00 p.m.

Earlier in the day she had stood on the mezzanine and watched everyone file into the Crystal Room. Ever since she had been kidnapped, with everyone she met she was always looking for something, some gesture, some familiar posture, a word, an inflection, an accent that would draw her back to those three lost days and what had happened to her.

Once, in Carlisle, she had heard a woman's high-pitched laughter, and it had drawn her memory to a room — not necessarily a room in which she had been held, but a room that had served as a stop along the way. When she had turned to look at the woman — a doughy redhead of forty with cigarette-stained lips — the feeling had gone. She understood then that the feeling would come and go. She only needed it to stay for a moment, during which she could take a snapshot. And remember.

Right now she had a job to do.

Lucy lifted her hand to knock but found she couldn't do it. Her arms felt weak and a little too light all of a sudden. She tried again.

'Housekeeping,' she said, knocking. She soon realized it had come out in a mousy whisper.

A louder knock. '*Housekeeping.*'

Nothing.

Now or never.

She took out her section card, swiped the lock, and stepped into Room 1208.

★ ★ ★

The room was empty.

She wasn't supposed to close the door, but sometimes they closed on their own and her supervisor was well aware of this. This was one of those times. Except that Lucy closed it herself.

She had lugged everything she needed into the room and had piled it on the bed. She breezed through her checklist. She had never worked so fast in her life.

This was crazy. What was she doing? This was all in her head. She had created a fantasy here — from the moment she'd heard about the Dreamweaver it had all been some crazy dream. The fact that a girl had been killed in this room was just a sick and tragic and horrible coincidence.

Mr. Adrian Costa had no special abilities, no special powers. The man was a charlatan, and he was lying to her. Just another long con.

Lucy flew through the rest of her duties, clocking the room at something superhuman, like fifteen minutes. When she was finished she felt a little better. A clean fresh room had that effect on her. Now she could leave.

On the way out she saw that the bottom drawer in the dresser was slightly open. She looked at the door, then back.

Before she could stop herself she eased open the drawer. Inside were three folded dress shirts. There was something glossy beneath them. She pushed the shirts aside, and saw it.

At the bottom of the drawer was a picture of her mother.

55

Byrne sat in his van. On the way to Chestnut Hill he had planned it all out: how he would present himself, how he would talk to Christa-Marie, how he would get the information he needed from her. He would walk in, the veteran investigator, Mr. Cool, Master of the Universe, and walk out with what he needed.

He had failed miserably.

He was leaving without one shred of information. He wondered what his next move would be. He could talk to Michael Drummond or Paul DiCarlo in the DA's office. They, in turn, would get in touch with Benjamin Curtin, and the request would be made to have Christa-Marie come into the city for a formal statement.

Byrne could all but see the attendant circus.

As soon as he started the van he saw Adele Hancock crossing the wide driveway. Byrne lowered his window as she approached.

'She wanted you to have this.'

Adele Hancock handed him a sealed CD. The cover photo was a picture of Christa-Marie at a café in Italy. Behind her was the Basilica di Santa Maria del Fiore.

'She told me to tell you that if you want to know her, you should listen to this.'

'What do you think she means by that?'

Hancock offered a thin smile. 'If you have a few years to spare, I could probably scratch the surface of that question for you.'

Fifteen minutes later Byrne found himself on the expressway. He couldn't head back to the city. Not yet. He had another stop to make.

★   ★   ★

Inside his head the urges combusted. One urge told him what he had to do, what he should do. The other told him what he ultimately *would* do.

Heading west, he opened the CD and pushed it into the player. In moments his world was filled with the soaring majesty of Christa-Marie Schönburg's cello.

56

Tommy Archer had never gotten used to the smell. Probably never would. This did not bode well for someone with a dream of one day owning his own beauty salon.

Today's offending odor — there were so many from which to choose in this line of work — was the cloying aftermath of the perm he had just finished doing on old Mrs. Smith. The perm smell was mostly ammonia, which, if he remembered correctly from his chemistry classes, came from ammonium thioglycolate.

Tommy just called it skunk.

He always told his customers that, seeing as the perm solution was very alkaline, the best way to get rid of the smell was with an acid-based product like tomato juice. He told them to apply it to their hair, leave it on for ten to twenty minutes, then shampoo and rinse.

His customers all thought he was some kind of genius when he explained this to them, but it was pretty basic science. Still, he let them believe what they wanted to believe. In his twenty-six years there hadn't been too many people who considered Tommy Archer a genius. Especially his father. On the other hand, considering what he had once done for his father, he had earned the man's undying gratitude, if not his respect. Not that the man would ever show it.

While getting the perm smell out of hair was

one thing, getting the smell out of the tiny shop, the sum total of six hundred square feet that made up Country Cutz (inarguably the worst salon name in the history of the business), was something else.

Even though the temperature was around forty-five degrees, Tommy opened the two windows overlooking the street. Mrs. Smith had been his last customer for the day.

Tommy popped a tape into the player behind the register and began to sweep up. He felt a chill cross the salon. It was getting near the holiday season, which meant more work, more money, but it also meant that the loneliness would begin to descend again. He was the poster boy for Seasonal Affective Disorder.

★   ★   ★

He was not allowed to smoke in the shop. After the floor was swept and the sinks rinsed, with combs and brushes cleaned, he stepped outside and lit a cigarette. Dark already. The main street of the town was all but deserted. The lights from Patsy's Diner two blocks away and the Aamco shop across the street were all that were on.

'Are you still open?'

Tommy nearly jumped a foot. He turned to locate the source of the voice. There was a man standing right next to him. As in *right* next to him. He hadn't heard him walk up the sidewalk.

The man wore a dark overcoat.

Tommy glanced at his watch. 'Actually, we close in about five minutes.'

377

The man ran a hand over the back of his hair. 'I was hoping to get a quick trim. You see, I have a wedding reception tonight — I'm the cool uncle, the one with the big wallet — and, while I could probably show up in a rainbow wig, I do like to make an entrance.'

Tommy looked again at his watch, as if the answer was going to be there. He liked the man's style, though, and the *big wallet* reference was clearly meant to imply some sort of huge tip. Plus, it wasn't like he had anywhere to go. His little hamlet didn't exactly have a thriving gay community, or even a seedy part of town. All he had to look forward to was a bottle of cheap Orvieto and the DVD box set of the second season of *Fericho. Thank God for Netflix.*

He glanced at the man. *Nice eyes. Nice smile.*

'Just a trim?'

'Yes,' the man said. 'And I'm willing to pay double the going rate.'

'That won't be necessary,' Tommy said. 'Besides, what would I do with all that money in a dump like this town?'

★　★　★

The man didn't really need too much work, but if Tommy understood anything — about both himself and most of the people he had ever styled — it was that personal grooming was just that. Personal. Everyone had a right to look exactly the way he or she wanted.

'Nice little town you have here,' the man offered.

Tommy snorted. 'Yeah, well, it is if you don't mind living in a place where you call the wrong number and end up talking to that person for an hour anyway.'

The man laughed. 'I'll bet it's not *that* bad.'

Tommy took out his hair dryer, blew the hair from the man's shoulders. When he was done he dusted the man's neck with powder.

'So, you're going to a wedding reception?' Tommy asked.

'Yes,' the man said.

'Whereabouts? Over at the Legion Hall?' Tommy took off the cape. He picked up his brush, brushed off the last stray hairs from the man's shoulders and neck.

'No,' the man said. 'This is at the Crystal Room.'

Tommy had never heard of the Crystal Room. 'Is that around here somewhere?'

'It's in Philadelphia.'

Tommy shrugged. He figured that the man was on his way across the state. They got a lot of travelers here, being so close to the Flight 93 memorial. Tommy wondered how the man had managed to find the shop.

The man stood up, straightened the crease in his trousers. 'I really appreciate this. I feel like a new man.'

A new man, Tommy thought. *I wish.*

'It was my pleasure.'

The man slipped on his coat. 'How much do I owe you?'

Tommy told him. The man doubled the price, as promised.

★ ★ ★

At just after eight Tommy locked the shop. As
per his explicit instructions, he left the register
open, drawer out, under a solitary spotlight.

He walked quickly to the parking lot. The
temperature had dropped in the past hour or so.

'Thomas?'

He spun around. He saw no one, just the
long-shadowed street.

Thomas? Who the hell called him Thomas?
The last person to call him Thomas had been his
ex, Jeremy. But that had been in York, and that
was three years ago.

'Hello?'

Silence.

Tommy stepped back around the corner. A car
trundled past, one person inside, never glancing
his way. He looked both ways down the street.
And saw him. The man he had just given the
trim to. Except now the man was wearing a dark
jumpsuit, zipped to the throat.

'*Benvenuto al carnevale.*'

The man lifted something into the air, an
object about the size and shape of a large
old-school garage-door opener. Tommy heard a
loud crackling sound, smelled something burning. Then his legs went south.

★ ★ ★

In a van. Moving.

Tommy blanked out. Came back.

He could not move his head.

The van was stopped. The man climbed into the back, put on a pair of thin latex gloves, shut the doors. Classical music was playing on the car stereo. Violins or something.

Tommy heard something else. It sounded like a drill.

Tommy screamed.

57

Byrne stopped for coffee in North Philly. He washed his face and hands in the bathroom. Fatigue was a shambling monster within. When he slipped back into the van he turned on his cellphone and saw that he had five messages. All from Jessica. He called her. 'Where are you?' Byrne asked.

'I'm at Jefferson Hospital,' Jessica said.

'*Jefferson*? Why?'

'I ran into an old friend of mine today.'

'What are you talking about? Who?'

'Lucas Anthony Thompson.'

'*What*? How?'

Jessica gave him a brief recap, starting with the suicide of Joseph Novak, the voicemail from the dead, the existence of Novak's journal, and the assault by Lucas Thompson on her. Byrne took a moment to absorb it all.

'Man, I leave the city for one minute,' he said.

'Tell me about it.'

'Is Thompson in custody?'

'No,' Jessica said. 'He's dead. And Novak's journal is gone.' She filled him in on the rest of the details.

'Where did it happen?'

Jessica told him.

'That was the Kimmelman crime scene, wasn't it?'

'Yeah.'

'Have they moved him yet?'

'Yeah. CSU is all over the place.'

'I'm going to stop there,' Byrne said. 'When did they say you could get out of there?'

'About an hour or so. Vincent is with Sophie. Can you pick me up?'

'I'll be there.'

58

Byrne arrived in front of the hospital at about nine-thirty. Jessica was waiting, forced to sit in a wheelchair — which made everything seem so much worse than it was. Spotting his van, she got out of the chair, crossed the driveway, and slid into the passenger seat.

'You *look* okay,' Byrne said.

'I *am* okay. You know how it is. You break a fingernail and they want to do exploratory surgery. Keeps the premiums up.'

'What did they say?'

'I'm fine. No concussion. They said I'll have a headache for a day or so. They want to see me again in two weeks.'

Byrne drove slowly before pulling into the small temporary parking lot. He put the van in park. 'Tell me more about this.'

Jessica tried to organize her thoughts. It was a little difficult after getting her brain scrambled. She told Byrne what she remembered about Joseph Novak's diary.

'He wrote that he was beholden to someone,' she said.

'His word? Beholden?'

Jessica nodded. 'He wrote: *All Saints Day. It is done. I know now that I will be forever beholden to him.*'

'All Saints Day. November 1st.'

'Yeah.'

384

Jessica also told him about the photograph in the back of the journal.

'Any idea who the woman was or where it was taken?' Byrne asked.

'None. I didn't recognize the place.'

'And the word *hell* was on the back?'

'Yeah. Just that. Hell.'

They fell silent.

'Now it's your turn,' Jessica said. 'What happened up in Chestnut Hill?'

Byrne told her about his conversation with Christa-Marie. Jessica had the feeling that her partner was not telling her everything, but that was his way. He would tell her only what she needed to know at this moment.

'She said there are going to be more killings,' Byrne said. 'She said that she could help us.'

'And that was it? No details?'

'No details.'

'Did she sound . . . how do I put this . . . '

'Nuts?'

'Yeah. That.'

'I'm not sure,' Byrne said. 'Yeah, I suppose she did. A little. But I'd like to talk to her one more time before all hell breaks loose with her. You know as well as I do that the second I put this on the record they're going to send a half-dozen shrinks up there. She'll shut down completely.'

The rain picked up again. For a few moments there was only the sound of the music from the stereo and the staccato impact of raindrops on the roof of the van.

Byrne turned in his seat, put his hand on hers.

'You sure you're okay?'

'Good to go,' Jessica said. 'Never better.'

Byrne just stared.

'Okay, I may have been better once. I think it was the summer my cousin Angela had that Thai stick.'

Byrne smiled. He squeezed her hand, put the van in reverse. Jessica leaned forward, turned up the stereo. 'This is beautiful. Is this who I think it is?'

Byrne reached behind her seat, picked up the CD case, handed it to her.

'This is what we're listening to?'

Byrne nodded. 'Yeah. Christa-Marie's nurse gave me that. She said Christa-Marie wanted me to hear it.'

Jessica looked at the CD player, saw it was track two. She looked at the case. Track two was *Nocturne in G Major* by Chopin.

'It's incredible,' she said.

When the track was over she played it a second time.

★ ★ ★

As they pulled out of the parking lot, Jessica read the liner notes.

'This was recorded here in Philly, you know,' she said. 'At the Prentiss Institute.'

'That's the music school, right? The conservatory over on Locust?'

'I think so.'

Jessica looked at the back of the CD. At the bottom was a brief list of credits.

386

'Kevin.'

Byrne looked over. Jessica handed him the CD, pointed to the last line of the liner notes.

RECORDING ENGINEER: JOSEPH P. NOVAK.

59

Once a stately mansion, the Prentiss Institute of Music was an impressive early-1900s Georgian sandstone building, across from Rittenhouse Square on Locust Street. In the world of classical music it was considered by many to be Philadelphia's version of the Juilliard. Many members of the Philadelphia Orchestra had studied at Prentiss. While most of the courses of study were at the college level, they also maintained a prep school. A number of principal players of major orchestras around the world had gotten their training at Prentiss.

Because of the prestige of the school, and the late hour, Byrne had put in a call to the DA's office. The office had then placed a call to the school and gotten Jessica and Byrne an appointment to speak with someone.

★ ★ ★

The dean of the Prentiss Institute of Music was Frederic Duchesne. In his forties, Duchesne was tall and sharp-featured, had thinning blond hair, hazel eyes, and an air of rumpled elegance. He met them at the front door of the institute, locking it behind them, and escorted them to his office, a large white-paneled room off the reception area. The room was cluttered with sheet music on stands, stacks of CDs, as well as a

388

variety of musical instruments in their velvet-lined cases. On the wall was a large framed copy of the school's charter. Duchesne offered coffee, which Jessica and Byrne declined. They sat.

'We appreciate you taking the time to talk to us,' Byrne said. 'I hope we're not keeping you too late.'

'Not at all. I sometimes don't leave here until midnight. Always something to do.' He absently straightened some papers on his desk, then stopped, perhaps realizing it was hopeless. He turned back. 'It's not often we get a visit from the police.'

'We just have a few questions,' Byrne said.

'I assume this has something to do with Joseph Novak.'

'It does,' Byrne said.

Duchesne nodded. 'I saw it on the news.'

'What can you tell us about Novak?'

'Well, as I understand it, Mr. Novak was loosely associated with Prentiss for ten years or so.'

'He was an employee?'

'No, no. He freelanced as an engineer for various recordings. The institute hires a number of different technicians based on the project.'

Byrne held up the CD he had gotten from Christa-Marie. 'He worked on this project?'

Duchesne put on his glasses. When he saw the CD he smiled fondly. 'That was recorded more than twenty years ago. Novak didn't record the original. He worked on the remastering.'

'Were you acquainted with Joseph Novak?'

'We met once or twice. I never worked with

389

him personally, no.' Duchesne shook his head. 'Terrible tragedy what happened.'

'When was the last time you saw him?'

Duchesne thought for a moment. 'It must be two years now.'

'You've had no contact since?'

'None.'

'Do you know how many recordings he worked on here?'

'Not off hand,' Duchesne said. 'I can get that information for you.'

Byrne glanced at his notes. 'I have just a few more questions. I'm afraid some of them are probably going to seem pretty basic.'

Duchesne held up a hand. 'Please. This is a place of learning.'

'Can you tell us a little bit about the institute?'

'You want the tourist version or the potential-donor version?'

'Tourist,' Byrne said. 'For now.'

Duchesne smiled, nodded. 'The institute was founded in 1924 by a woman named Eugenie Prentiss Holzman, and is known worldwide as one of the leading conservatories. It's difficult to get into, but the tuition is free. A number of the current members of the Philadelphia Orchestra are faculty here, as well.'

'How many students do you have?'

'Right now, around one hundred sixty.'

'And this is all free?'

'Well, not the private lessons.'

'Expensive?'

'Very,' Duchesne said. 'The hourly fee can be quite high.'

Duchesne continued, relating how Prentiss recruited its students, what the general curriculum was. He also name-dropped some of the more famous alumni. It was an impressive list. When he finished he reached into his desk, produced a pair of large full-color booklets, handed one to Byrne, one to Jessica. The publication was called *Grace Notes*.

'Prentiss publishes this quarterly,' Duchesne said. 'Inside you'll find all the background you need.'

Jessica and Byrne thumbed through the booklets. Byrne held up his copy. 'Thanks.'

Duchesne nodded.

'I do have one last question, if I may,' Byrne added.

'Of course.'

'When it comes to orchestral music — symphonies — is there always a book?'

'A book?'

'Like in musical theater. Someone writes the book, someone writes the music, someone else writes the lyrics.'

'I think I may know what you're asking. You want to know if symphonies have a *story* behind them. A narrative.'

'Yes.'

'It's a difficult question,' Duchesne said. 'And one that's been a topic for discussion and debate for a long time. I believe what you're talking about, insofar as instrumental music is concerned, is called program music.'

'Program music has a story?'

'Yes and no. In its purest form, program music

can be a mere suggestion of a narrative.'

'So a piece of music that follows a narrative approach might not be particularly coherent?'

Duchesne smiled. 'Tell me, detective. Where did you study music?'

'A little honky-tonk at the crossroads.'

'With the esteemed Mr. Johnson.'

'Yeah, well,' Byrne said. 'I made a different deal with the devil.'

Duchesne took a moment, thinking. 'To answer your astute question, yes. For the most part. There are a few exceptions, one being Vivaldi's *Four Seasons*.'

Jessica tried to listen closely but the only sound she could hear was the conversation flying over her head. She knew that Byrne took cryptic but detailed notes. She hoped he was getting all this. She was completely lost when it came to classical music. Whenever someone mentioned *The Barber of Seville* she thought of Bugs Bunny.

'Are there any symphonic poems, program music, that involve the use of animal imagery?'

'My goodness. Many.'

'Specifically a lion, a rooster, a swan, or a fish?'

'Perhaps the most famous of all. *Carnival of the Animals*,' Duchesne said without a moment's hesitation. 'It is a musical suite of fourteen movements. Much beloved.'

'The movements are all about animals?'

'Not all,' Duchesne said.

'Who was the composer?' Byrne asked.

'*Carnival of the Animals* was written by a great proponent of the tone poem. A French Romantic composer named Camille Saint-Saëns.'

'Do you have information on this that you might let us borrow?' Byrne asked.

'Of course,' Duchesne said. 'It will take me a little while to collate all of it. Do you want to wait?'

'Can you fax it to us as soon as you have it all together?'

'Sure,' Duchesne said. 'I'll get right on it.'

Jessica and Byrne rose. 'We really appreciate this,' Byrne said, handing the man a business card.

'Not at all,' Duchesne replied. He walked them to the door of his office, through the reception area, to the front doors.

'Were you here when Christa-Marie Schönburg studied here?' Byrne asked.

'No,' Duchesne said. 'I've been here for almost twenty years, but she had left by then.'

'Did she teach here?'

'She did. It was only for two years or so, but she was quite something, as I understand. The students were madly in love with her.'

They descended the steps, reached the side door of Prentiss.

'Perhaps this is something you are not at liberty to discuss, but does any of this have something to do with Ms. Schönburg?' Duchesne asked.

'No,' Byrne said, the consummate liar. 'I'm just a fan.'

Duchesne glanced over at the wall. Jessica followed his gaze. There, next to the door, mixed into a precise grouping of portraits of young musicians — violinists, pianists, flutists, oboists

393

— was an expensively framed photograph of a young Christa-Marie Schönburg sitting in a practice room at Prentiss.

★ ★ ★

On the way to the van — parked just off Locust Street on a narrow lane called Mozart Place — they walked in silence.

'You saw it, didn't you?' Jessica finally asked.

'Oh yeah.'

'Same one?'

'Same one.'

In the decades-old photograph of Christa-Marie next to the door she wore a stainless steel bracelet with a large garnet stone inlaid.

They had seen the same bracelet on the shelf at Joseph Novak's apartment.

60

The Audio-Visual Unit of the PPD was located in the Roundhouse basement. The purview of the unit was to provide A/V support to all of the city's agencies — cameras, TVs, recording devices, audio and video equipment. The unit was also responsible for recording every public event in which the mayor or police department was involved, providing an official record. The detective divisions relied upon the unit to analyze surveillance footage as it related to their cases.

In this regard there was no one better than Mateo Fuentes. In his mid-thirties, Fuentes was a denizen of the gloomy confines of the basement studios and editing bays, a fussy and geometrically precise investigator who seemed to take every foray by detectives into his world as an unwelcome invasion.

Recently promoted to sergeant, Mateo was now commander of the unit. What had passed for punctiliousness when he was Officer Fuentes now bordered on the obsessive.

When Jessica and Byrne arrived in the basement, Mateo Fuentes was holding court in one of the bays off the main studio, chatting with David Albrecht.

'So, you prefer the L-series lens, then?' Mateo asked.

'Oh yeah,' Albrecht said. 'No comparison.'

'No ghosting?'

'None.'

Mateo smirked. 'So, if I mortgage my house and sell all my possessions, I might be able to buy a rig like this?'

'You might be able to *rent* one.'

Both men looked over at Jessica and Byrne. Albrecht smiled. Mateo frowned. It appeared that the two detectives were harshing his vibe. A few minutes later the rest of the team arrived — six detectives in all, plus Sergeant Dana Westbrook.

Mateo was outnumbered.

'And so to business,' Fuentes said. 'Ready?'

The detectives gathered around David Albrecht's camera. The LCD screen was about four inches diagonally, but Mateo had hooked it up to one of the fifteen-inch monitors from the Comm Unit.

Mateo fast-forwarded through footage of the West Philly location until he came to the sequence showing the parking lot where Jessica had been assaulted.

The video showed Jessica walking out of the diner and into the parking lot. Ordinarily this would have been a moment for hoots and hollers, for a bout of good-natured ribbing. Everyone was silent. They knew what was coming.

On the screen Jessica made a call on her cellphone, then pocketed the phone. She leaned against the wall of the building, and opened the diary. She pulled something out of the back. This went on for a full minute. Cars passed in the

396

foreground. A mother walking with her three small children stopped in front of the lot. The woman adjusted the jacket on a two-year-old girl, who wanted nothing to do with it. They soon moved on. Jessica continued to read.

A few moments later Thompson emerged from behind the building. It showed him sucker-punching Jessica, the diary flying from her hand. Two loose pieces of paper lofted on the wind. Everyone watching winced. The second blow took Jessica down. Thompson paced for a few moments, strutting. The audio was from across the street, just the sound of traffic. His words were unintelligible, but his gestures were not.

'There,' Albrecht said. He hit a button on the small remote in his hand. The video froze. Albrecht pointed to the right side of the screen. There, just beyond the corner of the building, was a shadow on the ground, the unmistakable shadow of a person. Albrecht restarted the video. Thompson stood over Jessica's body, but all eyes were on the shadow. The shadow didn't move.

He's watching, Jessica thought. *He's just standing there watching what's happening. He's not helping me. He's part of this.*

When Thompson got close to the corner of the building a pair of arms reached out, over his head. A second later the arms descended and Thompson all but disappeared, dragged off his feet with enormous force.

Albrecht rewound the video, played it again, this time frame by frame. The arms were dark-clad. The subject wore dark gloves. When the hands were over Thompson's head Albrecht froze the video. Silhouetted against the white of the garage behind the building, it was possible to see what the man in shadows had in his hands. It was a wire. A long loop of thin wire. He slipped the wire over Thompson's head and around his neck, yanking back and pulling Thompson from the frame.

The screen went black.

'I want a copy of this sent to Technical Services,' Dana Westbrook said. 'I want this broken down frame by frame.'

'Sure.'

'I want tire impressions from that lot and the area behind the building,' Westbrook said. 'See if we have any police cameras on that street.'

Before Westbrook could say anything else, Dennis Stansfield came down the stairs in a hurry. He bulled into the center of the room.

'Detective?' Westbrook asked. 'You're late.'

Stansfield looked at the floor, the ceiling, the walls. He opened his mouth, but nothing emerged. He seemed stuck.

'*Dennis?*'

Stansfield snapped out of it. 'There's another one.'

★   ★   ★

The scene was a Chinese takeout on York Street, in a section of Philadelphia known as Fishtown. A longtime working-class neighborhood in the northeast section of Center City, running roughly from the Delaware River to Frankford Avenue to York Street, Fishtown now boasted a

398

number of arts and entertainment venues, mixing arty types with the cops, firefighters, and blue-collar workers.

As Byrne and Jessica threaded through the cordon to the area behind the restaurant, Jessica dreaded what she was about to see.

★   ★   ★

A pair of uniformed officers stood at the mouth of the alley. Jessica and Byrne signed onto the crime scene, gloved up, and walked down the narrow passageway. No one was in a hurry.

The call had come in to 911 at just after nine p.m. The victim, it appeared, had been dead for days.

Garbage bags had been piling up behind the restaurant for weeks. Apparently the restaurant owner had an ongoing feud with the private hauling company, and it had become a matter of principle. Pushed against one wall were more than a hundred bulging plastic bags, ripped and torn by all manner of vermin, their rotting contents spilling out. The foul smell of the decomposing body was masked by a dozen other acrid odors of decaying meats and produce. A trio of brave rats milled at the far end of the alley, waiting their turn.

★   ★   ★

At first, Jessica didn't see the victim. CSU had not yet set up their field lighting, and in the dim light of the sodium street lamps, combined with the meager yellow light thrown by the security light over the back door to the restaurant, the flesh of the corpse blended in with the trash and pitted asphalt. It was as if he had become part of the city itself. Stepping closer, she saw the body.

Light brown skin. Nude and hairless. Head shaved bald. The body was bloated with gases.

The entire team was present, along with Russell Diaz, Mike Drummond, and now a representative of the mayor's office.

They all waited for the ME's investigator to clear the body for investigators. Tom Weyrich was taking a day off. The new investigator was a black woman in her forties whom Jessica had never met. She examined the body for wounds, made her notes. She opened the victim's hand, shone her Maglite, and everyone saw the small tattoo on the middle finger of the left hand. It appeared to be a kangaroo. Photos were taken from every angle.

The ME's investigator rose and stepped back. Stansfield walked forward and gently removed the white paper band that was wrapped around the victim's head.

The dead man was Latino, in his late thirties. Like the other victims he had a slash across his forehead, but this time the puncture wound was over his left eye. His right ear was shredded into a scabrous tangle of blood and ruined cartilage.

Byrne saw the victim's face, turned, and took a few steps away, his hands in his pockets.

What was *this* about? Jessica wondered. Why was he stepping away?

'I know him,' Drummond said. 'That's Eduardo Robles.'

All eyes turned to Kevin Byrne. Everyone knew that Byrne had been trying to get the grand jury to indict Robles in the death of Lina Laskaris. And now Robles was a victim of their serial murderer.

'This is where she died,' Byrne said. 'She was shot on the street and she crawled back here to die. This is the Lina Laskaris crime scene.'

* * *

On York Street, the media crews swarmed. In the mix Jessica noted CNN, Fox and other national news outlets. Among them David Albrecht jockeyed for position.

Five victims.

61

Byrne got in the van and drove. At first he had no idea where he was going. But soon he found himself on the expressway, and not long after that back in Chestnut Hill, looking beyond the high iron fence at the huge house.

He saw a light in a window, a shadow cross the elegant silk drapery.

Christa-Marie.

Closing his eyes and leaning back in the driver's seat, he returned to that night in 1990. He and Jimmy Purify had been grabbing a bite to eat. They had just closed a double homicide, a drug murder in North Philadelphia.

Had he really been that young? He'd been one of the newer detectives in the unit then, a brash kid who carried over the nickname of his youth. Riff Raff. He wore it with the expected cocky Irish swagger. They called Jimmy 'Clutch.'

Riff Raff and Clutch.

But that was ancient history.

Byrne glanced up at the second floor, at the figure in the window. Was she looking out at him?

He picked up the file next to him on the seat, opened it, looked at the photos, at the body of Gabriel Thorne lying on the floor, the bloody white kitchen where all this had begun.

He had met earlier in the day with a man named Robert Cole, a man who ran an independent lab that sometimes took contracts from the department when rush forensic services were needed. He had seen Cole testify a number of times. He was good, he was thorough and, above all, he was discreet. Cole had promised Byrne a rush job on what he wanted.

Byrne flipped through the case file. He looked at his signature at the bottom of the form. A much younger man had wielded the pen that day. A man who had his whole career, his whole life, ahead of him.

Byrne didn't have to look at the time of arrest, the moment he had placed Christa-Marie Schönburg in custody. He knew.

It was 2:52.

62

In the night, when hotel guests are asleep in their beds, the dead roam the halls. They ride the elevators, take the back stairs, slip into rooms and stand at the foot of your bed. They sit on the edge of the sink when you take your shower. They watch as you make love, as you stuff the free toiletries and soaps into your luggage, thinking yourself so clever. They watch as you view late-night porn.

Stacy Pennell walks these hallways, her small feet barely making an impression on the soft carpeting. Guests come and go, but Stacy stays on, her final words circling in Room 1208 like sorrowful little birds.

Soon she will be set free.

63

Jessica Jogged down Third Street. At this early hour the running was not as bad as she'd thought it was going to be. Traffic was sparse, and the only people on the streets were those opening their bakeries and coffee shops, city crews, other joggers and cyclists. The hard part of running through a city was the uneven sidewalks, the curbs, the occasional stray dog.

There was a light drizzle, a condition that the weather report said would end by mid-morning. Jessica wore her rain gear and an Eagles ball cap. She was wet, but not soaked. The temperature was in the high forties. Perfect jogging weather.

As she turned the corner onto Wharton she thought about her and Byrne's meeting with Frederic Duchesne. She thought about the photograph on the wall of the Prentiss Institute, the picture of Christa-Marie Schönburg wearing the bracelet they had seen in Joseph Novak's apartment.

This morning they would get the background information on *Carnival of the Animals*, and they could begin to work on what might be the killer's twisted method.

She turned the corner and saw someone standing in front of her house. Again. She slowed up.

405

This time it was not Dennis Stansfield. It was Kevin Byrne. As Jessica approached she got a better look at him. She had never seen him look worse. His face was drawn and pale. He hadn't shaved. He was wearing the same clothes he'd had on yesterday. And he was just standing in the rain. He didn't seem to be looking for her, didn't seem to be doing anything. He was just standing in the cold rain, holding a large envelope in his hands. Just a few feet from where he stood was an awning that would have provided him shelter.

Jessica came to a stop, then walked the last few yards.

'Hey,' she said, catching her breath.

Byrne turned to look at her. 'Hey.'

'Want to come in? You're getting soaked.'

Byrne just looked up at the sky, letting the rain fall on his face.

'Come on inside,' Jessica said. 'I'll make some coffee, get you a towel.'

'I'm okay.'

Jessica took him by the arm, led him under her neighbor's awning. She shook the rain off her ball cap, brushed some of the water from Byrne's shoulders. 'What's up?'

Byrne was silent for a few moments. He pointed across the street, at a novelty sign in the window of a row house. It read PARKING FOR ITALIANS ONLY.

Jessica offered a smile. 'South Philly. What are you going to do?'

Byrne turned the envelope over and over in his hands. The moment drew out. 'I don't think I know how to do this anymore, Jess.'

406

He looked down the street, remained silent. Lights flickered on in some of the windows. Another morning in Philadelphia.

Jessica turned him to face her fully. 'There are two dozen people working these cases. Every resource available is on this. We're going to shut him down. Take the day. I'll call you every hour on the hour. If something breaks I'll — '

'We heard from the lab,' Byrne said, interrupting her. 'From Irina. We have a fix on the murder weapon.'

'Well, that's good, right? That's a good thing.'

'The killer is using strings from an instrument.'

'An instrument?'

Byrne looked down the street, back. 'The wire is a string from a cello, Jess. He's strangling them with a string from a cello. That explains the animal hair on the wire. It's horsehair from the bow.'

The implications of this were deep, and Jessica knew now why her partner had been up all night. There could no longer be any excuse for not bringing Christa-Marie Schönburg in for questioning. There were too many connections.

Jessica knew she had to tread lightly. 'How do you want to handle this?'

Byrne said nothing. A city street-sweeper trolled slowly by. They took a step back, closer to the building. When it had passed Byrne turned to her.

'When I walked into that house, twenty years ago, I felt something, you know? It was my first case as a lead investigator, and I had it all in my hand. I saw the body, the weapon, the blood. I saw the suspect, I knew the motive. I saw it all in one second. One big picture, no parts.' He looked at Jessica. He was on the edge. 'I said to myself *this is what you were meant to do.*'

Jessica wanted to jump in. It wasn't the right moment.

'I don't see it like that anymore,' Byrne said. 'Now it's all in pieces, and I'm scared that I made a mistake. I'm scared I can't do it anymore.'

'You're wrong, Kevin. I have no doubt that you can do this. I don't know anybody who does this better. But you know what scares *me*?'

'What?'

'What scares me is that this killer might go underground. That he might finish this up and disappear forever.'

'He's not done.'

Byrne said this with such finality that it stopped Jessica cold. 'What do you mean? How do you know?'

Byrne held up the large envelope. It was soaked. He didn't seem to care. 'This came in at four o'clock this morning.'

'What is it?'

Byrne pulled the document out of the envelope. But he didn't look at it, didn't hand it to Jessica. He just let it get wet. 'A body was found yesterday in a town called Garrett Corners.'

'How does this concern us?'

'It looks like it's connected,' Byrne said. 'We have to go there. We're expected.'

64

The Dreamweaver was waiting for Lucy with his door open. He gave her a start. Again, he looked different. Even younger than the day before. He stood a little straighter, and his clothes looked new.

'Lucy,' he said, gesturing for her to step inside.

She almost gasped. The place was all but empty. The only thing left inside was the stand. The Dreamweaver booth.

'Are you moving somewhere?' Lucy asked.

'Yes. Quite soon.'

She wanted to ask what this was all about. She had a million questions, but she decided to wait. What was most important was to go back under, to slip back to that horrible day in 2001 and see the man's face, the man who took her somewhere and at the same time took her memory, her life. The man who was staying in Room 1208. The man who knew her mother.

'Today we are going to sit inside,' he said. 'Is that all right?'

Lucy pointed to the booth. 'Inside there?'

'Yes. Today we go all the way back.'

Lucy took a deep breath. 'Okay.'

Mr. Costa opened the door. Lucy took off her coat and stepped inside. It was like a confessional. Inside was a small bench. She sat down. When Mr. Costa closed the door, it was pitch black. She heard him sit down on the other side.

He began to speak, and —

— suddenly she was back there. The darkness around her did not change. But she sensed that she was under. It was different from the first two times because this time she knew. It was like when you were dreaming and you *knew* you were dreaming, and therefore you could not be hurt. For the first time in nine years, she felt strong.

★　★　★

Are you alone?

No.

Who is there with you?

Another girl. A girl my age. Her name is Peggy.

Tell me about her.

She has on a spangly dress. And make-up. She's too little for make-up.

Are you wearing make-up?

I don't know. I can't see myself. But I am wearing high heels. They are big for my feet.

What is the other girl doing?

She's crying.

Are you crying?

No. I don't cry.

What else do you see?

I see candles. Candles and moonlight.

Why do you see moonlight?

Because I am running now. I'm running through the trees. The smell of apples is everywhere.

Is it an orchard?

Yes. It's an orchard.

Is the other girl with you?
No, but I see her. I see her up by the lake.
What is she doing?
She's not moving.
Why is she not moving?
I don't know.
Can you see the man's face?
I can't. But I know who he is.
Is he the man in Room 1208?
Yes. It's him.
You are certain?
Yes.
Did you place the note in his room? The note you wrote here last time?
Yes.
Good. Now I'm going to ring a bell for you. Is that okay?
Yes.
Can you hear the bell?
I can hear it.
It's a special bell, Lucy.
A special bell.
There is no other sound like it.
No other.
When you hear this bell at the hotel, there is something you have to do. Something you have to do for me.
Okay.
You will tell no one about this.
No one.
Remember the bell, Lucy.

411

65

The drive across southeastern Pennsylvania was energizing. The rain had stopped and it was a bright and sunny day. A lot of people think that the best place to view fall colors in the United States is New England, and they have a point. But the rolling hills of Pennsylvania, painted in scarlet and gold and lemon yellow, might well give New Hampshire a run for its money.

For a long time neither Jessica nor Byrne said much. Both were lost in the events of the past four days and the possibility of a break in the case, a break located far out of their jurisdiction.

Before leaving Philadelphia, Jessica had gotten Byrne to stop at his apartment, shower and shave, change clothes. He looked like two-thirds of his old self again.

★   ★   ★

They stopped for coffee on the way. When Jessica got back in the car she remembered something she had been meaning to ask her partner. It was about as far removed from the case as she could imagine.

'You didn't happen to find a piece of green yarn in your van, did you?'

'No,' Byrne said. 'Are you talking about the yarn that was around the box with your mom's things in it?'

412

Jessica nodded. The thought of having lost the yarn made her sick. 'I looked everywhere, asked everyone. It's gone.'

'Maybe it'll turn up.'

Jessica didn't hold out much hope for this. It was only ten cents' worth of yarn, but it had belonged to her mother. And that made it priceless.

★   ★   ★

The town of Garrett Corners was a notch on the map off I–80, set among rolling farmland. If you lived here, and you wanted something that could not be obtained at the local general store, hardware store, or pair of diners, there were a few larger towns within thirty or so miles where you could find a Wal-Mart, a Lowe's, or a Bed, Bath & Beyond. Dinner on Saturday night or special occasions was at Max and Erma's or Outback.

The police department of Garrett Corners was three officers strong. In addition to the standard duties involving processing civil matters such as court orders, writs and orders of possession, there were mortgage foreclosures and township auctions. Rarely did they deal with homicide.

The town itself was an intersection, twenty buildings deep in four directions. The municipal building was a featureless block of limestone, housing the police department, courthouse and public agencies. It was every small-town city hall east of the Rockies. Jessica and Byrne were instructed to meet the chief of police, a man named Rogers Logan.

413

*   *   *

The woman at the desk was in her fifties and had a lacquered, highly complex hairdo, cantilevered to one side. She also had about her an air of small-town bureaucratic efficiency that told Jessica there was no doubt who ran the office, if not the lives, of the three police officers stationed there. Her name was Helen Mott. There was a plate of Halloween-themed cookies on her desk.

Jessica and Byrne announced themselves, showed ID, and took a seat on the worn oak bench across the room. Jessica scanned the walls. Affixed to them with yellowed tape were mostly outdated posters for D.A.R.E and other community drug and outreach programs. After a few minutes the door to the back opened, and a man walked out.

Rogers Logan was a fit sixty: military flat-top, big hands and farmer's shoulders. He walked with a purposeful gait. Behind him was a young woman in full uniform and Sam Browne.

'I'm Chief Logan,' he said. 'This is Officer Sherri Grace.'

Handshakes all around.

Officer Grace was in her late twenties, stout and surly. She was maybe fifteen pounds over her prom weight, and Jessica knew why. Cop hours and cop food would do it to you if you didn't fight it hard. Jessica waged the battle every day. Still, Officer Grace wore it well.

'Can I get everyone some coffee?' Grace asked.

'Sure,' Byrne said.

'How do you take it?'

414

'Like it comes.'

Grace winked and left the office.

'Coffee maker's fritzed,' Logan said, hooking a thumb over his shoulder, a sheepish look on his face. He probably figured that in Philadelphia the police department issued espresso machines and milk frothers to every squad. Little did he know. The first thing Jessica noticed when she walked into the office was that they had the same make and model of fax machines.

They retired to the squad room, which amounted to two desks pushed up against each other, a pair of large corkboards on the wall, a conference table pushed into the corner, along with five or six dented file cabinets.

A minute later Officer Grace returned with three cups of coffee in chipped ceramic mugs. The outside temperature had dropped a few degrees, and the mugs billowed with steam. She put the cups down on the desk, then put a cardboard box filled with packets of non-dairy creamer, sugar, Equal, Sweet'N Low and plastic stirrers on the table.

'I'm off to patrol,' she said. 'Nice meeting you all.'

Giving Byrne a little extra wattage in her smile, she left the office.

The coffee rituals came to a close. It was time to get down to business. Logan, the country gentleman, gestured to Jessica to take his chair. Jessica smiled, declined. All three of them stood as Logan described the victim.

'His name was Thomas Archer. Twenty-six years old. Lived over in Kelton, right near the

415

county line. He worked in the beauty salon over there.'

'Where was he found?' Byrne asked.

Logan moved over to a map on the wall, a map of Garrett Corners and surrounding townships. He pointed to a small green area just a short distance from the county line. 'He was found here, in the Shadyside Cemetery. As you can see, the cemetery is on both sides of the creek. Tommy was found on the southern end, near the mausoleum.'

At the word *cemetery* Jessica and Byrne exchanged a look. All they had really known on the way up to Garrett Corners was what the telex had told them, namely that there was a homicide victim with a possible connection to the Philadelphia murders.

'Who found the body?' Jessica asked.

'Body was found by the mail carrier. He was doing his afternoon route and he noticed a pack of dogs circling something in the cemetery. We've had a few problems with meth labs out here in the past couple of years, and where there's meth labs there're mean dogs. Mail carrier figured they'd gotten loose, called it in, and we went out to check it out. County game warden scooped up two of the dogs, others got away. The dogs had been at Tommy, but not too bad.'

'Where is Mr. Archer now?'

'The body was taken to the coroner's office in the county seat. They do all our autopsies, what few we need done.'

'Do they know how long the body had been there?' Byrne asked.

416

'Hard to say until they give it a good going-over. Not that long, though.'

'Do you have photographs of the crime scene?'

'Yeah,' Logan said. 'Unfortunately, I do.'

Logan led them to a small area off the squad room, which served as storage space for fax paper, toner, and other supplies. A folded crib leaned in one corner. Logan flipped on the overhead fluorescents.

One wall was dedicated to racks of official forms. The town might have been small, but it rivaled the PPD for forms needed. In the center was a folding conference table. Most of the table's contents were bunched to one side, and a pair of large manila envelopes sat in the middle.

Logan opened the envelopes, slid out the photographs. He arrayed them side by side on the table. The longer shots showed a rural cemetery. The close-ups were of the body. It was a sight with which Jessica and Byrne were all too familiar.

Jessica looked closely at the victim. The signature was identical to the bodies found in Philadelphia. The body was nude, and shaved clean of all hair. The band of paper was wrapped around the head, just barely covering the victim's eyes. There were three bloodstains on the paper, one lateral, one circular, along with the mutilated ear. The body was sprawled on a hillside, surrounded by low headstones. The left leg was clearly broken.

'Does this dovetail with the case you're working?' Logan asked.

'It does,' Byrne said.

417

'We'll need copies of these photographs, if that's all right,' Jessica said.

Logan retrieved a stack of envelopes from the top of a nearby file cabinet. He picked up two of them. 'I anticipated that. There's duplicates of everything in here.'

He handed the envelopes to Jessica. 'Thanks.'

The three of them went still for a few moments, each of them taking in the horror displayed before them in full color.

'When was your last homicide?' Jessica asked.

Logan ran a hand over his chin. 'Well, even though it's been a few years I find it a little hard to talk about. And mind you, I was in Vietnam. Two tours. Saw quite a bit. This one shook me good.'

Jessica and Byrne remained silent.

'We haven't had but two murders here in all the time I've been on the job. One was a domestic that went tragically wrong. Everyone saw that one coming, I suppose. Those two were at it for years. The other was little Peggy van Tassel.'

'Would you mind telling us the details?' Byrne asked.

Logan sipped his coffee. Jessica noticed a slight shake in his hand. He put the cup down, rattling it slightly on the worn Masonite surface. 'Little girl, eleven years old. Father worked for the county in the water department, mother was a teacher at Jefferson Middle School. Only child. Peggy went to school one day, never came home. We put the word out and by that evening we must have had two hundred volunteers for the

418

search. We found her by Iron Lake ten days later. She'd been molested, stabbed to death. Whoever did it cut her pretty bad.' Logan cleared his throat, reached for his coffee, thought better of it. 'She had on make-up, and a woman's fancy dress. Not a dress that was for a grown woman, mind you, but a small one. One that was her size. The folks at the state crime lab said it looked like it was made for her. State police took the case.'

The idea of the killer making a dress for the little girl gave Jessica a chill. 'Was the case ever closed?' she asked.

Logan shook his head. 'There was a man who was questioned in that case. That man's name was George Archer.'

'Archer?' Byrne asked.

'Yes, sir. Tommy Archer's father. George was a state trooper for a few years, but as I understand it he was shown the door,' Logan added. 'Insubordination was the official line, but there were rumors.'

'Rumors of what?' Jessica asked.

'Like yourselves, I try to deal in facts, ma'am. If it's all the same, rumors should live and die just that. Rumors.'

Jessica nodded. *Fair enough.*

'Why did the state like George Archer in this case?' Byrne asked.

'George had been seen talking to Peggy a few days before she went missing. In fact, that's where we found Tommy Archer's body. Right near Peggy's marker.'

Jessica looked at Byrne, then back. 'He was

419

found near her plot at the cemetery?'

'Yes, ma'am.'

Logan went through the photos on the table. He picked one up. In it, the body of Thomas Archer was visible on the right side of the frame. To the left was a clearly marked headstone.

MARGARET VAN TASSEL
APRIL 6 1990 — SEPTEMBER 21 2001
'OUR BELOVED PEGGY'

'Do you think any of the girl's family might be involved in this?' Byrne asked.

Logan shrugged. 'I suppose anything's possible. But as I understand it her family were travelers. I think they moved on a long time ago.' Logan sat on the edge of the table. 'A few years later the FBI came around again, questioned George in another case, up round your way. It was a cold case.'

'The case was out of Philadelphia?' Byrne asked.

Logan nodded. 'I believe it was.'

'Do you remember any details about the case?'

'No. It wasn't ours. But I do remember that they also talked to Tommy, who swore that George was with him all during the weekend in question, right up at the house on the farm. I'm not sure that George was there, but that was Tommy's story and he stuck to it.'

'I'd like to take a look at the report on that original homicide,' Byrne said. 'The van Tassel girl. Can you reach out to the state police and have them fax that to us?'

'Consider it done.' Logan glanced at his watch. 'I've got a few things on today. If there's anything else we can do for you, let Helen know and we'll take care of it.'

'We'd like to speak to George Archer,' Byrne said.

'I'll give you directions.' Logan scribbled a few things on a legal pad, tore off the sheet, handed it to Jessica.

'You can't miss the sign,' he added. 'Archer Farms.'

Jessica and Byrne thanked Logan for his time and consideration. On the way to the parking lot Jessica turned, asked the chief one last question.

'What do they grow up there at Archer Farms?'

'Apples, mostly,' Logan said. 'They have about fifty acres of orchards.'

66

The house was a large, aging Dutch Colonial on a hillside, not so much the archetypal farmhouse but rather a house built on a farm, remodeled many times over the years. It was surrounded on three sides by apple trees as far as the eye could see. In addition to a triple garage there were two outbuildings; one small, perhaps for lawn and maintenance equipment; one large, perhaps for mechanical harvesters, straddle trailers, and the storage of harvest totes.

The air was heavy with the sugary-tart smell of the fruit.

Jessica pulled over on the drive, stopping about fifty yards from the house. Nothing moved. There were no vehicles in sight.

'Does it get quieter than this?' Jessica asked.

Byrne just looked at the house, at the acres of trees. There was a porch light on, but no lights were visible through the windows.

Jessica had a hard time reconciling the bucolic vision in front of her with what she had seen in the past four days, or with the story she had heard from Rogers Logan. Still, there could be no denying that the murder of Thomas Archer, who at one time had lived right here, was connected to the brutal homicides in Philadelphia.

She looked at Byrne. 'Ready?'

Byrne hesitated for a few moments, then nodded.

Jessica crossed the gravel drive, looked in the grimy garage-door window. Inside she saw a pickup truck on the right-hand side. It looked to be a five-year-old F-150. The other two bays were empty. There was a thin layer of dust on the truck. There had been rain in this part of Pennsylvania in the past three days. Chances were good that the truck had not been out.

She and Byrne then walked over to the porch. The place was eerily quiet. They were about three hundred yards from Route 68, and it seemed that even the sound of the occasional car passing by did not reach them.

The right-hand side of the porch had a rick of well-seasoned firewood, stacked in a rusted wrought-iron rack. The door was ringed with a grapevine wreath, strung with autumn mums and small gourds.

Jessica looked through the window in the door. She saw no activity. She knocked, listened. Byrne moved across the porch, next to the window that looked into the living room. There were sheer curtains over the opening.

Jessica knocked again, put her ear near the door. Only silence.

Walking around to the back of the house, they found a tilled vegetable garden, turned for the season. A small green-water pond sat at the bottom of a gentle hill. The back porch was smaller than the front, but boasted a pair of new Adirondack chairs. They climbed the steps, looked inside. Inside was a mud room of sorts, one that led to a large kitchen. There were no cups or plates on the table, none in the sink.

Jessica knocked again, waited. The house appeared to be unoccupied.

'Let's check the garage,' Byrne said.

They walked over to the triple garage, around the side where there was a smaller door. It was unlocked.

Byrne stayed outside while Jessica pushed open the door, stepped in. The garage was dark and dusty, smelling of axle grease and the ever-pervasive sweetness of apples. The cloying smell was even stronger in here. One wall was lined with garden and farm tools — rakes, half-round shovels, hoes, mattocks, pickaxes. The other wall boasted a collage of license plates and street signs.

Jessica walked over to the truck. She placed her hand on the hood. The engine was cold. She then took a Kleenex out of her pocket, opened the driver's-side door. The rusty hinge moaned, and she stopped. It had been so quiet that the sound went through the garage like a scream. She eased the door all the way open. There were no keys in the ignition, and the cab was relatively clean. A pine-tree-shaped deodorizer dangled from the rearview mirror.

On the seat was a small pile of papers. Jessica held the Kleenex tightly, sorted through them. There were a pair of flyers for a recent Oktoberfest in Kelton, a coupon for a free car wash. There was a brochure for tours of Philadelphia. At the bottom was a postcard depicting a beach in South Carolina. *Greetings from Edisto Island.* Jessica flipped the card over, angled her Maglite.

Looking forward to seeing you and everyone at Société Poursuite! I'll be staying at the Hyatt Penn's Landing. Look me up and we'll have a drink.

It was signed, simply, R.

Jessica glanced at the date on the postmark. It was from the previous Friday.

She slipped the postcard back where it had been, closed the truck door, and walked out of the garage. She told Byrne about the postcard.

'It looks like he might be at the annual meeting of the *Société Poursuite*.'

'That's the group that handles the cold cases, right?'

'And these are all — '

'Cold cases,' Byrne said. 'Melina Laskaris, Marcellus Palmer, Antoinette Chan, and Peggy van Tassel are all open investigations, just the kind of thing a group like *Société Poursuite* would look into.'

Jessica nodded, thought for a moment. 'Logan said this guy used to be a state trooper. Maybe he's a member.'

'That convention is this week.'

It occurred to both of them at the same time.

'He's in Philly,' Jessica said.

'He's in Philly.'

425

67

In July 1998, at a small Italian restaurant in Queens, New York — an old-school trattoria on Astoria Boulevard called Theresa's — a man named Paul Ferrone, a retired NYPD detective, met with two of his oldest friends.

The three men had been meeting at Theresa's every month for the past four years, mostly for two reasons. One, Theresa Colopinti's chicken with peppers was the best in the city of New York. More importantly, the second reason was that these three men genuinely enjoyed each other's company.

After their entrée plates were cleared, they began to talk about murder, as was their custom. Cold-case murder. Paul Ferrone's two friends — Matt Grayson, a retired forensic dentist from Newark, New Jersey, and Eli O'Steen, a retired judge from Brooklyn — had been thinking about forming a group that did this sort of thing with regularity, a group that would expand beyond the three of them.

On that night they created an association called *Société Poursuite*, an homage to the Vidocq Society, a similarly themed group named after a nineteenth-century French detective named Eugene Francois Vidocq.

Similar in some ways to the Vidocq Society, *Société Poursuite* — which translated as Pursuit Society — now boasted more than three hundred and seventy members worldwide. And since its inception on that summer night in 1998, it had contributed to the solving of more than sixty homicides around the world.

The group met every month in New York City, with their annual conclave held in a different major city on the east coast each October, rotating between New York, Philadelphia, and Washington D.C.

This year their eleventh annual conclave would meet in Philadelphia, at the Le Jardin hotel. On the final night, an evening which would include a five-course meal prepared by the hotel's Michelin-starred chef Alain Cochel, there would be a speech by the Attorney General for the Commonwealth of Pennsylvania.

★   ★   ★

When Jessica and Byrne arrived at Le Jardin they were met in the lobby by the hotel's director of security, John Shepherd.

Shepherd had been a homicide detective in Philadelphia for more than twenty years. When Jessica had come into the unit, it had been Kevin Byrne and John Shepherd who had showed her the ropes. While Byrne taught her — indeed, in many ways was still teaching her — how to work a crime scene, it was John Shepherd who taught her how to walk into an interrogation room, how to position her body at first so as not to intimidate, how to walk that gossamer-thin line between treating someone like a suspect and like a witness, how to coax that first lie out of their mouths, and then, an hour or two later, how to slam it back in their faces.

The PPD had lost a great one when he retired.

John Shepherd, turned out in a smart navy blue suit, opened his arms. 'Jess,' he said. 'Beautiful as ever.'

They embraced. Even though they were still on the same side, they were no longer on the same team, and shows of affection were now allowed. 'We miss you, John.'

Shepherd looked at Byrne. 'And if I wasn't head of security here, I'd have to *call* security on this shady-looking character.'

The two men did the handshake, shoulder-bump, back-slap, I-swear-to-God-I'm-not-gay thing. *Men*, Jessica thought. God forbid they should show emotion in public. Cops were the worst.

'You look good, Johnny,' Byrne said.

'Underworked and overpaid.'

Shepherd did look healthier than he ever had. Anytime you could get away from cop food and cop hours, you looked better. Tall and Denzel-handsome, now in his salt-and-pepper fifties, Shepherd looked relaxed, and in charge.

He led them to the other side of the lobby, to the other side of a tall frosted-glass panel that somehow managed to keep the noise of arriving guests out of the tastefully appointed lounge.

They stood at the far end of the bar, away from everyone. Without asking, three cups of coffee, with creamers on ice, were put in front of them.

'So what are you up to?' Shepherd asked.

'Keeping the peace?'

'Disturbing it whenever possible,' Byrne said. 'How are things here?'

'Had a door pusher last month.'

A door pusher was one of the more unsophisticated breeds of hotel criminal. He was a guy who got into the hotel, went to upper floors, and simply pushed on doors to find one that was unlocked, or improperly closed or, God help the room attendant, left open by housekeeping. These were guys who always had a record for B & E, generally nonviolent types but a real nuisance in hotel security work.

'You take him down?' Byrne asked.

'Guy hit the Sheraton Society Hill in March, moved over to the Hyatt Penn's Landing in May. We had him on tape, but he was slick — ball caps, glasses, packing his waist to look heavier. Wore a suit one time, sweats and sneaks the next. We got him, though.'

They kicked the cop talk around for a while, until Shepherd moved his stool closer and lowered his voice. 'Now, I know how magnetic and incredibly charming I am, but I think y'all are here for another reason.'

Byrne took a moment. 'There's a convention here. We think we might have a connection to a case we're working.'

Shepherd nodded. 'The serial?'

'Yeah.'

'Lay it out.'

Byrne told Shepherd the details.

'And his name is George Archer?' Shepherd asked.

'Yeah.'

'Hang on.'

Shepherd left the bar, returned a few minutes later. 'No one registered here under that name. Maybe he's staying somewhere else. Do you have a description on the guy?'

'Not yet,' Byrne said. 'We have a request in to the state police. But they may not even have a picture. The guy was questioned, but he was never arrested or charged.'

Shepherd nodded. He'd been right where Jessica and Byrne were.

'Can you reach out to some of the other hotels, see if they have a George Archer?' Byrne asked.

'No problem. I'll make a few calls.' Shepherd pointed to the other side of the lobby. 'They're setting up in the Crystal Room right now. It's going to be a big deal tonight, even bigger tomorrow.'

'Do you have cameras in there?'

John Shepherd chuckled. 'Is the pope . . . what is the pope now, by the way?'

'German.'

'Doesn't sound as good as Polish, does it?'

'No.'

'We have cameras,' Shepherd said. 'Come on.'

★   ★   ★

From the outside, the Loss Prevention office at Le Jardin looked like any other room in the hotel. Unremarkable door, heavy-duty key lock. In the center of the hallway outside, which itself was off-limits to hotel guests, was a smoked-glass dome cam.

Inside was a small outer office, which led, through another secure door, to a larger room in which two people were working.

Shepherd spoke to a young woman at one of the desks, wrote something on the pad. While he was showing Jessica and Byrne the surveillance capabilities of the hotel, she would be putting in calls to the security directors of the surrounding hotels, looking for a guest named George Archer.

★ ★ ★

In front of them were two thirty-inch high-definition monitors, each divided into six windows. According to Shepherd, one operator kept an eye on them at all times, two people per eight-hour shift, rotating every two hours.

Jessica scanned the monitors. The one on the right had six windows up that showed the huge atrium, viewed from the mezzanine level. A dozen people or so had congregated near the center of the room. A man and a woman, middle-aged, stood at the front desk. An elderly woman chatted with the concierge. A few seconds later the view shifted to the parking lot and front entrance. A limo idled at the front door as a pair of young bellmen pulled a number of large suitcases from the trunk. Another bellman leaned into the passenger window of a waiting cab.

The software rotated the windows, floor after floor, with a view of the elevators constantly in

431

the upper right-hand section of the screen.

Shepherd sat down, clicked a few keys, and more than sixty small windows lined up on the two monitors. 'We've got two dome cams in every hall, clock cams in all the personnel spaces, half-zone weatherproof bullet cams in the parking lot, and four state-of-the-art 360-degree pan-and-tilt domes in the atrium and lobby, watching the desk and the money room. Not too much goes on here that we don't see.'

'This is a real voyeur's delight,' Byrne said.

'Wait until you see the bathroom cams,' Shepherd said, with a wink.

Jessica and Byrne had done a lot of work with the Audio-Visual Unit of the PPD, as well as the communications unit, which monitored the PPD street cams, for which Philadelphia was getting more and more funding.

Shepherd brought up the Crystal Room on a split screen. There was a man at the lectern, clearly an employee of whatever company was providing the PA and sound systems for the event. He performed a sound check.

'So the people in this society used to be either cops or prosecutors?' Jessica asked.

'Not at all,' Shepherd said. 'Some were in forensics, some worked for medical examiners' offices, some of them were never on the job at all. There are pretty tight membership rules and dues, which are kind of steep, so they keep out the lowlifes and the thrill seekers.'

'There goes my shot at membership,' Byrne said.

'Believe it.'

'Are they any good at what they do?' Jessica asked.

Shepherd nodded. 'That's my understanding. Every case they take on has to be formally presented to them by a bona fide agency. They don't work with the FBI or the NYPD, but just about everyone else of note has presented something.'

The three of them watched the monitors for a while, the constant rotation of views from within and without the hotel. It was a relentless flow: staff, guests, visitors, deliveries.

Was one of them their killer? Jessica wondered. Would she know him if she saw him?

* * *

When Jessica and Byrne returned to the Roundhouse, Jessica checked her messages. Nothing case-breaking. She checked the fax basket. There was a five-page fax from Frederic Duchesne, as promised. It was a detailed description of *Carnival of the Animals*. She brought it to her desk.

Jessica got onto the *Société Poursuite* website. In addition to a brief history, its mission statement, and an explanation of what the group was about, there were lists of its members, officers, past officers, and sub-chapters around the world. It was clear that the group chose its cases carefully, perhaps with an eye on choosing only those that had a chance of resolution.

The menu at the bottom offered links to other sites and to message boards.

'Check the message boards,' Byrne said. Jessica clicked over. There were a few dozen ongoing topics. One was a discussion of current trends in forensics. Another was a discussion of the disposition of homicide cases around the world. There was a discussion of ideas for cases for the group to tackle. This board had more than four thousand entries. Jessica clicked over, and as she scrolled through the posts her skin began to crawl.

One by one the entries appeared. They were all there. All the original homicides had been suggested as cases in which the group might be interested. Melina Laskaris, Marcellus Palmer, Antoinette Chan, Margaret Van Tassel. And they were all suggested by one user. The user name was *css1835*.

Jessica got on the phone to John Shepherd, asking him to talk to someone from the group about the criteria for posting. A few minutes later, Shepherd called back.

'I talked to the president of the group,' Shepherd said. 'He says you don't have to log in or be a member to post something on that board. He says that it would discourage people from coming forward.'

'So they have no record of who this 'css1835' might be?'

'No,' Shepherd said. 'Sorry.'

Jessica thanked him, hung up. She looked back at the screen. Whoever was doing this was connected to, or had an interest in, *Société Poursuite*. Was it George Archer? Was George Archer *css1835*?

Jessica looked at the material she had received from Frederic Duchesne.

Camille Saint-Saens — css — had been born in 1835.

★ ★ ★

At six-thirty Dana Westbrook stepped out of her office, into the duty room. 'Kevin?'

Byrne turned to look at her. 'Yeah?'

'Could I see you for a minute?'

Byrne crossed the room, dropped his weapon in his file drawer, and walked into Dana Westbrook's office.

68

When Byrne walked into the office he was more than a little surprised to see that, in addition to Sergeant Westbrook, there were Michael Drummond from the DA's office and Inspector Ted Mostow. In the corner, arms crossed, smug look in place, was Dennis Stansfield. Russell Diaz held down the other chair.

'Inspector,' Byrne said. 'Good to see you, sir.'

'How've you been, Kevin?'

'Better days.'

'How's the baby?'

Byrne shrugged, more or less on cue. 'Ten fingers, ten toes.'

It was an old expression, one that meant all was well with whatever case you were working on. In homicide you responded that way whether the case was going well or not.

Byrne nodded at Michael Drummond. 'Mike.' Drummond smiled, but there was no warmth in it. Something was wrong.

'Please, have a seat,' Westbrook said. Byrne took a chair near the windows.

'As you know, Detective Stansfield is working the Eduardo Robles homicide,' Drummond began.

Byrne just listened. Drummond continued.

'In the course of his investigation he discovered the existence of a surveillance camera on the opposite side of the street, just across

436

from the Chinese restaurant. After watching footage from the time frame in question, and running the plates on the six vehicles parked on the street, he contacted and interviewed the owners. All but one checked out, and had solid alibis for where they were that night at that time.'

Byrne said nothing.

'The sixth vehicle, a black Kia Sedona, belongs to a man named Patrick Connolly.' Drummond fixed him with a stare. 'Do you know a Patrick Connolly?'

Byrne knew that Drummond, along with everyone else in the room, knew the answer to that question, along with most of the questions he had not yet heard. Byrne had been on the other side of the table too many times not to know the game. 'Yes,' he said. 'He's my cousin.'

'When Detective Stansfield interviewed Mr. Connolly, Connolly told him that he had loaned the minivan out, that he had loaned the vehicle to you. Is that true?'

'Yes,' Byrne said. 'I borrowed the van six days ago.'

'Were you driving it the night in question?'

'I was.'

'Were you in Fishtown that night?'

Again, Byrne knew that everyone knew the answer to this question. No doubt they had spoken to patrons of The Well, people who had put him in the bar that night. 'Yes.'

'Do you recall seeing Mr. Robles that night?'

'Yes.'

'Did you have a conversation or interact in any way with Mr. Robles on that night?'

Byrne had begun to answer the question when Inspector Mostow interrupted. 'Kevin, do you want your PBA representative in here?'

The Police Benevolent Association provided legal advice and representation for police officers.

'Is this on the record?' Byrne knew the answer to that question — there was no court reporter, he had not been sworn in, and no one was writing anything down. He could confess to the Lindbergh kidnapping in this room, and it could not be used against him.

'No,' Drummond said.

Byrne looked over at Stansfield. He knew what the man was trying to do. This was payback. The two men locked eyes, matching wills. Stansfield looked away. 'Then let's put it on the record,' Byrne said.

Drummond took a few seconds, looked at Inspector Mostow. Mostow nodded.

Drummond gathered a few papers, spirited them into his briefcase. 'Okay, we'll meet back here in the morning,' Drummond said. 'Eight o'clock sharp.'

Stansfield piped in. 'Inspector, I really think that we should — '

Mostow shot him a look. 'In the morning, detective,' he said. 'Are we clear?'

For a moment, Stansfield didn't answer. Then, 'Yes, sir.'

Byrne was out of Westbrook's office first. Every detective in the duty room had their eyes on him.

As Byrne crossed the room to get a cup of

438

coffee, Stansfield followed him.

'Not so much fun, is it?' Stansfield said.

Byrne stopped, spun around. 'You don't want to talk to me right now.'

'Oh, now you don't want to talk? It seems you couldn't keep your mouth shut the past few days about me.' Stansfield got a little too close. 'What were you doing in Fishtown that night, detective?'

'Step away,' Byrne said.

'Doing a little cleanup work?'

'Last time. Step away.'

Stansfield put a hand on Byrne's arm. Byrne pivoted, lashed out with a perfectly leveraged left hook, his entire body behind it. It caught Stansfield square on the chin. The impact sounded like two rams butting heads, echoing off the walls of the duty room. Detective Dennis Stansfield spun in place, went down.

And out.

'Ah, *fuck*,' Byrne said.

The whole room shut down for a moment, drawing a collective breath. Stansfield didn't move. *Nobody* moved.

After a few moments Nick Palladino and Josh Bontrager slowly crossed the room to see if Stansfield was all right. Nobody really cared all that much — no one in the room would have denied that he'd had it coming — but it didn't serve the department too well to have one of its own sprawled spread-eagle on the floor in the middle of the homicide unit duty room. Witnesses, suspects, prosecutors, and defense attorneys came through this room day and night.

Jessica glanced at Byrne. He rubbed his knuckles, picked up his coat, grabbed his keys off the desk. When he got to the door, he turned, looked at Jessica, and said: 'Call me if he's dead.'

69

The row house on 19th Street, near Callowhill, was immaculate. Beneath the front window was a pine flower-box. In the window was a candle.

Byrne rang the bell. A few seconds later the door opened. Anna Laskaris stood there, apron on, spoon in hand, a look of confusion and expectation on her face.

'Mrs. Laskaris, I don't know if you remember me. I'm — '

'God may have taken my looks and my ability to walk more than three blocks. He didn't take away my brain. Not yet, anyway. I remember you.'

Byrne nodded.

'Come, come.'

She held the door open for him. Byrne stepped inside. If the outside of the row house was immaculate, the inside was surgically precise. On every surface was some sort of knitted item: afghans, doilies, throws. The air was suffused with three different aromas, all of them tantalizing.

She sat him at a small table in the kitchen. In seconds there was a cup of strong coffee in front of him.

Byrne took a minute or so, adding sugar, stirring, stalling. He finally got to the point. 'There's no easy way to say this, ma'am. Eduardo Robles is dead.'

Anna Laskaris looked at him, unblinking. Then she made the sign of the cross. A few seconds later she got up and walked to the stove. 'We'll eat.'

Byrne wasn't all that hungry, but it wasn't a question. In an instant he had a bowl of lamb stew in front of him. A basket of fresh bread seemed to appear out of nowhere. He ate.

'This is fantastic.'

Anna Laskaris mugged, as if this was in any doubt. She sat across from him, watched him eat.

'You married?' she asked. 'You wear no ring, but these days . . . '

'No,' Byrne said. 'I'm divorced.'

'Girlfriend?'

'Not right now.'

'What size sweater you wear?'

'Ma'am?'

'Sweater. Like a cardigan, a pullover, a V-neck. *Sweater.*'

Byrne had to think about it. 'I don't really buy a lot of sweaters, to be honest with you.'

'Okay. I try another door. When you buy a suit, like this beautiful suit you wear today, what size?'

'A 46, usually,' Byrne said. 'A 46 long.'

Anna Laskaris nodded. 'So then, an extra large. Maybe extra-extra.'

'Maybe.'

'What's your favorite color?'

Byrne didn't really have a favorite color. It wasn't something that crossed his mind that much. He did, however, have *least* favorites.

442

'Well, anything but pink, I guess. Or yellow.'

'Purple?'

'Or purple.'

Anna Laskaris glanced at her huge knitting basket, back at Byrne. 'Green, I think. You're Irish, right?'

Byrne nodded.

'A nice green.'

Byrne ate his stew. It occurred to him that this was the first time in a long while he was not eating in a restaurant or out of a Styrofoam container. While he ate, Anna stared off in the distance, her mind perhaps returning to other times in this house, other times at this table, times before people like Byrne brought heartache to the door like UPS. After a while, she stood slowly. She nodded at Byrne's empty bowl. 'You have some more, yes?'

'Oh God, no. I'm stuffed. It was wonderful.'

She rounded the table, picked up his bowl, brought it to the sink. Byrne could see the pain in her eyes.

'The recipe was my grandmother's. Then her grandmother's. Of the many things I miss, it's teaching Lina these things.'

She sat back down.

'My Melina was beautiful, but not so smart always. Especially about the men. Like me. I never did too well in this area. Three husbands, all bums.'

She looked out the window, then back at Byrne.

'It's a sad job what you do?'

'Sometimes,' Byrne said.

'A lot of times you come to people like me, give us bad news?'

Byrne nodded.

'Sometimes good news?'

'Sometimes.'

Anna looked at the wall next to the stove. There were three pictures of Lina — at three, ten, and sixteen.

'Sometimes I am at the market, I think I see her. But not like a grown-up girl, not like a young woman. A little girl. You know how little girls sometimes go off on their own, in their minds? Like maybe when they play with their dolls? The dolls to them are like real people?'

Byrne knew this well.

'My Lina was like this. She had a friend who was not there.'

Anna drifted away for a moment, then threw her hands up. 'We have a saying in Greece. *The heart that loves is always young.* She was my only grandchild. I will never have another. I have no one left to love.'

At the door Anna Laskaris held Byrne for a moment. Today she smelled of lemons and honey. It seemed to Byrne that she was getting smaller. *Grief will do that*, he thought. *Grief needs room.*

'It does not make me happy this man is dead,' Anna Laskaris said. 'God will find a place for him, a place he deserves. This is not up to you or me.'

Byrne walked to the van, slipped inside. He looked back at the house. There was already a fresh candle in the window.

★ ★ ★

He had grown up in the mist of the Delaware, and always did his best thinking there. As he drove to the river Kevin Francis Byrne considered the things he had done, the good and the bad.

You know.

He thought about Christa-Marie, about the night he met her. He thought about what she had said to him. He thought about his dreams, about waking in the night at 2:52, the moment he placed Christa-Marie under arrest, the moment everything changed forever.

You know.

But it wasn't *you know.* He had played back the recording he'd made of himself sleeping, listened carefully, and it suddenly became obvious.

He was saying *blue notes.*

It was about the silences between the notes, the time it takes for the music to echo. It was Christa-Marie telling him something for the past twenty years. Byrne knew in his heart that it all began with her. It would all end with her.

He looked at his watch. It was just after midnight.

It was Halloween.

THREE

RONDO

70

I listen to the city coming to the day, the roar of buses, the hiss of coffee machines, the clang of church bells. I watch as leaves eddy from the trees, cascading to the ground, feeling an autumn chill in the air, the shy soubrette of winter.

I stand in the center of City Hall, at the nexus of Broad and Market streets, the shortest line between the two rivers, the beating heart of Philadelphia. I turn in place, look down the two great thoroughfares that cross my city. On each I will be known today.

★   ★   ★

The dead are getting louder. This is their day. It has always been their day.

I put up my collar, step into the maelstrom, the killing instruments a comfortable weight at my back.

What a saraband.

Zig, zig, zag.

71

The massive stone buildings sat atop the rise like enormous birds of prey. The central structure, perhaps five stories tall, one hundred feet wide, gave way at either end to a pair of great wings, each of which bore a series of towers that fingered high into the morning sky.

The grounds surrounding the complex, at one time finely manicured, boasting Eastern Hemlock, Red Pine, and Box Elder, had fallen fallow decades earlier. Now the trees and shrubs were tortured and diseased, ravaged by wind and lightning. A once impressive arched stone bridge over the man-made creek that ringed the property had long ago crumbled.

★   ★   ★

In 1891 the archdiocese authorized and built a cloister on top of a hill, about forty miles northwest of Philadelphia, establishing a convent. The main building was completed in 1893, providing residence to more than four dozen sisters. In addition to the vegetables grown on the nearby fifteen acres of farmland, and grain for the artisan breads baked in the stone ovens, the fertile land around the facility provided food for shelters throughout Montgomery, Bucks, and Berks counties. The sisters' blackberry preserves won awards statewide.

In 1907 four of the sisters hanged themselves from a beam in the bell tower. The church, having trouble attracting novitiates to the nunnery, sold the buildings and property to the Commonwealth of Pennsylvania.

Five years later, with four new wings built onto the original building — including two tiered lecture halls, a pair of autopsy theaters, a state-of-the-art surgery, and a non-denominational chapel built into one of the apple groves — the Convent Hill Mental Health Facility opened its doors. With its two hundred beds, sprawling grounds, and expert staff, it soon gained a reputation as a thoroughly up-to-date hospital throughout the eastern United States.

In addition to its main purpose — the treatment and rehabilitation of the emotionally disturbed — the facility had a secure wing maintained and staffed by the Commonwealth of Pennsylvania Department of Corrections. In its twenty beds slept some of the most notorious criminals of the early twentieth century.

By the early 1950s the facility's funding had begun to dry up. Staff were laid off, buildings were not maintained, equipment became outdated and plagued by time and disrepair. Rumors of inhumane conditions at Convent Hill circulated. In the 1970s a documentary film was made, showing deplorable and sickening conditions. Public and political outrage followed, with a million dollars being pumped into the coffers.

By 1980 Convent Hill had once again been forgotten. More gossip of corruption circulated, as did tales of incalculable horror. But the public can only be outraged about something for so long.

Convent Hill closed for good in 1992 and its inmates and patients were moved to other state-run mental health facilities, as well as to correctional facilities throughout New York and Pennsylvania.

Over the next eighteen years the grounds were bequeathed to the elements, the vandals, the ghost-hunters and derelicts. A few attempts were made to secure the facility, but with its nearly two hundred acres and many points of entry, much of it surrounded by forest, it was impossible.

The fieldstone wall near the winding road that led up to the entrance still bore a sign. As Kevin Byrne and Christa-Marie Schönburg approached, Byrne noticed that someone had altered the sign, painting over it, rewording the message. It no longer announced entry to what had once been a state-of-the-art mental-health facility, a place of healing and rehabilitation, a place of serenity and peace.

It now announced entry to a place called Convict Hell.

★   ★   ★

As they drove the twisting road leading to the main buildings, a thin fog descended. The surrounding woods were cocooned in a pearl-gray mist.

Byrne thought about what he was doing. He knew the clock was ticking, that he was needed

452

back in the city, but he also believed that the answers to many of his questions — past and present — were locked inside Christa-Marie's mind.

'*Will you come back on Halloween?*' she had asked. '*I want to show you a special place in the country. We'll make a day of it. We'll have such fun.*'

A special place.

Christa-Marie wanted him to come here for a reason.

Byrne knew he had to take the chance.

★   ★   ★

Once they crested the hill the ground leveled off, but the fronts of the buildings were still somewhat obscured by pines, evergreens, and barren maples. The walkways were crosshatched in rotting branches, matted with fallen needles. The arched entrance was flanked by two massive rows of Palladian windows. The roof boasted a main cupola, with two smaller watchtowers.

As he parked the van Byrne heard the call of larks, announcing an impending storm. The wind began to rise. It seemed to encircle the stone buildings like a frigid embrace, holding inside its many horrors.

★   ★   ★

Byrne got out of the vehicle, opened Christa-Marie's door. She gave him her delicate hand. They walked up the crumbling steps.

The two immense oak doors were secured by large rusted hinges. Over the years the doors had been marked with epithets, pleas, confessions, denials. To the right of the entry was an inscription carved in the weathered stone.

Christa-Marie turned, an animated look on her face.

'Take a picture of me,' she said. She smoothed her hair, adjusted the silk scarf at her neck. She looked beautiful in the pale morning light.

Taking a photograph was the last thing Byrne had expected to do. He took out his cellphone, opened it, framed Christa-Marie in the doorway, and snapped.

A moment later he pocketed his phone, put a shoulder to one of the huge doors, pushed it open. A cold breeze rushed through the atrium, bringing with it years of mildew and decay.

Together they stepped over the threshold, into Christa-Marie Schönburg's past, into the infernal confines of Convent Hill.

72

The dead walk here. The dead and the insane and the forgotten. If you come with me, and hear what I hear, there is much more than the whistle of the wind.

There is the young man who came here in 1920. He had been wounded at St. Mihiel Salient. He bleeds from both wrists. 'I am going home,' he says to me. 'First to Pont-a-Mousson, then home.'

He never left.

There is the solicitor from Youngstown, Ohio. Twice he has tried to take his life. His neck is deeply scarred. He cannot speak above a whisper. His voice is a dry wind in the night desert.

There are the two sisters who tried to eat each other's flesh, found in the basement of their Olney row house, locked in an embrace, wrapped in barbed wire, blood dripping from their lips.

They gather around me, their voices lifted in a chorus of madness.

I walk with my lover.

I walk with the dead.

73

They strolled arm in arm through the hallways, their heels echoing on the old tiles. A powdery light sifted through the windows.

Overhead was a vaulted ceiling, at least thirty feet high, and on it Byrne saw three layers of paint, each a dismal attempt at cheerfulness. Lemon yellow, baby blue, sea-foam green.

Christa-Marie pointed to a room off the main entry. 'This is where they take you on arrival,' she said. 'Don't let the flowers fool you.'

Byrne peeked inside. The remains of a pair of rusted chains, bolted to the wall, lay on the ground like dead snakes. There were no flowers.

They continued on, deeper into the heart of Convent Hill, passing dozens of rooms, rooms pooled with stagnant water, rooms tiled floor to ceiling, grout stained with decades of mold and long-dried blood, drains clogged with sewage and discarded clothing.

One room held six chairs still in a semicircle, the cane seats missing, one chair curiously facing away from the others. One room had a three-tiered bunk bed bolted to the floor over a decayed Oriental rug. Byrne could see where attempts had been made to tear away the rug. Both ends were shredded. Three brown fingernails remained.

One room, at the back of the main hallway, had rusted steel buckets lined against the wall, each filled with hardened feces, white and chalky with time. One bucket had the word *happy* painted on it.

They took the winding staircase to the second floor.

In one meeting room was a slanted stage. Above the stage, on the fascia, was a large medallion made of crisscrossed black string, perhaps an occupational-therapy project of some sort.

They continued through the wing. Byrne noted that many of the individual rooms had observation windows, some as small and simple as a pair of holes drilled into the door. Nothing, it seemed, went unobserved at Convent Hill.

'This was Maristella's room,' Christa-Marie said. The room was no larger than six by six feet. Against the wall, a long-faded pink enamel, were three threadbare stretchers. 'She was my friend. A little crazy, I think.'

The massive gymnasium had a large mural, measuring more than fifty feet long. The background was the rolling hills surrounding the facility. Scattered throughout were small scenes, all drawn by different hands — hellish depictions of rape, murder, and torture.

★   ★   ★

When they turned the corner into the east wing, Byrne stopped in his tracks. Someone was standing at the end of the wide hallway. Byrne could not see much. The person was small, compact, unmoving.

It took Byrne a few moments to realize, in the

dim light, that it was only a *cutout* of a person. As they drew closer, he could see that it was a plywood pattern of a child, a boy perhaps ten or twelve years old. The figure wore a yellow shirt and dark brown pants. Behind the figure, on the wall, was painted a blue stripe, perhaps meant to mimic the ocean. As they passed the figure, Byrne saw pockmarks in the plywood, along with a few holes. Behind the figure were corresponding holes. At some point the figure had been riddled with bullets. Someone had drawn blood on the shirt.

They stopped at the end of the hall. Above them the roof had rotted away. A few drops of water found them.

'You know at the first note,' Christa-Marie said.

'What do you mean?'

'Whether a child has the potential to be a virtuoso.' She looked at her hands, her long, elegant fingers. 'They draw you in. The children. At Prentiss they asked me a hundred times to teach. I kept refusing. I finally gave in. Two boys stood out.'

Byrne took her hand. 'Who are these boys?'

Christa-Marie did not answer right away. 'They were there, you know,' she eventually said.

'Where?'

'At the concert,' she said. 'After.'

There was a sound, an echoing sound from somewhere in the darkness. Christa-Marie seemed not to notice.

'That night, Christa-Marie. Take me back to that night.'

Christa-Marie looked at him. In her eyes he

458

saw the same look he had seen twenty years earlier, a look of fear and loneliness.

'I wore black,' she said.

'Yes,' Byrne said. 'You looked beautiful.'

Christa-Marie smiled. 'Thank you.'

'Tell me about the concert.'

Christa-Marie glided across the corridor, into the semi-darkness. 'The hall was decorated for the holidays. It smelled of fresh pine. We debated fiercely over the program. The audience was, after all, children. The director wanted yet another performance of *Peter and the Wolf.*'

Byrne expected her to continue. She did not. Her eyes suddenly misted with tears. She walked slowly back, reached into her bag, retrieved a piece of paper, handed it to Byrne. It was a letter, addressed to Christa-Marie and copied to her attorney, Benjamin Curtin. It was from the Department of Oncology at the University of Pennsylvania Hospital. Byrne read the letter.

A few moments later he took her hands in his. 'Will you play for me tonight?'

Christa-Marie moved closer. She put her arms around him, her head on his chest. They stood that way for a long time, not moving, not speaking. She broke the silence first.

'I'm dying, Kevin.'

Byrne stroked her hair. It was silken to his touch. 'I know.'

She nestled closer. 'I can hear your heart. It is steady and strong.'

Byrne looked out the window, at the fogbound forest surrounding Convent Hill. He remained silent. There was nothing to say.

74

Jessica could not find her partner. She had stopped by Byrne's apartment, visited all his familiar breakfast and coffee haunts, checked his favorite watering holes, hoping not to find him. She had not.

Byrne had not called into the unit nor, more importantly, shown up for his deposition, his on-the-record statement about his whereabouts on the night Eduardo Robles had been killed. Jessica knew that the inspector had smoothed it over with the DA's office, but it was unlike Byrne in any number of ways, not the least of which was his commitment to keeping his word.

Jessica spent the remainder of the morning reading through the material on *Carnival of The Animals*. There were indeed fourteen movements, not all of them devoted to animals. One was called *Fossils;* another, *Pianists;* yet another, *Finale*. For some reason the killer had chosen eight of the movements. But they were all there, and it was all making slow sense.

Beyond this, all these victims were related to cold cases. They were all suspects in homicides. Or suspected of complicity in homicides.

The connection to a group like *Société Poursuite* and a man named George Archer could not be overlooked.

All these people were in some way culpable. In the eyes of their killer, they were all guilty of something. But why *these* people? What linked them? Why the cases of Antoinette Chan, Marcellus Palmer, Marcia Kimmelman and Melina Laskaris? Why not any of the other hundreds of unsolved cases sitting in the dusty books on the shelf?

★   ★   ★

At one o'clock Jessica put a call into the Department of Motor Vehicles. If George Archer had a driver's license in the Commonwealth of Pennsylvania, they would be able to get a photograph.

She skipped lunch and spent the early afternoon on the phone with the lab and the DA's office. Michael Drummond was in court, but his secretary promised Jessica that he would get back to her.

By four o'clock she learned that there was no one named George Archer registered at any hotel in the greater Philadelphia area.

She also put in a call to Chief Rogers Logan in Garrett Corners. At her request Logan paid a visit to Archer Farms.

George Archer had not returned to his house.

★   ★   ★

As the first half of Jessica's long day wound down, there were no new leads. The three other lead detectives — Josh Bontrager, Nicci Malone, and Dennis Stansfield — were all on the street, chasing down their leads. Josh had interviewed members of the Chan family. All had concrete alibis. Nicci Malone had taken the morning to drive to Weirton, West Virginia to speak to Marcellus Palmer's son and daughter-in-law. She learned nothing of value. God only knew what Stansfield — obsessed now more than ever with Kevin Byrne — was doing.

It seemed the Byrne/Stansfield conflict had settled for the time being. There would probably be some kind of fallout from the incident, but it wouldn't be tonight. The homicide unit had a few other things with which to be concerned.

* * *

Jessica arrived home around five-thirty, made a quick dinner for her and Sophie. After dinner Sophie modeled her Snow Fairy costume. She looked adorable.

Outside, the wind picked up, swirling leaves in the street. Perfect Philly Halloween weather. And there was never a shortage of atmosphere or things to do in Philly on Halloween.

There was the Ghost Tour, which took participants on a candlelight excursion to Society Hill and Independence Park. There was the tour of Eastern State Penitentiary, once voted the number one haunted house in America. Then there was the Mutter Museum, and the home of Edgar Allan Poe.

But if Philadelphia was attached to its horrific past, it was nothing if not creative. Jessica had already seen news footage of people trick-or-treating in pink body suits, with a band of paper wrapped around their heads. The new favorite costume in Philly, it seemed, was the victim of a serial murderer.

Jessica took Sophie out for trick-or-treating early. This year was different from previous years. Trick-or-treating among row houses was a frontal assault. Within an hour, they hit a hundred or so houses. Sophie returned with a pair of bulging pillowcases.

★ ★ ★

While Sophie divvied up her swag on the living-room floor, Jessica showered and prepared for her undercover assignment at the hotel.

Before she left the house, she caught her reflection in the hallway mirror. *Not bad,* she thought. The simple black dress was okay, if a little tight. Time to ease up on the cannoli from Termini's.

The hard part, of course, was the gun. Though in many ways the perfect accessory, most designers did not allow for the bulk of a weapon when creating a line. It was never the Smith & Wesson collection for Dior, or Vivienne Westwood presents Frocks with Glocks.

Just to be on the safe side, she packed a small duffel with jeans and a hoodie, stowed it in the car. She had no idea where this night would take her.

★ ★ ★

The team met in Le Jardin's Loss Prevention office. There were ten detectives in all, including

Josh Bontrager, Dennis Stansfield, Nicci Malone, and Nick Palladino. Most were in plain clothes, the remaining few had on PPD windbreakers.

They were briefed by John Shepherd on the layout of the floors, the location of surveillance cameras, the hotel protocol for emergencies. They went briefly over the program for the evening, which included a lavish dinner, a number of speakers, along with a keynote address by the attorney general for the Commonwealth of Pennsylvania. In addition, in the smaller meeting rooms there were various panels and demonstrations. According to Shepherd, excluding front- and back-of-the-house staff and personnel, there were close to one thousand people in the building.

Every so often Jessica glanced at the door. Byrne had not shown.

After John Shepherd had completed his briefing, Dana Westbrook addressed the task force. They had received more than seventy DMV photographs of men named George Archer. None were registered to the man at the Archer Farms. The sheriff's office, in addition to detectives from the Pennsylvania State Police, were showing the photographs to neighbors and vendors in the area, trying to match the photo with the man who ran Archer Farms.

★ ★ ★

For the first hour Jessica worked the reception table, just outside the Crystal Room. The double-length conference table was draped with white bunting, and carried a few hundred name tags, programs, and pins bearing the slogan *He escapes who is not pursued.*

As people filed by, Jessica watched their movements, their behaviors. Overall, it was a rather staid-looking group. Conservatively dressed, quiet in demeanor, polite in manner. In the course of an hour she handed out more than fifty name tags.

At eight o'clock three men approached from across the lobby, one of them quite inebriated. They were in their forties, white, casually dressed. As they got closer, the shortest one — the drunk one — did his best to focus on the table, on the name tags, and finally on Jessica.

'Whoa!' he said, reeling a little.

'Welcome,' Jessica said.

'My name is Jukka Tolonen,' the tall blond man said, introducing himself.

'Jay Bowman,' said the other. Jessica scanned the table, found the name tags she was looking for, handed them both a tag and a program.

'Thanks,' the two men said in tandem, both sounding a little embarrassed for their friend.

'You know,' the drunk one said, 'I've been coming to this convention for, I don't know, five years? Most of the women look like Mrs. Marble.'

Jessica was pretty sure the man meant Miss Marple. 'What's your name?' she asked.

The man looked at his friends. 'You hear that? She asked my *name*, dude. She's hitting on me!'

'I think she wants to give you your name tag,' Tolonen said. He had an accent. Maybe Finnish.

'Oh.'

The drunk man made a production of

reaching into his pocket for his wallet. He pulled it out, made a bigger deal of extracting one of his business cards, a big smile on his face as if this were the cleverest bit ever. 'It looks like I'm somebody named Barry Swanson,' he said. 'Like the frozen dinner.'

Like the frozen adolescence, Jessica thought. She handed Barry Swanson his ID and a program. Swanson immediately dropped it all on the floor. Tolonen picked up the material, clipped the name tag on his wobbly friend.

'Sorry,' Bowman said to Jessica. 'He's a forensic chemist. He doesn't get out much.'

Jessica watched them walk away, wondering how crimes ever got solved.

* * *

When Jessica was relieved by a member of the task force, a detective out of West Division named Deena Yeager, she walked over to the front desk, surveyed the crowded lobby. David Albrecht had not gotten permission to film inside the ballroom, but he was allowed to shoot footage in the lobby and out on the street. Jessica saw that he had snagged some talking-head interview time with some pretty heavy hitters.

Just about everyone in the room had some connection to law enforcement. There were retired detectives, prosecutors, forensic professionals of every discipline, men and women who worked in the processing of fingerprints, hair and fiber, blood, documents. There were pathologists, anthropologists, psychologists, people who worked in behavioral science and mathematics. She'd heard there was a small contingent from *Keishicho*, the Metropolitan Tokyo Police Department.

She saw Hell Rohmer and Irina Kohl, pretending to be merely colleagues. It didn't take a seasoned detective to detect the occasional brush of hands, or the more than occasional longing glance. She saw judges, lawyers, bailiffs, along with a handful of ADAs.

She did not see Kevin Byrne.

75

Lucy Doucette stood at the end of the hallway on the twelfth floor.

Her shift ended at six-thirty, but she asked Audrey Balcombe if there were any credits to be had and it turned out that three of the guests had requested housekeeping twice a day. She imagined these people were in some kind of lab or forensic work and had a serious germ phobia. Regardless, she was able to stay on for an extra two hours. Now she was just killing time.

Lucy knew that the moment she swiped her card in the electronic lock on the door to 1208 it would go on the record. She was scared out of her wits to go back in there, but she had been scared so long it just didn't matter anymore.

She looked over her shoulder. The hallway was deserted, but Lucy knew she was not alone, not technically. She had once been in the main security station and had seen the big monitors. All staff knew where the closed-circuit cameras were. At least, the cameras they knew about, the obvious ones on the ceiling. At the end of each hallway was a sideboard and a mirror, and Lucy always wondered if the mirrors were two-way mirrors and maybe had a camera behind them.

Before she could stop herself, Lucy knocked on the door to Room 1208.

'Housekeeping.'

Nothing. She knocked again, repeated the

468

word. Silence from within. She leaned closer to the door. There was no sound of a TV, a radio, a conversation. The general rule was two announcements, then enter.

Lucy tried one last time, got no response, then swiped her card, eased open the door.

'Housekeeping,' she said once more, her voice barely above a whisper. She slipped inside, let the door close behind her. It shut with a loud and final click, meaning that the lock had irrevocably registered that she was in Room 1208.

★   ★   ★

The room looked exactly the same as it had the last time. The minibar was untouched, the bed had not been slept in, the wastebasket beneath the desk was empty. She peeked into the bathroom. Nothing had been disturbed in there, either. The toilet paper was still in a point, the soaps wrapped. Sometimes the nicer guests tried to hang the towels back the way they were, but Lucy could always tell. They never got them exactly right. She could also tell if someone had taken a shower or bath, just by the smell, the damp sweetness of body gel and shampoo that hung in the air.

She stepped back to the door, put her ear to it, listened for sounds in the hallway. It was silent. She walked to the closet, opened the door. The garment bag hung there like a body at a gallows. She reached out slowly, turned over the ID tag, her hand shaking.

THIS BAG BELONGS TO GEORGE ARCHER.

Lucy felt a chill ripple through her body. His name was George Archer. All these years she had tried to imagine her kidnapper's name. Everyone had a name. Whenever she read a newspaper or a magazine, whenever she watched a movie or a TV show, whenever she was in a place like a doctor's office or the Bureau of Motor Vehicles and someone said a name out loud she wondered: *Is that his name?* Could that person be the man in her nightmares? Now she knew. George Archer. It was, at the same moment, the most benign and the most frightening name she'd ever heard.

She closed the closet door, walked quickly over to the dresser, her heart pounding. She eased open the bottom drawer. The same shirts were inside — one blue, one white, one white with thin gray stripes. She mind-printed the way they were arrayed in the drawer so she could put them back in precisely the same manner. She bunched the three shirts together, lifted them. They seemed almost hot to her touch. But when she looked beneath the shirts, she saw that the picture was gone.

Had she imagined it?

No. It *had* been there. She had never seen that particular photograph before, but she knew where it had been taken. It had been taken at the ice-cream parlor on Wilmot Street. It was a photo of her mother, and her mother was wearing the red pullover sweater that Lucy had taken from Sears at the mall.

Lucy turned, looked at the rest of the room. It suddenly seemed foreign, as if she had never been here before. She put the shirts back in the drawer, arranging them carefully. She noticed something in the pocket of the shirt on top, the blue one. It was a piece of paper, a piece of Le Jardin notepad paper.

Lucy slipped her fingers gently into the pocket, took out the paper. It read:

Meet me here on Sunday night at 9:30. Love, Lucy.

It was her handwriting.

It was a note she had written and had left in the room for Mr. Archer to find.

She looked at her watch. It was 9:28.

The room began to spin. It felt for a moment as though the floor beneath her was about to give way. She slammed the drawer shut. It no longer mattered if she didn't get everything back the way it was supposed to be. The only thing that mattered was getting out of this room.

She recoiled from the dresser as if it were on fire, and suddenly heard —

— the bell.

Her bell. Her *special* bell.

Lucy felt calm, completely at peace. She knew what she had to do, what she *must* do. She walked to the hotel room door, propped it open. Then she entered the closet, closed the door, sat on the floor.

Once inside she smelled apples, pipe smoke, the essence of George Archer, the essence of evil. But this time she was not afraid.

As footsteps passed by the closet — two sets, a few minutes apart — the night closed in around her, and Lucy Doucette remembered it all.

471

'It's okay, Eve,' he said. 'There's been an accident. I will take care of you.'

He held out his hand. On it he wore a ring in the shape of a snake. The air was thick with smoke, the sky darkened from it.

'What kind of accident?' she asked.

Mr. Archer opened the door to his car. Lucy got in. 'A plane crash,' he said. 'A bad plane crash.'

'Where's my mom?'

'She wants me to watch after you. She's going to go help the people where the plane crashed.'

'My mom is?'

'Yes, Eve.'

Mr. Archer started the car.

* * *

He led her down the narrow wooden steps, through a small door into a drafty room with stone walls. The room was lit only with candles. It seemed as though there were hundreds of them. The room smelled like bad perfume and fermenting apples. Even the dust and cobwebs were cold.

When Mr. Archer left, and Lucy heard the door at the top of the stairs lock, she saw that there was another girl sitting there. She was about Lucy's age, eleven or so, but she was wearing a grown-up dress. It was spangly and short, and had straps over the shoulders. The girl's face was smeared with make-up. She had been crying for a long time. Her eyes were red and puffy.

'Who are you?' Lucy asked.

The girl shivered.

'I'm . . . I'm Peggy.'

'Why are you here?'

The girl did not answer. Lucy looked at the girl's arms and legs. There were deep purple bruises on them. Then she looked over and saw a second dress hanging from one of the pipes in the ceiling.

*   *   *

A long time passed. Hours and hours of which Lucy had no mind, no memory. Days of darkness.

On the third day she took a bubble bath. The bathroom was in a small room off the cellar. The walls were a pink enamel. The sink had gold-colored faucets.

When it was dark Mr. Archer came downstairs to get her. He brought her up to the dining room for the first time. The table was set for grown-ups. Wine glasses and more candles. Lucy found herself in her own grown-up dress, and wearing high heels that were too big for her. Mr. Archer was dressed up like a man in an old movie. He had on a white bow tie. He walked to the kitchen.

Lucy looked at the window. She walked across the room, edged it open, slipped through.

'Eve!' Mr. Archer yelled.

Lucy ran. She ran as far and for as long as she

473

could, through endless apple orchards, tripping and falling, scraping her knees and elbows, mushing the rotting apples beneath her. She looked over her shoulder, watching for Mr. Archer. She didn't see him. She soon came to a large pipe that emptied into a lake, crouched down inside, waited. She didn't know how long she was there. Hours and hours. She must have cried herself to sleep, because the next thing she knew there was a light in her face.

'It's okay,' the man with the flashlight said.

But it wasn't. It wasn't okay.

★　★　★

They talked to her for hours, but Lucy didn't say a word. What happened to her was locked away inside.

Her mother took her home. Time passed, and the man with the ring in the shape of a snake faded from her mind but took up faceless residence in that nest of fear inside her, flying overhead in the darkness of her dreams.

At night she would hear him humming, she would hear the sound of the car door slamming, the creak of the old wooden steps, the softness of his voice, she would hear —

The bell.

The bell rang again.

It seemed to come from far away, as if it were at the end of that long drainage pipe in which she had crawled. For the briefest of moments she smelled the sewage, felt the dampness of the air. Then it was gone.

474

Lucy looked around. It took a while for her to realize where she was. She was in the hotel. Le Jardin. She knew every inch of this place. She looked around the dark closet, felt overhead.

How much time had passed? She didn't know. She stood, opened the closet door, stepped into the room. The air had changed, changed in a way you could only know from being in a place day after day, knowing its walls, it ceilings, its corners, its very presence.

The door to the hallway was closed. Lucy looked at her watch. She hadn't been gone long. She had to get out of this room. Mr. Archer could be back any second.

She turned to leave, but suddenly felt lightheaded. She sat on the edge of the bed for a moment. Her mind began to clear, but something was wrong. Something felt wet underneath her. She got up, looked at her hands. They were coated in bright, glossy scarlet. She turned around and saw, in the dim light, the form under the blood-soaked sheets.

Lucy felt the contents of her stomach come up inside her throat. She backed away, certain that her heart was going to explode. She could no longer hold it in. She vomited on the floor.

Then she looked at the telephone on the desk. It seemed a mile away. The smell of her own vomit reached her at the same time as the metallic smell of blood. She was going to be sick again.

She ran to the bathroom.

76

Jessica watched the show from the back of the Crystal Room. The speaker at the lectern was a pathologist from Toledo, formerly with the Ohio Bureau of Investigation. He was talking about a cold case that took place in a suburb of Toledo in 1985, a case involving a woman and her elderly mother who were bludgeoned to death with a long piece of steel, believed to be the support beam of a single bed frame.

Behind the lecturer, photographs of the crime scene were projected on a screen.

Jessica watched the photographs come and go. She realized that the man could have been from Tucson or Toronto or Tallahassee. In some ways it was all the same. But not to the families of the victim. And not to the investigators whose task it was to root out the people responsible for the crime and bring them to justice. She had been at it long enough, and knew enough people in her line of work, to know that an unsolved crime eats away at your soul until it is either closed or replaced by a new horror, a new puzzle. And even then it does not disappear, but rather makes room.

She thought about Joseph Novak's diary.

What was his connection? All she could find on Marcato LLC was that it had been formed nearly fifteen years earlier, and listed as its primary business the publishing of music. Joseph

Novak, by all accounts, had a partner. But no one at any bank had any record of anyone other than Novak.

'Detective?'

A man's voice. Close. Jessica spun around. It was Frederic Duchesne, the dean of Prentiss Institute. He had approached without a sound. Not good. She was distracted, which meant she was vulnerable. She took a deep breath, tried to fashion a smile.

'Mr. Duchesne.'

'I'm sorry if I frightened you,' Duchesne said.

Frightened wasn't the word, Jessica thought. Provoked would be a better term. 'Not a problem,' she said, meaning something else. 'What can I do for you, Mr. Duchesne?'

'Frederic. Please.'

'Frederic,' she said. She glanced around the room. All was well. For the time being.

'I was wondering if you received the material I sent.'

'Yes, we did. Thank you very much.'

'Do you have a moment to talk?'

Jessica glanced at the clock over the door. It was just slightly little less rude than looking at her watch. She had a little bit of time. 'Sure.'

They walked to a quiet corner of the room.

'Well, when you were in, your partner asked about program music. Symphonic poems.'

'Yes,' Jessica said. 'Do you have further thoughts on this?'

'I do,' Duchesne said. 'Aesthetically, the tone poem is in some ways related to opera, the difference being that the words are not sung to the audience. There are examples of absolute music that contain narrative of sorts.'

Jessica just stared.

'Okay, what I'm getting at is that, while there may be nothing in the music itself, a lot of times material has been written as an adjunct to the music — a poetic epigraph, if you will.'

'You mean, written after the fact?'

'Yes.'

Duchesne looked out over the room, then back.

'Are you a fan of classical music, detective?'

Jessica sneaked a covert glance at her watch. 'Sure,' she said. 'I can't say I know too much about it, but I know what I like when I hear it.'

'Tell me,' Duchesne began, 'do you ever go to concerts?'

'Not too often,' she said. 'My husband is not a big classical-music fan. He's more of a Southside Johnny guy.'

Duchesne shot a quick glance at Jessica's left hand. She never wore her wedding ring — or any jewelry, for that matter — when she was in the field. Too many opportunities to lose it, not to mention having it give away your position when you needed silence.

'That was terribly forward of me,' Duchesne said. 'Please forgive me.'

'No harm done,' Jessica said.

'No, I've made a fool of myself. Mea culpa.'

Jessica needed a way to wrap this up. 'Mr. Duchesne — Frederic — I really do appreciate this information. I'll pass it along to the other detectives working the case. You never know. It might lead to something.'

Duchesne seemed to be a bit flustered. He was probably not used to being shot down. He was not bad-looking in a Julian Sands kind of way, cultured and refined: probably a hell of a catch in his social circle. 'Please feel free to call me anytime if you think of something else that might be helpful,' Jessica added.

Duchesne brightened a little, although it was clear he realized what she was doing — trying to placate him. 'I certainly will.'

'By the way, what brings you here tonight?'

Duchesne pulled a visitor badge out of his pocket, clipped it to his sport coat. 'I've done some work as a forensic audiologist,' he said. 'Strictly on a contract basis. My specialty is physical characteristics and measurement of acoustic stimuli.'

You never know, Jessica thought. She extended her hand. They shook. 'Have fun.'

As she watched Duchesne walk across the room, her cellphone vibrated. She looked at the screen. It was Byrne.

'Kevin. Where are you?'

All she heard was the hiss of silence. She wasn't sure Byrne was still there. Then: 'I've got to go in for more tests.'

It didn't register. 'What are you talking about?'

Another pause. 'They read my MRI. They want me to go back for more tests.'

'Did they say what it was about?'

'They don't want you back because everything is all right, Jess.'

'Okay,' Jessica said. 'We'll deal with it. I'll go with you.'

More silence. Then Jessica heard a bell on Byrne's end. Was that the sound of an elevator? 'Where are you?'

No answer.

'Kevin?' The silence was maddening. 'When do they want you to — '

'The original homicides. The cold cases. It was right in front of us. I didn't get it until I was driving up the parkway.'

Byrne was talking about Benjamin Franklin Parkway.

'What do you mean? What's on the parkway?'

'I drove by the hotel, and it all fell into place,' he said. 'You never know what's going to make sense, or when it's going to happen. It's what ties them together.'

Jessica got an earful of loud static. Byrne said something else, but she didn't understand it. She was just about to ask him to repeat what he'd said when she heard him loud and clear.

'There's a package for you with the concierge.'

The concierge?

'Kevin, you have to — '

'It's the music,' he said. 'It's always been about the music.'

And then he was gone. Jessica looked at the screen on her phone. The call had ended. She called Byrne right back, got his voicemail. She tried again. Same result.

There's a package for you with the concierge.

She walked out of the Crystal Room, across the lobby to the concierge desk. There was indeed a package for her. It was a pair of nine-by-twelve envelopes. Her name was on them, scrawled in Byrne's handwriting. She stepped away, looked inside each envelope. Files, notes, photographs, charts. It was not the official file, but rather a second one that Byrne had been keeping.

She raised Josh Bontrager on the handset. A few minutes later they met in a small meeting room on the first floor. Jessica closed the door, told Bontrager about her phone call from Byrne. Then she opened one of the envelopes, put the material on the table.

★ ★ ★

The first four pages on the top of the pile were photocopies of the death certificates for Lina Laskaris, Marcellus Palmer, Antoinette Chan and Marcia Jane Kimmelman.

Why had Byrne dropped off this information? She'd seen all of it before. What was in here that he wanted her to notice?

Jessica scanned the pages, taking in the relevant data: Name, date of birth, address, parents, cause of death, date of death.

Date of death.

Her gaze shifted from document to document. 'It's the dates, Josh,' Jessica said. 'Look.'

Bontrager ran his finger down each page, stopping at the entry for date of death. 'Marcellus Palmer was killed on June 21. Lina Laskaris and Margaret van Tassel were killed on September 21. Antoinette Chan was killed on March 21. Marcia Jane Kimmelman was killed on December 21.'

481

'Those are all the first days of the seasons,' Jessica said. 'The killer picked these cases because the original homicides took place on the first days of spring, summer, fall and winter.'

'Yes.'

'This is what Kevin meant when he said it came to him when he drove by the hotel. He was talking about the Four Seasons.'

The next documents in the file were copies of the photographs of the animal tattoos *in situ*. Jessica put the photographs side by side, six in all, spread across the table. 'These are all animals in the *Carnival of the Animals* by Saint-Saens.'

They looked at the photographs left to right. Six tattoos, six fingers. Six *different* fingers.

There was one other item in the first envelope. Jessica reached in, slid it out. And they had their answer.

Inside was a small booklet, about the size and shape of a *Playbill*. It bore a date from 1990. Jessica looked at the cover.

CHRISTA-MARIE SCHÖNBURG, CELLO
AN EVENING WITH SAINT-SAENS AND VIVALDI
SELECTIONS FROM *THE FOUR SEASONS*,
CARNIVAL OF THE ANIMALS AND
DANSE MACABRE
ARRANGED FOR THE CELLO BY
SIR OLIVER MALCOLM

Jessica opened the booklet. The program began with brief selections from each part of *The Four Seasons*. After that were selections from *Carnival of the Animals*.

482

Et marche royale du Lion was the lion. *Poules et Coqs* was the rooster. *Tortues* was the tortoise. *L'Éléphant* was the elephant. *Kangourous* was the kangaroo. *Le Cygne* was the swan. *Aquarium* was the fish. *Volière* was the bird.

There were eight selections in all.

'Someone is recreating her last performance,' Jessica said.

Bontrager pointed to the last part of the night's program. '*Danse Macabre?*' he asked. 'What do you know about it?'

'Nothing,' Jessica said.

Bontrager sat down at the computer, launched a web browser. In seconds he had a hit.

The wiki entry gave them the basics. *Danse Macabre* was written by Camille Saint-Saens originally as an art song for voice and piano. What had Duchesne said?

'*A lot of times material has been written as an adjunct to the music — a poetic epigraph, if you will.*'

'See if there's a narrative that goes with this,' Jessica said.

Bontrager did a search. He soon got hits. 'Yeah,' he said. 'There is. It was originally a poem by a guy named Henri Cazalis.' Bontrager hit a few more keys. In a moment the poem appeared on the screen.

The poem began:

> *Zig, zig, zig, Death in cadence,*
> *Striking a tomb with his heel,*
> *Death at midnight plays a dance-tune,*
> *Zig, zig, zag, on his violin.*

It all began to make sense. *Striking a tomb with his heel* explained the bodies found in the cemeteries, their legs broken. *Zig, zig, zig* was on Joseph Novak's computer. Jessica's gaze continued down the page, a symmetry forming.

Zig zig, zig, Death continues
The unending scraping on his instrument.
A veil has fallen! The dancer is naked.

Jessica thought: *The dancer is naked.* The shaved bodies.

'Is there an explanation for this?' Jessica asked. 'Some sort of source material?'

Bontrager scrolled down. 'It says the poem was based on an old French superstition. Hang on.' He did another search. He soon had the synopsis of the original superstition.

'According to the superstition, Death appears at midnight every year on Halloween, and has the power to call forth the dead from their graves to dance for him while he plays his fiddle. His skeletons dance for him until the first break of dawn, when they must return to their graves until the next year.'

The two detectives looked at each other, at their watches. It was 9:50.

According to what they were reading, there were two hours and ten minutes left. And they had no idea where or whom the killer was going to strike.

Jessica opened the second envelope. Inside were six transparencies. The clear plastic sheets

484

were 8½ by 11 inches. At first it was not clear what was printed on them. Jessica looked at the lower right-hand corner of one. There she saw a number she recognized as the homicide case file number. She soon realized that it was a transparency of the forensic photograph of the wounds to Kenneth Beckman's forehead, a photograph of the white paper band that encircled the victim's head.

Jessica took the transparency, held it up to the white wall. There was the Rorschach blot of blood on the left, which had come from the mutilated ear, a shape she had originally thought of as a rough figure eight. There was the straight line across the top, as well as the oval of blood underneath. In this format, a photographic transparency, the blood looked black.

Why had Byrne made these into transparencies?

She held up the next sample. The second transparency was from Preston Braswell's head. It was identical. She looked at the third sheet, this time the evidence photograph of Eduardo Robles. Identical. There was no doubt in her mind, or in the mind of anyone else investigating these homicides, that the signature for each of these murders was identical, and all but confirmed a single killer.

Except that they were *not* identical.

'Josh, bring that lamp closer.'

Bontrager got up and pulled the table lamp across the desk. Jessica sorted through the transparencies, her heart beating faster. She put them all in the order that made the most sense at that moment.

'Turn off the overhead light.'

Bontrager crossed the room, shut off the fluorescents. When he returned, Jessica held the stack of transparencies up to the bright lampshade.

And then they saw it.

There were five lines, but they were in slightly different places, one above the other. The puncture wounds were in different places, too. On the left side, the bloodstains left by the killer's mutilation of the victims' ears formed a stylized clef.

'My God,' Jessica said. The clarity was almost painful. 'It's a musical staff. He's writing music on the dead bodies, one note at a time.'

Bontrager sat back down. He entered the search phrase: '*Danse Macabre sheet music.*'

In seconds they had a visual representation of the sheet music. The two detectives compared the samples with the transparencies. They were identical. The killer was carving the final measure of *Danse Macabre* on his victims.

He was done with *The Four Seasons*. He wasn't *quite* done with *Carnival of the Animals*. There were two notes yet to write in the measure.

Jessica glanced back at the poem. The answer was in there. She read it all again.

Her stare fell on a phrase in the middle.

A lustful couple sits on the moss
So as to taste long-lost delights.

Is the lustful couple Christa-Marie Schönburg and Kevin Byrne? Is their killer taking them back to the night they met?

Jessica looked at her watch. It was 10:00. They had less than two hours to figure it all out.

And Kevin Byrne was nowhere to be found.

77

Lucy hid in a small room off the ladies' locker room in the basement, near the rear of the hotel. There were two other women in the room. They spoke animatedly in Spanish. Lucy did not understand the words, but she didn't have to. There was something going on in the hotel, and Lucy had to figure that they had seen the blood in the hallway.

Meet me here on Sunday night at 9:30. Love, Lucy.

She had to leave. They were going to discover what had happened, if they had not already done so. They were going to check the lock on the door to Room 1208 and think that it was her. Plus, there were all kinds of ways to know that someone was in a room, scientific things. She had wiped down everything she remembered touching, but she couldn't have gotten all of it.

She listened to the other girls in the locker room. They would soon be going on shift. When the locker room was empty, she would slip out the back door.

What had she done?

78

Jessica and Bontrager stood in the gift shop off the lobby. Jessica had briefed Dana Westbrook on their findings and Dana in turn briefed the rest of the team.

Jessica thought about the people milling around the lobby and the lounge, drinks in their hands. Something nagged at her. She couldn't put her finger on it.

'I want to see that guest list again,' Jessica said.

'Hang on. I'll get it.'

A minute later Bontrager returned, handed her the small stack of papers. She put it down on the gift-shop counter.

Her stare moved down each of the pages. She didn't know what she was looking for. She scanned the list of cities. Pittsburgh, Los Angeles, Montreal, Sao Paulo, Zurich, Cincinnati.

She leaned against the desk, took out her iPhone.

She remembered the crime-scene photos. There was something about one of the photographs. She scrolled through the photos she had taken. Nothing jumped out. There were photos of the Federal Street scene, shots taken at the Mount Olive Cemetery. There were also photos taken of the alley where Eduardo Robles was found, as well as the paupers' graveyard in the Northeast. The last roll was pictures taken in and around Garrett Corner, Archer Farms, as well as pictures she had taken of the state police file on the murder of Peggy van Tassel.

She had three pictures of the crime-scene photos. The scene was bloody and stomach-churning. One photo was a close-up of the girl's stomach.

Jessica zoomed in on the picture, on an area where the girl's killer had bitten her. As she got closer she saw that it was not one of the bite marks, it was a bruise instead. She increased the size one more time. The image was beginning to blur, but it was still clear enough. The bruise looked to be in the shape of a snake.

A ring?

Had she seen someone tonight wearing a ring in the shape of a snake?

Yes. A man wearing a ring of that description was one of the three men who had come up to the table, one of the Three Stooges. It was not the inebriated one, Barry Swanson. Nor was it the tall Finn.

What was the other one's name?

She remembered. She saw the name tag in her mind's eye. It was Jay Bowman.

Bowman.

Archer.

Jessica walked the perimeter of the Crystal Room, her heart racing. Table after table. She didn't see him. She walked to the other side, her eyes scanning, searching. No. He was not here. She hurried out to the lobby. The man calling himself Jay Bowman was not to be found. She got on her comm. In seconds she had John Shepherd.

'There's a guest here. He's registered under the name Jay Bowman.'

'Hang on,' Shepherd said. Twenty long seconds later: 'We've got him. Room 1208.'

★ ★ ★

The service elevator was agonizingly slow. For a moment Jessica considered getting off and taking the stairs, but that would probably delay her. Josh Bontrager and John Shepherd were taking the passenger elevator, which was on the other side of the hotel. On the twelfth floor they would be able to form a loose perimeter. There were now uniformed officers stationed at every exit on all the floors.

When she got out on the twelfth floor she passed a handful of guests. Two women about her age, dressed provocatively as French housemaids. A shorter man dressed as a wizard. A pair of boys about ten. None of them were George Archer.

She met up with Bontrager and Shepherd at the end of the hallway leading to the east wing. They moved down the hall, ears attuned to the sounds coming from the rooms. They reached Room 1208. Silence from within. Jessica made eye contact with the two men.

Bontrager knocked. No response. He knocked again.

Shepherd stepped forward, touched the electronic card to the top of the lock. Jessica and Bontrager drew their weapons. Jessica nodded. Shepherd swiped the card, turned the handle,

491

and pushed open the door.

Jessica rolled into the room first, her weapon high. There were no lights on. She reached out, felt along the wall, found the switch. It turned on a single light overhead, along with an under-cabinet light on the minibar across the room.

'*Police*,' she said. No response. She stopped just short of the bathroom door. She nudged it open with her foot. Bontrager flanked her on the right. He reached around the corner, turned on the light.

The bathroom was empty.

They edged forward, deeper into the hotel room. Jessica saw it first. There was a small pool of blood drying on the carpet in front of the desk. Next to it was the unmistakable stain of vomit. She touched Bontrager's arm, nodded at the stain. Bontrager saw it too.

They counted a silent three. Jessica rolled into the main part of the room first, her weapon raised.

It was a slaughterhouse. Blood slathered the walls, the floor. A spray of crimson dotted the window overlooking Seventeenth Street.

Josh Bontrager stepped forward, opened the closet. It was empty. He looked under the bed. 'We're clear,' he said.

Jessica holstered her weapon.

The body on the bed was covered with a single sheet. There was a full body print on the sheet, painted in blood. Josh Bontrager got on the far side, Jessica the near. They each grabbed a corner of the sheet, pulled it back.

George Archer had been savaged. His throat was cut from ear to ear. His chest was crushed.

492

There were bite marks across his stomach. There were also bruises across his thighs, bruises in the shape of a snake ring.

The ring sat on the pillow next to his head. It was caked with skin and hair, bits of drying flesh.

Jessica stepped forward, checked the dead man's fingers. No tattoos.

John Shepherd got on his two-way, raising the head of the hotel's security detail. 'Lock the building down,' he said. 'No one goes in or out.'

*　*　*

The lobby was in chaos when Jessica entered. There were a dozen uniformed officers deployed at exits, elevators, and service hallways. The restaurant's doors were closed. Inside Jessica saw patrons at candlelit tables, elegantly dressed, sipping their wines, perhaps figuring that, if you had to be locked down, being locked down inside a Michelin-starred restaurant with one of the most extensive and lauded wine cellars in the state was not such a bad thing.

Inside the Crystal Room, in an attempt to keep the crowd at ease, a member of the protection detail made his way over to the attorney general's table, tapped his watch. The AG got up calmly, shook a few hands, but quickly walked out a door at the back of the ballroom.

Jessica had changed into her jeans and hoodie. On her way out of the ladies' room she heard from Shepherd in her earpiece.

'Jess. One of the wait staff saw something near the rear service entrance. Just east of the kitchen.'

'What did she see?'
'Blood.'

★ ★ ★

Jessica and Bontrager met John Shepherd in the kitchen. Shepherd pointed out the handful of red dots leading to the rear entrance.

Shepherd stepped forward, swiped a card. They entered the area near the loading dock. A PPD officer was deployed behind the building. When he heard noise he spun around, his hand on his weapon. He was young, in his mid-twenties, a little spooked. Jessica showed her badge, and the kid looked quite relieved to have a detective on scene.

'How long have you been here?' Jessica asked

'A minute or so,' the officer said. 'I just got the call.'

The blood spots trailed over to a parking space, then disappeared.

'Did you see anyone leave?'

'No, ma'am.'

Jessica stepped back into the service area, looked at the door to her left.

'Where does this lead?' Jessica asked.

'Women's locker room.'

Jessica pushed through the door, her weapon low. The locker room had three benches, a row of sinks, a single shower, a pair of toilet stalls. Jessica checked them all. The room was empty. She looked at the inside of one of the toilet-stall doors. There was a smear of blood there.

Whoever they were looking for was gone.

79

In the Loss Prevention office Jessica stood behind John Shepherd. He rewound the video files. The recordings shuttled between different views, so there was a six-second rotation between each of four cameras on the twelfth floor. Even in a hotel as pricey and profitable as Le Jardin, they did not have the resources to devote a hard drive to each of the scores of cameras in and around the property.

Shepherd rewound the recording to when Jessica and the other detectives came to Room 1208, then kept going. A handful of people backed up to their rooms, as well as the stairwell at the end of the hallways. Shepherd carried on until he saw one of the room attendants exit the room backward, then retreat down the hall. He stopped, played it forward.

In normal time the view showed the room attendant walking down the hall, toward Room 1208. The attendant was female, petite and slender, with her light-colored hair in a braid. Here the view began its rotation, shifting to the area near the guest elevators.

'Do you know who this is?' Jessica asked.

'Hard to tell,' Shepherd said. 'I know a lot of the room attendants — most of them, in fact. But from this angle it's difficult.'

When the view returned to the eastern hallway, they saw the attendant stop in front of

1208 for a few seconds. She didn't knock, she didn't try the door. She just stood there, perhaps listening. The camera then cut away to another view, again to the elevators, where it stayed for six seconds. No one came or went. It then cut to a view of the other end of the hallway, the western wing. Two women came out of a room there. The next cut was to the service elevators. Empty. Back to the young woman in front of 1208. The recording caught up with her as she knocked on the door. There was no audio, but Jessica could see her lips move. In the split second before the cut-away she lifted her hand, and appeared to swipe a card in the electronic lock.

The recording moved again to its other locations. No other people were visible.

They watched the rotation for the next minute and saw no activity. When they returned to the eastern hallway they saw a man heading away from the camera. He was in costume, a wizard's costume. He moved slowly, so that by the time he reached 1208 the camera had rotated. When the camera returned he was gone, and the door to the stairwell was just closing.

'Shit,' Shepherd said. He rewound the recording with the joystick, and toggled it back and forth. There were no details visible. It was impossible to tell if the man had entered the room or just passed by. With his hat, long coat and what appeared to be gloves on his hands, there were no identifiable details.

Shepherd pointed to the time code in the lower right-hand corner of the frame.

'Right around here is when we went up,' he said.

A minute later Jessica saw herself and Josh Bontrager walking down the hall. A few seconds later Shepherd joined them. They went inside the room.

'I'm going to interrogate these locks,' Shepherd said. 'I'll be right back.'

While Shepherd was gone Jessica toggled the video back and forth. She saw nothing new. She looked at the menu down the right side of the screen. She saw that one of the selections was the rear loading dock. She clicked over. It was a static shot from above one of the three docks behind the hotel, showing the loading bay, a pair of Dumpsters, and the hotel's shuttle bus parked in a space. There was no movement. In the upper right-hand corner she could see a sliver of Seventeenth Street.

She was just about to click back over — she was certain that John Shepherd didn't want her messing around with the computers — when she saw a view that she had not seen before. It was above the side door to the loading dock, the man door, not the huge corrugated steel door. The view cut away, but before it did she saw something. She ran it back.

There was no mistake. It was Kevin Byrne standing near the mouth of the alley.

Jessica checked the time code.

Was this when Byrne dropped off the package with the concierge? If so, what was he doing at the rear of the hotel?

Jessica heard the door open in the outer office.

497

She clicked back to the paused recording at the beginning of the clip of the twelfth floor. Shepherd reentered the office.

'I interrogated all four locks along the path,' Shepherd said. 'The lock on 1208, the service elevator, the security door leading out to the loading dock, and the door on the dock itself. All four locks register the same card. It is signed out to one of the room attendants. Lucinda Doucette.'

Why is that name familiar? Jessica thought. 'Do you know her?'

'Oh yeah,' Shepherd said. 'Sweet kid. Shy.'

'Do you have a photograph of her?'

'Sure,' Shepherd said. He moved to another computer terminal, tapped a few keys. He input Lucinda's name and a few seconds later her ID page came up. He hit *print* and the color printer began to cycle. Seconds later, Jessica was looking at Lucinda Doucette's young face. Jessica knew her. She was the young woman at the Hosanna House, the one who'd been sitting at the little table with Carlos.

Jessica had no choice. She called in an all-points bulletin on the girl.

Shepherd hit a few keys, printing off one hundred copies of Lucinda Doucette's photograph. 'We need to get this to all the sector cars in the area.'

When John Shepherd grabbed the printed photos and left the office, Jessica's cellphone rang. It was Nicci Malone.

'Nicci. Why aren't you on channel with this?'

'I'm not in the hotel anymore.'

498

'What do you mean? Where are you?'

Nicci gave her the location. It was a few blocks away.

'What's going on?' Jessica asked.

Detective Malone hesitated. 'You better get over here right away.'

80

Lucy walked up Sansom Street in a fog, stepping from shadow to shadow. Everyone who passed her was a danger. They all knew what she had done. She could see it in their eyes. There was traffic, conversations, street sounds all around her, but she didn't hear the sounds. All she heard was the white noise in her head, raised to an insane volume, the static of her impending madness.

What *had* she done?

All she remembered was the bell. It had rung twice.

What did it mean?

She kept walking. Block after block passed. Walk. Don't Walk. Red light. Green light. There were people all around her, but they were ghosts. The only person who lived in her world right now was a dead man. A man lying under the sheets, soaked in blood.

All that blood.

At 22nd Street her legs felt as if she could not take another step, but she forced herself, she knew she had to keep moving.

When she reached the corner of Sansom and 23rd something jolted her out of her dark reverie. There were police cars all up and down the streets, their lights flashing on the walls of the buildings. Groups of people were gathered on the corners, chatting with each other, pointing at the church. Lucy had walked this way many times. She was pretty sure that there was a small cemetery next to the church. What was going on?

It didn't matter. It had nothing to do with her. She knew what she had to do. She knew who she had to call. She crossed 23rd Street. There was a policeman standing in the middle of the street, directing traffic away from the church. Lucy pulled up the collar on her coat, angled her head away from him. As she passed, she chanced a glance. He was looking right at her. She quickened her pace, made it across the street. When she had gone half a block she stepped back into the shadows, glanced back. The cop was still looking in her direction.

Lucy ran. She tried to get her bearings. The river was just a few blocks to her left. Ahead was Chestnut, Market, Arch, Cherry.

Cherry.

There was only one place for her to go.

★   ★   ★

Lucy stood in front of Apartment 106, her breath coming in hot, painful waves. She had run nearly six blocks and her sides ached. She tried to calm herself, to catch her breath. She could hear the sound of a television coming from one of the other apartments on this floor. Somewhere a dog was barking. She knocked softly, but there was no response. She tried again. Nothing.

She tried the doorknob. It turned in her hand.

She pushed open the door, and stepped into Mr. Costa's apartment.

* * *

The flat was completely empty. This time, even the Dreamweaver booth was gone. The floor had been swept, the walls were bare. She could smell the cleaning products — Spic 'N Span, Lemon Pledge, Windex, Scrubbing Bubbles.

Lucy moved slowly through the living room, glanced into the tiny kitchen. The old appliances remained, but that was it. There was no dinette table, no chairs, no dishes in the sink, no strainer. She turned back to the living room. On the right was a door that she figured led to a bedroom. She stepped lightly, but the old wooden floor still creaked under her weight. She stopped, waiting for the light to go on, for Mr. Costa to appear suddenly as he was likely to do. But it didn't happen. Lucy inched open the door to the bedroom. It too was empty. No furniture, no clothing, no personal items of any kind. There was a single window overlooking the street. That was it.

But it wasn't.

There was something on the wall. A small picture in a frame. Lucy reached over, flipped the light switch, but it didn't work. She crossed the bedroom, pushed the curtain to the side. A wedge of illumination from the street lights across the road spilled into the room. She took the small picture from the wall, angled it toward the borrowed light. The photograph was old, kind of blurry. It was a picture of a little girl, no more than two years old. She sat on a beach. In front of her was a bright red plastic bucket. In her hand was a small shovel. She squinted at the sunlight. She wore a floppy flowered sun hat. Chubby cheeks, chubby knees.

Lucy knew the face, the eyes. The last time she had seen those eyes they had been red with crying.

It was Peggy van Tassel.

Lucy's hands began to shake. She tried to plug it into everything that had happened in the past few days and she could not. Then she tried to put the picture in the pocket of her coat but it wouldn't fit.

She knew what she had to do. She would get to the nearest phone and call Detective Byrne. The longer she waited, the worse it was going to get for her.

Before she could take a single step, she heard the floorboards creak, felt the warm breath on her neck. Someone stood right behind her.

'Police,' the man said. 'Get down on the floor and put your hands behind your back. Do it now.'

Lucy felt her legs go soft. The photograph slipped from her grasp. It crashed to the floor.

'Now,' he repeated.

Lucy got down on the floor, next to the shattered glass, put her hands behind her back. She felt the man take her arms by the wrists, then slip a plastic band around them, tighten it.

He left her there like that for a full minute. She dared not turn to look at him. She heard him pace around the room. Then he spoke.

'Can you hear them?' he asked softly.

Lucy didn't know what he was talking about. She tried to listen hard, to figure out what he meant, but there was only the roar of terror in her head.

'The dead are all over the city,' the man continued. 'Tonight it belongs to them. It always has.'

A few moments later the man shone a flashlight on the broken photograph on the floor, spotlighting the little girl's face. He held it there for a long time.

'You could have saved her,' the man said. 'You could have saved her and you did nothing.'

Lucy's mind began to spin. This man was not the police.

She was pulled roughly to her feet. She felt the man's breath right near her ear.

'You're as guilty as George Archer.'

81

The St Demetrios Orthodox Church was a long rectangular building with a single cupola. Behind it was a graveyard, a small neighborhood cemetery, easily a hundred years old. There was a waist-high brick wall surrounding the courtyard, which was accessible by a double wrought-iron gate. In the light thrown from the headlights of the sector cars and departmental sedans, the headstones cast long shadows over the grounds, as well as onto the walls of the row homes on either side. The flashing lights projected images nearly ten feet tall, giant specters overseeing the dead.

As Jessica approached the scene, Nicci Malone came jogging up to her side. Nicci pointed to a young couple standing near one of the sector cars. They looked terribly frightened.

'These two were walking up the street about a half-hour ago. They said they were not really paying attention but when they got here to the edge of the block they saw someone walking in the shadows to the center of the cemetery. They said it was a man carrying something heavy over his shoulders.'

'Did they get a good look at the guy?' Jessica asked.

Nicci shook her head. 'Too dark on that side. But they still watched what he was doing. They said he dropped the parcel to the ground,

505

unwrapped it. When they saw that it was a body, they froze. Then they saw the man position the leg, propping it up on one of the low headstones.'

Jessica knew what came next. She remained silent.

'Then, according to our witnesses, the man jumped high into the air and came down on the leg. The woman said she heard the sound of the breaking bone all the way on the other side of the cemetery.'

A news helicopter roared overhead. Jessica wondered what this grotesque display might look like from above.

'What about the vehicle? Did they get a look?'

Again Nicci shook her head. 'They were both pretty much over the edge at this point. We were lucky they had the wherewithal to call us.'

Jessica glanced at the street corners. She did not see any police cameras. This was not a high-crime or high-drug-traffic area. She looked at the walls of the stone church. She did not see any surveillance cameras there, either.

When she stepped into the gated graveyard, Jessica saw the corpse, the now-familiar signature. The body was nude, a white middle-aged male, shaved clean. There was a band of paper around his forehead. The left foot rested on the headstone. Jessica crossed over to the plot, aimed her Maglite at the dead body, and saw the sharp bone protruding from the skin, just above the left knee. She thought about the line from *Danse Macabre*.

506

Zig, zig, zig, each one is frisking,
You can hear the cracking of the bones of
the dancers.

Then Jessica leaned in, moved the victim's left leg a few inches, directed the beam of her flashlight at the headstone. At the top she saw:

O THEOS NA TIN ANAPAFSI

The name of the person in the grave was Melina Laskaris.

She angled the light to the victim's right hand, which was on the ground, palm up. On the ring finger she saw a small tattoo of a donkey. It was the seventh animal, which meant there was one more to go.

Before Jessica could stop her — and she didn't really want to stop her — Nicci Malone stepped forward, knelt down, pulled off the bloodied white headband. When Jessica saw the victim's face, the triangle was complete.

The dead woman was Lina Laskaris.

Her killer was Eduardo Robles.

The accomplice, the harmony in this horror show — the broken body sprawled before them in this crumbling graveyard — was Detective Dennis Stansfield.

82

He stood in shadows, just a block from the Le Jardin hotel, the sounds of his city all around him, the flashing police lights a few blocks away. He felt the hand on his arm.

'Kevin.'

Christa-Marie looked fragile, sculpted from moonlight. She raised a hand to his cheek, a warm finger tracing the lines in his face. She slipped her hand around the back of his head, leaned forward and kissed him, gently at first, then with a growing passion.

A moment later she leaned back, looked into his eyes.

'It's time, isn't it?' she asked.

'Yes,' Byrne said. 'Are you ready?'

'Yes.' She took his hand in hers. 'Take me home.'

83

'Jess?'

It was Russell Diaz. The city block had been taken over by law enforcement. Residents had begun to drift out of their houses. Endlessly, the helicopter flew back and forth, hovering overhead. Jessica looked around. David Albrecht was not to be found.

'You have a minute?' Diaz asked.

She did not. But she knew that this was coming, just as she knew what it was about. 'Sure.'

Diaz looked at his two men. 'Give us a second.'

The two officers walked a few feet away, leaned against Jessica's car. When Diaz felt they were out of earshot, he spoke.

'You know what I have to ask, don't you?' he said, lowering his voice.

Jessica remained silent. It was a rhetorical question. Diaz plowed ahead. Niceties were over.

'I need to talk to Kevin,' Diaz said. 'Have you heard from him?'

'Not since earlier this evening.'

'About what time was that?'

Jessica had to think about this. She had to be accurate. This was all going on the record. 'Maybe an hour ago.'

'He called you?'

'Yes.'

'Did he mention where he was going?'

Now she had to be careful. Byrne had not said anything specific. 'No.'

'Is he still driving that van?'

'I don't know.'

Diaz looked out over the gathering crowd, back.

'I want to show you something.'

They walked over to the unmarked police van. Diaz opened the sliding side door. Inside was a rack of electronic equipment, surveillance monitors, three locked gun racks. Diaz grabbed a laptop off the front seat, opened it, put it on the floor of the van. The screen instantly displayed a flow chart. On it were six different squares. Diaz clicked the first one.

Seconds later three separate documents cascaded across the screen. Jessica recognized them as PPD witness statements, presented in .pdf format.

'We have statements from three people who live on West Tioga Street,' Diaz said. 'Neighbors of Sharon and Kenneth Beckman. They all stated that they saw Detective Byrne at the Beckman house an hour before her son reported her missing.'

'She was next of kin, Russell. Both Kevin and I were there that morning. We made notification.'

'As you know, he returned a short time later. Did you accompany Detective Byrne back to the premises?'

'No,' Jessica said. 'He returned to follow up. We had received additional information.'

'What was the information?'

Diaz knew the answer to his question. He was testing her. 'That Kenneth Beckman was questioned in the murder of Antoinette Chan.'

'When did Detective Byrne return to the Roundhouse?'

'It had to be around three.'

'What did he say about the interview?'

'He said that Sharon Beckman didn't answer the door.'

Diaz took a moment, then tapped another square on the chart. This was the ME's preliminary report on Joseph Novak. 'The coroner puts the time of death for Joseph Novak at between eight p.m. and six a.m. Do you know where Detective Byrne was during those hours?'

This was getting so bad, so fast. Was Diaz making an attempt to establish some sort of conspiracy here?

'I do not.'

'Did Detective Byrne mention anything about seeing Mr. Novak again that day?'

'No.'

Diaz hit yet another button on the laptop. A grainy video began to play. It was the stationary image of a city street at night.

'This is PPD surveillance footage near the corner of Frankford and York.'

At the thirty-four-second mark on the video a man crosses the top of the frame, hesitates for a moment, walks off frame. A few seconds later, a second man walks across the frame, right to left. He continues off. Diaz rewound the recording. He pointed to the lower right of the image, at a van parked on the street. 'This tag is registered to a man named Patrick Connolly. He is Detective Byrne's cousin. Connolly stated that he lent this vehicle to Detective Byrne last week.'

Jessica looked closely. It was clearly the Sedona minivan. She looked closely at the whole image. 'I believe Kevin already acknowledged that he was there that night. This is not new information.'

Diaz hit *play*. The image scrolled by in slow motion this time. He freeze-framed it as the first man walked into the frame. 'This is Eduardo Robles.' He hit *play* again. Robles disappears off frame, walking down the alley, the alley in which his body was found. The second man enters the frame. Diaz froze the image again.

'Do you recognize this person, detective?' he asked.

Jessica noted that she had gone from *Jess* to *detective*. To another person it might have gone unnoticed. Not to anyone in law enforcement. 'No. Sorry. It could be anyone.'

'Not exactly.' Diaz hit a few keys, zoomed in. It increased the size of the pixels, but some things were obvious. Like the man's left hand. 'It can only be a white male, so it can't be 'just anyone'.' He pointed to something next to the figure. 'We took measurements on this stand-pipe. This person is over six feet tall. He is wearing a dark overcoat and a dark watch cap.' Diaz reached onto a shelf. He produced a photograph of Kevin Byrne, a picture that Jessica recognized instantly. It had been taken a year ago at a benefit in the Poconos. It was of Kevin and her standing with a bunch of kids. Kevin wore a dark overcoat and navy blue watch cap.

Jessica said nothing.

Diaz directed her gaze to the body on the ground across the cemetery from where they stood. 'Everyone was well aware of the friction between Detective Byrne and Detective Stansfield. Add to that the incident between them at the Roundhouse and you can see what I'm faced with, right?' Diaz closed the laptop, squared himself in front of her. 'I now have a dead cop, and Kevin Byrne is missing again.'

Diaz opened a second laptop. There on the screen were two microscope photographs of hair shafts. Diaz pointed to the one on the left. 'This is a sample taken from a brush belonging to Sharon Beckman.' He pointed to the example on the right. Jessica was far from an expert, but to her eye the samples were identical. 'This was found on the driver's seat of Kevin Byrne's van. They match.'

Jessica recalled the hair on Byrne's shoulder.

'*Did you get a haircut?*'

'*Yeah. I popped in and got a trim.*'

Jessica began to feel nauseated. She remained silent, which was just as well because she had no idea what to say. Diaz closed the side door of the van, signaled to his two men. They approached, stopped a few feet away.

'Look, Jess. If you were looking at this from the outside, you would see why we need to talk to Detective Byrne.'

Jessica knew that Diaz was right. In her career she had brought people in for questioning based on far less.

'I don't know where he is, Russ. I've left five voicemails for him in the past half-hour.'

'When was the last time you called?'

'Five minutes ago.'

'Want to try again?'

Jessica took out her phone. She put it on speaker, hit Byrne's speed-dial number. It rang twice, and his voicemail greeting came on. There was no point leaving a sixth message. Jessica closed her phone.

Diaz nodded. 'Detective Byrne carries a 17?'

He was referring to a Glock 17, the standard-issue service weapon for PPD detectives. 'Yeah.'

'Does he carry a second piece?'

My God, Jessica thought, her heart in free fall. She was betraying one of the most important people in her life. She wondered how Kevin would handle the same situation if someone was asking these questions about her. 'Sometimes.'

'Today?'

Jessica told the truth. 'I don't know.'

'Does he pack anything else?'

Diaz meant knives, spray, knuckles, batons. 'No.'

Diaz processed it all. He looked out over the burgeoning mass of people, then back at Jessica. 'You know him better than anyone. I know you are close. I know this has to be hard for you.'

Jessica said nothing.

Diaz handed her a card. 'That's my cell on the back. If you talk to Kevin, have him call me.'

Jessica took the card, said nothing.

'You know this is going to move forward, right?'

'I know.'

'It's better for everyone if he walks in the front door.'

Diaz hesitated a few moments, then turned and walked away.

★　★　★

Jessica looked out over the cemetery. In all, there were probably thirty or forty people on scene. Jessica knew most of them by name, yet she had never felt so completely alone in her life.

A few minutes later Josh Bontrager emerged from the crowd.

'You okay, Josh?'

'No,' he said. 'I am *not*.'

'What's wrong?'

Bontrager bowed his head for moment. 'He was my partner, and now he's dead.'

'Josh, he wasn't really your partner. You were paired with him for one case.'

'Doesn't matter. Today he was my partner. Today I let him down.'

Jessica knew what he meant. She had certainly let Kevin Byrne down today.

'And I didn't even like the guy.'

Jessica left Josh to his thoughts for a few moments. She then filled him in on everything that Diaz had said.

'That's ridiculous,' Bontrager said.

'I know.'

'What are we going to do?'

'I'm going to try to find him before they do.'

'I'll go with you.'

'No, Josh. I can't ask you to do that.'

'Well, with all due respect, I don't remember you asking. It's something I'm volunteering for. Okay?'

Jessica lowered her voice as a pair of CSU officers walked by. 'Josh, there's a good chance I'm going off the reservation here. There's a *very* good chance I'm going to lose my job tonight. Maybe worse.'

Bontrager took a few steps away, looked out over the scene. The medical examiner's blue and white van came rolling up slowly. They would soon be loading Dennis Stansfield's body into the back for transport. Bontrager turned back. 'Remember my first days on the job?'

Jessica remembered them well. They'd been investigating a case that eventually took them up the Schuylkill River into Berks County. Josh Bontrager had been on temporary assignment. 'I remember.'

'Kevin wasn't too crazy about me at first, you know.'

'It just takes a little time for him to warm up to people.'

Bontrager looked at her, offered a smile. 'Bechtelsville, Pennsylvania may not be a hotbed of intellectuals, but we do know people,' he said. 'I knew right away what a closed group this is. I was the new guy, and a really inexperienced guy at that.'

Jessica just listened. She had gone through a brutal initiation period herself.

'In those first few months I made a lot of mistakes.'

'You did fine, Josh.'

'No, it only looked that way. I can't tell you how many times Kevin took me aside and showed me the ropes. How many times he covered for me.' Bontrager put his hands in his pockets. He looked across the cemetery. 'Nobody wanted me to have this job. Not really. I heard all the jokes, you know. All the stuff said behind my back. People thought I didn't, but I did.'

Jessica remembered well the hard time Josh had gotten. It was always bad enough for the new guy in the unit, but doubly so for Josh Bontrager, considering his background.

'You toughed it out, Josh,' Jessica said. 'You've earned the right to be here. You're a damned good detective.'

Bontrager shrugged. 'Well, it was you and Kevin who went to bat for me back then. I wouldn't even be here if it wasn't for you guys. If I lose it all tonight, I can live with that.'

'It might get worse than that, you know. Much worse.'

Josh Bontrager looked at her. Sometimes, with his clear eyes, open smile, and seemingly untamable cowlick, he looked like a kid, some country boy who'd got off I–95 at the wrong exit and wandered into the city. Other times, like right at this moment, he looked like a homicide detective with the Philadelphia Police Department.

'The Amish have an old saying,' Bontrager said. ''*Courage is fear that has said its prayers.*'' He drew his Glock, checked the action, holstered it, snapped it in. 'I've said my prayers, Jess.'

517

Jessica glanced at the crime scene, then back. 'Thanks, Josh.'

'I'm going to lock my car,' Bontrager said. 'I'll be right back.'

As Josh walked across the street, Jessica thought about what Byrne had said.

It's always been about the music.

Before she could make a mental list of their options her phone rang. It was David Albrecht. She answered.

'David, now is not really a good — '

There was static on the line. 'What's going on?' he asked.

'What do you mean?'

'I heard the call go out. Is there another victim?'

'What do you mean, you heard the call go out?'

'I heard it on the police radio.'

'You have a scanner?'

'Well, yeah,' he said. 'Of course.'

Jessica hadn't considered this. It made sense. 'Where are you, David?'

'I'm following Detective Byrne.'

Jessica's pulse spiked. She waved Bontrager over. 'You're with Kevin?'

'I'm right behind him. He was parked near the hotel. I saw a woman in the van. I thought you guys were together. I followed.'

'Where are you?'

'Hang on,' Albrecht said. 'Let me check my GPS.'

A few agonizing seconds passed.

'We're on Bells Mill Road.'

Bells Mill Road cut through the northeast section of Fairmount Park, traversing the Wissahickon Creek just west of Chestnut Hill.

'Do you know where he's going?' Jessica asked.

'Not a clue,' Albrecht said. 'But I kind of like it that way. This is so — '

'Which way are you heading?'

'We're going east. Northeast, technically. My GPS says we're coming up on something called Forbidden Drive. Is that the coolest name of all time or what? I think I'm changing the name of my movie to *Forbidden Drive*.'

'David, I want you to — '

'Hang on.' A loud blast of static. The coming storm was playing havoc with the signal. 'He's slowing down. I'll call you right back.'

'David, *wait*.'

Dead air. Jessica hit the button to call right back. She got David Albrecht's voicemail.

She told Josh what Albrecht had said.

'He's on Bells Mill?' Bontrager asked.

'Yeah.'

'Where do you think they're going?'

'I don't know.'

Jessica put the location into the Google Maps app on her phone. Seconds later she had a map of the area. She really didn't know anything about that part of the park. She fished out her keys.

'Let's get on the road,' she said. 'We'll figure it out on the way.'

84

Bells Mill Road was a two-lane blacktop that spanned an area between Ridge and Germantown Avenues. At its western end, where it became Spring Lane, there were houses, but as it made its way into Fairmount Park it became wooded and dark. As Jessica and Bontrager drove, the night was cut only by the headlights of their car.

On the way Josh Bontrager dialed David Albrecht's number twenty times, getting his voicemail each time. At the same time Jessica speed-dialed Byrne's cellphone with the same result.

'Maybe Kevin left his phone somewhere,' Bontrager said.

Jessica thought about this. 'No. He turns it off sometimes, but he always has it with him. He's just not answering.'

Bontrager went silent for a few moments. 'Don't all phones have some kind of GPS in them?'

Jessica didn't know about all phones. 'What are you saying, Josh?'

'If we could slip through a warrant, maybe we could get a fix on Kevin's phone.'

Jessica had thought of this. But it meant bringing someone into the loop. There was no doubt in her mind that an APB on Kevin had gone out. Police were looking for him and his vehicle. If she reached out to someone to help find him, she would be taking the chance that it would leak, and it would all end badly.

She looked at her watch. It was 10:24. Time was running out.

She had no choice. She knew who she had to bring into this. She called Michael Drummond.

★ ★ ★

'This is Michael.'

'Michael, it's Jessica Balzano.'

'Hey, Jessica. How are you?'

'I hope I didn't wake you.'

'Not a chance. I'm stuck at a Halloween party,' he said. 'What's up?'

'I need a warrant for a cellphone track.'

Drummond was silent for a moment. 'What do you have?'

Jessica told him the bare minimum.

'Who's the target?'

Jessica had no choice here, nor did she have a cover. 'Kevin Byrne.'

Once again, Michael Drummond fell silent for a few moments. 'This is about your serial?'

Jessica knew she was now on the record with this. If she lied, it would all come down around her.

'Yes and no.'

'Spoken like a true politician. But I'm going to need a little more if I'm going to get a warrant. You know it has to go through the chief.'

All search warrants related to a homicide case had to be approved by the chief of homicide in the district attorney's office.

Jessica had no choice. 'He might be in some trouble, Michael.'

Jessica heard Drummond take a deep breath, exhale slowly. 'I'll need his phone number and his carrier.'

Jessica gave him the information.

'I don't know if I can get this through at this time of night.'

'I understand.'

'Let me see what I can do,' Drummond said. 'Where are you?'

Jessica told him.

'Are you alone?'

'I'm with Detective Bontrager.'

'Hang tight. I'll call you back.'

Jessica clicked off her phone. She stood in the middle of the road, in the impenetrable country darkness. The road stretched into the gloom in both directions. Dark, forbidding, unknown, silent.

85

Darkness.

They were moving. There was tape over her eyes and her mouth. Her hands were still bound together behind her back with the plastic band.

Lucy tried to listen to sounds around her. She heard the sound of the road beneath her. They were on a paved road, smooth, maybe an expressway, although she did not have the sense that they were traveling at high speed. Every so often she heard the sound of something passing. It was a distinct rhythm. *Light poles?*

Underneath it all was the sound of the heater fan. There was no music coming from the radio, no conversation. Then she heard humming. She didn't know the song.

Lucy rolled to her right, then her left. The movements were small but she could feel the plastic on her wrists shift a little bit each time. If she had strength anywhere in her body it was in her arms and hands. You didn't lift as many mattresses as she had without getting stronger.

Left.

Right.

She flexed her wrists, relaxed.

Little by little she felt the plastic start to give.

86

Drummond called back ten minutes later.

'Michael,' Jessica said. 'What do you have for me?'

There were a few seconds of silence. At first Jessica thought the call had been dropped. She looked at the screen. They were still connected. She put the phone back to her ear. It was now quiet in the background on Drummond's end. He had either left or stepped away from his Halloween party.

'I don't know how to say this, Jess.'

This was not good, whatever it was. 'Just say it, Michael.'

Another pause. Jessica heard the rustling of paper. 'I just heard from the Hudson County prosecutor's office. They issued a search warrant yesterday to the Mailboxes USA location in Jersey City.'

Drummond was talking about the location to which the tattoos had been mailed from World Ink.

'Do we have something?' Jessica asked.

'We do. But it's not good news.'

'What did they say?'

'They got the records of where the material was forwarded to from Box 1606. The tattoos from World Ink. The package went to an address in South Philly.'

Jessica waited. And waited. 'Michael.'

'It was Kevin Byrne's address. The tattoos went to his home address.'

Jessica felt the ground shift beneath her. She wanted to speak, but her breath had not yet caught up to her words. 'It's not possible.'

'It's the only piece of mail the location ever forwarded from this box, under this registration. It was sent about a month ago.'

Another long pause. Drummond continued. 'Half the department is looking for him, Jessica. If I take this warrant request to the chief they're going to use it to locate Kevin and bring him in.'

'Okay, Michael. I understand,' Jessica said. 'But I have a favor to ask.'

'What is it?'

'I need a head start. There's an explanation for all of this. I just need to get to Kevin first.'

Silence for a moment. 'I can't break the law, Jess. You know and I know that there is now a record of us having this conversation.'

'I'm not asking you to break the law. I just need some time. Besides, who's to say what we talked about? Maybe we talked about the Phillies.'

'How about that Chase Utley, eh?'

Jessica took a moment, her mind spinning. 'All I'm asking for is a little window. Kevin is innocent. Let me bring him in.'

The next few seconds were excruciating. Finally: 'If the office brings me into this I'm going to have to drop the hammer. You know that, right?'

'I know.'

'But maybe it doesn't have to be immediately.

Maybe I can't get a cellphone signal. Maybe my phone was off.'

Jessica felt a cool wave of relief. 'Thanks, Michael.'

'Good luck, detective.'

Jessica clicked off. She filled in Josh Bontrager on the parts of the conversation that he had not heard. She began to pace. The rain began to fall a little harder. She barely noticed.

'Okay,' Jessica said. 'The killer was working toward this night for a reason.'

'*Danse Macabre*,' Bontrager said. 'Midnight on Halloween.'

'Right. The killer is doing this for Christa-Marie. Why?'

Bontrager thought for a moment. 'If he is true to form he's going to kill one more person to fill in the last note.'

'If this is all coming down to Christa-Marie, there must be a connection.'

'She can't be a target, though. She was convicted of murder. She didn't get away with anything, not like the other victims.'

'Unless there's something we don't know about,' Jessica said.

'*I'm scared that I made a mistake*,' Byrne had said.

Jessica took out her phone again. She called a man named Gary Peters, a friend of hers who worked the city desk at the *Inquirer*. They got their pleasantries quickly out of the way.

'What do you need?'

'I need you to check something for me.'

'Shoot.'

'I need you to look up an obituary,' Jessica said. 'It would be in November 1990.'

'What's the name?'

'Gabriel Thorne.'

'Okay,' Peters said. 'What am I looking for?'

'I just need the notice.'

'Got it,' he said. 'Do you want me to fax it to you?'

'Can you email it to me?'

'Not a problem.'

Jessica gave him her email address. 'ASAP, okay?'

'On the case, detective.'

Two minutes later Jessica's phone dinged with the arrival of the email. She tapped it, opened it. It was a pdf file from the *Philadelphia Inquirer*.

Prominent Psychiatrist Dead at 58.

Jessica quickly skimmed the obituary, soon finding what she was looking for.

''Services will be held at St. Stanislaus, followed by interment at the Briarcliff Cemetery,'' she read out.

'Does it have an address?' Bontrager asked.

Jessica had to enlarge the image. Her eyes scanned the file. 'Here it is. It's at 122 Sawmill Road.'

They looked at each other. 'Any ideas where that is?' Bontrager asked.

'No,' Jessica said. 'Hang on.'

She tapped over to her Google Maps app, put in the address. Soon a map appeared with a big red push pin at the center.

'Oh *hello*.'

'Where is it?' Bontrager asked.

Briarcliff Cemetery was a small suburban graveyard that abutted a number of large estates. One of them belonged to Christa-Marie Schönburg.

★ ★ ★

They turned onto Sawmill Road. The darkness was complete. A fine mist coated the ground; the headlights barely cut through the miasma. The road was serpentine, and more than once Jessica had to slow the car to a crawl. According to the GPS the back entrance to Briarwood Cemetery was approximately a mile ahead.

They took a slow bend to the right.

'Stop!' Bontrager yelled.

Jessica hit the brakes. 'What is it?'

'Back up.'

Jessica put the car in reverse. She backed up slowly for fifty feet or so. As she did, she saw what had caught Josh's eye. On the right side of the road were tire tracks cutting through the high grass, leading into the woods. A pair of small trees had been recently knocked over and splintered. Jessica angled the car so the headlights shone into the forest. There, about twenty feet in, was a vehicle, its motor still running. The lights were off but they could see warm exhaust spilling into the cold night air.

Jessica looked over at Bontrager. They drew their weapons, exited the car, walked down the culvert, up the other side. As they stepped closer to the vehicle Jessica saw more of it. It was a van.

A familiar van.

87

Lucy Doucette remembered a time when she was about four or five. Her mother had worked for a few months at a Dollar General and the money had flowed in. They were rich. That Thanksgiving they had a Jennie-O turkey breast, gravy, Hungry Jack mashed potatoes. All her favorites.

The thought of it made her stomach clench. She could not remember the last time she had eaten.

She had made slow progress on the plastic band around her wrists. She wasn't anywhere close to being able to slip her hands out. Not yet.

Ever since the van had stopped, a few minutes ago, she had lain motionless. She didn't know where they were or what was happening. It was better to be still for the moment.

At first she thought it was her imagination, but she heard footsteps. Footsteps *approaching*.

Lucy held her breath.

88

They approached the van, weapons drawn. Jessica took the driver's side, Josh Bontrager flanked right, a few paces behind. The immediate danger was the threat from the back doors.

At the rear bumper Jessica stopped, raised her left hand, made it into a fist. Bontrager stopped. Jessica put her ear to the back doors, listened. Silence from within.

Jessica held up five fingers. Bontrager nodded.

Jessica crept up to the driver door, counted down silently from five. There were no lights in the van, so the side mirror did not reflect the inside. She held her weapon in her left hand, trained on the door, slid her right hand along the panel.

On four she opened the door, stepped to the left in attack stance, weapon leveled. The driver's seat was empty, as was the seat on the passenger side. Keys in the ignition.

Bontrager opened the passenger door on five, pointed his flashlight inside the van. Behind the driver's seat were a pair of side racks. Strapped into them were David Albrecht's equipment — tripods, equipment cases, lights, microphone stands, a short ladder.

Jessica flipped on the van's interior light.

There was no one inside.

Near the back doors they could see the video camera on its side. The camera was on, the blue

530

rectangle of the flip-out LCD screen glowed. Jessica took a single latex glove out of her pocket, snapped it on. She crossed to the back of the van, opened a door. Reaching in, she tilted the camera back onto its side. There had to be two dozen buttons.

'Do you know how to operate one of these?'

'Sort of,' Bontrager said. 'I took the video of my cousin's wedding last year.'

'There's video at an Amish wedding?'

'My cousin left the church. She married English.'

Bontrager put on a glove, looked closely at the camera for a few moments. He hit a button. They heard a whirring sound, then a click. The side of the camera opened.

'There's no tape,' Bontrager said.

Jessica scanned the back of the van, looking for a tape. Then she went back to the front of the vehicle, searched through the console and the glove compartment. Empty.

'Sometimes there's a memory card,' Bontrager said. He clicked a few more buttons. Different menus flicked by on the LCD screen. 'Yeah, the card's still in there.'

Bontrager thumbed a few more buttons, the screens ticked by. He hit a button. A video copied to the memory card began to play.

There were only twenty seconds or so of video and audio, but it was chilling. The video showed someone walking up to the camera along a dark lane. The camera was shaky, showed the figure from the shoulders down.

'It's you,' a voice whispered. Was it Albrecht

speaking? Impossible to tell.

Without another word, the door of Albrecht's van was yanked open. The video spun into a collage of images: trees, night sky, the side of the van.

The image then became a stationary shot along the ground, showing Sawmill Road stretching out into the darkness. This continued for a few moments before the screen went black.

Bontrager stepped a few paces away from the van, pointing his flashlight at the ground. 'Jess.'

Jessica walked over. On the trunk of a fallen tree was a small pool of blood. A few more drops on the grass led deeper into the woods, over trampled branches.

Weapons in hand, the two detectives stepped into the forest.

89

Lucy couldn't move. She was lying on a cold stone floor. A draft was coming from somewhere. She had been yanked roughly out of the van, walked down some stairs, and deposited on the floor. Then she heard a door slam and a lock turn.

Then, nothing.

The good news was that her captor had not tightened the plastic band around her wrists. She still had a little slack. She rolled over and began to work on the band, flexing and relaxing her wrists. After a few minutes her lower arms began to feel numb. She stopped for a while, started again. After ten minutes or so it felt as if she might be able to begin to work her hand free.

When she had been dropped on the floor she'd felt a small puddle of water. She rolled over and over until she was on top of it. She angled her body so that her hands got wet. The water was freezing. She had never done well in science classes, but she figured that this might be a good thing, if it helped her hands contract and not the band.

She took a deep breath, bracing against the pain she knew was coming, and started to twist her wrists out of the plastic band. *No dice.* She wet her hands a second time. They were growing numb again, but she couldn't stop.

The third time she tried, she felt the band slip

over the base of her thumbs. With great effort she pulled her right hand out of the plastic band.

Lucy stood up, a little shaky, pulled the tape from her mouth. She gulped the cold air.

There was virtually no light in the room. With her hands out front, she felt along the wall. It was a small room, a cellar of some sort. Stone walls. There was a bench, a couple of old chairs. Everything had a deep layer of dust on it. She felt her way over to the door, listened for a while. Silence. As gently as possible, she tried to turn the knob.

Locked.

90

The trail of blood stopped about twenty yards into the woods, where the forest became thick and tangled before dropping into a steep gorge.

Jessica and Bontrager shone their flashlights into the ravine, but the beams were instantly swallowed by darkness.

'Albrecht is hurt pretty bad,' Bontrager said.

'If this *is* Albrecht's blood.'

Bontrager looked at Jessica, then back at the blood trail, which was quickly being washed away in the drizzling rain. 'You're right. We don't know if this is Albrecht's.'

'We have to call it in, Josh.'

Bontrager hesitated a second, no longer. He ran back to the road, called PPD dispatch, identified himself and their position. Dispatch would contact the closest emergency services agency and police K-9 units.

Jessica returned to the road. They stood on the shoulder.

'I'll stay here,' Bontrager said. 'I'll wait for the search team.'

'It's over, Josh. Even if Mike Drummond keeps his word, they're going to put all this together.'

Bontrager took a few steps away, thinking, turned back.

'Okay. Here's what happened. I was following a lead. I saw the vehicle, pulled over, discovered

535

the blood. I called it in. Before I could get back to my car I was ambushed. This is why I'm a little unclear on the details after that.'

'No one is going to buy that.'

'Maybe yes, maybe no. We'll worry about that later.'

Jessica considered the scenario. 'Are you sure?'

'Yeah,' Bontrager said, planting his feet apart. 'Make it look good.'

Jessica took a step back. 'Josh . . . '

'I know you box, so try not to kill me.'

Jessica put on one of her wool gloves, hesitated. This was getting deeper and deeper. 'Are you *sure* sure?'

'You're talking me out of it.'

Jessica reared back and threw the punch, pulling it a little. It caught Bontrager on the right side of his jaw. Bontrager reeled back, nearly toppling over.

'Wow.'

She had bloodied his lip.

'Jesus Christ. Are you okay?'

Long pause. 'I'm fine. I may never sing with the opera again, but I'm fine.' He reached down, gathered some dirt from the side of the road, scuffed up his suit coat.

Jessica looked from the van, back to Josh, then up Sawmill Road. According to the map she was about a mile away.

She wanted to tell Josh to call or text her, keeping her in the loop, but it was not a good idea. That would put everything on the record.

'You sure you're all right?'

Bontrager rubbed his jaw, which was already starting to swell. 'Go.'

Jessica checked the action on her Glock, snapped it back into her holster, and started down the road.

91

The smell of just-turned earth fills my senses. Each shovelful brings with it a plaintive voice: a plea of innocence, a shout of unrepentant pride, a wail of sorrow. I hear them all.

With the swing of his crimson hammer Kenneth Beckman took Antoinette Chan to the other side. His wife Sharon had helped. They too smell the earth now, rich with fur and blood and bone. They are joined by Preston Braswell, Tyvander Alice, Eduardo Robles, Tommy Archer, Dennis Stansfield, so many others. The earth always reclaims.

Tonight, in this place, white skeletons pass through the gloom. They are all around me.

There is one more note to play. I hear the player coming, creeping through the night. I push the sounds of murders past from my mind, listen for the footfall as it approaches.

There. Can you hear it?

I hear it.

One more note.

My instruments are ready.

92

Jessica walked down the road in a darkness so pure and complete that she could not see her own feet. The drizzle made the going even slower. Her only guide to the road was the white stripe on either side, along with the compass app on her phone, which she was reluctant to use. It seemed to put a spotlight on her. According to the GPS, she would be coming up on the parcel in a few minutes.

She passed a drive every so often, a gravel lane that snaked back into the woods.

When she came to the rear entrance to the Briarcliff Cemetery she saw that it was unmarked. Instead there were two fieldstone pillars, connected by a chain with a padlock on it. On one of the pillars was a rusted sign warning that trespassers would be prosecuted. Jessica clicked on her Maglite, aimed it at the ground, and headed into the cemetery.

★　★　★

The only good thing about walking through the woods was that she was now somewhat sheltered from the rain. Before long she came up to the southern end of the graveyard. She couldn't see far, but she did see lights in the distance. There appeared to be three large houses, perhaps a quarter-mile apart. She continued down the access road, passing crypts, monuments, row after row of manicured graves and expensive headstones. This was a world apart from the Mount Olive cemetery.

At eleven-thirty she reached the far end of the cemetery, the area that abutted the rear of Christa-Marie Schönburg's house.

Just as she was about to cross the field, to the rear of the property, her Maglite found a headstone bearing the legend:

DR. GABRIEL THORNE
HEALER AND FRIEND

The grave had recently been dug up.

★ ★ ★

As Jessica got closer she was overwhelmed by the size of the house. It was a three-story Tudor, half-timbered, with cross gables and a steeply pitched roof. Two massive chimneys rose at either end, both topped with chimney pots. A large deck jutted out over the backyard.

★ ★ ★

She could hear nothing but the rain.

Jessica studied the windows in the back of the house. There were faint lights in three of them. She watched for movement, for shadows. She saw none.

Jessica put her two-way handset on silent,

crossed the backyard, and stepped onto the rear deck.

* * *

The sliding glass door was locked. Jessica walked down the steps, rounded the house to the east wing. She tried to lift the windows. All were shut tight.

She had no choice. She found a fist-sized rock in the garden, stood atop the air-conditioning unit, broke out the window in the first-floor bathroom.

* * *

Once inside, she ran a towel through her hair, wiped her face. She opened the bathroom door. Straight ahead was a long hallway, leading to a large foyer and the front door. She left the bathroom, walked slowly down the hallway. To the left was the entrance to a small pantry, beyond that the kitchen.

Soft music played somewhere in the house.

Jessica saw that most of the rooms were lit by candles, dozens of them casting a pallid yellow light in the cavernous spaces.

She made her way cautiously down the hallway, watched by the eyes of dead ancestors peering down from huge oil paintings overhead. In the dim candlelight, objects waxed and waned — the occasional sideboard, end table, armoire. Each held danger. Jessica drew her weapon, held it at her side.

She approached a room, its door ajar. There was only darkness within. She edged up to the room, slowly inched the door open with her foot.

In borrowed candlelight she saw shapes in the room. A pair of bookcases, a sewing machine, a chair. There were two other doors. She could not clear them. There was no time. She had to take the chance.

She moved deliberately, right shoulder to the wall, sweat trickling from her shoulders, down her back.

Before she turned the corner, into what she was certain was the main hall, she stopped, tuned her ears to every sound. The music continued: a string quartet. Beneath it she heard a woman's voice, humming the melody.

Jessica took a deep breath, rolled the corner, her weapon held low.

Someone stood at the foot of the grand staircase, not fifteen feet away from her. It took Jessica a moment to adjust her eyes.

Kevin Byrne.

He was at the base of the steps, splendid in a dark suit, white shirt and deep burgundy tie. Above him was an enormous crystal chandelier. Jessica looked at Byrne's hands. He held a single white rose.

No, Kevin.

Please, no.

Before she could speak, Jessica looked up to see Christa-Marie at the top of the stairs. She wore a long black dress and a simple strand of pearls. Her hair was soft and luminous, a brilliant silver. She was radiant. She descended slowly, her slight hand on the railing, never once taking her stare from the man at the foot of the staircase.

When she reached the final step Christa-Marie paused.

Kevin Byrne handed her the white rose.

93

There is beauty so rare and ephemeral that it has confounded the poets for centuries. Byron, Shakespeare, Keats, Wordsworth — all failures. This is the beauty that is Christa-Marie. From the first moment I saw her she has owned my heart, taking it around the world, then into the deepest confines of hell.

I have never asked for it back.

I've always known that we would have this one last moment together, this moment when our hearts would once again be joined.

94

Christa-Marie stood face to face with Byrne.

Jessica watched, mesmerized by the tableau as Byrne took Christa-Marie by the hand and led her to the center of the hall, beneath the exquisite chandelier.

A new song began, a waltz. They danced.

As the strings played, Kevin Byrne and Christa-Marie Schönburg moved in beautiful, fluid lines, as if they had danced together all their lives. When they were finished, Byrne took Christa-Marie in his arms and kissed her.

The scene was so surreal, so unexpected, that Jessica found she had been holding her breath the entire time. She snapped out of it. She had a job to do.

She opened her mouth to speak.

She didn't get the chance.

The front door burst open, the sound of the battering ram echoing through the cavernous space. A pair of SWAT officers rolled into the foyer, their AR-15 assault rifles high. They were followed by Russell Diaz and two of his men, all three of them with weapons drawn. They ran down the main hall toward Byrne and Christa-Marie.

Diaz reached the couple first, stopping a few feet away. He pointed his weapon at Kevin Byrne.

'Down on the ground!' Diaz shouted.

Byrne edged slowly away from Christa-Marie, his hands out to his sides.

'Get down . . . on the fucking . . . *ground!*' Diaz repeated.

Christa-Marie stepped back, a look of horror and confusion on her face. The house was suddenly filled with silence. Byrne eased himself to the floor, put his arms out to the side. Two uniformed officers pinned him down and pulled his hands behind his back. They handcuffed him.

Seconds later, more people streamed through the door — Michael Drummond and Dana Westbrook among them. A dozen more officers spilled into the house.

Byrne was read his Miranda rights. As they took him into custody, Jessica put her weapon on the floor. She stepped into the foyer, her hands held high.

95

Lucy felt her way back to the long bench. She had stopped a few moments earlier, having heard muffled shouts from somewhere far away. Or had she? She didn't know. But all was silent now, and she had to get on with her business.

There were two drawers. She opened them, felt around, discovered some sandpaper, an oily rag, book matches, a pair of short screwdrivers. She felt the tips. One slot head, one Phillip's.

On top of the bench were a few more rags, along with a small stack of papers, some dried-out magazines. There was also an old lantern. Lucy picked it up, gave it a shake. There was liquid inside — she immediately caught a whiff of old kerosene.

She went back to the drawer, found the matches, opened one pack. They were damp. She tried them anyway. One by one, they smeared on the flint strip. Not even a spark. She found another pack, felt the matches. The top row seemed damp, the back row less so. She peeled off the top row of matches. She picked up one of the old magazines, tore off a page, rolled it up.

She tried the first match, got a spark, but the paper didn't light. On her third try she got a flame. She held the lit match to the rolled-up paper, got a torch going. She then pushed down the lift lever on the lantern. The wick caught, and the room was suddenly bathed in a warm glow. Lucy had never been more grateful for anything in her life.

96

There is a moment, almost sexual in its feeling of release, when a police detail winds down. Most of the time during this period of deceleration, in the minutes and hours after an arrest, there is a lot of handshaking and backslapping and fist-pumping in the air; never a shortage of gallows humor. But not this time. The personnel who made their way through this enormous Chestnut Hill mansion found no joy or happiness in this arrest. This was one of their own.

*　*　*

Kevin Byrne was in custody and en route to the Roundhouse. Christa-Marie Schönburg had been taken to Mercyhurst Hospital as a precaution. Her private nurse, Adele Hancock, had been at the opera. She was contacted and was on her way to meet Christa-Marie.

Before long it was Jessica, Dana Westbrook, and Michael Drummond, along with a few officers, searching and securing the house. Soon it would be November 1, All Saints' Day, twenty years to the day when Christa-Marie had been arrested in this very place.

*　*　*

Westbrook took Jessica aside. They stood in silence for a full minute, neither of them finding the right words to say. 'We'll sort this out,' Westbrook said. 'There's a hell of a lot about this I don't understand.'

Jessica just nodded.

'Kevin's arrest warrant came from on high,' Westbrook added. 'I had no choice but to serve it. You know that, right?'

Jessica said nothing. She could not get the image of Kevin Byrne in handcuffs out of her mind. The two of them had made so many arrests over the years, hunted down and brought to justice so many bad people, that she could not fathom Byrne being on that side of it all. The thought was beyond nauseating.

'So, I'll see you at the Roundhouse?' Westbrook asked.

Jessica looked at her watch. 'Give me an hour.'

'You got it.'

Westbrook took a few more moments, placed a hand on Jessica's shoulder and, perhaps trying and failing to find words, crossed the large atrium, stepped through the front doors and left.

Jessica glanced across the hall, at the steps which she had seen Christa-Marie descend earlier. She had to clear her mind. She had to think.

'Do you want me to drop you somewhere?'

Jessica turned around. It was Michael Drummond.

'Josh has my car,' Jessica said.

'Okay,' Drummond said. 'As soon as that scene is clear I'll send him back.'

550

Drummond stepped away, made a quick phone call. When he was finished he made his way over to where Jessica stood.

'I'm sorry it came down this way,' he said.

'I don't have much to say to you.'

'What are you talking about?'

'I just needed a little time, Michael. That's all. A little time.'

'I didn't make the call, Jessica.'

Jessica looked up sharply. 'You didn't? Then how did the fucking cavalry just happen to show up?'

'Police work, detective.'

'What are you talking about?'

'Russ Diaz followed up with Kevin's cousin Patrick. It turns out that Mr. Connolly's van had a LoJack installed.'

The LoJack was a recovery system that allowed police to track and recover a stolen vehicle.

'Russ called it in as a routine stolen vehicle, and got this location,' Drummond continued. 'I had nothing to do with it.'

Jessica's anger and rage did battle with her embarrassment for assuming that Drummond had dropped a dime.

'And just so you know, I talked to Detective Diaz,' Drummond said. 'Kevin is going to be handled with respect. I won't stand for any cowboy shit.'

Jessica had so much to say that nothing would come out. What she really wanted to do was scream.

'We're going to need your full statement

tonight,' Drummond added.

Jessica nodded. She picked up her service weapon, slipped it into her holster.

'I know this is hard for you, detective, but the good news, for the people of Philadelphia anyway, is that this nightmare is over.'

The feelings inside Jessica began to swell. The one feeling missing from all of it was doubt. She had no doubts about her partner. Her work, the task of proving Kevin Byrne's innocence, started right now. Before she could make a move she noticed someone standing to her left.

'Ma'am?'

Jessica turned. Standing there were two patrol officers from the Fourteenth District. The one talking to her was a big kid, twenty-three or so. He was pale as a ghost, but his hands were steady. 'The house is clear, ma'am.'

Jessica looked overhead, at the high ceiling, the large rooms. 'Are you sure? It's a big house, officer.'

The kid looked a little unnerved, then turned to look behind him. Four more officers stood there, and a pair of detectives from North that Jessica recognized. The kid was saying that a total of eight police officers had searched the house and that it was empty.

'I'm sorry,' Jessica said. 'It's not a good night.'

'No, ma'am,' the kid said. 'There are two locked doors — one in the attic, one in the cellar. Other than that, the structure is clear.'

He waited a few moments, perhaps to see if there was anything else. Jessica shook her head. The officer touched the brim of his cap, and together, single file, the eight cops walked out.

As the sound of the sector cars disappeared down the driveway, Michael Drummond put on his coat. He looked at Jessica, but remained silent. He walked through the door, closed it behind him.

The house was still.

Jessica was alone.

97

Lucy put the lantern on the bench and got her first real look at the room. It was smaller than she'd thought. There was no window. It had been bricked in a long time ago. Dust and cobwebs were everywhere. There were mouse droppings along the wall.

Peggy.

Lucy closed her eyes, tried to blot it all out.

She looked at the doorknob. It too was caked with dust. She picked up an old rag, cleaned it off. It was an old-fashioned white porcelain knob, set into a cast-metal plate. She felt along the neck behind the knob, and found the set screw. She angled the screwdriver behind the knob found the slot, gently turned. A few seconds later the set screw fell out. She carefully pulled off the knob, holding the spindle tightly. She didn't need the knob on the other side falling to the floor and making a racket. Then she went to work removing the plate. Four screws. Although she could not see that well, it looked like the screws in the plate were nearly stripped. She'd have one chance to get them out.

She looked at the head on the screwdriver, which was also rounded, dull with age and use. She put the screwdriver into the slot, put all of her weight behind it, doing her best to keep the tool perpendicular to the door.

She took a deep breath and tried to turn it.

Nothing. She backed off, tried again. This time she felt purchase.

The screw turned. Not much, but it turned.

Yes, Lucy thought.

A lock was just a device with moving parts, right? If there were moving parts, Lucy Doucette could handle it.

She set about her task.

98

The house was silent in a way that no small space could ever be; silent like a presence. Every so often its tranquility was broken by rain hitting the huge windows in the great room or a branch scraping a gutter.

Jessica had lived most of her life in a place too small, a place where the extra closet or tiny room was a premium. This was a fact of life in a Philadelphia row house. But this place — with its high ceilings, tall doorways and cavernous rooms — was too much. She didn't think she could ever live somewhere like this, although the likelihood of that happening was somewhere between never and *absolutely* never.

As she peered out of the front windows, anxious to get back to the Roundhouse, her phone rang. She jumped at the sound. She hoped it was going to be Josh telling her he was on the way. It was not. It was a number she did not recognize. She answered.

'Hello?'

'I'm calling for Detective Byrne.'

It was a man's voice.

'Who am I speaking to?' Jessica asked.

'My name is Robert Cole. I'm trying to reach Kevin Byrne. He gave me this number as a backup.'

'I'm his partner, Detective Balzano. Is there something I can help you with?'

'I have that report he wanted.'

'The report?'

'He had me red-ball a DNA test. Cold case.'

'I'm sorry,' Jessica said. 'What agency are you with?'

Cole went on to tell her that he ran a private, independent lab, and the work he had done for Byrne was off the record. He also told her that the job was the twenty-year-old homicide case of Gabriel Thorne.

'How much of the file do you have?' Jessica asked.

'I have copies of everything.'

'The crime-scene photos?'

'Yes.'

'Can you send me the DNA summary and the photos of the crime scene?'

'Sure,' Cole said. 'I can send the photos now, but it will take a few minutes to scan the DNA summary. It's on another computer.'

Jessica gave him her email address. Thirty seconds later the file arrived on her iPhone. Jessica tapped the file, opened it.

Cole had sent her four photographs. The first photograph was of the hallway in which she now stood. The fact that it had been taken twenty years earlier, in the precise space she now occupied, gave her a chill.

The second photo was of the kitchen. And it was a horror show. Gabriel Thorne's body was supine on the white tile floor, lying next to the kitchen island, a pool of blood beneath him, his chest butchered.

Jessica walked down the main hall, stopped at

the kitchen, turned on the light. The room had not changed. Same island, same white tile, same light fixtures. She scanned the photo and the real room, item by item. They were eerily identical, right down to the color of the kitchen towels on the rack next to the sink.

The other two photos were of the floor leading into the pantry, which was just off the kitchen, and the music room just off the pantry. The music room too was identical, except that now the cello in the corner did not have blood on it.

According to the brief summary attached to the photographs, it was believed that Christa-Marie Schönburg had stabbed Gabriel Thorne in the music room, then followed him into the kitchen. When he collapsed, she had continued to stab him in the chest.

Jessica tried to imagine the scene that night. She could not. But she knew what she had to do. If she was leaving shortly, locking the house behind her, she had better snuff out the candles in the music room. One by one she blew out the dozen or so candles, the scent of burned paraffin filling her head.

When the room was dark, lit only by the gas lamps on the deck at the rear of the house, she walked back into the hall, checked her watch. *Where the hell is Josh?* She called him, got his voicemail.

* * *

Jessica's phone rang again. She answered, but the call began to drop out. She ran down the hall toward the front door, but was still unable to get a signal. By the time she made it across the great room, she was able to hear. It was Robert Cole.

'Did you get the photos?' he asked.

'I did.'

'I'm having some trouble scanning the DNA report. I could keep trying, or I could just read it to you. Which do you prefer?'

'Read it to me.'

Cole read her the report. As he did, Jessica felt a cold finger run up her spine. It turned out that, in addition to Gabriel Thorne's and Christa-Marie's blood on the murder weapon and the floor of the kitchen, there were two other distinct DNA profiles found.

In other words, two other people had been present on the night of the murder.

What did it mean to the case? What did it mean to Christa-Marie's guilt on that night so long ago?

Jessica felt gooseflesh break out on her arms as she listened to the rest of the report.

She thanked Cole, hung up, her mind spinning.

This changed everything.

She stepped back to the front doors, opened them, fully expecting to see a sector car from the Fourteenth District at the gate. There was none. This was strange. The house would not be searched for evidence and cleared for at least twenty-four hours, and a police presence was standard procedure.

She keyed her two-way handset, spoke into it. No response.

559

What is going on?

She closed the doors, walked back into the main hall.

That was when Jessica Balzano heard the music.

99

As Jessica moved across the great room the music grew louder. It took her back to the first time she'd heard this piece in Byrne's van, the nocturne by Chopin.

She soon realized it *was* coming from the music room, but it sounded live, not recorded. It sounded like someone was playing the cello in that room.

'The house is clear, ma'am.'

From across the hall she noticed candlelight illuminating the room, candles she had just put *out*. As she approached the entrance, peering around the doorway, she saw someone sitting in a chair at the opposite side of the room. It was Christa-Marie. She held the beautiful cello between her legs and was playing the nocturne, her eyes closed.

It made no sense.

Why is she back? Who let her come back?

Jessica drew her weapon, held it at her side, rounded the door-jamb, and saw a second figure standing in the shadow of the short hallway leading to the kitchen.

It was someone she knew very well.

100

The figure in the hallway did not move. Christa-Marie continued to play, the notes rising and falling with the sound of the wind outside. As the piece came to a crescendo Jessica stepped fully into the music room.

'Is it now?' the figure in the hallway asked.

Jessica did not know how to answer. Too many things could go awry with the wrong answer.

The figure emerged from the shadows.

Michael Drummond had changed his clothes. He now wore a navy suit with thinner lapels. It was a style that might have been popular with fifteen-year-old boys when Drummond had been a guest, and probably a student, in this house.

There was something bulky in one of his suit-coat pockets. Jessica watched his hands.

'Teacher is mad at me,' Drummond said softly.

Jessica glanced at Christa-Marie. She was lost in the music.

'Is it now?' Drummond asked again.

'No,' Jessica replied. 'It's then, Michael. It's Halloween night, 1990.'

The notion registered on Drummond's face. His features softened in a way that told Jessica that his mind was returning to that night, when all things were possible, when love burned brightly in his heart, not yet tempered by the horror of what was to come.

'Tell me about that night, Michael,' Jessica said. She began to inch closer to him.

'We went to the concert. Joseph and I.'

'Joseph Novak.'

'Yes. When we came back, he was here.'

'Doctor Thorne?'

'Doctor Thorne!' Drummond spat the name like an epithet, glanced into the kitchen, then back. Jessica circled closer.

'What happened?' she asked.

'We argued.'

As Jessica closed the distance by another few inches, she noticed a shadow to her left, right near the entrance to the kitchen, just a few feet from where Michael Drummond stood. She looked over. So did Drummond. Someone was standing there.

'Joseph?' Drummond asked.

But it wasn't Joseph Novak, of course. Somehow, Lucinda Doucette was standing there. Lucinda Doucette from the Hosanna House and Le Jardin.

In one fluid motion Michael Drummond reached for Lucy, pulling her close to him. He now had a straight razor in his hand. He flicked it open.

Jessica leveled her weapon. 'Don't do it, Michael.'

'Zig, zig, zag.'

Everything Jessica had seen in Drummond's face, everything that told her he might be ready to give all this up, was gone. What stood before her now was a feral, calculating killer.

'Let her go.'

Drummond held Lucy even more tightly. Jessica saw the young woman's legs start to sag.

'I have a little more work to do,' Drummond said.

'Not going to happen.'

Drummond brought the razor up in a flash. The gleaming blade was now less than an inch from Lucy's throat. 'Watch.'

'Wait!'

Drummond glanced at the clock. It was 11:51.

'There's no time left,' he said.

'Just put down the razor. Let her go.'

Drummond shook his head. 'Can't do it, detective. There's one note left to play.'

'We'll get you help,' Jessica said. 'It doesn't have to end this way.'

'But it *does*, don't you see? This must be completed.'

Jessica glanced again at the grandfather clock in the hallway. 'It's not midnight yet. Let her go.'

'Look how many unfinished symphonies there are. Beethoven, Schubert. I am not going to leave a legacy like that.'

Jessica looked at Lucy. The girl was going into shock. Jessica knew she had to keep the man talking.

'Why these people, Michael? Why did you choose them?'

'They got away with murder, Jess. Surely you can understand that. They won't be missed.'

'They had families,' Jessica said. 'Sons, daughters, mothers, fathers. It's not up to us.'

Drummond laughed. 'We can't do it all, you and I. I've watched it for years. Police do their jobs, prosecutors do their jobs. Still people get away with it. Tonight all these people dance with the dead. Eddie Robles, Kenny Beckman, his sow of a wife. So many more.'

'What about George Archer?'

Drummond smiled. 'I'm not guilty on that one, your honor. But believe me, it wasn't for lack of effort. I tracked him for years. Ever since I got out of law school.'

'Who, Michael? Who killed him?'

'Do your job, detective. I did mine.'

Drummond leaned away from Lucy, the razor moving away from her throat momentarily. Jessica sighted down her weapon. She had a shot.

'Then why Lucy?' Jessica asked. 'She's innocent.'

'No, she is *not*.' On the word *not*, Drummond pulled Lucy closer. Jessica no longer had a line of sight. 'It's because of her that Peggy van Tassel is dead.'

'I don't understand.'

'Little Lucy could have told the police about George Archer. She didn't, and who knows how many other little girls Archer killed? This little piggy is part of the problem.'

Drummond stopped at the doorway to the kitchen. 'That's far enough, detective. Put your weapon down.'

Jessica did not move.

11:54.

'Do it *now*.'

'Okay, Michael,' she said. She lowered her Glock to the floor. 'It's down.'

Jessica glanced to her left. Through the

doorway she could see the bare feet and rolled-up trousers of a body on the floor, a few drops of blood on the tile. She also saw the knife on the counter. It was the precise scene from that night twenty years earlier, a re-creation of the murder of Gabriel Thorne. Except that there was a new twist. There was a band of white paper and a red candle on the counter.

Jessica looked again at the kitchen floor.

Is this David Albrecht's body?

The horrors were piling up.

'Look,' Jessica began. 'Dr. Thorne is already dead.' She pointed to the kitchen.

Drummond glanced into the kitchen, at the body on the floor. He looked back at Jessica. His mind was gone, lost in some kind of vortex between the night of Thorne's murder and now.

'It really is *then*?' he asked.

'Yes.'

Drummond began to nod rapidly. 'He was going to take her away, see,' he said. 'For good. That's why he had to die.'

'I understand.'

Drummond turned slowly toward the stereo cabinet behind him, touched the *play* button.

Christa-Marie seemed to return to the moment. She began to play a new piece, plucking one of the strings — the same note, twelve times.

'What is *Danse Macabre* without the chorus?' Drummond asked. He turned up the sound.

A moment later, beneath the resonance of Christa-Marie's cello, was a mix of sounds — street sounds, sirens. Beneath it all a chorus began to sing:

Zig, zig, zig, Death in cadence,
Striking a tomb with his heel,
Death at midnight plays a dance-tune,
Zig, zig, zag, on his violin.

But somehow the loudest part of this new background was the sound of a baby cooing.

'The dead own the world tonight,' he said. 'Listen to them. I've been collecting their voices for years.'

11:56.

The voices began to grow in volume. Screams, shrieks of terror, death wails.

'Look,' Jessica said. She circled to her left. She had to get into the kitchen. 'My gun is down, Michael. I can't hurt you. The doctor is dead. Let the girl go. We'll talk.'

'It's not about me. It's never been about me.' Drummond began to sweat. He waved the razor around, bringing it perilously close to Lucy's face. The chorus of screams grew in the background. Christa-Marie's playing increased in volume.

The lady, it's said, is a marchioness or baron-
ess
And her green gallant, a poor cartwright.
Horror! Look how she gives herself to him,
Like the rustic was a baron.

'She gave herself to him,' Drummond said, pointing at the body on the floor. 'She doesn't have long, you see. It had to be done.'

'Who doesn't have long?'

'Teacher. She's dying. That's why I had to write faster.'

Drummond took one step backward, into the kitchen, dragging Lucy with him. 'Listen to them all,' he said. 'Can you hear?'

'I hear, Michael.'

11:58.

Jessica moved forward.

'What about Gabriel Thorne?' she asked, gesturing to the body on the kitchen floor. 'Christa-Marie didn't kill him, did she? It was you, wasn't it? You and Joseph Novak?'

'Thorne was in love with her. He manipulated her.' Drummond shook his head, his eyes filling with tears. 'Joseph was weak. He was always weak.'

'But you let Christa-Marie take the fall.'

Tears ran down his cheeks. 'I've had to live with that for twenty years.'

Drummond backed to the center of the kitchen as *Danse Macabre* neared its final glorious section.

From somewhere beneath the cacophony came a man's voice:

'Michael.'

★   ★   ★

Inside, where the music lives, in that gilded hall, I watch and wait. Teacher knows what I must do.

There is one note left to play.

One final note.

568

At the sound of the man's voice everything slowed. Drummond held Lucy even more closely. Slowly, he lifted the straight razor to his own forehead and drew it swiftly across. Bright crimson blood washed his face, spilling onto Lucy.

Again, from somewhere: 'Michael.'

Drummond hesitated for a moment, his head cocked to the sound. 'Dr. Thorne?'

One more note.

One more voice.

Drummond looked at Christa-Marie, playing furiously in the music room.

They push forward, they fly; the cock has crowed.
Oh what a beautiful night for the poor world!

Midnight.

Michael Drummond lifted the razor high into the air. He pulled back Lucy's hair, exposing the white of her throat.

'Teacher . . . ' he said.

As he brought the razor down Jessica saw the body on the floor move.

It was not David Albrecht.

Detective Kevin Byrne rolled to his right, raised his Glock 17 and fired, slamming a single bullet into Drummond's head, just above the man's right eye. Thick gobbets of bone and brain tissue burst from the back of Drummond's skull, onto the white-tiled wall.

Drummond collapsed face down onto the counter, onto the band of cloud-white paper, his bloodied face painting the sheet in a grotesque parody of a musical staff. His body slumped to the floor.

Jessica looked into the kitchen, the sounds of the discharged weapon ringing in her ears. As she stepped into the corner of the music room, and embraced Lucy Doucette, she met Byrne's gaze. He was covered with blood, not his own. He had been lying in wait. He looked at her, but his eyes saw something else, perhaps something that had happened in this room a long time ago, something that had just now come to a close.

The Echo Man was dead, his symphony now complete.

101

For the second time this night, the Philadelphia Police Department processed a crime scene at this address. Dozens of personnel moved like silent ghosts through the now brightly illuminated spaces.

* * *

Outside, Jessica and Byrne stepped into the shadows. When they were alone, out of earshot, she turned to him, her anger at being left out of the loop seething within her. 'You've got about five fucking seconds to start explaining all this.'

'I know you're upset.'

'I'm way past upset,' Jessica said. 'When did you set all this up? Yesterday?'

'No,' Byrne said.

'Bullshit.'

She paced. Byrne gave her time.

'Jess, trust me on this. The arrest was real. Diaz and his team had evidence that the tattoos were mailed to my address. They also had hair and fiber evidence from my van. They came in hard to get me. I was completely blindsided.'

'What the hell were you doing here?'

Byrne looked at the house, then back. 'I'm not sure my answer is going to be good enough for you.'

'Try me.'

Another pause. 'I knew the answer to all of this was locked inside Christa's mind. I knew time was short, but I had to work that angle.'

Jessica just listened, deciding not to tell Byrne that she already knew about the evidence Diaz had. But she now realized that it was Drummond who had planted the evidence, hoping to buy himself more time tonight, counting on the arrest of Kevin Byrne.

'When we got to the Roundhouse they patted me down,' Byrne said. 'They took my cellphone. Russ Diaz started scrolling through the calls I'd made today. He also saw the folder that holds the photographs. He saw this.' Byrne held up his phone. 'I hadn't really looked at it before. When I did, it all fell into place.'

Byrne tapped the screen, showed Jessica a picture. In it, Christa-Marie stood on the steps of a huge stone building. Next to the scarred oak doors was an inscription. Byrne tapped the screen again, enlarging the words.

What you leave behind is not what is engraved in stone monuments, but what is woven into the lives of others.

Jessica looked at Byrne. 'This is what Drummond said at his leaving party.'

Byrne nodded.

'And this picture was taken at Convent Hill,' she added.

'Yeah.'

Jessica recognized the place. It was in the photograph that she had found in Joseph Novak's journal. The photo captioned with the word *Hell*.

'Drummond had been to Convent Hill to visit Christa-Marie. That was where he got the inscription. From the Roundhouse we called the Prentiss Institute and had them look through the records. Michael Drummond studied with Christa-Marie. Both he and Novak were her students on the day when Gabriel Thorne was murdered.'

Jessica took a step away, absorbing the new information. She turned back, her anger far from dissipated.

'I had my weapon out, Kevin. More than once.'

'I know.'

'Something could have gone really wrong, really fast.'

Byrne pointed to the six SWAT officers gathered on the grounds. They had a direct line of sight to the eastern side of the mansion, the side where the kitchen and the music room were located.

'At no time were you in jeopardy, Jess. They had Drummond in their sights through the windows. If he had made a move toward you they would have taken him down. We just hoped it wouldn't be before he talked. We had to get him to make the admission.'

'Why? What are you talking about?'

Byrne held up a CD in a crystal case.

'What is that?' she asked.

'It's the whole event. Christa-Marie has a very sophisticated recording studio upstairs. The music room has six microphones in it. Mateo is up in the studio now. He's like a kid in a candy store.'

'You're saying everything that happened in there was *recorded*?'

Byrne nodded. 'When Drummond got here tonight he slipped upstairs, into that room, started the whole process. It's all on here. Christa-Marie playing *Danse Macabre*, including the background of Drummond's sick recordings of death screams. He finally got his magnum opus.'

Jessica's head was spinning. 'What about Lucy?' she asked. 'I don't care how good the SWAT guys are — Drummond had that razor at her throat.'

Byrne looked away for a moment as the ME's transport van pulled into the long drive. He looked back.

'We didn't plan on Lucy,' he said. 'I had no idea she was here.'

★ ★ ★

Ninety minutes later, with the house sealed and guarded, Byrne was waiting for Jessica in the large circular drive. They would head back to the Roundhouse to begin the long process of piecing together the horrors of the last few weeks.

Jessica stepped through the front door, closed it behind her. She looked at her watch. It was 2:52.

It was All Saints Day.

102

There was no shortage of media interest. For the still photographers and videographers alike, the Tudor house at Chestnut Hill was a feast of images. It would probably be on the list of horror tours next Halloween. The road in front of Christa-Marie Schönburg's house was crowded with national and international media. Two days after the horror, the numbers were still growing.

For the police, the whole story would take far longer to assemble.

The investigation revealed that Michael Drummond and Joseph Novak had both attended Prentiss, had both taken private lessons from Christa-Marie Schönburg. Over the years the rivalry between the boys had grown, not for first chair in an ensemble but rather for the affections of Christa-Marie.

On Halloween night 1990, it came to a head. Although investigators might never know exactly what had happened, they believed that Michael Drummond and Joseph Novak killed Gabriel Thorne that night. Drummond, being the dominant one of the pair, held this over Novak's head for the next twenty years.

The two men formed a small, unprofitable company, through which they published limited-edition reproductions of sheet music, penned

575

reproductions in the composer's hand. The paper they used was Atriana.

When Drummond, who had taken a job at Benjamin Curtin's law firm — Paulson Derry Chambers — learned of Christa-Marie's illness, his own psychosis led him down a path of destruction, a reign of terror that would be felt for a long time.

It was Michael Drummond who had supplied the forged visitor's pass and clothing to Lucas Anthony Thompson.

Real-estate tax records traced back to Drummond led to a small commercial building in South Philly. Police found his killing room full of recording equipment, as well as a cache of nearly two hundred CDs and audiocassettes — all meticulously dated — of street and human sounds, some of them of people in their death throes. It would be months, maybe years, before police forensic audiologists would be able to make sense of the recordings, if ever. Michael Drummond had been building to this dark dénouement for a long time.

At Josh Bontrager's direction K-9 officers from PPD found an unconsious David Albrecht at the bottom of the ravine on Sawmill Road. Albrecht had lost a lot of blood, but paramedics reached him in time. Investigators were certain that he had been attacked and left for dead by Michael Drummond, but Drummond would escape this charge posthumously.

None of this explained the murder of George Archer.

Lucy Doucette, in her statement, told police

about the man she had met. The man who called himself Adrian Costa. The Dreamweaver. Police checked with the management of the apartment building off Cherry Street. The landlord said that a man had rented Apartment 106 for six months, paying cash in advance. He gave police a vague description.

They had showed Lucy the video recordings made on Halloween Night at the hotel, recordings of the hallway on the twelfth floor. Jessica had freeze-framed the image of the man in the wizard's costume and mask passing by the camera.

Lucy said she couldn't remember.

Jessica had also visited Garrett Corners again, researched the name Adrian Costa. No one with that name had ever been registered as a voter or resident of the area. The people knew the reclusive van Tassels to be travelers, carny people. The only photograph of the family was nearly fifteen years old. When Jessica revisited Peggy van Tassel's grave, she looked at the two plots next to it. One was the grave of a man named Ellis Adrian. The other was the last resting place of an Evangeline Costa.

Was the Dreamweaver Peggy van Tassel's father?

From what the investigators could gather, it appeared that Florian van Tassel had tracked Archer for years but had not known for sure that it was Archer who had kidnapped both Peggy van Tassel and Lucy Doucette back in September 2001. As the Dreamweaver, van Tassel enticed Lucy to submit to hypnosis

577

sessions during which van Tassel determined that he had been right. George Archer had killed Peggy. It seemed that van Tassel also gave Lucy a post-hypnotic suggestion to leave a note for Archer in his room, drawing him up there at 9:30p.m., then instructed her to open the door to Room 1208 at the right moment.

The enhanced video taken from the twelfth-floor hallway that night showed the man dressed as a wizard — believed to be Florian van Tassel — with an old-style school bell in his hand.

While all of this was circumstantial, it wasn't until forensic results started to come in that police issued an arrest warrant for Florian van Tassel, aka The Dreamweaver. Blood belonging to George Archer was found on the old photograph left behind in the room where the Dreamweaver had met with Lucy Doucette.

The George Archer file sat in a file cabinet at the Roundhouse.

The case remains open.

103

Byrne sat in the small lunch-room at the back of the Roundhouse. The four-to-twelve shift had already come and gone and were out on the street. Byrne, who had been on administrative leave since the shooting, sat by himself, a cold cup of untouched coffee in front of him.

When Jessica entered the room and approached him she saw something else on the table. It was Byrne's fifty-cent piece.

'Hey, partner.'

'Hey,' Byrne replied. 'You finish that FAS?'

A Firearms Analysis System form was a trace request sent to the Bureau of Alcohol, Tobacco, Firearms and Explosives.

'All done.' Jessica slid into the booth across from Byrne. 'You heading home?'

'In a while.'

They sat in silence. Byrne looked tired, but not nearly as tired as he had looked recently. He'd gotten the results from all his follow-up tests. There was no tumor, nothing serious. They said it was a combination of fatigue, poor diet, insomnia, with a Bushmills chaser. Jessica glanced at the menu displayed over the counter in the corner, and thought about how eating in this place might be part of the problem.

579

Byrne looked up, at the scarred booths, the plastic flowers, the line of vending machines against the wall, at the place to which he had come to work for more than twenty years. 'I didn't do my job, Jess.'

She'd known this was coming, and here it was. Everything she planned to say vaporized from her mind. She decided to just speak from her heart. 'It wasn't your fault.'

'I was so young,' Byrne said. 'So arrogant.'

'Christa-Marie confessed to the crime, Kevin. I wouldn't have handled it any differently. I don't know any cop who would.'

'She confessed because she was ill,' Byrne said. 'I didn't dig any deeper. I should have, but I didn't. I turned in my report, it went to the DA. Just like always. Boss says move on, you move on.'

'Exactly.'

Byrne spun the coffee cup a few times.

'I wonder what her life would have been like,' he said. 'I wonder where she would have gone, what she would have done.'

Jessica knew there was no answer to this, none that would help. She waited awhile, then slipped out of the booth.

'How about I buy you a drink?' she said. 'It's fifty-cent Miller Lite night at Finnigan's Wake. We can get hammered, drive around, pull people over, do some traffic stops. Be like old times.'

Byrne smiled, but there was sadness in it. 'Maybe tomorrow.'

'Sure.'

Jessica put a hand on Byrne's shoulder. When she got to the door she turned, looked at the big man sitting in the last booth, surrounded by all the whispering ghosts of his past. She wondered if they would ever be silent.

104

He found her behind the hotel. She was sitting alone on a stone bench, on her dinner break, an untouched salad next to her. When she saw Byrne she stood up, hugged him. He held on as long as she wanted.

She pulled away and turned, brushing off the bench for him. *Ever considerate*, Byrne thought. He sat down.

They were silent for a few moments. Finally Byrne asked, 'You doing okay?'

Lucy Doucette shrugged. 'Just another day in the big city.'

'Did you have any problems giving your statement?' He had put out the word that she was to be treated with kid gloves. The report back was that she had been. Byrne wanted to hear it from her.

'Yeah,' she said. 'But if I never go back to a police station for the rest of my life, that will be okay with me.'

'About that other matter,' Byrne said, referring back to Lucy's detainment for shoplifting. 'I talked to the DA's office, and to the owner of the store on South. It's all smoothed over. Just a big misunderstanding.' Because Byrne had intervened before Lucy was charged there would not be a record.

'Thanks,' she said. She looked at Byrne, at the bench, at the surrounding area. 'Where's your man bag?'

'I'm not carrying it anymore.'

Lucy smiled. 'Were you getting grief from your fellow officers?'

Byrne laughed. 'Something like that.'

A wink of silver caught Byrne's eye. It was a small heart-shaped pendant around Lucy's neck.

'Nice necklace,' he said.

Lucy lifted the heart, ran it along the chain. 'Thanks. I got it from David.'

'David?'

'David Albrecht. I went and saw him in the hospital.'

Byrne said nothing.

'We're kind of in this thing together, you know?' Lucy said, perhaps feeling the need to explain. 'I guess he's going to be okay?'

'The doctors say it looks good.'

Lucy dropped the pendant, smoothed it against her uniform. 'He's got some offers on his movie, you know.'

'I heard that,' Byrne said. 'So, are you guys an item?'

Lucy blushed. 'Oh *please*. We're just friends. We just *met*.'

'Okay, okay,' Byrne said.

'*Gosh*.'

Two young women walked by, no more than eighteen or nineteen, smartly dressed in their crisp new Le Jardin uniforms. They eyed Lucy with something akin to awe.

When they passed, Lucy looked at Byrne. 'Rookies.'

They sat in thoughtful silence. The autumn sun warmed their faces.

'What are you going to do, Lucy?'

'I don't know,' she said. 'Maybe go home for the holidays. Maybe go home for good.'

'Where's home?'

Lucy Doucette looked up at the hotel, down Sansom Street, then over at Byrne. In that moment, for the first time since he'd met her, she looked a lot more like a woman than a little girl.

She said: 'A long way from here.'

105

The women sat around the small table, a game of gin rummy in progress in front of them. Between the ashtrays, Styrofoam cups, cans of Diet Pepsi and Diet Mountain Dew, the bags of pork rinds and barbecued chips, there was hardly room for the cards.

When the petite young woman in the oversized blue parka walked into the room, Dottie Doucette stood up. Dottie was terribly thin. She looked older than her forty years, but a light had come back to her eyes, her friends all said. It was faint, they averred, but it was there.

When Lucy hugged her mother, Dottie felt as if she might break.

Lucy wanted to ask her mother about George Archer. She had talked to some of the women who had known her mother when they were younger, and she'd learned that Dorothy Doucette had gone out with George Archer a few times. That was probably when the man had put his eye on Lucy. Lucy knew that her mother felt guilty for so many things. Dottie Doucette did not need this burden now.

Dottie let go, wiped her eyes, reached into her pocket. She showed Lucy her chip. Six months sober.

'I'm proud of you, Mama.'

Dottie turned toward the women at the table. 'This is Lucy, my baby girl.'

The women all fussed over Lucy for a while, and Lucy let them. She'd stay on for a month or so, taking a room at a boarding house in town, in exchange for housekeeping duties. From the moment she got off the bus, she knew that she would not be staying forever, just as she knew that in many ways she had never left. Not really.

Her mother slipped on the pilled sweater that was draped over the back of the folding chair. Lucy recognized it as one she had stolen from the JC Penney's a long time ago. The sweater was getting on in years. Her mother needed a new one. Lucy promised herself she would buy it this time.

'Take me for a walk?' Dottie asked.

'Sure, Mama.'

Out in the lobby, Lucy helped her mother on with her boots. As Lucy was tying the laces, she glanced up. Her mother was smiling.

'What?' Lucy asked.

'I used to do the same thing for you when you were small. Funny how life comes full circle.'

Yeah, Lucy thought. *Life's hilarious.*

They walked, arm in arm, down the path that led to the town park. The temperature was falling. Lucy bunched the sweater around her mother's neck.

Winter was coming, but that was all right. In the end, Lucy Doucette thought, the sunshine was inside. And now that she remembered everything, she could begin to forget.

106

She had cooked for twenty. Like many Italian Thanksgiving gatherings, the meal began with a full pasta course. This time, Jessica and her father made Jessica's grandmother's fresh ravioli, the filling a delicate and savory balance of beef, pork, and veal.

For the first time, Sophie helped serve.

By six o'clock the men were sprawled around the living room, snoring away. Tradition called for them to be awake by six-thirty and ready to take part in Round Two.

At ten after six, Jessica opened the front door. South Philly was alive with the holiday. She looked left and right, didn't see Byrne's car. She wanted to call him, but she stopped herself. He had a standing invitation every year, and this year he'd said maybe. With Kevin Byrne, when it concerned events like this, 'maybe' usually meant no. But still.

Jessica was just about to close the door when she looked down. There, on the front steps, was a small white package. She picked it up, closed the door, walked over to the kitchen. She slit open the Scotch tape with a knife. Inside was a ball of yarn. Green yarn. When Jessica brought it into the light she saw that the yarn was the same shade as the oddly constructed cable knit sweater that Kevin Byrne had been wearing around the Roundhouse of late, a sweater, he told her, that had been knitted for him by Lina Laskaris's grandmother, Anna.

Jessica checked on her family. The men were still in a turkey-and-Chianti-induced coma; the women were doing the dishes and sneaking cigarettes out back. Then Jessica walked upstairs into the bedroom, closed the door behind her.

She unspooled the yarn, brushed back her hair, gathered it. She took the yarn, tied her hair into a ponytail, checked herself in the dresser mirror. The autumn had long since taken back the highlights bestowed by summer. She turned to the side, and for a moment had a memory of her mother tying back her hair with green yarn on her first day of school. How much youthfulness the world had then, how full of energy it had been.

She could use some of each.

As the new mother to a rocketing little two-year-old-boy, Jessica was going to need all the vitality and vigor she could muster. The papers had come through a week earlier, and Carlos Balzano was at that moment downstairs charming the entire family.

Jessica looked one final time at the yarn in her hair. In some ways, it was just as good as the original.

No, she thought as she turned out the light and descended the steps. In some ways it was even better.

EPILOGUE

For every light there is shadow. For every sound, silence.

In this massive room the silence was complete. Considering that there were nearly twenty-five hundred people in the Verizon Center, it was all the more profound.

The last note of *Sinfonia Concertante* sifted through the hall, and the applause began.

As the conductor turned to the audience, Byrne saw people noticing Christa-Marie, heard their whispers. The story had broken wide a few weeks earlier, the account of Christa-Marie's innocence in the murder of Gabriel Thorne. Byrne could not imagine the courage it had taken for Christa-Marie to come to this place on this night.

Soon the applause turned from the stage and was offered to the woman in the tenth row. A soft spotlight found them. The conductor walked to the footlights and bowed. The orchestra rose to its feet.

Byrne didn't know how much time together they had left, but he knew that he would be with Christa-Marie until the end. More than that, he wondered how it sounded to her. He wondered if it sounded the same, if it meant what it had meant twenty years ago when she had been the brightest star in the heavens.

Kevin Byrne took Christa-Marie's hand and

held it as the applause grew, the sound echoing across the deep chasms of memory, the vast and merciful landscape of time.

ACKNOWLEDGMENTS

Special thanks to:

Meg Ruley, Peggy Gordijn, Jane Berkey, Christina Hogrebe, Don Cleary, Mike McCormack, Kristen Pini, and the great team at the Jane Rotrosen Agency.

Kate Elton, Susan Sandon, Georgina Hawtrey-Woore, Jason Arthur, Rob Waddington, Emma Finnigan, Claire Round, Glenn O'Neill, and everyone at Random House UK.

Darin Brannon, Tara Klein, Francis Gross, Jane Sembric, Ray Villani, Douglas Bunker, Diana Richardson, Sandra Brancaleone, and Tacy Dooley.

Jennifer Kallend at the Curtis Institute of Music; Evan Evans at Le Meridien Philadelphia; Emily McCarthy at Ritz Carlton Philadelphia; Frank Thompson at Sheraton Society Hill.

Gino Rafaelli for his kindness and time, and the librarians at the CH-UH libraries for putting up with my many requests.

Detective Eddie Rocks, Sgt. Joe Rosowski, Lt. Edward Monaghan, and the brave men and women of the Philadelphia Police Department.

Mike Driscoll and the staff at Finnigan's Wake; Patrick Ghegan, Dom Aspite, Joe Sickman, Bob Mulgrew, Al Kurtz, John Dougherty, Vita and Adjani DeBellis, and the rest of the Philly crew.

My father, Dominic Montanari. Nine and change, Pop.

The city of Philadelphia and the Commonwealth of Pennsylvania for letting me create hotels, institutions, and townships, and for letting me move streets, buildings, and neighborhoods. I promise to put everything back where I found it.